I've travelled the world twice over,
Met the famous: saints and sinners,
Poets and artists, kings and queens,
Old stars and hopeful beginners,
I've been where no-one's been before,
Learned secrets from writers and cooks
All with one library ticket
To the wonderful world of books.

© JANICE JAMES.

HESTER VERNEY

From the age of fifteen, Hester Verney has been forced to make her own way in the world. A child of the harsh, bleak fenlands of late nineteenth-century England, Hester is a beautiful and independent girl whose modest contentment is shattered by the inarticulate devotion of her employers' son, Chad Langtoft. When she rejects his suit, Chad's love turns to bitter resentment. Hester is forced to seek employment elsewhere, and meets two men who will further influence her life's course.

Books by T. R. Wilson
in the Charnwood Library Series:

MASTER OF MORHOLM

T. R. WILSON

HESTER VERNEY

Complete and Unabridged

CHARNWOOD
Leicester

First published in Great Britain in 1993 by
Headline Book Publishing Plc
London

First Charnwood Edition
published November 1994
by arrangement with
Headline Book Publishing Limited
London

British Library CIP Data

Wilson, Timothy
    Hester Verney.—Large print ed.—
    Charnwood library series
    I. Title II. Series
    823.914 [F]

    ISBN 0–7089–8796–6

Published by
F. A. Thorpe (Publishing) Ltd.
Anstey, Leicestershire
Set by Words & Graphics Ltd.
Anstey, Leicestershire
Printed and bound in Great Britain by
T. J. Press (Padstow) Ltd., Padstow, Cornwall

This book is printed on acid-free paper

For Dave Marzy

The romance growing up in the interstices of a mass of hard prosaic reality.

THOMAS HARDY

Part One

1895

1

HESTER VERNEY was fifteen when she made the first important decision of her life. She made it in the chill dead middle of a spring night, sitting on the settle by the empty hearth, and sipping herself awake with cold black tea. Her father had made that settle with his own hands, from bog-oak dug up out of the fen fields; and as was the way with bog-oak, the settle had warped, so that the polished seat sloped at an angle along its length. To sit on it for more than a moment was to feel oneself sliding, slowly, gradually, steadily, from one end to the other; and by the time Hester had completed this progress, she had made her decision.

Her father had woken her a few minutes before, coming with an oil-lamp into the bedroom she shared with her sister and brothers and urging her in a whisper to shake a leg; and while the younger ones slept on above, she had dressed and come downstairs to find the family's few possessions wrapped up in bundles, her father's old horse standing in the shafts of the cart outside the open door, and all the signs of a flitting, familiar to her from earliest memory.

"I'm got to go, gel," her father said, still in a whisper, though there was half a mile of bare pitch-black fen between them and the next house. "There's rent owing summat cruel.

3

If they'd just be patient, then they'd git it, sooner or later; but they wun't be patient — so they wun't git it at all, and that ain't my fault."

Hester was used to her father's fractured logic, and she only said: "Where to this time?"

Her father rolled up the pegged rug from the floor and tied it with string; then stood pensively contemplating a crate that contained a dozen fish-kettles, packed in straw. "I still reckon I could find a use for these," he said. He had bought them from a market trader in Whittlesey and had been unable to sell a single one: they did not fit over the turf fires of fen cottages.

"They're no good," Hester said. "Anyway, the handles come off."

"Detachable," her father said mysteriously.

She was properly awake now: she finished the tea. "Father, where are you going to go?"

"I'm finished here. I don't seem to git a run o' luck here." Her father picked up the oil-lamp, tried to pick up the crate as well, needed both hands, set down the oil-lamp on the floor. "I reckon I need to mek a clean break. A clean sweep. A new broom." The metaphors entangled him for a moment, and he went and, uncertainly, picked up the broom from the hearth. "No," he said, putting it back, "what I mean is, I'm gitting off the fen altogether. I shall try me luck over Leicester, where your aunt Netty is."

Hester stared for a long moment into the dregs of her tea. Then she stood, picking up the oil-lamp before her father kicked it over, and looked at him in its pasty light. A smile came and went on his face.

"Your aunt Netty's a good woman, Hester," he said. "She's been pressing me to go over there for long enough. I know you don't git along with her all that special — "

"I'm not coming, Father. No, not on account of Aunt Netty. Even though she looks at me like summat that crawled out of a drain. And she always smells of tar-water. And even though," she added, warming to her theme, "she carries on like she's the Queen just because she's got a skerrick of old Nottingham lace on her table and some pretend flowers under a glass bowl what look like they come off a gravestone — "

"Not to everybody's liking," her father said, shaking his head.

"But anyhow, it's not her. I said to meself last time we had to flit that I weren't going to do it any more; and I'm decided."

Her father reached up to scratch his head, found he was wearing his hat, and scratched that instead. "I know it's not been much of a life for you lately, gel," he said. "Racketing about from pillar to post. I just don't seem to be able to hold on to money these days. But once we git over to Leicester, mek a fresh start — "

"It ain't that. Father, I'm got friends here," Hester said. "I'm been gitting good work at Langtoft's farm. Mrs Langtoft's been teaching me dairying and everything. I don't want to chuck it all up again."

"I know, gel. I know. I'm been thinking of

that. But I'm got to go, you see. There's Artie Gill an' all, carrying on all unreasonable reckoning I owe him money. Well," he added, conceding a minor point, "I do owe him money. But the point is, I seem to have lost all me reputation round 'ere."

Hester could have told him that his reputation was all too intact; but she was too fond of him for that and, even leaving aside loyalty, she was like him in several ways. She did not think much the worse of him for being chronically unreliable: while he was hopelessly improvident, he was also affectionate; and if there was no god but the one god, Respectability, then she was quite as much a pagan as he.

"And then there's Mrs Puddock, you see," her father said, "gitting the wrong idea"; and he coughed delicately and took down the brass candlesticks from the mantelpiece.

Mrs Puddock was a widow who kept a good table and, it was said, had no objection to men getting their feet under it. She was the latest in a series of single or widowed women of a certain age with whom, in the course of several years' flitting from place to place around the fens, Hester's father had become tenderly involved. It was never his intention to begin these decorous affairs. He was a man of susceptible temperament and natural gallantry; and though he was a vague and ungainly creature, there was still a sort of distressed handsomeness about his perenially hopeful face and blue eyes, which these ladies seemed to take to; and one widow at Chatteris, from whom he had beaten a hurried retreat, had evinced a startling tendency to lay hold of him by his side-whiskers, and call him a Saucebox.

"She's a charming woman, Mrs Puddock," her father said, "but I do think our association will have to come to an end." For he never meant anything by these entanglements: they were born of the same airy romanticism of spirit that had made him lease an osier-bed and try his hand at making baskets, because he said his French Huguenot ancestors had done so, or set up a cart selling lemonade to the Irish navvies working on the new railway cut, because he thought some of them might be Temperance. And besides, in that same spirit he was faithful to the memory of Hester's mother, dead seven years since. "You see why I'm got to go, don't you, gel?"

She nodded. "And you see why I'm had enough of the flitting, don't you, Father? You know how Mrs Langtoft is always asking me to go and live in at the farm. With a room and everything — she's always right kind to me — it'd not be like going into service. And that's what most gels of my age are done by now."

"They're very good sort of people, the Langtofts," her father said. He was still absently holding the candlesticks. She took them from him, and packed them in a box. "Ah, I suppose it had to come sooner or later. The young 'uns'll miss you, Hester."

"Well, I hope so. I mean — you know what I mean. But there's Becca twelve now, and starting to earn soon, and Georgie and Arnold able to shift for theirselves. Besides, Father — I know you won't say it, so I will — I'm another mouth to feed, ain't I?"

"Thass never been a consideration wi' me, gel," her father said solemnly. And with some truth, for his children were always hungry. "Well! Your aunt Netty'll be sorry not to see you. I know that'll be better for the young 'uns, being close to her — she's a rare hand wi' children, my sister Netty."

Hester held her tongue. She knew about Aunt Netty's hand: it was large, hard and red, and always seemed to be descending on your ears. If she had any uneasiness about separating herself from her family at last, it was at the thought of the young 'uns coming into that rather slapping orbit of Aunt Netty. But at least they stood more chance of being fed, and of being turned out smartly. Hester had never been one for playing the little mother — that was for story-books — the young 'uns being accustomed to setting out for school with no more than a cat-lick and a slice of bread-and-seam in their hands. She would miss them — there was a lump like a potato in her throat at the thought of saying goodbye — but her mind was made up. She had truly had enough of the moonlight flits, the shifting and bolting and hiding under the table at the bailiff's knock. They had been nearly a year now at the cottage on Hinching Fen: she had friends, good work at Langtoft's farm, a feeling of home. The fen was her place.

"Now you're sure the Langtofts'll tek you in?"

"I'm sure. Mr Langtoft'll likely be astir soon, he's usually up at five. I can git a bed at Lizzie Gosling's if they're not ready for me."

She helped her father carry the bundles out to the cart. The old horse turned his neck to watch them, indifferently, as if nothing could surprise him any more. The fen night was a great void around them, punctured here and there with stars.

"Better wake them young 'uns, and lay the bed in the bottom of the cart. We should git as far as Peterborough by daybreak." Her father was whispering again, as if the silent blackness teemed with lurking creditors. "Don't really like to flit without saying goodbye to folks. Tell the truth, I'm afraid they'd be asking me not to goo. They'll find they miss having a good higgler about the place — you'll see." He adjusted the halter and went on, as if speaking into the horse's ragged ear: "Funny, saying goodbye to you like this, gel. I s'pose it means you're growed up — and I can't quite believe it somehow."

Hester smiled, gave him a kiss, and refrained from saying that living with him, she had had to grow up well before time, and this only set the seal on the process.

The young 'uns, in various states of sleepiness and protest, were roused from bed: the oat-flight mattress was placed in the cart, and Georgie and Arnold, after sitting up and blinking like two bewildered owls for a few minutes, had burrowed down and gone to sleep again by the time the cart was moving. The fen-drove that led to the high road was in an atrocious state

9

after spring rains, but they had been through all this before and slept soundly despite the lurches and bumps; and Becca sat beside Hester with a look of resignation at this familiar reality and of having just been roused from some very different dreams.

Dawn was the merest phosphorescent presence, like some vast ghost haunting the eastern horizon, when her father pulled up the cart at the corner of a drove. "I'll let you down here then, gel. You give my best to the Langtofts, and tell 'em I'm sorry I didn't git chance to say goodbye to 'em proper-like."

Hester climbed down. Her father handed her the carpet-bag containing her worldly goods.

"Be a credit to me, now. And any trouble at all, you know where we are. I s'll write you, though you know I ain't much of a penman. Your mother were always the one for writing. She could spell any word you cared to name. Excepting cottage, I seem to remember. That one always seemed to trip her up. And I tell you what — as soon as I git set up, and mek a bit o' money, I s'll send you the train fare, so's you can come and visit. That'll be summat to look forward to, wun't it?"

She was glad at the last to see her father floundering back to his old, hopeless optimism; even though its effect was to make the tears that had been standing in her eyes fall at last. She kissed her sister, promised to write, and watched the cart go creaking away. Colour was leaking into the sky; and all around, out of the formless dimness, fields and dykes and trees were stealing

10

into view, as if they had been away somewhere in the empty night, and had just that moment come stealthily back. Abruptly, Hester was a little frightened: by nothing physical, but by an idea; the idea that she was alone. All at once she saw her life as a thing belonging only to her: as something precious that was being thrust into her hands. She picked up her bag and began to walk down the long drove to Langtoft's farm, with the world of the wide fens taking on shape around her, as if she were just that moment being born into it.

2

HINCHING FEN covered half a thousand acres of the great flat basin known as the Bedford Level. It was a place sufficient of itself. The towns of Huntingdon, Peterborough and Ely were all at a distance that would have been accounted convenient in a district less poor, isolated and elemental: as it was, the fount of such amenities as the folk of Hinching Fen enjoyed was Stokeley, a diminutive market town a couple of miles down the river, consisting of a ruined abbey, an enormously wide High Street, and a nest of houses with deep roofs and long dormer windows that gave them the look of having low foreheads, and of glowering at each other in suspicion. For the rest, the land was all, and the land was low, black, peaty, strange, and precious; and given half a chance the water would take it back.

Such were the horizons of Hester's world for the next three years. Langtoft's farm lay in the middle of the fen: a geographically imprecise expression, but one readily comprehensible to any fen-dweller — for to live in the fens is always to live in the middle of them. The farmhouse was a square building of brick and tile, not large, with a crow-stepped gable-end facing the east wind that came like a battering-ram over the fields. The farm was worked for the most part by the Langtofts alone; and while Hester earned her keep, with an allowance of pin-money when times were good enough, and was trained up much as any female farm-servant would be, she was from the beginning encouraged to count herself part of the family. No one in that part of the country was rich; and those few big farmers who did go in for ceremony, and yellow gig-wheels, and lace curtains, elicited more contempt than respect.

Mrs Langtoft took Hester under her wing. There were three sons in the house, but Mrs Langtoft's only daughter Mary had died from diphtheria in infancy and, as she confided to Hester, she missed having a girl about the place. Often she spoke of her 'Meery', and what a shame it was they never raised her.

"Ah! I could just picture my Meery looking like you now, gel," Mrs Langtoft would say, as Hester came into the kitchen glowing from the winter's morning. "She'd have been just your age — and just your colouring too, I reckon, if she'd ha' lived."

This colouring of Hester's was one which her father would no doubt have attributed to the Verneys' French blood, of which he was so proud: others — in a land where the plough turned up the paved causeways of Caesar's legions, and the 'ole Romans' were spoken of as familiarly as great-grandparents — might have harked back further. In fact it was a complexion not uncommon in the fens: and whether or not she had inherited the blue eyes from the Danes who had sacked Stokeley

Abbey, the very fair, almost waxen white skin from the free-born Saxons who had made their last stand here against the Norman tide, and the pure black hair, blue-black in sunlight, from the French Protestants who had sought refuge from persecution in this watery land, in Hester the ensemble was both peculiarly native and striking.

She came into her looks late. The needy, harum-scarum life with her father had meant that the physique of a child had persisted into her sixteenth year, and it was the influence of Langtoft's farm that effected a transformation, rapid as the forcing of a hothouse flower. Poverty at such small family farms was held at a distance only by unremitting labour, but held it was, and the food that came to Mrs Langtoft's scrubbed deal table, while plain, was substantial. There was home-cured bacon and ham, there was home-baked bread, there was fresh milk, there were potatoes and greenstuff in plenty, and there were also Mrs Langtoft's formidable puddings, known as water-wallopers, which could take the edge off the keenest appetite. When the winter weather was raw and savage, and the fen, as Mr Langtoft said, was 'as blea as nowhere on God's earth, not excepting Roosia', you always came indoors to the blaze of a good turf fire; and when the rain drenched those naked shelterless fields, there were always clean dry clothes to change into, stitched by Mrs Langtoft and herself in the evenings by the light of the oil-lamp. Merely the absence of those deprivations to which she had long been

14

accustomed was enough to send Hester's body shooting from girlhood to young womanhood, and seeming to omit adolescence in between — a pleasant enough omission, indeed, though perhaps as a consequence a certain healthy element of self-doubt was lacking in a nature otherwise open, generous and tolerant.

It would have taken a more saintly girl than Hester — emerging thus from a gawky and harassed youth, schooling constantly interrupted by the vagaries of a father who was a large child himself — not to feel a newly satisfying sense of self. "I see you, gel," Mrs Langtoft would say, as Hester hovered before the polished milk-pan hanging on the dairy wall, "admiring yourself there. You'll see the devil over your shoulder one of these days!"

But it was a feigned sternness: Mrs Langtoft liked to regard the girl as her protégée, and it rather comforted her than otherwise to witness the flourishing promise that 'her Meery' would have enjoyed in her place. And Hester examined her image with perhaps as much genuine pleased surprise as outright vanity. The reflection showed her an oval face, high-cheekboned, and dominated by a pair of eyes large and limpid enough for the cloister, the force of which was partly disarmed by dark slanting brows, expressive of scepticism: whilst, in strong contrast, the tilt of her nose and upward curve of her lips might have come from a portrait of one of Charles II's lazily humorous mistresses. With her dark hair bound up to reveal small ears and a fair neck, she had something of the erect shapeliness of a flower — no exotic bloom, but a country flower as English as Chaucer. Hester gazed, and was what the Chapel called ensnared by the flesh; but in spite of Mrs Langtoft's warning she did not see the devil over her shoulder. What she did begin to notice, after she turned eighteen, was the face of the Langtofts' eldest son Chad observing her. But when she turned round, he would always be walking away, or busy with something. Beyond those odd covert stares there was no alteration in his manner towards her; and as hers was a mind very much at ease, and never inclined to burden itself with unnecessary reflection, she scarcely gave the circumstance a second thought.

It was the more natural that Chad should remain in the background of her consciousness, in that it was Mrs Langtoft around whom life at the farm revolved. Everyone worked hard: Hester; Mr Langtoft whose name was Charles and was therefore known as Wag; Chad who was twenty and Jacob and Will who were in their early teens; but Mrs Langtoft was the oil in the engine. She was a small, neat, round, black-eyed woman, sturdy as a Shetland pony, utterly tireless, and deft and quick in everything: she even had a habit of rapid blinking, as if there were a lot of blinks to get through, and not much time to do them. Her square red hands were never still: they wound wool or worked stitches while she waddled from place to place or waited for a pot to boil; and when the cat jumped on her lap of an evening, her fingers would stroke and scratch to such an alarming degree that it was almost as if she had half a mind to unpick him, and start him all over again. The work of the farm was unceasing, and at times like harvest it rose to frenetic pitch, and in Mrs Langtoft there was a fear that if they let up for a moment, everything would collapse. She had burning memories of the terrible distress of '79, when some on the fen had survived on potato peelings and turnip tops.

"Git on!" she would say. "Git on, will yer — you want to end up on turnip-tops?" She was fond of her menfolk, but she confided to Hester that they were useless articles, and needed driving: and if they showed signs of lingering at the breakfast-table, and reluctance to turn out, Mrs Langtoft would charge amongst them as if she were a ball and they were so many skittles, and scatter them off to work.

With her Hester learned all the tasks of the distaff side of the farm. She milked, she made butter, she baked bread, she tended the pigs; she scrubbed the brick floor of the big kitchen, she black-leaded the range and scoured the hearth with red ochre, she heaped the laundry into the great boiler on washing-days when the house ran with steam that made it more damp than ever; and at harvest she worked with the others in the fields, tying the sheaves that Mrs Langtoft raked. Always at these times Mrs Langtoft seemed to be far ahead of her, clad despite the heat in the invariable black high-collared dress, wielding the rake with her short arms that never tired. 'Come on, git on!' she would say, if the men leaned

17

on their scythes for a few moments. 'Never git done at this rate. Tek us a month o' Sundays at this rate.'

The work was exhausting, but Hester — while she would gladly do nothing and lie in the sun all day given a chance — found she thrived on it. She became supple as a young tree. Her legs, from the awkward stalks of neglected girlhood, grew long, straight and strong by dint of walking about the sprawling distances of the fen: her arms were as firm as apples. Her skin, subject to that East Anglian climate of sustained sunlight tempered with cool wind, was infused with colour sufficient to ripen but not coarsen it. Between rough twill sheets she slept the profound satisfying sleep of those who trouble not in the least about what the next day will bring; and to a disposition already conditioned, by life with her father, to taking nothing very seriously, was added a cheerful sense of the ridiculous and a readiness to laugh. 'You'll see, my gel,' Mrs Langtoft would say, 'the wind'll change one o' these days and your face'll get stuck like it!' But again it was a severity she did not mean, for she could not deny that laughter suited the girl's face, and that there was a peculiar charm in the way that a little glimpse of pink tongue showed against her white teeth.

Hester's wants were few; but as she turned eighteen, and the reflection in the milk-pan began to arrest her attention more strangely and pleasingly, they seemed to sharpen, and to pierce her in the form of sudden wishes for some item of adornment beyond the capability of her needle. A silk ribbon, a strip of lace, a feather to trim her Sunday straw hat, some mother-of-pearl buttons that she had seen on a blouse at chapel — such things appealed to her with an absurd urgency. Stokeley was where they were to be had, but that meant a four-mile walk across the fen, or waiting until Mr Langtoft went over to market in his waggon, and both of these were contingent on the farm being able to spare her. The easiest way to procure luxuries was by the tallyman.

Mrs Langtoft did not approve of the tallyman. He was known as 'Rob' Risby, from the abbreviation of his name painted on the tailboard of his cart, though some said the epithet had a more sinister significance. He came regularly out from Stokeley to tour the widely scattered fen cottages, offering for sale a variety of goods from clothes to trinkets to crockery, all to be paid for on an 'easy' instalment basis which made them the more tempting to folk who lived always on the margins of poverty. Hester limited herself to combs and beads, and once a bangle that produced a bright green stain on her wrist; but many women on the fen were inveigled into buying things on the tally that they could not afford, and this roused Mrs Langtoft to fury.

"Silly davils!" she snorted. "Putting theirselves in debt for a bit o' trumpery! They ain't got the sense they were born with. It meks my blood boil."

But the real reason she was so vigilant against Rob Risby was her husband. Mr Langtoft

19

was sadly susceptible to the tallyman. If Mrs Langtoft were the first to spot Risby's cart coming up the drove, all was well: she would go running out of the house, flapping and shooing as if he were some species of large despoiling bird, and crying: "You git away! You'll do no good here! We don't want no kickshaws!" But if for some reason she was not at hand, then Mr Langtoft was helpless, a fly to the tallyman's web.

"He's got me again, gel," Mr Langtoft would say to Hester, coming into the house bearing an umbrella, a shoe-tree, or a bed-valance with huge purple roses on it. "I dunno how it is. It's summat about the way he talks. I go all sort of weak-like."

It was not that Rob Risby dazzled him with patter: far from it. Hester watched and listened from the kitchen window one day, when Mrs Langtoft had gone to call on a sick neighbour (only a mile's walk), and the tallyman's cart drew up outside the yard where Mr Langtoft was working. She saw the farmer straighten up and frown, and then march up to the gate as if he were resolved to be firm.

"We don't want nothing off you," he said, in quite a stalwart voice. "So you're wasting your time, thanks all the same."

Rob Risby got down from the cart, throwing the reins over the pony's head. "Morning, Mr L. How're you keeping?"

"I'm all right enough," Mr Langtoft said suspiciously, keeping his hands on the latch

20

of the gate. "But like I say, we don't want nothing today."

The tallyman nodded. "Just as you say, Mr L. If you don't want nothink, you don't want nothink. I thought as I'd pass the time o' day, any road." He was a thin, hollow-chested, worn-looking man, with sparse pale hair, a feeble whisker, and a voice of reedy timbre that drooped off into a frequent sigh. "I won't deny I'm got a little trifle here as I thought you might want to look at, at least: I brought it out special on account o' you; but it don't matter."

"Why, what's that, then?" Mr Langtoft said, still gruff.

"We-ell," the tallyman said, with great reluctance, pulling a small parcel from his pocket, "it's rather a nice thing, you know; a pair of sewing scissors, very dainty, Sheffield steel, and in their own little case of morocco leather, with spaces an' all for needles. Soon as I saw it, I thought of Mrs L, her being such a smart needlewoman as everybody knows, and likely to appreciate such a thing, which there's not everybody would. I like things to go where they're appreciated, you see, and so I was even thinking of letting it go for two-and-sixpence, which is doing myself down summat chronic."

The little case was held out, negligently, and Hester saw a sort of paralysis creep over Mr Langtoft's face as he gazed at it. Then he seemed to rally, and shook his head. "No," he said stoutly, "not interested."

Rob Risby's forehead wrinkled in pain. "Have I made a mistake, d'you think, Mr L? Does it

seem a little shoddy? I try never to buy shoddy
— not that there's some who wouldn't notice
either way — but there's some folks whose
judgement I rely on — and I'd hate to think I'd
offered summat in the way of an insult — "

"No, no," Mr Langtoft said, uncomfortable
now, "I didn't mean that, you know. But — "
he bit his lip — "we can't afford it."

"Well, Mr L," Rob Risby said, "you're got
me. Two shillings it is."

"Eh — ?"

"Oh! I know it's worth more than that. But
I can't fight you, Mr L. You're too strong for
me, and thass a fact. You might as well tek it
for one and ninepence — " here the tallyman's
gloom deepened terribly, and he fetched a great
sigh — "and just kill my poor ole wife off
altogether."

This imputation of murderous designs against
Mrs Risby threw Mr Langtoft into alarm. "Why,
whatever do you mean?" he said. "What's the
matter?"

"It's the stomach, poor soul," Rob Risby said,
"it's always been her trouble, and this time . . . ."
and his weak voice faded completely.

Mr Langtoft, in a tone of dismay, hoped it
was not very bad?

"It *is* bad," the other said, judicially. "I wish
I could deny it. There's only certain foods as she
can tek at all. I says to her last night: Mother,
could you fancy a bit o' fish? I could, Robert,
she says — but we ain't got the money to buy
it, have we? And I had to say no. Ah, that
would be nice, she says, a bit o' fish — say

22

whiting, or hake, nothing fancy — and you know, Robert, I feel better just a-thinking on it. Thass a little harmless fancy we go through, you see, Mr L: sometimes we pretend kidneys, and sometimes we make-believe bacon — and so we bear up." He swallowed, and fixed his eyes on the distance.

"Well, now, look here," Mr Langtoft said, "I didn't say I wouldn't tek it for two shillings, you know."

"Now thass a funny thing. I says to my poor ole wife the smorning: Mother, bear up, I says, because I'm gooing to see Farmer Langtoft today, and if there's one man on the fen as has got a reputation for fair dealing, and sense, and recognising the value of independent tradesmen with a living to make, then he's that man." Rob Risby shook Mr Langtoft's hand, with an appearance of deep humility. In a moment the transaction was done, and Mr Langtoft was in possession of the scissors-case, and actually looking as if he felt he had come out of it rather well. The tallyman began to put up the tailboard of his cart; then paused, and turning back to the farmer with renewed dejection, took something else from his pocket.

"I don't suppose for a moment, Mr L," he said, "you'd consider investing in a couple o' these?"

"Smelling-salts?" Mr Langtoft laughed: he was confident again. "What would I want with them?"

The tallyman seemed to wince at the laughter, and shook his head. "Well! I promised our Nelly

I'd try. I can't do no more . . . I suppose it won't be long now."

This mention of Nelly threw Mr Langtoft again into discomfiture. "Why, who's Nelly?"

"Our youngest, Mr L. Sick abed now. It's the lights, you see. Rising. Mother reckons it's on account of how she were frightened by a balloon going up at Pete'borough Fair when she were carrying her. Anyhow, I'm afraid we shan't raise her. Oh! bless you, Mr L," he went on sympathetically, as Mr Langtoft showed great agitation of mind, "it's nothink as can't be cured. Don't think that. But it's a question of paying for the medicine, you see. Afore I come out the smorning, Nelly sat up in her little bed, leaning on one hand — the other hand was holding her doll, you see — leastways it's nearly a doll — it only lacks the head — and she makes shift to sort of imagine the head there, if you follow me — and so she bears up. There's a lot of imagination in our family, Mr L . . . if nothink else . . . She sat up, and she says to me, Daddy, shall you git the medicine today? And I says, not wishing to lie to her: Nelly, that depends on me mekking a bit o' money — and that all depends on the customers, you see. And she says, Daddy, why wun't them customers give you a bit o' money — are they very bad men? And I says no, Nelly — they ain't bad. I won't believe that of 'em . . . "

A few minutes later Mr Langtoft was standing, crestfallen, on the threshold of the kitchen. Besides the scissors-case and the smelling-salts, he was holding a cigar-box and something dusty

24

in felt and wool which he explained to Hester, dubiously, as a 'pen-wiper'.

"D'you think Bess'll be awk'ud with me?" he asked, without hope.

Hester, struggling to maintain an expression of the utmost seriousness, said she was afraid so.

"Beggared if I don't think he plays on me, that one," Mr Langtoft said. "Well, I s'll git a dusting-off for this." It was a curiously appropriate phrase, for Mr Langtoft being a loose, baggy, shapeless sort of man, and his grizzled hair and bedraggled moustache seeming to trap everything from corn-chaff to wood-shavings, he was a standing affront to the neat habits of his wife, who was unable to come near him without dusting him down, and plumping him up, and generally rearranging him.

At the scullery door Hester listened to Mrs Langtoft's lamentations on her return; and when Mr Langtoft made a despairing effort to justify the smelling-salts, saying they might rouse the old horse when he was sluggish of a morning, she had to cram her apron into her mouth to stop herself bursting out laughing. It was just then that a shadow fell across the doorway to the yard, and she saw Chad standing there.

"What you laughing at?" he said.

His expression was so mistrustful that she sobered a little. She explained.

"Oh! that," he said. He continued to stand in the doorway, tapping his muddied boots on the step, looking at her and not quite looking at her. Hester swallowed another laugh, and began to work the pump.

"Should you like it if somebody bought you things?" Chad said abruptly.

"I don't know — nobody ever has," Hester said.

"But would you though?" Chad said, in his dogged way.

"Well — not smelling-salts."

"Not smelling-salts. I don't mean nothink like that."

"Well, I should like it, of course," she said; but as she turned from the pump Chad was already gone.

She did not think anything of this at the time; nor did she recall the small indications of a shifting in Chad's manner during the last few months. They touched her consciousness like breath on glass, condensing and evaporating in a moment. There seemed nothing remarkable in the fact that he often appeared suspicious of her laughter, as if fearing it was directed at him. Chad had always been the slowest to laugh of the household, seldom sharing the high spirits of his younger brothers, moving quietly about the farm somewhat in a circuit of his own, and often inclined to be touchy. If she had been observant, she might have detected a note of intensity in what she took to be his normal silences and stares; his fastening, terrier-like, on the most trivial remarks and not letting them go. But to Hester's spontaneous nature was added the characteristic egotism of youth, which arranges other people into a mere concomitant pattern, like so many planets to the sun of self: and it was not until the long frost which began after

26

Christmas of her nineteenth year, that she was forced to review the pattern, and confront its disruption.

★ ★ ★

It was Uncle Bevis who started it.

He came out to the farm in his dashing little gig, on a bitter bright February morning, when there was cat-ice at the edges of the dykes, and the ploughed fields sparkled as if they had been sugared. Hester was in the kitchen boiling up pig-taters, and Mrs Langtoft was mixing the pudden, when they heard the smart clop of hooves and the crunch of wheels, followed by a familiar voice roaring out: "Whup, Chaddy, bor! Mind when you tek 'old on her — she's as lively as a cricket the smorning!"

Mrs Langtoft snatched off her hessian apron. "There's Uncle Bevis — pass me my clean apron, Hester gel — and goo and call in Wag and them boys. And fetch out the nodding-cake we made yis'dy — I'm sure Uncle Bevis will tek a slice."

It was notable that whilst the family were always at some pains to receive Uncle Bevis properly, none of them looked forward to his visits with much pleasure. He was a relation of Mrs Langtoft's, who had done well for himself as a butcher, and had a bay-windowed house in Stokeley, with its own set of railings. He liked to present himself in the character of a sportsman, and to speed off in his gig to the races at Huntingdon, and to clink tankards with horsey persons in the bar-parlours of inns hung with hunting-prints; and there was a hint of breezy condescension in his periodic descents on the Langtofts' farm to, as he put it, 'gee them up'. He had an apparent compulsion never to call anyone by their plain name, but always to lend it a jolly and, as it were, sporting aspect; and while 'Hester' had defeated him for a while, he had at last triumphantly modified it to Hetty — which made her want to scream every time.

But, he was a person of consequence: and so Hester called in Mr Langtoft and his sons, who were dyke-roding at a small distance from the house; and she was just fetching out the nodding-cake, a confection of pastry, sugar and currants of which Uncle Bevis was known to be fond, when Mrs Langtoft cried: "There! I knew I should ha' laid a fire in the Room. Goo and mek it up, Hester — there's turves enough."

The big, warm and cheerful kitchen was where the family lived: the Room was an icy parlour, a small square frigidarium where a row of upholstered chairs were preserved, as if they were of fresh composition, and liable to go off. But just then Uncle Bevis came in, stamping and blowing, and hallooed out: "No, no, Hetty, not for me! Don't trouble for me — a comfortable kitchen fire suits me — no pampering. Well, Bessy, and how do I find you?"

He was a big man, this uncle Bevis, made bigger by a suit of eye-catching check, with a great close-cropped ginger head, a fox-coloured moustache, plump red ears, hands like hams, and a substantial seat which he turned to the fire. Everything about him was large, ruddy, and obtrusive; and even when he was not talking, there was a continual noise about him, from the jingling of watch, watch-chain, seals, buttons, studs, and silver and copper money in all his pockets. He threw down his stiff bowler hat, which left a red weal round his forehead, and clapped his hands at the old dog lying in the corner. "Come here, then, Towser! Come here, you old davil!"

The dog (whose name was Dan, not Towser) tried to slink away, but was forced to submit to the jovial mauling that Uncle Bevis, who boasted of a way with animals, thought all dogs rejoiced in — just as all horses were to be heartily slapped, and cats picked up by the scruff with a facetious shout of 'Meow!' "Ha ha, you rascal!" he said, rolling Dan about on the floor, whilst the dog, who was gentle and not at all rascally, looked as if he wished he were elsewhere. "You would, would you? I know you, you davil."

The dog was saved at last by the entrance of Mr Langtoft and his sons. "Whup, Jakey! Whup, Billo!" Uncle Bevis cried, and proceeded to his usual greeting of the boys, which was to punch them on their upper arms, laughing the while, and making boxer's feints. "The old fellow keeps you at it, eh? No rest for the wicked — and they don't come much wickeder, I'll be bound. Eh?" For he considered he had a rapport with boys too; and after a further series of playful cuffs, head-butts, and shoulder-slappings, he squeezed his rump at last into the Windsor chair, and regaled them with accounts of fist-fights and ratting, until the tea was made.

"So, Waggy, and how do you get along?" Uncle Bevis said, between mouthfuls of nodding-cake.

"Not so very bad," Mr Langtoft said with caution. "But I wish this here frost would goo. It's the davil to plough, and there's gret old cracks forming in the dykesides."

"You're at the mercy of the elements — thass your trouble out here. Always fighting the elements. Thass what's good about setting up in town. Not that I couldn't put up with it here meself," Uncle Bevis added, for fear of seeming unmanly. "Why, I thrive on it — I can spend a day up to me knees in snow and think nothing of it — "

(Mr Langtoft stirred, as if he did not think much of it either.)

"It'd be no hardship for me — but there's my wife to consider." Uncle Bevis's wife was a shadowy figure, who never went out, but had headaches in a darkened room full of caged birds.

"And how do you go along, Uncle Bevis?" Mrs Langtoft said.

"I can't complain, Bessy — I can't complain," Uncle Bevis said, jingling excessively, and throwing out his stomach. "I'm thinking of setting up another gig — nothing fancy. Old Chancy Lowe, who keeps the livery stables, gives me a fair bargain. I wonder you don't trade in that old cart of yours, Wag, for summat a bit sprucer."

"I'm thought about it," said Mr Langtoft,

30

though he had not, "but it don't seem practical, with the droves the way they are in winter."

"True — true. But bless you, while there's a long frost there's skating — ain't you seen it? It's froz all across Milney Wash. I see a whole issue of folk skating there just yis'dy. Why, where's the point in living on the fen, without going skating? Chaddy, bor — " Chad had just come in from seeing to the pony — "you can skate a bit, can't you?"

"Ah," Chad said. "I ain't been this year, though. Don't seem to git time."

"You want to mek time — frost most likely wun't last much longer. What about you, Hetty? Ain't you ever skated?"

"No," Hester said. "I never learned." The peripatetic life with her father meant she had missed out on such things.

"Why, you can't call yourself a fenlander if you ain't skated," Uncle Bevis said. "I was a beggar for the skating-matches when I were a lad — maister used to box me ears for sloping off to 'em — 'cos, you know, I were only a 'prentice then: no bigger than Billo here — " here Will came in for a few more cuffs, and had his hair rubbed the wrong way — "and twice as skinny. I used to go to Bury Fen where the races were — and I remember tekking part once, and beating the chap who were reckoned to be champion — only they disqualified me, on account of I were too young."

"Perhaps you could teach me, then, Uncle Bevis," Hester said, not without mischief.

"Wehrr, I'd like to, gel, but I ain't kept it up

31

these last few years — my wife, you see, she reckons it ain't safe, so I left off for the sake of her nerves."

"I know I'm got an old pair o' skating-pattens what'd fit the gel, somewhere," Mrs Langtoft said. "We used to go when we were courting, Wag — d'you remember? — and you had to hold me up the whole time." She patted her husband's arm affectionately — for she was fond of him, albeit he was a useless article — and even with this gesture she was unable to resist giving him a prod and a dust, and rearranging his waistcoat.

"There you are then!" Uncle Bevis said. "Chaddy bor, you could teach Hetty here skating. Why, it puts Blood in you — there's no exercise like it!" And he made a pair of great fists, and performed a mime, expressive of skating into a head wind, at an unlikely speed.

"Ah, that'd be nice for you, gel," Mr Langtoft said. "You don't git a lot of outings. Should you like that?"

"All right, then," Hester said, for she was willing to try anything once.

"What d'you say, Chad?"

"I don't mind," Chad said.

"Let's see," Mr Langtoft said, "you could go tomorrer — "

"Not tomorrer!" Mrs Langtoft said, in a pouncing way. "Sunday tomorrer — not on a Sunday." For Mrs Langtoft, as was usual on the fen, was Chapel, and embraced that subtle interpretation of the Day of Rest, which precluded doing anything on it that might be

32

nicer than working. "Besides, we're got the preacher coming to dinner tomorrer. We're got a missioner coming all the way from Spalding to our chapel, Uncle Bevis, and it's our turn to give him dinner."

"That'll be a treat for him, Bessy, as ought to inspire him to highest eloquence," Uncle Bevis said; while Mr Langtoft looked at the fire, and seemed to suffer a temporary lowering of spirits. "But any road, what's against this evening? The moon's near full, and there'll be folk galore there, and bonfires on the ice, I shouldn't wonder."

There was nothing against that evening; and before Uncle Bevis left, he treated them to balletic demonstrations (on the kitchen floor) of how to bend the knees, and how to turn, and how to stop, and how to figure-of-eight — all of which manoeuvres apparently involved treading on people's toes, and elbowing them in the face. "Ah, you'll tek to it like a natural, gel!" he assured Hester; and having already punched the boys goodbye, he modified the gesture in deference to her sex in the usual way, by digging his hands in his pockets, and bumping her sideways, as if he were trying to break down a door.

"Poor ole lot — I reckon they wouldn't do nothing if I didn't goo and gee 'em up now and then," Uncle Bevis said to himself as he rattled away in his gig.

"Uppity ole fool — I bet he never skated in his life," Mr Langtoft said to himself as he went back to work.

★ ★ ★

Chad Langtoft was a fair-haired young man, with light eyebrows and eyelashes, and that fairness of skin that tends at times almost to a tender rawness, and on which a flush of embarrassment or anger shows up like blood on snow. His frame was a light, fine-boned one, though wiry and strong; and with pronounced cheekbones where the skin seemed thinner than ever, and very transparent blue eyes: altogether he gave the impression of lacking a layer somewhere, and of going too naked into the world.

Whether or not as a direct consequence of this, an extreme caution marked his manner. He would never give an opinion: 'I don't mind,' he would say: 'Whatever you like,' or ''S all right enough'; yet it was a kind of indifference that did not suggest equanimity or self-possession. It was almost, Hester thought, as if an opinion, a thought or a feeling were a secret thing, and might betray him if it were let out.

So it was no surprise to her when Chad said, that afternoon as they were getting ready to go skating: "You don't have to go if you don't want."

"No, I want to," she said. "I don't know how I shall get on, but I'll have a go. Don't you want to go?"

"Oh! I don't mind."

So as the afternoon darkened, she changed in her small attic room, putting on woollen stockings and a knitted scarf, which constituted

34

all her winter wear; and pinned her hat with a long silver pin, which had been sent to her as a present by her father a year or so ago. Since then he had faded further from sight: her sister and brothers were all earning their keep in Leicester, at shoe-factories, and living with Aunt Netty, while her father had disappeared north, apparently with some quixotic scheme of becoming a fellmonger, though he never could bear the sight of a dead animal. More and more her life before Langtoft's farm seemed like an incoherent dream, in which her own identity was as vague as a phantom. She looked at the plain little room and thought, 'I've been happy here': and at the same time the thought was flavoured with a little unaccustomed dissatisfaction — for to pass from a state of happiness, to an exterior perception of it, is to render it finite and conceive its end. Pessimism was no part of Hester's character, for the simple reason that she never thought of the future at all; but just for a moment, rather as she had done at that moment when she had said goodbye to her father at the corner of the drove, she glimpsed a large space about the contours of her life, and wondered how it was to be filled.

The sun was low when she and Chad walked to Milney Wash, traversing the bone-hard fields, and crossing the dykes by the narrow bridges made of railway sleepers. Chad, with a muffler added to his usual outfit of white duck trousers, jacket over sleeved waistcoat, and neckerchief, seemed sunk in a great shyness of her — as if they had not been living and working side by side for three years.

"Chad, what's Uncle Bevis's wife like?" she asked him, uncomfortable at the silence. "You ever seen her?"

"I'm seen her in Stokeley once," Chad said. "Not to speak to."

"It'd be funny if he were frit on her, though, wouldn't it? I mean, him mekking out he's so manly and all — it meks you wonder. I'll bet thass what it is. I bet when he gits home he has to knuckle under, and do everything she says, and she teks a broomstick to him."

It pleased her to find she had made Chad laugh: he looked better when he laughed.

"Father says there's a chap like that lives over at Forty Feet Bridge," he said. "Goes down the Labour In Vain and sups hisself silly and talks big all night 'bout how he's the master in his house and then when he gits home his wife's waiting for him wi' the coal-shovel."

It was a long speech for Chad, and again she was pleased at having drawn him out. "Shall you be master in your own house when you git married, Chad?"

His guard came up again. "How d'you mean?"

"Well . . . " She hadn't meant anything really. "You know — wear the trousers."

"Oh! I don't know."

It was a subject, in fact, on which she herself had views both decided and cloudy. Decided, because she was never going to call any man 'maister', as some women on the fen still referred to their husbands; and as far as

36

she could see, once it got to broomsticks and coal-shovels, you might as well give in and each go your ways. Cloudy, because at the core of her practical nature she was intensely romantic, and conceived of love as transforming prosaic reality, not merely overlapping it, and certainly not emerging from it.

The noise of exhilarated voices reached them before they were in sight of Milney Wash, such is the carrying power of sound on the fens; and when they arrived they found several score of people, skating on the expanse of water-meadow which was frozen to an even smoothness, lined here and there with cracks which showed that the ice would bear safely. The sun was close to the horizon, and in its declension had scored a great brazen trail in the sky, deepening to fiery orange where it traced the ribs of cloud, and shedding over the scene a biting metallic radiance. There was a pure cold suspension in the air, which seemed to lend its quality to visual perception, so that the very shadows on the ice were crystalline in their definition, and the figures of the skaters were outlined with an aura, like silhouettes beaten out of copper.

There were a lot of people there whom they knew, from the scattered cottages and the odd hamlets, scarcely rising to the status of villages, around the fen. On the edge of the field someone had lit a brazier and, dotted about on the ice, incongruously, were a few chairs, both for sitting on to fasten your skates and for beginners to hold on to. The sound of the skates, now deep and grumbling, now shrill, was exciting, and

37

Hester thought it looked very easy.

Her friend Lizzie Gosling, whose father kept the Hinching Fen mill, came gliding over as she was putting on her skates.

"Hester Verney — I'm never seen you skating before."

"I'm never done it before. Chad's going to teach me."

Lizzie Gosling was a plump, dark, deceptively sleepy-looking girl, with a pretty sceptical mouth, who could give such sharp answers that the boys did not quite know what to make of her. She blinked her heavy lids at Hester and then at Chad, and nearly-smiling as always said: "I shall have to see this. Didn't you bring a cushion to stick on your behind?"

"I'm sure I can do it if you can, you ole haybag," Hester said, in the affectionate terms which they always used with each other. "Come on, Chad. Let's show her."

She teetered upright and Chad took her hands crosswise. She went about a yard before she fell down.

"Graceful," Lizzie said, in her dry way. "Very pretty, that."

For some time after that Hester remembered only getting up and falling down, with a few wildly wobbling upright interludes. After the first few falls it ceased to hurt and, what with the relentless inevitability with which her bottom hit the ice, and the deadpan comments of Lizzie, she could not stop laughing.

"Go again," Chad said. "Try again."

"It looked so easy!" Hester said, and the

frost-smoky horizon wavered in her tears of laughter, and then swooped as she fell down again.

All around them other people were laughing as they slipped and overbalanced and collided; but Chad did not laugh. All the time he went doggedly on, skating with competent strokes, and helping her up; until at last she staggered, exhausted, to a chair.

"I reckon it's harder work than lifting taters!" she gasped, wiping her eyes. "Never mind Uncle Bevis's fancy turns — I can't even stand up!"

Chad crouched down, with his arms on his knees, his eyes on the other skaters.

"S'll we go home now, then?" he said after a moment.

She looked at him in surprise.

"Well," he said, seeming to study the composition of the ice at his feet, "if you're only going to laugh, and not do it properly."

"I can't help it," she said. "It don't matter, does it?"

"I don't like being laughed at, thass all."

"Chad, I weren't laughing at you! I was laughing because o' falling down." She did not know what to say to him: his hostility smote her like a wave. In the rich apricot rays of the setting sun, streaming level now across the ice, his cheeks were stinging red: while conversely, all colour seemed to have left his pale eyes.

"Evening to you, Hester. Evening to you, Chad."

The voice belonged to Henry Wake, who came skating over to them with his hands behind his back. He did this with great dignity, as befitted a man who was superintendent of the chapel Sunday School, and had no doubts that everyone shared his good opinion of himself.

"Not seen you here afore, Hester," Henry Wake said. "Correct me if I'm wrong."

"It's my first time," Hester said. "I'm not gitting on very well!"

"Ah, it'll come — it'll come. I think you'll find that you're keeping your feet too far apart. Bring 'em together as soon as you feel you git your balance, as it were. I think you'll find this is where you're going wrong." Henry was a man approaching forty, rather lacking in height and length of limb and breadth of shoulders, and with little sharp features curiously crammed in the middle of his face, so that there was something about him suggestive of the last loaf in the baker's oven, made with such dough as was left over. He was only an ordinary one-hoss farmer, but his work for the chapel and a smattering of education which made him talk, as folk said, like a newspaper, gave him at least in his own eyes a certain prominence on the fen. "Ain't that right, Chad? By-the-by, you'll be having the missioner for dinner at yourn tomorrer, I believe? Ah, I reckon he'll do us proud, this one. He's got a high reputation for a sermon, straight from the heart, as it were. He used to be the drunkenest man in Spalding — I think you'll find my information's correct on this point — till one day the spirit moved in him, and he were plucked as a brand from the burning. They say he wrestled with himself for two days

40

and a night, not excepting mealtimes. Now, Hester! Don't say you're give up already."

"No," Hester said, getting up. "I'm going to have another go. Come on, Chad. I want to try."

Chad, after a moment, took her hands again. She wobbled forward, trying to think of unhappy things so as not to laugh.

"That's the way," Henry Wake said. "I'd advise you to keep your head well forward — I'm been skating for thirty years, and I think I can speak with some authority on this point. Knees bent, knees bent!"

This time she kept her balance for some thirty yards, and all at once her legs seemed to stop their wild juddering and to relax. Chad swung her round in a wide arc, and then held her just by one hand as they glided back towards Henry Wake.

"I did it, I did it!" she cried.

"Better — much better," Henry said. "A word of advice from the right quarter, you see. If I might be allowed one more suggestion — as skating is summat I know about, as it happens, there's no point in pretending it's not — keep the back straight as you lean forward, and then I think you'll find you git on a lot better."

Lizzie Gosling rejoined them as Henry lifted his hat and skated away. "Yes, I saw you," she said, "wonders'll never cease. Henry giving you lessons, an' all."

"Oh, ole Henry Wake. It's Chad here who's taught me. Come on, Chad — let's go again."

She said this out of a simple desire to please

Chad, who had seemed hurt at her not trying, and also because she was beginning to enjoy it now. It seemed however to startle him, and to bury him in abstraction again, so much so that he lost his own balance and fell.

She went down with him, laughing. "There, now we're even," she said: and at last got him to laugh too.

"I can never tell whether you're mekking fun or not," he said, as they skated again.

"Well, you want to just mek fun of me back," she said.

He frowned. "I can't, though."

The sun had gone down. A crisp turquoise twilight hovered over the flat levels, and there was the first breath of wind, like the twanging of a great cold string in the air. They skated on for some time, as Hester's confidence grew. At last one of her skates needed oiling, and they went over to the brazier, where a man named 'Sunny' Daintree was mending and oiling skates for coppers. He was a molecatcher, and a gravedigger besides, and anything else he could turn his hand to, and was known as Sunny because of his gloomy disposition.

"Mekking a few bob, Sunny," Chad said.

"It's summat, I suppose," Sunny said. He was bald, pink, smooth, and ageless, like a cherub who had fallen and known great woe; and, incongruously, he had a chirping voice that seemed made for cheerfulness. "I can't see it lasting, meself."

"Think we're in for a thaw, then?" Hester said.

"It wouldn't surprise me," Sunny said.

"Well! it'll be nice to have a bit of warm weather, any road."

"I don't know." Sunny shook his head. "Last time I remember a frost like this, there was terrible flood after it. You couldn't go to bed for fear of waking up drowned. It wouldn't surprise me if that happened again. I wouldn't be a bit surprised." He turned the skating-patten over in his seamed hands, as if it were a poignant relic prompting reflections too deep for tears. "Well, thass the best I can do wi' that."

It was quite late when they made ready to go home at last, and stars, like small chips of frost themselves, were breaking out in the sky. They walked slowly back across the fields. The exercise, the tension and relaxation, the pure cold air, had left Hester feeling both tired and exhilarated; and when she remembered that tomorrow the preacher was coming to dinner, she exclaimed aloud in sudden despondency.

"It's always so stiff," she said. "I hate sitting all stiff and formal like that." The members of the chapel took turns in having the travelling preachers to dinner, and it was a great event in the Langtoft household, marked with unaccustomed formality. While it was this that chiefly repelled Hester, she was also something of an unregenerate spiritually. If she would not exactly go so far as to say all religion was just cant and hypocrisy — her particular hates — it was only because Mrs Langtoft was devout, and she liked Mrs Langtoft. It was typical of her to thus make the personal the arbiter of her judgements. "After all, the preacher's only an ordinary chap like anybody else," said she. "Thass the point of going to chapel and not church, ain't it?"

"Well," Chad said, "you'd never have the vicar to dinner, anyway."

"Thass true," she said. Nobody, saint or sinner, liked the vicar of the scattered parish, who lived in a big house on the edge of the upland, and always spoke to you as if he were breaking bad news to an exceptionally dim-witted foreigner. "Do you believe in it all, though, Chad? You know — when they go on about the flames burning for ever more, and how we're all going down there, every one on us, unless we repent."

"Yes," Chad said, with unusual promptness and conviction. "I believe it."

"What, even if we're just sort of ordinary sinners — you know, haven't done any murders or thievings — just swearing and missing chapel and things like that?"

"I believe it," Chad said again. And then, shortly: "It's what's in your head."

She thought of what had been in her head lately that might consign her to the flames: wishing nosey old Mrs Onyett who had called her flighty would fall in the dyke, envying Lizzie Gosling that lace-fronted blouse that would look so much better on her, watching with interest that handsome young carter stripping himself down to wash at the pump . . . Well, after all, if you couldn't call your thoughts your own . . .

"You did enjoy it, didn't you?" Chad said.

"Enjoy what?" she said, with a guilty start.

"The skating. It was good, weren't it?"

"Oh! yes. It was lovely. Mind you, I shall have a few bruises in the morning where I shan't be able to see 'em. Shall we go again?"

"If you like," he said. "If you want to. I mean, you did enjoy it, didn't you?"

"Course I did."

"Good. We'll go again some time then. If you'd like to."

He was an odd one, she thought: she would have to tell Lizzie about this. But she had a suspicion of what Lizzie, in her dry way, would say. She would say Chad was sweet on her; and at the same time she remembered the glances in the milk-pan, the silences . . . But Chad? — Chad who had scarcely ever spoken to her, who had barely paid more attention to her than to any other fixture of the farm? She disbelieved it, and was obscurely flattered in the same moment.

Hester at this time had two trivial characteristics that were yet indicative of much: she could fall fast asleep in a matter of seconds in any place and at any time of the day, and she could dismiss an uncomfortable thought from her mind and genuinely forget about it. The latter was a kind of mental double-jointedness, and she exercised it now, as she walked down the drove with Chad. It was an ability that a worrier might have sorely envied; and it had never occurred to Hester that it might be anything but an unmixed blessing.

★ ★ ★

A bird's-eye view of Hinching Fen on Sunday morning would have disclosed a multitude of little processions, marching out from cottages and along droves, and all appearing to converge on an insignificant little brick building fronting the high road that crossed the flat land like a line drawn on a map. A short flight away, north and south, the same bird might have observed the sublime ruins of two great abbeys, which (supposing the bird to have been alive to such impressions) rendered the brick building even more insignificant, and its attraction more inexplicable.

To the people of Hinching Fen, however, the Wesleyan chapel was 'their' place. It was on a manageable and human scale; and in that landscape, where there were no hills, not many animals, few trees, and fewer houses, the human figure bulked large and important in the unobstructed view, and was genuinely the measure of all things. An experience familiar to fen-dwellers on foggy days was the apparent spectacle of giants walking towards them across the fields: an optical illusion in which a person of normal stature appeared to loom hugely, by some strange distortion of perspective produced by the misty air and the level distances. But it was a distortion appropriate to life on the fen, and to that intensely individual character perhaps expressed by Andrew Surfleet, the oldest man in Hinching Fen (and some said the silliest), when he described his one visit to

Cambridge thus: 'Ah, I couldn't abide it, bor. There was so many people I couldn't look at 'em all.'

The opportunity it presented for having a good look at each other was, of course, one of the secondary attractions of the chapel. Turn-outs were impeccable. Dresses spoke of the tremendous labour of flat-irons heated on turf fires: children looked as unhappy as only stiff collars and tight boots could make them; and about the heads of the men there was a sort of a general righteous ache of hard hats pressed down like lids on oiled hair. And busying himself everywhere was Henry Wake, nodding, greeting, patting children's heads, and drawing attention — by means of coughing and rubbing it with his handkerchief — to the brilliance of the brass pulpit rail, which he had spent the morning polishing.

Mrs Langtoft too had been devout since dawn, and through breakfast had practised hymns in her ardent contralto: it was odd to hear that sturdy bright little woman asserting, as she raked out the oven, that she Thirsted, she Pined, and she Died. But when the chapel congregation threw themselves into the hymns, it was always old Andrew Surfleet whose voice could be heard lifted in a quavering falsetto above everybody else. He was an ancient peering pippin of a man, with an innocent dewy face framed by a white beard, and, as the saying went, not much oil in his lamp; but he dearly loved a good sing, and he allowed for his shortness of breath by a novel system of punctuation. "'Hide me. O.

My Saviour. Hide. Till the. Storm of. Life is past.'"

Hester, even with her ability to fall asleep virtually at will, had been thwarted at first by the hardness and uprightness of the pine pews, and by one's extreme visibility; but she had evolved a method whereby, when the time for the sermon came, she placed her chin on her chest and clasped her hands as if she were absorbed in the profoundest spiritual meditations, and was thus able to snooze quite comfortably. On this occasion, however, the sight of the visiting preacher arrested her. He was an elderly man with a dead white face, black eyebrows, a sharp red nose, and gappy teeth, so that on looking up at the pulpit she had the bizarre impression of being harangued by a snowman. But what was most transfixing about him was the way he could not keep still. It was plainly true, as Henry Wake had said, that this reformed sinner had once been the drunkenest man in Spalding; and if salvation had sobered him, set his feet upon a rock, and washed him in the blood of the Lamb, it had done nothing for his DTs. His hands did not simply tremble. They were a blur. When he gave the psalm the Bible capered in his fingers as if it were alive, and nearly went flying over the pulpit on to Henry Wake's reverent head. Hester knew she was done for if she did not control herself now: she took a pin from the collar of her blouse and prepared to jab herself with it if the laughter threatened to burst out.

The sermon, without notes and straight from the heart just the way folk liked them, contained the expected references to the preacher's former iniquities. "I were a boozer," the preacher cried. "I testify to it. I looked on the wine when it was red, I were a brawler, I were raging. I did reel to and fro, and stagger like a drunken man, which I was, and I lifted up my hand against my old woman, and I did clobber her. And I dwelled in the tents of wickedness." He was able now to steady his hands on the edges of the pulpit; but this did nothing to moderate the twitching, the convulsive wink, the ticking cheek, and a motion of the head as if he were continually seeing something startling over his left shoulder. "The heat of the flames was already on me, and the fiend's hands were already clawin' hold of me. And the heat of them flames is terrible, the heat of them flames is like a burning fiery furnace, like the burning fiery furnace where them three men were thrown, in the Book of Daniel. And them three were Shad-hat, Meese-hat, and a Dibnibo."

Hester jabbed the pin in her finger, while to her right an expression of perplexity formed on Mr Langtoft's face. The preacher himself hesitated, but then casting his wandering eye over the heads of the congregation, and perhaps fortified by the pervasive atmosphere of Hats around him, repeated the names. "Shad-hat, Meese-hat, and a Dibnibo. And what happened to Shad-hat, Meese-hat, and a Dibnibo, when they was chucked in the burning fiery furnace? Did they burn? Did they swelter, and roast, and frizzle? No. They was saved."

"Ah!" said Andrew Surfleet, who was given to

49

pious interjections, though sometimes they were only twinges of rheumatism.

"And why was Shad-hat, Meese-hat, and a Dibnibo saved? Because they served the Lord, thass why. And can you say the same, all on yer? When the time comes, shall you be saved like Shad-hat, Meese-hat, and a Dibnibo, or will the flames tek you, and burn you up to ashes, except they won't, see, cos you'll just go on burning for ever, and never gitting any less?"

"Ah!" said Andrew Surfleet again, rather uncertainly; and began chewing his beard.

"There's only one way," the preacher said, fixing them, as far as he was able, with a steady gaze. "There's only one way to avoid the flames what's waiting for you. There's only one way to be saved, I tell yer. And that is — " he stretched out his arms, and in a paroxysm of shakes reached his peroration — "*to put yourself in the safe hands of the Lord.*"

Hester stuck the pin in her finger till it drew blood, and managed to convert the yelp into an "Amen!" that made Mrs Langtoft smile on her, and think the spirit had moved in that heathen girl at last.

★ ★ ★

The preacher was not a man for small talk. He came stumping back to the farm in a stern silence, as if still brooding on the word of the Lord. Mr Langtoft, in his friendly way, inquired of him: "Had much snow over Spalding this year?"

50

"There wun't be no snow in the next world, brother," the preacher said, knitting his black brows. "Nor ice neither, nor hail . . . Nor slush," he added grimly.

"There now!" Mrs Langtoft said with satisfaction, and seemed to think so poorly of her husband for lowering the uplifted tone, that she dusted him down in quite a bitter manner.

After that Mr Langtoft's spirits visibly sank. He was a temperate man, and preferred to take his religion in moderation. He was well aware that his wife preferred it in stronger doses: but he did not mind that, as long as it stayed in the chapel and did not come home with them. The preacher, however, had other ideas. He was fired up with salvation; and in expressing it, he still had all the boozer's belligerence.

They sat down to dinner — pudden first, meat after, in the old fen way — and Mr Langtoft had just picked up his knife and fork when the preacher burst with a groan into a long extempore Grace.

"Look down on us, Lord, seated at this board all set about wi' food and the fruits of the earth what come from out of your bounty and what we don't deserve, none on us, poor wretched sinners, full as we are of fancies, and greed and sloth and worldliness, and thinkin' on our stomachs instead of your blessed mercy . . . "

It was perhaps an unfortunate chance that the preacher was seated directly opposite Mr Langtoft, so that the prayers seemed to have him as their especial object. Certainly Mr

51

Langtoft appeared disconcerted at this great volley of sinfulness coming straight at him, especially when his own stomach, stimulated by the smell of pork, gave a great growl.

The Amen came at last, when even Mrs Langtoft had begun to reach out a finger to see if the pudden were still hot; and after that things went better for a time. The preacher was fully occupied with his knife and fork, which in his unsteady hands made a clashing like a fencing-match, and then with getting the food to his mouth without that recurring urge to look over his shoulder. Mrs Langtoft said what a nice job Henry Wake had made of the chapel, and Hester chipped in with a remark about Henry Wake's old horse not having the farcy after all, and gradually the conversation seemed to be moving away from the holy at last; when all of a sudden the preacher, facing Mr Langtoft, and with the righteous light in his sunken eyes, exclaimed:

"Do you know what it's like to have Nails driven through your hands and feet?"

Mr Langtoft hastily swallowed a lump of pudden. "Well," he said with an air of being helpful, "I got a tin-tack in me thumb once."

This was clearly not the right answer, and Mr Langtoft intercepted a crushing glare from his wife.

"Our Lord knew them pains," the preacher said.

"Ah, so He did, so He did!" sighed Mrs Langtoft.

She and Hester began to clear the plates, and

Hester went to draw the pork and the tater-net out of the pot.

"That was for us He bore them pains," the preacher continued, while they dished up. "And do we care!"

"Hark at him!" Mrs Langtoft said to Hester in an admiring undertone.

The addition of gravy to the meal was unfortunate. Jacob and Will, seated on either side of the preacher, came in for most of his. Jacob, a stoic at fifteen, carried on gravely eating in spite of the brown rain showering on him, but Will, the youngest, began to look more discontented at each splash, and seemed about to protest when the preacher paused again, and demanded,

"Have you ever had a Spear thrust in your side?"

Mr Langtoft, who could hardly have been expected to suffer such a mishap, still looked uncomfortable at the omission.

"Our Lord did," the preacher said, exhibiting mashed greens between his teeth. "He knew what it were like. But do we care? Do we think on it? No! We laugh, we carouse, we frolic about, and kick up our heels!"

Mr Langtoft looked as guilty as if he had been doing all those things at that very moment.

"And what about the scourging! Think o' that! The laying on of whips!"

"Well, after all," Hester said, with some idea of protecting Mr Langtoft, "you can't be thinking of such things all the time. It ain't natural."

53

Across the table Chad lifted his eyes to her in surprise at her daring.

"Ah! I was such a one as you once, my gel," the preacher cried. "I was defiled with my own works, and went a-whoring with my own inventions. I warn you. You'll be chastised with scorpions."

"Why, I don't even know what a scorpion looks like," Hester said.

"Summat like a spider, I reckon," Mr Langtoft said. "With a sting."

The preacher's eloquence, thus challenged, seemed to falter. He applied himself to his dinner, contenting himself with a truculent stare all round the table at intervals, until his plate was clean: and when Mr Langtoft mildly inquired if he would take a little more pork, the preacher stood up and intoned: "Be not tempted to gluttony, that meks us like the beasts of the field. Thank you, Lord, for the meat we have et, the pudden likewise, what you give to us, and look wi' mercy on them among us as mocks and blasphemes, and dances among the wash-pots, and save 'em from the wrath to come."

"Won't you stay for a drop o' tea?" Mrs Langtoft said.

"I'm got a long walk ahead of me, on the Lord's business," the preacher said; and picking up his hat, and getting it on by making a sort of dive into it head first, he marched to the door.

"You're got a nerve, answering the preacher back," Chad said, while Hester cleared away, and Mr and Mrs Langtoft saw the visitor out.

"Me? I reckon it's him as has got a nerve,"

she said indignantly. "He never said a word of thanks — giving it all to God — it were me and your mother as cooked it. Wash-pots and scorpions, I never heard such stuff."

Mrs Langtoft was full of praise for the preacher, and shook her head at Hester's obduracy. "Do you better to tek some of his words to heart, my gel," she said, "stead o' fleering. You'll know — it'll come home to you!" But Mr Langtoft sat himself down by the fire, and lit his short 'nose-warmer' pipe, and looked relieved to be contemplating flames of an earthly nature.

Sunday or no Sunday, there were still chores to be done; and after washing up in the scullery, Hester went out to feed and water the hens. Crossing the yard back to the house, she found Chad standing there, holding up his hands and looking at the sky.

"It's raining," he said.

"Oh! so it is," she said. Murky, mud-coloured cloud stretched from horizon to horizon. Chad's eyes were baleful. "What's the matter?" she said.

"Can't you feel it?" he said. "Temperature's gone right up."

She noticed it for the first time. "Well, old Sunny Daintree was right then — it is a thaw. About time too."

"Don't you see?" Chad said. "The ice on the washes'll be melting. There won't be no more skating."

"Oh! of course," she said. "What a shame. I was just getting on, as well."

Chad's face was almost tragic as he stared at the lowering sky. "I can't believe it. I were so looking forward to it."

"Still," she said, wishing to cheer him up, "shows it's spring. There's Stokeley Fair at Easter — there's something to look forward to."

"Will you go to Stokeley Fair with me, then?" he said, quickly.

He looked so miserable over the loss of the skating, that she said promptly, "All right, Chad. Thank you for asking me."

"You sure? It don't matter. You needn't, if you don't want."

The gloaming light showed her his face now withdrawn in the old indifference. It was the face of a man who doubts himself, even as he mistrusts others. For a moment she wondered if she were doing the right thing; but then after all, she thought, it was a pity about the skating.

"Stokeley Fair," she said.

3

THE thaw that set in marked the end of that winter, and the flood-waters where skaters had laughed and shrieked rang again with the honking voices of wild geese. The cessation of frost meant the beginning of the turf-digging season; and Chad Langtoft, like other young men wishing to do a little work on his own account, hired a half-acre of peat land, and began to stake it out and prepare it. Turf-digging — the digging out of rectangular blocks of peat to sell as fuel for cottage fires — was an occupation that many old men in the fen had pursued seasonally all their lives, with the result that some of them were permanently bent double, and never saw the sun unless they lay on their ruined backs like beetles. Chad, as a beginner, consulted old Andrew Surfleet as to the best methods; and he was full of his plans, which he confided to Hester.

"I reckon to get a hundred thousand turf out of that plot," he said. "Thass what I reckon. Prob'ly I shall only manage five hundred a day to start with — while I git my hand in, like."

He went over these computations endlessly. Rambling down these paths of arithmetic, he lost his inarticulacy with her. "Git up to a thousand a day, mebbe, when I git used to it. Reckon to git about seven bob a thousand nowadays. Course, there's the cost of boating them away. Thass about two-and-six a thousand." He became entangled in his calculations, until it was just as if he were talking to himself. But he was not: he was talking to her, and it seemed that it was only in terms of such abstractions that he could do so freely. The exception was the subject of Stokeley Fair, which he brought up regularly yet always with a great show of nonchalance.

"We still going to Stokeley Fair, are we?" he would say, in the middle of some task about the farm, as if it had just happened to occur to him.

"Oh! yes. Well, unless you're thinking of tekking somebody else."

But it was impossible to rally him like that. He was too serious; and when she spoke there was something dog-like in the way he hung on her words, though the suggestion was of a dog more cowed than docile.

It was not easy for Hester to comprehend him, though she tried. Always there was about him an uneasy coolness: a dull turmoil. His was one of those natures which are slow to commit themselves, but once committed, fasten like a badger's jaws.

And so while his attentiveness to her was obvious it was also, as it were, not obvious at all: it expressed itself merely in an intensification of his guarded manner. Anyone else might have noticed nothing — which provided her with an excuse (which she was very willing to take) for not thinking about it. They were only going to Stokeley Fair together; and she easily succeeded in convincing herself that he contemplated this as casually as she did.

In truth Hester did not know what she felt. Her father, the higgler, had been notorious for his tendency to take his cart round ten miles in pursuit of some chimerical job involving cut-glass rather than go a mile down the road and pick up some beer-barrels: and she was so far her father's daughter in that, for all her dislike of effort, she would often make the most laborious mental detour to arrive at what she wanted to think, rather than take two steps to the unlovely truth. When the day of Stokeley Fair came, and they set out across the fields, she was aware that plenty of girls on the fen would have been well pleased to consider themselves as in a position to make a catch of Chad Langtoft, even as she felt a little weariness at his beginning to talk again of his plans for the turf-digging; but she kept these two thoughts separate.

It was windy as they walked. The wind here was part of the landscape, as physical as earth: it was possible, turning out of it, to lean on it for a moment like a shooting-stick. The sails of the Hinching Fen mill, black on the skyline, were whirling round as if to outrace the coasting clouds. They passed a group of men dyke-digging, in long stout boots and 'slops', the old-fashioned smocks still to be seen in the world of the railway and the telephone as they had been in that of the stagecoach; and Hester felt that special pleasure of going on a jaunt when others are working. (Mr and Mrs Langtoft were to follow with the boys later: when Will had demanded why they couldn't all go together, his mother had shushed him.) Without need for words they gave a wide berth to the ruins of a farmhouse that had burned down: one of the 'haunts' with which the fens abounded had been seen there, a ghostly horse running in circles. Hester, if you had asked her whether she believed in ghosts, would have said no, but there was no point in looking for trouble.

The chief business of the fair, the buying and selling of stock and seed and tools, and the hiring of labour, had been disposed of earlier in the day; and when Hester and Chad arrived in Stokeley a mass of side-shows, stalls and entertainments had taken possession of the High Street. The great width of this thoroughfare, sufficient for a Parisian boulevard and given an even more expansive aspect by the river running alongside it, bore testimony as eloquent as that of the pure picked bones of the Abbey to the fact that Stokeley was a decayed place. From the days when it had stood as a wealthy island above the drowned fens, and been reckoned with in the counsels of kings, it had undergone a kind of reverse historical process, settling down at last as a pottering market town of a few thousand souls, and consoling itself, perhaps, with the reflection that its name was writ large on maps of the realm when Birmingham and Manchester were blank spaces on the parchment.

"Hey-up there, Chaddy bor! Halloo, Hetty gel!"

A bright check suit, with Uncle Bevis inside it, emerged from the crowd. Laughing like a fusillade of blanks, he slapped a meaty hand on Chad's neck and shook him from side to side, and then butted Hester like a shunting-engine. "So, they let you come off that ole fen for a change, eh? Well, what do you think of it?" — this with a smirking modesty, as if the fair were all his own work. "Not a bad show this year, though it's all a bit prettified for my taste. Now in my young days, we used to git a lot of real Romany folk, and they were Rousers. Why, you couldn't call it a proper do till the stallholders had had a free-for-all on the last night. Broken heads ten a penny — you thought nothing of it. There were one Terror name o'Mealy Jack who could pick up a cart on his own and chuck it in the river — I'm seen him do it. I tell you what though — " he took hold of Chad by the waistcoat — "you want to come over the boxing-booth, bor — there's a lad there from Pondersbridge tekking 'em all on. Very smart little fighter — sharp, very sharp." He danced about on his toes, like a frisky carthorse. "Course, it's nowt to the boxing we used to get up to in my day — a fight were a fight then, and I'm had blood pouring out my nose an hour at a time and thought nothing of it. Still, it's worth a look."

"No, ta, Uncle," Chad said with discomfort. "We're got other things to see."

"Ah, goo on! You'll mebbe see him git beat."

"Why don't you tek the lad on yourself, Uncle Bevis?" Hester said.

"Wehrr, I wouldn't mind, gel," Uncle Bevis said. "Matter of fact there's nothing I'd like better. Only there's my wife's nerves to consider, see, and I don't reckon they'd bear it if she knew I'd been boxing and up to me old tricks."

"Well, we wouldn't tell her, would we, Chad?" Hester said.

"Aah, ha ha ha!" Uncle Bevis went on laughing for an unnecessary time. "Wehrr, it'd git back to her though, in a town like this, you know — where everybody knows me. Ah well, I'll leave you to it, then."

"Phew, I'm glad you got rid of him," Chad said.

"Wehrr," Hester said in Uncle Bevis's accents, "we didn't want to go and watch some silly beggars knocking each other about, did we, Chaddy bor? Let's git some whelks."

They made the tour of the stalls, and Hester followed up the whelks with peppermint twist and then hot peas — "she's got cast-iron guts, that gel!" was a frequent exclamation of Mrs Langtoft's. Chad hovered at her side with his peculiar, soft, cat-footed gait, continually solicitous, in his brusque, uneasy way, about what she wanted to do. It was nice, after all, to be made a fuss of, Hester thought: even though Chad's attention seemed more possessive than considerate. They had a go at the Aunt Sally, and the coconut shy, and went into booths to see a waxwork of the beheading of Anne Boleyn watched by a cheerfully smiling Henry VIII, and a peepshow rather ambitiously representing the Charge of the Light Bridgade with the horses running like greyhounds, and seeming to have too many legs. The greatest attraction was a tent where a phonograph was to be heard, and outside this they met Henry Wake and Andrew Surfleet.

"Quite a remarkable invention, that," Henry Wake said urbanely, tipping his hat to Hester. "Simple enough once you understand its principles, mind you — but our friend here was quite shook up by it."

Old Andrew Surfleet, dressed in his best outfit of half-high hat, red neckercher, and shiny trousers with the gusset somewhere around his knees, shook his head and chewed a few snowy strands of beard. "Well, I thought it were some sort o' trick at first, like when I went to see the hoss with its head where its tail should be, and all it was was an ordinary hoss standing with its arse to the manger," he said. "Then when I found it weren't a trick, and that voice were really coming out of summat like a sewing-machine, I felt a bit peculiar. I wun't deny my hand went to my fairy-stone, sort of without thinking." Some old fen people still carried holed stones called fairy-stones, as a protection against witchcraft. "Still, I don't feel so bad now Enry's explained it to me."

Henry Wake fairly beamed condescension. It was a great satisfaction to him, Hester thought, to know someone like Andrew Surfleet, who some said was so daft he'd stick his head out of the window to see if it was daylight, and who believed whatever Henry told him. "Yes, I'm got a certain grasp of these things," Henry said, "don't know why, just one of them matters I happen to understand pretty well. It's the 'lectric that accounts for it, you see — thass the elementary principle you have to bear in mind — the 'lectric. I think you'll find I'm correct."

"The 'lectric, you see," Andrew Surfleet repeated. "I wouldn't ha' thought of that."

"Why, where's the electric come from, then?" Chad said doubtfully.

"Oh! it's conducted, you know," Henry Wake said. "Conducted. I can't really go into more detail than that just now."

They went into the tent, and heard from the machine an excruciating soprano voice intoning 'Twinkle Twinkle Little Star'.

"There weren't no electric there!" Hester said; but when they came out Henry and Andrew had moved on.

"He'll say anything, that Henry Wake," Chad said. "Down the Labour In Vain one night some chaps got a dead sparrer and painted it all wi' blue paint and then showed it to Henry and asks him if he's ever seen one of them before. 'Ah,' he says, 'I'm seen them flying about Holme Woods, and they're called sky-blue warblers.'"

Then Hester saw a fortune-telling booth, and wanted to go in.

"I dunno," Chad said. "Mother reckons it's heathen."

"Only if you believe in it. Come on."

An old man with a shock of white hair and silver earrings read her palm, his jaws working and munching. Suddenly he made a noise like a pot boiling over. "Tssss! You're going to cross some water."

It was impossible to go more than a couple

of miles across the fens without crossing water, but she let that pass.

"There's fortune coming."

"Good fortune?"

"Tssss!" He ran his finger round the heel of her hand. "There's a journey — quite soon. There's money, plenty of it. There's gold, and long life. But you'll wear an eelskin wedden ring, gel."

"Oh, I want to do better'n that!" she laughed. There were still older women on the fen who wore wedding rings made of a coil of dried eelskin, their husbands having been too poor to afford a real one.

"Eelskin wedden ring," the old man repeated. "You'll wait for gold."

"Oh! well. Chad, you have a go."

"No, not me," Chad said, in his most cumbrous way, flushing. "I don't want to know."

"It's only for fun," she said as they left the tent: though the circumstance of the eelskin wedding ring had made a deeper impression on her mind than she pretended. Hester was as little acquisitive as it was possible for a person to be: her imagination was kindled not by the prospect of gold or otherwise, but by the sheer tantalising mystery of her future, and the shapes, fair and foul, that might be waiting there. "Don't you wonder how your life'll go, Chad?"

"I don't want to know. Leave it dark," Chad said.

"So there you are, you two!" Lizzie Gosling appeared, and gave them both one of her

65

long, searching, I-could-say-something-but-I-won't looks. "Where you been hiding yourselves?"

"Well away from you, you ole fishwife," Hester said. "Couldn't you git nobody to bring you, then?"

"I'm here with my brother," Lizzie said. "He's in the dancing-booth. Ain't you been in there? You want to come and see — there's Sunny Daintree having a dance."

The dancing-booth was a long tent of striped orange canvas, which filtered the light of late afternoon, so that the interior swam in a warm haze resembling the dim congealed atmosphere of dreams, thickened further by clouds of sawdust rising from the boards that formed the dancing-floor. A fiddle and concertina provided the music which was just audible over the stamping of the dancers and the clapping of the spectators, gathered in narrow aisles on either side of the floor; and standing atop an upturned barrel an old man called out the steps in the nasal carrying voice of a cattle auctioneer. The dancers were a very mixed set: here was a flash of beauty in eye or lip, there a glimpse of grace transforming plainness, and on all sides an enthusiasm and pleasure atoning for the absence of either; youth danced beside age, and girth and leanness trod the same measure. But even in such a harmonising of incongruities the figure of Sunny Daintree was conspicuous. It was often observed, apropos of his bow legs, that he would not stop a pig in a passage; but more remarkable than that was his utterly doleful expression even as he turned, skipped, and pranced to the Cross-Hand Polka, his round face a lugubrious moon in the laughing half-light.

The concertina shimmered a last chord: the dancers dispersed. "Step up," cried the old man on the barrel. "Step up and tek your partners for Speed the Plough."

Hester turned to find Chad edging away: some of his friends were calling to him from the other side of the tent.

"I just got to say hello to them ole boys," he said.

"Don't you want to dance?"

"Oh! I can't dance. You do it — you go on."

It was twopence to go on the floor. Hester did not lack for partners, and she even had a turn with Sunny Daintree, to 'Toast to King Gustav.'

"I never knew you liked dancing, Sunny," she said as they bowed to each other.

Sunny sighed deeply.

"I can't abide it," he said, whirling her round.

Out of breath at last, she rejoined the spectators. Chad was still with his friends; but she noticed how he seemed to just inhabit the edge of their circle, and whenever they broke out in laughter he was always the last to join in, as if he first sought to reassure himself that the laugh was not against him.

Lizzie Gosling was at her side. "Fell out already?" she said.

"Don't be daft."

Lizzie's face teemed with irony. "It's not anything serious, then?"

"How do you mean?"

"Well, you coming to the fair with Chad. I mean, there's nothing in it, is there?" And before Hester could answer she added, "I didn't think so. Not you and Chad. Mary-Ann Cole was saying the other day how she's fishing for Chad — reckoned she wouldn't need more'n a twitch to land him."

"Mary-Ann Cole!" Hester said. "Her! She's got a face like a hoss looking over a gate."

Lizzie was all dark glinting amusement at this. "True; but if there ain't nothing in it, why should that bother you?"

"I didn't say there weren't nothing in it — I never said that," Hester said, finding herself thus in a position she had not intended, and, typically, deciding she might as well stay in it.

At that moment Chad came over. As he left his friends, one said, "Going to dance, then, Chad?" and another, with a whoop of laughter: "Chad, he can't dance to save his life!" It was an ordinary enough piece of banter, but Chad's whole face and neck flamed in a moment.

"Come on Chad — got twopence?" Hester said, taking his arm. "We're not had a dance yet. You taught me skating — I'm sure I can teach you dancing — thass much easier." She was not given to analysing her impulses, and a generous wish to save Chad's face was so much the chief constituent of this one, that the minor ingredient of putting the absent Mary-Ann in her place was scarcely detectable, at least by herself.

"Choose yer partners!" called the old man on the barrel.

His eyes fixed on her with a sort of morose struggle, Chad said: "I'm no good at this"; but he went unresisting on to the floor with her.

"Just do what I do," she said, and all through the dance, which he managed no worse than anyone else there, his eyes remained riveted on her, just as if they were balancing on some terrible height, and he would be lost if he looked down.

For her part Hester liked to dance, enjoyed the music, and was lifted — by the holiday and by the tent's orange glow that made of the figures of the dancers something strange and visionary — into a mood of inclusive warmth: if she had ever been drunk she would have recognised the sensation.

One dance was enough for Chad; and she was hot and thirsty. They left the dancing-booth, and she refreshed herself at a lemonade stall. The westering sun was firing the roofs of the little town, but the fair was still crowded with people, some having just arrived after long walks from remote places on the fen: the smell of paraffin from oil-lamps joined the medley of fish, gingerbread, calliope-steam, liquorice and manure. They saw Henry Wake and Andrew Surfleet again, at a thimble-rigger's stall; and Henry Wake turned to them and shrugged.

"I wish you'd help me persuade him," Henry said. "He's lost near two shilling already."

The thimble-rigger's equipment consisted of three tiny cups and a dried pea: after switching the cups around with an apparent negligent slowness he invited Andrew Surfleet again to select which of the cups the pea lurked under. "You're been watching pretty close, granfer," he said, "I reckon you're got it this time."

Old Andrew gazed long at each cup, tasting his beard. "Why," he said, putting his money down, "thass got to be the one."

The thimble-rigger whipped off the cups. "Ah, hard luck, granfer — I thought you'd got me."

Henry Wake clucked his tongue. "Andrew, Andrew — now will you be satisfied?"

"Well, beggar me," Andrew said smiling. "Would you credit it? There's that bloody ole pea up tother end. Beggar me. Beggar my ole boots." It was of course a trick: the thimble-rigger secreted the pea each time under his long horny thumbnail.

"Come away, my friend," said Henry Wake, who did not approve of gambling.

"Well, I'll just have another goo," Andrew said.

"You're being done, Andrew — it's not under any of 'em," Hester said, while the thimble-rigger attempted to look injured.

"Ah, I suppose so," said Andrew, unperturbed, and turned his innocent smile on them. "I'll have another goo, though. Why, thass quite a treat just to watch him dew it."

Chad had left her side during this: she found him calling to her from a fenced enclosure. "Hester. Come and see."

There was a small, scraggy, elderly bear in a cage. There were bald patches on its fur from rubbing against the bars.

"Watch," Chad said. He picked up a handful of gravel and tossed it into the bottom of the cage: the bear pounced at once on it, leathery nose snuffling, then looked up at them with small, weak, baffled eyes.

"He thinks it's summat to eat," Chad said. He repeated the action. "See? He does it every time — he don't learn."

Hester, in spite of the years on the farm, was uncomfortably humane towards animals: she always had to absent herself when the pig-killer came round, and could not abide to see anything in a cage. Cruelty affected her so much that it caused a horrible tightness, worse than tears, in her chest; and the onset of this, when she had been feeling so happy, undid her completely. Chad was still laughing and tossing the gravel as she turned and stalked away from him.

"Wait — wait, what's the matter?" Chad came after her.

"Look here; I shan't stop wi' you, if you're going to do things like that," she cried.

Chad looked startled, then alarmed. "I didn't hurt it — there weren't no harm in it."

"Teasing it like that!" She could not look at him: she brushed a tear away.

"Here — wait — I'm sorry. I never meant — I just thought it'd mek you laugh. Thass all. I just wanted to mek you laugh."

His expression was really stricken. "Oh, it don't matter," she said.

"I'm sorry . . . I could git some cakes or

summat and feed it if you like."

He was so remorseful that her feeling of pity partly transferred itself to him. "No — it's all right," she said. It was something of a relief, all the same, to have the attention diverted from her by a little boy who in plain desperation began to pluck at her skirts, and declare himself lost.

"Who was you with, then?" she asked, bending down. "Your mam?"

"Me sister," the child said, making herculean efforts not to cry. "I can't find her. Mammy says we weren't to stop out long. I went on a swingboat and I were sick."

A few more inquiries established that the boy lived in the town, though he didn't know where, except that it was 'near the 'Orse'.

"There's a pub over the river called the Nag's Head," Chad said. "I should think thass what he means." So they escorted the child over the bridge and down to the south end of the High Street, where his excited pointing at the signboard of the Nag's Head confirmed Chad's conjecture, and he was able presently to recognise his front door. The woman who answered thanked them and confided in an aggrieved voice: "I told her to tie a bit o' string to him!"

The water-meadows at the edge of the town were close by here, and a path led behind the houses to the ruins of the Abbey, spectral in the dusk. Chad said, "Shall we go and have a walk round the ole Abbey?"

"All right," Hester said. She didn't mind; and she was a little ashamed of herself for having the vapours just now. Like one of those drippy girls who piped their eyes at the slightest thing, she thought — like Mary-Ann Cole or somebody. Still, the plight of the bear grieved her.

The noise of the fair faded behind them as they took the path to the Abbey Green, and was lost in the ever-present boom of the fen wind. A slight sensation of going uphill — which a native of a less level country would not even have noticed — indicated that this had once been an island of firm ground standing above a virtual swamp, in the days when the monks had first raised here their great stone standard of faith. Standing sentinel to the remnants of the Abbey itself was a ruined gatehouse, where pilgrims had once waited to be admitted to the presence of the Abbey's relics: it was reduced now to the barest portal, yet so strong was the imprinted sense of those parts of the structure that were gone, like the itch of feeling in an amputated limb, that to pass under it was still to have an impression of entering a place. The Abbey proper reared up in spare profile against a steep chasm of clouded sunset: the large, asymmetrical fragment of west front was joined by the arch of a vanished window to a single shattered column so that it appeared like an old man leaning on a stick. Moss-grown gravestones were planted in the grass at its foot, so old that the carving on them had been weathered away completely, and they seemed to be melting back into the living earth from which their mother-stone had been hewn. Hester and Chad walked down the nave, open to the sky, and haunted by no voices now but those of the rooks that quarrelled in the bare galleries above.

"I want to ask you summat," Chad said, in his flat way, as they emerged at the open end, where trees were raving in the wind.

"Yes?"

Chad paused in his stealthy tread. "Well," he said, "I want to ask you if you'll git engaged."

She nearly, very nearly, said "Who to?" Perhaps it might have been better if she had. But her habitual flippancy was constrained, heathen though she was, by the solemnity of the setting; and just for that moment the romantic in her was seized, really in the abstract, by the sheer idea of a proposal amongst Gothic stones and creeping shadows.

"How do you mean?" she said instead.

"I want you to git engaged to me."

"Me? But — Chad — "

"I want you to. I been meaning to ask you. You got to — you got to."

She looked at him, his taut slight figure and his face half-sullen, half-seething. Dusk lay like a thick net over the gaunt spaces of the Abbey; but enough light remained, if he had had eyes to see, for him to read her answer in her face. Though Hester's mouth, pretty and mobile, moved so naturally in mature curves of irony, she had singularly truthful eyes: they were still a child's, with a child's helpless candour; and they probably expressed her more than she knew herself.

"Chad — you can't really . . . . You don't really know me, it don't make sense. You got to git to

74

know people first . . . ”

He looked uncomprehending. “I don’t care about that. I made me mind up. Look. You got to. I’m gitting a ring — I’m gitting one off Rob Risby — proper, not eelskin like that ole gippo said — ”

“A ring?” She was astonished, but also dangerously flattered. “Oh, Chad, you shouldn’t do that — ”

“Well, you said you’d like to be bought things — you said it yourself, you can’t deny that.” He spoke with harsh challenge.

“But you can’t just buy a ring like that, without saying anything — ”

“I’m just said, ain’t I?” A rook took off with a dry flapping of dusty wings at the sound of his raised voice. He paced back a little way down the path, plucking at his collar as if it irked him. “You got to. I’m serious — I ain’t mucking about. I don’t want nobody else. You can’t just say no — think about it. Say you’ll think about it.”

“I don’t know . . . ”

He was standing facing her, perfectly framed by a dog’s-tooth arch, a solitary soaring bow of stone miraculously preserved on the thinnest of decayed columns. The afterglow in the sky behind it deepened to red as she looked at him, turning the toothed mouldings inside the arch fiercely black and sharp; and suddenly, irrationally, the image terrified her. He seemed to be standing unaware in a sinister mouth, a great fanged maw about to close on him. “Chad — come away from that arch,” she said.

75

He did not heed this, and remained where he was. "Say you'll think about it."

The jagged mouth gaped, red-rimmed.

"Just say you'll think about it."

"Oh! all right — yes, I will — just come away from that arch." She covered her strange panic with a forced laugh, saying as he came forward: "It looks so broken-down, I thought it might fall on you or summat."

"How long?"

"Eh?"

"How long you going to think?" And before she could answer he went on: "Two days. Till Monday. How about that?" Again there was something dog-like in his gruff insistence. "Two days."

Did she really need two days to think about an answer she already knew deep down? Well, she had said she would think about it — it was done now. And it would postpone it, after all . . . Hester both benefited and suffered from a moral nature that was decidedly not strenuous. As she was generous in her judgement of others, she was correspondingly lenient to herself: she was inclined to give herself the benefit of the doubt, and rely on the universal alibi of meaning no harm. No one had ever asked her to get engaged, moreover: it seemed mere courtesy to give it consideration, rather than a flat no . . . "All right," she said, and he looked so relieved that she felt she had done the right thing.

They said no more about it. Chad only repeated once: "Two days, then". The business

76

seemed to have exhausted him. They left the Abbey to the rooks and the wind; and on returning to the fair they found Mr and Mrs Langtoft and the boys newly arrived, and went round the fair with them all over again. She acted, she supposed, quite normally, though her mind kept fetching up with a bump against the thoughts: A proposal! Fancy that! And so much for Mary-Ann Horseface! And, occasionally: But I don't love him.

★ ★ ★

The two days passed: Chad was the same as ever, that is, subdued, with a sort of muffled edge about him; and on the Monday morning he returned to the turf-fen to continue preparing his digging. Hester's mind oscillated between wishing she had never got into this, and thinking: 'Ah — well — it won't hurt.' This was a mental habit she had picked up from Mr Langtoft, who was a great bodger: he would perform a perilously makeshift repair on a cart-axle or a coulter, and when asked whether it was safe he would contemplate it with his head on one side and say, 'Ah — well — it won't hurt.' She was equally reluctant to give Chad the pain of a refusal, and to give herself the pain of making it.

At mid-morning Mrs Langtoft told Hester to go and take Chad his dockey.

"Oh — can't Jacob go, or Will?"

"Wha' for? Git on, git on, gel. You mek my blood boil." Mrs Langtoft was sharp on

Mondays, suffering from the pious equivalent of a hangover from the intoxicating devotions of the day before. "Stand slummocking there. You'd end up on turnip-tops, the whole issue of yer, if it weren't for me."

Hester placed Chad's dockey — a hunk of bread and cheese, a sliver of pickled pork, and a 'hungin' or onion — in the basket and went out. It was a goodish walk to the turf-fen, requiring a roundabout route to find the sleeper-bridges across the dykes, or places where they were narrow enough to jump; and after a while she was singing under her breath, for it was a spring day of magnificent pearly sky, and along the green dykesides there were wild violets and marsh-marigolds. She was healthy, she was young, she was fed, and for the moment there did not seem very much in the world that could threaten her. As she crossed the brimming main drain she could see the figure of Chad in the turf-fen beyond, with the sun on his pale hair: he straightened up, saw her, and remained stock still, watching her, as she approached.

"I'm brought your dockey, Chad," she said — rather unnecessarily: but he was staring so. "I say, you're gitting on well now — have you started the digging yet?"

"No. I'm just finished paring. It just wants a bit o' cleaning and levelling yet."

The half acre of land was marked out with pegs, and the top layer of earth had been removed by the sharp hodding-spade on which Chad was leaning. At the edge of the pit he had already prepared a flat surface, the staddle, where the blocks of peat would be stacked. She examined all this for some time, while Chad did not touch his dockey, but watched her. They were alone in a vast arena of black earth and blue sky, with only the muttering wind, the old gossip of the fen, beside them.

"Two days is up," Chad said.

"I know. Thing is, Chad — "

"I give you the two days. I didn't pester you — you can't say that," he said, with his smothered belligerence.

"I know."

"Say yes then. Say you will. You know how I feel."

"But thass it, you see," she said, snatching at this. "I don't. I mean, you just up and say let's git engaged all of a sudden, and — "

"You think I don't mean it, then? Is that what you think? You think I'm mucking about?"

"I dunno. You ain't thought about it, Chad. I mean, you only imagine it's me you want." She hesitated: her honesty censured this as a weak argument. "You know, there's loads of girls who — "

"I don't want them. I ain't bothered about them. It is you I want. I'll prove it yer. I'll show yer I mean it. I'll prove it — you got to — " He slammed the hodding-spade down: its sharp blade slid into the peat like a knife into flesh. "If you don't believe me — if you're just mekking fun — "

"I'm not mekking fun," said she, with truth.

"I'll show yer. What can I do? — I'll prove it — " Then in the midst of his grim flounderings

79

he seemed to strike on the very thing that had released him into articulacy before. "See this peat? I reckon to cut seven hundred turf when I git started tomorrer. Seven hundred, thass a fair number for a start-off, they reckon. Here's betting I can do two thousand. I'll dig two thousand turf tomorrer — I'll do it — I will. Then will you believe me?"

"Whatever do you mean?"

"Just what I say. That'll be my proof. Will you believe me then? Two thousand turf in one day. For you."

She stood in amazement and confusion. "Oh, but, Chad — "

"Three thousand then!"

There is no malice in spring violets and blue skies, and they are seldom the instruments of unlucky fate: but just then it might have been better if Hester's walk to the turf-pit had been a trudge through grey November, for the flowers and the brilliance had got into her head, which at the soberest of times was inclined to lightness and rashness. And as Chad stood there making his wild bet and stabbing the spade into the peat, Hester's first thought was of fairy-stories her mother had told her as a girl: stories where the hero won the girl's hand by the performance of some tremendous and bizarre task. Imagine her being in a fairy-story! There was an irresistible novelty in that, to a girl inured by austerity to the grindingly prosaic. Her second thought was of what a thing it would be to tell Lizzie . . . Between these two, a third thought — of what would happen if she agreed — was quite squeezed out; and her instinctive conviction that Chad would never manage the task obliterated it completely.

"Three thousand! Say the word and I'll do it!" cried Chad.

"Oh! all right then — I'll believe you if you can do that."

"And you'll git engaged to me then?"

He had not forgotten that part of it, even if she had in the astonishment of the moment: she faltered; but then, after all, it was so ridiculous . . . "Go on, then."

Chad clapped his hands once: then sat down and began eating his dockey as if she were not there.

★ ★ ★

He was still out in the turf-fen that evening when she walked over to Lizzie Gosling's.

"Three thousand turf, eh?" Lizzie's black button eyes glittered. "Let's see — my brother Jack's been turf-digging for a couple o' years now. He reckons to do two thousand on a good day."

"Oh, I know he won't be able to do it. But ain't it the queerest thing? I nearly went through the floor when he said it. 'Cept I weren't standing on a floor."

"Three thousand . . . Well, he might manage it."

"Goo on!"

Lizzie's wry bud of a mouth expressed a world of cynical possibilities. "He might. Depends how serious he is about gitting you."

"Oh, but thass what's so daft! He's got hold of this silly idea he wants to marry me . . . But he can hardly find a word to say to me. He stares and stares and gits mardy if I mek so much as a joke."

"Oh, yes, I know what you mean. But still. What if he does do it?"

Hester actually felt the muscles of her face relax as the smile faded from her face. "But it's a joke — it's just so ridiculous . . . Ain't it?"

"*I* think it's a good 'un. Best I ever heard," Lizzie said, and gave one of her most satisfying laughs.

"Well, there you are then."

"But," Lizzie said, her eyebrows mounting right up her head, "I wouldn't say a sense of humour was Chad Langtoft's strong point — would you?"

Hester made her way back to the farm. Giving Lizzie the news had not been as much fun as she had expected. Clouds like ragged witches were sweeping the dimming sky, and a wish came to her that it might rain tomorrow — then Chad might not be able to do the digging. Not that it mattered really — he couldn't do three thousand, surely? That was the trouble with Lizzie Gosling — you could never tell whether she was serious or not.

The little star-like eyes of the flowers on the dykesides were closed now; and the gaiety of the joke seemed to have worn off a little too.

"Well-a-well, who'd ha' thought it!" Mrs Langtoft was beaming when Hester came in.

"You pair certainly kept things quiet, I'll say that."

Hester glanced over at Chad, eating his supper by the light of the oil-lamp. He did not look up.

"Seems we'll be hearing some news tomorrer then," Mr Langtoft said, smiling over his pipe.

"Mind! We'll say no more now," Mrs Langtoft said. "Not while it's time tomorrer. I declare though, it's quite a romantic sort o' fancy, ain't it — reminds me of when we were courting, Wag, d'you remember? — and you climbed on the sail of the mill and went all the way over, hanging on, just to show off to me, and I begged you not to, though I were tickled in a way." She gave her husband an affectionate pummel, smiling on Hester all the while. "Just fancy — still — we'll say no more now. Not while it's time."

Hester made her excuses straight after supper and went up to bed. She could not believe it. Chad had marched in and told everyone that she was going to marry him. He had announced it flat: with the turf-digging task as a sort of flourish on the contract.

She did not undress: she wasn't ready for sleep — she had some thinking to do. Oh, but she hated thinking . . . She had taken one boot off, when she heard Chad's familiar creeping tread on the stair, and she went hopping out to the landing.

He was dressed to go out, and was just descending the stairs. He looked spruce, and almost cocky.

"Where you going?"

"Just down the Labour In Vain for a spell."

"Look here — what'd you have to go and tell all about it for?"

His face flushed up in an instant, making his eyes pale. "Tell what?"

"Me marrying you — all that."

"Well, you are, ain't you? You said. You can't back out now. You said. You said."

"I know — but I didn't mean — "

"You said. You said." He repeated the words like a private charm: he suddenly gripped her arms in a convulsive movement, his fingernails digging into her skin. It was the first time he had touched her like that, and it was not a pleasant touch. "You can't back out. You said. You said."

"All right, I said — no call to go blabbing it — "

He let go of her. "You reckon I won't be able to do it, don't you? Well, I'll prove it to yer. You'll see." He turned and padded down the stairs.

★ ★ ★

It did not rain: the next day dawned bright and fine. Chad had gone to the turf-fen at first light. He had not stayed long at the Labour In Vain, the pub in the hamlet of Milney St Mary, for he had gone there not to drink but to tell everyone that he was promised to Hester Verney: the Labour In Vain performing for Hinching Fen a function analogous to that of the main drain, and serving as the channel through which all the news of that scattered parish flowed.

Hester remembered not only her mother's fairy-tales but the stories she retold from little yellowback novels which her father, full of pride at her scholarly accomplishment, got for her from the market whenever there was spare money. In these stories men with long aristocratic names and varying styles of whisker competed for the favours of a heroine who was always, throughout her trials, implacably single-minded. *Single-minded* hung round those heroines' necks like the fabulous necklaces with which the whiskered lords were continually presenting them. That Hester was unconvinced by these stories had much to do with the fact that she was not at all single-minded herself. Those single-minded heroines, she reflected, would never have got themselves in this position.

She woke feeling optimistic — the whole thing was after all so absurd and fantastical there could be no harm in it whatever happened: began to feel uncomfortable under Mrs Langtoft's significant nods and smiles; and set out at mid-morning to take Chad his dockey feeling dreadfully uneasy.

She began to see, now, that it would have been fairer to Chad to have turned him down flat straight away, at the Abbey. But at the time that had seemed the very opposite of fair to him. Anxiously examining her motives, she was unable to acquit herself of frivolity in taking up his challenge, but her wish to be fair was quite genuine; and so was her desire to avoid hurting him. She still did not want to hurt him, but an easy middle way seemed to be petering out before her eyes, and dark extremes closed in on either side of her.

On drawing near to the turf-fen she was relieved, at first, to see some other folk there: and then dismayed when she realised that the gaggle of children, Henry Wake, and Jass Phelps must have gathered about Chad's pit for the sole purpose of witnessing something that had been bruited all over the fen; an idea that was confirmed by the universal gaze of speculative interest that greeted her arrival.

Chad however hardly glanced up, but continued with his digging. He was dressed in shirt sleeves and sweating-cap, and there was already a great stain under his arms. The peat was dug in blocks, called cesses, of about six by four by eight inches, marked out in rows of three by a wooden gauge pressed into the surface: and the cesses were turned off the spade on to the staddle in neat rows, three at first to make a firm foundation, and two above. Veteran turf-diggers took pride in the precision of their stacks; but though Chad's were not as tidy as they might have been, they were already large, and the cut surface of the pit seemed to be growing at disturbing speed.

"I'd advise you to eat summat, Chad," Henry Wake said, observing the dockey-basket. "I think you'll find you git on better. It replaces the animal salts, you see. You mustn't lose your animal salts."

"In a minute," Chad said.

"Is there any cheese in that basket, Hester?"

Henry said. "Cheese is a very feeding food."

"People reckon as sugar gives you strength," Jass Phelps said. "So they reckon. *I* don't know."

Jass Phelps was the landlord of the Labour In Vain: he had come over in his little donkey-cart. He was a sleek man of fifty with a dropsical belly, dainty hands and feet, and a crown of oiled hair looking as if it were painted on; with a snub nose and, as it were, a snub mouth and snub eyes too, as if his face were permanently pressed up against a window-pane — and indeed, being of voraciously inquisitive character, he could be said to be habitually pressing himself up against his neighbours' business, and trying to see in. "I suppose some people might reckon three thousand in a day's too much to ask of anybody," he said, glancing sidelong at Hester: he seemed to feel that his curiosity was somehow mitigated by inserting it crabwise, in arch generalities. "Or perhaps I'm got it wrong. *I* don't know."

"We-ell, turf-digging's not a thing I'm ever turned me hand to, meself," Henry Wake said, "but I'm known quite a few turf-diggers in me time, and I'm observed the process pretty closely, so I reckon I understand it as well as anybody, no point in mekking out I don't: and I think you'll find three thousand's well within the bounds of possibility. I think it is, you know."

"You'll mek yourself ill if you don't eat summat," Hester said quietly to Chad. He turned off a last row of turf, spat out his sucking-pebble, and picked up the dockey-basket. He ate standing up, quickly, looking at his stacks.

"I suppose you could ask," Jass Phelps said, "who's going to count 'em? And I suppose some people might wonder what's going to happen if they're just a few short or something o' that kind. I don't know, perhaps that don't matter. It's nothing to do with me."

"Oh! if there's a disinterested witness required, I'll be quite happy to step in," Henry Wake said. "A 'judicator you call that, you know, but we'll say witness. Not," he said, smiling pleasantly at Hester, "that I think it'll come to anything as strict as that."

Hester found she could not smile back. Chad had finished his dockey, bolting it down, and picked up his spade again.

"Well! I'm got things to see to," Henry Wake said. "Better git back. I shall drop by later if I may. It's not the sort of thing you see every day, this."

"People might say this is what you call a labour of love, ain't it?" Jass Phelps said, staring sideways at Hester. "Or summat like that. I suppose some people might think it's all a bit peculiar. *I* don't know."

As it was early in the season, with the spring floods not long past, there was water slopping about in the bottom of the pit, icy with all the stored coldness of winter; and Chad's lower hand, grasping the base of the haft, was raw scarlet. Birds, attracted by the prospect of wriggling eatables turned up by the spade, were continually alighting round the edges of the pit. Hester was sure she saw irony directed at her from their small gemstone eyes.

As she watched Chad digging, mechanically, with morose intensity, Hester seemed to feel the chill touch of the water herself — a cold invasion of misgivings. Not once did he look her way, and that unnerved her. She went away, and was glad to be given the job that afternoon of taking the cow round the droves and dykesides to get a little early grazing, a task of which the solitude usually irked her. She lingered, and found herself reluctant to return to the farm at dinner-time.

"I'm been out to see Chad," Mrs Langtoft said. "He ain't half gitting on. You can't top the Langtofts for wukk when they put their minds to it." For all the irritable impatience and the turnip-tops, Mrs Langtoft nourished a fierce family pride. She enjoyed the privilege of calling her menfolk useless articles, but woe betide anyone else who should slight them: there was something of the mother cat about her, and sometimes it seemed that only her lack of stature hindered her from picking them up in her mouth by the scruff, and taking charge of them that way. Hester did not find these thoughts encouraging. "Now you get your dinner ate, gel, and when it's settled you can tek Chad's out to him — he ain't coming back here for it."

Hester watched her wrapping the pork dumpling in a cloth. "Oh, but he can come home for his dinner, surely. He'll just mek himself ill. It's silly!" She spoke lightly: but a heaviness of foreboding was on her. The day was beginning to seem like one of those dreams in which familiar faces turn alien, and the world becomes a series of jagged distortions.

Mrs Langtoft looked at her in surprise. "Why, you're an odd one, you are. I'd ha' thought you'd be flattered. I declare it's made you go all shy, and I'm never seen *that* afore. Chad knows what he's about, don't you fret."

The walk to the turf fen was becoming a *via dolorosa* for her. This time when she was within sight of it she heard a voice haling her, and Peggy Chettle caught up with her.

"Wait for me, gel. I could tell it were you from other side of the drain. Tell your walk. I can always tell folk by their walk. You walk straight and stick your chest out. Why not — stick 'em out, if you're got 'em. I wish I had a bit more on the sideboard meself, still they did their job, I'm raised four boys and one of 'em drives a hoss-omnibus."

All of Hinching Fen and many surrounding parishes knew Mrs Chettle, or would know her eventually; for she was of that indispensable race of matrons piquantly known as first-and-lasters, who acted as midwives to the newly arrived and layers-out to the newly departed, and sometimes ministered to minor illnesses in between, in the absence of doctors repelled by the poverty and remoteness of the region. She was a stout and hardy woman, very cheerful about her trade in all its aspects, with a permanently strenuous stride, suggestive of ploughing through droves in all weathers and not minding a bit. Two wings of grizzled hair framed a flat face more honest than comely, split by a great healthy horsey smile like one almighty tooth, and adorned by wiry black eyebrows of almost manly thickness. She did pretty well out of her work, and was always smartly turned out — a straw sailor hat, and tailor-made walking dress with leg-of-mutton sleeves: but there was nothing of vanity or frippery about her. Rubbing shoulders daily with mortality as she did, Mrs Chettle's social manners were inevitably marked by the frankest intimacy — made manifest by her habit of standing very close to you and constantly touching you, in a familiar manner not entirely pleasing, with pink brisk hands that always seemed to have just been washed after doing something.

"I heard the news the smorning," Peggy Chettle said, thrusting her smile in Hester's face, and kneading her arm in her fingers. "So I thought I'd come and tek a look for meself, thinking this'll perhaps be summat to remember in after years, and say I was there. Who knows, I might even be recalling it in my professional capacity with you, at the proper time, that would be quaint, wouldn't it? And I'm got to git over and see Coggy Onyett who got kicked in the stones by a cow, though he wants it kept quiet, daft beggar, as if it were some sort of shame to be kicked by anything less than a hoss, and he's such a shy morsel, he won't show the damage, though anybody can see it, and Mrs Onyett's had to cut an extra gusset in his britches to mek room — so it was in me way, like, so I thought I'd tek Chad a dab o' neat's-foot-oil, knowing how the diggers suffer terrible with their hands at the start o' the season, gret blisters and cracks you can put your finger in, still, what's a drop o' pus here or there, when you're soaring on the wings of love!"

There were more people gathered round the turf-pit, Hester saw as they approached: the stacks of cesses had mounted, and from the top of one a tassel fluttered in the breeze — signifying a thousand. At the sight of it Hester swallowed, and tried to hide her dismay from the midwife's benevolently devouring gaze.

"You're looking a bit peaky yourself, gel." Mrs Chettle squeezed her hand, and confidentially laid her chin on her shoulder a moment. "I'd say it was green-sickness, if I didn't know you better; you was never the lent-lily sort. Now if it's summat as you think you can't speak of, you know, then you come to me and we'll see you through it, bless you, I'm birthed dozens of 'em what were in the belly before the banns, and they drop out just the same way."

"Oh, I'm all right, Mrs Chettle, thanks all the same," Hester said: but this last had hit home direct as an arrow, and had the effect of clearing much that was confused. That she — that she and Chad . . . Impossible! She had got to know him better, and understand him a little, and had enjoyed the skating and the fair, and been flattered by his attentions, all very light-hearted . . . but as for feeling anything like that for him . . . The shock of it went through her like a physical jolt, right down to the soles of her feet. She seemed to behold for the first time the chill, dour aspect of Chad's passion, and something within her recoiled, with uncharacteristic violence.

She remembered an outing to the hills-and-hollows at Barnack — ancient quarries whence had come the stone of Peterborough Cathedral — when she had begun to run, laughing and exhilarated, down a steep slope, and then had found her own momentum carrying her on, frighteningly, against her will, faster and faster. The same helpless sensation came upon her now. If only she could just speak to Chad alone, sensibly, without all these people around, watching and making things worse!

She handed him his dinner, and saw that his hands were indeed cracked and blistered. Peggy Chettle moved in. "I'm brought you a spot o' salve for them hands, Chad, no, you put them coppers back, I wouldn't think of mekking a charge, not for such a special occasion as this, any road you'll most likely be needing all your money afore long. Now it wants rubbing in deep and then you'll find it eases you, mind, wait while you're et your dinner fust, you don't want none of it gooing down with your dumpling, else you'll find it coming out tother end afore you can shift your braces."

Lizzie Gosling was among the watchers. Hester took her aside.

"I can't believe it, Lizzie. I never thought he'd tek it this serious."

"Gitting near his two thousand, I reckon."

"He'll mek himself ill," Hester said, watching Chad, having swallowed his dinner like a gannet, set in again. "I don't want that!"

"What's his mam and dad think about it all?"

93

"Oh! I don't know, really." She was afraid she knew too well: they had taken Chad's cause to heart.

The day waned; and as they knocked off work more people came across the fields to watch Chad's labours in the turf-pit. Such a thing was worth seeing, not simply in itself but because there might be a tale in it, and this was important. The existence of the folk of Hinching Fen was bare and plain in the extreme: they lived out lives of narrow poverty in clay-lump cottages, and in the featureless landscape there was little to beguile the eye but the giant kaleidoscope of sky; and remote from modern communications as they were, the oral transmission (and embroidery) of stories, forming an ongoing local epic, was a vital sweetener in a meagre diet of experience.

"There weren't nothing like this in my day," old Andrew Surfleet remarked to Sunny Daintree. "You just poddled up to the gel you wanted and ast her to be promised to you there and then. That were usually on the way home from church — afore the chapel were built, like — I don't know why then 'specially, I suppose it were because you'd had a good wash, and she could see what you looked like without your muck. And if she didn't tek to yer, she said no."

"If you were lucky," Sunny said, darkly.

"I had to give up the turf-digging, meself," Andrew said. "It were gitting so as me fingers had been gripping the spade so long, they wouldn't uncurl when I got home, so I couldn't eat me dinner: 'less me missis helped me, and she weren't very patient at it, she used to keep poking the next bit o' pudden in me mouth afore I'd swallowed the last beggar. Ah! not that it'll hurt a young feller like Chad, in the prime o' life."

"Ooh! dear." Sunny Daintree sucked in breath. "I wouldn't goo so far as to say that. I knew a young chap once as were lifting taters, and it were past supper-time, but he'd took it in his head that he wanted to git 'em all up that day: so he carried on, and overshot his strength — and his ole mother come out with a lamp and found him there laying dead amongst the taters like he'd been pole-axed."

"No! What killed him, then?"

"Why, it were the wukk: summat just bust inside him. Ooh! dear. He were about Chad's age. I tell you, if Chad was to fall down dead at my feet now I wouldn't be a bit surprised. I wouldn't bat an eyelid."

At dusk the Langtofts themselves went out to the turf-fen; but Hester was not with them. She had made an excuse some time earlier of taking Chad a can of tea, and had hidden herself in the barn.

"Oh — it's not my fault if he goes and gits the wrong idea!" she said aloud, making a mouse scuffle in the straw: then paced up and down, and admitted to herself, silently, that it probably was her fault. A moment of light-mindedness had induced her to accept the outlandish challenge; and still she could scarcely believe that such a momentous weight

95

of consequence should be poised on that tiny apex.

It was her misfortune to come into collision with a nature like Chad's: a nature singular and colourless, embracing no diversity, which the belated presence of a passion stained a uniform dull hue; and disabled by a crucial dislocation between feeling and expression. Hester could no longer deceive herself as to the reality of his feeling: but that grim, blank way in which he was labouring in the pit gave her an idea of its quality too, and it did not suggest warmth.

She sat down in the straw. It occurred to her that there was simply no one to whom she could turn: and if she had been prone to self-pity, she would have bewailed her loneliness. As it was, she admonished herself for hiding. "Well — you did it — you're got to face it," she said to herself; but still she lingered in the barn, until she could scarcely see her hand in front of her face; when she was roused by a voice in the yard, calling "Hallo there!"

It was Henry Wake. She left the barn.

"Ah, there you are, Hester — I'm come to fetch you to the turf-fen — Mrs Langtoft were going to send young Will, but I volunteered to nip over meself — I'm always been a tidy runner, I don't know why it is, I think I'm right in saying stamina's the word for it. Well! He's done it, gel — he's done it: three thousand. I did a quick count-up meself, not one by one, you understand, but I think I've a pretty fair eye for these things."

"I'd better come then," Hester said faintly.

Henry, in his urbane way, gave her his arm. "Whole issue of folk stood there watching as he cut the last one — seems to have quite captured the imagination. Might make a nice little item for the *Hunts Post*, if it were written out properly — I'm a fair hand with a pen meself as it happens, it's one of them things you're born with — "

"No, Mr Wake — don't do that."

He stopped in surprise, and peered at her in the gathering darkness. "Why, Hester, what is the matter?"

"Oh, this is going to sound awful — but the thing is, I never meant all this to happen — he would keep insisting so, and then he made this silly bet, and I thought it was funny so I said go on then — but he's so terrible serious and he went round saying I were going to marry him — and now I wish I'd never got into it."

Her choice of Henry Wake as confidant was dictated simply by the pressure of feelings that had been building up all day and now could no longer be restrained: in fact she might have done worse. It was known all over Hinching Fen that Henry Wake, for all his big talk, was as tender as a chicken; he could not bear the sight of distress, and someone else's troubles would afflict him as if they were his own. People put up with a lot of his bumptiousness, on account of this quality which he believed he kept hidden. And so he peered anxiously into Hester's face, and his hand went to his handkerchief.

"Oh! dear," he said. "Dear me, I — this rather puts a different complexion on things.

I'm sorry, Hester, I had no idea . . . " He gave her the handkerchief, and studied the distance while she made use of it, looking as if he might need it himself.

"I'm been thinking about it all day," she said. "I'm got to tell him. I know folk'll think badly of me."

"I'm rather afraid they might," Henry said.

"But think how much wuss it'd be if I went and got engaged to him for such a daft reason," cried she. "That wouldn't be no kindness to him, would it? Not when I — well, I don't love him. Thass the thing. And he'd find it out."

"Ah," Henry said; and stroked his little moustache.

"It'd be a mockery. I know I shouldn't have took him up on it — but wouldn't it be a disgrace to go through with it, and mek two people miserable for the sake of a pile o' turf?" As she spoke she was afraid this would seem a mere cobbling-together of an excuse — yet at the same time she knew she was absolutely right. All the while in the barn she had been fending off this harsh conclusion: it had pain on its side, but truth too, and she must embrace it.

"It'll mean going back on your word," Henry said reflectively. "But like you say — the alternative's a lot wuss. Oh! dear." Timidly he patted Hester's hand. "Well, you must do what's right, Hester. Better to settle it now than later. I shan't judge you — though I'm afraid some people will; but then it's been a bit of an excitement for them, like, and they'll be sorry at being disappointed." He expressed these views with a gentle tentativeness, far more convincing than his usual assertive parade of learning. "Never mind. It'll be all right. Truth's always best, I reckon, in the long run."

She believed him — for her habit of lying to herself was really the superficial evasion of a rather frighteningly honest nature: but the trouble was she had always lived her life in the short run. And suddenly that had become a dark thicket of difficulty.

"Do you want to come now?" Henry said. "I could go back and mek an excuse for you if you like — I could say you're got headache. I could say you're indisposed," he added, with a flash of genteel inspiration.

"No," she said, laughing in spite of herself at that ladylike phrase while the odours of the farmyard wafted around them. "No, thank you, Mr Wake, I'm got to come." She had hidden enough.

It was almost full dark when they reached the turf-fen; but Mr Langtoft had brought a storm-lantern, the light of which revealed a dozen or more people standing around the pit, and the long walls of stacked cesses with the three tassels waving — at her — in the night breeze. There was a cheer as she approached, and a few ribald comments.

"There now," Mrs Langtoft said, coming forward and taking her hand in a motherly, or mother-in-lawly, way, "didn't I say nobody could wukk like a Langtoft when he sets his mind to it?"

Peggy Chettle had returned, and having made

Chad sit on the edge of the pit had her hands up the back of his shirt and was rubbing ointment into the muscles. "Never mind your modesty, dear boy," she said, "I'm past fretting about such things meself, why, I have me hands in funnier places than this every day and it don't mean no more to me than kneading a bit o' dough. Now I'm putting plenty on, so you'd best sleep on your front tonight else you'll be sliding about in bed like an eel on a wet oilcloth." Her great teeth shone at Hester in the lamplight. "Not that you'll feel much like sleeping, I shouldn't think."

"See?" Chad said to Hester.

"Well, I'm sure we're all had a very interesting time," Henry Wake said, "but Mrs Wake'll be putting a lamp in the winder for me by now, so I reckon I'll be going, and I'd suggest we all do likewise."

"Ah! you're right, Henry," Mrs Langtoft said, "there's a couple of people here wants leaving alone, so let's all say goodnight. Come on, Wag," and she collected her husband from the edge of the pit with both hands like a wheelbarrow, and having rearranged the load a little, turned him round and trundled him home.

The spectators left: their voices dwindled, very slowly, into the wind-rippled silence of the fen night. The lantern was left behind. Chad picked it up and held it close to Hester's face.

"You never saw me cut my three thousand," he said.

"No."

He brought the lamp a little closer. "So now you believe me," he said.

"Yes, I believe you," she said. Her heart began to pound horribly: suddenly she felt like an animal caught in a snare. Part of her longed to equivocate, to sidle out of it, even to give in — an engagement, that was nothing, engagements had been broken before . . . But it would not do. "You're done wonders, Chad. I ought to be right proud, I know — "

"What d'you mean, ought to be?" Suddenly the lamp was right in her face, hurting her eyes: he had caught something in her tone.

"Well, I am — I mean it's very flattering you doing this — but it still don't mek any difference to what I feel. Or what I don't feel. Thass why I can't get engaged to you, Chad. I'm sorry I took you up on it, I know I shouldn't have. I'm sorry."

"But I'm done it," he said, as if not understanding. "Look — I'm done the three thousand. Dad counted — Henry Wake counted. I'm done it."

"Oh, but you don't marry someone just because they pile up a load of turf!" she cried, unable to suppress a note of exasperation.

"You said you would." The lamp was unsteady in his hand: its light fell in ghostly smears on the black walls of turf, so that they seemed to face each other in some sunken prison-vault. "You said — you said you would."

"Only because you were daft enough to suggest it! What sort of a person would really

101

marry someone because of a thing like that?"

"You got to! You said! You said!" Chad's face, so cautious of expression, betrayed his fury obscurely: the rising flush of blood merged with the shadows of fatigue until it looked horribly bruised.

"No, Chad. I can't. It's no good. I don't — " It seemed too hard to say *I don't love you* — those cruel words, so stark and deathly; but even as she hesitated to give him this pain, he grasped the unsaid. He stared at her for two more seconds, and then hit her in the face.

Such essentially passionless natures as Chad's, once infected, know moderation. He might have reflected that his was the moral advantage, having kept his side of the bargain while she had broken hers; but because of that emotional equivalent of tunnel vision from which he suffered, he hit out and forfeited the advantage with a single stroke of the fist. Hester staggered back, more in shock than pain, and nearly fell.

"You said," Chad repeated, dully, then dropped the lantern on the ground and walked away.

Afterwards she wished she had hit him back; but at that moment she was immobilised not only by shock but by a feeling curiously akin to relief: relief that it was all with utmost cleanness finished, settled, done with — at least where she and Chad were concerned. She knew, however, that those few violent moments in the dark turf-fen had irrevocably changed her relations with the Langtofts: she was their dependant, and utterly vulnerable; and she was afraid to go back to the farm.

At last she wiped her eyes, and made her way, carrying the lantern, over to Lizzie Gosling's, where she explained the mark on her face by saying she had walked into a low tree branch in the darkness. Lizzie bathed it in an eloquent silence.

"What's going to happen now?" Lizzie said, as Hester finally prepared to go home.

She shook her head. "I don't know."

Mrs Langtoft met her at the door of the farm; and at once she knew that Chad had told his tale.

"Now git in here, gel, and tell me the truth! You gone and broke your promise to Chad, is that it? You gone and led him on and then broke your promise? Well, come on, out wi' it!"

"Where is he?" Hester said.

"Gone down the Labour In Vain. Terrible state he was in — *that* shows it — he's never been a drinker before. He never learnt that in this house. Well, what's it all about? Lord give me strength, you mek my blood boil!"

The boys had been packed off to bed. Mr Langtoft, looking more than usually perplexed, and also sad, sat in the armchair and patted old Dan.

"I never meant that promise," Hester said. "It started as a joke . . . He took it too seriously."

"Joke? What joke?" Mrs Langtoft snapped. "Mekking a joke of Chad? What on earth are you playing at?"

"I never really thought of gitting engaged to

Chad — you can't do that unless it's the right person — "

"Right person? What's wrong with our Chad?"

"Nothing, nothing. But I don't feel . . . " She went on to repeat the things she had said to herself, to Henry Wake, to Chad . . . but at some point she became aware that Mrs Langtoft, exclaiming, snorting, and pacing around the kitchen as if she felt its walls pressing in on her, was not listening.

"Never heard anything like it in my life — just git the winter over and now this — I thought he'd gone spare when he come in tonight — mekking a promise like that . . . " Her stalwart bosom heaved, and her magnified shadow revolved endlessly. All her loyal protectiveness of family burned in her, and for the moment she did not see the girl of whom she was fond and who had replaced her Meery, but an intruder and betrayer.

In the midst of this Mr Langtoft, speaking for the first time, said quietly: "What you done to your face, gel?"

"Knocked into a tree in the dark," Hester said, turning away from the light.

"Is this what we took you in for? Playing tricks like this?" Mrs Langtoft fumed on; and Hester grew weary as she realised there was nothing she could say that would penetrate the shell of Mrs Langtoft's possessive indignation. She was the villain and that was that.

An end was put to this hopeless wrangling at last, when Chad came in, drunk.

"Oh! Chad, you'll do yourself no good this

way," Mrs Langtoft said, fussing him into a chair. "Git the kettle on, gel, mek yourself some use. And look at them blisters! They want threading — pass me my sewing-box, Wag."

The huge blisters caused by turf-digging were treated by passing through them a needle threaded with wool, then leaving the wool inside to soak them dry. Chad, slumped in a chair, submitted to this operation silently, his eyes lowered.

"Drink's no answer, my boy," Mrs Langtoft said, as she tutted and shook her head over the blisters. "You won't git it sorted that way."

"Folk were having a rare old laugh at me down the Labour In Vain," Chad muttered. "A rare old laugh."

Suddenly Mrs Langtoft shot at Hester a glance that hurt her — for instead of being reproachful it was hateful. "Look what you're done!" she said.

"We can git it sorted," Mr Langtoft said. "Surely we can git it sorted."

"I tell you what," Chad said, lifting his eyes to Hester at last, "I wouldn't have you if you paid me! Thass what! Not if you paid me, you ole slut!"

"Now then," Mr Langtoft said, "no call for that. We can git it sorted."

But even as he spoke Hester knew that it could not be sorted: that here, among the lamplight and the needles and the hot water, the possibility of reconciliation was receding moment by moment. And in a white glare of instantaneous truth she saw what those few moments of trivial foolishness had led to — the end of her days at Langtoft's farm.

"Just hold your hosses a bit," Mr Langtoft was saying. "Remember we're all got to git along together here."

"We what?" Mrs Langtoft was crushing. "What peace are we ever going to git with her around? Playing tricks — leading people on — "

"Well, then, I shan't stay," Hester said, with deliberate dignity. The sight of Chad's blisters had renewed her sense of guilt — but one can only bear so much reproach without sinking into self-contempt, and Hester did not think so badly of herself as that. "I shall go as soon as you like."

"Thass the best idea I'm heard yet," said Mrs Langtoft, with stabbing bitterness.

Hester took a candle and went up to bed. She had not yet begun to undress when there was a tap at the door. It was opened slightly, and Mr Langtoft stood in the gap, not looking in.

"You all right, are you, gel?" he said softly.

She said yes.

"All a bit of a to-do, ain't it? I don't know what to say. You shouldn't have done it, gel. Well, I s'pose you know that. I shan't say no more. Trouble is — " he dropped his voice to a whisper — "I'm afraid I don't reckon Bess is going to come round, you know. If it were just up to me, like . . . " He left a pregnant pause.

"I know," Hester said. "I don't see how I can stop here, any road. Not now."

"Ah. It ain't that we're not fond of you, gel. You're been a good worker, and all, and I wouldn't ha' wanted you to go. I like a quiet life meself, and if I thought there were a chance of gitting it sorted . . . " His voice trailed off.

"Thank you, Mr Langtoft," Hester said. "I'll go. I'll go tomorrow."

★ ★ ★

The morning brought no alteration in the facts of the situation: no alteration in Hester's mind, and most importantly none in Mrs Langtoft's.

The truth was, Mrs Langtoft's liking for Hester had been deep and genuine; and for some time there had been at the least an unconscious willingness on her part to look on the girl as a future daughter-in-law. The sudden realisation of this prospect, and its more sudden demolition, had produced in her a combustion of feeling — and its most fiery element was that jealous family pride, taking the form of an indignant rhetorical question: "So she thinks Chad Langtoft's not good enough for her?" Her husband was forced to listen to several animadversions on Hester's family, who she said were as poor shabby an ole lot as anybody on the fen and nothing to be proud of, but he knew as well as she did there was nothing in them — they were just smoke from the flame of her disappointment and resentment. The flame was too strong and fierce to be damped down by reflection: and the sight of the baleful, hung-over Chad scarcely able to

107

eat his breakfast for the blisters on his hands, was oxygen to it. "You still sticking to what you said last night, gel?" was Mrs Langtoft's abrupt greeting of Hester, spoken as it were out of the back of her head; and the girl scarcely needed to reply. It was plain that she and Chad could not remain in that house together — and there was no question of who should go.

Mr Langtoft drooped untidily about the farm all morning, could settle to nothing, and at last went up to Hester's room where she was packing her few clothes and possessions.

"This all seems a bit hasty to me, gel," he said, plucking miscellaneous straws and seeds from his moustache. "Twouldn't be so bad if you was just going home to your folks — but you ain't got no folks near, have you?"

"I don't know where Father is now," she said. "It don't matter, though. The Goslings'll put me up for a time, while I look for work."

"Ah. Well, I'll give you a good word, gel, wherever you go — just tell 'em to refer to me." With great difficulty he took a handful of shillings from his pocket and placed them on the wash-stand.

"Oh! Mr Langtoft — really, I ain't got money owing to me, you know, and I'm got a few bob — "

"I know, gel, but still, you tek it, you'll want a bit by you — you got to look after yourself — we ain't struggling quite so bad wi' winter done now, and there'll be extra coming in when Chad sells his turf — oh! well, we won't talk about that — any road . . . " and beaten about with various sorts of discomfort as he was, Mr Langtoft made a sort of hurried sidle out of the room, colliding with the door-jamb as he went.

"Give her how much?" Mrs Langtoft said when her husband at last told her. "Hm! One thing's for sure — we s'll end up on turnip-tops yet." But, more significantly, she did not object.

The packing did not take long. A walk over to the Goslings' secured her a temporary berth there — Lizzie, being the capable only daughter of a not very capable widower, having a good deal of say in the household. Hester had no wish to linger out her farewell to the farm. Life with her father had been a continual round of flitting, but this was different: she had come to regard this as home; and to tear herself quickly and sharply from it, she felt, was the only way of limiting the pain, and making the severance bearable. It still seemed scarcely possible that, virtually overnight, the earth should have shifted beneath her feet like this. The material aspect of her predicament would have daunted a temper less buoyant than Hester's — for she had lost a good job, and was now thrown on the world without means: as it was, her chief sorrow was at the loss of friends. She did not love Mrs Langtoft the less for what had happened, and she might almost have run to her and begged to be allowed to stay, but for one thing: wrong as she had been to agree to Chad's wager, she was sure she had done right in the end.

She went out to the fields to say her goodbyes to Jacob and Will — their respective ages manifest in their reactions to this drama, in that Jacob understood it too well and could hardly look at her, and Will did not understand it at all. Returning, she met Chad in the yard.

She was not much of a hater: the sight of him now produced little more than a weary aversion, insignificant beside her sadness. Perhaps therein lay the essential misfortune of their association — that it was curiously difficult to feel anything much towards him.

"You going then?" he said.

"I reckon it's best," she said. "Don't you?"

Still he gave her his dogged, watchful look. He said: "I meant what I said, you know. Last night."

Meant what he had said? Ah — that. She allowed herself a grain of bitterness. "Oh! well, don't worry about it, Chad. I'm never going to pay you. You can be sure of that."

★ ★ ★

The news of Hester Verney's broken promise and of her leaving the Langtofts' farm under a cloud did not take long to permeate Hinching Fen, and it formed the chief topic of conversation at the Labour In Vain that night.

This public-house was the most prominent feature of Milney St Mary, a hamlet which was really only a sort of brief inhabited interlude along the course of a fen causeway — as if the road, tiring of its ruler-straight transit across the flat miles, had momentarily broken out in houses. The peat which formed the soil of this district was notoriously liable to shrinkage, with the result that not only was the road elevated several feet above the fields, but the foundations of buildings were unstable: and so the few dwellings of Milney St Mary had settled at various angles to the perpendicular, with an effect of leaning towards each other in promiscuous and raffish attitudes. The Labour In Vain, a long double-fronted building with a stout chimney-breast at each end, had suffered a variation on the common fate by subsiding in the middle. This not only gave its exterior a broken-backed appearance, but meant that to walk across the bar-parlour was to be aware of a listing sensation, suggestive of a heeling ship — an experience alarming to strangers, and giving rise to wild speculations on their part as to the strength of the beer. For the same reason chairs and tables had had to be tailored to the declivity of the floor, by the sawing off of odd inches from legs to make them level: and it was not an uncommon occurrence for jugs and tankards to make a slow sliding progress to the edge of the shelves along the walls, and be seen teetering there, as if in two minds whether to throw themselves off. To these basic appointments the Labour In Vain superadded an extravagant piece of décor, hanging above the great open hearth fire and running the whole length of it: a painting in oils, representing sheep, stags, and cows all in unlikely proximity to a thunderous waterfall, with a storm and a sunset going on for good measure; the whole blackened monstrosity covering a great deal of wall, and seeming to have been chosen on that dependable old principle, If You're Going to Have One, Have a Big One.

The coming of spring meant more work, and hence more money around, and so the bar-parlour was well-filled. It was expressive of the rough democracy of the fen that labourers like old Andrew Surfleet rubbed shoulders with farmers: including Henry Wake, who overcame his Methodist disapproval of liquor to the extent of supping a half-pint or two, simply for the sake of the gossip.

"There's some as reckons there's more to it," said Jass Phelps, the landlord. "Reckons as she was in a certain condition. So they say. *I'm* not saying that, mind you."

"Why, what condition's that, then?" Andrew Surfleet said.

"Expectin', you daft ole beggar," grunted an old turf-digger named Artie Gill, a cross-grained fellow whose eyebrows met in the middle, mirroring his moustache and giving his face a sinister symmetry.

"Oh! that." Andrew Surfleet — who took his beer warm — watched as Jass Phelps plunged the hot poker into the mug, and thought deeply. "No! Surely not. She'd never have turned him down, in that case. That'd be tother way around."

"I'm sure there's no suggestion of that," Henry Wake said. "No call to bring that into it."

"Funny sort of business, all the same," Jass Phelps said, scratching the arched back of one of his cats. He was a man who loved cats, hated children, and believed the worst of people with an almost religious faith. "She were always a flighty sort, so they say. Always giving the glad-eye one way or tother. Thass what I'm heard. *I* don't know."

"Oh! she's young, you know," Henry Wake said. "Young and a bit giddy. No more than that."

"Thass Chad I feel sorry for," said Andrew Surfleet, with the steam from his beer all over his beard. "I'll never forgit his face when he come in here last night."

"You weren't here last night," growled Artie Gill, "so how could you know?"

"Ah — no, but — I'll never forgit it, from how Jass there, and Sunny here described it — you saw him, didn't you, Sunny?"

"Ooh! dear. Did I." Sunny Daintree felt in his moleskin waistcoat for his tin watch — a frequent consultation which invariably seemed to indicate that it was later than he thought. "I thought he'd gone spare, for definite. I wouldn't have been a bit surprised to be fishing him out of the dyke the smorning." He sighed. "With a pole."

"Terrible pity," Andrew said. "Not that Chad's such an easy chap to feel sorry for, somehow: he seems to have got there before you, if you see what I mean."

"It's the gel I feel sorry for — losing a good place like that," Henry Wake said. "And no family to fall back on. I'll tek half a pint of Barceloneys, Jass, if you'll be so good."

"Ah — the family. You might say it's only what you'd expect from a daughter of Ben Verney — we all knew what *he* was like — not that I'm saying anything against him." Jass Phelps served Henry with a half-pint of Barcelona nuts, by the direct expedient of emptying them on to the table.

"I shouldn't wonder if he's come to grief by now," Sunny Daintree said. "If he were laying in Lincoln gaol I wouldn't be a bit surprised."

"Come now," said Henry, "he were a bit unsteady — no more than that."

"Ah! but thass just what's coming out in the gel," Sunny said. "You tek a gel on to wukk at your house, you want her steady. Ooh! dear. A gel gits that sort of reputation and she's done for. She might as well just tip herself in the dyke and have done with it."

"They reckon Bess Langtoft took a strap to her," Jass Phelps said. "Buckle-end."

"I don't feel we should judge when we don't know all the facts of the case," Henry Wake said uneasily. "And if she weren't quite sure, it would have been a shame to marry him — and then the pair of 'em be unhappy."

There was a delicate sort of silence, punctuated by a few coughs: for it was known that Mrs Wake was a little on the harsh side, and would make Henry's life seven kinds of hell if he so much as got mud on the boot-scrapers.

"Well, Hester's made her bed now — she must hope it's a soft one, though I'm afraid she'll find it hard," Andrew Surfleet said.

"Your missus is in bed with a quinsy, you

were saying, Andrew?" Henry Wake said quickly — for Chad had just come in.

"No!" said Andrew, slow to catch on. "I never said that. The ole gel were right as rain the smorning. Well, she were!" he protested, as Sunny Daintree trod on his toes.

"Evening to you, Chad," Henry Wake said. "Turning a bit misty out there, I reckon, or perhaps it's clearing."

"Well, now you mention it she were looking a bit poorly," Andrew said belatedly.

Chad ordered a pint of beer, drank half of it in one go, and then sat down at the table with Henry, Andrew and Sunny, causing them to shift in their chairs, nod, hum, look at their beer, and all start talking at once: "Mole-catching season's nearly done, Chad, tell your father — " "Preacher from Chatteris at the chapel this week — " "My ole gel's got the quinsy, Chad, did you know — " until Chad silenced them with a belligerent sort of smile, drawing from his waistcoat pocket a small packet of gauze.

"See what I'm got here?" he said, and unwrapped a plain silver, or silver-coloured, ring. "Got that off Rob Risby."

Jass Phelps craned over the bar to see like someone at the scene of an accident, and there was silence, broken only by Andrew Surfleet piping: "Thass nice!"

Chad held the ring aloft, with a general stare at everyone. "And I'm here to tell you I'm not bought this for nothing. There's half a dozen gels hereabouts who'll be glad to put that on — mebbe Mary-Ann Cole, mebbe Kate Dyer,

115

mebbe somebody else — I'm not made me mind up."

"Course, you know, it might not fit all on 'em," Andrew said helpfully, "fingers being what they are," and had his foot trodden on again.

"So, if you're all been chuntering over what I'm going to do, now you know," Chad said, his cheeks very pink, "and you needn't trouble yourselves any more."

"Very wise, Chad, very wise," Henry Wake said. Privately he did not think it wise at all . . . but, for once, Henry held his peace.

4

HESTER'S stay at the Goslings' could not be of long duration. The tiny cottage was already overcrowded, with Lizzie's father and three brothers all as sturdily well-built as Lizzie herself: the money Mr Langtoft had given her would not pay her keep for long; and moreover Mr Gosling tended to take Chad's part, giving her the frostiest of welcomes, and when she overheard some disapproving remarks about her being Ben Verney's daughter all right, she knew she would have to go as soon as possible.

Unable to find work in the immediate vicinity, she sought it further afield by means of Rob Risby the tallyman, who asked around for her on his travels. At last he brought her the address of a farm the other side of March where a female servant was wanted.

"Five pound a year!" Hester said in dismay. "Why, I'd be nothing but a slavey!"

"Ah, thass the way of it," Rob Risby said, feeling his whisker. "There's precious little wukk about. I should know. My table don't see meat from one week to the next. I caught my missis a-kissing the pig tother day. 'Robert,' says she, 'I'm trying to remember what pork tastes like'."

Hester had deep misgivings about a place offered on such parsimonious terms: but she

117

did not need Mr Gosling's surly reminders that beggars could not be choosers. The urgent necessity of securing a living, which only her own hands and wit could supply, pressed upon her; and her native optimism, reasserting itself, did the rest — the place surely couldn't be *that* bad. She wrote, and received a pencilled reply engaging her, and telling her to '*Come next Mundy, bring cloths & boots, caps providid.*'

So a new life awaited her. It was not a great distance from Hinching Fen — a matter of twelve miles — but that was far enough to entail a complete separation from the place she thought of as home, and the people that made it so. It was a barren prospect for Hester, who by nature would trade riches for a friendly face. And yet her feelings about leaving were not unambiguous — because of the very thing that had overturned her fortunes. She knew that on Hinching Fen a certain opprobrium attached to her as a result of what had happened with Chad. There were as many varying views on that, of course, as there were people; but she frequently intercepted glances of wary disapproval, and conversations faltered and stopped as she walked by. Pride she normally had little use for, but she certainly had no intention of donning sackcloth and ashes for what she had done. She still maintained it would have been a far greater disgrace to have bound herself to a man she did not love for the sake of a wild bet; and it seemed to her that folk were rather too automatically ready to blame the Woman in the case. Hester was no self-tormentor. If she was irresponsible, it did not extend to refusing to accept the consequences of her own acts: indeed she was far more willing to do that than to think badly of herself. Her heart was sore at leaving, but her self-respect provided an opiate. If she were to be burdened here with the unmerited reputation of a cruel flirt, then perhaps it was all for the best.

To travel to her new place of employ required a roundabout railway journey, from the little halt at Stokeley to the main-line station at Peterborough, and thence to March, a small fenland town which had been hoisted into prominence by the siting there of a great concourse of railway marshalling yards. Lizzie Gosling saw her off at Stokeley. Elastic as Hester's nature was, at the last moment she tasted a rare despondency. "Oh, Liz," said she, half laughing and half crying, "am I going to end up like my ole father — flitting about like a flea in a colander for the rest of my life?"

"Well," Lizzie said, biting on tears, "you ain't got a moustache quite like his, any road. Git on, gel. You'll be all right."

A whistle shrieked, and steam enveloped the two girls. Lizzie said goodbye, giving Hester a hug and one of her most speaking looks — this one saying I-really-don't-know-what's-going-to-become-of-you-but-you-know-you've-always-got-a-friend-in-me.

A train ride was a novelty for Hester: the price of the ticket had absorbed almost all her money, and the two shillings left plus the contents of her two carpet-bags constituted all her worldly possessions as she watched the edge of the upland country, clothed in unfamiliar woods and sheep-pasture, slip by on the way to Peterborough. "Here I go again," she said to herself, recalling the day she had stepped down from her father's cart at the end of the Langtofts' drove. Having changed at Peterborough she arrived at March, deep in black fen country again, in the early afternoon. Her enquiries after Gore's Hole Drove met with uncomprehending stares until she found an old man sitting in the spring sunshine in the market-place.

"Noo-oo, you won't git a carrier going out there," he told her. "You'll have to try and walk it, I reckon. Whass your legs like, gel?" he said with a meaningful look over her.

"They start at me behind and go down to the floor," she said.

"Ah! well, they'll dew. You tek the Rings End road and keep going. You'll git there, eventually. I'd offer to carry them bags for yer, but I should want one hand free, at least."

"Dream your dreams, granfer."

She was inured to walking long distances, and scarcely noticed the first few miles: she was still fresh when she came to the drove turning. But the drove went on, and on. This was remoteness: and the place seemed to have a micro-climate, for while the rest of the country was dry, the drove was a morass of puddles and ooze. Huge black fields surrounded her, tinted with the merest shade of green growth. When at last the farmhouse did come in sight it seemed for something like an hour to squat on the horizon, and never get any nearer.

At last she found herself knocking on the door, and looking up without enthusiasm at a patched tiled roof, and tottering gutters, and windows grimily opaque that gave the place a blind look. She knocked for some time before the door was finally, cautiously opened by a little old woman, with moist rheumy eyes, a snuffly nose, and a dribbling lip, all swathed up to the chin with a tight winding of shawls and scarves, as if she were inclined to be leaky, and had to be lagged.

"We don't want nothing," the old woman said; and waved a rusty poker in Hester's face.

"I'm Hester Verney. I'm come about the job."

"We don't want nothing, I tell you!"

"I wrote to you," Hester said. "About being the farm-servant. You said to come Monday."

"Oh! that. No, we got a gel. We already got a gel — she come asking on Sat'dy so we took her on."

Hester was astonished. The old woman was starting to close the door. "Wait a minute — you offered me that job. You told me to come today — "

"Oh, I can't help that," the old woman said, wetly. "We wanted a gel quick, and this one were handy. Any road, now I look at you, you wouldn't have done at all. A gret thing like you. We wanted a proper young gel, fresh, what we could train up. I should think you're probably got set in all sorts of ways of your own."

There was a grim resonance in those words *fresh* and *train up*, taken in conjunction with

121

the ramshackle state of the farm. A skivvy — just out of school, and too frightened to protest at being treated like a slave — Hester knew the pattern. An awful prospect — yet she had no other . . . "But I'm come all the way from Hinching Fen," she said. "I'm spent all my money on gitting here. Don't you see — I counted on this job — you offered it me!"

"I can't help that," the old woman said. "Folk should stop where they are. Thass none of my business if folk choose to go gallivanting. No, you wouldn't have done for us at all. We don't want no gadabouts!"

The door was closed. For some moments yet Hester did not apprehend the gravity of her predicament, occupied as she was with thinking of those stinging retorts that always come to mind too late, contemplating arson, criminal damage and assault and battery, and furiously pulling faces at the spot where the old woman had been standing. It was only when she turned round at last, and looked at that drove stretching away to infinity, that her spirits really sank.

"Oh! piss-emmets," she said, and began the long trudge back.

She would have to find something: she had not sufficient money to get back to Hinching Fen — and what was there for her there? She couldn't stay at the Goslings' any longer. Family — well, she had lost sight of her father, who had disappeared north in search of new windmills to tilt at: there remained Aunt Netty, in charge of her younger siblings a long way off in Leicester. No: there was to be no question of turning to

Aunt Netty, even if she were in a position to get there. She could just imagine that lady's sour triumph in being sought out for help by the girl she had always characterised as Heading For a Fall.

A couple of hours of daylight remained. There must, she reasoned, be more farms in this fertile area, and there was at least a chance that one of them might be in need of female labour. She tramped down more droves, each seeming longer than the last, as if the farms had been deliberately sited to be as far from human contact as possible; and indeed, one or two of the people here were so accustomed to isolation that company simply frightened them, and they could barely find a voice to answer Hester's inquiries. She had no luck: no girls wanted; labour had been taken on at Easter. One woman advised her to go down to the nearby village — "it's only a step," she said, ominously. "You're more likely to find work there than out here."

She went, moving like an automaton now: and found the village a straggle of cottages hugging the banks of the Old Nene. The same negatives met her. Exhausted and hungry, with darkness coming down, she turned to a waterside inn called the Ferryman, the chief building of the place, with several barges tied up at the landing-stage: seeking now only rest and food, and undeterred by the palpably seamy character of the inn. This was discernible even at the outer door, through which was exhaled a great breath that was curiously smoky, steamy, fishy, beery, earthy, and oath-y, all at once.

The parlour of the inn was a long, low-raftered room with windows at the end overlooking the river. The windows were open but it seemed none of the smoke was going out: it simply filled the room as water fills a tank, and to Hester's stinging eyes it seemed that the stuffed fish in cases on the walls were swimming in it. Her first thought, as the babble of talk reached her ears, was that some sort of violent quarrel was going on, for every second word seemed to be a curse: but a few moments' observation revealed that the watermen, standing in groups or hunkered round tables, were on the best of terms, and that it was merely a convention that conversation should be conducted in a stream of cheerful obscenities, some of them physiologically impossible. She was not, as she had first thought, the only woman there: several women of her own age (or at any rate wishing to appear so) were joining in the colourful exchanges, seeming by the unbuttoned state of their blouses to feel the heat excessively; and by the window one was seated on a waterman's knee, or in that region, and was responding to the confidences he whispered into her ear by a reiterated squeal of: "Y'mucky bugger! Y'mucky bugger!"

Squeezing through a sort of corridor of waistcoats, caps and laughing mouths, she found an empty table and ordered a mug of beer and a meal of bread and cheese. She sat with her feet on her carpet-bags and ate voraciously. A few watermen turned to look round at her: she was dressed pretty much in

124

any working-girl's best, a straw boater-style hat, short jacket with high-necked blouse and plain skirt, buttoned boots; but perhaps even that was a little smart for this place, and one brick-red face with a covering of whiskers like a luxuriant growth of mould loomed down and asked if he could buy her a drop of wet.

"No, ta," she said, keeping her left hand out of sight, "I'm waiting for me husband," and the whiskers vanished.

She finished the bread and cheese. It was very short commons compared to what she had become used to at Mrs Langtoft's table, and the landlady passing her just then with a tray, she caught a seductive scent of eel stew. No, she told herself, you can't have none of that — your money's nearly gone, and you'll need a place to sleep tonight — do you hear . . . ? She heard, but did not obey, and was soon digging into a plate of stew, steaming with thyme and sage.

Replete, she sat back, sipping the remainder of her beer, and addressed herself to the problem of what was to become of her. Her money would now only extend to the barest night's accommodation — some cheap lodging-house, which she would probably have to trudge back to March to find. 'I should have throttled that ole ratbag at the farm,' she thought: and as she thought pleasantly of this, and about asking the landlady if she had any skivvy work, washing-up, anything, she found her attention being caught by a conversation going on at a table behind her.

" . . . Farm over Whittlesey way — load of

phosphate of lime. Promised to git it over there tomorrow. Now how am I going to manage?"

She turned to look at the speaker, who was seated in the chimney-corner. Oil-lamps had just been lit, and the curling smoke diffused their radiance, so that the interior of the inn was now clothed in a rich chiaroscuro: the man speaking was hidden in one of the pockets of shadow thus created, but he suddenly leaned forward into the light towards his companion as Hester turned to look.

"Not the first time I'm been left in the lurch like this," he said. "I wish they'd stick to it, when they tek the job."

"Whass a matter, bor?" another voice said from the bar.

"I'm got to git my lighters over Whittlesey, and my mate's done a bunk," the man in the chimney-corner answered. "Five lighters, heavy load to barrow, I can't manage it on my own. I were just asking Fred here whether he'll tek the job on."

"Not me!" said his companion. "I'm a landsman, and I'll stick to it. I went on me cousin's lighters once, just for a lark, and it were such terrible wukk I swore I'd never mourn about digging ditches again."

"Whass happened to your mate, then, bor?" the voice at the bar asked.

"Oh! he went mortaring after a gel, Outwell way," the man in the chimney-corner said, in tones of great disgust. "That were his excuse, any road."

Several ribald comments followed this, terribly

old and stale, but of the sort which men of all ages have taken to be a conclusive demonstration of virility. The man in the chimney-corner paid no heed, but sat staring into the smoke with a deep frown which was doubly expressive: evincing his present vexation, but also appearing plainly as a habitual mien, into which the contours of his face settled naturally. A peculiar immobility was also noticeable about him — he sat there amongst the crowd and movement and noise just as if, Hester thought, he was completely alone; and there was a short-sighted look about his heavy-lidded, dark brown eyes which might have been either physical or a further manifestation of that quality of seeming to inhabit his own circle of space, and to positively not perceive his surroundings. His colouring, naturally dark, was made more so by the typical tan of the waterman, accustomed to a life in the open air, and the large brown hands which tapped restlessly on the table-top were almost of a colour with the chestnut hair, roughly parted in the middle and slightly curling about the ears. His figure, dressed in corduroy trousers, waistcoat, striped shirt and neckerchief, was distinguished by its breadth and bigness of limb, with just a lingering suggestion of the gangling youth — enough to cause Hester to revise her estimate of his age down to twenty-four or -five. That first impressions should have suggested an older man was owing not only to the depth and sonority of his voice but to a certain rigidity about his strongly marked and clean-shaven features, as if he would deny them expression, and impression too, by conscious will.

"Ain't there anyone," he said, coming out of abstraction again, "some lad in the village, mebbe, who'd tek the job? I'm the master, mind: but he'd get a share of the profits, fair and square, and a berth and his meals."

"None that I know on," his companion said. "They're all wukking on the land. They're too daft, some on 'em, to blow their own noses — but they ain't daft enough to come off the farm and go breaking their backs on the lighters." And with a dismissive laugh he got up and went to the bar.

The man in the chimney-corner drained his beer, then ran his finger round the rim of his empty tankard, and toyed with it, as if debating whether to have another. In these few moments Hester made up her mind. She gathered up her bags and went and took the recently vacated seat opposite the waterman.

"Not interested," he said, barely glancing up.

"Nor am I," Hester said, "if it comes to that. But I'm interested in the job."

The waterman frowned at her, then made an impatient gesture. "You got it wrong, gel. I'm got a gang of lighters, I need a mate to work on 'em. Thass the job."

"Well, thass the job I'm asking for."

"Oh! git along. I'm not in the mood for joking."

"I'm not joking. You need someone to work for you and I need work."

128

"A man, I meant, a man," the waterman said, frowning harder.

"All right — but you can't git one — and I can work just as hard as any man. I'm done three years on a fen farm — I'm used to it. What do you say?"

"You?" The waterman glanced up and down her figure, then shook his head, his lips compressed, as if he could barely even bring himself to laugh. He got up. "Don't waste my time, gel."

She watched him go, threading his way through the crowd. Unlike the heroines of her mother's yellowback novels, Hester was not particularly proud: she had never, as far as she could recall, flung her hair out of her eyes in Fiery Resentment, or felt her cheeks Mantle (whatever that was) at an Insult. But she was unaccustomed to being found so unworthy of a second glance, which piqued her . . . and besides, what she had said was perfectly true. Her desperate need for any job had made her speak out: being dismissed as unequal to this one made her more determined to get it.

She picked up her bags and went out after the waterman. It was full dark now, but fine and starlit, and she presently descried him walking down the towpath behind the inn, and then stopping to look at the river where several lighters were tied up. He pulled out a tobacco-pouch and began filling a pipe, visibly falling into that rapt absorption of solitude that she had already noticed in him; so that he started when she spoke.

"These your lighters, are they?" she said.

"Oh! it's you." He continued to pack the pipe. The starlight, and the soft margin of illumination from the windows of the inn, showed her his uncommunicative profile, and the shapes of the fen lighters, low open barges of a peculiarly native type, moored by the landing-stage.

"I weren't joking," she said. "I'm looking for work and I don't mind if it's heavy. I'm young and fit and I got no ties. I don't know much about lighters but I'm willing to learn. You said you need someone bad, and you can't git anybody here. So why not?"

The waterman put the tobacco-pouch away, and faced her at last, turning his whole body in an aggressive presenting of himself. "Now why on earth," he said, "should you want to do this job?"

"Like I said — I need the work. Down on my luck. Nothing strange about that, is there?"

The waterman grunted, studied her for a few moments, then said: "Wait here," and turning away from her descended a boarding-plank on to the first lighter, locating the plank in the dark with a conspicuous negligence. With the same casualness he traversed the narrow strip of deck running the lighter's length and from the stern drew out a wheelbarrow and shovel. In a very few seconds he had loaded the barrow with lime from the hold, and was wheeling it down the deck and then up the boarding-plank to the landing-stage, his clay pipe fixed in his mouth. He set the barrow down in front of Hester.

"Now let's see you tek it back," he said.

Just in time Hester stopped herself from saying she might get her clothes dirty. She grasped the handles of the wheelbarrow and carefully, refraining from tugging, took the weight. It didn't seem too bad. The waterman stepped out of her way as she steered it along the towpath and on to the boarding-plank. The river being low and the landing-stage high, the plank descended at quite a steep angle: gravity suddenly took hold of the barrow and nearly pulled it out of her hands, and only by setting her arms as taut as cables was she able to control it. The water twinkled underneath her as she crossed the sagging plank, trying not to look down. The barrow seemed somehow to have got heavier by the time she reached the deck: her arms juddered as she slewed it round, but she kept her balance, and with a conscious briskness she trundled it down to the stern. Upending the barrow to tip the load into the hold caused her to go rather red in the face, but she felt she presented a tolerably composed appearance by the time she rejoined the waterman on the landing-stage.

"Well," he said, smoking, "thass the easier part, of course — barrowing downhill. You'd be barrowing up high banks mostly."

"Fair enough."

He continued to contemplate her, his hands on his hips. She returned his gaze steadily.

"You harness a hoss?" he said abruptly.

"Do that in me sleep," she said — with perhaps a little unconscious mimicking of his manner. It was a job she had done, just

131

occasionally, at the Langtofts'.

"Powerful lot of walking you have to do — leading the hoss."

"Well, I'm never kept a carriage, you know."

The waterman sighed and frowned down at his lighters. Reading his thoughts, Hester said: "You can't manage on your own — I heard you say. And there's nobody else offering, is there?"

From the inn a blowsy, boozy gust of laughter came floating on a smoke-scented breeze, dying away in the purer air. The river made quiet lappings to itself round the struts of the landing-stage.

"All right," he said. "Look here. I need someone for the job, so you'll have to do, though I never heard of a woman doing it. You got to be serious, mind — no skipping out if you find you don't tek to it: I'm got loads to deliver, and I'm late as it is. Still game?"

"Oh, yes!" said she: elated by having won her point, and for the moment beguiled by the sheer novelty of the position she found herself in. She had a strong regard for the capabilities of her sex, and it pleased her that she was doing what women had never done before.

"Rules," said the lighterman. He pointed to the first lighter, where there was a cabin amidships. "Thass my cabin — there's a little stove there for cooking on — you'll git plenty to eat. My mate used to have one of the bunks, but thass no good for you. There's a cabin on number four — full o' taters at the moment, it ain't been used much — you'll have to sleep on that. I ain't carrying no passengers, mind. You do the work proper, and you'll git your share of the profits, same as anybody else: but like I say, it's a man's work, and you'll have to live as a man. No frocks. It ain't practical, and besides that I don't want folk thinking I'm got a gel faffing about on my boats. I'm got some ole trousers and a moleskin jacket somewhere, and a cap — I s'pose you can put your hair right up?"

"Oh! yes," she said — she didn't fancy cutting it off.

"Well, we'll have to sort all that in the morning — we'll not be sleeping yet — I do a lot of travelling at night. Not changed your mind?"

"No," she said: and really she did not see why she should. It could hardly be worse, after all, than life at that old crone's farm would have been. Her decision had been made with characteristic celerity — but part of the reason for that promptness was that little daunted her. Hester's conception of the world, and of her relations to it, was still imaged forth as a slate on which she might write broadly what she chose, and as yet she did not envisage this principle acting the other way round. "I reckon I can do it. If *you* ain't changed your mind."

He shook his head, and looked hard at her. "I dunno. I must be mad. I want my head seeing to. Still, have to mek the best of it."

"Well, at least you can be sure of one thing — I ain't going to do like your last mate and go mortaring after some gel."

He did not respond. "Come on. We'll go and fetch the hoss."

The inn, like most of its kind, had stabling for the lightermen's horses. Theirs was a strong and thickset beast, and submitted with the utmost placidity to the collar and bridle under the waterman's hands: but when he suggested that Hester lead him out, and she began to do so, the horse kicked and bucked like the very devil.

"Here, here — you ain't up the stick, are you?" the waterman said.

"No, I ain't!"

"Only it sends him funny, that — he knows it somehow. Whoa, steady Boss."

"It's just he ain't used to me, thass all," Hester said; and she kept a tight hold of the bridle and crooned some nonsense words that Mr Langtoft had always used to his team. The horse ceased kicking, but shied at passing through the amber shafts of light coming from the inn windows, and she had to lead him round.

"He'll git used to me," she said as they went down to the towpath. "I'll bring him round — I'll git him to like me — you'll see."

The waterman watched her with an expression of profound scepticism. "Think pretty well of yourself, don't you?" he said.

She was not accustomed to being assailed so frontally. She seemed to come up against a large hard arrogance, like some bulky obstacle in the darkness, and it irked her. "Well," she said, "I don't see why I should be ashamed of myself, instead. Do you?"

"We'll see," he said dryly.

"Any road — my name's Hester Verney, and I'll let you call me Hester, and I come from Hinching Fen."

Mine's Jonathan Eastholm; and I don't come from anywhere in particular; and you'll call me captain, or skipper — 'cos thass what I am."

★ ★ ★

The waterways of the fens, along which the gangs of lighters carried their goods, comprised a mixed network of the Rivers Ouse and Nene and their tributaries, and artificial drainage channels, of varying age, and testifying to the long and still continuing struggle to free the land of its burden of water. The route that Hester and her new employer took that night led from the Old Nene into the straight cut known, from its width, as the Twenty Foot. Leading the horse, she found that he soon lost his nervousness of her, seeming glad of any company in the lonely darkness. She soon found, too, the impracticality of her normal clothes. Though the weather had been dry, the towpath along the high banks, with their soft soil, was in that permanent condition of mud known locally as slub, which coated the hem of her skirt in no time, and then seemed to creep on upwards as if possessing a life of its own. In places the fences of the surrounding fields came right up to the bank — and coming across one without a gate, but only a stile, she stopped: only to hear Jonathan Eastholm bellowing at her from the lighters: "Don't let the rope go slack, damn

135

you, I lose steering-way! Jump him over it — he's used to it!" And indeed the horse, though not appearing to relish the effort, cleared the stile quite easily. Then there was a bridge — which necessitated untying the horse, and trotting him over the top, while the lighters drifted through below, and then retying again on the other side, with the rope all wet and slippery, the horse skittish from his few moments of liberty, and Eastholm cursing at her to git on. Everything seemed slimy, damp, difficult, and frustratingly laborious; and add to this the wind which came howling down the straight funnel of the Twenty Foot, always full in her face of course – the fens being the only place in the country where two people can be observed walking in opposite directions into a head wind — and altogether Hester saw the sun rise on her first day on the lighters in a state of the severest dejection and exhaustion.

By that time they had passed into Whittlesey Dyke, and it was necessary to untie again while the lighters passed through a lock. Waiting on the towpath with the horse, she leaned her head against his neck, and could almost have fallen asleep there and then.

"Hoy, look alive there!" Eastholm called. "Tain't a pleasure cruise!"

"Aye, aye, captain," she said under her breath, except that captain was not the word she used.

Soon after that, however, to her intense relief, they moored just below another bridge, and the waterman proposed some breakfast. There was grazing for the horse on the bank, and Hester was glad just to place her aching bones on a canvas stool in the doorway of the cabin on the house-lighter, and smell the bacon frying in a blackened trivet on the little oil-stove.

"Out of eggs just now," Eastholm said, producing bread and a parcel of butter from a foot-locker, and knives and plates from another. "We'll mebbe git some from the farm where this lime's going. Git that ate, and I'll brew some tea in a minute."

Hester was not particular, and was too weary just now to take much notice of her surroundings; but she did notice that everything was surprisingly clean and neat in a spartan sort of way, and that the tiny cabin seemed to contain most domestic necessities; though getting at them entailed on Eastholm's part a complicated set of manoeuvres, dictated by the impossibility in the confined space of opening more than one drawer at a time, and requiring him to squeeze his long limbs into unlikely postures. Extracting a box of cutlery from underneath the bunk compelled him to lie on his side, and swing his great legs round so that his boots touched the wall, as if he were going to walk up it like a fly. That he was plainly unaware of the incongruous appearance of this, demonstrated further what Hester had observed from her first sight of him – that he was a creature of solitude, who carried that quality with him into company, as a fish in a glass bowl inhabits its own miniature element amidst the alien one that surrounds it.

A great wedge of lean bacon, and a slab of

137

bread and butter which the waterman cut as if he were sawing wood, with tea in a mug like a pint-pot, did much to revive Hester's spirits — as did the thought of that dingy farm, and the sort of victuals that moist old woman was likely to serve up. Eastholm, having disposed of his meal very much as he stowed away the utensils in his cabin, occupied himself with sorting appropriate clothes for Hester.

"You git these on," he said. "We'll be delivering to the farmer upstream in a bit, and I don't want it looking like I'm carryen some fancy-piece with my cargo."

"Well, you could always pretend I was your wife," Hester said.

Eastholm gave a grunt, something like "Pah!" and, collecting the plates, rinsed them by the simple expedient of lowering them over the side in a net.

The cabin on the fourth lighter was the barest hatch, with an earthy smell of the vegetables stored under the bunk. Here she stored her bags, and changed into the clothes he had given her. The coarse calico shirt and the moleskin jacket fitted well enough, their roomy folds being filled out by Hester's figure, for as Peggy Chettle had remarked, she had plenty on the sideboard: but long-legged as she was, she could not compete with the waterman in that respect, and she had to roll the bottoms of the trousers up into great cuffs that flapped as she walked. Her hair she gathered up into the flat cap, and finished off the ensemble with a silk square scarf of her own, tied as a neckerchief.

138

She went down the towpath, trying to walk like a man (however did they manage it?), to where Jonathan Eastholm was harnessing the horse, and drew his attention to the trousers.

"Ah! well, they'll have to do for now," he said. He clucked his tongue. "You still don't look like a chap really."

"Well, I ain't going to wear a beard, if thass what you're thinking."

Eastholm shook his head and turned back to the horse. "I dunno. I want my head seeing to."

★ ★ ★

So Hester Verney, having left Hinching Fen to be a farm-servant, found herself a waterman instead.

The men who plied the gangs of lighters around the fens were the survivors of a much more numerous breed, having their origin in the days when the waterways were the easiest, and in some cases the only, means of transport in that remote part of the kingdom. The antiquity of their trade was sufficiently exhibited in the very design of the lighters, which was traceable to the shallow-drawing boats of the Vikings, who had penetrated the channels a thousand years ago to lay waste to the fenland abbeys. The lighters were flat-bottomed and rounded at bow and stern, forty feet in length and ten feet wide, sturdily built in oak with deck planking of elm, and coated with pitch: they were not equipped with rudders, the leading lighter in the gang being steered by a pole, and the following lighters linked by seizing-chains and a system of ropes which kept them aligned. These craft, though reduced in number, were still a familiar sight despite the coming of the railways to the fens; the lightermen surviving by working at cheap rates, and carrying heavy local loads — sand, bricks, clay for stabilising the peat soil, and in particular the ubiquitous turves for domestic fuel. A spirit of comradeship accordingly existed among them, as Hester soon found when they passed a gang coming in the other direction. "What you carryen?" was the standard greeting shouted across the water — accompanied, as was the reply, by a volley of curses casting vivid aspersions on the other's parentage, eating habits, and sexual endowment: the whole, however, as mechanically harmless as the passing of remarks on the weather.

Having delivered the load of lime at Whittlesey on time, they were at last permitted a rest, and Hester lay down in her clothes in the musty bunk and slept a drugged sleep. In the afternoon Jonathan Eastholm outlined their itinerary.

"Load o' tiles to pick up at Yaxley, and mebbe some turf; then back down the Twenty Foot, through Outwell, through Denver Sluice, down the Ouse, down Brandon Creek and back, down to the clay-pits at Ely; round Pope's Corner, up the Old Bedford, and down the Forty Foot to Stokeley."

They proceeded via the King's Dyke; and it was suggestive of the persistence of the past in this land that the King in question was

Canute. The banks were tree-lined here, the interlacing branches bristling with new green buds: spring growth quickened in the fields below. Everywhere was transfixed with the light of the limitless sky, to a bright glassy stillness. In such conditions, rather than at night, the possibility of those ghostly apparitions common in the fens seemed tinglingly present; and time appeared a porous membrane, through which at any moment the past might leak, and the carved prows of the Norse longboats be seen nosing round the bend in the stream, or the tramp of the legions be heard on the ancient wind. The horse pricked up his ears at the brilliance of the day; and Hester felt that life on the lighters had, after all, strong charms, and that she had rather fallen on her feet.

She continued to feel this over the next few days. Unfortunately, this optimism alternated with times when it seemed hell on earth.

It was him that was the trouble — him with his great stern frown of scepticism, always watching her for a mistake. She was soon on good terms with the horse, who was pretty well accustomed to the places where he had to jump a stile — and there were places too, where if he could not negotiate the obstacle and the banks were not high, the lighters would be brought in to the side and the horse would jump on to the first one, sailing on for a few yards as if it were the most natural thing in the world before leaping back on to the towpath. But still there were occasions when Hester would start woolgathering, and the horse would very willingly dawdle too — and soon the shouts of the captain would alert her, in withering terms, to the fact that the tow-rope was slack.

"Wake your bloody ideas up there! I'm damn near into the bank! Bugger my ole boots, I never see the like of it. Whoever told you you could be a waterman?"

"You did!" she cried back.

Then there was her first experience of barrowing goods up the high flood-banks which carried many of the fen waterways above the level of the land. The trick, of course, was to take the barrow up the plank at speed, the momentum carrying you through without that horrible wobbling, sagging moment in the middle: but this was a lesson more easily apprehended than put into practice. She was afraid of dropping the load into the water, she was afraid of dropping herself into the water, she was afraid that her arms would come out of their sockets, and she was afraid that Jonathan Eastholm, impatiently waiting behind her with the next barrowload, would see all these things; and the resulting paralysis of caution made her more clumsy than she was. At Yaxley she lost control of a barrowload of tiles just as she reached the bank: it overbalanced, and a few of the tiles smashed as they hit the towpath.

"Cack-handed sort of ole boy you're got there, ain't it?" said the man collecting the tiles.

"Oh! you have to tek what you can git," Eastholm said. He unloaded his barrow, then told her to follow him to the cabin. A piece of slate was nailed to the cabin wall, on which he noted details of loads and payments: and here he chalked the letters H.V. and a minus sign. "Them tiles are coming off your pay," he said. "Probably a bob's worth. We'll call it ninepence," and he chalked the figure up.

Then there was the long heavy shower of rain — which was snug to hear drumming on the roof of the boathouse, but less fun to slop through leading the horse. Eventually, with the rain coursing off her hat and her trousers clinging round her legs — how did men bear to wear them? — she pulled the horse up and trudged back to the first lighter.

"Whass up?"

"I'm gitting soaked! Can't we moor for a while?"

"Just for a drop of rain?" Eastholm was standing on the deck with all his perpendicular sturdiness, gripping the steering-pole, bareheaded and with his shirt plastered down to his square torso by the wet so that its contours showed through like a Roman breastplate. "Git along."

"Well, ain't there a bit o' tarpaulin or summat I can put over my shoulders?"

"Coh! give me strength," he muttered, and presently an old oilcloth was flung in her direction. "Goo on, we're losing headway."

The clearing of the rain, thankfully, threw everything into a different aspect. The long straight channel of Bevill's Leam stretched ahead like a spear aimed at the horizon: the sun glittered on the water; a pair of swans drifted by, pure white and unruffled. It was impossible not to wonder at the ingenuity and aspiration of man, wrenching this inimical landscape to his own purposes, and to feel a sort of proud solidarity with those whose past labour, so often heartbreaking, bore renewed fruit in each crop that was lifted from the jealous fields. But for all her exhilaration, there he was still behind her, watching out for a slip, and getting out his tobacco in that slow thoughtful way that infuriated her.

But when they moored things were better. He caught a fine bream in his bow-net, and they cooked it on the oil-stove, and there was a wonderful quiet between the high banks roofed over with red-ribbed sky. He had told her that she would have to live as a man on this job; and that certainly extended to the meals, which were huge and satisfying, and which he dispensed with a rough liberality.

"Here — git that down you. Goo on — tek some more. Plenty where that come from."

At these times all the brusque urgency of work subsided in him, and he sat on the canvas stool in a kind of massive repose that had in it something suggestive of the large elements of water and earth with which he was so plainly at home. He looked about him at the changing colours of the sky with a dwelling eye, as if he were conning the pages of a book, and his voice sank to a deeper register as he placed his hands on his knees and remarked on their progress or the weather. "Wind's shifted. Reckon it'll be fair tomorrow. Git through Outwell afore sun-up."

"Well, I'll say this — " she wiped her plate

with bread — "you git fed as well here as on the ole farm."

"How'd you lose your work then?" he said. "Farm go bust? — I know a lot do, on the fen."

"No . . . it weren't that." She watched a cluster of wild duck fly overhead, briefly traversing their roof of sky as sparrows will pass through an open warehouse; and her mind suffered the mental equivalent of a sigh. It was a pity, after all, that a part of your life should be finished, cut off as if it had never been: was it always to be like that? Sadness touched Hester's shoulder, and for a moment she could not brush it off. "It were one of them personal things — a disagreement. It's a shame, because I liked the work, but you can't go on once that sort of thing happens."

The waterman nodded, slowly, and seemed to look down a deep well of thought. He took the pipe from his mouth and said with deliberation: "It's gitting all involved and tangled up wi' feelings that causes half the trouble in the world."

"I suppose so," she said. "But then you can't just live life all on your own, can you? Thass no way to live."

The look he gave her was more of surprise than anything else. "It's the *only* way," he said. He knocked out his pipe, stood up and stretched. "Well, I reckon I'll gi' meself a bath."

"Oh! Where do you do that?"

"Why, where d'you think?" And he gestured over the side.

"Oh! I see."

For some moments she did not understand the uneasy frown he gave her. At last he said: "Well — you git up tother end, if you want to do the same."

"Ah — sorry."

She went down the towpath to the other house-lighter, smiling to herself: he was as modest as a girl! A splash, and some satisfied baritone gasps, indicated that he had gone in. She considered going back and saying she had forgotten something — but she more than suspected he was not amenable to that kind of teasing.

Her amusement at his unexpected pudency, however, gave way at the first touch of the water on her bare legs to amazement at his hardiness: it was freezing! She contrived to bathe herself with piecemeal splashings, and with the help of a bucket to wash her hair. She was combing it, and despairing of ever getting it dry, when he came down the towpath to fetch a bait for the horse. He was all in a glow, and not shivering in the least.

"Ain't you got a mirror anywhere?" she said.

"What would I want a mirror for?"

"Well! not to look at your beauty, thass for sure," she said. But again, these sallies simply rolled off him, leaving him as unmoved as the icy water had done.

"We'll git going in a minute," he said, digging in the tub of oats and bran.

"All right," she said. She looped her hair into a great bunch, combing it over her shoulder.

She wished there was a mirror: when she had it down you could really see the sheen on the black, almost indigo in the sunlight. Suddenly she noticed he was staring at the long sweep of hair. Well, she thought, consciously spreading it out, he wasn't completely made of stone after all.

"I hope all that stuff's going to go back in your cap when it's dry," he grunted, going away.

He took his cold plunge whenever the opportunity was furnished by a quiet stretch of water. It was part of that same stoical impassivity that made him stand out on the deck in the east wind in no more than shirt and waistcoat; that enabled him to barrow the heaviest load of turves without so much as an extra puff of smoke coming from the clay-pipe jammed in his mouth; and that manifested itself in a complete indifference to her own shivering dips into the water from the other end of the gang. Of course, she would soon have told him where to go if he had tried to sneak a look — but still it was a little provoking to feel that for all he cared she might just as well have been the man into which the borrowed clothes imperfectly transformed her.

She hated the sight of those turves — and not simply because of the memory of the awful débâcle of Chad's wager. Delivering them a few at a time, to cottages close to the waterside, was not without its novelty: Eastholm would throw them up to her from the lighters, and she was deft at catching them; and occasionally housewives would come down to the towpath, and hold out their hessian aprons to catch them as he tossed them up. But mostly, alas, they were dealing in hundreds. Back on the Old Nene towards Outwell they were sailing between high flood banks; and pushing a barrow of a hundred turves up these was like pushing a boulder up a hill. And the fact that whenever she thought she had taken the last load, there always seemed to be one more waiting for her, added to the sisyphean quality of this nightmarish labour.

And him, of course — always watching her with his arrogant eye and his sceptical scoffings.

"Stop watching me — you put me off!" she exclaimed once.

"Watching you? I have to watch you — Lord knows what you'd do if I didn't."

It was at Outwell that it happened, at last. There was a big load to deliver, and half-way through the muscles of her arms felt as if they were drawn out like soldering-wire. "Just let me have a rest a minute," she pleaded.

"A rest? What for?" Eastholm said. "I don't want a rest."

"But my arms ache — I'm afraid I shall drop 'em if I carry on."

"Pah! Do as I tell you, and git on."

Muttering some words she had learned from the watermen under her breath, Hester manoeuvred the barrow on to the plank and gritted her teeth to go at it at a run. Half-way across she realised she had lost her momentum — it was just as she feared — the barrow wobbled wildly — she could not hold it — her wrists gave way, and the load of turves toppled into the water, Hester just managing to save the barrow from following them.

"Coh! bloody hell fire me," Eastholm said. "I reckon you did that on purpose!"

Hester opened her mouth to protest: could not speak for sheer indignation.

Eastholm put down his barrow and walked slowly to the cabin. "Better chalk that up, hadn't I? Shilling a hundred."

She had always thought 'seeing red' was just an expression: in that moment she knew better. She was even-tempered by nature, but something about this man made her hackles rise; and somehow all her strength came back. She waited till Eastholm had emerged again from the cabin. Then she trundled the empty barrow back to the lighter, loaded it with another hundred turves, wheeled it half-way across the plank, and calmly and deliberately tipped the whole load into the water.

Eastholm's mouth was open: she saw she had got to him, and she swelled with black, devilish satisfaction. She walked past him into the cabin, picked up the chalk, and wrote another shilling on the slate.

"*That* was on purpose," she said, dusting her hands.

They finished the delivery in silence: sailed on a little way in silence, then moored, in silence, for supper. Hester gave the horse his feed, and came back to the house-lighter to find bacon on the stove, and Eastholm standing looking down at it, his tobacco-pouch in his hands.

She turned the rashers over, whistling, and aware of a pair of glowering chocolate-brown eyes fixed on her.

"That were a bloody daft trick you played," he said.

"Well — next time you'll know what to expect," she replied — her anger by no means over.

"Next time? Any more o' that and I'll dump you on the bank and leave you there — where I should have left you in the first place!"

"Try it! You wouldn't git anybody else to put up with you!" The sight of him aloofly filling his pipe was too much: he even conducted a quarrel from a lofty height! Wildly she snatched the tobacco from his fingers and tossed it over the side. "And I'll chuck that in the river an' all if I feel like it!"

"Why, you little beggar — " He seized a broom-handle. "I'll tek this to you — "

"Don't you hit me wi' that! I'll hit you wi' this!" she exclaimed, grabbing a wooden shovel and brandishing it.

He hit her with that, and she hit him with this. She came off best: for while he only paddled her behind with the broomstick, she brought the shovel down on the back of his neck much harder than she intended. "Oh no!" she said, dropping the shovel, and convinced for a moment that she had killed him; but he straightened up, rubbing the back of his neck, and swearing in surprise.

"Did I hurt you?" she said.

"Well, that was the idea, weren't it?" he said,

throwing the broomstick down. They stared at each other a moment: then Eastholm picked up the pan of bacon and began slopping it out on to plates.

"Here," he said gruffly.

"Thank you," she said, with equal shortness: and they ate their meal in silence, each selecting one of the high featureless banks to gaze at throughout, as if it were a view teeming with absorbing detail. This restful repast over, she returned to the towpath, and he to the steering-pole, to move on for an hour or so before finishing for the day.

Along the towpath, besides flag irises and purple loosestrife as high as the horse's withers, there was a thick spring growth of reeds and thistles. Hester was in that sullenly smarting state in which we tend to barge about with a sort of masochistic defiance, and if we get hurt, well, that just shows how cruel the world is: and so she ploughed through the foliage as if she had the strength of the horse, with the result that one tangled clump of knife-edged reeds fairly lacerated her bare leg just above the boot. When they tied up for the night, it was bleeding heavily; and as Eastholm was putting the kettle on the stove for a last brew of tea, he noticed the blood.

"What you done to your leg?"

"Nothing."

Unceremoniously he pushed her on to a stool and yanked up her trouser leg. "I'm got summat for that," he said. "You don't want it turning nasty."

"It ain't anything much," she said.

He ignored that, and went into the cabin, where he underwent his familiar contortions to extract a tin from under the bunk. She watched him crushing some leaves in a bowl, adding a little hot water, and mixing. There was a piquant contrast between the big-hewn character of the man and the nimble nicety with which he performed these actions: in spite of herself she smiled.

"Right, come here." He knelt and pulled off her boot, and applied the poultice with more gentleness than the size and work-roughened texture of his hands suggested.

"What is it?" she said.

"Water-bitney," he said. "Grows all down the river."

Hester was particularly susceptible to small pleasant sensations, one tincture of them being sufficient to colour her whole mood: and so the soothing of the poultice, taken with the unfamiliar sight of the russet crown of Eastholm's head — a part of the body that communicates a peculiar vulnerability — was sufficient to relax, mellow and generally transform her straight from ill-humour to content with no gradations in between.

"Feels nice," she said.

"It's good stuff. That'll all be healed up tomorrer."

"I'm sorry I hit you with the shovel," she said.

Eastholm sat back on his haunches. "Well . . ." he said, and then seemed to make a mental

152

swerve. "I ain't sorry I hit you with the broom — you deserved it."

★ ★ ★

The peacefully unvarying panorama of level horizons, dykes, and cloudscapes scumbled here and there by the smoke of pumping-stations, was interrupted after Outwell by a stop-and-start passage of locks and sluices, culminating in the great engineering feat that acted as the heart to the fenland's arteries, Denver Sluice. It was as they lay up in the late evening waiting for a passage through Salter's Lode that Hester, just about to catnap on her bunk, heard the sound of music, small and faint above the lapping of the water. Having been accustomed all her life to the home-made music of poor fen chapelgoers, she immediately recognised the timbre as that of a concertina.

She got up and went down the towpath; and saw Jonathan Eastholm sitting in the doorway of his cabin, his back against the jamb, with a concertina of ancient appearance, with a turkey-necked look about its leather bellows, on his knee. He was working his way, with terrific concentration, through the melody of 'Tom Bowling': his performance being of that pluckily amateur kind which the ear follows with a sympathetic suspense in apprehension of a wrong note. Hester, liking a tune, and no more able to play an instrument than fly, heard its halting progress through with pleasure: struck too by the altered appearance of Eastholm, who bent over the concertina with something of the perplexed, encumbered look of large men when engaged on small tasks of tenderness with babies or animals.

"That was nice," Hester said.

Eastholm nearly jumped out of his seat. "What you doing there?"

"Listening. I didn't know you could play that."

"I can't — I can't play it, really." He shoved the concertina out of sight, as if to deny the very fact of its existence. "It's just an ole thing I'm got — it ain't anything." He had gone red in the face, and seemed thoroughly and disproportionately embarrassed by the whole thing. "Ain't you going to git some sleep? Don't want you dragging your feet in the morning."

She went back to her cabin, framing to herself a sketch of his character headed by the word Impossible.

★ ★ ★

With the passage of Denver they left behind the locks and sluices, and entered the River Ouse, wending its way south through a sea of rich earth on which Ely Cathedral, in the limpid dawn, could be glimpsed like a distant galleon. Here the waterway was busier, and Hester more conspicuous: other lightermen called greetings to Eastholm, and asked who he'd got working for him; watermen outside riverside taverns and at ferries watched her leading the horse with the frank curious stare of the isolated country

154

district; and once a fisherman on the towpath asked her the time.

"Whass a'clock, bor?"

"Bout half arter," she muttered, pulling her cap down.

They were to make a diversion down the tributary known as Brandon Creek to deliver turf. The venerable Ship Inn commanded the turning into the Creek, and they moored here to eat some dinner — fish again, cooked on the stove.

"Can't we go up to the Ship to eat?" Hester said.

"No we can't," Eastholm said. "Likely to be a whole issue o' chaps I know there, and they'll soon want to know all about you."

Even as he spoke, a man sitting underneath the trees on the grassy plot before the inn stood up and hailed him: "Jonathan! Is that you, you ole bugger?"

Hester found herself being abruptly bundled into the cabin. "Here, what's to do?" she cried.

"Git in there and lay low. Thass Shush Hubbard coming over — I'll never hear the last of it if he cottons on you're a gel."

"Well, I am! It's nothing to be ashamed of."

"Just git in and stay out of sight."

"Why's he called Shush?"

"Because he don't, thass why — he's got the biggest mouth between here and Boston Stump. Every tale you ever hear started with Shush Hubbard. I'll try and git rid of him."

He shut the cabin door on her, and presently

she heard the usual cuss-strewn exchange of greetings, with a great yelping laugh that could only be Shush Hubbard. She sat down on Eastholm's bunk and peered round in the semi-darkness. There was a narrow shelf above her, stocked with a handful of books: *Old Moore's Almanac*, for the tides, *Pilgrim's Progress*, the Bible, *Robinson Crusoe* and *Paradise Lost*. The further shaft of light thrown on Eastholm's character by this mini-library was not without interest: she was tantalised by a glimpse into a bafflingly inaccessible personality; but there was insufficient physical light for her to read in the books, and she grew bored. Outside the conversation went on, dominated by the deafening counter-tenor of Shush Hubbard: "What you carryen then? — *Are* you? — Down Brandon, then? Ah, *I'm* been up Burwell — few bricks, poor ole load, *poor* ole load" — all interspersed with the shrieking laugh, which seemed not to derive from anything funny, but to be a kind of reflex like the rattling of a jester's bells. Boredom, instinctive dislike of self-proclaimed wits of Shush Hubbard's sort, and hunger for her dinner got the better of her: she pulled her cap low over her face, opened the cabin door and went out.

Shush Hubbard and Jonathan Eastholm were standing on the towpath close to the lighter; and the latter, turning, threw Hester a wild glance, with more than a dash of murder in it. Shush Hubbard — a plump ginger specimen with a mouth which bisected his face like a split in an apple — raised his eyebrows and said, "Who's that then? That your new mate?"

"Ah," Eastholm said, through clenched teeth. "Thass it — Jack — thass his name."

"How do," grunted Hester, stumping over to the stove with hunched shoulders. She slapped some of the cooked fish on to a plate and squatted down on a stool with her back to them. "Scuse me — got to git some bloody grub down me — I'm that hungry I could eat a dish o' pigshit wi'out a spoon." And she began gobbling the fish down with appreciative smacks and slurps.

There was a moment of surprised silence, and then Shush Hubbard said: "Been on the lighters long?"

"Not long — used to wukk on the wharf up at Lynn," she growled. "Chucked it in when I saw a chap git caught by a load o' timber right in the knackers — sod that for a lark, I says."

Shush Hubbard let out a gurgle of laughter, though a little uncertainly. "Whass he like to wukk for then, ole Jonathan here?" he said.

Hester risked a glance round, seeing what appeared to be a carved statue of Jonathan Eastholm standing on the towpath, with a most lifelike expression of smothered anguish. "Ah! he ain't a bad ole bugger," she said. "Bit of a tight-arse, you know — put a foot wrong and he gives you a look as black as a coalman's cods — but he ain't bad." She spat out a fish-bone.

"Ah! Right." Shush Hubbard's laugh trailed off again. "Well, I reckon I'll goo and git meself another drop of beer. Yew coming for one, Jonathan?"

"Er — no, ta all the same, Shush."

"What about you, Jack?" Shush Hubbard said.

"Not that bloody ole beer they serve here," Hester said. "You might as well drink a pot o' piss and cut out the middleman."

"Ah! Right." Shush's laugh faded completely. "Cheer-oo then." He started down the towpath, and then she heard him say to Eastholm — with a totally ineffectual attempt to lower his voice — "I say, Jonathan, that ole boy you're got wukking for you — he's a bit foul-mouthed, ain't he?"

Hester carried on eating — aware of Jonathan Eastholm's footsteps coming slowly up the boarding-plank, and ready to seize the shovel again if it came to it.

He sat down on the stool opposite her, picked up a plate and served himself with fish, cut a slice of bread, put both down on the deck, and burst out laughing.

It was a pleasant sight to see. The set, curtailed lineaments of his face broke up: he gave himself up completely to the laughter, which afforded an instructive contrast to the forced hootings of Shush Hubbard — it was a young laugh, the laugh of a boy still inhabiting the deep-chested figure of the man, and gladly breaking out as if he had been suppressed a little too early and a little too strictly. Tears started to his eyes, and he slapped his legs helplessly, and at last choked and half-strangled.

Hester jumped up and slapped his back. "I made you laugh! Hooray! I did, I made you laugh!" she said, her hands on his shoulders.

He groaned, wiping his eyes. "Oh, you little beggar. I never thought I'd see somebody shut Shush Hubbard up — I never did."

"So my name's Jack, then, is it?" she said. "What made you pick that? — Jack's as good as his master?"

He made to shake a fist at her, but was still too weak. "I dunno," he said. "Whatever happened to my quiet life?"

★ ★ ★

They moored that evening at Littleport, having returned from Brandon Creek to the Ouse. Littleport had a bad name in the fens: seventy years ago it had been the centre of food riots, as a result of which six men were transported and five publicly hanged for refusing to starve quietly; and perhaps the fact that these sentences were meted out under the merciful authority of the Bishop of Ely was not without influence in the turning of the fen folk to the chapel. If the loved and respected lord and clergyman were ever to be found outside the pages of novels, they were not to be found in the fens — where the deepest pride in lineage still attached to an ancestor who had fought for the good old cause of Oliver Cromwell.

No wronged shades, however, troubled their peace as they tied up at a tree-fringed mooring below the town. It was an April evening of rare beauty, with a sky bearing both the colour and something of the bloom of rose-petals, reflecting in the water with yet softer hue, and casting glancing shadows amongst the trees. Hester had found flour and dried fruit amongst Eastholm's miscellaneous stores, and had contrived to make a nodding-cake, which they ate hot from the pan, sitting on the deck and watching the river banks dissolve into violet shadow. There was scarcely a sound beyond the quiet croppings of the horse on the grass; and it was possible to sense the broad unpeopled distances that lay on either side of them, and to receive the impression of the primeval, paradoxically, in this man-made landscape — to taste that ancient loneliness, of when humankind was few, and the world vast.

"Hark at that quiet," Hester said. "We could be on a little island in the middle of the sea — like in that book you're got — *Robinson Crusoe*."

"How'd you know I'd got that?"

"I saw it in your cabin — when you shut me in."

"Oh! then," he said, and gave a retrospective chuckle.

"Thass what it's about, ain't it? I remember being told about it at school."

"There's more to it than that — but thass the main bit, and the best bit." With a sudden uncoiling of reserve he said: "I must have read that a score of times — can't git enough of it."

She was going to make a remark about him being quite a scholar, but stopped herself. It was by no means unheard of for men in the fens, isolated in mills, farms, boats, to turn

160

despite ill-education to a little store of books; and besides, she did not want to inhibit his newly expansive mood.

"How's he end up on this island then?" she said. She was sitting directly on the deck, her back comfortably against the outer cabin wall — sitting just how you liked, she decided, was one advantage of wearing trousers. "Tell me what happens."

"Well . . . " Jonathan scratched his head, the hair quite coppery in the rays of dusk. "He's shipwrecked on the island, the one survivor. It's all uninhabited, though there's goats what he kills for meat and skins, and he manages to salvage some tools and things from the wreck: and he meks a pet of a parrot, and teaches it to say his name. But he has to do everything hisself, all alone, from scratch — all these things you don't think twice about: growing corn, mekking bread, mekking an oven to mek the bread; he's only got hisself to rely on. And so you watch him struggling with this, and then conquering it — and realising that you can manage all on your own, quite apart from all the world. That everything you need's in yourself. Just in yourself."

His voice had assumed the tones of a dreamy incantation: his eyes were not seeing her.

"It sounds awful — I'd go stark mad," said she, with conviction.

"Oh! well, some other people visit the island eventually — cannibals. And he saves one of their victims, and he stops with him. Course he don't speak English or anything. He names him

161

Friday, because thass the day he found him."

"There — thass what you should call me."

"I found you on a Monday."

"Well, Monday then — Jack Monday, how's that?"

"Ah! well, the thing is about poor ole Friday — Robinson Crusoe kept him as a slave."

"Sounds more and more like me all the time!"

Jonathan smiled as if he could not help himself, and took out his pipe. Hester saw this with unease — remembering she had thrown his tobacco in the river. "How'd you git started on the lighters then?" she said quickly.

"Started wi' just two — hired 'em, and carried stuff for the brickyards at Whittlesey. I'd been working on the land till then. I saved all my harvest money to put the deposit down — I'd got my heart set on the lighters, see, so I worked every day of an eight-week season."

"It don't run in the family then? Your dad weren't a waterman?"

"No." He looked at the pipe, put it away. "He were a banker over Wisbech way." This description did not indicate that the Eastholms had fallen from high estate — a banker in the fenland context being not a man in charge of vaults but a worker engaged on the repair of waterway embankments.

"He ain't around now, then?"

"No," Jonathan said, with that attentive look in another direction which indicates that a subject is closed.

"So you ain't got a home then — apart from the boats?"

"Just the boats," he said. "Everything I'm got's in these five ole buckets. Oh, I know folk reckon there's not much future in 'em any more — the railways finished a lot of the trade. But it's the life that suits me. Always summat new to see — but you only look on, and don't have to git mixed up in it, and go on your way when you're seen enough."

All of a sudden a heron, which must have been standing motionless in the shallows all this time, took off with a great ponderous noise of wings, seeming to make a palpable disturbance in the air, and becoming in a moment an elongated silhouette diminishing against the sky.

"Creaky old hernshaw," Jonathan said. "They always look ghostly to me — a ghost of some other bird, mebbe."

"You ever seen a haunt?" Hester asked.

"I don't know. I'm seen summat odd: I'm often thought about it. I were tied up just this side of Huntingdon one morning. It were a bright day, birds singing, everything plain and ordinary — not when you'd expect to see a haunt, I suppose. I were sitting up on deck, like this, and peeling a few taters, when I saw a little boy running along the bank up above. I'm tried since then to think whether I saw him come from anywhere in particular, but I'm not sure. He were a boy, but he had long curls, and he were wearing skirts — summat like a pinafore, which I thought were strange. He were sort of laughing, and cheerful-like; I couldn't hear any

163

sound, but then he were a little way away from me. He kept looking over his shoulder, as if there were somebody following him. Then he went down to where there was this patch of reeds on the edge of the bank, and he seemed to sort of dip down — whether he'd fallen, or jumped in the water, or what, I couldn't tell. I never heard no splash: but I jumped up and ran down the towpath, to see if he were all right. I looked and looked, but I couldn't find no sign of him."

Hester let out a breath, and found the back of her neck tingling. "D'you reckon that was a haunt?"

"Like I say — I ain't sure. But I believe in 'em, all right." He looked at her sharply. "Whass up?"

"Nothing. Just you're the last person I'd have thought of as believing in 'em."

Suddenly he looked displeased, and was curt. "Well, you don't know me, do you?" he said.

"I suppose not. But you don't seem to want anybody to know you, any road," she said — curious about him, and not meaning to be rude.

"Mebbe I don't." His face contracted into the old frown, then he gave his dismissive grunt: "Pah!" and stood up. "Come on, Jack Monday — git up off there and git the kettle on for tea. I never saw such a lazy article."

★ ★ ★

They had much business at Ely: unloading of fertiliser and several thousand turf, taking on of

164

gault from the Roswell clay-pits and a load of cinder and gravel to go to Stokeley. Eastholm drew up the profits of the run so far, and gave Hester her share — at the same time wiping off the debits he had chalked up in the cabin.

"Why'd you do that?" she said.

"Why? Because I want me head examining, thass why. Tek it before I change me mind."

He had provisions to buy in the town, too; and while he was gone Hester slipped up to a little dry-goods shop on the waterside and bought him an ounce of tobacco. It was nice to have money in her pockets. What she was a little tired of was having pockets: she had an urge to wear some decent clothes again.

They moored for the evening near Waterside Quay, beneath a row of massy chestnut trees just breaking into blossom, with a crazy huddle of ancient warehouses on the other side, staggering down into the river on decayed struts like invalids taking the waters.

"Here," she said, presenting him with the tobacco. "Present from Jack Monday."

"Whass this?"

"Fairy dust, whass it look like?" She grinned at him. "Tek it before I change me mind." She had been feeling guilty about that tobacco: she had always abhorred pettiness, and had been disturbed to discover it in herself.

They had stabled the horse at the Cutter Inn, whence Hester had caught a tantalising whiff of good food and drink and a lively intimation of company. Jonathan was about to light the oil-stove when she said: "Oh, can't we go up to the Cutter for summat to eat? It looks good there. I'm fed up with the boats. Let me put my glad rags on and mek a night of it."

"That money burning a hole in your pockets already, is it? Oh! goo on then. No stopping late, though: we're got to make a start tonight, to git to Earith in the morning — d'you hear?"

"Yes, master," she said happily, and ran off to change.

She put on her best stiff-boned blouse, with at the neck a little cameo brooch that Mrs Langtoft had passed on to her, and a pair of earrings that she had got from Rob Risby the tallyman, which he said were garnets, meaning they looked a bit like garnets, from a distance, if you half-closed your eyes, and had had a drop to drink — and which Mrs Langtoft said were a bit trollopy . . . but then what did an old married woman know about looking nice? She fastened her hair above her ears, as best she could, with a bowl of water as her only mirror, and decided she ought to turn at least a few heads tonight, if those ratty old haybags she had seen at the Ferryman were anything to go by.

Jonathan was waiting on the towpath for her.

"Bet you'd forgot I could look like this, hadn't you?" she said.

He stared at her.

"Suppose I had," he said.

He dug his hands in his pockets, and spoke little as they walked up to the Cutter. Every now and then he gave her an abrupt sideways glance, with something like affront in his eyes at her altered state. It seemed to throw him into

166

difficulty. The ease with which he had spoken to her last night of the haunt and of Robinson Crusoe was replaced by his old, short, bristling manner.

The first thing she saw in the Cutter Inn was a large pier-glass on the wall, which sent her spirits higher. It was like meeting an old friend to see a clear reflection of herself, free of that wretched cap and old moleskin jacket. And she did look all right! She scarcely noticed the meal of chicken and ham pie they ate, except that it was rather salty and gave her a thirst. The bar-parlour was noisy, and full of watermen: not just lightermen, but denizens of the quayside quarter of the little city; and she was on her second mug of beer when some acquaintances of Jonathan's hailed him, and they began a familiar conversation bewailing the state of the trade.

Hester considered herself not unused to light liquor: at the Langtofts' she had drunk the home-made wine to which Mrs Langtoft, like others on the fen, somehow considered her Methodist views on temperance inapplicable; she was accustomed to a drop of small beer on fair-days and feast-days, and felt she knew her limit. In short, she was soon thoroughly tipsy. After staring in perplexity for some time at a girl her own age, and having the stare returned, she at last recognised her as someone she had known years ago, when her father in his wanderings had settled briefly at nearby Sutton-in-the-Isle: and they fell on each other with all that superheated warmth of acquaintance renewed in the cups. The girl, whose name Hester never did remember, introduced her to her two female companions, whose names she did not catch, and they were soon all firmly bonded in conviviality. Suddenly Jonathan Eastholm's head appeared over her shoulder, seeming to bend from a great height.

"Don't forgit — no stopping late. We got to git moving. D'you hear?"

"Oh! all right," she said: she was sure it was not late yet.

"Is that your chap?" whispered one of the girls.

"Him?" said Hester. "Why, he ain't interested in anything that ain't shaped like a boat and got three layers o' pitch on it." And as they laughed she went on, more in soliloquy than dialogue: "It's all self with him. He don't see no farther than his own nose."

At some point someone began playing the upright piano that stood in the corner, and a man was prevailed upon to sing — not that he seemed very reluctant. This was a man of abbreviated stature, dressed in a suit of startling check that even Uncle Bevis might have baulked at, and brought up to reasonable height by a tall bowler hat. It soon appeared that the hat was an indispensable adjunct to the singer's performance, his repertoire being of the comic-sentimental kind, and the final vibrato cadence of 'Polly Perkins' being given a most affecting pathos, by his raising the hat perpendicularly off his head, and waggling it in the air with his eyes closed. He followed up this triumph with the 'The Death of Nelson', clasping the

168

hat impressively to his heart, and then signalled his transition to the comic mood by setting the hat on his brow at a racy angle, and making motions suggestive of riding a galloping horse. All this Hester saw and enjoyed through a haze of what she took to be tobacco-smoke, until three young men who had been nudging each other for an unconscionable time came over to her and her companions and offered to buy them a drop of wet; and she soon found herself flirting with them. What a relief it was, after all that dour grind of lock-gates and turves and hard boots and hard bunks! None of the three men was up to much — but it was delightful to feel herself admired and appreciated at last.

Her attention had been diverted from the singing for some time, in half listening to an interminable anecdote told by one of the three young men, who was attempting familiarity by proxy, by caressing the back of her chair, when the piano introduction to a song struck her with a peculiar recognition. The singer expressed a nautical mood by placing one hand on his stomach and the other in the small of his back, and crooned: "'Here, a sheer hulk, lies poor Tom Bowling . . . '"

Hester listened raptly: the melody, sweetened perhaps by her own tipsiness, seemed to fairly wrench her heart from her breast; and all at once she recollected that it was that same tune that Jonathan had pieced out on the concertina, alone in the evening. "Oh! I say, Jonathan — thass your song," she said, "there's the song you were playing the other night." She turned to where she had last seen him. He was not there. How long was it since she *had* seen him? She had rather lost track of time. She evaded the tentative grasp of the young man, who had forgotten the punchline of his story, and made a struggling, squeezing circuit of the packed parlour.

"'His form was of the manliest beauty,
His heart was kind and soft . . . '"

Eastholm was nowhere to be seen: he must have gone back to the lighters. Hester groaned inwardly. She supposed it was getting rather late: but how dreary to have to go back to work, just when she was feeling human again . . .

She left the inn; and the cold night air reproached her, with a dizzying slap in the face, for having that extra drink. She walked down to the moorings, and stood looking at various unfamiliar shapes of boats under the chestnut trees, until her mind numbly registered the fact that Eastholm's lighters were not there.

He had gone on without her. Disbelief was followed by fury, to be succeeded again by disbelief. She began walking down the towpath, exploring in her mind various alternative scenarios — but of these even the least unlikely was that all five lighters had suddenly and noiselessly sunk to the bottom. No: he had gone on. "I'll murder him," Hester said to herself, stumbling as she hurried in the dark.

She had passed the railway bridge, and left the environs of Ely behind, by the time she discerned the squat outline of the rear lighter on the dim river ahead; and then, beyond that, the white shirt sleeves of Jonathan Eastholm leading the

170

horse. Confirmation converted her anger into the form of new energy: she ran; the speed of her sudden approach startled the horse, and seemed to startle Eastholm too, who had a job to hold him.

"What's the 'nation idea of that — going off and leaving me behind?" she cried.

"Whoa, steady there — it's all right," Eastholm said — to the horse, not to Hester. To her he presented a face of which the arrogant neutrality was perceptible even in the dark. "I told you not to be late," he said. "I told you we'd got to be moving tonight. Tain't my fault if you don't listen."

"You could have said! You didn't have to just go off like that!"

"Look here — you work for me, and you work by my rules. You shouldn't need telling — it ain't my business to go chasing you up."

"Oh, you — you ain't human, I swear you ain't!" His harshness seemed the blankest affront to her melting mood of a few minutes ago. "You're got no more feelings than your ole boats!"

"I'm got a bloody living to earn, thass what I'm got — small chance wi' you around. Now tek hold of this hoss, and git going — I want to see Pope's Corner by sun-up."

She glared at him — he glared back; but the darkness intervening, they faced each other as it were insubstantially, like two irate ghosts, and after a moment she reached up to grasp the horse's bridle. What seemed at first a reluctance on the animal's part to take the strain quickly revealed itself, in the tension of the tow-rope, to be something more serious. Turning back, they found that the lighters, having lost steering-way, had drifted into the reedy shallows of the bank — the case being made worse by the jambing-poles getting caught up in the tangled scrub that came to the water's edge.

"Stuck," Eastholm said. "Look at 'em — stuck fast. You satisfied now?"

"Me? Thass your doing — tekking off on your own with nobody to steer."

"I wouldn't have had to, if you'd done as you were told."

Abruptly he put an end to these recriminations, flinging off his boots and stockings and clambering down into the shallow water, where he began clearing away the weedy obstructions from poles and ropes with his bare hands. Pausing, he stared up at her.

"Well, don't just stand there."

"You don't think I'm gitting down there in these clothes?"

"Change 'em then! Coh — I swear to God I'll never crew up with a woman again. I must have been mad."

In a sort of savage compression of mutinous feeling Hester changed in her cabin into the hated men's clothes and then joined Eastholm in the water. It came up to her waist: it was bitterly cold, silty, weedy, reedy, and scummy; the river that was so sparklingly innocent in the sunlight became in darkness a sink of clammy unpleasantnesses, nameless sticky and slimy things that clung to her skin and were the more repulsive because they could not be seen. Her foot slipped on the muddy bottom and gave her a ducking; overhanging branches raked across her face; she skinned her hands on the thick ropes and on the pitchy hulls of the lighters. What am I doing? she asked herself once — what am I doing, working like a slave up to my neck in freezing filthy water in the middle of the night? — when there's people down at the inn living a normal life?

"Shove harder!" Eastholm commanded, as they put their shoulders to the hull of the first lighter, and strained to heave it out of the silt. "Goo on, push!"

"I am pushing!" she wailed: the lighter shifted: she lost her footing again, and went under. The water sang in her ears, and then Eastholm dragged her out with one strong arm, and deposited her on the bank.

Convulsed with shivers, Hester pulled a clump of stinking weed out of her hair, then sat back aching and exhausted, aware that something alive was wriggling on her upper leg. Eastholm, having freed the waterlogged tow-rope, heaved himself up by his arms, like a muscular Triton, on to the bank. She regarded him standing there, and his great robust dripping figure seemed an emblem of imperviousness to her misery. "I shall never git dry — and when I do I shall go down with rheumatics," she lamented, with more feeling than logic. "What a way to live!"

"You shouldn't have took the job on if you can't manage it," he said. "I told you it was a man's job."

"Man's?" All the toil and discomfort of the lighters seemed to boil up within her and condense in a single protest, a cry in the chill comfortless dark. "Man's? This life? This is no life for a human being at all — it's no life for a dog!"

"It's my life, and it's always suited me," Eastholm said, after a moment — his words simply a flinty articulation, without emphasis.

"Well, you're welcome to it," Hester said, hauling herself to her feet. She hugged herself, and tried to stop the wild chattering of her teeth. "I'm had enough."

"So you're backing out then, are you? Just what you said you wouldn't do — leave me in the lurch half-way through the run — "

"Oh, no," she said. "I'll carry on to the end of the run — as far as Stokeley, weren't it? Yes, I'll do that. I'll keep my side of the bargain — I shan't let you reproach me with that. But then thass it. I'm finished. I'll try my hand at road-mending or summat. It'll be a holiday after this."

"All right." He turned away, and his expression, if any, was lost to her. "Goo and lead the hoss, then. Quicker we git to Stokeley, quicker you can pack in."

"I don't suppose you'll be sorry to see the back of me, any road," she said. "Will you?" This little coquettish fishing was no adulteration of her resolve to go, which was as genuine as her wretchedness: it was rather the tic of a still irrepressible vitality.

"Well, you said it," Eastholm said.

He presented to her his broad back, shoulder-blades outlined where the wet shirt clung. Hester looked around for something to throw at it, but something more than her weariness prevented her. To her own surprise she plumbed a momentary desolation: the surprise being not so much that she had not Jonathan's good opinion, but that she really cared, pig as he was, to have it.

* * *

Hester, like many pliable personalities, could adhere to an idea with dogged persistence once she had set her mind to it. The compensations of life on the lighters made themselves felt during the rest of the journey to Stokeley — interludes of charming peace, with fish popping to the surface of the water and the cry of wildfowl across the sunlit Ouse washes, strewn with marsh-marigold; but these little persuasions could not compare in eloquence with aches, blisters and chills, nor with the voice of Hester's inward resentment. Enough was enough: though one thing might have changed her mind. A soft word of commiseration, apology — anything — from Eastholm, and her hard resolve might yet have been flipped over on its back like a turtle; but nothing of the sort was forthcoming from the waterman, who accepted — indeed seemed to welcome — her decision with finality. He conducted himself for those two days pretty much as if she were already gone — that self-containment which she had

175

first noticed about him merely deepening a shade into finished introspection.

So a bright morning found them leaving the Forty Foot and approaching the familiar environs of Stokeley: the Abbey's ruined beauties rising above the low roofs, and painfully reminding Hester of those rash moments with Chad which had been the unwitting beginning of this odyssey of hers. The last load to be delivered was of cinder and gravel to a horse-dealing establishment in the town, of which the exercise paddock came down to the towpath; and the banks were sufficiently high and the barrows heavy enough to dispel any traces of regret in Hester's mind, leaving only a grim thankfulness that this was the last time.

A little crushed-looking groom, with bow legs and sorrel hair all flat on his head as if he had been curry-combed, superintended their unloading of the cinder and gravel in a corner of the paddock; but as Hester tipped out the last load, an elderly woman came from the direction of the house, beyond the row of stables, to inspect the goods: her proprietorial manner, and loud insistence that they'd better not be diddling her, proclaiming her as the owner of the establishment. Hester, considering her obligations finally discharged, sat herself wearily down on the edge of her barrow whilst the old woman haggled with Eastholm, and pondered her next move. She was without work again. There might be something in Stokeley; but if not, she would go and throw herself on Lizzie Gosling's mercy once more — the journey having brought her back to the old district of Hinching Fen — and from there she would have to swallow her pride and write to Aunt Netty. Horrible thought! — and redolent of defeat: but the compass of her options was so contracted. There must be something wrong with her, she thought: here she was with no home, nobody, nothing — no eye to pity, and no arm to save, as they said on the fen; and quite downcast, she buried her head in her hands.

"We're laying an exercise track for the horses, for all weathers," the old woman was saying to Eastholm. "Paddock's a mess in winter. Could do with someone to help lay the gravel. You interested?"

"Can't help you, I'm afraid," Eastholm said. "I'm moving on."

"What about you, boy?" the old woman said. She carried a long walking-stick, less it seemed to support her figure, which was noticeably upright, than as a brandishing instrument; and as she spoke she gave Hester a hard poke in the ribs. "You afraid of a bit of hard work?"

Hester did not greatly like being poked in the ribs, and the imputation just then touched an equally tender spot. "No, I ain't," she said, "but I'm had enough of loading and barrowing, and I'm finished with it. And I ain't a boy — I'm a girl," and she snatched off her cap and pulled down her hair with a feeling of liberation.

The woman stared, thumped her stick on the ground as a horse will stamp its hoof, and let out a shout of hard laughter. "Well, damn me, so you are! Damn me — I never saw the like of it!

What's a gel doing working on the lighters?"

"I took it on because I had to — temporary-like," said Hester, rising with an assumption of dignity, and picking up the empty barrow.

"Well, damn me!" the old woman said again; and she continued to laugh, and exclaim, and stare after her, as Hester and Jonathan wheeled the empty barrows down to the paddock gate and out to the riverside.

Hester went into her cabin for the last time, threw off the water-man's clothes, changed into her walking-dress, packed up her two carpet-bags, pinned on her hat, and emerged again to find Jonathan Eastholm waiting for her on the towpath.

"Not changed your mind then?" he said.

"No," she said. She looked up at him in surprise — his hair was white. "Whatever's that?"

"Eh? Oh, that — " He brushed a hand over his hair: it was blossom which had fallen from an apple tree at the end of the paddock.

"Thought for a minute I'd made you go grey," she said.

"Here — here's your share of the money." He dropped the coins into her hand, and bent his frown upon her. "How you going to manage now?"

"Don't suppose that bothers you much, does it?" she said; and then, relenting: "I'll git work in Stokeley. How you going to manage?"

"There's a berth up past the bridge — I'm tying up there for a while. I'll find somebody proper to do the job at Stokeley market, mebbe."

Somebody proper indeed! Till then she had been ready to say farewell to him on friendly terms: they had been through some experiences together, after all; but now she glared at him, and her glare was about to translate itself into scathing speech, when they were interrupted by a loud "Hem!" from the paddock gate above the towpath. A maid, in the form of one great starched frilled affronted stare, was standing there, and addressing Hester said in frosty accents: "Missis says WOULD you be so good as to step up to the house as she'd like a word with you IF you wouldn't mind."

"Me? If it's about laying that gravel, I — oh, well, beggars can't be choosers. All right."

She turned back to say goodbye to Eastholm; but he was already walking away from her, down the towpath to the horse, brushing the blossoms from his bowed head.

"Well — and ta-ta to you too," she said tartly under her breath: though it gave her a queer pang to see him go like that. At last she picked up her bags, and followed the ramrod back of the maid through the paddock gate and up to the house.

"What's it about, then?" she asked, as they crossed a stable yard, watched by the elegantly protruding heads of horses in loose-boxes.

"Oh dear don't ask ME I'm sure I don't know I'm only the MAID," said the maid, in terrible capitals.

"Who's the missis, then?"

"Oh dear me Mrs SAUNDERS is the name of the mistress of the household as such," the maid said, leading her in through a back kitchen, and pausing on the threshold to wipe her feet on the mat with such pointed emphasis that she looked like an exceptionally unsubtle mime artist doing the same.

Hester was conducted into a parlour, furnished with an eye more to massiveness and durability than refinement, where the elderly woman was seated in a wing chair before the fire, grasping her stick before her.

"Ah, there you are, gel! And you *are* a gel — I can see that for sure now. Well, well, that's the funniest thing I ever saw — when you whipped that cap off and gave me a mouthful out there. You could have knocked me down with a feather. Come a bit closer — let's have a look at you. Pretty gel, too! Don't mind me asking you in here — but it's tickled me so, I had to get to the bottom of it." All this was delivered in a powerful, indeed booming voice, which not only betokened strength of character, but suggested that the lady was somewhat deaf, and so assumed that everyone else was. "There must be a story behind this, I said to myself — gel like you doing work like that. Go on — sit yourself down, you look worn to a shade — go on, and tell me."

Hester complied: it was very welcome to find herself the subject of kindly interest at last, and moreover she glimpsed a chance, given the size of the establishment, that she might beg a little work here. She gave an outline of her career which glossed over the reasons for her leaving Langtoft's farm, and which at several points caused Mrs Saunders to break again into sharp-edged laughter.

"And you've been swanning about in men's britches, with a lot of hard-swearing watermen! Oh! I shall have to tell Gideon this one — I shall have to write and tell Lyle. It'll tickle him to death."

"Well, I needed the work, you see," Hester said, blushing a little but laughing too. "And I thought if men could do it, I'm sure I could just as well. If not better."

"Ah! you're right, there, gel," Mrs Saunders said, thumping her stick on the floor, and disturbing an indiscriminate basketful of fur by the fire, which resolved itself into two drowsy tortoiseshell cats. "Don't ever let them tell you otherwise, though of course they will. A woman can get through a day's work while a man's still wondering which side of his mouth to put his 'bacca in. Look at me — finest horse-yard in the country. Gentlemen and ladies of the aristocracy come to Saunders' for their carriage-horses and hunters — and that's *Mrs* Saunders and they know it. Optional extras, men," she declared. "I've buried two husbands, I have — " the dismissive tone in which she added this, suggesting that in thus disposing of them she had not regarded their decease as a necessary preliminary.

"I had to pack it in, though," Hester said with honesty. "I'm not afraid of work — but I just couldn't tek that life any more."

"Oh! they're a rough set of men on the river, right enough," Mrs Saunders said. "That's no place for you. Still, I like your spirit — I like that. I can't abide these mincing chits of gels you get nowadays, frit to step in a bit of muck. I hope he dealt fair with you — that waterman — eh? No funny business."

"Oh! no — nothing like that," Hester said. "I might just as well have been a man."

"Eh! you in those trousers," Mrs Saunders said, with a reminiscent chuckle: then fixed Hester with an acute look. "You got any work to go to now?"

"No," Hester said. "I was going to look for something in Stokeley — service, or anything."

Mrs Saunders's eyes, glinting amidst shrewd wrinkles, dwelt on Hester for some moments. Hester decided the best thing was to gaze straight back.

"You know what a companion-help is?" Mrs Saunders said abruptly.

Hester said yes: and tried not to betray her jolt of astonishment at what seemed to be coming. Amongst girls of her class, going as companion-help was the very best sort of service: lady's-maid was nothing to it. Many were the tales of girls on the fen who had gone as companion-helps to rich widows or genteel spinsters, and been left fortunes — though of course there were tales of the opposite sort, in which the employers turned out to be old dragons, and made the girls' lives a misery. Hester held her breath.

"Well, I've been looking out for a companion-help for a while," Mrs Saunders said. "I've buried two husbands like I said, and there's just my two sons now, and one of them's away. I'm a busy woman still, with the yard to see to, and there's a few things I can't manage. Folk say I'm going deaf, though I reckon it's just that they mutter; and I'm getting arthritis in my hands, which is a nuisance when you want to be well turned out, though I've never been one for titivating. Anyway, I've worked hard for nigh on forty years, and I reckon I've earned the right to be waited on. I didn't know whether I'd find a gel as would suit me: I had one call about the position the other week, but she was such a mousy thing she got on my nerves after five minutes. I make my mind up quick when I meet folk, and I either take to them or not; and I reckon you might do. I like a gel with a bit of pluck, and not afraid of rolling her sleeves up. Perhaps I've got you wrong — or perhaps you don't fancy the job — what do you say?"

"Oh! Mrs Saunders — I dunno what to say. Thank you!"

"Should be a step up from the lighters. Won't be soft, mind you: I'm particular, and what I say goes: we'd best have a month's trial. You'll have your own bedroom — you won't be expected to share with a maid or anything like that. You'll get your keep, and an allowance for clothes, and a bit of pocket money: I don't believe in throwing money at gels of your age, it only turns their heads. Well then! Tell me your name."

"Hester Verney, ma'am."

"You needn't ma'am me — Mrs Saunders will do. Well, Hester Verney: it's a good position — do you want it?"

Did she want it! Even the mention of a bedroom, after the musty bunk on the lighters, fell on Hester's ear like a promise of oriental luxury. There were lines round Mrs Saunders' mouth that suggested she could be a Tartar . . . but all in all, it was a piece of the greatest good fortune. Jobs like this were not going begging: Hester's head began to swim as she took it in, and she could not help smiling as she said: "Oh! yes, please, ma'am — I mean Mrs Saunders."

"Good. You've got sense in your head. No more cap and trousers, eh?" She checked herself in another chuckle, and said with a thump of her stick: "Mind, there's one thing I won't put up with, and that's canoodling. I won't have canoodling and spooning under my roof — you hear?"

"Oh, yes, Mrs Saunders," Hester said. She wasn't too concerned about that just at present — and that could surely be got round, anyhow.

5

HESTER was allowed one day off per fortnight. She used the first of these to go by carrier's van out to Hinching Fen to visit Lizzie Gosling, and give her the news of her alteration in fortune. Wearing a new velvet-edged cream frock bestowed on her by Mrs Saunders, she surveyed the familiar landmarks, which she had last beheld under the shade of obscure disgrace; and she would have been less than human if she had not felt a little pulse of triumph, and vindication, though she was amply conscious that she owed her new vantage to nothing more than luck.

"Mrs Saunders of Stokeley — I'm heard of her. What a turn-up!" exclaimed Lizzie. "There's gels on the fen'd give their eye teeth for a job like that. Course it depends — what's she like?"

"Well, she's nice to me, mostly. She's a masterful sort of woman, though, and got a terrible temper when she's roused. You have to tread careful. But I'm got my own bedroom — and I git clothes, and I eat at table with her, and everything!" Hester concluded with uncontainable elation.

"Well — talk about falling on your feet. I don't suppose you miss the farm, do you?"

"Oh! well — I think about it sometimes. I wouldn't mind going over and saying hello to

Mr Langtoft, but I suppose I can't do that . . . Folk are still talking about it, I suppose?"

"Not so much now. There's always summat new to gossip about. Fact is, Chad Langtoft's turned to courting Mary-Ann Cole, and they reckon there'll be an announcement any day now."

"Has he indeed?" Hester spoke grimly. "Well, good luck to 'em."

The days at the farm seemed very far off to Hester now. Not only had the mode of her working life wholly changed, but she was living in a town for the first time. Stokeley was small as towns went: to the birds that alighted in its gardens it represented no distinguishable habitat from the fields in which they chiefly lived, and the pollen clouds of early summer blew straight down its wide High Street. But the town's distinct separation from the country consisted not so much in its modest concentration of bricks and mortar as in its function. There was a world of economic specialisation within its small bounds, with at least one tradesman for every trade imaginable, rising to a rarefied upper atmosphere of the professions in the odd solicitor and schoolmaster. On the fen the absence of large manorial landlords and the universal struggle to earn a living placed everyone pretty much on an equality: on walking into Stokeley, one entered the labyrinth of class. And Hester soon found that in this world where everyone was striving for importance, Mrs Rachel Saunders, her new employer, was very important.

She had not always been so. Her father, who had barely been able to write his own name, had kept a decayed inn on the Great North Road, a dozen miles to the west on the edge of that foreign country known as the upland. But for the stable, with a few ponies and carts for hire, it was practically an ale-house. Rachel, on her father's death, had taken on the stable side (in both senses) of the business; had united her knowledge and instinctive understanding of horses with the capital of her first husband, and found herself at his early death the proprietor of a small horse-dealing yard. The move to Stokeley followed her meeting and marrying her second husband, Saunders, a native of that town, who also possessed a store of capital which it took his wife's acuity to put to good use. Two children and seven years later, he followed his predecessor to the churchyard, leaving Mrs Saunders a well-set-up widow holding in her capable hands the reins of a large and profitable horse-dealing business, located in a sturdy three-storey brick house by the river, with two rows of stables, yard and paddock, and an auxiliary cottage for grooms, as well as an outlying farm property. The whole formed a realm of which she was absolute monarch — her wealth and force of character giving her a sort of suzerainty over much of the town as well.

Hester learnt most of this history from the servants rather than from Mrs Saunders herself. She was a proud woman, and in spite of her frank and down-to-earth manner she did not encourage familiarity — as Hester quickly learned, when some initial democratic casualness in her own demeanour was sternly reprimanded. One piece of equine argot which Hester quickly picked up was 'Plenty of Bone': this seemed to be a good thing in a horse, and if Mrs Saunders' opinion of herself was anything to go by, a good thing in a person too — for she was a big woman, tall and bulky, with the cast of figure called statuesque, though the sort of statues she brought to mind had more of Mars than Venus about them. Her long, strong, dark-complexioned face had no curves in it, and was graven with firm lines: two especially deep ones ran from the sides of her straight nose to the corners of her mouth — and, as Hester soon learned, if the science of palmistry had extended to the face, these might have been aptly christened the Lines of Awkwardness. Her hair, scarcely greying though she was getting on for sixty, was severely parted and bound up in plaits at the back of her head; and Hester, who had seen many prints and peep-shows representing the terrible Red Indian chiefs, could well picture Mrs Saunders in fringed buckskin at the head of a company of braves, and felt that if she had been, the settlers of America would never have stood a chance.

The binding up of these plaits every morning was one of Hester's tasks, as was assisting at Mrs Saunders' dressing, and the care of her wardrobe, which consisted chiefly of a hulking platoon of black bombazine frocks, with several black fur-trimmed capes, heavy as pieces of armour, for outdoors, rigid high-button boots which were tortured every night on a boot-tree but refused to yield, and for evening wear some ropes of pearls, so weighty to manipulate that it was like handling anchor-chains. A portable writing-case was also in Hester's charge, in which to Mrs Saunders' dictation she made various memoranda, and fired off endless notes to tradesmen, very seldom of the complimentary sort. She likewise officiated at the making of tea, which Mrs Saunders drank strong and black throughout the day; accompanied her on shopping trips, dealing with the terrified clerks and cashiers who were beneath that lady's notice, and plucking her out of the path of advancing waggons — Mrs Saunders serenely assuming that what she could not hear did not exist; dispensed her medicines, which she took in large quantities and did not believe in; interpreted for her the 'mutterings' of people who did not shout loudly enough to penetrate her deafness; acted as a partner for her nightly, and highly competitive, games of rummy; fetched and carried, and generally performed any little task for which the fluctuating arthritis in Mrs Saunders' hands incapacitated her; and received, when no one else was available, her blasts of bad temper.

These were frightening. They rose, like bubbles to a calm surface, without warning.

"I want my spectacles," she would say. "Look in my ridicule." (Meaning her reticule — which was the size of a small flour-sack.)

Hester looked. "I can't find 'em."

"What do you mean, you can't find them?" Suddenly Mrs Saunders was snarling, fierce, terrible. "Look, gel, look!"

"Oh! I remember — I put 'em down on the night table upstairs."

"Well, don't just stand there! Go and fetch them! What in the name of all the saints do you think you're doing?" Mrs Saunders' mighty voice shivered the ornaments on the mantelpiece. "Look alive!"

The heroines of her mother's yellowback novels would not have stood for this: they would have gone all spirited and lifted their chins and tossed their hair and so on. Hester soon knew better, and simply rode out these brief storms. There was nothing personal in them: Mrs Saunders breathed occasional fire, and if you happened to be in the way, you got scorched. The most concentrated salvoes were reserved for tradesmen, who were all, every one, out to diddle her. They were criminals of monstrous artfulness. To hear her talk, you might suppose that the tradesmen of Stokeley were in the habit of meeting by night, in ceremonial conclave, to plot the sole ruin of Mrs Saunders.

One of these was Uncle Bevis, the butcher. It was significant of Mrs Saunders' prestige that Uncle Bevis himself, not the manager who looked after the shop, came to the house at her summons. Hester met him in the hall.

"Wehrr, beggar me — what are you doing here, gel?"

Hester explained her position. Uncle Bevis stood there holding his bowler hat, and looking doubtfully into it, and seeming to shrink inside his check suit.

"Not a bad place, eh — 'cepting the mistress is a bit of a fire-eater, eh? Ah, there's no harm in her, you know — I'm known her for years — we understand each other." But he did not say this very loudly.

"She's waiting to see you," Hester said.

"Is she?" Uncle Bevis essayed a ghastly sort of smile at this prospect, and scratched his fat shaven neck. "Good sort of mood, would you say, gel?"

Hester sharply sucked in breath, and looked noncommittal.

Uncle Bevis was not invited to sit down. He endeavoured to make light of this, as if standing in the middle of the room suited him best of all things in the world; but his hands seemed to incommode him, as if he longed to put them in his pockets, and jingle.

"I suppose you meant it as a joke, did you?" Mrs Saunders said, with an alarming lack of preamble.

Uncle Bevis smiled at the word joke, saw that wouldn't do, and turned solemn. "Why, what's that, then, Mrs Saunders?"

"Sending us horsemeat instead of beef — us dealing in horses as we do."

"Horsemeat?" Uncle Bevis tried bluster. "Now, now, steady on — I can assure you there's never been any of that in *my* establishment."

"Well, it certainly wasn't beef," boomed Mrs Saunders: it was futile even for Uncle Bevis to attempt to compete with her in volume. "Some folk might say sending a side of horsemeat

191

instead of beef's bad enough; but then some folk are strict; I'm the forgiving sort myself. I've buried two husbands, and both of them were always telling me I'm too soft — I suppose it's my nature. But when the meat's off as well, I think I've got a right to complain — what do you think?"

"Off, Mrs Saunders? Meat supplied by my establishment? Oh, now, I say — "

"High as old game!" Mrs Saunders cried, with a thump of her stick. "When they brought it in even the flies walked out! I suppose you think because I'm a poor old widow-woman you can fob me off with that sort of muck. Take advantage of me — poison me into the bargain — why not! I dare say you'd like to see me dead — I dare say it'd please you — I dare say you'd Laugh!"

Uncle Bevis denied these aspersions in a very humble, shuffling, sweating, and small-boyish manner.

"Well, I've put up with a lot. I've put up with burying two husbands, and arthritis in my hands so I can't hardly take the top off an egg, and having my good nature traded on, and having tradesmen diddling me every which way. But I shan't put up with this any more. I shall have to take my custom to Mason's. I dare say they'll rob me like the rest, but perhaps I won't be poisoned."

A few minutes later Hester was showing Uncle Bevis to the door. He looked a broken man, and scarcely had the energy to give her one of his genial punches. He had just managed to hold on to Mrs Saunders' custom by means of an abject apology, a promise to do better and an offer, grudgingly accepted, of a joint of beef gratis with a couple of chickens thrown in. He mopped his brow with a handkerchief and looked at Hester in wistful appeal.

"That beef weren't so bad really — was it, gel?" he said in a whisper.

"Not really," she said.

There had been nothing wrong with the beef: a little gristly, merely, by the high standards of Uncle Bevis's meat — a man can be a fool and good at his trade. The remarkable thing was that Mrs Saunders really seemed to believe that there had been something wrong with it: she grumbled afterwards to Hester that that fat fellow had better not diddle her again. Every egotism is sustained by its delusions, and those of this highly realistic woman were that everyone was trying either to do her down, or affront her by canoodling under her roof.

She hated canoodling — or spooning, or poodle-faking, or making sheep's eyes, or carrying on: all her words for loving dalliance were mocking and a little contemptuous. Hester had to accompany her on periodic forays into the servants' quarters of an evening, when she would burst in on the grooms and maids in the hope of catching them up to something; and it was a by-blow of her deafness that she was convinced people were always murmuring endearments behind her back. "What are they saying?" she demanded of Hester, if she saw a maid pass a word with the stable-boy;

and Hester would have to repeat the most innocuous commonplaces about tea being ready. Mrs Saunders' detestation of this most natural of human predilections seemed to originate in plain incomprehension.

"What do they want to do it for?" she protested to Hester. "Making up and carrying on. Billing and cooing. I don't see the point of it all. I just don't understand why they want to do it — " an assertion which the rather glum faces of her buried husbands, staring sadly out from framed photographs above the mantelpiece, seemed to corroborate.

Hester never saw any canoodling amongst the servants — with whom, as a glorified servant herself, she had much to do. Judy, the parlour-maid who had taken against her so emphatically on her first meeting, did not relent: she had a habit of stiffly placing herself in Hester's way, and then noticing, and exclaiming: 'Oh do pardon ME I'm SURE': and she was no more encouraging to men. The kitchen-maid was more of an age to be interested in dolls than chaps. The two grooms and the stable-boy, who slept above the tackle-room across the yard in a leathery ambience of saddles and bridles, spoke a strange language which sounded saucy, until you realised that they were referring to horses when they rhapsodised about sloping shoulders, good withers, sweet-itch, snaffles, wisping her over, and Damp Legs. The domestic arrangements were presided over by the cook-housekeeper, a sallow matron named Mrs Dawsmere.

Mrs Dawsmere did much to make Hester feel

at home in the first difficult weeks, when she was in sore need of a friend. She was a kindly soul whose view of the world was obscured by a fog of superstition. Hester, living on the fen, had unconsciously picked up a few of these — never put shoes on the table, turn your money over when you see a full moon. For Mrs Dawsmere, the whole of life was a terrible maze of omen and augury.

"Don't put that down there!" she cried, as Hester brought Mrs Saunders' tea-tray down to the kitchen.

"What's the matter?"

"The spoons are crossed — cross your spoons, and you'll come to want. Oh! no — don't turn 'em that way — see your face in the back of a spoon, and you'll never marry."

Hester laughed. "How would it be if I just chucked 'em out the window?"

"You laugh, gel. You want to be careful — specially wearing that brown."

"I thought it was green that was unlucky?"

"Ooh! Brown as well. Wear brown above your waist, and you'll never suckle your children. There's truth in these things." In fact there seemed to be so many unlucky colours that Mrs Dawsmere was forced to wear nothing but a shadowy grey. "Don't put your feet on there!"

"Why not?"

"Rest your feet on another's chair, and they'll never again be sitting there."

"Is it all right to put 'em on the fender?"

"Ooh! Spit on your shoe if you do — spit the devil away," Mrs Dawsmere said — the devil in

195

her cosmology seeming to be a feebly persistent little nuisance, who had nothing better to do than pop up in tea-cups and fireplaces, and be endlessly repulsed with salt and spit. She cleared the tea-things away, disposing of them in various auspicious attitudes, and suppressing a yawn — it was doubtless unlucky to yawn when your hands were wet, or something. She always looked tired: probably, Hester suspected, because going to bed involved so much treading on the right stairs, and taking off the right pieces of clothing first, and touching wood, that before she was finished it was time to get up again.

Domestic life at Mrs Saunders' was subordinate to the horse. The furnishings of the big high-ceilinged rooms were, like the mistress, burly and solid — great chairs and tables of oak and mahogany with shin-catching legs, thick cretonne drapes sagging under their own weight, thumping brass lamps with swollen heads — but the only adornments were of an equestrian character. There were glass cases full of cups won by Mrs Saunders' horses at shows, statuettes of horses, paintings of horses, books about horses — the very leather of their bindings seeming to whiff of the saddle. When Mrs Saunders occasionally took a horse out to ride — arthritis permitting — she became a centauress in riding-habit and hard hat. For Hester horses and ponies had always been convenient four-legged machines for pulling ploughs and carts — and now lighters; when she walked down the stable-yard past the protruding heads she could not tell which were new arrivals and which had been sold: it was one undifferentiated stream of horseflesh. For Mrs Saunders, it was poetry.

Her son Gideon, and the head groom, did the day-to-day work — travelling to shows and fairs to buy; breaking in; training for riding or draught or carriage-work; negotiating sales — but Mrs Saunders' was the guiding hand. She inspected each new arrival, and could tell its height at a glance, for she knew how many hands high her chin was. Every morning she went out to the stables to cast her eye over the daily operations, the mucking out and feeding, the grooming, and then the saddling up for exercise; and she was always snatching the broom or the bowl of oats from the stable-lad's hands, and doing the job herself. She grabbed muzzles, to peer into that most unlovable orifice, a horse's mouth, and ensure that the teeth had not been filed down to make the animal seem younger: she put hoofs over her knee like a blacksmith, and barged fearlessly into loose-boxes with notorious kickers. Periodically she went out in the trap to look at the stock at grass in a meadow on the upland near Holme, driving the trap herself, with Hester accompanying her. Mrs Saunders was at her most queenly on these outings, her hat tied on with a veil, her gauntleted hands waving condescending greetings to trembling tradesmen. This was an occasion when her deafness sustained her dignity, for though the little fat pony broke wind stertorously all the way, Mrs Saunders remained heedless and serene — only once remarking, above the trumpetings, that the country smelt very rich today.

It was all a strange world to Hester, but an interesting one; and once or twice it afforded her a glimpse into a much higher sphere. Whilst the yard dealt chiefly in stock for farm work and tradesmen's carts, they handled carriage-horses and hunters too for the shires to the west; and rich gentry who would not so much as tie their own bootlaces came in person to Mrs Saunders. Hester, rather to her surprise, was specifically told to be present when Mrs Saunders received these influential customers: afterwards she thought that lady was seeking to impress by thus displaying her own waiting-woman. One of these customers was actually a Sir Something; another was a lady whose name was prefixed with The Honourable, though Hester couldn't see what was honourable about her, except that she had gloves that buttoned right up her arms, and a whole dead bird on her hat. There was, after all, some sort of fairness in the world, Hester thought: for though these people had all the money, they talked like congenital idiots.

Someone who was always present at these occasions was Mrs Saunders' eldest son Gideon.

Gideon was something of a dandy — something, but not much. His lilac suede gloves and double-breasted waistcoats had an air of belonging to someone else: he seemed rather to lurk within his chimney-pot collars than to wear them. His hair had a habit of sticking up at the back, which no amount of macassar oil would remedy, and when he paused, as he often did, before mirrors,

198

he seemed to hover in a brooding region between vanity and doubt. A new mother-of-pearl tie-pin, patted at frequent intervals, cried out for comment: Hester obliged, saying, "Oh! I do like that tie-pin"; Gideon said, "Oh! that," appeared to have forgotten it, patted it again, then glowered suspiciously at her as if fearing mockery; and further convinced Hester that she and Gideon were never going to hit it off.

He was a thin sandy man of thirty, with small eyes and an undernourished moustache marooned on a long expanse of upper lip. His prominent Adam's-apple was offset by an absence of chin — just as if he had swallowed it at some point in his nervous chewings and munchings, and it was now only to be seen forever bobbing up and down his hairless throat. His mother called him Giddy (which he was far from) except when they were receiving that top-drawer company, when she addressed him as Gideon in awful tones. Leaning with uneasy negligence on the mantelpiece, Gideon hung on every constipated word that fell from the lips of Sir Something or the Honourable Dead-Bird, his face frozen in a half-smile of ingratiation; and sometimes he would fling himself rashly into conversation:

"Shall we see you at the Norfolk Show, I wonder, Sir Leonard?"

"Gideon," Mrs Saunders would say, her voice coming down like a guillotine, "go and bring the mare in out of the paddock." And off, crushed, he would go.

His subservience to his mother was complete.

It had given him a sort of habitual furtiveness, so that he even ate his breakfast eggs as if they were so much humble pie, and drank his tea as if quite prepared to be told to stop doing it. He was busy all day, training and riding, clipping new stock, and travelling often to horse fairs and auctions; but Mrs Saunders poured him only a half measure of responsibility, and none of that strong liquor authority at all. One morning he brought home from the station a horse he had bought that was no bargain: it turned out to be lame in the left front foot, which the dealer had concealed by the old trick of bruising the right front foot too, thus disguising the favouring. Mrs Saunders was scathing. "You ever throw money away on such a pig in a poke as that again," she said, "and you can do the stable-lad's job, and I'll promote him to yours. He couldn't do worse." Gideon's ears went crimson — but it was Hester he glared at. He was used to his mother's browbeatings, but not to having them witnessed by this newcomer; and as he plainly dared not resent his mother, he seemed to transfer the resentment to Hester — and it was no good her trying to look away, and appear not to have noticed his humiliation at all.

"Ooh! she can be terrible sharp with Mr Gideon," Mrs Dawsmere said in the kitchen that night. "With Mr Lyle, too, though it's not so bad for him, because he don't seem to mind it, and just laughs it off. Mr Gideon teks it more to heart."

"I wonder he don't just up and start on his own," Hester said.

"Well, it wouldn't be easy for him. He's hardly got a penny to bless himself with." Mrs Dawsmere lowered her voice. "Oh! I know he's got all them fancy clothes — and that smart hunter what he goes to hounds with, though thass mainly to git business — but what I mean is, she gives him an allowance for things like that — very strict — he has to go cap in hand and ask for every last sixpence. Why, there ain't a nail in this whole place what ain't in her name alone, and Mr Gideon and Mr Lyle won't git a morsel of it till her time's up — and mebbe not then if they don't behave theirselves. Such a masterful woman as she is — she'd burn the whole place down to spite 'em, if it meant getting her way. Oh! God forgive me for saying it — " And Mrs Dawsmere incapacitated herself for some moments crossing her fingers, touching wood, and performing some complicated charm involving a lump of coal, the sugar-bowl, and seven human hairs.

"I know how close she is with money," Hester said. "She bought me a frock to wear when she's got company, but when I asked her for some pocket-money she nearly bit my head off."

"Ah! She gives me my wages like they're a favour," Mrs Dawsmere said, having warded off the evil eye for a few moments. "But thass just it — there's no wage at all for her sons. I'm heard her say to 'em: what d'you want money for? — you git everything you need here. So they're cheap labour for her, you see. And there's poor Mr Gideon been walking out with Miss Phoebe Purefoy for five years — her father's the corn merchant up Infirmarer's Street."

"Five years! Why, don't they want to git married before it's too late?"

"Thass just it — there'd be such a to-do if Mr Gideon was to git his courage up and try and git married — Coh dear! I daren't think of it!"

"What about Lyle?" Hester said.

"Oh, Mr Lyle's never give no trouble that way, not yet. I don't reckon she'll ever let either of them go, though. Not her."

Well, Hester thought, they must be a poor pair if they'll let one self-willed old woman stand in the way of their happiness. She felt she could perhaps believe it of Gideon: any temptation to sympathise with Gideon Saunders was obviated by the unpleasantness of his character. Privately Hester thought he resembled a weasel. He never laughed but with a cackle of spite; he jealously guarded a dignity he did not possess. To her he adopted a sneering condescension when Mrs Saunders was not around, though she could put up with that: what repelled her was the way he sucked up to those brainless blue-bloods and bullied the stable-boy, whom he addressed with seigneurial disdain; and he made a very sanctimonious fuss when one of the grooms got drunk one night, though Hester often detected on his own breath the smell of surreptitiously supped whisky. But the younger son, Lyle, was an unknown quantity to her — except through his letters to his mother, which it was Hester's job to read out to her.

Lyle Saunders was in Belgium, living with

an eminent horse-dealer in Brussels, and establishing a Continental trade link for the Saunders yard: he had already sent over several pairs of magnificent Percherons which had made the other horses in the yard look like pygmies. His letters were frequent, informative and affectionate; and after Hester became Mrs Saunders' amanuensis for her replies, there was always a friendly mention for her. '*I hope you are not ill-treating that companion of yours, Mother. If she is half as nice as her handwriting I look forward to meeting her. I dare say you let her sleep on the cinders, and feed her on potato peelings: I don't suppose there are many princes round Stokeley way but you never know — there might be the odd prince out on Chatteris Fen, down on his luck, and lifting carrots with his crown on — so you'd better watch out.*'

"Daft beggar," Mrs Saunders said, laughing and tutting at herself for doing so. "He always was as daft as a brush."

It was an odd sensation for Hester to be writing and reading letters to and from a person she had never met. She found herself looking forward to the arrival of those envelopes with the funny foreign stamp and violet ink: and wondering greatly what Lyle looked like. She could of course have asked Mrs Dawsmere, but she did not do so, perhaps from fear of being disappointed — he might look like Gideon.

She had entered her fourth week of employment at Saunders' horse-yard when Gideon's paramour, Phoebe Purefoy, was invited to Sunday tea — or at least, Gideon tentatively announced that she was coming, and Mrs Saunders acquiesced with an ominous silence. Sundays there were not characterised by the strong devotions of the Langtofts' farm. Mrs Saunders was Anglican — on taking Hester on, she had sharply demanded of her whether she were church or chapel, which was like asking a cat whether it preferred turnips or parsnips — and apart from the mandatory visit to Stokeley's old abbey church, where she gorgonised various tradesmen as they tried to hide behind their hymn-books, she chiefly marked the Sabbath with vast meals, so that the big house was all a-swelter with roasting and baking from dawn to dusk. Tea was a gargantuan affair of ham and potted meat and pork-pies and fruit tarts; and contemplating the laden table on the day Phoebe Purefoy was expected, Hester thought there was something specially daunting about it all. Everything was weighty in Mrs Saunders' house: the great cut-glass salad-bowl could only be moved by putting both arms around it, and the cake-stand was like an altar; and all the clumsiest, most stiff-necked china and cutlery seemed to have been got out for this occasion — as if with the intention of confounding Phoebe Purefoy with sheer weight of crockery. That her welcome was not to be a genial one Hester had already gathered, when helping Mrs Saunders to dress: "I'd better put on my best, I suppose," she had said, "seeing as we've got Miss coming to quiz us."

At four o'clock Gideon came in attended by a sort of supernumerary shadow, which gradually detached itself and became a young lady dressed, with Gideon's gingerly elegance, in a tight-waisted dress and a zouave jacket over puffed silk sleeves. She was introduced to Hester, and gave her a little cold apologetic hand, as if she were purchasing with a ten-shilling note from someone who had no change; and in the same shrinking manner greeted Mrs Saunders, who intoned in a voice like a gong: "I hope I find you well, Miss" — giving this title a terrible bitterness — and led them straight in to tea.

Phoebe Purefoy, by the equine standards prevalent at Saunders', must have been judged deficient in Bone. If Mrs Saunders was a good strong hack, Phoebe Purefoy was a soft-mouthed pony, sufficient only to pull an old lady's dog-cart. She was a very well-washed young woman, apparently in some peril of being washed away completely, with neat coils of buttery hair and a pretty heart-shaped face that continually blushed, not in becoming touches of pink, but with a brick-red glow: Hester sitting opposite her could almost feel the heat. It was clear that her attitude to the world was deferential, not only from the way she seemed to wind herself placatingly round the table leg, but from a habit she had of murmuring 'Thank you' at arbitrary moments, in a sort of universal propitiation. Hester already knew Mrs Saunders well enough to see that, quite apart from her general disapproval of canoodling and all its works, Miss Purefoy was not the sort of girl to please her: what converted worse to worst was the fact that Gideon's sweetheart had a very soft and low voice. And what Mrs Saunders could not hear, did not exist.

"Mother," Gideon said, "Phoebe's father was telling me his carriagehorse was sickly, and he had a farrier in from Chatteris, instead of old Reeves. Found him much more reliable." Mr Reeves, the Stokeley veterinary surgeon, was not found very satisfactory: rather to the disadvantage of his professional authority, he was frightened of animals. "What was the man's name again, Phoebe?"

"Ashley, I believe," Phoebe said. "Which is rather odd because that's my mother's maiden name, though there's no relation, but it shows what a small world it is, as they say. Of course she came from — "

"Reeves ought to retire and let a younger man in — that's what he ought to do," declared Mrs Saunders, cutting across Phoebe's cooings like an axe through cobwebs. "The man's got a few bob — he's diddled enough out of me." She munched loudly: Mrs Saunders had all her own teeth, and seemingly a few more.

"Father thought at first that what the poor horsey had was something called glanders," Phoebe said — making, Hester surmised, a valiant attempt to tailor her conversation to Mrs Saunders' interests. "I always thought that was a place but apparently not. They do say you learn something every day. It turned out that the horsey only had — "

"Hester," Mrs Saunders said, "did I tell you I've run out of my liver pills? Anyway, I have. You'll have to run over to Robson's after tea and get me some more."

Phoebe being placed on her right, behind a monstrous glass vase of irises, Mrs Saunders was able to stare chewingly straight ahead, and not see her. Perhaps in an attempt to counteract this, Phoebe leaned forward across the table in a wriggling manner, and said, "Oh, do you suffer from the liver, Mrs Saunders? So does my father — sometimes he's hardly able to stir out of the house — though Mother says that's a good thing in a way as it stops him overworking which he's rather inclined to do — so as they say it's an ill wind that blows nobody any good — " seeming thus to habitually fall back on the proverbial, for sheer fear of committing herself to a personal opinion.

"Pass me the cress, Hester," Mrs Saunders said — for, of course, she could not hear.

"Do you ride, Miss Purefoy?" Hester said, feeling sorry for her.

"Oh! I've been learning to — thank you — Giddy has been teaching me for a year or more but I'm afraid I don't get on very well. At least, I can get on all right, but somehow I can't make the horsey go where I want it to — I keep clicking my tongue and saying giddy up — which is quite a funny thing when Giddy's standing by because he says 'Up where?' — pretending he thinks I'm talking to him, you see — and we do laugh — thank you."

"You're improving all the time," Gideon said. "Just takes a bit of confidence."

"Oh! well, I'm sure Giddy — thank you — I feel very confident with you helping me."

"That hackney you bought's a sticky trotter," Mrs Saunders thundered at Gideon, visibly shaking him out of canoodling mood. "You still hoping to drive that at Peterborough Show? I doubt it'll be trained in time. Got a bit of a wooden mouth too, if you want my opinion."

"What does that mean — a wooden mouth?" Phoebe said.

A large black-clad patch of silence met her.

"It means the horse doesn't respond very well," Gideon said.

Mrs Saunders' resolute deafness persisted to the end of the meal. By that time Phoebe Purefoy seemed herself to doubt whether she actually existed, and appeared to catch sight of her reflection in the hall mirror with a start of surprise. A short interval in the parlour followed, during which Phoebe was obliterated again, by being buried in the most massive of the wing chairs, and towered over by a giant potted fern. She very soon took her leave, quite beaten down by overpowering furnishings, and utterly defeated by Mrs Saunders' determination not to know she was there at all.

Gideon went too, to see Phoebe home. Hester saw a glitter of triumph in Mrs Saunders' deep-set eyes, but all the old lady said was, "Bah, it wears me out, entertaining all this company. Well, go on, gel — step over to Robson's and get me my pills."

"Mr Robson perhaps won't like being disturbed on a Sunday."

"Won't he indeed! I don't know who Pop Robson thinks he is to put on airs. The day he got married they had to have a midwife as a bridesmaid just in case. Go on, don't dawdle."

Robson was a pharmacist, whose shop was at the other end of the High Street. The town was quiet at the glimmering candle-end of the spring day: nothing moved on the river, and there were only a few strollers, wearing Sunday hats and faces. Hester lingered on the narrow stone bridge, looking down at the green water steeped in sky. Suddenly another head appeared beside the rippling image of her own.

"Oh! it's you," she said, finding herself face to face with Jonathan Eastholm.

"Hullo," he said awkwardly. He seemed unchanged since their last meeting: shirt-sleeved, brown, hard-lipped, frowning as he looked at her as if she were a bright light: though she had forgotten just how much height and breadth there was to him.

"You back in Stokeley, then?" she said. "Well — I can see you are."

"Moored down by the Abbey. Moving on soon," he said. "Fact is — I'm glad I saw you."

"Are you? Well, that's a first, any road."

"Ah — I just wondered — whether you were all right. Whether you'd got work."

"Oh! yes. I had a bit of luck." She told him of her job with Mrs Saunders: though the meditative gaze he threw down at the water below made her wonder if he was listening.

"So you're all right then?" he said at last.

"Yes," she said. "Thank you." Now I'm sounding like Phoebe, she thought. "Are you?"

209

"Eh? Oh! yes." He continued to stand there, like some muscular excrescence grown out of the bridge. "I just wondered. As long as you're all right." And then, abruptly, he walked past her.

"Goodbye," she said; and went on to Robson's, thinking to herself that her absence from the lighters had done nothing to improve Eastholm's command of the social graces. All very well to go asking her now if she was all right, she reflected as she returned home with Mrs Saunders' pills (huge pink bullets that she swallowed in horse-like quantities): it might have been better if he'd been a bit more solicitous when she was wearing herself to a frazzle on those wretched lighters. But perhaps that was what was behind the odd little scene — a belated guilt on his part at the way he had treated her.

Gideon had just arrived back before her, and was closeted with his mother in the parlour. Hester went up to her room to change out of her walking-dress, and was half-way down the staircase when she was arrested by a great wail issuing from the parlour.

She ran in, and found Gideon standing on the hearth-rug, plucking his lip, his face as white as flour: and Mrs Saunders in her chair, emitting another moan of lamentation. It seemed she had had one of the cats on her lap when stricken with this loud grief, and in the absence of an apron had buried her face in the animal, and was sobbing into it — the cat reacting to this unexpected turn of events by peering over its shoulder and looking exquisitely displeased.

"Whatever's the matter?" Hester said.

Gideon shot her a bitter glance, as if her being privy to this was another mark against her. "Nothing," he said unconvincingly.

"No! it's nothing," Mrs Saunders groaned, muffled with cat. "Just my own son turning against me — that's all."

"I'm not turning against you, Mother," Gideon said. "I'm only saying what we want to do — I didn't mean — "

"Oh! you do what you like," Mrs Saunders said. "You just carry on. I've had my time — just leave me here to die, seeing as that's what you want."

"That's not what I want, Mother — "

"If I was a horse you'd shoot me — you would!"

"Mother, I wouldn't — "

"And it'd be kinder. It'd be kinder if you'd just shoot me here and now. Your father's old gun's in the tackle-room — you might as well go and get it. Hester, fetch me my smelling-salts."

"You haven't got any smelling-salts," Hester said in surprise.

"Even my help's against me!" wailed Mrs Saunders. The cat had had enough and bolted from her arms. "And Tipsy as well. I wish I were dead."

"Mother," Gideon said, "please don't take on like this. I only suggested . . . I never meant — "

"I know what you meant! Help me to bed, gel." Mrs Saunders struggled out of her chair and leant on Hester's arm, though her touch did not feel noticeably weak. "My son doesn't want me around any more — I may as well get out of his sight."

Hester accompanied her upstairs. "Mrs Saunders, what is the matter?" she said — though she had a fair idea.

"Draw the curtains, gel. Shut out the light. I can't bear it. I'm fit to fly. What's the matter? Me — that's what. I've done my best for my boys, but they don't want me." She went down on the bed like a dropped sack of oats. "Giddy came back from seeing Miss home and marched straight up to me and stabbed me in the heart. Or that's what it felt like. He says he wants to get engaged — him and Miss. Engaged. You know what that means. Oh! I don't know why he had to come and tell me — seeing as he's made his mind up. Just to crow over me I suppose — just to rub salt in the wound — just to see me weep." All this in a loud voice, conspicuously audible to Gideon tapping at the door outside. "I thought I'd a bit of life left to me — I thought my boys would allow me that, after all I've done for them. But no. He wants to just chuck me away like an old shoe. Don't let him in, gel! He doesn't want to see me anyway. The only way he wants to see me is in my shroud — and he will soon — it'll not be long."

★ ★ ★

Mrs Saunders took to her bed. This, Hester learned from Mrs Dawsmere, was not a new

212

strategy where a conflict of will with her sons was concerned; but she pursued it with grim application. For three days the curtains remained closed and Mrs Saunders lay in stately despair: the face of a stony martyr, above a black crocheted bed-jacket, scrutinised the ceiling. Meals were sent away untouched, and only Hester was allowed in the shaded room. Gideon came periodically to knock on the door and plead with his mother.

"Let me in, Mother — please. Just let me explain. I only wanted — that is, we only wanted — to ask your permission — "

"We, he says!" cried Mrs Saunders. "Oh! it's We now. Well, that says it all. I suppose Miss wants this bedroom, does she? Well, I'm dying in it as fast as I can. I'll be leaving it soon. That should be some satisfaction to you."

He came back again. "Mother, listen. All I meant was that we — I — was thinking about an engagement. Nothing more than that for the time being — "

"For the time being! Ah! I know. Just give it a little while, you said to Her, and then we can get rid of the old nuisance. I know. Well, I'm trying to save you the trouble, son. You'll be shut of your burden soon."

"What's she doing in there?" Gideon said to Hester, when she came down for dinner.

"Just lying there," Hester said.

"I wish she'd just listen for half a minute," said Gideon in his whining way, gnawing at his lips.

But she is listening, Hester thought: she's

listening to every word you say. And none of it's any good. She's not going to meet you half-way, or one-tenth of the way: that's the point. She won't be satisfied till you and poor old Phoebe have surrendered completely. And then you'll be walking out for another five years . . . Hester would have counselled him to stand up to her, but she knew Gideon would be uppity if he thought he was being given advice by a paid servant; and besides, it was not easy to feel for someone who had so little that was likeable about him.

On the third day Gideon came supplicating to the closed door on another matter — business. A wealthy customer had taken a fancy to that grey hunter, and was prepared to pay any price — but they had half promised the animal to that lady from St Ives . . . what was he to do? Such knotty decisions had always been taken by Mrs Saunders, and Gideon was helpless. His mother had ensured this helplessness, of course, by exactly that tactic of never allowing him responsibility. Hester had to admire her shrewdness.

"But what shall I tell him, Mother?"

"Oh! don't ask me, son," Mrs Saunders said mournfully from the bed. "You don't need me now — you said so yourself. You're the one who knows it all. I'm just a makeweight about the place. Ask your Miss — she's the important one, apparently."

Gideon gave a wretched little groan, and his footsteps died away down the stairs.

"I hope he's not such a fool as to turn that

214

offer down," Mrs Saunders said to the ceiling.

There was discussion in the kitchen that night. Judy the maid, vengefully sewing, said it was only to be expected when folk would get involved with Attachments: the head groom recalled a time when they had a stallion that was so savage nobody would go near it, except Mrs Saunders herself, and she just slipped a halter over its head like a ribbon on a kitten, and said he wouldn't put it past her to starve herself to death up there; Mrs Dawsmere said this was the longest she had ever gone. Hester was about to say that if Gideon had any sense he would call her bluff, when Gideon himself appeared at the top of the kitchen steps.

"Hester — will you come please — Mrs Saunders is getting up — and Mrs Dawsmere, boil a couple of eggs and make some toast and tea . . . "

Hester found Mrs Saunders sitting up in bed and dabbing her eyes with a handkerchief. "Ah, there you are, gel," she said in a weak voice. "Pass me a clean handkerchief out of that drawer, will you?"

Hester did so: though neither the first handkerchief, nor Mrs Saunders' eyes, seemed at all wet.

"You will eat something now, won't you, Mother?" Gideon said, sitting down in the chair by the bed.

"I'll try and swallow a morsel," Mrs Saunders said. She turned a marmoreally tragic face to her son. "I did hear you right, didn't I, Giddy? — because you know I'm a bit troubled in the ears. I couldn't bear to think I'd heard you wrong." She glanced briefly at Hester — who realised she was being used as a witness. "Just — just tell me again."

"Yes, you did hear me right, Mother," Gideon said, with a glance of his own at Hester, not at all friendly.

"Tell me again."

"I shan't say any more about — I promise I shan't say any more about getting engaged."

"Or think it?" Mrs Saunders said, her voice noticeably less weak.

"Or think it. I shan't get engaged. You're to forget it ever happened." In Gideon's demeanour as he said this there was more than a little of the reprimanded schoolboy, which formed a droll contrast with his man-of-the-world collar and two-tone shoes. Hester was amused: but with a twang of distaste. Poor Phoebe! So he had unconditionally surrendered. She knew one thing — she wouldn't put up with that sort of pusillanimity in a man.

Mrs Saunders exhaled a sigh. "I suppose you think I'm a silly old woman."

Silly's not the word I'd use, thought Hester, as she went down to fetch the eggs and toast.

"Oh! I shall never manage all this," Mrs Saunders said, on being presented with the tray. But she did, pausing only to complain that the eggs were overcooked. Within an hour she was up and dressed, and ramping about the house and stables, setting to rights everything that had been neglected during her absence from its affairs. "Can't take my eye off things for two minutes," she declared: while Hester followed in her wake, dispatched hither and yon to fetch and carry and to tell Judy this and Mrs Dawsmere that, and barely able to keep up with this elderly woman who a short while ago had been ready to turn her face to the wall. By the time Hester retired to bed, she was more weary than she had been since she had worked on the lighters.

Sinking into bed, she was reminded of the strange meeting with Jonathan Eastholm on Stokeley bridge. There were still times, if she woke in the night, when she thought for a moment she was still on the lighters, and seemed to hear the lapping of the water round the bows. Now an idea occurred to her — perhaps he had found no one else to do the job, and had been about to ask her to come back! Now that *was* funny.

★ ★ ★

The elderly man who was Hester's replacement on Eastholm's gang of lighters was an experienced waterman who could do the work in his sleep, and sometimes seemed to. Not only was he capable but he was extremely taciturn: he could go a whole stoical day without uttering more than a couple of monosyllables. All in all Eli, as he was called, was an eminently suitable companion for Jonathan Eastholm. And Jonathan Eastholm found that he hated him.

At first, Jonathan thought he knew how to account for this. He must be suffering from an attack of the Old Goblin. This was a

217

term that he had privately framed for himself to express the fits of fierce melancholy that seized him from time to time. Such a mood assailed him without warning, and had done so ever since he had reached manhood: the mood seemed to both darken and intensify his vision, so that the simplest external events rasped against his consciousness like sandpaper, and the disregarding flux of the world suddenly bristled with menacing import. At such a time the not uncommon sight of a stray dog drowned in the river, for example, filled him with black thoughts: cruel aimless presences stalked his dreams, and the hand of an injudicial dispenser of suffering seemed discernible behind all the processes of the universe; he found himself both tending to a cosmic pessimism, and deprived of the sense of proportion that would have allowed him to laugh at himself for it. The way in which this mood overcame him, as if it were some extrinsic visitation rather than an inner state of feeling, caused him to give it the name of the Old Goblin: and he believed it must be the Goblin's unwelcome presence that was making him sharply dissatisfied with Eli, with the lighters, with himself, with everything.

And yet it did not have the familiar malicious features of the Old Goblin. It looked somehow different.

Jonathan Eastholm was not born complete, fully formed and alone out of the waters of the fens, though such was the impression he often gave, and perhaps chose to give. Scarcely anyone knew his history: he did not care to tell it. Its leading event was the death of his father when he was a boy, and his mother's subsequent remarriage. His father being a man kind only in his cups, and seldom then, and given to augmenting the miseries of poverty by a liberal use of the strap on both wife and son, there could only be the prospect of better times in the acquisition of a stepfather who seemed demonstrably fond of his mother, did not drink, and was a market-gardener in a small way, in the orchard country around Wisbech. Such was the supposition of the boy Jonathan — who, it turned out, was the one unwanted factor in this comfortable equation. The market-gardener wanted a wife: he did not want a ready-made son, already growing tall, and with a deplorable habit of eating. The memory of the methods by which his stepfather had signalled to his young and vulnerable self that he was to get out and not come back remained fresh to Jonathan yet, in his twenty-fifth year, but he would never let that memory out. A similar pain attached to the memory of his mother, too crushed and ineffectual to protest at her son's treatment — a treatment which did not last long, for Jonathan put an end to it by leaving: he would not plead or cling. While other boys, even on the ill-educated fens, were still at school, he went to work on the land, at a good distance from the home he could no longer claim. The crucial junction of feeling at which he found himself at this time of his life might have been expressed in three words: 'All right: alone.' But he did not say them to anyone; for the resolution embodied

219

in those words precluded trust, confidences, or communication.

His years of labour on fen farms, where his strength and endurance became a byword, were terminated as he had related to Hester, by his scraping up enough money at last to hire his first lighters. This was a life that had long attracted him by virtue of its complete independence. By this time all his ties were gone. His mother had died in giving birth to his stepfather's child, which had outlived her but a few days. His stepfather, perhaps finding the management of his business a strain, perhaps remorseful, had soon afterwards invited Jonathan back. Jonathan was having none of it. The self-reliance which had been forced upon him, he had now come to embrace: the solitariness that had been grafted on to his personality was now an ingrained part of it, as a living tree will grow round a nail. He loved his life on the waterways of the fens, and wanted nothing better.

He prospered modestly on the lighters, having few wants and no dependants. He earned a name for driving a hard but scrupulously fair bargain. That he never at any time engaged in the mildly shady dealing that most watermen did, was attributable to a fastidious and rather severe sense of what could only be called honour — an abstraction he valued the more, because he had been treated with the opposite. Probably the same causes lay at the root of his somewhat sternly judgemental attitude to others. He had grown to a young man with only a limited tolerance of human frailty, who was more surprised than gratified when people behaved well.

The books which Hester had observed in his cabin had for some time been his closest companions, and with his formal education having been early terminated, he schooled himself to learn their ways with much labour and struggle. *Pilgrim's Progress* and *Robinson Crusoe* he knew virtually by heart: *Paradise Lost* he had begun several times, always retiring defeated by its difficulty, though never without a sort of swimming wonder and a sense of having glimpsed something as elusively glorious as the vaporous galleries that opened up momentarily in the vaulted clouds of the fen sunset. He dearly loved a song, too, but was disabled by a conviction that this was somehow unmanly of him, and a sort of shame clung about the old concertina he had bought and taught himself to play. It was an uncompromising version of maleness that Jonathan Eastholm had constructed for himself: it combined with that rigorous code of honesty which made him intolerant of those who did not come up to similar standards, and with the sheer habit of being alone, to make him cold and short in company. Added to this was an aggressive species of egalitarianism natural to horizontal landscapes, which historically has made flat lowland countries the most anti-aristocratic; and it was no wonder that he was known as an unapproachable customer. If his great generosity, a warm lining to a rough topcoat, was less well known, it was partly because he was always afraid of its being abused.

There was more than a touch of the ascetic about him, as Hester had discerned in his addiction to cold plunges — and in deference to her he had moderated a habit of semi-nudity, which had once led him forgetfully to enter a neat little waterside shop clad in only his trousers, to the screams of the maiden lady behind the counter. In his moral scheme simplicity assumed the value of the highest good: he was uncomfortable in towns, and of the sophisticated appurtenances of technical civilisation he made use of little more than the printed book and the oil-stove. To see Jonathan Eastholm standing on the deck of his house-lighter whilst in the background a steam-train beetled across the fen, was to see the juxtaposition of two different worlds, and to feel that this oaklike figure had more in common with his Saxon ancestors than with his coevals speeding on their coal-driven, steel-thewed way. That he was impervious to cold and wet and discomfort did not generally mean that he was insensible, but that he was occupied with his own thoughts, which in his solitude came to represent a much nearer reality. In another age and clime Jonathan might have submitted himself to the disciplines of the Spartan mess, the monastic cell, or the bare feet and begging-bowl of the mountain mystic; but these would have lacked the elemental pleasures that constituted the charm of the life he had made for himself. Such were the sight of cornfields waving under moonlight; the orange-tipped flight of swans against the fiery cold of a winter sunset; the fatly buoyant shapes of ducks on the water, scarcely troubling themselves to hustle out of the path of the lighters, as if he and his boats appeared to them as no more than gently gliding aspects of the natural landscape. Lying flat on deck and looking up at the stars, which on a summer night could seem as near to the terrestrial observer as cottage lights, he felt there was nothing more to be asked of life. What was most disturbing about his new mood, was that he no longer felt that. Somehow, relish had departed, and Jonathan's palate began to taste the jaded dregs of discontent.

Having been ground in the mill of some pretty hard experience, Jonathan Eastholm considered his development complete, and did not believe he had anything more to learn about life. Womanhood belonged only to the irrelevant margins of his actuality, and the taking on of Hester Verney as a temporary workmate had not seemed to threaten this. He had been heartily glad to get rid of her — and once she was gone he could not stop thinking about her.

He thought, repetitively, maddeningly, of everything that had happened while she had been on the lighters, until that short time seemed to stretch and fill half his past life. What an infuriating little beggar she could be! — the way she had chucked those turves in the river, just to get back at him! He should have known she was that sort from the moment she came and took the empty chair opposite him that night at the Ferryman — there was

223

something about her mouth — even when it was not smiling it seemed just about to. The devilish sort. He hated that sort. But then the way she had outfaced old Shush Hubbard — that was a good one. And then that wonderful clear still evening at Littleport, when she had got him talking about *Robinson Crusoe* . . . How had she done that? His pleasures were personal and private — a part of himself: it alarmed him, the way she had drawn him out, and tempted him to share them.

Still, she was a giddy beggar — and fancied herself something rotten — always after a compliment. Well, she *was* pretty, no doubt about it, but he wasn't going to play that game. Nosy too.

"Git used to anything, I suppose," he said to the horse — it was no use speaking to Eli, that was like talking to the wall. "Miss an ulcer when it's gone."

He had got used to her, in a way — which was why it had been such a shock for him that last night at the Cutter when she had suddenly appeared in her woman's clothes again. There had been something baffling and dismaying about her beauty, and the realisation that he had been so close to it all this time: that these distracting eyes, lips, and other things had been smuggled into the jealously guarded confines of his independence. He could not have described the way he had felt that night as he walked up the towpath to the inn beside her, looking the way she did, except that there was something in it of pain, of being probed and invaded. His silence that night had belied a great internal noise of tocsins and alarums, manning of battlements and raising of drawbridges.

She represented something quite new in his view of the world. As a native of the fens, and travelling constantly about their high-banked waterways, Jonathan was accustomed to contemplating far horizons: his eyes dwelt often too on the detailed foreground, in the pages of a book; but towards the middle distance of life he had developed a certain blindness, which found a correlative in the short-sighted look of his eyes. Now, occupying this former blankness was the figure of the girl, even more vivid to him since she had gone, so that he found himself staring at the canvas stool on the deck and thinking, "That's where she sat — just there — I can see her now."

"Whass up?" said Eli — who was sitting on the stool. This was a long speech for him.

"Oh! nothing," Jonathan said: but he knew something was, very gravely, up. These feelings were strange to him: he was adrift and without bearings. The books he had read gave him no guidance, being of the stern kind, puritan not cavalier. In this benightedness, he at first mistook the specific for the general, and sought a solvent for his unrest in making a night of it with some fellow-watermen at a riverside inn where the girls were known for their friendliness — thinking that what ailed him was a late manifestation of a trivial urge which he had hitherto dismissed as a fool's game. But the laborious flirting in the smoky parlour bored him within a few minutes: he supposed, in the abstract, that the girls were pretty, but their dull talk and sheepish faces repelled him; and he very soon sloped off.

The experience was useful, however. It threw into stronger relief the figure of the one girl, the unique girl, and compelled him to confront the implications of the way this figure haunted him. She was the first thing he thought of when he woke: at intervals during the day he suffered something like mental palpitations when the image came to him unbidden of some element of her, such as the way her pink tongue showed against her teeth when she laughed. (He thought of this, of which Hester was unaware, rather than her hair, of which she was so vain: the things people love about us and the things we expect to be loved for seldom coincide.) And he came out of his reveries to see the plodding horse, and the river banks, and another lock ahead, and the familiar crabbed face of the lock-keeper leaning on his gate, and it all seemed dismayingly aimless and tasteless.

She had broken up his carefully constructed life, and he half hated her for it. He seemed to lose his identity. The precincts of self in which he had loved to dwell were no longer an ample habitation containing all he needed, but an airless prison, from the walls of which his sole voice resounded in dullest echoes.

"Well, this can't go on," he said to himself. "I shall have to do something." For Jonathan the accession of these disturbing feelings was not an occasion of joy in itself: the springs of his nature were still too tightly wound for that; he sought the restoration of the lost equilibrium. "I shall have to marry the girl," said he. "Thass all there is to it!"

It was all an infernal disruption, not what he had intended for himself at all, but he was lost without her, and there was no help for it. His mind leaped forward from perplexity to decision with characteristic directness, and with never a glance to right or left, wherein he might have seen the more dubious aspects of his case — those shadowy regions of contingency in which most lovers dwell, touched by subtle winds of fear and hope. The recognition of his longing, and the possession of its object, appeared to him as successive stages linked by a straight smooth path. The fact that he and Hester Verney had fought like cat and dog virtually throughout their short association seemed an insignificant eddy against the tide of his will.

It would be unfair to Jonathan to state that he scarcely thought of Hester's possible feelings at all: even the most altruistic love, looked at in a certain light, is mere indulgence of self; and besides, the moment of his decision was immediately succeeded by his asking himself the question: would she have him? In this he was deeply influenced by her final verdict on life as a waterman: 'This is no life for a human being at all — it's no life for a dog!' These words had burned into Jonathan like a cattle-brand: they stayed with him through all the restless, empty days following her departure, until the awakening of his feelings for her, and their prospective resolution, became inextricably linked with them. She had left because she found the hardships of the lighters intolerable. She would never marry him whilst that was the only life he could offer her. The lighters would have to go. She would want a house.

★ ★ ★

Habituated as he was to living at the pace of a dawdling barge-horse, Jonathan could also be extraordinarily swift both in the making of his decisions and their execution — a speed facilitated by his austere circumstances, untrammelled by ties. When Hester met him on Stokeley bridge, his choice was already made — he had been asking after her in the town that day — and only the fact that his plans were not quite complete had prevented him speaking out there and then. He had already concluded a deal to sell his gang of lighters to a small Whittlesey brickyard, who were seeking to do their own transporting: and he had a house in view.

That the house was not finished did not daunt him. It stood at the end of a long drove on Hinching Fen, a tiny cottage built of clunch and thatch — with only half a roof, and windows yet unglazed, and a bare earth floor. It belonged to an acquaintance of his, a former waterman, who had found himself in possession of five lighter-loads of building materials when the dealer for whom he was carrying them defaulted, and so had decided to realise a long-cherished dream of settling down as a one-hoss farmer. At the depressed prices typical of these remote spots he had bought a building-plot and hired a few acres, begun his house and his new life, and found the whole business intolerable within a few months, so that he had not even the heart to finish the building, and was rained on through the gaping roof while his heart hankered for the freedom of his old brawny, boozing, rootless ways. He was desperate to sell up, and could hardly wait to get Jonathan to the solicitor's in Stokeley, and be rid of the place, stock and all.

"I'll be honest with you, Jonathan bor," he said. "It's the loneliness I can't abide. Thass a different sort of being-on-your-ownsome from the lighters, somehow: I hope you can tek to it."

Jonathan was not listening. He was looking round at the four walls, and picturing bringing here the girl whose image gave him no rest. A house: a house was the one thing needful; she would want a house. It did not occur to him that he might be starting from the wrong end. The sheer idea of a house had become so firmly linked in his mind with the success of his suit, that he considered them as good as married by the acquisition of it.

He would purchase it. The sale of his lighters would only just meet the cost: he negotiated a further advance of money from the proprietor of the brickyard, who knew him well, and trusted him. Such a wrenching and uprooting of the massive solidity of his nature had these new

229

emotions caused that he was able thus, in the space of a few weeks, to completely transform the conditions of his existence with equanimity, and even with impatience that the processes of law did not allow it to go through more quickly. But there was nothing else for it: the life of the waterways had formerly defined his personality, but it did so no longer — he was like a scripturalist scuttled by Darwin — he would have been living a lie.

There was ten days' hiatus between the brickyard's entering into possession of his lighters, and Jonathan's entering into possession of the half-finished cottage. For that time he lodged there with his friend, and threw himself into the working of the few acres — only half of them planted — as the latter had never found the energy to do. One fine May morning, however, he left the seed-drill and the hoe, put on his best neckerchief, and set out to walk across the fen to Stokeley.

* * *

Gideon Saunders' wild gesture of rebellion had ended in defeat and capitulation. He knew better than to dispute the terms of the peace. But if his subjugation to his mother was complete and unprotesting, his resentment of Hester, the witness of his humiliation, became more sharply defined. A needling slyness entered his manner to her. He would seek the newspaper when she was looking at it, and then on her offering it, say airily, "Oh! no, don't mind me, I wouldn't dream of troubling you." He delighted to bring her messages from Mrs Saunders: "Mother says would you go down to Robson's for her embrocation. Sorry to put you to such trouble. It's a hard life, isn't it?" Hester met all this with a brilliant glassy smile which seemed to satisfactorily unnerve him, and indulged herself with private fantasies of sneaking into his room when he was asleep and snipping off his ridiculous moustache.

From the absent son, Lyle, there had been no communication for a while, so when a letter with the familiar Belgian stamp arrived one morning, Hester took it straight out to the yard, where Mrs Saunders and Gideon were watching the clipping of a young bay that had just been fetched from the station. This was the first stage in a process at which the Saunders establishment was adept — the transformation of unpromising horseflesh. After the clipping, which left just a saddle of longer hair on the back, came the trimming and thinning of the tail, the plaiting of the mane, the burning off of whiskery hairs round muzzle and ears, and then a long course of brushing and currying. The plainest animal came out of the Saunders stables sleek and shapely — and, of course, fetching a higher price.

"There's a letter from Mr Lyle, Mrs Saunders," Hester said, handing it to her. She turned away so as not to see the application of the twitch to the bay's nose. This was a cord tightened round the flesh between the nostrils with a pole: its effect was to numb the horse, so that it would not feel the painful pulling out of hairs, but it

231

always made Hester's eyes water to see it.

"Ah! I thought as much — he's coming home. Lyle's coming home — d'you hear, Giddy?" Mrs Saunders said.

"Oh, is he?" Gideon said without enthusiasm.

"He's coming — when's that say, gel? I'm hopeless without my spectacles — read it."

"He says the end of next week," Hester said. Lyle had made an arrangement with an English-speaking agent in Brussels, the letter disclosed, who would maintain their contact with the Percheron dealer: the latter was closing up his house for the summer. "'The Dielmans have been very kind to me'," Hester read, "'but oh how I long for English cooking. I keep dreaming about hills of Yorkshire pudding and mountains of Cheddar and lakes of onion-sauce.'"

"Ha-ha!" Mrs Saunders' big hard laugh made the horse jump. "I knew that would happen. They're not as bad as the Frenchies, but still, they're not English, and they do funny things with food. Mix it up together, so I've heard, instead of cooking it separate like civilised folk. Oh! we'd better get ready for him. His room's been shut up all this time. Hester, go and tell Judy to have Mr Lyle's room swept and aired — clean laundry and a fire to take the mustiness off — I want everything homey for him when he comes."

In the kitchen Mrs Dawsmere was delighted with the news. "Thass always nicer when Mr Lyle's here. There's more of a smile about the place somehow. That'll be a treat to see him. Oh! now I'm done it — I'm counted me chickens — and him having to cross the water as well — I shall have to sleep with me stockings on tonight, else he'll never git here."

"Hem!" said Judy, who had just answered a knock at the back kitchen door. "Pardon ME I'm sure, but it appears there's a Person who wants to see you."

"Me?" said Hester. "What sort of person?"

"OH I'm sure I don't know I'm only the MAID after all it's none of MY business," Judy said on one long plain-song note, gliding past Hester as if she were on wheels, and adding out of the back of her head, "It's always been MY understanding that the staff weren't allowed FOLLOWERS but there I dare say it's nothing to do with ME."

Hester went to the door. She was astonished to see Jonathan Eastholm standing there.

"Oh!" she said.

"Hullo," he said. "I wanted to speak to you."

Hester pulled the door to behind her. "What about? I'm not supposed to have people calling here, you know. Mrs Saunders'll have my head."

"It's urgent." He frowned on her. "Don't they ever let you out?"

"Well — I'm got my day off on Saturday — "

"Right then."

"But I'm going to see Lizzie — my friend — on Hinching Fen. I go on the morning carrier."

"Where's the carrier leave from? Spread Eagle yard, ain't it? Right. I'll meet you there. Day to you."

233

* * *

On Saturday morning Hester walked down
Stokeley High Street to the Spread Eagle inn
in a condition of perplexity which two days of
wondering had done nothing to elucidate. Could
it really be that Eastholm wanted her to come
back? She knew little enough of him, but she
did know he was far from stupid. Did he really
believe that she would give up this comfortable
job for the purgatory of the lighters? It was
baffling.

The Spread Eagle was a large inn which had
formerly served as the centre for such coaching
trade as the little town had enjoyed. Now its
capacious yard, entered by an ivied arch, was
the depot for carriers' vans and the gigs of
marketing farmers; but the inn still wore a
mellow and sleepy look, as if it had scarcely
awakened from a dream of former days, and
high up on the forehead of its gable-end there
was a sundial marked in vague gradations from
seven to five, and seeming to say that if there
were any more precise ways of measuring time,
it didn't want to know about them. The latticed
windows were open to the spring day: from the
upper storey there was a flapping of sheets and
dusters, and from the lower a murmur of talk
from farmers smokily taking refreshment in the
parlours, which the sunlight never seemed to
penetrate, and left as cool, congenial dungeons.
Along the outer gable wall there was a high stone
bench, and here sat a row of women waiting for
the carrier, some who had come in early from

the fen to sell a few eggs or a little butter, others setting out on visits to relatives: hopping down from the bench now and again to rearrange something in their baskets, or to shake out their black shawls or re-pin their black bonnets, hopping up again and chatting all at once, like so many inky-plumed and cheerful crows. At the other side of the yard was a solitary cherry tree, leaning at a slouching angle, as if it had imbibed the beeriness of the spot through its roots, and was permanently foxed: an old wooden seat was fixed around its base, with below it a smooth circular groove in the earth, worn down through long years by the shuffling feet of sitters there; and here in the bright sunshine Hester sat and composed herself to wait for the carrier to Whittlesey which passed through Hinching Fen on its circumambient way.

The carriers were more reliable than prompt, and you would have to be pretty late to miss one. A couple of the vans were standing in the yard, their horses stabled in the inn's stalls. They were broad four-wheeled carts, open-ended, with plank seats along each side for passengers and a wooden top. Parts of the fenland were served by the railway, and within the environs of such places as Cambridge and Peterborough the horse-omnibus had lately appeared; but the mass of ordinary folk depended for local transport on these sturdy waggons, which would have been recognisable in their essentials to their ancestors of the Tudor age. The carrier himself did more than just drive the van: for isolated cottagers he was a link with the wider world, fetching miscellaneous shopping from the towns, and carrying in his roomy pockets an item of ironmongery to be mended, a pair of boots to be hobnailed, a couple of plucked chickens to be sold. As a consequence his journeys were slow and roundabout in the extreme: a typical carrier's detour would take him a mile down a drove to deliver a broom-handle to a cottage — the presentation of the broom-handle itself being performed with all the deliberation and ceremony of Black Rod. But no one seemed to mind the slowness; and Hester had once heard an old woman declare, as they rumbled to a halt outside her cottage after three hours had brought them as many miles: "Well — here we are already! All this flying about meks your head spin!"

Hester had been sitting only a few minutes when she saw the tall form of Jonathan Eastholm appear in the archway, and walk purposefully in her direction. It was the first time she had seen him wearing a hat — a peaked cap, which he swept off as he approached, less it seemed from gallantry than because it irked him. He ran a large brown hand through his hair, and stood looking down at her from the great height, for all the world as if it were she who had asked him for this meeting, and he was wondering why.

"I wish you'd sit down," Hester said uneasily. "It meks my neck ache looking up there." And indeed the upright size of him, interposed between her and the morning sun, created a patch of shade in which she was entirely enclosed.

"No," he said. "I don't think I'll sit down."

"Oh! well — shall I stand up then?"

Jonathan shook his head. "I wanted desperate to speak to you — "

"Well, I don't know — one minute you can't wait to get rid of me, and the next you're seeking me out again."

" — And now that it's come, I don't know how to do it," he concluded, paying no heed to her interruption.

All sorts of vague surmises had begun to crowd in on Hester: but persisting in her first idea she said, "If it's about going back to the lighters, then you needn't ask. I'm got a very good job at Mrs Saunders' — I know you give me a job when I was down on my luck, but that don't mean — "

"I'm sold the lighters."

"You never have!"

"I'm sold 'em, and bought a house. A cottage on Hinching Fen — with a bit of working land. It wants the odd finishing touch, but it's a house, fit to mek a fair life in. I worked on farms for years — you know that — I can manage it."

"I'm sure you can," she breathed — quite taken aback. She could scarcely picture him separated from the waterways. "But I thought you loved the lighters."

"You hated them. That was no life for a dog, you said. I knew you'd never go back to them, so I bought a house." Jonathan pronounced this as straightforwardly as if he were talking of buying a loaf of bread. "It ain't a bad little place — come and see it before you decide, if you like."

"Decide what?"

"Why," he said with difficulty, "I wanted to ask you to marry me, you see."

Part of her mind knew he was quite serious; but another part reacted with disbelieving flippancy. "So," she said, "you have a woman for a week or two on your ole boats, and then you suddenly fancy you want a wife, eh?"

"I'm never wanted a wife," Jonathan said reflectively. "Not till now. I don't know as I want one now, come to that. It's all come on me so sudden and I'm not sure I like it. But that don't matter." For a weird moment she thought he was going to kneel, but he only dropped down on his haunches — the sun's rays streaming in again where his figure had blocked them — so his head was level with hers. "I can't get on without you, you see," he said with grim earnestness. "I don't know how it's happened, but I'm all of a mess. I'm tried to put it out of my mind but I can't — it's made me fit for nothing. So that's why I bought the house, see. For you to live in. The lighters were no good. I knew you'd want a house."

A suffocating sensation overcame Hester: utterly unprepared as she was, she panted like an animal tensed to flee. "I don't want a house," she found herself saying, with some inconsequence.

"Well, thass a story!" Jonathan declared. "You couldn't abide the way we lived on the lighters — thass why you packed it in. And I suppose it ain't much of a life for a gel. But the house now — thass different."

238

"I don't understand you," cried Hester. "Do you mean to say you're gone and sold up, and got a house on the fen, just because you took it into your head that — well, that I might marry you?"

"I didn't tek it into my head. You put it there."

"I never did no such thing!" said she, sharply, for there was accusation in his tone.

"Well, I don't know what else to call it. I never wanted this to happen. I never thought I'd git caught like this — but it's happened, and there's no help for it. I'm got to have you."

For the moment any incipient feeling of flattery or gratification at this avowal was eclipsed in Hester's mind by indignation. The disaster of Chad and the turf-digging rose vividly before her: here it was repeated! A pile of turf, a pile of bricks — these men seemed to think she was a piece of property, and they had only to put down a material deposit to secure her.

"But you shouldn't have done this thing," she faintly said. "Thass not the right way — you should have asked me before."

"Should I?" It seemed quite a new idea to him, and he bent his eyes thoughtfully on the ground at her feet. "Well — I never thought you'd have me the way I was, see — with the boats, and no home. Still!" Jonathan stirred, and fixed her with a penetrating look. "I'm asked you now — never mind which way about. It's done now. Come and see the house — I know you'll like it."

"No — I mean, I dare say it's very nice

239

— but there's no point in me going to see it." There was something overwhelming in his rugged ardour — alarming too: her palate shrank from such a concentrated essence of decision.

"Why, you want to see what sort of a place you'll be living in, don't you?"

His choice of tenses pricked her — releasing her confused feelings into the safer channel of vexation at his arrogance. "Oh! what a fellow you are! Who said I'm going to be living in it?"

"You did — just now — you said I should have asked you to marry me before."

"Oh, but what I meant was, you should ask a person such a question before you go and get a house for 'em — I didn't mean I'd say yes," exclaimed Hester, conscious that this statement, though perfectly true, had a coquettish sound. Her fear on this point was confirmed by Eastholm, whose frown deepened. "Well," he said, "after all that, what *do* you say?"

Hester looked distractedly around the innyard as if for guidance, but the carts, the heaped baskets and beer-barrels wore only the smug, stupid look typical of the external world at such critical moments. She groped for the lightness and clarity in which she trusted, but his presence cast her into doubtful unease: he made her feel terribly unsure of herself, and she did not like that. "I don't know what I can say," she said. "You're the last person in the world I'd have expected to ask me."

"Why, I'm not an old codger, you know,"

240

Jonathan said, with a little pique.

"Oh, but you never even said a single nice thing to me!"

He shrugged, as at a supreme irrelevance. "I suppose so — but then I'm no good for that sort of canoodling."

There was that word again! It infuriated her. What was so wrong with the small change of love, that it had to be dismissed so?

"But whass that got to do with anything, any road?" he went on, with honest scepticism. "I dare say it's true — I dare say I'm not like other chaps in that — " this with rather more pride than humility. "Perhaps I'm more serious about things. Thass why I bought the house."

"Oh! you and your house! Really, you must think pretty well of yourself if you went and bought that, never even thinking I might say no." Her indignation, which had begun as the froth from a troubled swirl of emotions, took solid form. "And you reckoned it was me who fancied meself! Why, I think it's men who are the vain ones."

"But I did it for you, damn it."

"To get me, you mean — to possess me. Well, I won't be bought like that."

"Beggar me! you are a skittish one." Jonathan had subsided to his knees now, though more for ease than in the posture of a suppliant. "I don't understand you. What more can a man offer you than what I have?"

"Well," said she, hesitating, and trying to look elsewhere than the large expanse of striped shirt and braced thighs that still filled her view, "well

— there's love, you know."

For the first time his eyes left her, and a little of the air seemed to seep out of his tight resolution of manner. Then he rose to his feet and, placing his hands on his hips, spoke with such deep-toned emphasis that Hester seemed to feel his voice as a perceptible reverberation through the ground. "Now look here," he said, "I'm gone to a deal of trouble for you — I'm give up my occupation, and everything that mattered to me, and staked it all on one chance."

"But I never asked you to!" cried Hester, both distressed and angry.

"Never mind that — I won't be put off. I'm dealing fair with you, and I expect you to deal fair with me. It's a good offer — tek it or no."

"Oh, dealing — you talk like you're trying to sell me a hoss! I declare you're the most pig-headed man!"

"Well: mebbe — I won't be made a game of," Jonathan said sharply. "I s'll only ask you once, you know."

"Oh, I'm honoured!"

Jonathan snapped his fingers. "A man must be a fool to put hisself through this, and set hisself up as an Aunt Sally for a gel," said he, as if giving rein to a compelling bitterness. "I'm always thought so, and it goes hard with me to do it: I never thought I would, till you come along."

Hester might have been disarmed by this tribute to her power — had it not been couched in such unflattering terms, which seemed to

242

transfer all the virtue to his part. And she was being represented as a mere destroyer: it was so unjust! "Well, if it's such a pain to you, why do it?"

"Because I can't help it," he gruffly replied, and his glare was so baleful she could not meet it. "You're made a proper mess of me. You going to give me your answer?"

"I already have, haven't I?" she said, with some asperity, for she felt herself more accused than appealed to. "You must be more pig-headed than I thought if you can't see that." She was the least pitiless of girls, but at that moment it hardly seemed to her that she could hurt such a flinty surface as he presented to her.

"Very well then." Jonathan, instead of putting on his cap, screwed it up in a ball and crammed it into his pocket as if he had no more use for it. "I'm asked you — I shan't ask again."

With no word of goodbye he walked away, with a certain slow deliberation, as if he were carefully carrying something — perhaps a large vessel of pride, from which he did not choose to spill a single drop.

★ ★ ★

A further twenty minutes' wait for the carrier ensued, but this and the journey itself were fused for Hester into one long brooding abstraction of thought, such that she stared for a couple of hours at the wedge of moving scenery between the two passengers opposite, and saw not a leaf of it. She was profoundly upset, but could hardly tell why. Some vulnerable part of herself seemed to have been laid bare and scarified. Her dominant sensation was one of regret: but it was regret not so much for what had happened as for the pattern of which it seemed a specimen — a pattern which had her as its protesting centre. It was not entirely the twist of perversity in Hester's nature that enabled her to feel, directly after a proposal of marriage, that nobody valued her. She considered that she had good grounds for feeling slighted. Practical as she was, she had a certain contempt for the material — perhaps inherited from her father — and she could only see the matter of the house as a proposition of barter, with herself as the complementary item.

Canoodling — what was wrong with canoodling? Jonathan had made it sound like a diminution of love — or whatever hard, immutable version of love he countenanced — instead of its expression. Hester was as susceptible as most mortals to the pleasure of making conquests — but in this case the conquest seemed a highly ambiguous one: it was as if he had made a grudging concession to the overmastering elements, like lighting a fire against the cold. Perhaps it was this elemental aspect about him that nonplussed her. She could understand a man wanting to kiss her, but not a man wanting to build a house for her: she could frame no conception of sincerity that would include them both.

"And even then, I don't reckon he said a single nice thing to me," she mentally grumbled. "No — he didn't — it was all as if I'd done him a wrong. Arrogant — that's it — I wish I'd used that word to him." The idea of what it would be like to have Jonathan saying nice things to her was quite swallowed up in her resentment that nobody did.

She tried then to dismiss the whole thing — he had said that was the end of it, and besides it meant nothing to her anyhow: but that this was not true was illustrated by her decision, as she alighted from the van at last, to say nothing to Lizzie about it. Lizzie would mock. Somehow she found the experience, far from being superfluous, had alerted her to a consciousness of lack within her — a lack which Eastholm's brusque proposal had highlighted by its very failure to fill it in the right way. Hester wanted to enjoy the sensation of being loved, not be violently presented with love as an achieved fact. If there was a certain sophistry and self-justification in this reasoning, it was perhaps because Hester felt an uneasy need to go all round the houses in order to avoid the thought of that one house, bought for her; and to avoid a suspicion, subversive to her view of life, that even bricks and mortar might be an emblem of passion.

6

THE day before Lyle Saunders' return was expected, Mrs Saunders and Gideon made a visit to a wealthy gentleman at Warboys who was offering for sale a desirable thoroughbred that had been a racehorse. This was clearly a deal, and a social contact, that could not be trusted to Gideon alone. Before she left Mrs Saunders gave Hester a shopping-list of various small items requisite for her younger son's return: this occupied her morning. Hester enjoyed going into Stokeley's shops nowadays — the authority of Mrs Saunders clung about her, and when she walked in the shopmen flapped like hens before a vixen. Back at the house, she applied herself to the laborious task of pressing Mrs Saunders' lace jabots, tippets and bands, all of intensest black. Coming downstairs from putting them away, she stopped. It occurred to her that she was all but alone in the house: it was Judy's half-day, and Mrs Dawsmere inhabited the kitchen like a cuckoo in a cuckoo-clock, emerging only at rare and prescribed intervals. The staircase on which she paused set the tone of massiveness that characterised Mrs Saunders' house: it comprised enough wood for a small plantation, in colour like petrified chocolate, with newels crowned by great brown footballs. Hester never ran her hand along the broad, highly polished banister without a sort of tactile speculation about what it would be like to slide down it: and here at last was an opportunity to find out.

She went down the first time side-saddle: it was disappointing — she had to hang on so awkwardly. As there was no one to see, she hitched her skirts up between her legs, and slid exhilaratingly down astride the banister.

"Whee!" she said — *sotto voce*, as a gesture to decorum. She came to rest by a collision of her behind with the newel-post — that was less pleasant; but she scrambled down, and ran up the stairs again to repeat the exercise. This time she essayed to twist her body at the end of her descent to avoid the posterior impact: lost her balance; and would have landed in a heap on the hall rug had not a pair of hands come from nowhere and stopped her fall by seizing her round the waist.

Hester let out a shriek of surprise — also of surprising volume — the hands of her supporter left her waist, and went to his own ears. "By the left!" he exclaimed. "You must be Hester — now I know why she picked you — I'll bet she can hear you *quite* plain!"

With the echo of her scream still springing about the hall, Hester turned to the speaker. She found herself looking into the amused blue eyes of a loose-knit young man, somewhat above medium height, dressed in a light suit and turn-down collar with a straw hat, which he removed to reveal a crown of short fair hair, slightly curly. Though there was nothing in his features reminiscent of Mrs Saunders or Gideon except for the pronounced curve of his mouth, she knew him at once to be Lyle: something about his looks immediately recalled the tone of his letters. His was a notably open face, with something gently mocking about the upward configuration of the eyebrows; and an odd little smile, mostly cheer, with a moiety of melancholy, like a spring sky brushed with cloud. There was an assurance in it which curiously communicated to Hester as reassurance, as if she had long known him.

"Well, even if you're not Hester," he said, after she had stood mute for some moments in embarrassed confusion at the way he had found her, "I'm Lyle Saunders, and how do you do." He proffered his hand.

"Yes — I'm Hester — I mean, how d'you do." She shook his hand, and said: "But you're not supposed to be here till tomorrow!"

"That accounts for my welcome. Are you the only one here?"

"Just me. Mrs Saunders and Mr Gideon have gone to Warboys to look at a horse."

"Oh! well, it don't signify. Fact is, I was able to get a night packet across, and then I got a train straight from London, rather than hang about there. My luggage is still at the station — I just walked up from there — funny, I don't feel a bit tired." He turned to close the front door, which was still standing open from his sudden entrance, and came back to Hester. "Well, I feel like we've met already, through those letters, and d'you know your face is very much as I pictured it. Not that your *face* was my first introduction to you . . . "

Hester, most unusually for her, blushed. "I don't know what come over me," said she. "I didn't think anyone would see."

"Oh! your secret's safe with me. *I've* been pulling faces at myself in the glass, on the train journey — it whiles away the time — I think this was the best one," and he grotesquely sucked in his cheeks and screwed up his eyes, looking not unlike a caricature of Gideon. "What d'you reckon?"

"Why, you don't look any different," Hester said.

"I see. One of these sharp women. Come on, let's go to the kitchen, I'm starving. Everybody well? Mother still fit?"

"Yes — excepting the arthritis, of course — I'm afraid she can't hardly fasten a button some mornings."

"Sad," Lyle said. "Why an active woman like Mother, eh? Still, she's got you now — I'm glad about that — I wanted her to take on a help before I left. What about Giddy? Still walking out with Phoebe Purefoy?"

"Yes — well, at least, I presume so . . . I think perhaps Mr Gideon or your mother had better tell you about that."

"Oh! dear, like that is it?"

They descended to the kitchen, where Mrs Dawsmere was so delighted to see him that she spilt salt with impunity, and could not find a bad omen anywhere. "You're looking thinner, though, Mr Lyle," she said. "I was afraid they wouldn't feed you proper over there."

"Not feed me! You should see the way the

Belgians eat. Thumping great sausages and sticky pastries every hour of the day. Huge tankards of beer you can hardly lift. And that's just the ladies. I'm starving now, though — what can I eat?"

"Oh, I'm afraid dinner won't be ready for a couple of hours yet," Mrs Dawsmere said. "I know there's a couple of kippers, if you want something hot — "

"Can't wait for that — let me forage in here," Lyle said, with his head in the larder. "Can I chew on this mutton-bone?"

"Oh, yes, sir — I was going to give it to the cats."

Lyle made his meal standing up at the kitchen table, gnawing on the mutton-bone, with a plate of radishes and bread and butter, and spoke of his life in Belgium. "Quite a rich sort of place. Crops growing on every inch of ground, and some of the farmers make our fen-folk look like paupers. You see 'em driving about in these enormous wagons, with horses like elephants."

"Did you manage to speak the language, sir?" Mrs Dawsmere said.

"I got by with a bit of French. Of course, some of them speak Flemish instead, and I couldn't follow a word of that."

"Fancy. You'd think one foreign lingo would be enough for 'em," said Mrs Dawsmere, as if they had two out of mere perversity.

"What were the people you were staying with like?" Hester said.

"Mr Dielman is about five foot nothing, with a little pointy beard. Mrs Dielman is about six foot

250

tall and six foot round. But somehow they've got two daughters — they always seem to be either at Mass or confession, and one of them wants to be a nun."

"Oh! Papists!" cried Mrs Dawsmere, with a native disgust unmodified since the days of Cromwell. "I hope they didn't try any tricks with you, Mr Lyle — trying to mek you one of 'em. I've heard things about them Nuns."

"No, I was too much of a benighted heathen for that," said Lyle, amused. "Mind you, I would have followed the eldest girl practically anywhere, if not quite to the convent. She was a dazzler."

"Why, what's she want to go and hide herself away in one of them places for, if she's so pretty?" Hester said, feeling somehow piqued.

"Well, her eyes weren't fixed on worldly things," Lyle said, with a glance of some interest at Hester. "Certainly not on me. Ah! I'll go — " There was knocking at the front door. "That'll be my luggage."

The driver of the station brake brought Lyle's bags into the hall, one of which Lyle seized and carried into the parlour, saying, "Hester, come and see what you think of these. Presents for Mother and Giddy."

In the parlour Lyle sat himself down on the rug and began to rummage eagerly in the bag. "Now then. This for Giddy. You should see the Brussels shops — all gilt and velvet and cherubs with fat behinds. D'you think he'll like that?" It was a boot-jack inlaid with silver. "I suppose he still wears those crippling tight boots? Sorry

251

— shouldn't ask you that really." But he gave her a droll look, which established the matter of Gideon's vanity between them, without either of them mentioning it.

"I'm sure it's just the thing," Hester said.

"And this for Mother."

It was a dressing-case, again inlaid with silver, and it was the most luxurious thing Hester had ever seen. "Coh," she said. "Coh."

"I'm glad you like it. I dare say it'll be mostly in your hands, what with Mother's arthritis. I've got some fancy Belgian chocolates for Mrs Dawsmere and Judy somewhere — where are they — hope they're not squashed. Anyway — this is for you, Hester. Now you see my problem. I didn't know what you looked like. For all I knew you might have been a right old gargoyle, instead of — well, the way you are. Anyway, I thought I couldn't fail with Brussels lace. I hope it's all right."

From a wad of foreign-looking wrapping paper came forth a lace fichu, of unendurable delicacy.

"Oh dear," Hester said.

"What's wrong?"

"I can't take this."

"Eh?"

"Well — what I mean is — I don't know you."

Lyle burst out laughing. "True. But I shouldn't let that stop you, if you like it. Anyway, you *are* going to know me, aren't you? I mean, now I'm back."

"Shall you be stopping here permanently, then?"

"I should think so. We've got the contact on the Continent now, and it's a lot of work for Giddy to manage on his own here. Give me England, anyhow. I got fed up with rolling my Rs. Letter Rs, that is. Ha! I've been waiting to use that joke. You do like it, though, don't you — the lace?"

"It's lovely," Hester said. "Thank you very much."

"That's all right then." Lyle suddenly yawned like a cat. "Phew, I think I am tired after all. Hope you don't mind if I go to sleep. Can't be bothered to shift all that luggage yet. Would you wake me in an hour, if Mother and Giddy aren't back by then?"

He took off his jacket, climbed up on the sofa, curled on his side, and fell asleep in a few moments. Hester had thought she was the only person who could do that. She lingered in the parlour to have another look at him, with that slight uneasy feeling of guilt attached to observing a sleeping person. It was not enough to say that the face, fair-complexioned with a pleasant straight nose, was a boy's face — Gideon's could often be that: rather it was, unlike Gideon's, the face of a boy when he thinks no one is looking at him. What strange differences there were in families! There seemed nothing of Mrs Saunders in him at all, and he appeared the temperamental opposite of Gideon.

"But then, after all, you don't know him," Hester told herself — feeling, however, that she did. She went upstairs to admire herself in

253

the lace fichu, in Mrs Saunders' dressing-table mirror, and presently heard the sound of the trap entering the yard.

"Mr Lyle," she said, going into the parlour. "Wake up." She shook him by one warm, shirt-sleeved arm. "Wake up — your mother's here."

Lyle sprang up with his hair in a mess. "Ow! My leg's gone to sleep," he exclaimed, and ran with a hopping, hobbling, pins-and-needles stride out to the hall.

"Lyle!" Mrs Saunders' voice must have been audible at the other end of Stokeley. "You beggar! We didn't expect you till tomorrow!"

"Hullo Mother — hullo Giddy." Lyle kissed his mother and shook hands with Gideon: there were greetings, laughter, inquiries. Out of the blue, Hester was assailed by sadness. Though she had seen the unedifying spectacle of Mrs Saunders' possessiveness, still there was real warmth and affection here: and she felt a little forlorn. No one ever kissed her affectionately. She was momentarily brushed, in fact, by the claw of the Old Goblin, though she did not know it.

"Well, my son," Mrs Saunders said, "I suppose you've met my help, then?"

"She was just coming down the stairs when I walked in," Lyle said, and Hester caught the faintest wink.

"Ah, she's not a bad gel," Mrs Saunders said, all the lines of her face deepened in a big harsh smile. "You have to watch her, though."

"Oh! I'll watch her," Lyle said.

254

★ ★ ★

Life at the Saunders yard was different following
Lyle's return. Formerly there had been an odd
sort of balance between Mrs Saunders, who was
a vivid physical expression of the idea of will,
and Gideon, who was a colourless distillation
of submission. Beside these two elements, Lyle
was an ambiguous alloy. It was very soon clear
to Hester that Mrs Saunders tyrannised her
sons indiscriminately: she was quite as severely
dictatorial to Lyle as to Gideon, and he had
barely settled in when he was set to work;
but there was something pliable about him,
something india-rubbery rather like the smile
of comic irony often to be seen on his mobile
lips, that meant he was not ground down as his
brother was. He was adept at the soft answer,
even when his mother berated him at length for
his bad habits.

"You've got settled into your bad habits,
you have," she stormed at him. "That's what
happens when you don't have my eye on you.
You go all to pot. D'you hear?"

"You look just like the Queen of Belgium,"
Lyle said dreamily, and kissed her hand.

"Get away with you! I'll give you kings and
queens — " But he had already gone off,
chuckling.

Lyle's bad habits were not far to seek, though
they were of a sort which Hester, for one, found
forgivable. He could work hard enough — once
you had got him out of bed, which, Mrs
Saunders said, was like trying to prise a brick

255

out of a wall. While he could be gently ironical about Gideon's attempts to be a masher, he had a weakness for clothes himself, and was always appearing in new neckties. He had a frank liking for a drink, and on one of his first evenings back home, took Gideon down to the Nag's Head to make a night of it: they returned very late and convivial, and Hester was woken by a strange muffled yodelling which she afterwards learnt was the sound of Gideon being rather ill into the water-closet. Mrs Saunders was very sharp with a somewhat grey and chastened Lyle in the morning; but it was better, Hester thought, than those secret tipplings of Gideon's. Lyle's general friendliness towards Gideon, which met with a decidedly mixed return, somewhat surprised Hester. That this proceeded too from a certain indolence, and that Lyle preferred amiability because it was simply less strenuous, she dimly discerned; but she was far from thinking any the worse of him for that, and her prejudice in his favour had material grounds, in that her position in the household improved in comfort following his return. He was always taking thought for little things that would never have occurred to Mrs Saunders — that the fire should not be allowed to go out simply because there was only Hester in the room, that she might want some paper to write a letter, that she might be introduced when folk called rather than left sitting there like a piece of furniture.

"Huh! you'll spoil the gel, you will," Mrs Saunders said. "She fancies herself as it is."

"Better to spoil her than lose her," Lyle said.

"Anyway why shouldn't she fancy herself? Blow your own trumpet, I say."

"Ah, I know you say that!" Mrs Saunders said. "You kept me waiting five-and-twenty minutes this morning — you with your titivating."

"Well, after all, it was Colonel Napier we were going to see. You need to be turned out like a gentleman for the Master of the Fitzjohn Hunt."

"You need to arrive on time, not five-and-twenty minutes late!"

Lyle laughed at himself for this, but it did not stop him doing the same again. This was a characteristic, Hester thought, that was more Verney than Saunders — Lyle, though candidly averse to effort, would nevertheless go to enormous trouble dressing himself to the nines, if the fancy took him, just to go down the street. Similarly, he took a liking to a chest of drawers that was standing in the spare room, and decided he wanted it in the bay window of his bedroom. One of the grooms came up to help shift it: they measured the bay window, measured the chest of drawers, measured again.

"No — I'm afraid it won't fit," the groom said.

"No," Lyle said, "I suppose it won't." He looked again at the bay. "But then — perhaps if it stood out a bit — I think it might, you know."

"I reckon it's too narrow, sir."

"Too narrow — it is, you're right. Silly idea." He measured again. "Still — you know — I think it might squeeze in." And in the end

257

nothing less than the laborious shifting of the chest of drawers from one room to the other, and the demonstrated physical impossibility of its going into a space six inches narrower than its width, would satisfy him.

He called it optimism: Mrs Saunders, pig-headedness. Hester inclined to his side. She was prepared to make a good deal of allowances for a person who made her laugh. The seed of flippancy in her own nature had borne bitter fruit in the dark turf-pit that disastrous night, but that did not mean she wished to uproot it: hers was no parable mentality, eager for a large dividend of precept from the small investments of experience. Lyle's capricious attitude to life was one she understood. She recognised the way that boredom came upon him, not by degrees, but instantaneously, in the manner of young animals: he would abandon a whole project in momentary lassitude. Mimicry diverted him in the same way. Walking down the stairs quite normally, he would suddenly become Gaffer, a creaking tottering character he had invented who spoke with a whistle through his teeth. "Ah! beggar theshe old shtairsh. Play merry hell wi' me jointsh. Hark at 'em popping. Like a load of ole sheed-podsh. You shtand there laughing, gel. You'll be old yourshelf one day." His sudden humours were always catching her unawares. One evening she was sewing, and Lyle was reading the newspaper. All at once she became aware that he had gravitated to a seat near her, and was regarding her solemnly with his chin on his hand.

258

"Whatcha doing?" he said, hushed.

"What's it look like I'm doing?" she cried, beginning to laugh.

"Sshh!" he admonished, finger to his lips, though there was no one around. "I won't tell anyone," and he tiptoed back to his chair, and read the newspaper with ferocious concentration.

When rich and influential customers came to the yard, Lyle was usually on his best behaviour: he did not lack that most salient feature of the Saunders physiognomy, a nose for business, and he was a ready flatterer. But then one morning came Mr Maurice Pimlott, who while not a Sir was the son of a Sir — six feet two of genial vacancy wrapped in a dove-grey frock-coat, with a painted-on smile like that of a marionette, and no back to his head; who was, he said, after a soft-mouthed Anglo-Arab with well let down hocks. Though this flower of the nation's élite was a valuable customer, it was difficult for Hester at least to keep a straight face when he was talking; and when young Mr Pimlott took tea with the Saunders in the parlour, Lyle began to catch Hester's eye, and a little devil entered him.

"So you've been in Belgium, I understand, Saunders," Mr Pimlott said, manipulating with difficulty the complexities of cup, saucer and spoon. "That must be a devilish queer sort of place."

"Very queer indeed," Lyle said, gravely. "One gets used to some things, you know: but it was the sun I couldn't get used to — rising in a different place. The sun rises in the west there,

259

as I'm sure you know, Mr Pimlott, because of the latitude; and I just couldn't take to that."

"By Jove, does it really?" Mr Pimlott sucked tea from his moustache. "Where *is* Belgium, exactly?"

"Quite near Africa," Lyle said, deadpan.

"Yes — of course — near Africa. I suppose they don't wear clothes like ours, do they?"

"Well — pretty much the same as ours," Lyle said. Hester risked a glance at him: his eyes met hers for the merest instant, but his face remained utterly sober as he went on, "Except for the unmarried women over forty, that is — they don't wear anything at all. Except a sort of apron, for modesty. It's some curious old custom left over from the Dark Ages, and the Belgians aren't too keen on its being known — but it's sanctioned by tradition, you know."

"Oh, quite." Mr Pimlott pondered: giving him the appearance of a man who begins to suspect he is sitting on something nasty. "Don't they get awfully cold?" he at last said.

"Well, it's a very hot climate, you see — tropical — being near Africa," Lyle said.

"Shall you be going to the Huntingdon Show, Mr Pimlott?" boomed Mrs Saunders, who had caught enough of this through her deafness to find she did not like it.

"Yes, I believe so, Mrs Saunders." The young man turned back to Lyle in fascination. "I say — people are *white* over there, aren't they?"

He's going to say they're green, thought Hester, with her hand over her mouth: he's going to say they're green, and I'm going to scream.

"Oh, yes, they're white," Lyle said. He paused. "That's the Russian in them, you see. The country used to belong to Russia — and some of the older men still wear fur hats and boots, in spite of the heat. Tradition, you see."

"Oh, quite. I've a great respect for tradition." Mr Pimlott pondered again. "Still, they're queer, these places. Aprons, eh? Damn me."

Gideon cut in then, and diverted the visitor's fragile mind to the safer subject of hunting till his departure. But as they stood in the yard to see him off, Mr Pimlott turned to Lyle before climbing into his gig, and said, "Those aprons, now — what are they made of?"

Lyle, almost thrown for a moment, seemed to cast wildly about in his mind.

"Seaweed," he said.

Hester had a fit of coughing, whilst Mr Pimlott nodded reflectively. "By Jove," he said. "Jolly interesting — but awfully queer. No: you've convinced me, Saunders — the diplomatic service would never have done for me."

"You'll see," Mrs Saunders reproached Lyle, after Mr Pimlott had left, "one of these days you'll be so sharp you'll cut yourself."

"By Jove," Lyle said, giving Hester a smile of Pimlottesque foolishness. "Will I really?"

★ ★ ★

One morning Mrs Saunders sent Hester out to the paddock to fetch Lyle: he was to accompany them on a charity visit to some of Stokeley's poorer townsfolk, to whom she was a staunch if rather browbeating benefactress. "Tell him not to keep me waiting," she said. "Now means now."

Outside the spring sunlight had all but attained to the high brightness of summer, and the callow green of the new leaves on the apple trees around the paddock seemed to deepen visibly in the warm air. From the paddock there was a strong and rank smell of bruised grass and earth, being trampled into a yet juicier compound by the thudding hoofs of a young cob, which had shown the most prolonged resistance to bit and bridle, and had yet to be broken in to a rider. Lyle and one of the grooms were standing at the paddock gate, watching the skittish trottings of the animal, and conferring.

"I'm going to give him another go," said Lyle, who was in riding-breeches and boots. "I think he's quietened down a bit. Hullo, Hester."

Hester gave him her message.

"Oh! I'll be along directly," he said. "I just want to try this chap again — I think he's getting used to me. Don't come into the paddock, will you, Hester — his hoofs fly a bit."

Hester needed no persuading. The cob, though it had been given the typical Saunders gloss, yet had something wild and swarthy about it: the innocence of its long eyelashes did not disguise the dark glitter in its eyes, even as it submitted to be caught and held by the groom. Lyle patted its neck and spoke cheerily to it, measuring it with his eye, and looking very slight beside its thick black quarters: then all at once he swarmed up on to the cob's back

262

like a man besieging a rampart. The horse gave a great galvanised twist in the air, describing almost a full circle, and landed only to spring up again, and career at zig-zagging angles across the paddock in a series of buck-jumps, each fiercer and more frenetic than the last. Lyle, braced backwards in the saddle, hung on, and even seemed, with his clenched rictus of effort, to smile grimly. The muscles of his thighs were so taut that they seemed quite as anatomically delineated, through the riding-breeches, as the rippling sinews of the horse, so that rider and mount might have been one infinitely steeled and compelling creature. The strenuous snorting of the horse's mouth and nostrils produced a cloud of moisture in the sun's rays that enveloped the two like a film as they bounded and plunged about the paddock; and this added to Hester's impression, derived from the balletic arch of the cob's back and the way it kept its feet almost daintily together, together with Lyle's stylised posture, of a weird dance — something at once graceful and violent. She watched in a suspense of troubled fascination.

Suddenly horse and rider, unpredictable as a jumping-jack, were right over by the fence where Hester stood: automatically she recoiled at the frantic rolling eye and staring neck-veins of the horse, and the spray of froth that rained on her; then the cob twirled again, the pounding of its hoofs perceptible as a vibration through Hester's feet, and Lyle twisting in the saddle was unseated at last. He grasped at the pommel for a moment, could not hold it, swore, and slid off, landing heavily on the grass, and straightway rolling out of reach of the prancing hoofs. His roll took him a little too far, and he struck the side of his face against the lowest bar of the fence.

"Oh! you've gone and broke your head — I knew you would," cried Hester, falling on her knees beside him, "it ain't safe!"

Lyle sat up and tenderly touched his upper cheekbone. "Ow! Silly bloody thing to do. Go through all that and then go and knock my own silly bloody head against the fence. Sorry — pardon my Belgian — ladies present."

"Don't worry. I should think I can swear as well as you."

"I'll bet you can as well." He smiled at her, then winced.

"Oh, does it hurt?" She touched his shoulder. "You ain't cracked a bone, have you?"

"Just bruised, I think. But you can kiss it better if you like."

"Indeed I won't!" She let go of him.

"Well, I thought you might like a treat."

"Huh!" She had caught this emphatic exclamation from Mrs Saunders. "I can git them ten a penny."

Lyle got to his feet. "Ow — I think I'm bruised somewhere else as well — "

"Don't you say it!"

They went into the house, where Mrs Saunders rounded on him. "There you are — hurry up! Go and get changed. Keeping me waiting till bull's noon. And you, gel, go and get your hat on."

They raced up the stairs. Hester was ready in a few moments: there was no sign of Lyle when she came out on the landing.

"Hester!" Mrs Saunders bellowed from below. "Tell that son of mine to hurry up — he needn't titivate himself for where we're going."

She went to Lyle's bedroom door, which was ajar: he was scrutinising his face in the mirror on the wall.

"I hope it won't mark," he said, touching his cheek. "There'll be girls on both sides of the Channel mourning if my looks are spoilt."

"Well, here's one who won't be," Hester said.

There is a peculiarly enhanced intimacy in the meeting of eyes in a mirror. The solitude of self is startlingly broken, and the two reflected seem bound in a common consciousness, seeing themselves and each other in one closed circuit of vision. Lyle held Hester's eyes in the glass for some moments, then smiled: then ceased to smile, and turned to the bureau by the bed.

"Hester — look here — I want you to have these. I brought 'em back from Brussels. Look. I had to have them." He held out on the palm of his hand a pair of jet earrings, like black pendant raindrops.

"I — I can't tek them," she said.

"You're a rum one. Why not?"

"I just can't . . . You already give me one present."

"Oh! that was because I brought everybody a present. That was just formal — I didn't even know you then. These are different. Look — I'll

265

be honest. When I saw them I had no idea of a girl to wear them — I just bought them sort of on the off-chance. Now I know what you look like — and you're just the one to wear them." He held them for a moment by her hair. "You've got the colouring — everything. I want them to go where they'll suit."

"But I can't," she said. "It wouldn't be right — "

"Oh! right, wrong — who cares about that? I want you to have them. Go on — else I'll give them to Phoebe Purefoy."

"I don't know when I'd be able to wear them — your mother likes me turned out plain."

"That doesn't matter. The best gifts are useless ones. Now then — mind your blushes — I've got to get changed."

"Oh yes — sorry." She left the room: and on the landing found, without quite knowing how, that she had taken the earrings on to her palm.

★ ★ ★

Early summer saw the beginning of the show season, an important time for the Saunders establishment, which entered horses and ponies at all the various agricultural shows around the fenland. Gideon and Lyle were continually busy schooling animals to be ridden and driven in the ring. Lyle had particular hopes of a smart dappled pony he had named General Blucher, and spent hours with it in the paddock, preparing for the Huntingdon Show. Hester frequently watched him: sometimes sent out to take a message from Mrs Saunders, more often drawn of her own accord.

"I believe you'll be sorry to see that pony go," she said to him.

"Oh! well — you mustn't get too attached to them," he said, stroking the General's nose. "But we're going to win a cup together first — aren't we, old fellow?"

"All that effort for a cup!" said Hester — who, despite a couple of months in the Saunders ambience, still viewed things equestrian in the most prosaic light.

"Ah, but it's not just the cup — it's the acclaim. When I'm riding in the ring, I like to pretend I'm taking part in a tournament — knights of old and all that. Where the victor receives a kiss from a lady fair. You know. Some filly in a pointed hat."

"A lady fair at Huntingdon Show — you daft beggar."

"I know. Lady Fitzjohn usually presents the cups — pointed head, more like. Moustache like Giddy's. Tell you what — I'll claim a kiss off you if I win the cup."

"I'd sooner kiss General Blucher!" she said.

"No, you wouldn't. He's not your type. Anyway he can never have children. Oh! go on, Hester — promise — it'll spur me on."

"I just don't know what to mek of you. Go on then, Sir Lancelot. First prize only, mind. If you git second prize, there's no kiss from me."

"What then?"

"Kiss from Judy."

"Ech, now I've got to win!"

Both Gideon and Lyle, with several horses to display each, were at the showground early on the day: Hester drove over later with Mrs Saunders in the trap. Mrs Saunders' arthritis making it sometimes difficult for her to handle the reins, she had lately been teaching Hester who, having taken charge of Mr Langtoft's farm cart occasionally, was a ready pupil; and this was the first occasion on which Hester was the driver for the entire journey.

"I don't know," Mrs Saunders sighed. "Only just sixty, and I can't even drive a little dumpling of a pony."

"Oh, but Mrs Saunders," said Hester, who knew how to butter her up, "thass only right you should have things done for you — having got to your position. Specially at the show — you don't want folk thinking you're a farmer's wife or some such."

"True, gel: true — I reckon I've got a bit of respect due to me. Well! I hope we shall win a fair few prizes today. That pony of Lyle's looks a certainty."

This was a subject on which Hester did not know what to think: she attempted to solve that problem by not thinking about it at all. She and Mrs Saunders took their seats in a small stand at the edge of the main show ring, beside the presentation dais. A feeble white-gloved waving at the edge of Hester's vision resolved itself into Phoebe Purefoy, sitting with her father a few seats along.

"Hello there — how d'you do — thank you

— lovely day — they do say flaming June, don't they?"

Hester greeted her, and said to Mrs Saunders, who was fixedly staring at a spot of sky, "There's Miss Purefoy, Mrs Saunders, saying hello."

"I see her!" Mrs Saunders said out of the corner of her mouth, and added with vicious indignation, "Hello, is it! I know what she means by *that*!" And she continued her resolute study of the sky whilst poor Phoebe helplessly pantomimed civilities across the intervening row of hats and knees.

Lyle's fantasy of the show as a medieval tournament did not quite accord with the large hoardings advertising cow-cake and fertiliser, or the bowler hats and furled umbrellas; but the colour of the marquees, the flags rippling against the blue sky, the rich grass that surely merited the word greensward, and the mixture of voices — the broad ones at the rails speaking in Anglo-Saxon terms, of Hosses and Kine, whilst the clipped accents on the dais talked of Stables and Cattle, recalling Norman French — established the show as a recognisable descendant of those occasions. And Hester, sitting through the displays of pony-and-trap and sulky-driving with amiable disinterest, felt her blood quicken at the sight of Lyle riding into the ring, quite as much as if he had been clad in mail, with a scarlet cross on his chest.

She had seen him practising on General Blucher a score of times, but never had the two seemed more elegantly, gracefully fused than now: and she seemed to feel herself moving with them, through every step of their routine, and holding her breath against a slip. She wished to catch Lyle's eye, but it was impossible here: the situation was the reverse of when they had looked at each other in the mirror, and she felt herself receding from him into the mass of the encircling crowd, as alien and separate as if they had never met. Her suspense was sharpened when the time for the judging came, and she barely noticed Mrs Saunders tugging at her sleeve.

"What are they saying? I can't hear a word. What are they saying, gel?"

"They're judging the riders — Yes, it's Lyle! First prize!"

"Oh! the riders," Mrs Saunders said. "I knew he'd get that. That don't matter." It was the value of a prize pony that mattered to her; and soon enough, the chairman of the judges announced first prize in the pony class to General Blucher. "There! I knew he would!" Mrs Saunders cried. "Good old boy, Lyle! — I knew he was schooling a champion. That pony'll fetch a blinder of a price. Hester — go and tell Lyle congratulations — he'll be in the enclosure — and say he's not to take any offers. They'll be at him like flies round jam. Tell him to say we've had an offer — two fifty — that'll push 'em up. Quick now."

She found Gideon in the Saunders' partition of the enclosure, with their horses. He had won a blue rosette for carriage-driving, and was in high spirits — or some sort of spirits: his whisky-flask protruded from the pocket of his hacking-jacket. "Lyle?" he said. "Yes, he's over there," and he gave her an unpleasant smile. "If you can get near him."

Lyle was receiving the congratulations of two young women whom Hester did not know. She stood around for a minute, like a fool, before she could attract his attention.

"Hester — hullo — this is my mother's companion — Miss Bowen, Miss Blythe."

"How d'you do. Mrs Saunders says congratulations, and — er — "

"Oh! I see. Excuse me a moment, ladies."

He took Hester to one side, and she gave him Mrs Saunders' message. "Two fifty, eh?" he said. "Well, if she says so. See him go, Hester? I hardly had to guide him."

He was happily smiling, and gazing directly at her as he said this, but there was nothing whatsoever to suggest that he remembered the promise attached to the winning of first prize. "Tell Mother I'll be along to see her soon," he said, and went back to the two young women, one of whom was examining the silver cup and getting fingermarks all over it. No — he had forgotten! She noted the two women — turning on all the charm — oh Mr Saunders this and la Mr Saunders that — she knew the type. The giggly sort, who made fizzing noises through their teeth when they laughed. She thought he'd have better taste.

The vehemence of her own reaction to this disconcerted Hester and made her a stranger to herself all the rest of that day. She was a stranger to herself because she was for the first time feeling something like jealousy — a large emotion springing from small and trivial causes, in direct contrast to the usual straightforward progression of her feelings. "You all right, gel? You're quiet. Not got the curse coming on, have you?" Mrs Saunders said, in her plain way, when they drove home. She had not; but it felt not unlike that.

The Saunders establishment had made several good deals that day: Lyle and Gideon went out in the evening to celebrate. "Landlord of the Nag's Head getting all our profits," Mrs Saunders grunted, but without malice: she was in a good mood. Everybody was, it seemed, except Hester. They had the nightly game of rummy. Sometimes of late Lyle would join them for this. He had several flashy ways of shuffling the cards, which never quite came off, so that they ended up fluttering all over the floor. "Oh, it does work, though," he would say, scrambling for them, "let me have another go — "

"Get on, you great fool-jabey!" Mrs Saunders would say, clipping his ear.

Hester went up to bed and, inhibited from sleep by some vague shape of discontent, pillow-punched for an hour or so. She scarcely seemed to have been asleep a few minutes when she was woken by a thunderous banging noise. She thought for a moment it was Gideon and Lyle, coming back soused again; but country living had given her the ability to tell the hour of the night quite precisely by the shade of the sky, and a glance at the window told her it was well past three — too late for that. She put on her dressing-gown and went out to the landing. Someone was lighting an oil-lamp in the hall: the illumination revealed Lyle, dressed in shirt and trousers.

"What is it?" Hester said.

"Just a horse got cast in the stable. Giddy's up. Tell Mother, will you? — and tell her we'll deal with it — don't let her get up, it's a bit nippy."

Hester did as she was bid, and then went down to see if there was anything she could do to help. In the stable-yard light was streaming from one of the stalls, whence came the banging: the two grooms, coats thrown over their nightshirts, hurried towards it. The unsettled occupants of the other stalls were shuffling and whinnying in the darkness. For a horse to get cast was a not uncommon occurrence: the animal, enjoying a roll on its back in the stall, found itself unable to turn on its side and get to its feet again because it had edged too close to the wall, and the noise it made in its struggles was enough to wake the household. Looking in at the open stall, Hester found that it was a young mare that had got cast. Lyle and Gideon had already fetched ropes from the tackle-room and were tying them on to the flailing legs.

"Take hold of this lamp, will you, Hester?" Lyle said. "She'll have it over in a minute. Hold it high — that's it. All right, Tom — let's pull her over."

Lyle, Gideon, and the two grooms wrapped the ropes round their arms, braced themselves against the opposite wall, and with much heaving and straining, pulled the mare over to the centre of the stall so that the animal was able to get to its feet. The grooms quietened the mare with their peculiar crooning stable-talk whilst Lyle and Gideon untied the ropes and ran their hands along its flanks to check for damage.

"She's all right," Lyle said. "There, you silly old devil. Don't do that again."

They returned to the house, yawning, Hester carrying the lamp, and Lyle and Gideon drooped back to bed. On the landing Hester heard Mrs Saunders call to her, and opened her bedroom door a little.

"No damage done, is there, gel?"

"No, everything's all right, Mrs Saunders."

She closed the door, and crossed the landing to set the lamp on a small table there. Lyle emerged from the shadows. His hair was the colour of dull gilt in the lamplight.

"It wasn't old General Blucher, anyway," he said softly. "He wouldn't do anything so daft."

"I suppose not," Hester said. Her limbs still had the kittenish weakness consequent on awakening from sleep, and the lamp wobbled as she set it down.

"Now then," Lyle said, standing quite still, "I think you owe me something, don't you?"

"Eh? Oh! that. I thought you'd forgotten about that."

"No, I hadn't forgotten."

"You didn't seem in much of a hurry to claim it," said she, hearing in her own voice a pettish resentment she could not control.

Lyle's expression was unperturbed. "Ah, at the show, you mean? That was no good. Not in front of those two old cats. No pleasure in that."

Hester felt herself outfaced: and had a sensation too of being suspended between intense wakefulness and drowsiness.

"Oh! well," she said, trying to sound careless. "If you still want it."

"Only if you do."

She did not answer; and a moment later the white shirt had advanced towards her out of the darkness, like a moving patch of moonlight, and Lyle's lips touched her own.

"First prize," said he. "Good night," and light and quick as a panther, he disappeared back into his own room.

★ ★ ★

The following Saturday was Hester's day off: mentioning this at breakfast, Lyle said, "I suppose you go and see your family?"

"I'm got no family local," Hester said. "I go and visit my friends on Hinching Fen."

"Someone fetches you?"

"Oh! no. I go by the carrier."

"Mother!" Lyle said. "You mean to say you make the poor girl travel on those lumbering old carriers? I should think half her day's gone by the time she gets there."

"Why, what else should she go by — magic carpet?" said Mrs Saunders. "I wasn't ashamed to use the carriers when I was a girl — I don't see why she should be. She's only a paid help."

"Well, you're not going by carrier today, Hester," Lyle said. "I'm taking you in the trap. I was going to take it out today anyway — that grey we bought wants more schooling."

"Huh!" Mrs Saunders said. "I wonder you don't take her in a coach-and-four — with a footman to boot! She'll start to expect it, I'm sure, the way you're going."

"Oh, I'll hit her with a stick every now and then, so she doesn't get proud," Lyle said.

"I took a stick to you when you were a lad," Mrs Saunders said grimly, "but look how you turned out."

"I was an angelic child, you know, Hester," Lyle said confidentially. "Mother had to cover me up when I went out to stop rich ladies stealing me and making me their own. Crusty old men used to burst into tears at the sight of my curls — and thieves turned reformed characters with one look at me, and devoted their lives to the church."

"Bah! He could wriggle his way out of anything — that's what he was like," snorted Mrs Saunders. "And he's no different now. If he fell in the river he'd come up with a fish in his mouth."

The trap was soon waiting in the yard, in all its compact smartness, with polished brass side-lamps and whip-socket and black-and-white check seats. The grey pony, which Lyle was schooling as a carriagehorse, was a much leaner and more wiry animal than their own steady dumpling, and was restless to be off.

"Up we go," Lyle said, handing Hester up, and then stowing a wicker basket on the backboard.

"What's in that?" she said.

"Cow's eggs," said Lyle, taking the reins. "Now then, old girl!"

The pony sprang forward, and they were borne briskly out of the yard and down the High Street, pedestrians stopping to admire the whirl of the red wheels as the trap whisked by, and a draught-horse stationary in the shafts of a dray turning its heavy head slowly at their passing, like age contemplating youth. In a few moments they had left the arches of the Abbey behind; and Hester suddenly marking the road they were taking, said, "You're going the wrong way — you want the other road for Hinching Fen."

Lyle slackened the reins, and said: "Oh! you want to go there, do you?"

"Why — what else?"

"I thought you were coming for a day out with me. I've got a picnic lunch in the basket — I asked Mrs Dawsmere to make it up for me."

"Well! you *are* a story."

"Not really. I'll take you to your friends' if you like; or you can stay with me. Which is it to be?"

He turned his face to her, haloed by his straw hat, and all at once she laughed, reaching up and pinching his nose between her finger and thumb.

"Ow! what's that for?"

"Thass to be going on with. Come on then — the picnic it is."

"I shall cry if you're going to knock me about."

"Oh! git on and drive."

He did so, clamping his hat down on his head and with a grin setting the pony off at speed, so that Hester was thrown backwards in her seat. It was a clear summer day, warm and windless, and the pony was full of vigour, scarcely noticing her light burden. The merest dab of Lyle's whip sent them bowling along, the wheels below seeming rather to skim the ground than actually revolve on their axes, and a vortex of onrushing air funnelling between Hester and Lyle, so that a third person seemed to be sitting there, rubbing against their shoulders.

"Can't you slow down a bit?" Hester cried.

"Can't hear you."

"Slow down!"

"Why? It's the pony — not me," he said — at the same time giving the reins a flick. "Anyway, it's grand, isn't it?"

The straight road ran directly parallel with the high banks of the Forty Foot, which traversed the open fen like a backbone in the earth. Fields of pale olive-green wheat rippled away to the encircling horizon, on which in the bright air landmarks could be seen at such distances that a couple of miles' progress along the road could be made with no apparent change relative to the position of a far-off steeple or barn: so that they seemed at the same time to be plunging along at furious speed, and standing still. Starlings fluttered up from the roadside in fright, just as their ancestors had done at the spiked wheels of Boadicea's war-chariots; and butterflies were caught up in the momentary turbulence of their passing, spinning helplessly for an instant in dusty whirlpools of air before being deposited again on the flowered verges. At some point Hester — unable now even to protest, as the whipping air snatched the breath from her open mouth — passed from fear to exhilaration, though this feeling was not without its coppery tang of alarm: at some point too she had put her arm about Lyle's shoulders, as the most convenient means of holding on, and when he suddenly pulled on the reins, tugging them to a slewing halt on the grass of the verge, she was compelled to cling to his neck to keep her balance, and was thrown full against him.

"Hester — I declare you've got designs on me," he said, looking down at her gloved hand clasped close to his face. Her recent indoor occupation, and the regenerative power of youthful flesh, had rendered the former farm-servant's skin as white and smooth as a lady's, so that the two inches of wrist between sleeve and glove appeared like a splash of milk against Lyle's navy jacket. Before she could move he had bent his head and kissed the exposed skin; and her heart still beating fast as it was from the excitement of the ride, she seemed to feel the pulse of her own blue veins against Lyle's mouth, like the ticking of a watch.

"Here," she said, drawing back from him, "you're already had your prize."

"Oh, that was *your* prize."

"You conceited davil!"

"Not enough, eh? Have another one?" said he, and kissed her lips.

Hester felt the kiss as something warm, sweet and bright — like some detached aspect of the deep blue summer air in which a lark was singing. Her happiness came to her with a curious unsurprise: it was not at all the proverbial happiness too deep for expression — it made her smile. She looked at him through eyelids half-closed against the sunlight, so that his face was fringed like a cameo by the glowing nimbus of her own lashes. "You are a davil," she murmured.

"Ah, you like me, though, don't you?"

"Sometimes."

"Only sometimes?"

"Well — I was mad as fire with you the other day — flirting with them two old cats at the show."

"Aha! Hester, that's a confession!"

"No — I only meant — "

"Too late," he said, kissing her again. "Secret's out. Jealous, eh? Why, they didn't mean anything at all."

"Thass what you say."

"Well, I wouldn't take *them* out for a picnic. Strait-laced little misses they are — Phoebe twice over. No fun at all."

"Oh! I see — not the sort you can tek liberties with — not like me — thass what you mean. Well you're wrong there." But almost before she had finished speaking she suffered a sort of mental flex of impatience at herself, for there was something perfunctory about this coquetry now

280

that she had been brought to acknowledge what had been inexorably stealing on her ever since Lyle had come home — and so she effectively contradicted her words with an eager embrace which took him by surprise and sent his hat rolling on to the grass.

"By the left," he said, when he had recovered his breath. "I don't feel safe with you!"

"Oh! I won't hurt you. Now where you going?"

"To get my hat."

"I'll git it," she said, springing down from the trap. She got to the hat first, and put it behind her back.

"You Pampered Jade — Unhand My Boater," Lyle said in his theatrical voice.

"Say please."

"Please."

"No."

She ran up the bank. Lyle came after her as Gaffer, knees wobbling. "Ooh! I shan't get down from here. Not with my anklesh. I shall go arshey-vershy. You young beggar! Thish were all fieldsh when I were a lad. And you never had to lock your door in them daysh."

Hester made as if to skim the hat into the water.

"No! please — Hester — no, not my best hat!"

She put it behind her back again. "Give us a kiss then."

"Another one? She's insatiable."

At last they returned laughing to the trap: drove on till they found a dry place shaded

281

with a few rare trees by the waterside, and got out their picnic, sitting on carriage-rugs spread on the ground, whilst the pony cropped the grass and was teased by flies. The precipitancy of the drive and the chase with the hat was now replaced by a brilliant stillness; and when Hester lay back on the grass, after eating with her usual appetite, the only movement to be seen was directly above her, where a few white clouds travelled in a slow arc from horizon to horizon; the fens at such times offering a perceptible intimation of the spherical nature of the earth, which their very flatness seems curiously to reinforce.

Propped on his elbow, Lyle leaned over her and tickled her face with a blade of grass.

"What a bit of luck, meeting you!" he said.

"True." She felt utterly, blissfully relaxed with him: not a cell of self-consciousness in her whole body. "Lucky boy."

He stretched out his legs in his feline way. "Folk are so serious, aren't they?"

"Terrible serious." She snatched the blade of grass from his fingers, and poked it down his collar. "Wouldn't it be funny if Gideon came along now, and saw us?"

"Mr Gideon to you, serving-wench."

"Yes, Mr Lyle."

"Oh! just My Lord will do."

She put one hand to his face, and held it there. "It's an odd sort of situation, ain't it?"

"How odd?"

"Well. Funny. Tricky."

"Oh! it would be, I suppose — to serious

282

people. Which we're not. I knew you were my type when I saw you sliding down that banister."

"I don't know what I'll say to your mother if she asks me whether I'm had a nice day."

"Well, you are having a nice day, aren't you?"

"Oh! fair — fair to middling. But you know what I mean."

He subsided beside her, placing his hands behind his head and tipping his hat over his eyes. "Just fib. It's easy. I've been fibbing all my life, and it's never hurt me yet."

"You'd better not fib to me!"

For answer he merely curled his lips in a smile, his eyes invisible beneath the brim of his tilted hat.

"Oh! Lyle," she said, "just think — it's a whole fortnight till my next day off."

"Trust a woman to think of that, when this one isn't even over! Anyway — a fortnight — that's years away — that's practically infinity. I can't think that far ahead. Besides, there's always a way round things, my dear. Always."

"Is there?" Scarcely listening, she laid her head on his gently rising and falling chest, gazed at the sky, and felt herself to be closer to that blue ether than to the earth below.

★ ★ ★

Jonathan Eastholm tended not to measure time in weeks. Though he had read much in the Bible, so that its accents often coloured his speech, he had little time for church or chapel, which divided time by Sundays; and the solitude of his life on the lighters having estranged him from the workaday world, and made the moon his chronometer, he habitually thought in fortnights — thus unconsciously evading fifteen hundred years of Christian history, and perpetuating the mental forms of the ancient Druids. When that June fine weather came, he had been precariously established as a one-hoss farmer in the little half-finished house on Hinching Fen for nearly four fortnights.

Even the poorest cottager from the upland shires might have been aghast at the bareness of his situation; and there were moments when even Jonathan's mind, schooled to hardship, staggered a little at the consequence of his reckless action. When he had first seen the house, he had viewed it in the light of a bower to bring a bride to; and so that vision had transformed it, and cloaked with romance the rough edges of reality. The failure of his suit — worse, its revelation as the purblind fantasy of a beleaguered egotism — had lifted the spell, and forced him to contemplate what he had done. Three things kept him from despair in the first days: the resilience of his own nature, the kind weather which eased a prospect that in winter would have been grim indeed, and the fact that, the lighters being untenable now by their sheer force of tormenting association, he would have had to change his mode of life anyhow.

The floor-space of the entire cottage was about the size of a prosperous tradesman's drawing-room. The single downstairs room, the house-place as it was called locally, had a brick floor and an open hearth for a turf fire, along with a few sticks of furniture which the former owner, Jonathan's friend, had left behind him, having no use for them on the boats to which he had returned with hungry eagerness. A ladder-stair led to the room in the roof, which when Jonathan moved in still gaped with unfinished thatching, so that sparrows popped in and out, as if the house were no more than a negligible interruption to the sky: the windows too, at first, were only shuttered. Jonathan slept on a straw palliasse on the floor. The cottage was damp, of course — most fen cottages were; but this was particularly so, owing to its very recent and flimsy construction, and the thinness of its foundations on the peat. In consequence, the walls were inhabited by crickets, which after dusk made the whole place ring with their stridulations, and disturbed Jonathan's rest by making wild Cossack leaps over his body, and sometimes landing on him, with a disagreeable scratchiness. He countered this in an old fen way, by obtaining a young hedgehog scarcely out of the nest, and inducing it with libations of milk to become a house-pet. The hedgehog found the cottage a very comfortable berth, and its nightly trundlings around the walls soon reduced the cricket infestation; though if nature roused him in the night Jonathan was always careful, for both their sakes, lest he set his naked foot on the creature in the darkness.

As he lay on his straw bed, his large limbs

disdaining clothes in the warm nights, Jonathan bore something of the appearance of a warrior of antiquity, taking his statuesque repose within arm's reach of sword and shield. Bone-weary from the day's work as he was, he always thought long, staring at the ill-laid rafters above, before going to sleep: thinking being something he had always enjoyed, as an active process. The silence of the fen pleased him, as did the sense of being his own master, and he felt that this new life promised some satisfaction. Still, troubled currents moved in him, swirling about the thought of Hester Verney, and the strange effect she had had on him. At times he could scarcely believe that he had been such a fool as to propose marriage, and all it entailed: that he had actually contemplated exchanging the purity of independence for the tainted pleasures of a cloying proximity. At such times the chance meeting with the girl at the Ferryman assumed the dimensions of a vast mistake in his life, engineered by a capricious fate which owned no higher aims than the vexation of mortals, and the confounding of their attempts to order their existence. But at other times, the image of the girl continued to haunt him in a peculiarly remote way, as if those eyes, that mouth, that laugh had only existed in one of those dreams which linger long after waking, and during which one seems to have been living in a parallel universe. He was not a good liar to himself, and could not deny that these latter times were the more frequent.

In fact his disappointment had changed

Jonathan, more perhaps than he yet knew, and the change was not without benefits. There was something of liberation. The soul of the boy had been purposefully smothered on the day he left his stepfather's house, and the premature manhood on which he had entered had the slightly showy and unnatural quality of all forced growths. Now he had received a severe knock, and its effect was to release some of that buried youth, which was not without poetry. He had elevated self-sufficiency to a religion, of a stern and jealous kind: now the revelation that he was vulnerable after all left him a freer if more bewildered man, doubt replacing dogma. Most importantly, the disappointment he had suffered was notable for its sheer commonness: he had loved and known rejection, and so at a stroke found himself involved in the universal experience of humanity — which hitherto he had tended to regard, if not to despise, as an alien and irrelevant abstraction. The dammed springs of sympathy and generosity began to play again on his too long arid nature. He was carrying in his heart an image of beauty glimpsed and lost, which worked its age-old alchemy upon him; and the true man was beginning to emerge from the hard chrysalis of the persona.

Strangely enough, Jonathan seldom wondered what she might be doing now, or thought of seeking her out again. Her rejection had been absolute, so it seemed, and he was used to thinking in absolute terms. That he had gone about it all wrong he now knew, but that did not mean he knew of a right way to go about it, nor that he cared for a second time to expose the tender tissue of his pride to the lacerating scalpel of feminine scorn; and that element of the Spartan in him told him the only thing to do was to abjure the sight of her, and give himself up to work.

Work was, in any case, a pressing necessity, for the loan from the brickyard owner could only be repaid from the harvest of his first crop, and his friend the previous owner had only half-heartedly cultivated his few acres. He had sown some potatoes, which came as stock with the property, but Jonathan had done most of the planting, rather late, on land that had not been well ploughed. Of course, only the completest beginner could fail to get a crop from the rich peat: it was the very fertility that was the problem. Weeds were rampant: Jonathan, labouring with mattock and hoe, often thought he could see them growing out of the corner of his eye: even tall, thick-bladed reeds sprang up. However, he was no beginner, having done farm-work since boyhood. What he chiefly lacked was materials. He began as a farmer with one horse, stabled in a lean-to, a rusty plough and harrow, and a few other dilapidated implements which his friend had left behind him. That ingrained and rather rigid independence of his baulked at seeking help from neighbours; but he soon found it generously offered. This perplexed him at first, for he had yet to recognise that nobility did not only reside in an aloof self-reliance.

There was great interest in him, he knew, as a newcomer to Hinching Fen; but fen folk not being of the sort to impose themselves, and Jonathan keeping himself very much to himself, there was virtually no contact. The little world of the fen, its only landmark the windmill which Jonathan's front window framed exactly like a Dutch landscape painting, was spacious enough for him to avoid company if he chose. He seldom went to Milney St Mary, the village; a long drove separated his house from the high road; the nearest cottage was half a mile away. All this allowed him to embrace solitude as devoutly as he had on the lighters. One morning, however, he was returning from a walk far afield in search of mushrooms, his favourite food, when he caught sight of a youth standing by the boat-dyke, throwing his cap forcibly on to the ground, and bursting into noisy tears; and Jonathan could not pass by on the other side.

"Now then, boy," he said, more gruff than he intended, from sheer lack of use of his voice, "whass up?"

The youth, a tall stripling in that raw state of adolescence where the elbows and knees seem to belong to some maturer individual, beheld Jonathan through a mask of tears, and cried, "Oh, mister! Look what I'm gone and done! Oh, 'ell! I let Molly git in and now she can't git cut!"

Below, Jonathan looked into the large helpless eyes of a cow which, led round the dykesides for grazing, had obviously climbed down into the dyke to drink, and now found it could not climb out again. The animal had its hindquarters in the water, and looked like a person demurely testing a bath.

"Thass my fault!" the youth bellowed. "I were dreaming again — mairster tells me off for dreaming — but I done it again — mairster'll have me guts for garters — I wish I were dead!" And seizing his cap, he threw it down on the ground once more, then picked it up and crammed it on to his head, as if he were a candle, and he were trying to extinguish himself.

"Who's your master, then?" Jonathan said.

"Mr Wake, mister. Oh, 'ell!"

"And where's his farm?"

"Oh — way uvver yonder," the boy said, without any accompanying gesture, as if 'yonder' were a sufficient direction in itself.

"Well, now, stop roaring, do," Jonathan said. "You stay here, while I go back to my place, and fetch a spade and a bit o' rope. We'll soon have Molly out, and she won't come to no more harm than a wet behind amounts to."

The boy gazed up at Jonathan as if he were some superhuman being sent to his aid, and he was still rooted in the same awed posture when Jonathan returned, bearing over his shoulder a hodding-spade and shovel and a coil of rope.

"Now then," Jonathan said, clambering down the dykeside using the spade and shovel like crampons, "I'll see if I can dig out a bit of a slope for her." He cast one end of the rope around the cow's neck. "Catch hold of tother end — whass your name?"

"Charlie Smeeth, sir."

"You needn't sir me. They ain't knighted me yet. You give her a pull when I say."

The dyke walls were in a soft condition, and it did not take long for Jonathan to dig out a rough ramp, shallow enough for the cow to manage; but the animal merely looked round at him with bovine obtuseness, giving an apologetic moo, and had to be encouraged to scramble up by the youth's tugging on the rope, and Jonathan giving her rump a hearty slapping.

Once this crisis was over, and Molly was safe, Charlie Smeeth gave a remarkable display of emotional volatility, by bursting into a great high-pitched laugh of relief, with the tears still wet on his cheeks, and throwing his cap repeatedly into the air, as if headgear was a sort of auxiliary channel for the expression of his feelings. "Hooray! I thought Molly was drownded. Hooray for you, sir!"

"Well," Jonathan said, not without amusement, "don't go dreaming again, will you?"

"Oh! no. Oh, 'ell!" said Charlie. "I'm got to git back to mairster — and I'm ages late now, and he'll want to know why, and what I'm been up to — and I dursn't tell him! Sir, will you come wi' me, and tell mairster? Please, sir!"

"Well, you are a dippy beggar," Jonathan said frowning, but as the round eyes of the boy seemed to presage further tempests, he said, "Oh! come on then. I don't know. I never see such a panicky article."

"Yes, sir. Thass what mairster says. He told me to try tekking deep breaths — but all it did was mek me heart go pitter-pat even wuss — and once I even keeled uvver and went head-fust into the pig-bin, because I'd sucked all this breath in and not let it out — so I don't do that no more, sir."

"Don't sir me," Jonathan said, between laughter and annoyance. "Well, next time you feel yourself going panicky, try repeating a bit of poetry to yourself, just in your head."

"Don't know any, sir. We used to have a bit at school, but I never got none, because I used to sit at the back, on account of the stink coming off Daddy Lucas — that were the schoolmaster, sir — he was as old as the hills, and I don't reckon he ever got a wash any more, because he used to bottle summat chronic — and he hadn't got much of a voice either, just a sort of wheezing, so I never heard nothing."

"Hmm. D'you know any psalms?"

"I know The-Lord-Is-My-Shepherd-I-Shall-Not-Want."

"Well, try that. Let's hear you say it."

In this way, driving the cow before them, they came to the drove which led to Charlie's master's farm, and found Henry Wake coming down the drove to meet them.

"There you are, Charlie Smeeth!" he said. "And me thinking you'd run away to sea! What's it all about?"

"Please, Mr Wake — I had a bit o' trouble — and I axed this mister to come and explain, because he got Molly out of the dyke."

Charlie told his tale, wrenching his cap into various illustrative attitudes.

"Now, Charlie Smeeth!" Henry Wake said.

"Do you mean you're fetched this neighbour here, who I don't know the name of, but I shall be glad to, out of his way for this, besides putting him to so much trouble?"

"No trouble," Jonathan said.

"Well, you're good enough to say so, neighbour," Henry Wake said. "Only if I know Charlie Smeeth here, you're had a teasing enough time on it. Charlie, what am I told you about dreaming, and gitting in a panic, and how one follows another? And look! here's our neighbour all drenched up to the thighs, on account on it."

"Oh! that," said Jonathan who, between the lighters and the damp cottage, was as seldom dry as a frog, and had not even noticed it. "Tisn't anything."

"Well, here's my thanks, any road," Henry Wake said, holding out his hand, which was as slight as a cat's paw in Jonathan's. "I think I'm right in saying you're our neighbour at the new cottage. I'm Henry Wake — everybody calls me Henry — I think you'll find I'm pretty well known around these parts — " this with an air of modestly refraining from saying why.

Jonathan introduced himself, and on Henry Wake's inviting him to step up to the house for a pinch of tea, declined, saying he had to get back to his work.

"Of course you have," Henry Wake said. "And here's this boy been keeping you from it. Charlie, when will you learn? Well, I'll walk as far as the high road with you, if I may, neighbour."

So Henry Wake, taking three brisk steps to his one, accompanied Jonathan on the way back, talking volubly. The conversation turning naturally on farming, Jonathan was soon perforce confessing his deficiencies in tools and other necessaries, and Henry Wake offered him help with alacrity.

"I know I'm got a coulter in my shed — you must have that. I'm got onion-seed too — plenty to spare. As for a long-handled rake, I'm pretty sure Wag Langtoft's got one he could lend you."

Jonathan was embarrassed, wishing he had not said anything, and afraid of seeming to cadge. But it appeared that this was only in his own mind, not Henry's: the latter came right to the cottage with him, and took great pleasure in assessing what he needed. "Don't lay out capital on tools — not while you're just starting," he said. "I can help you to them. I say, that roof's a bit of a nuisance, ain't it?"

Jonathan had covered the unthatched gaps with rick-cloths. "Thass another thing that'll have to wait, I'm afraid," he said.

"I think I'll ask Sunny Daintree about that. He's our molecatcher — he turns his hand to all sorts of things out of the mole season. I reckon he's done a spot of thacking in his time."

"Well — I'm really not able to lay out money at all just at the moment."

"Don't worry about that. Sunny's not the sort to dun you for money if you ain't got it. I'll see how busy he is."

From this moment, Jonathan's relations with

the people of Hinching Fen changed, willy-nilly: he became a known quantity, and an object of practical interest. Sunny Daintree came ambling over one evening, with ladder and reed-sheaves, and laconically began patching up the roof.

"I shall pay you, soon as I'm able," Jonathan said.

"Oh! no," Sunny answered from the roof, in a voice like the sigh of wind through grass. "Thass a poor ole world if you can't do a neighbour a service. We're only here the once, you know; and we never know when we'll be took. It always comes when you're not expecting it. We might be took tomorrer — both on us. I wouldn't be a bit surprised."

"You're right there, Sunny," said a little white-bearded old man, who had been approaching down the drove for an enormous length of time, like a clock-hand reaching the hour. "How do, bor," he said to Jonathan. "I'm your next-door neighbour — " meaning he was the inhabitant of that nearest cottage, a mile down the road " — I'm come to watch ole Sunny thacking your roof." For in the fens any such operation assumed the character of a public spectacle, and it was accounted natural to go along and watch it.

"This won't be a proper job, mind," Sunny Daintree said. "I'm only a bodger at thacking, and I dare say a real thacker would turn up his nose at it. But there ain't been a real thacker on Hinching Fen since Mucky Strode died. And he was an example, the way he was took. Right in the middle of a big swear he was, when an apple-plexy hit him, and he were took straight up to answer for hisself before you-know-who, with that on his lips. Ooh! dear. Terrible swearer he was. He could swear for ten minutes without repeating a word — couldn't he, Andrew?"

"I'm heard him meself," said Andrew Surfleet (for it was he). "It were quite a thing to hear him, in a shocking sort of way. Not that I understood half of the words he used. And when 'Enry Wake explained 'em to me, I still didn't. I'm always got by with a few damns and beggars, meself, and never felt the need of owt stronger. Thass like when Farmer Mather give us a drop of brandy one day, on account of his wife had give birth to two twins: I couldn't tek to that sort of drink at all, for it gits you drunk straight away, and you don't git the pleasure of feeling it creep up on you; and then you're got to the headache before you know where you are. Well, bor, I reckon you're doing a fair ole job wi' that thacking — I wonder you don't tek it up proper."

"No," Sunny said, "I git by wi' the molecatching, and the grave-digging when I'm wanted. Matter of fact, I were up at the churchyard yis'dy, mekking hole for that chap over Milney Bank passed away Friday. He'd worn the same weskit for twenty-five year, you know: and then on the Thursday he bought hisself a new one off the tallyman, and the very next day he were took. Ooh! dear. Thass what you git for vanity, you see. Any road, the vicar was wittling at me to dig the hole a bit deeper. Now you know, you dig too deep in that peat and the hole just fills up wi' water: but there were no telling him. So I did as he said, and they lowered the coffin in, and down it went wi' a gret splash like a bucket in a well. Ooh! dear. I could have told 'em that would happen. Git one big shower of rain, and I wouldn't be a bit surprised to walk in the churchyard and see all the coffins floating about like a load of ole boats. I wouldn't bat an eyelid."

Presently another visitor came down the drove, with much greater speed than Andrew Surfleet. Peggy Chettle, bearing her great toothy smile before her like a torch, gripped Jonathan's hand quite crushingly. "How do, dear boy. Thought I'd come and see how Sunny's doing, and mek meself known at the same time — not that you'll be wanting me yet, me being the midwife and you being a single man I'm heard, though how long that'll last I'm not sure — " genially fingering the open throat of Jonathan's shirt, and peeping down it — "not long I reckon — no spare fat there, just like a washboard, what would you give to have a figure like that, eh, Andrew Surfleet?"

"Aye — a tidy figure of a man," quavered old Andrew — he and Jonathan together looking like an illustration of the extremest variations possible to the human body. "Not that I reckon I could tek to being quite so tall, meself: things must look so different from up there."

"Now, then dear boy," Mrs Chettle said, "you may be big as a Grenadier Guard, and such a pair of calves as, dear me, quite a pleasure to look at 'em, but you git an ague on that chest, even though it looks like two pillows on a bed, and before you know it you'll be weak as a seven-month delivery, and ther's nothing worse for the ague than a damp floor — so I says to Chettle the smorning, I shall tek that chap at the new cottage some of my horehound tonic, and here it is." Peggy Chettle seized Jonathan's hand, and pressed a small bottle into it. "You tek that regular, and you'll stay as strong as, well, as strong as you are, dear boy, carryen sacks of taters on your back like they were a couple of young 'uns not yet breeched, and looking at you I dare say we'll see that before long, dear me, such a breadth of back, quite like one of them ancient chaps you see in pictures, driving chariots with nothing on."

"Thass very kind of you," Jonathan said awkwardly, pocketing the bottle. "Thank you."

"Don't speak of it, dear boy. Now you feel badly any time, you come to me, the nearest doctor's in Stokeley and he charges a guinea just for tekking his gloves off, and though birthing babies is my business, and laying out of course, I know a bit about most ailments, and don't feel shy on account of me being a woman, why, I'm been seeing to Chettle's little trouble for years and it don't mean no more to me than peeling a mushroom. Well. I'm sure you'd keep me talking here all day, but I shall have to git on. I've only stopped on me way to Mrs Binns who's gitting near her time, her first, a bit over-anxious she is, merest gripe of wind and she's laying on the floor with her legs up, goodbye, all!"

"She ain't a bad soul, Peggy Chettle," Sunny

Daintree said when she had gone. "She do rather talk, though."

"Ah! she do. You can do wuss than tek her remedies, though, neighbour," Andrew Surfleet said. "She cured my rheumatiz years ago. Course, it's come back since then."

So Jonathan went to bed that night beneath a whole roof; and the timing was fortunate, for there was a shower of rain before dawn. He was grateful, but confused. His independence seemed to be slipping away from him: and he still associated that independence with selfhood. He had read *Robinson Crusoe* not as an allegory of hard-headed Protestant man overcoming his environment, but as a romance of ideal life, the sort of uninvolved and uncompromised life he had fought to attain ever since he had been turned out on the world alone. But now that was being undermined. Perhaps it was the business of Hester Verney that had started it: his conscious mind still sought to stigmatise his falling for her as an infiltration of weakness, rather as the watermen held that hot baths enfeebled you. But his certainties were gone. He had always proudly refused to lay himself under obligation: now he came up against the fact that to proudly refuse Henry Wake's offer to tools was mere churlishness. Andrew Surfleet began to call in to see him every evening on his way home from work; and Jonathan came up against the fact that, in spite of himself, he looked forward to the company.

Sometimes Jonathan would be out in the field when Andrew dropped by, and the old man would take up the hoe or the rake and potter around lending him a hand. "Ah, it wun't hurt me, bor," Andrew said when Jonathan protested that he must already have done a hard day's work. "I'm been digging gault for Farmer Mather all day, which is a stale sort of job when you git a lot on it, and doing this is just like having a skerrick of jam to tek the taste away." Once he came when Jonathan was eating his tea — a plate of cold potatoes left over from his dinner (which had been a plate of hot potatoes). Andrew Surfleet seemed to grow thoughtful at this: and the next day when he called, he said, "You swack your hat on your head, bor, and come along of me. My missis has got a pork dumpling waiting, and it'll tek three on us to eat it."

Jonathan's first instinct was to refuse with thanks, but the thought of the lump of dry bread and cheese on his larder shelf got the better of him, and he found himself going along to Andrew's cottage, deploring his own laxity.

"Ah, course, you don't wear hat, do you?" Andrew said. "Well, we're all made different, and I dare say your head don't git so cold up there. They reckon it gits colder, higher you go, but I can't see that meself, seeing as it's nearer the sun."

Mrs Surfleet was a dainty old woman even more diminutive than her husband, with white hair as fine as cobweb combed in two wings over her head. Seated at their little table, Jonathan felt himself rather too prominent in point of knees and shoulders, and afraid to move his feet for fear of treading on someone. How many years this venerable couple had between them he could only guess, but neither was at all impaired in hearing, and their conversation was all in gentle cooing undertones, so that Jonathan had a strange sensation of having squeezed himself into a dovecote: Mrs Surfleet in particular did everything with the utmost quietness, and once or twice he was startled when a disembodied voice like a gnome's whisper spoke in his ear — "Ha' bit more. Goo on. Tek bit more" — and he found that she had crept unseen to his side and was shyly offering him the rest of the dumpling. The meal was very good, and was lent extra savour by Jonathan's perception, as he looked round at the bare scrubbed house-place, unadorned but for a piece or two of pewter and some pots of musk and geraniums, that his hosts had never had a penny to spare all their lives. It was natural, perhaps, that one so full of years as Mrs Surfleet should refer to him several times as a 'growing boy', though if he had grown any more he would have broken his chair in two: and when he left, thanking them for their hospitality, she tugged his sleeve and softly entreated him, "Mind the road," though between their two houses the incidence of traffic was about one slow farm-cart per week.

Such marks of generosity strengthened Jonathan's resolve to work every moment of the day, so as to be in a position eventually to reciprocate. But even his diligence was circumscribed by the hours of daylight. One night in June, when the descent of darkness

301

found him still not ready for sleep, he took a walk down to Milney St Mary, and outside the Labour In Vain he paused. The pub was a temptation he had so far successfully resisted, but tonight he was transfixed by something more insidious than the odours of smoke and ale. There was music playing within. Jonathan had sold up his old concertina, along with practically everything else, when he left the lighters; and had been starved of music ever since. There had, typically, been a touch of the anchorite's renunciation about this — but now, standing in the dusty road outside the glowing window, on which shapes moved as in a shadow-play, Jonathan gave himself up to sensual indulgence, and listened with a throbbing heart. It may have been that his encounter with Hester Verney had deepened this susceptibility which he had always been a little ashamed of, and given it a more tender resonance: certainly he hearkened to what was in truth an indifferent performance, on a kit-fiddle in need of tuning, as if the melody were wafted to him from Arcadia. A gusty wind, which had been getting up since sunset, boomed about his ears and impeded the music: so, thrusting his hand in his pocket to make sure he had twopence for a glass of ale, Jonathan went in.

He was greeted at once by Henry Wake, who was standing on the hearth before the enormous painting. "Evening, Jonathan. I thought I saw you outside the window just now — just in silhouette, as it were, but thass not a build as one can mistake," he said civilly.

Jonathan, a little embarrassed that his lingering

outside had been observed, ordered his beer and joined Henry at the fireplace. The music was being played by Artie Gill, the old turf-digger, though attention to it among the drinkers seemed to have passed its zenith: Artie Gill having this in common with amateur musicians throughout the ages, in that he seldom cared to play when he was asked, and when he did play he would not leave off.

"You've an ear for a tune, neighbour, I can tell," Henry Wake said. "I've a tolerable ear meself, no point in pretending I haven't: when we lack an instrument at chapel I'm often called upon to give the note for the hymns, and I'm seldom far out. Hark at that wind rising!" he added, as a gust moaned down the chimney, and scattered some unswept ashes in the grate.

"Hope we're not in for a blow," remarked Sunny Daintree, who was sitting on a bench by the wall, the slope of the floor causing him to lean at a compensating angle, like a man taking a corner in a fast buggy. "Not with the new crops just up. It wouldn't surprise me. It were black over Will's mother's the smorning" — this expression not signifying a particular locality, but being a variant of yonder.

"Jonathan, I don't believe you're met Chad Langtoft, are you?" Henry Wake said, gesturing to a thin fair young man at the bar. "Chad's got something to celebrate today — he's got hisself engaged to Mary-Ann Cole, and they're gitting married as soon as ever is. Chad, this is Jonathan Eastholm."

Jonathan gave his congratulations. Chad

Langtoft, with a slightly glassy stare of beer and elation, said, "Come to the wedding, neighbour. It'll be a good do, I tell you. And tek a drink on me now."

"Much obliged to you," Jonathan said. "I'm got one here barely started, thanks kindly."

"Oh! well, if you say so," Chad said, with a covert look at Jonathan, as though he suspected a snub.

"When's it to be then, Chad?" asked Sunny.

"Right after harvest, I reckon. No point in waiting, is there?"

"Unless there's summat up as won't wait," grunted Artie Gill, pausing in his fiddling to dunk his mouth in beer.

"Why, whoever said anything of that?" Chad said, turning round taut as a whipcord, and flushing a terrible red.

"No one, no one, Chad," soothed Henry Wake. "Just Artie's joke, and not a good one. I'm sure we're all looking forward to the wedding, aren't we?"

"Ah!" said the company in unison. "If we're spared," added Sunny Daintree.

"Well, I'd better git off hum," Chad said. "Don't want to start wedded life set in bad habits," and, rather unsteadily, he took his leave.

"So it's a forced job, then?" said Jass Phelps, the landlord, when Chad had gone.

"No-oo!" said Sunny. "That were just Artie, stirring trouble."

"It's nice for the lad, I reckon," Henry Wake said. "He's soon got over Hester Verney, as it's

304

turned out, so thass a blessing."

"What's that about Hester Verney?" Jonathan said, abruptly roused from listening to Artie Gill's mournful rendering of 'Spanish Ladies' and presenting a face of such fierce interrogation that Henry Wake jumped.

"Why, nothing, neighbour," Henry said timidly. "You know her, then? Chad Langtoft had a taking for her, thass all; but now he's found hisself another gel."

"Oh," Jonathan said, relapsing into meditation. "Yes, I know of her."

"Hester's left the fen now, of course, and gone Stokeley way. Lizzie Gosling sees her odd times," Henry said. "A very nice gel, I always said. But I reckon Mary-Ann Cole's more suited for Chad."

Presently Henry announced he was off home, and Jonathan, regretting the way he had alarmed him, elected to walk with him. He could find little to say. The simple mention of Hester Verney — the reminder that she really existed in the world, when in some odd way she had become for Jonathan an entity in a private mythology, with significance for him alone — had unnerved him, and thrown the world momentarily out of joint. In this agitation of mind, he noted as merely complementary the commotion in the sky, where the wind, veering to westerly, was driving before it a multitude of mangled clouds, which streamed headlong across the face of the moon as if in flight from some direful catastrophe.

"Gitting up," Henry Wake said, gripping

his bowler hat to his head. "It'll 'bate by morning, I reckon." Their ways parting, they said goodnight, and Jonathan proceeded deep in thought to his cottage, where he laid himself down in his shirt, and passed at length into an uneasy sleep, threaded through with fragmentary dreams. One of these jolting him awake, he looked round to see the sickly pallor of the fore-dawn steeping the room, and realised at last, from the sound's being repeated, that it was not a dream but an actual crashing noise that had roused him.

He lit the oil-lamp, which in the dim greyness glowed like rotting matter, and dressed himself. A snuffling alerted him to the presence of the hedgehog, which instead of going on its prowl, was curled in the farthest corner of the fire-grate, and winked its weak eyes at him. Jonathan opened the door, only to find it snatched from his hand, and flung with violence against the outer wall. Stepping outside, he thought for a moment he had blundered into some large yielding object: it was the wind, hurling itself against him with a solidity that seemed scarcely possible to mere air. He stumbled out, forced to turn his face so as to catch his breath, and found the source of the noise he had heard in two slates which had been lifted from the roof of the lean-to and dashed on the ground: inside his horse was unsettled, quivering all along its flanks, and rolling a wild eye at him as he spoke to it. A squawking chorus of alarm came from the chicken-coop: it seemed quite secure, but for safety Jonathan weighted the roof down with a couple of bricks. In the sky a fragile light was beginning to appear, dissipated by a confusion of scurrying clouds, so that it scarcely amounted to a dawn at all, but it was sufficient to limn the thatched roof of the cottage, and to reveal that Sunny Daintree's workmanship was standing firm against a westerly gale that seemed to shake the very chimney-stack.

Jonathan returned inside, and made himself a hasty and absent breakfast of bread and cheese with a pennorth of milk, his ear cocked all the while to the wind, which seemed to stretch all around in a multiform clamour, like the passage of some vast and ragged army across the country. A long interval of muttering quietness was succeeded all at once by a fortissimo shriek, which burst open the shutters at the window as if the gale had suddenly turned all its potent attention to Jonathan's cottage alone, and funnelling inside, set the pans that hung above the hearth clanging like so much percussion, and riffled in an instant through every page of the *Old Moore's Almanac* that stood open on the table.

Jonathan sprang up and heaved the shutters to, and then bound the latches together with twine. A tremendous diapason sounded down the chimney, as if a giant had blown across the mouth of a titanic stone jar. Throwing on his jacket and buttoning it to the chin, Jonathan went out to his fields.

A lemon-yellow morning was beaming fitfully through the wrack of cloud. Jonathan, trudging along with bent head, saw little rills of fine

307

black dust dancing along at his feet, and in these trivial signs read the terrible magnitude of what was happening. The wind was not, as Henry Wake had said, going to blow itself out. What might be no more, within the confines of a town, than a slightly perturbing gale, became in the open spaces of the fens the unchaining of an element. Across this flat land, scarcely broken by so much as a hedgerow, the wind walked at will, and in spring and early summer a westerly traversing the great plain could whip itself into a sheer frenzy of force. The danger in the phenomenon called a fen-blow lay not so much in the damage to human habitation as to the soil. Heavy clay land was resistant to the scourging of the gale, but here there was only light and vulnerable peat, which before Jonathan's eyes was being sifted in the wind's fingers and whirled into the air.

The soil-dust was beginning to choke him: he took off his neckerchief and tied it around his nose and mouth, screwing up his eyes at the gritty particles that were swirling and eddying about in miniature tornadoes. Drifts of lifted peat like rapidly forming dunes were beginning to obscure the field-path. The water in the dyke running alongside was blown into a furrowed pattern like the roof of the mouth, whilst a continual rain of pulverised peat dappled its surface. Looking out across his mangold-field, Jonathan saw the tender young plants fluttering and trembling in the blast.

He ploughed on. Uprooted shrubs were bowling across the fields, and he caught one full in the face. For a few moments he thought he was blinded, and when he opened his stinging eyes at last it was to the hallucinatory sight of the sun shining in a black sky. The soil-storm was sweeping across the fen in a silky curtain, and darkening the light of morning to the hue of an unearthly dusk. On the horizon he could just make out the shapes of a row of old pollard willows, bent over like saplings so that their topmost twigs brushed the ground, and the spinning sails of the mill.

Grainier fragments were striking his face now, and peppering the dyke, and he recognised seed — late seed that he had planted, and that the wind was simply planing off with the surface peat. He battled on, thinking of the potatoes, the turnips, the peas; but he knew there was nothing practical to be done. If rain threatened ricked crops, you covered them; if fire, you put it out: but if a fen-blow assailed the fields, you were helpless. He knelt down and lifted a seedling, and found the young leaves shredded by the flying granules of soil as if grubs had eaten them away. All across the young green of the field, specks of naked white were appearing where roots were being exposed by the clawing of the gale.

He turned back out of the blast in an impotent sort of fury, and saw a little figure tottering towards him up the field-path. It was old Andrew Surfleet, gripping on to his hat with both hands, his white beard turned to pepper-and-salt by the soil-dust.

"I'm been up Farmer Mather's," Andrew

shouted above the howling. "All his gates are gone down like a pack of cards. You sealed up your house, bor?"

Jonathan shook his head dispiritedly.

"Come on, then. That'll all be a davil of a muck if you don't. You can't do no good out here."

Jonathan followed him. In spite of the neckerchief, his mouth and nostrils were filled with dust. A few hapless starlings, their feathers clogged, whirred clumsily over their heads for a moment and then were lost in the turbulent murk, which mounted right into the upper air in teeming cataracts, closing out the rays of the sun like a thick gauze. On lifting a hand to push back his hair, Jonathan observed that the black coating on his skin continued up his arm even where it was covered by his sleeve: he pushed his fingers under his shirt, and found that his midriff was the same, and that his body must be as effectually covered with the soil-dust as if he had gone out naked.

They arrived at his cottage at last, and Jonathan found that though he had fastened the shutters and the door, everything within was covered with a fine black bloom, right down to the inner surface of the teapot and the edge of each page of *Robinson Crusoe*. Andrew Surfleet helped him seal the door-jamb and window-sill with rags. "Might as well stop it gitting any wuss," the old man said. "You can't keep it out completely, though. Even the crocks packed away in my missus's cupboard'll want washing after this."

Jonathan found he had not the heart to start clearing up: he felt ridiculously weary. He slumped in a chair, and listened to the shrill melisma of the wind and the endless scurrying of the peat, whilst Andrew puttered around putting things straight and lighting the turf fire to boil a kettle. "You got a pinch o' tea, bor? May as well have a drop. Farmer Mather sent me hum, there's no work doing today. Ah! we don't often git a blow this late on, but it happens. There ain't a beggaring thing you can do about it. Still, no cross, no crown, as they say."

They sat for some time drinking the tea and listening. The fury of the wind raved on, and its declension to a lower note was so gradual that only a brightening of the light in the shuttered room alerted Jonathan at last to the fact that the fen-blow was abating. He got up and opened the door: this time, it was not torn from his fingers. Followed by Andrew, he went out.

Dust still bleared the air, but the wind was tiring of its ghastly dance with the earth, and was relinquishing its partner by degrees, the soil sinking downward in hazy vortices, with brief scutterings as it subsided like the convulsions of death. The drove leading up to the house had disappeared beneath a drift of peat and seedlings — not his own: these must have been blown from the next farm, or further. Mechanically Jonathan walked out to his fields to see the damage to his crops. Except, of course, there was no telling where his crops were. They might have been amongst the mass of dislodged seedlings choking the dyke and strewn about the field-paths: they might have been hurled right over to the other side of Hinching Fen. Some few of the stronger young plants remained, half-buried in black dunes, shredded to tatters: the rest were scattered broadcast, their fertiliser with them. The wind had whisked off the cultivated layer of the fen like a tablecloth, and torn it to shreds.

"Ah! well, bor — never mind," Andrew Surfleet said, patting Jonathan's back — he had to reach up on tiptoe to do this. "You'll just have to drill again, like everybody else on the fen I shouldn't wonder."

Jonathan nodded. He had thought of that: had been thinking, indeed, all the time he was sitting slumped in the cottage. He already owed money, and had none with which to pay for new seed and fertiliser; and to drill all over again, this late in the season, would produce at best a much enfeebled yield, certainly nothing sufficiently profitable to pay off his debts. Moment by moment it was being borne in on Jonathan that, insecure seedling of a farmer as he was, this morning's work by a skittish wind had undone him, and it was doubtful that he would be able to keep the cottage and its holding. Reproachful thoughts of his rashness in buying it were not slow to occur to him, as he contemplated the prospect, perhaps measurable a few fortnights hence, of losing his cherished independence at last: but he thought too, with a certain wistful twist of humour, that it was fortunate that his proposal to Hester had been unsuccessful, and that the trials coming to him would not be rendered sorer by the torment of knowing he had embroiled her in them too.

The gusts were growing fitful now, and carelessly tossing down the last clouds of winnowed peat. Jonathan stooped and picked up a sliver of metal. It was a coin, of some antiquity judging by its abraded condition, turned up by the soil-storm: in the fens nature is her own archaeologist. Normally Jonathan was intensely interested in these finds, but after a glance he let it fall to the ground.

Andrew Surfleet reached up to pat his back again. "You come along o' me, bor," he said. "We'll see if my missus has got summat to eat."

7

THE summer when Hester fell in love drew on, marked by strong, dry and glassy heat, which seemed to burn with full maturity from the very first moment of dawn, and to subsist long after sunset, in the manner of a cooling brick oven.

The horses in the yard thirsted with heaving sides, and grunted with pleasure when the stable-lad came along with buckets of water, the merest splash from which brought sparrows darting down to fill their tiny bills and bathe their dusty plumage. Even the draped and vault-like rooms of the Saunders' house were stifling, and the dropsical vases and jardinières that stood in the windows were as hot to the touch as if they had just come out of the kiln. Hester's feelings were wrought up to intensest pitch in just the same way, and when she restlessly threw back the bedclothes and stared at the first torrid smears of sunrise, she hardly knew whether she laboured under heat or love.

From her earliest childhood Hester's emotional life had tended more to diversity than singularity, and flux rather than fixity. Instead of a home she had had a series of insecure habitations: in place of a mother and father, a vague gentle memory and a vaguer presence whose very insubstantiality eluded the grasp of anything stronger than affection; and her naturally keen and intelligent mind being denied a prolonged education, she had none of that attachment to an idea which makes saints and tyrants. So her feelings were warm, but diffuse: she would far more readily have sympathised with the pagans who saw a deity in every leaf and stone, than with her contemporary worshippers of the one God. And yet inside Hester, like a grown chick within the egg, there was the most ardent and partisan of romantics waiting to be born. Some people fall in love as dogmatically as others embrace politics or religion; and it was perhaps typical of Hester's streak of perversity that she, who valued lightness above everything, fell in love with Lyle Saunders so heavily that oblivion shrouded every other dimension of her consciousness. The spectrum of her emotions was refracted to the purest and fiercest ray. Lyle became her metropolis, to which everything else in life was an indifferent hinterland.

It was a truism to reflect that she had never felt like this before: more accurately, she had never felt anything this strongly before. She was a coaster who suddenly found herself in deep waters. Not merely the pleasures, but the luxurious pains of the lover were opened newly to her: the latter occurring not through quarrels, doubts or misunderstandings, but as a result of the difficult soil in which their affair took root. She was with Lyle for a great part of each day, and for a great part of each day she was forced to affect towards him the respectful formality appropriate to the son of her employer: to observe with equanimity the smooth hands which fitted her own so well, and never betray her urge to seize them; to watch the cat cross the room and sit on his lap, conscious of the stark impossibility of her doing likewise; to intercept his smile across the dinner-table, and yet stay fixed in her seat, instead of soaring up to the ceiling and careering about the dusty chandelier like a balloon. The strains this placed on Hester, who was not used to dissembling her feelings, were great: the compensations, as is the way with love gratified, both ample and dissatisfying. Her days off she spent entirely with him, but it was never enough. As she said to him, she was not greedy: twenty-five hours a day of him was all she wanted.

The season was favourable to a romance that was of necessity pursued mostly outdoors. Sunlight, blue sky, heat and burgeoning greenness formed the medium in which her love was cultivated, and it grew up as rapidly and sturdily as the wheat which stirred about them in tawny seas as they drove out in the trap. Hester's practical nature was turned on its head: the utilitarian landscape of the fen, which she had always associated with back-breaking labour, all at once became a picturesque setting for the drama of her feelings; she saw meads of asphodel in a field of mustard-seed, the scrubbiest orchard glowed like the garden of the Hesperides, and the enchantment of an idyll transformed the humble banks of the Nene. She was ready for these outings from dawn, and was reluctant to return at dusk: and though she told Mrs Saunders that she was visiting her old friends on Hinching Fen, in fact she neglected them most shamefully. There was no help for it. In her first exhilaration, friendship seemed to stand to love in the same relation as pap to solid food — impossible to savour the one after a taste of the next.

The minutiae of the process by which Hester surrendered a heart that had hitherto been given over to little more than frivolity were commonplace enough — insofar as any of the daily miracles of human life may be accounted commonplace. They went out in the trap, Lyle always driving recklessly fast, they explored the countryside, they talked, laughed, ate picnics. Lyle, who pecked erratically at food, liked to watch her eat. 'What an appetite!' he would say, admiringly, as she finished off the contents of the picnic-basket; and for the first time Hester began to be self-conscious, and tried to eat a little more daintily, without it being obvious that she was doing so. Why she should do this, when her appetite was one of the things he liked about her, she could not have said: perhaps she was touched by insecurity. Hester, who had always had a healthy sense of her own merits, discovered that the experience of being loved did not necessarily reinforce it. As the slightest comment on our physical appearance sends us flying to the mirror, Hester found that the apprehension of Lyle's loving her set off an anxious mental review of all her qualities: she submitted to endless examination a self that she had always taken for granted. The result, of course, was that disturbing feeling that her lover did not really know her at all; that she was two people; that what he saw was not what was within, and that at any moment the mask might fall. This unavoidable disjunction in human intercourse troubled Hester particularly because she was supremely honest. She valued Lyle's love so dearly that she could not bear to think it might be based on a false premise.

Lyle was amused at the pleasing torments she put herself through on this account. "But you must have known a lot more interesting girls than me," she would say.

"Interesting!" he laughed. "What a word! How do you mean — girls who smoke cigars, or do the Indian rope-trick, something like that?"

"No — you know. I'm never done anything, Lyle — nothing but donkey-work on the ole fen. Thass all there is to my life."

"Why, what do you think the young misses in the smart houses in Huntingdon have done in their lives? Sewed a few samplers and gone out with their mamas to sip tea with a lot of other young misses. I'm sure you've had a lot more worthwhile experience than that."

"They're got more education than me."

"Have they? What education do you suppose Phoebe Purefoy has, for example? A couple of chords on the piano, the names of the kings of England, and a few French verbs which you could pick up in a week or two, if you wanted, and if there was any point to it, which there isn't. Besides, Giddy and me never got much schooling. Mother had us working in the stable-yard practically as soon as we could read."

"Well . . . I wish I knew what you really think about me."

"What a wittler you are! My dear, I think — " suddenly he became young Mr Pimlott — "I think you're an absolutely *topping* gel."

Such questioning was also, of course, a way of hearing nice things about herself — a harmless lovers' subterfuge which Adam and Eve probably adopted: but Hester was quite in earnest. She desperately wanted to be loved, and feared being found unworthy. Having enjoyed a sturdy independence of mind for so long, her loss of it was the more complete — a girl who was forever falling in and out of love would have assumed more, and hungered less. All this did not mean that she spent all her time with Lyle in a gloomy fidget: she was happier than she had ever been in her life — indeed it seemed to her that only now had her large capacity for happiness met with its proper object.

Often she thought how intolerable the two of them would have seemed to a third person. They laughed at each other: they laughed at anything. They put on each other's hats. She plaited his hair like a stallion's mane, then sat back and screamed at the sight of him. He draped the picnic-cloth around him like a toga, and delivered an oration to the waterfowl. Once they called at an isolated farmhouse in hopes of buying some milk, and were greeted by a little mad old woman wearing a bonnet entirely covered with nodding wax cherries, who confided to them in a whisper that she could not sell them any milk because a Bear had come along and drunk it all; and after that Lyle only had to say the word 'Cherries' for Hester to be in danger of hysterics. Sometimes, for devilment, he would do so at home, even with Mrs Saunders or Gideon around. "Cherries, my dear," he would intone gravely, passing Hester in the hall or the yard, "cherries."

"What's the matter with you, gel?" Mrs Saunders cried.

"Got a bit of a cough, Mrs Saunders," spluttered Hester into a handkerchief.

"Huh! Don't give it to *me*."

It was typical of Lyle to sail close to the wind in this way. The convention they observed of giving no hint of their relationship at home was always at risk from a wink or chance familiar remark from Lyle. "Oh! I don't reckon anyone's going to notice," he said, when they were alone and she mentioned this. He kissed her fingers. "You worry too much. What do you do?"

"Worry too much. Ooh, you want a shave."

"So do you."

"I suppose your mother'll have to know eventually, anyway."

"Eh? Oh! yes. Don't mind about that." He subdued her fears with a kiss. When she was alone, however, they returned, with all the painful earnestness that had hitherto been conspicuously absent from her life. All sorts of shadows were newly fretting the clear light of Hester's personality, and not the least of these was guilt at deceiving Mrs Saunders. She tried to tell herself that it was the old lady's fault, after all, for being so unreasonable about canoodling; but she found it would not do, precisely because she was so serious about Lyle. She might have concealed a mere flirtation with an easy conscience — but this was much more than a flirtation. It was certainly conducted in that manner, because of the light-heartedness that was the natural mode of expression for both of them. But Hester was in deep: her heart seemed to throb distractingly from waking to sleeping, and she moved about the Saunders' house and yard in a state of disorientation. Everything there was defined by Lyle's presence. A footstep in the hall, and she was tensely listening lest it was that light and mercurial tread of Lyle's; on Gideon's birthday she scrutinised Lyle's characteristically lavish present to him as if it were for her; when a groom came to the door with a question, it was Lyle she automatically fetched, as if no one else lived there. With this glowing consciousness on her, to dissemble what was going on seemed not only treacherous, but downright fantastical — rather as if she should carry on with blithe normality when the house had turned upside-down and stood on its roof.

And so her proximity to Lyle was both a delight and a torture. He was cunning in manufacturing pretexts for them to be alone — even inventing a nervousness on the part of certain new-acquired horses, which only Hester's presence would quell; but there were long periods in which no such opportunity presented itself, and she was forced to yoke together the violent antitheses of lover and spectator. When he was not at work Lyle exhibited a sort of restless idleness. He would sleep on the sofa with profound abandon, as if he had just fought a battle, for a couple of hours, then rise abruptly with his face all creased and attempt as if his life depended on it some trifling task, like mending an old clock which Mrs Saunders was going to throw out anyway. He could remain in bed until it seemed he would never surface again, but stayed up the whole of one night with one of the cats while it gave birth to kittens, and then was bright as a bee all next day. Some evenings he went out to the Nag's Head, and came back with a high colour, and a conspicuously careful step; others he read the newspaper from front to back and back again, one slender leg over the arm of his chair, yawning and eating his way through a whole bag of grapes, which was the sort of nibbling food he preferred to orthodox meals. A year ago Hester would have thought herself daft to find in all this such a tantalising fascination. She would have thought herself daft, too, and rather contemptible, for having a sort of weepy tantrum.

It happened on her day off, when for the first time Lyle could not go out with her: Gideon, who was to have gone to an important auction, was ill with toothache and Lyle had to take his place. They were under the trees by the paddock when he gave Hester this news: she stood still for a moment, caught in a green net of glare and shadow created by the sun beaming through the branches, and all at once she felt crushed: an insupportable woe overcame her, and to her own astonished shame she was in tears.

"Oh! it's no good, this," she stuttered wretchedly. "We might as well give it up — there's no point to it at all."

Lyle looked as surprised as she was at this outburst. "Yes, there is," he said.

"No, there ain't," cried she, driven contrary by the pressure of disappointment. "It's nothing but hiding, and pretending, and sneaking, and it just spoils it." Such were the doubtful feelings that had been building up in her over the summer — something like a photographic negative of her happiness; but she had not anticipated expressing them like this. "Oh, Lyle, what I mean is — everything's so sort of underhand between us, and it makes it seem like it don't mean anything real and true — and it does to me."

"It does to me too, Hes," Lyle said. "Did you think it didn't?"

"No," she said, "no, no," scrubbing away her tears, and suddenly conscious of seeming to extort an emotional blackmail — a despicable proceeding. "I didn't mean that. I know it's not easy. I know you're got to go to the auction. I don't know what's the matter with me — I never git the miseries like this — honest."

"Poor old girl — you are in a state," he said tenderly, curling his arm about her waist. "It is pretty awful for you having to go without me for a day — that's enough to make any girl cry — but there'll be lots more days, you know."

"I do love you, thass the trouble," she murmured, "swell-head."

"That's no trouble. That's very handy, because I'm pretty keen on you too. What could be better? Ah, I know. You're afraid you're going to end up like Phoebe Purefoy, with nothing ever coming of it. Confess, now."

"Well," she said, a little prideful, "maybe — except I'd never wait for you for five years — sweet as you are."

He laughed. "Oh! yes, you would. But you won't need to. Don't you worry. I'm not going to give you up, Hes. Where am I going to find a girl to suit me like you do? Why, you're the only one I could bear to marry."

Hester swallowed, and almost choked. "Lyle Saunders! Is that meant to be a proposal?"

"Why not? We're right for each other, aren't we? Oh! don't shay I've got to get down on me kneesh. Not with my legsh . . . Tell you what. I'll marry you, if you'll marry me. Bargain?"

"You gret fool," said she, between laughing and crying. "You gret yawnucks. I'd say yes if I thought you were serious."

"Serious as I'll ever be. Don't cry any more, Hes. You look like the very devil when you cry." He touched her chin. "And I do mean it about getting married. You're the girl for me — don't think I don't know it. By the left, I do believe you're speechless! Now that's a first. Why, you didn't reckon I was a Trifler, did you?"

"Oh! I don't know what you are," she said, unable to do more than bathe in the moment, with Lyle's arm about her waist, and the sunlight scattering like gold treasure through the canopy of branches.

"Now no more of that stuff about giving it up."

"Wait a minute — I ain't said yes yet, you know."

Sternly he said: "Hester Verney, if you don't take up this offer, I shall go and chuck myself in the river, and you'll never see me again — except when they drag me out all slimy, and nibbled at by fish and other freshwater creatures; and then you'll spend the rest of your life in regret and remorse, and end up a mad old woman tippling gin, and wearing a hat covered with cherries. So, make your choice."

She was laughing, but her heart was full as though she would cry again: she was a very pincushion of stabbing emotions. "Oh! give us a kiss," she said. "I'd better say yes — no one else'd put up with you." Still, as he kissed her she heard the faint insistent note of doubt; and the honesty of her nature compelled her to express it. "It's not me that's the trouble, though, Lyle," she said, fixing his light blue eyes with her own, "it's your mother, ain't it?"

"Mother? Don't worry about that. Her bark's worse than her bite, you know."

She was silent: she thought they were both pretty formidable.

"Now, my love," he said, pressing her waist, "you're wittling inside — I can tell you are. You just leave it to me. I know my mother. I've known her all my life, funnily enough. All I've got to do is pick my time, and use my charm, et cetera, and everything will be all right. After all, she likes you, you know. She even likes me, in her way."

"But she don't like her sons gitting married," Hester said — clutching thus at a fugitive pessimism, even as Lyle's gaiety blew it away.

"She hasn't tried it yet, has she? I'll soften her up. Trust me."

Hester wondered whether even Lyle's powers of persuasion might meet their match in Mrs Saunders' obstinacy: but she did trust him; and now she had a fund of delighted anticipation, which she continually drew on and which never diminished. She spent her day off walking by the river, her feet scarcely touching the ground: nervously happy, and exulting that the Promise had come true at last. The Promise was a hazy embodiment of her optimism, which from her earliest youth had fulfilled in Hester's mind something of the function of religious faith. She had never known what form this distant vindication might take, but through every vicissitude, however dispiriting, of her life, the vision of it had hovered before her, a bright patch in the blur of futurity. And here it was — sooner than she had thought — in the quicksilver shape of Lyle. She could not let it slip from her hands. A hole-in-the-corner affair was no good — she felt too much. Nothing could have made her interrupt the pleasure of loving him but the fear — which had burst out in tears among the paddock trees — that it might never come to fruition.

But she did not press him, after that: the visions of what was to be were so beguiling as to suspend the uncertainty of the present hour, and her discomfort at deceiving Mrs Saunders was assuaged by the assurance that it was a temporary expedient: she could enjoy the sailing all the more, now she knew that land was in sight. Memories of what had happened when Gideon had raised the idea of marrying Phoebe she dismissed: Lyle was not Gideon; she knew Lyle's propensity for getting his own way, and had seen him gain concessions from his mother on other matters by catching her at the right moment. As it happened, she was wrong as could be in dismissing those memories — partly because while she waited for Lyle to make his move it was Gideon, of all people, who forced the issue.

It is simple enough to disguise a liking for someone — countless romances have begun with a long prelude of silence and cool looks; but it is practically impossible to disguise a dislike for someone. The most disingenuous face betrays itself — whereas Hester's might have served as an illustration to the phrase about the eyes being the windows of the soul. That said, she had always rubbed along with Gideon as well as she was able, and never meant him any harm. Hester's was as free from malice as it is possible for a mortal nature to be; but what was in her a mere trace-element was much more substantially present in Gideon — and it was active.

Afterwards, what happened seemed inevitable, as she retraced its stages in memory. She recalled a day when she had been shopping in the town for Mrs Saunders. Lyle was supposed to be taking the trap out that day, and when she saw it standing outside the tobacconist's, she assumed the boatered figure bending over the tail-board to be Lyle: she hurried across the street calling his name, and realised her mistake just as Gideon straightened up, turned, and gave her a tremendous stare, which did not moderate at her feebly and uselessly saying, "Oh . . . sorry — I thought it was Mr Lyle." Then there was the morning when, Mrs Saunders having complained to her that the parlour looked like a bear-pit, Hester tidied round: Gideon, coming in, protested that he could not find his papers.

"Did you put them away?"

"Yes — in the bureau."

"They'll be all mixed up now," Gideon grumbled. "They're important accounts. It's not your job to mess about with things like that. You should ring for Judy, it's the housemaid's business, not yours. Your job is to attend to Mrs Saunders — "

"Leave her alone, old man, can't you?" said Lyle, who was reading the newspaper. He spoke lightly, but his cheeks had gone pink.

"I didn't suppose it was your business either," Gideon said.

"Well, I'll make it so, if you don't stop going on at Hester," Lyle said, his eyes still on his newspaper.

"Oh! pardon me," Gideon said, looking narrowly at his brother, and then at Hester. "I seem to be the odd one out here."

It was curious, as Hester had noticed before, that Lyle was uncomfortable at quarrelling with

Gideon, even when the latter provoked it: he seemed to prefer to be affectionate even with no return, and at dinner that day he stood up for his brother. Gideon mentioned that he would not be here on Sunday for tea — he had been invited to the Purefoys'.

"Well, I've got Mrs Fowler coming," Mrs Saunders said, "and I want you here."

"Really, Mother — "

"You'll be here on Sunday. I'm telling you. That's the end of it," said Mrs Saunders, stonily.

"That wouldn't be fair on the Purefoys, if Giddy's accepted the invitation, Mother," Lyle said casually. "You know how you hate it when people cry off. I'm sure Mrs Fowler will understand — and I'll be here, and — "

"You'll both be here, I say so, and that's all there is to it," declared Mrs Saunders, glaring into the middle distance, and looking like a carving on a totem-pole, perhaps representing the Spirit of Pig-Headedness. "Judy, clear away."

But if Lyle radiated affection indiscriminately, Gideon's resentment seemed to work in the same way. Instinct told Hester that Gideon suspected them: instinct told her too that if suspicion became knowledge, they could scarcely rely on him not to convert it into credit. Sooner or later, however, Lyle's rather flagrant nonchalance made it inevitable that Gideon would observe something that could not be mistaken. It came sooner; the very day after the dinner-table row about the Purefoys. Lyle was exercising a mare,

329

and Hester was sent out to give him a message from Mrs Saunders. With an impulsive bravado, Lyle bent lithely right down from the saddle, like a circus-rider, to plant a kiss on her lips. She turned round from the kiss to look straight into the small eyes of Gideon, watching from the back window of the tackle-room.

★ ★ ★

"Get in here, gel."

Mrs Saunders was seated in her wing chair by the bare hearth, nursing her stick, her large feet up on the fender. The curtains were drawn against the bright August sun, embrowning the room, and for a moment Hester did not see Gideon's elongated form, standing like a footman behind her. It was the gleam in his eye that alerted her to his presence.

"Come here," Mrs Saunders said. "Let's get this sorted. Giddy, you leave us alone."

"Yes, Mother," Gideon said, dutifully, and without looking at Hester he softly went out.

"Now then, gel. All I want is the truth. Giddy saw you canoodling with our Lyle this morning: says he's seen such things before. You needn't deny it."

Gideon had allowed half a day to elapse before telling his tale — relishing it, Hester supposed — and Lyle had gone out in the meantime. She wished Lyle were here; but her first emotion was one of relief, that it had come at last, even so inopportunely. "No, I don't deny it, Mrs Saunders," she said.

330

"Well! What's it all about? He's been pestering you, is that it? I know what he's like. Thinks he's the cat's whiskers. If you've been afraid to tell me, gel, you needn't be: you shan't suffer for it: I'll just tell him straight off to stop bothering you. He'll do as I tell him. You're here to wait on me, not for him to amuse himself with."

"No, Mrs Saunders, it ain't that," Hester said. The old lady's eyes, ensconced in harsh wrinkles, drilled into her. Hester had repeatedly told herself that she wasn't frightened of Mrs Saunders: it was dismaying to find after all that she was. In all her life Hester had never had the slightest power, and now in Mrs Saunders she seemed to confront power incarnate. "The thing is — me and Lyle — "

"EH?" bellowed Mrs Saunders, the monosyllable rising through a whole chromatic scale. "MISTER Lyle — !"

"But thass it, Mrs Saunders — we ain't on that sort of terms any more, because, well, Lyle was intending to speak to you about it, you see — "

Thump went the stick on the floor. "He's got you in the family way! God help us, that's what it is! The silly young beggar, I'll skin him — "

"I'm not in the family way," Hester said hotly. "It ain't that at all. We want to git married, Mrs Saunders — we're in love and we want to git married, and he was going to speak to you about it, as soon as — "

"Huh! I know — he's *afraid* he's got you in the family way, and so he reckons he ought to

331

marry you — that must be it."

"No, it's nothing like that," said Hester, losing her temper, and with it her fear. "I don't know why you have to make everything sound so cold and nasty — I don't know why you won't believe that people can — well, can really and truly fall in love! It does happen!"

Mrs Saunders pointed her stick at Hester like a sabre. "You've trapped him. That's what you've done. You're that sort — you hook your claws in like our Tipsy, so they won't come out. Well! I knew you fancied yourself, but if I'd known you were one of that sort I'd never have let you through the door. You needn't think it'll work, gel. I didn't get where I am now just to see my son throw himself away on you. Lyle's got better things in view than that. He's had chits like you throwing themselves at his head before — "

"It ain't like that at all!" protested Hester, both indignant and pained: all that was precious to her was being pelted with muck. "Mrs Saunders, Lyle and me have been walking out, properly, on my days off: and he asked me to marry him, and I said yes: and he was going to tell you all about it — "

"Properly? What do you mean, properly? My son canoodling with a servant — a waiting-gel off the fen — what's proper about that? Lord give me strength. He must have gone off his head! Lyle, and you! Why, what can he get off you that he can't get for a shilling against the railings?"

"I'm glad I am just a servant-gel, if being

332

rich gives you such a dirty mind," Hester said with disdain.

"Now you listen to me, my gel. You've been treated well here, and allowed to sit at table with the family, and given clothes, and I dare say it's gone to your head, and given you ideas. You get rid of them ideas right now, and maybe we can work something out."

"There's nothing to work out," Hester cried, despairing of compromise. "Lyle wants to marry me, and he's a grown man — he can do as he likes."

"Can he?" All at once Mrs Saunders seemed to shift her ground. Her eyes glittered craftily. "All right, gel. Say he thinks he wants to marry you — I'll suppose that for the sake of argument. What do you suppose he's got to live on? Hm? You bringing him a dowry, are you — a little fortune you never told me about?"

"I don't care about that," Hester said, haughtily, and with truth.

"Well, perhaps I believe you there," Mrs Saunders said, softly for her. "I'll give you that. But Lyle, now! Is he really one for love in a cottage, do you reckon?" She shook her head. "I'll tell you what it is. I think this is one of Lyle's jokes. It's not one of his better ones, and I shall tell him so: he shouldn't tease a simple gel like you."

"Ask Lyle, then!" exclaimed Hester — and then, with a surge of relief and joy, she heard the sound of the front door. "There he is — you'll see!"

She ran to open the parlour door, surprising Lyle on the threshold. "Now that's what I call service," he began: looked into Hester's face, and took in the whole situation in a moment. "Ah," he said.

"Get in here, my son, and shut the door," Mrs Saunders said. "We're going to get to the bottom of this."

Lyle came in, very smart and cool — the heat never seemed to affect him — hands in his trouser pockets, reefer jacket unbuttoned. "Now what's up?" said he in his lightweight way, propping himself against the back of a chair, and smiling slightly on his mother, with his eyebrows tilting into that ironical curve. To Hester, in her rather fevered state, the scene looked like an angel confronting a gargoyle.

"There's nothing up with me, my boy," Mrs Saunders said. "There's something up with you, though, if half of what I've heard is true."

"Heard from who?" Lyle said. "Or is it whom — I can never work that out. Let me guess, anyway — Giddy. Well, he's saved me the trouble, though I somehow don't think that was his intention."

"Never mind that — you been turning this gel's head?" barked Mrs Saunders.

"She's been turning mine," Lyle said, with a cheerful glance at Hester. "Lord knows why — she could have her pick of chaps — "

"You mean to say it's true? You've been poodle-faking with this gel under my nose?"

"Oh, come on, Mother. You're no fool. What d'you expect? You throw a pretty girl and a rather handsome bloke together — and then you're surprised when they fall for each other. It's the most natural thing in the world," Lyle laughed, breezily inspecting his patent-leather shoes.

Mrs Saunders stared: gasped. "But she's a paid help!"

Yes, thought Hester — and your son's an unpaid help, and that's why you don't want to lose him. But she held her peace: she could see Lyle's mind working, and she was confident that for all the big guns his mother carried, he would disarm her.

"You know Hester, Mother. You know all her ways — and you like her, I know that. So isn't that better than if I'd suddenly brought home some miss you'd never heard of, all airs and graces and having a good look at you and making everybody uncomfortable? I know you're not sentimental: what you've got is bags of sense, and I know you'll see the sense in this."

"So she has trapped you," breathed Mrs Saunders.

Lyle laughed. "Why are women so uncharitable to each other? I haven't done anything against my will, you know."

"Then you're more of a fool than I thought!"

"Well, I dare say I am. I'm not the only one. Look around, Mother — there's fools going two by two through the church door every day of every week — and they don't come to any harm, do they?"

Mrs Saunders curled both her hands, gnarled

335

by arthritis, round her stick: Hester, looking at them, felt a moment of pity — one of those dashes of contrary feeling that season even the purest emotions; for certainly Mrs Saunders looked hateful, stubborn and despotic enough for anything at that moment. "So you've been carrying on behind my back," she muttered.

"Well, blame me for that, Mother," Lyle said. "That's exactly what Hester wasn't happy about: but as I intended telling you anyway — "

"Telling me what? What daft promises have you been making this gel? She reckons there's talk of marriage. Did you put that in her head?"

"You do make things sound dramatic. Anyway I am daft — you've always said so. You shouldn't be that surprised."

"Did you say you'd marry her?" thundered Mrs Saunders.

"Of course I did. Didn't I, Hes? Lucky to find anyone who'll have me. And we do want your blessing, Mother — that's why I waited: it's too important to just casually mention it over the rice pudding. I wanted to wait until you could give it a bit of thought and attention — because I know you, you're not half as awkward as you pretend. Hester's a fine girl — I'm mad about her — and I know you're fond of her. So come on — what do you say? Isn't it really a good thing all round?"

Mrs Saunders was silent for some moments. Then she levered herself out of her chair. "I'm going to my bed," she said. "No, not you, gel — !" as Hester moved to help her. "I don't want you near me. Ring the bell for Judy — Judy can help me."

"Oh! Mother, lie down here if you're going to, it'll be hot as hell up there," Lyle said.

"I can't feel any worse than I do," Mrs Saunders moaned.

Judy came, rigid with triumph, to take Hester's place and assist Mrs Saunders to bed. Mounting the stairs, the old lady exclaimed of a sudden: "I've nourished a viper in my bosom!"

Lyle gave a shout of laughter. "Oh! I wish I'd said that." He came back into the parlour and shut the door. "If she says never darken my door I'll scream. Oh! poor old Hes." He kissed her brow. "I'll bet she gave you a proper grilling, didn't she?"

"Both sides," she said, smiling with more confidence than she felt. "I'm done to a turn."

"That was a mean little trick of Giddy's, wasn't it?"

"I suppose it was bound to happen eventually."

"Of course it was. And I'm glad it did, in a way," said Lyle with energy. "Silly of me to have waited. I should have just spoken out straight — needn't have worried. It's turning out all right."

"Is it?" said she — uncertain whether or not he was joking.

"Yes, of course! We nearly had her just then, you know — oh, she tried not to show it — but she was weakening. Bless her, she took to her bed because she knew she was losing. Like I said, she's not as stiff-necked as she pretends. And it does make sense, doesn't it — you and me? Anyone can see that." He took her hand, and twirled her in a dance step. He was at his most blithe and engaging. "Giddy did us a favour, really. He sort of threw the idea of us at her, and so she didn't have time to think up any arguments against it. See?"

"Yes . . . "

"Doubting Thomas. I'll let her stew a few minutes, and then go up and see her."

Whilst Lyle was in his mother's room, Hester waited nervously in the parlour, staring into the sphinx-like eyes of the cats, who lay on the floor, boneless with the heat. At length he returned: a little more subdued, and irritably unfastening his collar.

"Phoo, it's like an oven in that bedroom," he said, flinging himself into a chair.

Hester sat opposite him. It was strange that now they could be alone with impunity, but could not enjoy it. "What did she say?"

"She says . . . " Lyle rubbed his hair. "She says if we'll break it off she'll think about not sacking you."

"Huh!" cried Hester. "As if I cared about that!"

"It's a good position," Lyle said, looking wryly at her.

"It's nothing," she said fiercely. "It's you I want."

He reached out and squeezed her hand, then leant back wearily. "Oh! Mother, Mother, why do you have to be so difficult . . . ? Well, she accepts that we're serious, Hes. She actually brought herself to speak of our marriage as a possible thing. That is, she says if I go ahead and marry you, she'll have nothing to do with me ever again — melodramatic enough: and, more to the point as far as Mother's concerned, I'll get nothing." He waved a hand round. "The horse-dealing business — all Mother's, you see. I don't get a penny of it if she chooses. And that's what she says." Frowningly he nursed his leg and studied the sole of his shoe. "That's what gets my goat — the way she thinks I'll care more about that than marrying the girl I love. Pretty insulting to both of us, that. She's a mercenary old stick, that's her trouble. Money before everything."

"She'd do it, wouldn't she?" Hester said. "If you went against her will. She'd cut you off. I can just see her doing it."

"She would," Lyle said, brooding; then he grinned. "Except that I'm going to win her over."

"But what if you can't?"

"O ye of little faith! Hes — you don't really think if it came to a choice I'd give you up just to keep a stake in the business?"

"Oh, no," said she passionately, reaching out for both his hands: there seemed blasphemy in the very idea.

"Well, it won't come to that anyway, my dear — because I'm going to have both."

At tea-time Mrs Saunders sent for Hester. The bedroom was stifling, and Mrs Saunders had all the blankets on. She lay huge and supine just as she had done when she had taken to her bed over Gideon and Phoebe. On her lip was a sheen of perspiration, which stubbornly she would not wipe off.

"Pull that chair up, gel. Judy, you leave us."

Judy exited, stiff as a clockwork toy, her chin pointing at the ceiling.

"Well, you've got your claws into him good and proper, haven't you? That boy never gave me any trouble before — and here he's been swearing he's going to stick by you — fleering in my face. I hope you're satisfied with what you've done."

"No, Mrs Saunders," Hester said, "I ain't. I never meant to make any trouble with you and Lyle, and that's God's honest truth. We can't help the way we feel — "

"If you think so much of him, then leave him alone! I suppose he's told you what'll happen if he carries on with it? I mean it. He marries you, and I'm finished with him. He won't get a penny. I know him — he thinks he can wheedle his way out of it. Well, he's wrong, gel: and I think you know it."

Hester was silent. She did know it: wish otherwise as she might, she could see that the old lady was utterly, fanatically in earnest.

"So you'll be doing him no favours, gel. You'll be the ruin of him, that's all there is to it. Oh, I know you're full of fine ideas now; you think it doesn't matter; you think canoodling's enough. How long do you suppose that fairy-tale's going to last, eh? Well, it'll be on your head when Lyle looks around him and realises what he could have had, and starts

340

complaining about the prospects he lost when he married you."

"I'll tek my chance," Hester said. "Is that all you're got to say?"

Mrs Saunders stirred angrily, plucking at the coverlet: she seemed to perceive that in this, at least, she was facing a will as strong as her own. "Damn it all, gel, who do you think you are? Can't you see that my son's got better things ahead of him than tying himself to you?"

"Better things? Like what? To be a slavey to you all his life?" cried Hester, determined to prick that monstrous selfishness. "Thass all you want for Lyle — and Gideon come to that! It don't matter whether I'm a servant-gel or one of them toffee-nosed misses who come here in carriages — you just don't want your boys to have any life of their own — and I reckon you're bloody lucky they don't hate you for it!"

It was out before she could stop it. Mrs Saunders' face went red, a thing she had never seen before.

"Well, you've finished it now, gel. You'd better start looking for a place, because I want you out of here by the end of the week. Giddy'll give you your wage, and then I want you out of my sight. I don't let anybody talk to me like that — least of all a little trollop I picked up out of the muck. I don't know where you're going to go — but I hear there's a street in Cambridge where gels of your sort ply their trade."

"Where'd you hear that from?" Hester said, getting up. "Your husbands?"

Somehow she managed to get to the bottom

of the stairs without falling — she was blinded with tears, and in the hall she ran into a warm obstruction, which turned out to be Lyle.

"Here, here, what's going on?" said he, looking closely into her face. "Hes — "

She could not speak: gently he guided her into the parlour and sat her down.

"What's she been saying to you?" Lyle said, kneeling beside her.

"Oh — we got into a bit of a row — silly," said Hester, who despite the openness of her nature was always curiously ashamed of being seen in tears. "It's nothing."

"Oh, yes, it certainly looks like nothing," Lyle said frowning.

"Well — she wants me gone by the end of the week. I don't care about that . . . but I ain't what she said I am!" she burst out, with fresh distress.

Lyle's lips had gone thin. "I'm not having this," he said. Absently he patted her hand and stood up. "I don't care if she is my mother — I'm not having her speak to you like that."

"Well — I did lose my temper as well," Hester said, wiping her cheeks.

"It's no wonder!" said Lyle, pacing. "About time somebody did lose their temper with her. No, no, she's gone too far."

"Lyle — she said to tell you that she means it — about you gitting no share in the business, and all that."

"Did she?" He stopped. "And now she's waiting to see which way I'll jump." He came back to her, kneeling again. "Well. What do

342

you think I should do?"

Hester put up a hand to smooth his tousled hair. "I think," she said, "you should stand up to her — and call her bluff — but then I'm biased, because I love you."

"You're right. Of course you are." He was on his feet again. "Damn it, I shall do as I like! We'll get married, and if she doesn't like it she can do the other thing. Pooh! she thinks she can scare me off with all this talk about cutting me off without a shilling. Don't you worry about that, my dear. I've got money of my own. Not as much as her, maybe, but I've got a good bit salted away. I did plenty of trading on my own account in Belgium that Mother never knew about — why, I've been doing deals on my own for years — else I *would* be a fool, like poor old Giddy. Dry your eyes, my girl, because it's all right!"

"They're dry," she said, jumping up and kissing him. "Oh, Lyle, do you really mean it?"

"Of course I do. Let her stay in her wretched bed. We're going to have our life together, Hes, and that's a promise."

"And you're sure you can manage? I don't like to think — "

"Bless you, love, there's money in an account in my name lying there in the bank in Huntingdon just waiting for us."

"And Lyle — " she held his shoulders for a moment — "you really don't mind, that you'll be cutting yourself off from your family and everything, just for me?" She spoke very seriously: there was a crucial importance in this. She wanted him, she would have him at any price: but to feel that she had torn him, reluctantly and acrimoniously, from his family; to feel that she had created an estrangement which he would find bitter — it would give a taint to the taste of her love.

"Pah! she asked for it," Lyle said lightly. "Anyway . . . it's not as if it'll be for ever, you know — even Mother couldn't keep that up."

"How do you mean?" said she, touched with misgiving.

"Eh? Why, what I mean is, some day she'll relent — that's all."

"But if she didn't, Lyle." She hated herself for pressing this point: she wanted to give in to jubilation. "Just suppose she didn't — ever — you won't mind? It'll be all right?"

"Of course! Time I broke the apron strings anyway. It's *you* that's more important, Hes."

She put her arms around him, surrendering to her happiness: too happy even to be troubled when he added, hugging her, "And besides — we'll surely patch it up, eventually."

★ ★ ★

All the next day, and the day after that, and the day after that, Mrs Saunders remained in bed. She did not call for Hester, or mention her at all except, as Judy exultantly informed her, to ask whether That Girl was still around, and to remind her to be gone by the end of the week. Hester was past the stage of being hurt by this:

344

she had had a certain admiration for the old lady's qualities, affection for her indeed, but they were no more. What was more disturbing was Lyle's expression of disappointment and frustration when he emerged from the curtained bedroom; but he always brightened on seeing her. "She thinks she's wearing me down," he said, "but oh no! Not this time."

Gideon was evasive, and kept out of Hester's way in particular: he had had the courage to make mischief, she thought, but not to face the consequences. But she met him on the stairs once, and she shifted across a little so that he could not hurry past her and had to stop. His Adam's-apple pumped up and down like a piston, and his little winking eyes avoided hers.

"I'm been meaning to say thank you, Giddy," she said. She had never called him that before! — he gaped in surprise. "You're done us a service, as it turns out. Now why don't you do the same by poor ole Phoebe, before she finds somebody else?"

He did not answer, and after a moment she let him go by.

Lyle told her, categorically, not to worry about that business of being out by the end of the week: anxious in spite of herself, she pressed him, but he only smiled and tapped the side of his nose. On the fourth day he was out all morning: returning at noon, flushed with heat, elated and mysterious, he beckoned Hester into the parlour and stood there smiling.

"What are you grinning at?" she said.

345

"Hester, do you still want to marry me?"

"No," said she, "I fell in love with somebody else this morning."

"Well, that's a pity, because — " he tapped his breast pocket — "I have taken out a marriage licence, and we are expected at All Saints', Stokeley, at eleven o'clock on Saturday."

Hester caught her breath. Surprise and joy were only the first of a whole flood of feelings: in that moment everything about her took on a sharp-etched, unforgettable look of enhancement; and she had an almost physical sense of leaving behind her old life for her new, as if a mooring-rope had been cut through.

"It is all right, isn't it?" Lyle said. "I'm sorry — did you want the banns and everything? I thought the way things are — "

"Is it all right?" she said. "Oh, Lyle, it's more than all right. You gret fool, I — I don't know what to say . . . " Helplessly, she looked down at her clothes. "D'you mind marrying me in this frock?"

"Well, I'd rather wear a suit. Ha, good one! Come on — " he seized her hand — "let's go and tell Mother."

"Now?"

"Of course!" His face was humorously artful. "And won't *this* fox her."

Judy opened the bedroom door. Lyle poked his head in. "Hullo, Mother. It's me and Hester, can we come in?"

"Not that gel!" boomed Mrs Saunders' voice. "Don't you bring her in here!"

"All right then, I'll stay here. I shan't come

346

in if my fiancée can't," Lyle said cheerfully. He took hold of Hester's hand. "How long are you planning on lying there, Mother? Only we're getting married on Saturday, and we'd like you to come to the wedding."

There was a silence from within the darkened room. Hester, not without a little grim satisfaction, pictured Mrs Saunders' face above the black bed-jacket.

"Is that all you've come for?" came the reply at last. "To make daft jokes?"

"No joke," Lyle said. "I've got the licence here — like to see it? All Saints' Church. Eleven o'clock. It's all fixed. I'm going, Hester's going — why don't you come too? Please."

There was a creaking of bed-springs. For a brief moment Hester thought that Mrs Saunders was getting up — Lyle smiled, as if he thought so too, and as if he had won; but almost immediately her hope was replaced by sombre suspicion. She remembered the intransigent glitter in the old lady's eyes, the deep intolerant lines that ran to the corners of her mouth; and she wondered whether she perhaps knew Mrs Saunders better than the fondness of a son ever could.

At last Mrs Saunders' voice came again. "You're a fool."

"Oh! I suppose I am, but it doesn't matter," Lyle said. "Come and see the fool get spliced, anyway."

"You can do what you like," Mrs Saunders said. Her tone was level, harsh, and completely controlled. "It's of no interest to me. I won't

347

see you wed: I won't see you after you're wed: you'll get nothing from me. I've done with you. That's all. Shut the door, Judy."

The door swung to. The smile froze on Lyle's face.

"Lyle," Hester said, "come away now." She touched his arm: it had gone rigid. "Come away."

Lyle was staring at the door. He suddenly struck it with his fist, and for the first time ever Hester — with disbelief — saw Lyle furious. It was unbelievable because his easy, supple nature had never seemed susceptible to anger, any more than a liquid could have a sharp edge. She knew then how confidently he had counted on this daring stroke to win his mother over: how stunned he was by the repulse. "All right then, Mother!" he shouted. "Damn you then! Lie there and rot, you miserable old crow! I'll make my own life!"

There was no sound. He struck the door again, jammed his hands in his pockets and stalked away. Hester followed him downstairs.

"Now what?" she said.

Lyle glared round at her abruptly: he hardly seemed to see her. "We get married, of course," he snapped, "and be damned to her. Let her go to hell."

It was satisfying to hear a son of Mrs Saunders say that — except that she herself almost seemed to have been forgotten in the revolution of the moment. "Well, in the meantime, where am I to go?" she said.

Lyle's expression softened: the stare of a

resentful youth left his eyes, and he was himself again. "Sorry, Hes. Don't look so worried. Let's go out this afternoon and buy some wedding clothes — a ring — the lot. Everything'll be all right."

★ ★ ★

Mrs Saunders declared her intention of remaining in her room until That Girl was out of the house: Lyle, restored to a buoyancy that expressed itself as frantic energy, laughed and said that suited them admirably. He rented a set of furnished rooms in Huntingdon as a temporary base, chastely establishing Hester there the night before the wedding.

"Furniture's pretty ghastly," he said. "There'll be no one to help you dress in the morning — damn, what a mess — I bet you never pictured your wedding-day like this, did you?"

"Help me dress?" she laughed. "Why, no one's helped me to dress since I was two years old. It ain't the wedding," she said, her eyes shining at him, "it's who you're marrying that matters." And she was happy: the informal spontaneity of it all accorded exactly with her temper. Away from the baleful ill-wishing of Mrs Saunders, her misgivings receded, her spirits rose, and her eyes were fixed on the immediate prospect, which was so radiant to the view that the past and the remoter future scarcely merited a glance.

A hired phaeton, tied with white ribbons, conveyed them to All Saints', Stokeley, the next morning: children ran cheering down the streets after it, old women stared with their customary affront at other people's happiness, and Hester was conscious — with a sort of half-measure of vanity — of being half of a handsome couple. Lyle had asked Gideon to come to the service, but he had made an excuse of obedience to his mother's wishes.

"Poor Lyle!" she said. "No family there. It don't seem right."

"Oh, pooh, I never like a lot of fuss at weddings. It's just between us, after all, isn't it?"

But waiting outside the church, to her surprise, was Phoebe Purefoy. She had heard the news from Gideon, she said, and she wanted to be there to wish them joy. They had both rather laughed about Phoebe in the past, and Hester greeted her with a guilty compensatory warmth: wondering if the girl perhaps saw a personal omen, hopeful or otherwise, in the marriage of a Saunders son, and thinking not for the first time that she could surely do better for herself than Gideon.

Hester's background was chapel, and though folk on the fen used the church for weddings and christenings, she felt herself to be on foreign ground there. The frowning parson seemed to know that she had no religious faith, and that the lips of a pagan mouthed the responses: the cool stony solemnity dismayed rather than uplifted her, and she inclined her shoulder so as to touch Lyle's arm, and be reassured of the warm presence of the one element in all

350

this that mattered to her. He returned the pressure: clearly churchiness did not oppress his elastic spirit. How wonderful it was to be with him, who took everything in his stride, and gaily side-stepped the craggier obstacles of the world!

They emerged from the gloom of the church into brilliant sunshine, and it seemed to Hester like surfacing from a dream into reality. Phoebe Purefoy apologetically scattered rice: Hester hugged her, and resolved to be more charitable to people in future. Their luggage had already been sent to the station, and they went straight there to begin the long train ride, first to Peterborough, thence to London and then Bournemouth, where Lyle had booked in a hotel for their honeymoon: a novelty in itself for Hester, who though she had covered just about every inland part of Anglia during her father's wanderings, had never seen the sea. Since he had struck his fist against his mother's door, Lyle had thrown himself single-mindedly into these preparations, and now he looked a little weary as he sat opposite her in the railway-carriage.

"Rubbish," he said. "Lively as a cricket. This is the best way of doing things, isn't it, Hes? I'm sure we've done right. I reckon it takes the bloom off it, making a long drawn-out song-and-dance about it."

He had a way thus of reasoning himself into approval of a *fait accompli*, which touched her. "It suits me best," she said. "Only thing is I can hardly believe it — all of a sudden I'm Mrs Hester Saunders, and yet I haven't changed. I just know I shall feel like a hussy when I walk in that hotel with you. It ain't *too* smart, that hotel, is it, Lyle?"

"Don't know — never been there. It was recommended. Why, you're not frightened of that, surely? Just look confident, and you can carry anything off."

"I suppose so," she said, smiling, but nursing secret dubieties about some uppity chamber-maid seeing her petticoats and combinations.

They ate on the train: the miles flashed by unheeded, and then there was London: the steam and smell and noise of a vast station, a brake-ride through glaring, horse-crowded streets, and then another vast station, and they were on their way to the south coast. Hester was too absorbed in Lyle, and in trying to comprehend the sheer incredible fact of their being married, even to notice the unfamiliar sight of downs and hills beyond the carriage window: everything passed her in a whirl; and it was with the profoundest disorientation that she found herself all at once in Bournemouth, in a soft-aired dusk, amongst pine-woods and cupola-crowned mansions, with lights winking on along the promenade — just about as far from the atmosphere of the fens as it was possible to be. The hotel was imposing enough, but nobody seemed to stare at her, and she loved the room, which had a view of the sea, rich red damask wallpaper, and a gaselier shaded with ruched silk. The dining-room was rather more intimidating, until Lyle looked over his shoulder to another table and, turning back to Hester, whispered, "Do you know what they're having for dessert, Hes? Cherries. Cherries, my dear."

"Lyle — don't you dare start me off!" she gasped, cramming her hand over her mouth. They were aching with laughter when they returned to their room. Lyle lit the gas, and hung his jacket over a purple crewel-worked fire-screen, which he said made him feel bilious.

"Hark at that," said Hester, standing by the window and running her hand along the sill in sudden nervousness. "The sea — don't it sound peaceful?"

He joined her. "That's not the sea," he said. "That's the wind in the pines, isn't it?"

"That it ain't."

"Yes it is — listen."

"Lyle Saunders," said she, turning her face to him, "I ask you, is this the time to be having our first quarrel?"

"Wrong time altogether."

"Well then . . . Thass more like it . . . "

★ ★ ★

August had burned into September, freshened by breezes but still hot and cloudless, when Hester and Lyle returned from the south coast to the fens to begin their married life.

The rooms in Huntingdon, on the top floor of an old house overlooking the little school that had seen the boyhood of Cromwell, were clean but drab, and Lyle was adamant that they would not stay in them a day longer than was necessary. He visited his mother immediately on

353

their return, and was met with a monumental huffiness, and a refusal even to mention the fact of his marriage. Hester was dejected by this — the honeymoon had been so happy that she had almost forgotten the extent of her mother-in-law's resentment — but Lyle snapped his fingers. "Pooh, she's got to keep it up, for pride's sake. Let her stew in her own juice — can't be bothered with her just now — we've got plans to make."

He was enormously sanguine about these plans. "It's not a bad little sum I've been salting away: now all we've got to do is turn it to good account. All sorts of possibilities." Each day he returned from visits to auctioneers and estate-agents, and each day it seemed he had a new project in view. "Now this is the just thing for us — seedsman's business in March. Nice brick-built premises, plenty of accommodation. What do you say?"

"Well . . . I can't really see you as a seedsman, Lyle."

"No? Well, we'll see. I reckon it would suit me just right." But on viewing the property, he changed his mind. "No — that would never have done. Imagine me trying to sell seed to a lot of shrewd old fen farmers! That was an awful idea."

Then there was a confectioner's shop in Peterborough.

"Does that appeal to you, then?" she said to him.

"Oh! yes — there's scope for a tea-room, you see — you could make it a really smart little place, get the carriage-trade when they're shopping." But the next day, the confectioner's was a wretched idea: poky little hole, dreary occupation, miserable profits, he didn't know how he could ever have considered it.

"What we really want, you know," he said finally, one day in October, "is a house with a bit of land. I'm not cut out to be a shopkeeper or anything like that."

"Thass exactly what I think," Hester said smiling.

"Do you? I should have taken your advice in the first place. Sarsby's had a couple of fen properties the other day, but they were small fry — just cottages — we can do better than that."

"Well, don't go bankrupting yourself, love — I'm not after a mansion. I only wish I brought a few bob to this marriage!"

"Bah, you're worth a fortune in yourself. We'll do pretty well, Hes. And even apart from this money — well, Mother won't hold out for ever, you know."

He said it lightly; and she replied, trying to be just as light: "We won't actually count on that, though, will we?"

"No?" He grinned. "Don't trust my charm to work on Mother in the end, then?"

"Oh! I'd trust your charm for anything," she said, briefly touching his face. "But — let's not count on it, eh?"

"Whatever you say, my love."

The very next day Lyle returned from Walton's, the land-agents, with the details of

355

a farmhouse on Hinching Fen, with seventy acres of land. He strode about in his excitement, rubbing up his hair into unlikely shapes, and painting a vivid picture of the prospect. "Brick-built house and outbuildings, barn — stock and implements — it's a going concern, not some run-down shell. Can't you just see me as an independent farmer? — answerable to nobody — yes, I should have done this years ago."

"It does sound nice," Hester said. "And I should certainly know my way round a fen farm!"

"Of course! It's made for you. Except you'd be in charge this time, love — not doing the donkey work. But now — this is the best part — 'extensive stabling and paddock'. You see? I could do what I know best — horse-dealing. Isn't that perfect?"

"It certainly sounds it. What — do you mean do the horse-dealing instead of the farming?"

"Oh! combine the two, you know — it'll work out — one will pay for the other, or the other way around — I don't know," he said, with his infectious laugh. "No need to cut off any options. Anyway, Walton's going to take us out there in his gig tomorrow morning."

Later, when Lyle had gone out to buy a newspaper, she studied again the details of the farm, written out on foolscap with auctioneer's flourishes. It was hard to address her mind to practical considerations: she was still all aglow with the sudden transformation in her life, and every morning when she woke her mind had to leap a mental ditch of disbelief that it had really happened so swiftly; moreover it was difficult to attach the idea of life with Lyle Saunders to the idea of everyday prosaic reality — it was like trying to nail down bubbles. For her part the opening chapter of married life had been so happy — the days and nights by the sea, able at last to enjoy the fun of being with him freely and without fear, seeming simply an intensification of their courtship — that she just wanted to prolong it under any conditions. Their material situation she saw in a neutral light: the only thing that could darken it for her was the shadow of Mrs Saunders. The old woman could burn the horse-yard down or give it to the Salvation Army for all she cared — at least then they would know where they were. What she hated was Mrs Saunders' using it as a standing reproach to her son for his folly — a physical reminder of what he had forfeited: and if possession of their own farm would negate that, then all the better.

Mr Walton, the land-agent, was a very fat pink moist man, bald, with the merest suggestion of features, like a great bowler-hatted tweed-smelling baby. It was quite a squeeze for Hester and Lyle to get into his little gig beside him, but he seemed used to taking up a lot of room, and as they drove out to Hinching Fen he talked too in a swaggering oracular voice, as if the broad countryside were his own house, and he were showing them round it.

"You'll observe, sir and madam, that we are traversing some of the finest peat land in the county. The productive capacity of this soil is not to be exaggerated. This may be amusingly illustrated, in the remark of the natives, to the effect that one may plant a walking-stick in the ground and it will sprout." Mr Walton offered this with a short peremptory laugh, as a limited gesture of condescension to the natives, who might be supposed from his tone to be an aboriginal residue imperfectly acquainted with the use of the wheel. "On your left, sir and madam, if I may presume to indicate, you will observe the Hinching Fen windmill, furnished also with a pumping-engine, providing a reliable system of drainage, and insuring against Inundations. To your right, various rustic operatives, and a cow being grazed on the stubble subsequent to the harvest: and ahead, the drove leading to the aforesaid deseerable property, which, sir and madam, we will proceed to view."

The drove, overgrown with grass, led between bare fields to a tiny thatched cottage, which exhibited boarded windows and other marks of desuetude. Mr Walton pulled the pony up short and, taking off his hat, mopped his spherical brow, staring.

"Good Lord," Lyle said, "you don't mean this is it?"

Mr Walton snapped his chubby fingers. "Pardon me, sir and madam — I see it now — I've proceeded down the wrong drove. I was deceived by the absence of landmarks and distinguishing features. No, no: this is quite another property, the merest smallholding

— just come on the market. Pardon me — we'll retrace our steps."

"Thank goodness for that!" Lyle said, as Mr Walton turned the pony about.

"Oh! I don't know," Hester said, craning round to look at the cottage, which seemed to her forlornly to watch them go. "It's quite a sweet little place. Shame to see it all abandoned like that."

"A deseerable property in its way," Mr Walton said, "but not appropriate to the requirements of sir and madam. The correct property, to which I shall convey you without further mishap, is a far more considerable establishment, boasting a panoply of conveniences. Ahead of us, observe a bridge constructed I believe of railway-sleepers, traversing the dyke."

Hester was observing something else — a glimpse of the turf-fen where Chad Langtoft had laboured. She suffered a pang at the memory of what a fool she had been; but it all seemed a very long time ago, and herself a completely different person; and the farm, it turned out, was a good distance further on, almost on the edge of the upland, and was not at all familiar to her.

"Ah, that's more like it," Lyle said as they approached down the drove. The farmhouse, a solid square Georgian structure, appeared gradually between a screen of mature and tortuously leaning trees, the leaves of which were beginning to turn. It was a building of two storeys, with a shallow hipped roof of tiles, a stout chimney-breast at one end, and angled bays either side of a central front door; but the first impression it gave was somehow of a peculiar tallness, an effect which Hester could not for a moment account for.

"You'll observe, sir and madam," Mr Walton said as they got down, "the advantageous situation, facing west, and protected by a fortuitous plantation from the ravages of the elements. Glazing, quite new. Gutters, in good repair. Birds," he added, waving a hand at the sparrows pecking before the threshold, "contributing to the rural scene or aspect. The steps up to the door do not indicate the presence of a basement. These are of recent date — the foot of the door having originally been parallel with the ground: but the shrinkage of the peat, common to this region, has lowered the level of the soil over the years, with the effect you observe."

"Ah, thass what it is," said Hester. The sinking of the earth had exposed a foot or two of the foundations of the house, which were whiter than the mellow brick above — it reminded her of a countryman's sleeve rolled up beyond the tan of the forearm — and that was why it seemed to stand proud of its surroundings in that curious way.

"Is it safe?" Lyle said.

"Oh! of course," Mr Walton said. "Many dwellings in the black fens are subject to such a change. This one, as you may observe, was built with deep foundations, as a precaution against just such an eventuality. Shall we enter?"

The farmhouse had not been long empty: the creaking floorboards seemed still to yield to the feet of the previous occupants, and there was a faint olfactory ghost of homely cooking in the big whitewashed kitchen with its long black range. Hester, brought up in the country, immediately felt more at home than ever she had in Mrs Saunders' varnished and antimacassared house — and how roomy it was after their digs in Huntingdon!

They inspected the yard and farm-buildings — stepping out of the back door with rather a jolt, for the doorstep was about two feet off the ground. All was in good repair. There was a block of brick-built stabling, and Lyle squeezed Hester's hand and gestured expansively. "See? Ample for dealing in a few draught-horses, maybe even riders. Keep my hand in till I'm back in Mother's good books."

"Oh! I shouldn't count on that," she said, retaining his hand and watching his expression: he had proudly burnt his bridges, yet still, laughingly, he believed one was intact. "The farm's the important thing."

"Oh! no. I'm not counting on it. Just saying — you know — it'll be something extra."

Mr Walton led them to the paddock: pausing, with conscious effect, to point out to their surprised eyes an ancient gate, the bottom of which, because of the lowering of the land, was several feet above the ground, so that a small pony might just as easily have passed under it as through it. "I imagine this is preserved more for novelty than utility," Mr Walton pronounced, huffing with genteel humour.

"It's a bit like a crooked house out of a

fairy-tale, ain't it?" Hester said aside to Lyle.

He chuckled. "You do like it though — don't you?"

"I do," she said. She was on home ground: the barn, the rick-staddles, the hen-coops met her eye with an effect like that of seeing a familiar face in a crowd.

"Just think — all ours," Lyle said. "Mr and Mrs Lyle Saunders, of the Crooked House, Hinching Fen."

★ ★ ★

The damage done to Jonathan Eastholm's precarious independence by the fen-blow was not put right by the glorious summer. He had replanted, at great cost — an advance from the seedsman sinking him further in debt: but the tardy harvest his ruined fields yielded was negligible. The loan of money made to him by the brickyard owner had been at a moderate rate of interest, but it was strictly short-term; and that gentleman, somewhat in low water himself, could not or would not postpone repayment, and wait for the doubtful prospect of next year's harvest. Jonathan, denied recourse to mortgage and the other financial devices of more sophisticated milieux, gazed down a winding, darkening tunnel of debt. His sharp sense of honour demanded what expedience suggested: he would have to sell up, satisfy his creditors straightway, and then see where he stood.

This was a bitter draught, but he took it at a swallow: he did not seek to linger out a struggle that could have only one end, for he was temperamentally averse to half-measures; and even losing his independence was more tolerable than gaining a name as a welsher and bad debtor. In many men this might have been humbug, but it pressed on Jonathan almost as a physical imperative. All the same, it was depressing to contemplate the work he had put into the little holding all coming to naught: to reflect that he had failed in an enterprise which had engaged so much of his energy, confidence and hope. It was with a resolute mind but a heavy heart that he turned the hedgehog loose to get its living, surrendered his title to the property to the land-agents, who had quickly snapped it up at a very fair price, and left the little cottage to the sad state of vacancy in which Hester had glimpsed it from Mr Walton's gig. The sale cleared all his various debts, leaving him solvent and unencumbered — an enormous relief that felt to Jonathan like the removal of a throttling collar — but without sufficient funds to pursue any occupation on his own account, as had long been his custom and desire. The notorious unpredictability of the fen soil had been the agent of an entire reversal of his fortunes, and he found himself in the self-same position as when he had been labouring on the land and striving to save enough for his first lighters.

Youth and strength are not perhaps the palliatives of despair that they ought to be, and Jonathan was hard put to it to fend off a fierce attack of the Old Goblin, who spoke desolate innuendoes about the relentlessly downward course his life seemed to be taking. But to his surprise he found he had allies against his old adversary. There would always be willing hands to help you support a burden of good fortune, but under a burden of ill-fortune you staggered alone — such had been Jonathan's somewhat cynical credo. It was proved wrong. The kindly interest of his neighbours did not disappear with his independence. There was a deep vein of fatalism in fen-folk: they knew that the dyked and embanked fields, so apparently tamed and harnessed, were at the capricious mercy of storm and flood, and so theirs was an instinctive sympathy with mortal frailty — a sympathy Jonathan, in his proud way, had so signally lacked. They commiserated, they condoled, and they encouraged: and it came as a revelation to him to find that this strengthened rather than enfeebled him. Others had suffered from the fen-blow — Henry Wake frankly confessing that he would only just survive this year — and it was a further revelation for Jonathan to find himself commiserating in turn. This simple experience forced on him an entirely new perception — that self-reliance and selfishness melted into one another, and you could cross the border without knowing it.

The surrender of the deeds of his little property left him without a home and without work: but he had already been offered a lodging by old Andrew Surfleet, who engaged too to ask Farmer Mather, his 'mairster', if he had any work for him. "That'll be hard, I know, having to work for another, once you're been your own mairster," Andrew said. "But Farmer Mather's an easy sort of man: and mebbe if you sort of mek-believe, and pretend thass your own ditch you're digging, that wun't sting so."

"Well, I'm been a labourer before, Andrew," said Jonathan, "and it won't hurt me to do it again."

And so that autumn he found day-work clearing dykes and digging gault — hard and exhausting work for which his large frame, as Farmer Mather's eye discerned, was admirably fitted: and took up his lodging in Andrew Surfleet's cottage. His bedroom beneath the roof-beams had once contained the Surfleets' three sons — now mere striplings in their fifties, living on the other side of the fens — but plainly they must have been built along the economical lines of their parents, and Jonathan had to move about with the utmost circumspection, for fear of putting his elbow through the window, or his head through the thatch. There was a feather bed, an heirloom of great antiquity and softness; but of such modest dimensions, that he had to take the precaution of folding the blankets under the mattress very tightly, and sliding into bed like a letter into an envelope, to prevent himself toppling out in the night. When he came stooping down the stairs in the morning, his stature seemed to strike Mrs Surfleet afresh each time and, recalling the legendary fenland giant, she declared it was like having Tom Hickathrift living with them.

Jonathan scrupulously paid a reasonable rent,

and shared at the Surfleets' table the plain diet of the fen labourer: bread, potatoes, onions, home-made lard, and salt pork made to go as far as possible by means of dumplings and puddings: once or twice he walked over to Stokeley market to buy for a few coppers a sheep's head, which made a rich broth called shackles. Whenever he left the house after breakfast Mrs Surfleet would be putting on her hessian apron for her day's work: when he returned at night she was always transformed by a clean white apron and a chignon bag enclosing her wisps of hair. Whilst she laid the table he went to fetch water from the dipping-hole at the dyke and washed himself from a bowl that stood on a stool outside the back door — Mrs Surfleet sidling past the window with her face averted, so as not to glimpse him with his shirt off. (When he had his bath in the tin tub on the kitchen floor, she always took herself off to sweep upstairs — Andrew confiding to Jonathan that she was as shy as a mouse, and she'd always done the same when *he* had a bath, for fifty years.) Often in the evenings, after supper, the Surfleets would set the oil-lamp on the table, and entertain themselves with the neat pile of newspapers that stood in a corner of the house-place. These were all rather old, and some of the yellower ones were rather history than news, but that did not diminish their interest for the old couple. Mrs Surfleet would draw a newspaper out at random, spread it out on the table, and read aloud from it — the ole girl, as Andrew remarked, being a rare reader, whereas he could only struggle his way through a few bits of the Bible that he knew reasonable well already. Mrs Surfleet exercised no editorial discrimination, and read her way through every column: Andrew blinking at the turf fire, listening with devout attention, and taking a personal sort of interest in the intelligence, as if he were hearkening to an intimate letter.

"'Indisposition of Prince Alexander of Teck'," read out Mrs Surfleet. "'His Royal Highness is reported to have been suffering from pharyngitis, which has restricted his public engagements. The royal physicians give a good account of his recovery.'"

"Oh! dear. Poor ole boy," said Andrew with feeling. "Thass a shame. Thass nasty, that is."

"'The celebrated actor Mr Henry Irving, whose notable impersonations of the tragic heroes of Shakespeare have formed the chief adornment of the modern stage and earned him the universal respect and admiration of connoisseurs of the dramatic arts, has been awarded a knighthood, and becomes the first of the thespian fraternity to receive such an accolade.'"

"Ah! thass nice for him," Andrew said, nodding approvingly. "I'm glad about that. Thass nice to git a bit o' credit. I suppose he'll be gooing to see the ole Queen, and she'll be tapping him with a sword — well, well!"

"'Accession of Tsar Nicholas the Second Celebrated with Ancient Formality in St Petersburg.'"

"We-ell, I wouldn't swap with him. He wants

to be careful. I remember the last one of them Stars — they blew the poor ole boy up. Riding along in his carriage he was — I'll never forgit that. No-oo, I wouldn't want to be a Star — I shouldn't feel safe."

Occasionally in the evenings Jonathan would walk with Andrew over to the Labour In Vain for a half. Here the topic of conversation, having moved on from the wedding of Chad Langtoft and Mary-Ann Cole, had for some time been Jonathan's own misfortune; but one night, to his secret relief, he found that it had been superseded by a savoury new morsel of information. Jed Gosling, the mill-keeper, had been drunk on duty once too often, and the Drainage Commissioners had given him notice.

"Found him laying flat on the mill-'us floor, dead to the world, with his head in a bucket," said the landlord, Jass Phelps. "So they say. Thass what *I'm* heard. *I* don't know."

"Ah! he'd always pour a pint atop of enough, Jed Gosling would," said Andrew. "He were bad enough at Chad Langtoft's wedding-feast — singing them songs wi' wicked rhymes, what made you blush for the chap who thought 'em up."

"It's a pity for young Lizzie," said Henry Wake. "She works hard, that gel, and does her best to keep the family going, and she's had less help than hindrance from Jed, I'm afraid. I don't reckon it's right to put upon your own child like that: I wouldn't do it — at least, in theory, as it were — Mrs Wake and meself not being blessed with issue."

There were various significant nods at this last, as at a subject better understood than expressed.

"Well, he'll wish that drink back in the barrel before he's done," said Sunny Daintree. "Git a reputation for supping on the job, and no mairster'll touch you with a long-handled rake. Ooh! dear. You might as well knock on the work'us door and have done with it."

"Does this mean the miller's job's going begging, then?" Jonathan said with interest.

"It does, neighbour," Henry Wake said, "and they'll want someone as soon as may be — Jed's to be finished by the end of the month. D'you fancy tekking it on, now?"

"I might, at that," Jonathan said.

"Ah! he's the very man," Andrew said. "You should see him digging in the gault-pit, with all the muscles standing out on his shoulders, like a galloping hoss."

"You're a tidy worker, Jonathan, we all know that," Henry Wake said. "I'd put my name to that, if called upon. Mind you, I think you'll find the Commissioners hoping for a man with a bit of knowledge of machinery: do you reckon you're got a bit of that?"

"Lock-gates and threshing-tackle is about as far as I go," Jonathan said meditatively. "But I can learn."

"Thass the spirit," said Andrew. "Why, if you could see him washing of hisself in the evening, you'd trust him to any job in Chrisseldom: I know I would."

"How should I go about applying?" Jonathan

asked, addressing himself to Henry Wake — more from a consciousness that he would be flattered to be asked, than a conviction that he would know.

"Well now — if you'll tek my advice," Henry said with boastful modesty, "you'll go to the Commissioners when they meet in Stokeley, and put your case to them straight. Farmer Mather's on the board, I believe — that'll stand well for you. They meet on the first Thursday each month — I think you'll find my information's correct."

"They had a special meeting about Jed Gosling," Sunny Daintree said. "Poor ole boy had to stand there afore 'em, and be now-thened and my-manned till he didn't know where to put his head."

"He were drunk even then, so I'm heard," Jass Phelps said.

"Course, milling's not a job as everybody'd tek to," said Henry Wake. "The pay's not a great deal — but then in fair weather, neither's the work, and you can do other jobs in between whiles."

"Not that Jed Gosling ever did," Jass Phelps said.

"And of course there's the solitude — minding the mill all on your ownsome, through the winter nights — that wouldn't suit everybody," Henry said.

"Suited Jed Gosling, he just used to sup," Jass Phelps said.

"You do it, bor," Andrew said. "We want a reliable man tending the ole mill. Miller

370

Eastholm — I can see that now."

The solitude of the miller's avocation was scarcely a disadvantage in Jonathan's eyes, and he was anxious for something more secure than day-work: moreover he had always found something pleasing in the sight of the Hinching Fen windmill, which seemed to unite beauty and utility in harmonious proportions; and so on the appropriate day he walked to Stokeley, and presented himself to the Drainage Commissioners as a candidate for the vacant post. The Commissioners were meeting at the Spread Eagle Inn, in the yard of which Jonathan had made his memorable error of judgement in laying his suit at the feet of Hester Verney: he cast a long and rueful look at the seat beneath the cherry tree that was the locus of that disaster, and wondered if there was ill-omen in this. But the Commissioners, who had just had a convivial lunch, were glad to be relieved of the trouble of seeking out a man for the job, by a man's seeking them out instead: an enormously fat florid farmer in a diamond-pinned cravat declared it made a change in these days, when nobody wanted to work, and then nodded off; Farmer Mather recommended Jonathan, and half an hour later he left the Spread Eagle entrusted with the job of running Hinching Fen's drainage mill, at the winter rate of twelve shillings a week, with the summer rate to be negotiated. Miller Eastholm he became — except that he disclaimed the formality of the surname, and was soon simply known to the denizens of Hinching Fen as Jonathan-up-at-the-mill.

Most of the fen windmills had been replaced by pumping-stations in recent years, and the Hinching Fen mill was provided with a steam-engine on the mill-house floor as an alternative source of power; but when the wind was fair, the traditional structure continued to do its traditional work, the thirty-foot sails operating the water-wheel which discharged the water from the dykes into the main drain, and preserved the safety of the fields of Hinching Fen. The mill luffed herself, the head turning into the wind by means of a fan-tail: Jonathan's job, in which he was coached at first by the mill-keeper of the adjoining fen, was to run the mill whenever there was a wind, keeping all the luffing-gear and striking-tackle oiled, and to stoke the boiler when it was necessary for the steam-engine to take over. Jed Gosling had taken to neglecting the mill unless the water in the drain were really high: Jonathan, anxious not to make the same mistake, was soon habituated to leaving his warm bed at the Surfleets' and tramping out to the mill at the first mutter of a rising wind.

Typically, Jonathan thought of the hardships and rewards of the job in terms that could only be called aesthetic. He found something satisfying to mind and heart in the mill just as he had in the lighters: mounting the five flights of stairs to the head with the oil-can, he dwelt with admiration on the symmetry of the gearing, the smooth movement of the great wooden cogs, the nice precision of the chain-hung weights which rose up and down to regulate the speed of the sails: the rhythmic revolutions of the great water-wheel impressed him with a sense of hypnotic fitness, like the figure in a Persian carpet. When he sat and rested a while with a pipe before the mill-house fire, the creakings and trundlings that echoed down the wind-shaft were like the comfortable stirrings of some large, benevolent animal. Jonathan began to love his work, and because he loved it he did it well.

There were long hours when there was little to do but be on hand, and these he filled with reading and thinking; but something — perhaps the tail-brass at the foot of the wind-shaft which gave a long reverberating organ-note when it needed oiling — put him in mind of music again, and set up the old longing for a tune, smothered during his recent troubles. He was still doing in-between work on the land, and had money to spare, so, with something of his former discomfiture at this weakness of his, he asked Rob Risby the tallyman whether he ever dealt in musical instruments.

"Oh! dear, yes," sighed the tallyman. "Any amount on 'em. Kit-fiddles, mouth-organs, banjoes, I'm carried 'em all in me time: 'cornet, flute, harp, sackcloth, solitary, dulcimer and all kinds of music', as scripture has it."

"D'you reckon you could lay your hands on a concertina?" Jonathan said.

"Say the word, miller, and it's done. A concertina you shall have — I shall bring it next week. If I'm spared," Rob Risby said. "Not that I can complain: my poor ole missis has got it wuss than me; and I'm not sure as the hoss ain't got it wuss than either on us." The tallyman did not specify what 'it' was, but seemed to suggest that it was chronic, contagious and fatal.

The concertina the tallyman brought was of the piano-accordion type, much more impressive to the eye than Jonathan's old squeeze-box, and his fingers itched to play upon the gleaming keys; but he was too embarrassed to do so whilst Rob Risby was still there. "Thass a handsome thing, miller," Risby said. "German, I shouldn't wonder, from that name on the side. All full of zeds and double-yews; and there's no one meks 'em better. I'm fond of a tune meself — it helps you forgit your troubles — for a little while any road," he added with a graveyard cough. "There's some people as don't seem to melt to music at all: as for me, the hairs are standing up on me arms the moment I hear it. There! it's such a pleasure to talk about with you, miller, that I almost hate to bring up the subject of a price. If it was just me, I'd let you have it cost; and if it was just my poor ole missis having to lay with her feet above her head, I'd hardly ask more; and even with my Nelly as she is, with her chest all bound up wi' brown paper till she can't sleep for the rustling, I'll only say three and six down, and ninepence a week, and I don't care if they do call me a fool for it."

"Done," said Jonathan, glad to be rid of him so that he might try the accordion out. He soon found, however, that the keyboard worked on a different principle to the studs, and he had a frustrating time of it, trying to conjure a melody from the instrument. Recalling Artie Gill, the old turf-digger who had played the fiddle at the Labour In Vain, Jonathan sought him out for advice as the only musical person he knew; though with little hope of success, as Artie Gill was known as a cantankerous fellow who would growl at his own shadow. But he found Artie flattered and delighted to be asked — there is a soft place in the flintiest man — and the old turf-digger went out of his way to call at the mill and instruct Jonathan in the rudiments of keys and chords; and thus two of the gruffest men on the fen could be found applying themselves to harmonising sentimental melodies, and mournfully declaring that o-ver rocks which are steep-est, lo-ove will find out the way.

Unexpectedly, Jonathan too found himself performing the role of a teacher of sorts — at first in spite of himself, and with no great faith in his abilities. Ever since Jonathan had helped him extricate the cow from the dyke, young Charlie Smeeth, Henry Wake's farm-boy, had regarded him in the light of an oracle, a prodigy, and a hero: during Jonathan's last hopeless days on his ruined smallholding, Charlie had come to offer his labour gratis whenever Henry Wake could spare him; and once Jonathan was established as mill-keeper, the lad was always turning up at the mill and asking if he could help.

Jonathan was often glad of a helping hand, especially when he had to run the engine: at busy times it was handy to have someone to mind the mill while he strode home to the Surfleets' for a meal or a wash; and Charlie Smeeth was so eager for this, that there was no question of taking advantage.

"Let me stoke the boiler, sir — goo on, do," Charlie cried, "I s'll mek a proper job on it, sir!"

"Well, thass a mucky job, Charlie, and I reckon you're done a day's work at Mr Wake's already. I don't want you overtaxing your strength."

"I'm strong, sir — I'm like a Ox, reely!" said Charlie, exhibiting arms of approximately the girth of a walking-stick; and proudly dug the shovel in the coal, and staggered with it to the stoke-hole, his face all red but gamely smiling.

But there were times when there was no work for Charlie to lend a hand with; and to Jonathan's perplexity, he would still remain there, looking up at Jonathan with his round eyes, and manfully trying not to be in the way, as if he could make his gangling limbs invisible by a mental effort of effacement. The comforts of the mill, besides the fire, comprised only a few square feet of swept floor, a mattress on which Jonathan snatched a little rest when he had to spend the night there, a shelf or two, and a couple of bentwood chairs, the rest of the space being occupied by the machinery. Charlie could never be persuaded to take a chair, but would prop himself against the wall, or squat on the floor, protesting against all the evidence of his bony and abraded joints, that he was as comfortable as anything. Jonathan was a man who could take any amount of companionable silence; but even he grew restive under Charlie's baleful gaze of humility.

"Won't your mam and dad be wondering where you are, Charlie?" Jonathan asked him.

"Ain't got a dad, sir," Charlie said. "Just me mam. And a uncle. Except he ain't," he added, looking with great concentration into his cap. "I know THAT."

"Ah," Jonathan said.

"They wun't be looking out for me, any road," Charlie said simply. "Me sister Edie might — but she knows I come the mill."

"Won't there be no supper waiting for you?"

"Shouldn't think so, sir — not unless Edie's got summat in. It don't matter — Mr Wake give me some apples and a slice of waiting-cake when I come away from work today. He often slips me summat to eat, Mr Wake does — except I always have to mind and not tell Mrs Wake, he says — her being the way she is."

"Don't sir me . . . I'm never seen Mrs Wake," Jonathan said. "I don't go to chapel, and that seems to be the only time she goes abroad. A bit severe, then, is she?"

Charlie twisted his cap as if he were wringing out a flannel, and said in a rush: "I git all panicky when she comes near me — she's so big, and she stares so and breathes through her nose — and her thumb bends all the way back — and there's all these hairs on her face, like on a peach, and I can't stop looking at 'em!"

"Calm down, boy. Think of a psalm like I told you."

"Yes, sir." Charlie gabbled The-Lord-is-my-shepherd under his breath.

"She don't treat you badly, does she?"

377

Jonathan said when the boy had recovered.

"Oh! no. Thass a good job I'm got at Mr Wake's: he's very good to me, and she don't have much to do with me. It's just I'm a bit afeared on her — and sometimes I reckon Mr Wake is too — if she shouts for him from the house, when he's out in the field, he goes a-running — and once she come out to the yard, scattering the chuckies wi' her skirts, and her face all scowling like one of them gurgle-spouts on the church roof — and she lifted Mr Wake's hat off, and hit him 'cross the head wi' a cowcumber — "

"She did what?"

"Yes, sir — thass what she did, and she says 'There's for you!', and then she marched back in — and Mr Wake put his hat back on all sad and mild-like, and he says to me, it'd perhaps be as well if I didn't mention what had just happened — and now I have — oh, 'ell!"

"Never mind, boy: I shan't tell anyone," said Jonathan, mentally revising his opinion of Henry Wake.

"Thank you, sir. We never said no more about it; but a day or two after, when I was having a panic, and me heart were scuttering away like a rat in the hay-loft, Mr Wake says to me, take care of your heart, Charlie Smeeth — and never give it away careless-like, in case you come to regret it later."

"Well . . . I dare say he's right there," Jonathan said, frowning at the fire, and suddenly swept by a cloud of nameless emotions.

"Oh yes, sir. He's got all sorts of learning,

378

Mr Wake — he reads in books when he don't have to, just like you do, sir — and he can read the words off a flour-sack without hardly looking at 'em."

"Why, surely you can read, Charlie?"

"Well — I wouldn't go so far as to say I *can't* read, sir," said Charlie dubiously, "only it teks a lot out of me, I'm that slow — I reckon I told you it weren't a very good schooling I got."

"I remember," Jonathan said.

"Same wi' writing — it's so long since I learned how, and stopped doing it — thass like when you work the pump, and the prime goes."

"Why, how old are you, Charlie?"

"Fifteen, sir — sixteen come Martinmas."

"I'd thought you were younger."

"Yes, sir — I'm all behind-hand wi' me growing, except uppards, and there ain't a hair on me face — and there's Mrs Wake all — oh, 'ell! I mustn't think of that!"

"Well, boy," Jonathan said, "I'll help you with your letters, if you like." He thought it a pity that anyone should lose out on reading: even in the rural sphere of the fen, illiteracy would hinder the boy; and an occupation would at least divert Charlie's unnerving attentiveness. So the wall of the boiler became a blackboard, on which Jonathan chalked Biblical texts and other simple phrases in his own strong, unformed hand, Charlie doing his best to read and then copy them. Often, as he said, Charlie's 'head wouldn't go', and he got into a panic; but Jonathan's recent trials had revealed to him unsuspected reserves of patience, and what began as a chore became a pleasure. He wanted to help the boy get on: though he hardly knew it, this represented another stage in the breaking down of his aloof self-sufficiency, for his self of a year ago might well have disdained such an involvement with a harsh declaration that no one helped *him* when *he* was a lad. He guided Charlie through some elementary arithmetic too: remarking that this would all come in useful if he had his own farm some day.

"Coh! I should like that, sir," Charlie said, contemplating a multiplication sum as if it were a work of art. "I shouldn't want for nothing more, then. And I'd keep pigs, and ducks, and rabbits and all, them loppy-eared ones. Uncle won't let us keep rabbits, you see . . . Thirty-six. Is that right, sir?"

"Quite right."

"I like the multiplying — it's the dividing that beats me down. Hester Vern."

"What did you say?" exclaimed Jonathan.

"I'm reading what it says there — Hester Vern — thass right, ain't it, sir?"

Jonathan looked, and saw that he had chalked the name on the boiler wall — now when had he done that? — and had imperfectly rubbed it out. "Yes — anyhow, that isn't anything," said he, hastily erasing it. "Well, stick at it, boy, and you may have your farm one day."

"I'm always dreaming about it, sir," Charlie said. "Just a little holding like Mr Wake's — or like yours, sir — at least, yours as was — that were such a 'nation shame! And

I should have Edie come to live wi' me, and keep house — 'cos she don't like it at home with Uncle there — which he ain't an uncle — nor an uncle wouldn't treat her the way he does — and she don't have to call him Uncle if she don't like, does she, sir?"

"No, Charlie, she don't," Jonathan said firmly: remembering his stepfather and thinking he would have to meet this uncle some time.

Autumn approached the margin of winter gently and temperately: the water in the drain was seldom high, and Jonathan had plenty of time for casual work on the land. He took all he could get, for he still meant to revive his fortunes eventually; and the available work being strictly limited at this season, he was doubly interested in the piece of good news Charlie Smeeth brought him one day.

"Edie's got herself a place in service!" Charlie said breathlessly. "Peggy Chettle saw there was boxes being carried into the big farm right over Upwood way — thass been empty half a year or more — and Edie went straight over yis'dy to find out if they wanted a servant-gal, and they were just starting to move in, and they says yes, and she starts next week!"

"You're pleased about that, eh?" Jonathan said — for Charlie's smile seemed to go right round to the back of his head.

"Not 'alf, sir! It's a good place, and she'll be free of Uncle, you see (which he ain't), and she'll be earning ten pound a year, all found, and she'll have a half-day every week, so I s'll be able to see her."

"Well, I'm pleased for Edie, Charlie: I'm sure she'll do well. Farm over Upwood way, you say? Well, I dare say they might be tekking on labour: I reckon I'll soodle over there and ask if there's any work going."

Following Charlie's directions, Jonathan walked over late that afternoon to the western edge of the fen, coming to the farmhouse a little before sunset. The front door, which had steps going up to it, seemed a little grand for his errand: walking round the side of the building he came upon a broad yard flanked by brick stables. At the door of one of these he saw a fair-haired man crouching with his back to him, apparently working on a broken latch: at the same moment the figure of a woman appeared from a rear door of the house. Jonathan sprang back as if he had touched electricity; some instinct made him retreat a little round the corner chimney-breast of the house, where he could not be seen. Slightly short-sighted as he was, he knew the girl immediately — her very gait, swinging and supple, transfixed him with recognition. Half-way across the yard, the girl suddenly stopped and then began to tiptoe towards the crouching young man, who was plainly unaware of her approach: Jonathan saw her smile of mischief, white teeth touched by a tip of pink tongue. There was sawdust on the ground around the man, and the girl, swift and deft as a cat — yes, he remembered that! — bent down, scooped up a handful and, seizing the man's shirt collar, emptied it down his neck. The man started and leapt up — lithe as she, it seemed — made a grab and caught her to him, pantomimed raising a fist, whilst she reached up and tweaked his nose. All the time they were laughing. The girl put her arms around the man's neck, her face against his. Jonathan could see the curved, laughing shape of her mouth outlined on the man's cheek.

He turned, and walked back the way he had come. At the end of the drove he stopped to wipe his face, for though it was cold he found he was covered in sweat. A sort of blankness had taken possession of his mind, and it was only now that he bethought himself of why he had come. Well: that was out of the question.

He set out for home, trudging along the high road. It was empty as a trail crossing a steppe: in its straightness it seemed to unroll before him like the expression of some mysterious and intractable purpose. The wind was in the west, and blowing steadily, though the dead leaves at his feet whirled and scurried in cryptic little patterns, as if obedient to some other and discriminating force. The sharpness in the air was that of November, which while cutting enough is different in quality from that of February: the early winter retaining even within its desolation something of the foregoing season, as if it were the decayed corpse of the summer, whilst on the other side of the solstice there is an assertive rigour, which seems to have no conception of kinder days — the presence of cold rather than the absence of warmth. On the horizon the sun was momently disappearing, and profound layers of shadow were invading the land: at the very last a fiery cusp seemed to pause on the lip of the earth, and the shapes of objects near at hand appeared to start forward; the bare trees by the road revealing for a complex instant every twig of their tracery before coalescing in a soft blooming of blackness. In the sky above the sunset the eye was bewitched by a swift succession of colours, exhibited all in their tenderest, most opalescent forms, like the same note played on different instruments, until the last embers of orange were extinguished in a metallic afterglow: whilst at the same moment, from the opposite quarter of the firmament, the first stars sparked into life from a bed of harsh and remotest green. The wind freshened as if freed by the promise of night: it ran with a long dry whistle through every stalk of wintry vegetation that clothed the banks of the high road; it snatched the white vapour of Jonathan's breath and tossed it over his shoulder. He was wrapped in incomplete night, his footsteps here and there involved in pockets of pure black, and through the soles of his feet the bumps and concavities of the road's surface became magnified to his sense of touch, like the tiny ridges of the teeth when felt by the tongue.

All this presented itself to Jonathan's consciousness with utmost intensity, and yet with a certain disconnection, as if he were an infant seeing for the first time. All his mental processes seemed displaced by a large mass of emotion, which he could only apprehend, and try to feel his way around as he felt his way along the road. Minutes passed him like seconds, and when he beheld the distant cottage lights of Milney St Mary, and nearer at hand an angular patch in the darkness which must be the mill, he almost felt that he wanted to simply go on walking, on into the night, until his mind somehow freed itself of its burden.

At the mill he lit the lamp and climbed the stairs to the head to oil the luffing-gear. The slow creaking of the great machine sounded hollowly up the tower, and the wind sang through the sail-vanes. All was well here, and Jonathan, descending again, stood at the mill-house door, calculating the time from the stars, and thinking that Mrs Surfleet would have supper ready and he ought to go home.

All this time he had not allowed himself to think of the vignette he had seen at the farm: he had kept it at a distance. It seemed foolish to do so any longer. Hester was married; Hester was happy: these were simple facts that he must negotiate. Perhaps, he thought, it was fortunate that he had been confronted with them at last. He had been carrying his feeling for Hester around with him without ever strictly inquiring what it was, or what he expected from it: it was like some large, strange, unwieldy talisman that he could not let go of, useless as it was. Jonathan was severe on himself: he had suffered, he had expanded, but he would still sacrifice poetry on the altar of consistency, and believe that he was not doing violence to his nature. Mixed in with this was a sort of superstition, which suggested to him that fate had led him to the farm and prepared that paralysing dumb-show in order to administer a hard lesson that he had been too long evading. Out of a complexity of emotion he plucked a simple imperative: he leaned against the door-jamb and stared into the night, and an observer of his stillness would never have guessed that he was making a momentous decision — forcibly, violently — as if breaking the talisman over his knee.

He went home, ate supper, and then accompanied Andrew Surfleet to the Labour In Vain for a drop of beer. Inevitably, the news had reached the public house that Hester Verney, Saunders as she now was, had returned to Hinching Fen to live at the Upwood farm, and was the topic of much discussion.

"Done well for herself — this Mr Saunders' mother's the richest woman in Stokeley, so they say," Jass Phelps said. "There — I always said Hester Verney'd git on."

"That you never," growled Artie Gill. "You always said she'd come to grief."

"Well, I'm glad for her," Henry Wake said. "And it'll be nice to have someone local there — someone we know."

"I don't know about that — she'll probably think herself too grand," Jass Phelps said with malicious relish. "Look down her nose at us — pretend she's never seen us afore — when *we* know what she's like, for all her airs. All red hat and no drawers, thass what some people say. Not that I'm saying owt against her, mind," he added.

"No, no — Hester never looked down her nose at anyone!" Henry Wake said. "I raise my glass to her — and her new husband; and I hope their married life will be as happy as — well — " he coughed — "as can be expected."

Jonathan raised his glass too: the company in the bar-parlour noticed nothing unusual in his demeanour. His decision had been made, the renunciation was complete, and he was determined to savour the serene pleasure of being heart-free. And yet that night he felt, in spite of himself, that a little of the glory had gone out of the world.

Part Two

1899

1

ONE morning in April found Hester at her butter-making in the dairy-shed of the Crooked House. This fanciful name for the place had become general on Hinching Fen; and it was never referred to as Saunders' farm.

The hour was early. The spring weather was exceptionally warm, and Hester had risen at dawn in order to do the butter-making before the mature heat of the day made it difficult. The rays of the climbing sun, obliquely penetrating the open door of the dairy, laid a bright triangle of gold on the brick floor: a few flies, prematurely roused by the early warmth, rotated drowsily with the light jewelling their wings. Hester turned the handle of the churn with a sure and practised hand — the training she had received at the Langtofts' had never left her — listening for the change in the sound of the squelching cream that indicated it had turned. From time to time she crooned a snatch of a song, though in a subdued voice, and with something more of wistfulness than gaiety. Just as her arm started to ache, and she began to think that the cream had gone to sleep, there was a soft satisfying thud within the churn: the butter had come. She gave it a turn or two more, then opened the lid to pour in cold water and wash out the buttermilk. At that moment the door of the house banged, and the farm-servant, Edie Smeeth, came galloping across the yard. Edie was fourteen: her height, which was mostly composed of leg, made her look older, as did the starveling thinness of her features; that, however, had been filling out since she had come to work at the Crooked House and eaten regular farm fare — so that altogether she was an odd mixture of childhood and womanhood. A neat black-curled head and bright black eyes gave her something of the look of an alert and pretty bird; and she had a quality of being intensely alive, her body containing a vitality sufficient for three or four persons if it were shared out; the energy required to shift a hundredweight of coal Edie put into closing a door, and she could not cross the yard without breaking into a galumphing run, embroidered with skips and hitch steps. She came bounding thus to Hester — who was fond of her and, being so recently a servant herself, found it practically impossible to act the mistress and order her about. The girl reminded her of herself too, as she was not so very long ago; and this made her both amused and sad.

"Ooh, missus, you're been a long while. Go to sleep, did it?" Edie cried, swinging her arms in unison back and forth, with a clap of her hands alternately fore and aft. "D'you want any help?"

"No, I'm all right, thank you, Edie," Hester said, lifting the shiny butter out and beginning to knead it.

"Don't it look a treat! Now, what did I come

to say? Oh! ah. I'm give the horsekeeper his breakfast, thass it, and shall I put breakfast on for you, missus? There's them taters from yis'dy, what'll fry up wi' some bacon."

"Oh! yes, please, Edie," said Hester, who was mightily hungry. "I could fancy that. Oh! wait a minute — is the master up yet?"

Edie shook her head, turning it through a hundred and eighty degrees, and most of her body with it. "Still abed, missus."

"Perhaps you'd better wait till he's up, then," Hester said reluctantly. Her stomach protested at the delay, but it wasn't fair to make the girl cook twice over. "Have you sorted the eggs, Edie? I shall be going to market today."

"I'll do it now, missus. That little Dorking's been hiding 'em again — sly ain't in it!" Turning to go, she whirled back again. "I knew there was summat else — there's Billy Onyett turned up for wukk, and he says is he to go a-weeding of the wheat today, only master didn't say yea or nay, and there's a hoe all rusted through in the head, and he's mended it best he can, only thass going to bust like a twist of barley-sugar any day now."

"Oh — I thought Lyle had . . . Well, anyhow — tell Billy to do the best he can: and when I go to St Ives today I shall buy a new hoe."

Left alone again, Hester finished the butter, making it up into pats and half-pats, and packing them up in muslin. She saved the buttermilk in a basin, and went to rinse her hands under the pump in the yard. The heads of four horses, protruding from their loose-boxes, watched her benevolently: two farm-horses and two ponies, one of which Lyle had purchased with the intention of training in carriage-work to sell at a profit, though he had not got round to it. The crazily leaning trees that surrounded the house resounded with the shriek of nesting birds. The horsekeeper appeared from the back kitchen door — stumbling and nearly falling down the two-foot drop from threshold to ground, which he never got used to — and Hester asked him to have the trap made ready.

Another hour had passed, during which she helped Edie in the kitchen, before Lyle came downstairs, yawning and amiably protesting that she should have woken him. They ate breakfast at the little table by the parlour window, Lyle picking at his bacon and finally abandoning it to bathe his lips again in tea.

"No letters for me?" he said.

"No, don't think so. Were you expecting one?"

"Oh! not really. Just to break the monotony, you know." He rumpled his hair and yawned, looking at her with a foggy smile. "By God, you do look healthy, love. You make me feel like something fished out of a well. How do you manage to get up so early?"

"Oh, the light wakes me, I think. You know the way it comes through your eyelids."

"Not if you put your head under the blankets," he laughed: then held his head. "Ow! I don't know what they put in that beer at the Labour In Vain. I only had a couple last night. That'll teach me, won't it?"

"Oh, I shouldn't think so!" she said, with the quietest of laughs on her own part.

"Ah, is that Walt getting out the trap?" he said, glancing out of the window. "I must have told him last night — damned if I remember doing it."

"No — I asked him: I was going to take the butter and eggs to St Ives' market this morning."

"Oh! that," said Lyle vaguely, pouring more tea. "Well — that'll wait, won't it?"

"But it's market-day, love."

"Yes — I suppose. But the thing is, I wanted to take the trap today — to school that bay. You know."

"Did you? Sorry."

"I meant to tell you. Didn't I tell you? Oh."

"I'm really got to go to market. The butter won't keep — "

"Yes, yes, I realise that." Lyle dipped his spoon in his tea and toyed with it, watching the dribbles.

"Why don't you come to market with me?" Hester said after a moment. "We could go together — and sort of make a day of it — "

"Oh! Lord, no — it would bore me to death," Lyle said with a cross laugh. "All those farmers talking shop."

"You are a farmer, love," she said lightly.

"Yes . . . but you know what I mean. Oh! well, in that case — "

"I shouldn't be back late," Hester said, "depending how busy it is — "

394

"Look, it doesn't matter," Lyle said, pushing away his plate.

"Have you got a buyer for the bay?"

"Oh! no! Nothing like that. Probably won't get one, not at the price I was hoping. Bit of a pig in a poke, to be honest." Lyle linked his hands behind his head and looked up at the ceiling. "That's what comes of doing things half-measures. Can't really deal in horses properly here — no up-to-date equipment — no exercise ring . . . Hes, does this butter and eggs business really make much difference? You can't get much for them."

"Shilling a pound for butter," Hester said. "It's a big help with the housekeeping."

He looked at her with an expression in which the frown cancelled out the smile. "You mean I don't give you enough?"

"No. It's not that, love. There's just so many little things that come up on a farm. Billy Onyett needs a new hoe — "

"Oh, that's what *he* says," Lyle said. "He's always got some complaint or other."

"But he does need one — and he's got so much work to do, everything's so forward this year, there's thistles and charlock and poppies and all sorts choking up the wheat . . . "

"Just a few weeds, my dear."

"Well, I know thass how it seems, love, but these are the things that matter on a farm — and if you just took a bit more interest — "

"Oh! all right," said he breezily, "don't keep banging on about it, my dear — " they were both employing that excessive number of endearments

395

typical of a marital quarrel. "I suppose we must be doing worse than I thought, if the butter and eggs are keeping us."

"We're not doing badly, Lyle," she said softly, "are we?"

"Oh! how should I know?" He left the table, plucking up the newspaper and sinking into an armchair.

Hester went upstairs to change. She took off her apron and put on a powder-blue tailor-made jacket over her blouse and tied on her hat with a veil. On the dressing-table she noticed the jet earrings that Lyle had given her when she was Mrs Saunders' companion. She had not worn them since their honeymoon — how long ago it seemed!

Coming down again she found Lyle still in the armchair, one leg hooked over the side in his boneless way — one of those unconscious physical quirks that can make the heart stop with love more effectively than the most eloquently amorous speeches.

"You look very nice," he said, putting out a hand to briefly caress hers.

"Lyle — are you sure you won't come with me?" she said.

"Oh! no," he said, conning the newspaper, "I don't suppose the farm can spare both of us."

She stared down at his tousled head.

"Well, aren't you going?" he said, turning a page. "After all that damn fuss about how you'd got to have the trap."

Edie had carefully loaded the butter and eggs on to the back of the trap, and Walt had harnessed up the pony: and off Hester went. The long drove was dry, the air was warm, and the scene as the pony and trap rattled out on to the high-road was one of ripening beauty. The fens of Anglia can be incomparably bleak in winter, when uplands enjoy the advantage of undulation which may soften even the bareness of ploughed fields; but in a favourable spring the same fens are as richly green as a Wessex vale and, in the dazzlingly pure light of that almighty sky, would defy the brush of a Dutch master. The theme of green, set forth by the crops that extend in a carpet as far as the eye can see, is taken up by the wild growth that shoots up along drove, dykeside, and roadway, and elaborated in a thousand variations by grasses, by reeds and rushes, by wildflowers: and such was the view that met Hester, seated high up in the trap above the fields, whence it seemed that there was not a square inch of earth from horizon to horizon that was not giving forth leaf and bloom.

An observer might have judged the smart young woman in the trap, expertly gathering the reins in her gauntleted hands, as complementary to the beauty of the scene, and even surpassing it: for there was a certain maturity of expression about that well-shaped face beneath the veiled hat, a touch of shade about the youthful contours, which gave a finish lacking in the vernal landscape. In fact Hester was trying not to cry, and not entirely succeeding; so that the road before her often dissolved behind a watery film, and several times she had to trust to the straightness of the road and the sureness of the pony, while she fumbled to wipe and blink away the sporadic tears.

She was crying because of the quarrel with her husband, but the deep pain of it lay not so much in the incident, as in the general tendency of which it was a part. It would not have been so bad if she could have viewed it as an isolated outbreak — a bump in a reasonably smooth surface. But it was not so, and that was why she was troubled. The quarrel, such as it was, had been simply an intensification of the normal conditions of their married life: a downpour in a drizzly climate.

She had been naïve, she supposed, when she married Lyle seven months ago: if she had not exactly believed that love conquered all, she had at least held that the possession of it robbed the world of much of its power to hurt. And indeed in that she was not changed: when she woke in the morning she did not regard the face on the pillow beside her with hate or aversion; her love remained, and she cherished it still. It remained, but it seemed to be dissipated in a thousand trivial drops. The wings that had lifted her to such heights of promise beat in vain against the hard front of circumstance: and poor Hester, whose worldly aspirations extended little further than a full stomach and an intact roof, felt herself ground in the mill of the material.

Yet there was nothing, in reviewing her life since she had knelt beside Lyle in the church at Stokeley, that she could seize on as a separable cause of regret. She had married the man she loved; they had begun their life together on a fen farm, the environment she knew and loved best: she would change none of it. She laboured under a sense of grievance which she could not or would not shape: on the one hand she stoutly believed that there was nothing in her own conduct that merited serious reproach, but on the other she left a wide margin of allowance around Lyle's behaviour; and so she hovered in-between, in a limbo of doubt, the most oppressive to her straightforward spirit. For the first time Hester was hearing the eternal note of sadness, and recognising that its timbre, resounding from the soul, was different from that of sorrow or suffering; and she saw her self of a year ago, with a mixture of envy and pity, as a mere unreflecting animal living in a world of the simplest sensations.

The name of the Crooked House, which she and Lyle had coined in the first careless days, might have taken on a sinister meaning: it was tempting to see it fatalistically as a place where everything went awry. But, confused as she felt, Hester had not lost her practicality. They had taken on the farm in high hopes, and she saw nothing intrinsic in their situation that should dash them. She liked the house: though they had been able to furnish it only sparsely, there would be lots of time to improve it; and the holding of peat arable land, intensively farmed in the fen way, should support them with ease. She was used to hard work, and threw herself into it all the more willingly in the knowledge that it was for she and Lyle alone. Nothing could persuade her that the farm was a bad thing — not even the belated revelation that Lyle had not really been able to afford it.

He had taken out a loan to make up the shortfall, a fact she only learned by chance on catching sight of a letter he had received from the bank. Her dismay at this he had shrugged off. "Oh! it's not much," he had said. "That's what banks are for, after all. It'll be paid off eventually."

"Oh but, Lyle — you never told me!" said she, with visions of bailiffs and bankruptcy courts.

"Why, I didn't want to bother you with it," he said, with his cheerfullest smile: at the same time moving away a little restively, as if to tell her that she needn't look so reproachful. "You wanted the farm, didn't you? No point in settling for some dingy cottage."

"Well, yes — but if I'd known — "

"Well, you know now, love, and don't worry about it." He remained good-humoured, but also seemed to suggest that he was being very forbearing in doing so.

Hester was left with a dual discomfort. The knowledge that the farm was not entirely theirs gave a new urgency to every task but, worse than that, her mind had laid hold of the horrible idea that she could not trust Lyle, before she could reason her way out of it. Reason hurriedly declared that he had not told her a lie — he had merely neglected to tell her some part of the truth, from the best of intentions: she was far too cut-and-dried about these things herself, and besides she ought to know that Lyle's was not a personality to be measured against a ruler

— that was one of the things she loved about him . . . Still the unease could not be rooted out. And there was something else she knew he often omitted to tell her — his visits to his mother, and what prompted them.

She had never for a moment supposed that he would not continue to call on his family, and to try to make it up with Mrs Saunders — it was only natural. But when they had married, she had earnestly sought assurance from him that if the estrangement should prove permanent (which it showed every sign of being — Mrs Saunders was unyielding), then he would accept that as a fair price to pay. He had given that assurance freely — of course he accepted that! But now she began to see that Lyle had never really believed he would have to pay that price. He had once told her, jokingly, that that old chestnut about not being able to have your cake and eat it was nonsense — he had been doing it all his life. Now Hester feared that it was more than a joke. It seemed that at each fresh rebuff from his mother, Lyle — instead of cutting his losses — redoubled his efforts to win her round. He no longer spoke laughingly of his charm working on her in the end: he seldom spoke directly about the matter at all. It had become a grim struggle. And what chiefly oppressed her about it was the fact that Lyle would go to a great deal more trouble in trying to find a way back to his mother's favour than he would in working the farm. Hester was well-placed to understand such a perverse misdirection of effort: it was a habit of mind she had been prone to herself — but now it dismayed her to observe it in Lyle. She knew he was dissatisfied with the farm, and that he could not begin to be satisfied with it while half his mind was still fixed — in spite of his denials — on the more substantial prospects of the family business.

It was for the same reason, she supposed, that he was so ineffably careless about money. They had enough to live on, if they did not throw it about: but it was precisely because of that vague hope of his mother which he never relinquished that Lyle did throw it about; and thus a comfortable competence became a deficiency. Had he accepted that there would never be any more, he might have lived within his means — instead he tried to live as if that phantom inheritance were already in the bank, and chafed when confronted with the more modest reality. It was in this way that life with Lyle — one of the attractions of which had promised to be a freedom from niggling mundanity — was full of fretting about money. The words of Mrs Saunders' prediction echoed in Hester's ears like a curse.

And yet she loved him; and to quarrel with him cut her like a slow razor. Indeed perhaps it was now, rather than during the idyll of their courtship, that she beheld the full magnitude of her love: what smote most sorely on her heart was the perception that Lyle was not happy, when she longed to make him so, and felt she would do anything to that end.

Hester wiped her face, and sat up more smartly: a cart was coming the other way.

Along with sadness she had discovered pride, and she would sooner have walked on fiery coals than permit her distress to be seen. After all, she told herself, flicking the reins, this wasn't like her — wittling and cry-babying. Hadn't she always been down-to-earth and realistic — and wasn't marriage to be viewed in that light too? Wasn't it natural that it should have its troubles and disappointments? (Even as she strove thus to be mentally bracing, Mrs Saunders' words mocked her: *How long do you suppose that fairy-tale will last?*) She could not reproach herself with having gone into marriage blind: her far from sheltered upbringing had led her to anticipate at least as much shade as light across any tract of experience. Complexity was a condition of life, and she supposed that included what the Chapel called the life of the flesh. Well, she accepted that: perhaps it was unreasonable to expect the initial intensities of feeling to persist; the everyday was a fine diluter of passion. But still . . . Hester was not an outright sensualist: a sense of humour perhaps precluded it — she thought, for example, that the designer of the human libido and the designer of the human foot must have been working at cross-purposes; but her nature was warm and responsive, and she did not see why the physical celebrations of honeymoon should have subsided so swiftly to such a complete indifference. That bewildered and hurt her.

Of course there was the question of children — and with Lyle worrying about money as he was . . . How that took the edge off everything!

It even made him irritable: he had seemed the least irritable of men before their marriage. Here lay something she had never expected to find, and she could not tell whether it was a common revelation of marriage or specific to their case — the fact that getting to know the person she had married was not a matter of penetrating further into known country, but of suddenly finding herself in unguessed-at and alien regions. That genial optimism which she had seen as the expression of Lyle's whole being turned out to be a somewhat thin and brittle crust on the surface of his character. The loss of a hen to a stoat, heavy rain making the drove impassable, the cost of a broken window: such small things seemed to gnaw at him, and pointing out that they were small made it worse. "God! it's all so damn trivial," he had said, "that's what gets me. Like being eaten alive by gnats."

Often — increasingly often — he escaped by going down to the Labour In Vain. Hester recoiled from an image of herself as the waiting, disapproving wife of the music-hall joke — but still she wished he would not do it so often. Of course, she had known he liked a drink when she married him, hadn't she? — at Mrs Saunders' he had been a frequent patron of the Nag's Head. And yet this seemed different — a retreat, an evasion.

No, Hester could not accuse Lyle of fostering any illusions about himself: that was why she shrank from acknowledging her own discontent, and why she flinched with a sort of guilt from the idea that instead of the broad open sunlit spaces

404

which she had associated with her husband's character, there were dark airless tunnels, and redoubling mazes that led nowhere.

Well, something was amiss with their life: so much was definite, and she could no longer deny that at least. She wished Lyle had come with her — but in a way it was good to be alone like this, and think it out. If something was wrong, then she would have to put it right. There was no alternative, unless to admit that her marriage had been a mistake — the thought was like a cloud passing across the sun, chilling her before she could dismiss it — no, that was nonsense! Once she would have said that the best way of dealing with problems was to ignore them and hope they would go away: even now a trace of that attitude remained to her (Hester's flippancy was just as sincere as other people's solemnity); but in this case she must not turn her face away — as it seemed Lyle was all too liable to. If they quarrelled again, she decided, she would not draw back from the brink: she must openly confront what was wrong, confront even her great fear — that Lyle felt trapped, and that he might begin to blame her for it.

Hester arrived at her destination less dejected, at least, than when she had set out: it seemed to her that that stifled feeling that had long oppressed her was a direct result of pretending that nothing was wrong, and while the ache of tears lingered, she breathed more freely. The approach to St Ives was picturesque enough to lighten the heaviest heart. The road in revealed a broad prospect of river meadows, where spindly lambs darted among the sheep like another species, and it seemed impossible that they should ever become such thick solidities as their elders: the little town was enisled in greenness and sparkling water, with the two church spires hoisting aloft like twin masts. Hester's was not the only vehicle crossing the venerable bridge with the stone chapel built on it, for St Ives — the place of the man with seven wives — had once been a great trading centre, and still boasted a market more substantial than the modest scale of the town might suggest. Before the bow-fronts of comfortable houses, as quietly handsome as a country parson's daughters, a busy drama of commerce was enacted. Livestock, which on this southern edge of the fens were more common, huddled together in pens, and trembled singly on the backboards of waggons; early vegetables, still with the coldness of earth on them, toppled from wicker baskets and rolled off the trestles; bowler-hatted farmers weighed grain and seed on their grooved palms, and shook their heads and stroked their side-whiskers despairingly, as if their trade were sheer agony to them, and they would rather do anything else.

Here Hester, going about her marketing, was strongly conscious of being a farmer's wife (a young and pretty one), and enjoying it. It suited her well. You were an agent in your own right, instead of subsisting in your husband's background, like poor old Uncle Bevis's wife. Most pleasing to her, it was not an 'uppity' position, which set limits to who you could mix with: at the Crooked House she had re-forged her links with Lizzie Gosling and other old friends — though there had been no reconciliation with the Langtofts, and she was thankful that their farms were on opposite sides of the fen. Even as Mrs Saunders' companion, she had had to stand within the circle of that lady's dignity: here she was on her own ground. If only she didn't feel that Lyle was pursuing this life on sufferance! She knew that he could make a success of it: he had energy and resource enough for anything, if they could be rolled into one lump, and not dissipated in fitfulness — and if he were not always mentally looking over his shoulder for that elusive side-road that somehow got there quicker.

Hester counted up her butter-money, and ruefully reflected that she was doing the very thing she had always laughed at as the summit of futility — believing you might change your spouse once you had married him. But she did believe they could be happy: and somehow she must make him believe it.

She had various things to buy besides a hoe — salt, paraffin oil, soap, yeast, a roll of chicken-wire, things that Lyle never thought of — and after she had tipped the boy who had helped her load them into the trap, she returned to a stall that had caught her eye earlier. What attracted her were the sheaves of cut tulips. In recent years tulips had begun to be commercially cultivated in large numbers in the northern fens around Spalding: and thus a flower that had its origin in ancient Persia, and had bloomed on the Hanging Gardens of Babylon, pouted its exotic mouth among daffodils in a homely Anglian market town. For Hester their beauty was enhanced by association, for her mother had loved them; she had often been haunted of late by a strange longing wistfulness for her childhood, which formerly she had been glad to leave behind. Why this feeling of weakness? Wasn't love supposed to make you strong? But she could not resist the tulips; and she set out for home with two large bunches atop the rest of the goods in the back of the trap.

The day had begun to cloud over a little, but it was warm and still; when she came in sight of Hinching Fen mill she noticed that the sails were barely moving. The waters had been high after the spring thaw, and Jonathan must be running the pump a lot. On passing the mill Hester always freshened the pony's pace a little. When she had come to live at the Crooked House the presence of Jonathan Eastholm in the neighbourhood had first surprised and then made her a little uneasy. Of course that time on the lighters, and his strange, sudden and contemptuous proposal, were a good while ago, and so much had changed in her life that it all seemed to lie on the further side of a great gulf of sundering experience — even though, most curiously, there were still occasions when she woke up in bed and in the first hazy moments believed she was lying on the bunk in the lighter-cabin, with the river murmuring beside it. But spacious as the fen was, she was bound to see Jonathan Eastholm around from time to time, and when she did she had the disturbing feeling that he despised her.

Why this troubled her so she could not say. With the Langtofts, she had fallen out with them, and that was that. She was sorry it had to be that way, but she really didn't care what they thought of her — it was all in the past. But it was as if Jonathan saw her in some way which no one else could; and somehow it seemed that his contempt for her sprang from his contempt for himself, for his extraordinary lapse, as a man might regard the crazed ruins of a folly on which he had squandered a fortune. When she saw him she felt vulnerable; she seemed to stand in a ruthless beam of light. All this really made no sense, she told herself; and yet the feeling was as convincing as disquieting, like some unperceived colour in the spectrum of her emotions. And so it was with a double alarm that Hester heard a cracking sound from the left-side wheel, right opposite the drove leading to the mill.

A great jolt rattled her teeth, and before she could pull the pony up the trap had slewed to one side: some of her parcels went sliding off the backboard and fell in the road. Jumping down, she found to her dismay that a spoke of the wheel had snapped off at the socket; the metal wheel-rim was buckled, and the two adjacent spokes were bowing under the pressure. Another glance took in the scattered parcels, and, most melancholy, the tulips all over the road: and another, the sight of Jonathan Eastholm coming out from the mill, whence he must have plainly seen the accident.

"Bit of trouble, I think," said he, frowning at the buckled wheel, whilst the pony peered over its shoulder, with an air of helpful attention.

Hester nodded in confusion, scarcely able to look at him; somehow it seemed the worst part of her distress that he should be the witness of it. "I don't understand," she said, "the trap was perfectly all right — Walt greased the axles this morning . . . " All at once the memory of her quarrel with Lyle afflicted her; she had insisted on having the trap, and here it was broken! "Oh! whatever will my husband say?" she murmured, before she could stop herself.

Jonathan looked at her with an expression of purest surprise. "Why, it's not your fault," he said.

"No . . . " How stupid she felt. "Will I — will it bear up, do you suppose?"

"Well, I'm no wheelwright." Jonathan bent to examine the wheel. "Rusted — I shouldn't trust the other spokes. You'd best not ride any further; it wouldn't be safe with the weight. Try leading the pony — go very gently." He looked down at the parcels. "You'd best not load up again either. I'll carry these for you."

"Oh, no — I can't let you do that — it doesn't matter."

"Why, you can't leave them all over the road," he said, in his short way, and began gathering them up in his arms.

She was reluctant to accept his help, but there seemed nothing else for it; and in her fear of Lyle's reaction to her bringing back the trap damaged, after that scene this morning, she found she could not think straight. "Will the mill be all right?" she said feebly.

"She won't run away," said Jonathan.

"Oh! don't trouble about them," she said, as she saw him picking up the tulips out of the dust: but he ignored her, and such as were intact he laid in the crook of his arm.

It felt strange indeed to be leading the pony and the limping trap with Eastholm walking along beside her, the parcels tucked under his capacious arms. Once this might have tickled her, but she felt herself crushed between his silent disapproval and the prospect of more trouble with Lyle. Out of desperation she said the first thing that came into her head. "Why do you call the mill 'she'?"

It came out more pert and inconsequential than she intended. Jonathan, by his frown, certainly seemed to think it so; but he answered carefully: "I don't know. Millers do, generally. I suppose it's the same as calling a boat she; and I suppose railwaymen do the same with an engine."

"But you wouldn't call a house she," said Hester, some part of her mind, in spite of herself, becoming interested in the question.

"No," he said. "But a mill, or a boat, seems to have a life of its own — and moods, too."

"Ah, thass it. But men have moods just as much as women, it seems to me."

"I wouldn't know," said he.

Hester was silent. The coolness of the miller's manner depressed her. It was not that she expected to find the flattering jealousy of the

411

rejected suitor: she had lost the coquettishness that might have looked for such a thing; and besides, Jonathan's suit itself had been so grudging and unloverlike that she suspected the only thing he now regretted was making it in the first place. No, what she felt was an acute form of that unease, which seemed all entangled with his opinion of her. Something made her long to say, straight out, "You hate me very much, don't you?" But she could not; and chilled by a specific dread of Jonathan's perceiving her unhappiness — he of all people — she suddenly burst instead into rattling cheeriness. "Well, ain't the spring being kind to us? You don't often get April days like this — course, the fields could do with a drop of rain — it'd be nice if we could just have the rain-showers at night, wouldn't it, and the sun all day — oh, I don't know though, I love the smell of rain on the land, you know, to stand at the door and sniff it, and you wouldn't get that if you were asleep . . . " She broke off. "Look, Jonathan — it's been very kind of you — you needn't come any further, I don't want to take you out of your way . . . "

He stared down at her. "Don't be a fool, missus," he said. "What's the point in bringing this stuff halfway?"

"Well, there's no need to snap at me!" she cried — wailed rather, more in wretchedness than anger. "You always were terrible hard on me!"

His glance fell keenly on her, as if he saw much; he seemed to refrain from comment, and shook his head, saying: "Well: never mind me.

Come on, it's not far now."

Hester was too perplexed by a sensation of having somehow given herself away, to say much more; and soon they reached the drove leading to the Crooked House. Edie Smeeth came flying out to them in the yard, and had to be pacified from a first impression that Hester had been flung from the trap into the ditch, and was walking wounded.

Jonathan gave Edie the parcels, and handed Hester the tulips. Holding the flowers in her arms, she suddenly thought to ask him whether he would like some of them, as a thank-you, saw at once it was inappropriate, and said hesitantly: "Jonathan — I think there's some ale in the kitchen — would you like some before you go?"

He looked at her with a fierce sort of astonishment. "Why, do you think I was just after a tip? What d'you think I am?"

"I'm sure I don't know," said she, stung — for she had intended no harm. "I don't understand you at all — and I reckon I never will!"

"I dare say: it doesn't matter," he replied coolly, shrugging. "I don't want no tip — thass all. Good day to you."

In the kitchen Edie Smeeth, unwrapping the parcels as if she were in a parcel-unwrapping race, said to Hester: "Weren't it lucky Jonathan-up-at-the-mill were around to help you, missus! My brother Charlie says he'll always go out of his road for folk — just like he did when Mr Wake's cow went in the dyke — and he'll never tek no thanks for it. And they reckon the mill's

413

much better kept now he's there — and he does all manner of work on the farms an' all, and never gits tired."

"Why, he's never asked for work here," said Hester. Did he dislike her that much?

"No, missus," agreed Edie, who (like many people) paid to others' remarks about half the attention that she gave to her own. "And my brother Charlie said Mr Wake said Jonathan-up-at-the-mill were quite an illegible bachelor, and thass a wonder he don't git married; only he don't seem interested, and just keeps hisself to hisself."

"Well — probably he thinks just a shade too well of himself," Hester said, going to the kitchen door, and looking sombrely out at the buckled wheel of the trap, while Walt unharnessed the pony. Of course, as Jonathan had said, it wasn't her fault . . . "Where's Mr Saunders, Edie?" she said in a small voice.

"Not here, missus — he went into Stokeley. Got a lift on Farmer Mather's cart."

"Oh . . . did he?" And had he gone to renew the hopeless siege of his mother's obduracy? She felt cold.

She helped Edie put supper on, and was in the parlour mending a petticoat when she heard Lyle arrive home. A few moments later the door opened, and she stared; a soldier stood on the threshold.

"What — Lyle, wherever did you get that?"

Grinning, Lyle marched in. He was clad in a soldier's scarlet tunic, with gleaming buttons, which in the wainscoted farm parlour looked

414

as outlandish as a sultan's cloak. He saluted smartly, clicked his heels, and bowed to kiss her hand.

"I've joined up, my dear. Taken the King's Shilling. Off to fight the dervishes, whatever they are. Oh! Hes, your face!" he said, laughing and falling onto the settle beside her. "You really believed it for a moment there!"

"I never did," said she, flushing, and slapping his knee. "You gret fool — I was just a bit flummoxed for a second, thass all."

"I'm sorry, love." He put his arm round her and kissed her. "I do wish I had a picture of your face just then, though. Well, how do you fancy me in uniform? I think I could rather take to it, you know. I reckon I look quite a Blade."

"What does that make me, a battle-axe?" she said.

"Very cutting! Ow, we'd better stop these puns, hadn't we?"

"I think we had," she said laughing. In fact his lean boyish figure did look well in the red coat. "Where on earth did you get it?"

"At Balsam's — you know, the dyer in Stokeley. 'Mourning Our Speciality'." He pulled a long face. "He comes creeping out of the back of his shop with his head on his shoulder and says 'Iss it a bereavement, ssir?' Anyway, that's my good news — I think I've sold him that bay pony. He's worth a mint of money, and he doesn't know a thing about horseflesh, so I ought to get a good price. That's a turn-up, isn't it? I knew today would be a lucky day.

And when I was in the back of his shop, I saw these discarded tunics — he gets them for a song and uses the cloth — and he let me have one when I took a fancy to 'em." Suddenly Lyle sprang up and strutted to the fireplace, tweaking an imaginary moustache. "Couldn't you just see me at that great ball in Brussels before Waterloo, eh? With all those titled ladies in see-through frocks, admiring my regimentals — as it were." He darted back and fell on one knee before her. "Lady Montmowency, you are a wavishing angel. Your shoulders are like marble — all cold and veiny. Will you gwant me a single night of bliss, before I go off tomorrow and thwash Boney?"

"Oh! not tonight," she said, "I'm got the Duke of Wellington coming, and it takes him half the night to get his boots off. Oh! come here," she said, kissing him warmly. "Perhaps I'd better tell you while you're in a good mood. The left wheel of the trap's broken — a spoke came off and the wheel-rim buckled . . . I'm sorry."

"Rusty, I should think. Did you manage to get home all right? Well, that can soon be fixed," he said blithely. "Oh! Hes, have you been worrying about that?"

"Well, a bit," she said lamely; her relief must have shown in her face.

"Daft girl. Anybody would think I'm some sort of tyrant who takes a strap to you. What's that you're sewing at?"

"Just a petticoat of mine — it wants mending."

"Pah!" said Lyle, "chuck it away, my dear. No patched clothes for us. I reckon my selling that bay is just the first of a — well, it shows things are on the way up for us. Don't you think?"

"Yes, I suppose so . . . "

"Never mind suppose, wench. Of course they are — I never doubted it. Pessimist, that's your trouble."

Hester did not propose to remind him of how different he had been that morning. She did not view married life as an exercise in scoring points, and at that moment she was happy just to have what she saw as the real Lyle back again.

"I wonder if I could mend that wheel?" he said.

"Oh, I don't think so, love. It wants somebody who really knows the job — "

"Pooh, I'll bet I can," he said, getting up with energy. "Just you see."

But presently he was back, wiping his hands and shaking his head. "No chance of that," he said. "Silly idea. Wants a wheelwright. That damned drove's in such a state, it's a wonder the trap's in one piece at all. Damn it, more expense. All these things just keep adding up . . . I don't see how we'll ever get out of the wood. It's like banging your head against the wall." He sighed. "Is it supper yet?"

After supper Lyle's brow cleared again. The night had turned chilly; he sat on the floor with his long legs stretched out to the fire — the floor was still his favourite seat — and leaned his head against Hester's knee. She stroked his hair, which sent him into a sort of cat-like trance;

417

and at last she nerved herself to ask the question that had been in her mind all the time.

"In Stokeley today," she said, very casually, "did you go and see your mother?"

She could feel the muscles in his neck go tense, but he answered, quite as casually: "Yes, I called in."

"How is she?"

"Oh! still the same." His fingers tapped a moment on her foot. "Didn't get much of a welcome, as you can imagine."

Hester licked her lips; her mouth had gone dry. "Why do you go?" she said. She knew why he went, but it had to be said.

Lyle's neck was like the skin of a drum. She saw his jaws working in the firelight; but at last he said lightly: "Don't know, really."

"I mean," she said with care, "there's no pleasure in just being ignored, is there?"

"None at all."

"When you never get any welcome . . . It would serve her right if you just stopped bothering."

He half turned to her. "You think I should?"

"I know it seems hard," she said, with a feeling of walking along a tightrope, "but it would save you the — the disappointment each time."

He reached up for her hand. "All right," he said. "Whatever you say, my dear. Whatever you say."

★ ★ ★

418

Jonathan had been suffering from a cold. On his constitution this had rather less than the effect of a tick-bite on a bull, but he had unwisely mentioned it to the Surfleets, with whom he still lodged, and so it had got round to Peggy Chettle.

She visited him at the mill, arriving on the bicycle in which she had newly invested. These machines were a novel sight in the fens, and children ran out of cottages to watch Mrs Chettle go pedalling hardily by — looking, in her ample divided skirt and leg-of-mutton sleeves, like a genial balloon on wheels. "It cost me a pretty penny," she confided to Jonathan, "but in my line o' work you need to be mobile, what wi' laying-ins coming at all hours, and laying-outs, well, not that they're in any hurry, God rest 'em, but best not to delay when the warm weather sets in. Now then, dear boy, Mrs Surfleet happened to mention as you weren't at the top of your form, so I thought I'd come and look you over, neighbourly-like."

Jonathan attempted to protest, with thanks, that he was quite all right.

"Oh! I know you young men, you reckon nothing short of a thunderbolt'll lay you low, but there's nothing worse than a spring chill if you don't cosset it. It'll go down in your lungs and lay there till you sound like Jass Phelps' donkey — ain't that right, boy?" Mrs Chettle added to Charlie Smeeth, who was visiting the mill as usual.

"Coh! I should know, Mrs Chettle," said Charlie, who was one of those people who

419

offer their ill-health as a matter for modest congratulation, "I git 'em in spring and summer and all, I do. They mek me ears go all clogged — I were deaf as a post once for a dozen weeks together, I was, till I ran up to the hay-loft one day and they unpopped, and Mr Wake said it was because of the alti-chewed."

"Now look here," Mrs Chettle said, taking Jonathan's hand in her own pink scrubbed one, and pressing a jar into it, "thass goose-grease, and you want to rub that all across your chest, well, p'rhaps not all across, my word, you'd need a bigger jar than that, but any road, rub it in well and then cover it with brown paper cut out in the shape of a heart — ah, I know that sounds a bit daft, but never mind — it may not be scientific but it works, like when I cured Chettle's little trouble with a piece o' lint and a clothes-peg. Now mind you use it, dear boy. Charlie Smeeth, you'll see he looks after hisself, won't you?"

"I will, Mrs Chettle."

"Well, Charlie, and how do you go on? I declare you're more of a long drink o' water than ever. When are you going to grow outards a bit, instead of uppards?"

"I dunno, Mrs Chettle," said Charlie, mournfully throttling his cap. "I keep trying, but I don't git no thicker — Mr Wake says if I was a plant he'd train me on a trellis."

"You'll be better when you git to twenty-one — third cycle of seven," said Mrs Chettle. "Well, I must be leaving you, I'm got to see poor ole Mrs Miles who should have delivered

420

a week ago, and her with her busts sticking out like chapel hat-pegs and enough milk for a school-treat, still, it'll come, you git one like that sometimes, they stay up there and it's like trying to pull a football through a knot-hole — just tek hold of my iron steed, will you, Charlie, while I climb on, I'm all right once I'm got going but it's mounting up thass the trouble, that reminds me of a joke but it's not for your young ears, cheer-o, both!"

Charlie was deeply impressed by the responsibility of seeing that Jonathan looked after himself: and insisted on going up to the head with the oil-can, and doing the rounds himself, whilst Jonathan sat by the fire.

"This is nonsense, boy," Jonathan said. "All because of a little sniffle!"

"Oh, but let me, sir — goo on — you know I like doing it!" Charlie said.

"Well, if it'll mek you happy. And don't sir me." Inactivity irked Jonathan, but he was in a brooding mood which had something of the Old Goblin about it, and by the time Charlie had come down again he had fallen into a deep abstraction from which he was only roused by the sight of the boy examining his own reflection in the opaque mill-house window.

"What's the matter, Charlie?"

"Oh! it's my beard, sir. My beard what I ain't got, I mean. It's like Mrs Chettle said — I don't seem to be growing proper at all."

"Rubbish, boy. I was no different from you when I was your age." In fact one of the reasons Jonathan kept so completely clean-shaven was that he did not have a very strong beard, and it had used to worry him just as it did Charlie.

"Weren't you really, sir?" said Charlie, with an expression that showed he longed to believe, but was forced to doubt.

"Thinner, if anything," Jonathan said, with a hyperbole more kind than credible, for Charlie had scarcely more breadth of body than a folded umbrella.

"But there's me ears, sir," said Charlie, in renewed despair, "sticking out like anything! Oh, 'ell!"

"Calm down, boy. Say your psalm. We're all made different, Charlie: thass what it is," Jonathan said, raking the fire and staring into the embers. "There's some things we can change about ourselves, but some we can't no matter how hard we try — because we're made that way. We're all got our little peculiarities, see: and when these chaps stand up in their wing collars and high hats, and tell us we all ought to work harder, or we ought to be good and not have so many children, or we ought to stop drinking and go to church, just remember they're got their little peculiarities too, though they're trying so powerful hard to mek out they haven't got a single one; and when somebody reckons he never had a doubt, or a secret, or a weak moment — why, he's a liar, and no less. See your own little peculiarities, and you'll look different on other people's." To a less appreciative ear than Charlie's, there would have been nothing remarkable in this philosophy — but it was remarkable in that it was quite new to Jonathan Eastholm, the harshly judgemental waterman who needed no one. A year or two ago he would have brusquely shied away from such ideas, and even now he groped at their incomplete form through a prickly mesh of self. "Any road," he said, hoping to turn the boy's thoughts to a more hopeful channel, "you're got plenty of growing yet. Tek your sister Edie — I saw her just the other day — look how she's filled out, and coloured up, in just six months."

"Oh, ah, sir, thass the best thing that ever happened," Charlie said, cheering up at once. "Edie loves it at the Crooked House: no more Uncle (which he ain't), and the way he — well, the way he used to behave; and all the grub she can eat. And she says young Mrs Saunders is nice as pie with her, and don't frighten her at all — not like Mrs Wake do me — oh, 'ell! And she says Mrs Saunders is allus giving her presents, bits o' clothes and the like, though she don't hardly ever have anything for herself."

"Don't she, Charlie?" Jonathan said, his eyes on the fire. "Aren't they well off?"

"Well, Edie reckons Mr Lyle Saunders put just about everything he'd got into that farm — but now he don't seem to want to mek a proper fist at it, and Mrs Saunders does all the work while he does all the spending — thass what Edie says — and when he's not riding about on his ponies, all fligged up to the nines, he's down the Labour In Vain — and he's always in a funny mood about summat or other, all strung up, like a dog that ain't had a walk all

423

day — thass what Edie says. And there's Mrs Saunders doing her best, and Mr Saunders not caring about nothing, and Edie says they're allus quarrelling about it — "

"Charlie, don't tell me any more," Jonathan said.

"Oh, sir — I didn't mean to tell tales," said Charlie in alarm. "Nor didn't Edie!"

"No, boy, I know. Still, best to keep them things to yourself, eh?" Jonathan looked at his turnip watch, without really noticing the time. "Reckon you'd better be off home to your supper now."

Charlie who, whatever his naïvety, had a tactful sense of when he was superfluous, quietly left. Jonathan climbed up to the mill-head and went over all the luffing-gear with rag and broom — the boy was always too liberal with the oil, though Jonathan chose not to tell him. At last he closed the boiler flues, scattered the ashes on the fire and, locking the mill-house door, set off home to the Surfleets.

He hoped he had not been short with the boy, but there was such a volume of thoughts pouring into his mind, and he needed to be alone to pump them out. When he had met Hester (how could he think of her as Mrs Saunders?) the other day, he had thought her greatly changed; but he had wondered then if he were seeing merely a reflection of change in himself. Now Charlie's words brought that scene back to the foreground of his mind from which he had consciously banished it, and forced him to consider what he had dismissed — that

Hester had looked an unhappy woman. Both halves of that epithet were significant of her transformation, for he had never conceived her being unhappy and he had never thought of her as a woman, rather than a girl. And that she most assuredly was now. The most strange and compelling symptom of her unhappiness, it seemed to him, lay in her beauty — and that was a word he would never have applied to her before: a beauty unaware of itself, and as far from mere prettiness as a night prospect of bare trees against snow. That slightly indrawn lower lip, and those slanting eyebrows, which had formerly seemed emblematic of sheer fun, had gained in subtle expression what they had lost in gaiety. Even in her voice he had detected a new timbre, a faint throb of disturbance which had not been there before.

His reactions to this ran a swift relay, from surprise to perplexity to confusion. Much had happened, of course, in the year since their ill-fated rendezvous at the Spread Eagle, but still that Hester should have changed so much seemed to Jonathan as untoward as if the mill had got up and walked about the fen; and he had had great difficulty in behaving normally when he had carried home her parcels. If she appeared to have entered new and sombre dimensions of emotion, his own feelings were more obscure. He had solemnly abjured all remnants of love for her on her marriage: half a year had passed, in which this conscious resolution had settled into a fixed habit of mind; and he supposed he was feeling something like the tugging unease of a person who has lost his faith, on revisiting a church. Her married state, and the apparent prosperity of large farm, pony-and-trap, and fine clothes, had emphasised the wide separation between them — they seldom met, and it was effectively as if they had never known each other; and this had helped him to build up a strong protective earthwork of indifference, which he was not sure he wanted breached in any way. If Hester Saunders was unhappy, it was none of Jonathan Eastholm's business: that was the only way to look at it.

He was able to acquit himself, at least, of any sensation of vengeful triumph at this discovery; and this was not magnanimity, conscious or otherwise: he simply did not feel it. Indeed, that was part of the puzzle of his feelings, and that night Jonathan, who was normally asleep before the pillow was warm, lay wakeful.

The next morning was a Sunday. It dawned overcast, but Mrs Surfleet declared it would clear. "There's enough blue to mek a sailor a pair of trousers," she said as she got ready for chapel, tucking her thistledown hair into an ancient poke-bonnet crowned with ribbons faded to the colour of dead leaves. While the Surfleets pattered off to the chapel, Jonathan followed his usual custom and went the other way, to spend the morning by the river which ran along by the Stokeley road. He did not hanker for the lighters, but the river still drew him as a patch of sunlight draws a cat: he loved the peace of the water-meadows on a Sunday morning, when most of the inhabitants of Hinching Fen were in their pews — and as Jonathan was if anything a pantheist, these open-air rambles could be seen as his equivalent of religious observance. This morning, however, on approaching his favourite spot where he would stretch himself out on the grass with a book or his thoughts, he found a party of children — the annual Sunday School treat. The Sunday School helpers were laying out picnic cloths and baskets, whilst the children ran about the buttercup-strewn meadow with squeals of release.

Jonathan drew himself off to a distance, and sat down by a clump of pollard willows to watch: childhood he found rather a wistful spectacle, his own having been terminated so prematurely; but his mild interest was suddenly sharpened by the sight of Lyle Saunders there, amongst the children. He knew that Lyle was not a chapelgoer, and it soon became clear that he had volunteered to come along and help amuse the children, because he simply enjoyed it. He had thrown off his jacket, and was giving the children piggy-backs, pretending to run right to the river edge, swerving at the last moment, and laughing as hard as they. Jonathan, watching, had to admire his patience: Lyle did not mind playing over again the same game which, in the manner of children, they wanted endlessly repeated: he submitted, with satisfying howls, when the smaller ones pummelled him and thrust grass down his collar; he drew the shyer ones into a game of blind-man's-buff, going first with the blindfold himself, and clowning by catching hold of a tree and pretending it was a person. Several little girls presented him with daisy-chains, which he put on with appropriate solemnity, and did not take off when the children sat down at last to the picnic lunch.

When Jonathan got up and left it was time for the sweets, which were distributed by being thrown and scattered in the grass, the children running to pounce on them: and Lyle was running and laughing with them, his adult voice standing out from the sound of their shrill ones by its finished quality, like a chord amongst random notes.

Jonathan made his way back to the Surfleets — but on impulse carried on past the cottage, and struck the field-paths towards the western edge of the fen, where the Crooked House was. Whilst he had done casual work on most of the farms in the area, he had avoided seeking it there — it seemed an unnecessary complication; but now he had a desire to see what the Saunders' fields were like. It was a compact holding, stretching from the main drain to the edge of the upland, which was clearly visible on the horizon, the peat giving way to the purple-tinged ribs of clay. A glance was enough to show him that the Saunders acres were not well kept. The young green wheat was struggling for room with weeds: the fields had not been tilled right up to the dyke-edge — a tempting omission given the risk of the plough-team going into the dyke, but terribly wasteful on rich fen land; and the dykes themselves were choked with reeds and scum, and could hardly be doing their job at all.

Well, after all, it was none of his business. About Lyle Saunders Jonathan had striven to make no judgement, or at least postpone it; but the fact was, from what he knew of him, he thought him a worthless hound. However, he would have thought that in any case, whether he were Hester's husband or not. And he could not deny the man's charm — he supposed they were well suited.

Jonathan trudged home. The sun had come out with a flourish, but his mood was dark. This marriage was a fool's game, he said to himself, and grimly he embraced his old self-possession — his mind darted to it like a fish released back into water. "Mind when you git married, boy," he said abruptly to Charlie Smeeth at the mill that night, "it's a fool's game — " surprising the boy, who had been thinking of nothing more romantic than whether to eat the apple-core in his pocket, or save it till later.

★ ★ ★

Jass Phelps, the landlord of the Labour In Vain, had found a comfortable increase in his profits of late. There was Mr Lyle Saunders, who (as Henry Wake put it) frequently favoured the establishment with his custom, and thought nothing of standing drinks all round for his neighbours. (The mistrust aroused by his slightly dandified clothes and waggish humour was quite overcome by this friendliness, and he was pronounced a fine fellow.) More surprisingly, the pub had a new regular in the shape of

429

Chad Langtoft. Formerly Chad had been a rare visitor: not only his chapel upbringing but the tepid caution that marked all his habits had made him one of the most temperate men on the fen; but now he was sometimes the first to arrive, often the last to leave, and usually went home very far from sober.

This of course did not go unnoticed or unremarked. When he was not there, the explanation for this change in him was discussed among the company, and the blame was generally assigned to his domestic situation.

"Two women in one kitchen — ooh! dear," Sunny Daintree said. "I always said no good would come o' that." For Chad had married Mary-Ann Cole with no separate home to take his bride to, and they were living at his parents' farm.

"Well, it needn't be, you know — depends on the nature of the parties," said Henry Wake. "But I'm afraid Bess Langtoft's not the sort of woman to tek kindly to anybody else having a say in the household. Still — connubial bliss, they say, but it's not all bliss," he added with suppressed feeling, studying his tankard, "not all bliss by any means."

"And there's Mary-Ann a bit of a spitfire when she's crossed," Sunny said. "Ooh! she's got a voice in her. I were moling one day in Wag Langtoft's field when she come out to call the boys in — you could hear her from Dan to Beer-sheba. I wouldn't be a bit surprised if Chad's smelt her fist by now."

"Some people might say he rushed into that

wedding," Jass Phelps said. "There was hardly any courting-time. Almost seemed like a forced job — you know. Not that *I'm* saying that."

"That don't matter how quick it is, if she's the right one," said Andrew Surfleet. "I'd only been walking out wi' my ole gel four weeks when we got wed. Mind you — her sister-in-law were my brother-in-law's second cousin, so that were different."

"All the same, I can't help thinking Chad was a bit hasty," Henry Wake said. "Took it into his head that he wanted to git married willy-nilly, and he's mebbe regretting it."

"Why, he'll mek things no better coming down here every night," said Jonathan, who had noticed what a truculent glare Chad could have in his cups, and who tended to sympathise with his wife. The girl that Chad had precipitately wooed and married was a healthy, broad-browed, wide-lipped creature who struck Jonathan as no more discontented than she was entitled to be. Occasionally, going at night back and forth to the mill, he would come across Mary-Ann waiting, white-aproned and sturdy, at the end of the Langtofts' drove.

"Not seen that husband of mine, have you, miller?" she said. "Tell him he's got a wife waiting at home, in case he's forgot, if you do." She would laugh: it was a mainstay of country jokes, of course; but looking at Chad drinking himself to a trance in the corner of the bar-parlour — Chad retreated to the corners as naturally as a trapped animal — Jonathan felt far from amused, and weighed in his mind some

431

heavy thoughts about marriage, and what a fool's game it was.

Jonathan was one of the less frequent patrons of the Labour In Vain, with his time circumscribed by care of the mill, and when he did go it was usually later on in the evening: when he walked over one night in April he found that Chad Langtoft was already up to his ears in beer. He was slumped forward across the table in a doze, his head resting on his forearms. Jonathan sat down by Andrew Surfleet, who made his one mug of hot beer last all night, so that it seemed to diminish as much by evaporation as potation. "Third night running he's been like that," Andrew whispered, with a nod at Chad. "And not even a crust of supper in him to mop it up — dear-oh-Lor!"

Jonathan was considering whether to wake Chad up — the young man was so prickly in his cups, and he wanted no quarrel — when the door was flung open, and conversation died away at the swaggering entrance of a young soldier, whose red tunic and brass buttons had the startling effect of a drawn sword in the dim smoky parlour. The soldier, his peaked cap pulled down low on his brow, a short cane under his arm, stepped smartly up to the bar and with a sweep of his hand across his glossy moustache ordered a pint of mixed. Jass Phelps, more snub-nosed and staring than ever, served him and said: "A fine night out, is it, sir?"

"Misty, my good man," said the soldier gruffly into his beer. "I dare say it often is in these parts."

432

"Were you perhaps looking for anywhere in particular, I wonder, by any chance?" Jass Phelps said in his most insinuating way, like a man peeping under a curtain.

"Nowhere in particular," the soldier said, dabbing with excessive care at the froth on his moustache. "I'm recruiting around here, you know: I wonder if any of these stout fellows would care to join the colours and defend our flag against the followers of the Mad Mahdi?" He turned to survey the company, his eyes invisible beneath the peaked cap, and suddenly pointed with his cane at Sunny Daintree. "What about you, my good fellow?"

"Ooh! no," Sunny said. "You'd not git me near no Mardies. I couldn't abide the heat of them places, for a start-off. I knew a chap once as had a son jined up and went out to India — he fell down dead in a swelter the moment he stepped off the boat."

"I doubt you'll do much recruiting around here, sergeant," Henry Wake said affably. "Fen-folk don't go for soldiers, as a rule."

"Not since Oliver Crumble's time, any road," Andrew Surfleet said. "They marched to ole Noll's drum, all right."

The soldier's well-made lips began to curve beneath the moustache. Jonathan knew there was something wrong with that moustache — it was too dark and smooth: it suddenly occurred to him what it reminded him of — a woman's hair. At the same moment Sunny Daintree's eyebrows rose like twin caterpillars to the peak of his bald head, and he exclaimed, "Why, thass

433

Mr Saunders, or I'm a Dutchman!"

Lyle Saunders pushed back his cap and gave a peal of laughter. "Damn it all, I knew this moustache wasn't good enough. Took me an age to paste it on, as well. Still, it worked for a while, didn't it?"

After a moment there was a general round of laughter at the joke, and Lyle ordered drinks for everyone. "Not a bad disguise at all, neighbour," Henry Wake said. "I hate to say it, but I'm afraid I saw through it straight away — I didn't say anything, not to spoil the fun, like."

Lyle began to tell them the story of how he had come by the tunic, when his glance fell on Chad, dozing in the corner. Suddenly he stopped, pulled down his cap again with a grin and, signalling silence with a finger at his lips, marched across to Chad and shook him by the shoulder.

"Now then, lad," he said, deepening his light voice to great effect, "look alive there!"

Chad's pale, sleep-creased face came slowly up, and he blinked with fuddled astonishment at the military figure confronting him.

"What happened to you today, then, my lad?" Lyle said, drawing himself up tall and tucking the cane under his arm. "You never reported to me at Huntingdon barracks this morning, and I have to come looking for you. What's it all about, eh?"

Chad licked dry, liquor-parched lips. "Eh?" he said. "What d'you mean? I don't know what you're on about."

"Come! Never mind that, my lad," intoned

434

Lyle. "You'll be telling me next you've never seen me afore. You'll be telling me next you don't remember what you did in this very public-house last night, in front of all this company. You'll be telling me next you don't remember taking the King's Shilling of me, and joining Her Majesty's army, as a private in the Huntingdonshires."

Chad stared as if mesmerised by the scarlet and the glinting brass that filled his view. "I don't know what you mean," he haltingly murmured. "I never did nothing like that — "

"Stow that, lad," said Lyle. "You may have had a drop to drink at the time — in fact I'd go so far as to say you were half-seas over; but you perked up when I came in here recruiting last night, and you stepped forward and said you'd join up to serve your country — swearing to it like a good 'un — and you gave me your signature on the papers; I've got 'em here — " Lyle patted his breast pocket. "So come along, lad: your kit's waiting for you at the barracks: we're off to fight the dervishes, who've been insulting of our Queen!"

Chad started to his feet with a clatter. His face was pasty and damp as a new mushroom. "Here," he stammered, "this ain't right — I don't remember nothing o' this! You can't do nothing to me — it ain't right — "

"Why, many a chap's joined up when he was in his cups, and never regretted it afterwards," Lyle said. "You'll feel better when you get your uniform on."

Chad, jammed against the wall, cast a wild and

sweating glance around at the others, who were silent. Jonathan, finding something unpleasant in the atmosphere, was about to speak when Lyle threw off his cap and yanked away the moustache, wincing even as he laughed. "Ouch! that hurt — serves me right, I suppose. Well, Chad, don't you know me now?"

Chad stared as if fearing he was the victim of some new trick. "Whass going on?"

"Only a joke, Chad," Lyle said, offering his hand. "I just played the same one on the others, didn't I, neighbours?"

"Aye, aye, he did that," several voices replied, a little hesitantly.

Chad did not take the proffered hand. "Well," Lyle said, undismayed, "you're a damn good sport, anyway — let me buy you a drink on it."

There was a heavy silence for some moments, while Chad continued to gaze at Lyle's cheerfully smiling face. "You rotten bugger," he said at last in a tight voice, flushing a flaming, painful red. "You rotten stinking bugger."

"Oh! well, I deserved that," Lyle said. "Have a drink on it anyway."

His smile refused to fade: Chad's tortured expression, with his lower lip drawn down to expose clenched teeth, was like a horribly distorted reflection of it.

"I wun't tek a drink off you — you rotten sliving bugger!" Chad cried, edging round the table.

"Well, all right then: I'm sorry — you always seemed the sort to take a joke in the right

436

spirit," Lyle said blandly, putting his hands in his pockets.

Chad's eyes, transparent as glass above his burning cheeks, travelled swiftly over all the watching faces: there was a suppressed snigger, which Jonathan recognised as coming from Jass Phelps.

"You think you're so bloody clever," Chad said, seemingly unable to look at Lyle any more, "well you ain't — you ain't, see — " All at once he barged and blundered his way out, as he did so knocking over a glass which by some chance did not break but rolled round the floor in curious frantic circles.

"Well! I must make a better sergeant than I imagined," Lyle said, picking up the glass. "Perhaps I missed my vocation — perhaps it's *me* who should join up — what do you think, neighbours?"

Lyle did not stay long after that: after a couple of drinks he said laughingly that he had a sergeant-major of his own at home, who would have him on kitchen fatigues if he wasn't careful, and wished them all goodnight. When he had gone the hum of conversation rose like the noise of a stirred beehive.

"Coh, if that don't beat everything since Coggy Onyett laid hisself down on top of Squire Hardwick's tomb all covered wi' flour and clasping his hands, and the gleaners coming home through the churchyard thought he were a statue till he upped and shrieked at 'em!" said Sunny Daintree. "And I'll bet their faces weren't half such an object as Chad's were just now."

"I thought for sure Chad was going to flare-up, like, and poke him one in the eye," Jass Phelps said with relish: adding piously: "Not that I allow that sort of thing in my pub, mind."

"Pah! no — not Chad," grunted Artie Gill, who habitually threw dust in the face of any speculation. "He's not the one to use his fists: he don't have the guts."

"A good joke — a good joke, I suppose," Andrew Surfleet said uncertainly. "I'm known such things happen real, mind. There was a Stokeley chap took the shilling in his harvest-drunk, and he were in the Crimea looking down the Roosian guns before his head had cleared."

"A good joke," Henry Wake said, "but Chad's not perhaps the appropriate individual to play it on, you know. He don't tek to being laughed at. I'll not say anything against Mr Saunders, him being a neighbour and all, and a very open-handed gentleman — but still, you know . . . " He glanced at Jonathan for corroboration.

"I'm glad he didn't try that trick on *me*," was all Jonathan said by way of reply, shortly.

★ ★ ★

Edie Smeeth had been dreaming of the hooky-man: Hester could tell that from the marks under her eyes, like thumb-prints of charcoal. They were clearing out one of the bedrooms of the Crooked House, which was full of decaying lumber left behind by the previous

438

occupants: it was a job Hester had long been putting off. Edie showed other signs of having had a sleepless night — she was only moving about twice as fast as the average person, for one — and at last gave herself away by dropping a box of bottles, for she was normally the most deft-handed of girls.

"I dunno what I'm doing!" she cried. "I'll pick 'em up — I'll pay for what's broke!"

"Don't be daft, Edie," Hester said. "They're just a lot of dusty old bottles that we were throwing out anyway. What strange things people keep! And you needn't pick them up, either — I'll do it — you sit down on that stool and rest a bit."

"I can't do that, missus — it's the middle of the day!" Edie said.

"Yes, you can. Sit down and keep me company. I can tell you're tired. Have you been having bad dreams again?"

Edie nodded, subsiding reluctantly on to the stool. "It didn't start as a bad 'un," she said, making a cat's-cradle of her fingers. "I dreamt I was picking flowers down by the but-dyke — gret armfuls of 'em, jonquils and hen-and-chickens and Bess-in-her-braveries — it was a lovely dream really — and then up comes the ole hooky-man all of a sudden out o' the dyke, and grabs hold o' me leg — and I woke up sweating like a hoss, and I couldn't go back to sleep again. Oh! it sounds daft in the daylight, don't it?"

"Nightmares often do," said Hester. "But that don't make them any better in the dark."

The hooky-man was a bogeyman with a practical purpose. Many unwary children had drowned in the numerous dykes of the fenland: mothers reinforced their warnings not to play by the dykeside with chilling references to the hooky-man, who would rise up and hook you in. That a girl of Edie's age, with a nature as clear as a vessel of rain-water, should still be having bad dreams about him, had puzzled Hester at first. But as she had gathered an idea of what Edie's home life had been like, with her mother's lodger or 'Uncle', she began to suspect that the hooky-man was the lingering expression of some less supernatural fear. It was encouraging that the dream was diminishing in frequency the longer Edie lived at the Crooked House; but Hester took care to ensure that Edie did not need to go home for anything, such as clothes and washing, and that her wages went into her own pockets and did not find their way to those of Uncle; and she had a large heavy warming-pan at the ready with which she was going to greet this uncle if he ever came round to object.

"Why, you don't have bad dreams, do you, missus?" Edie said.

"Well . . . sometimes," Hester said. Her rest had been disturbed of late, but not by anything she could picture or name: the thoughts of her waking life seemed to persist through her sleep in subterranean distortions which left her with an oppressed, unquiet feeling.

"My brother Charlie don't — but then he sleeps so hard, after wukking at Mr Wake's,

440

and then helping the miller, there ain't room for dreams."

"You see Charlie on your days off, don't you, Edie?" Hester said.

"Always, missus. We go to Stokeley together, if it's fine."

"Well if you ever get a wet day, and you want to meet Charlie, tell him he's welcome to come here — any time."

"Lor, really? Thank you, missus!" Edie, forgetting her injunction to rest, wriggled down from the stool and picked up the red soldier's tunic which Lyle, tiring of it, had thrown in here. "What's to be done with this, missus? Don't Mr Saunders want it?"

"I don't think so. We may as well keep it — something could be made out of the cloth. Lay it in the rag-box, Edie."

"Handsome, ain't it?" Edie said, holding up the coat to the sunlight which streamed in through the dormer window, producing that warm peppery atmosphere of closed-up rooms. "Billy Onyett says everybody was fooled when Mr Saunders went down the Labour In Vain in it last week — and Chad Langtoft made a right fool of hisself about it, they reckon."

"How made a fool of himself, Edie?" Hester said, pausing.

"Oh! I dunno — Billy Onyett weren't there hisself. I don't listen to his tales. It's summat as they're all talking about, any road."

After a few moments Hester went down in search of Lyle. She found him outside at the stables, the only part of the farm in which he

441

took an habitual interest, hammering a cross-beam on a rotten loose-box door.

"Just a bodge," he said as Hester came up. "Planks are like match-wood. One frisky kick and the door'll be down."

"Stubby don't kick, though, does he . . . Lyle," Hester said, resting her hand on his shirt-sleeved shoulder, "when you went down the Labour In Vain dressed in that soldier's coat — what happened?"

"Why, I told you. I walked in and fooled 'em into thinking I was a soldier, like I said I would: you let me cut a bit of your hair to make the moustache."

"Yes . . . " She could not suppress a smile at the thought of it; yet she was troubled. "But what exactly happened?" she said.

"This damn hinge is rusted through as well — I don't know how it's holding. Is there any part of this place that's not falling apart?"

"Lyle, what happened at the Labour In Vain — to do with Chad Langtoft?"

"What's this, training for the Inquisition?" Lyle said, straightening up and shrugging off her hand in doing so. "It was a bit of fun, that's all, like I said: God knows I need it."

"What sort of fun?" said she, soberly.

"How many sorts are there?" Lyle frowned at the hinges, picking off flakes of rust with his thumb. "I swear you're getting to be quite a prig, Hes. You used to like a joke and a bit of fun. I never thought I was marrying a maunge-gut . . . I wonder if there are any stronger nails in the tool-shed." He dusted his

442

hands and walked away from her.

Strange how it was always with the coolest, lightest, most offhand words that he could hurt her most! Hester stood still where she was for a moment, as if to bite down the pain of them; yet she felt it more than ever imperative that she should know what had happened. The memory of her own trouble with Chad over the turf-digging was more rueful than sore — after all, she had suffered for that; but there was something alarming in the thought that her husband had made a dupe of him, if that was what had happened: she feared that Chad was all too likely to see a pattern of persecution.

She must find out the plain faithful truth of what had gone on at the Labour In Vain that night; and instinctively her thoughts, seeking truth, flew to Jonathan Eastholm. Arming herself with an excuse that she wanted to seek Charlie Smeeth anyway, to tell him he should feel free to visit his sister at the Crooked House, Hester walked over to the mill that afternoon.

The sails were turning, with their long, creaking, communing notes, as if wood and iron were breaking into voice; and she found Jonathan leaning on the parapet above the mill-drain, watching the revolutions of the water-wheel. There was a curiously attractive smell here, compounded of timber, weed, fish, and the moss which depended in rank clumps from the paddles, like herbage from the mouth of a chewing cow; and always the air about the splashing wheel, seeded with infinitesimal water-droplets, seemed a degree or two cooler than everywhere else.

"Hullo there," Jonathan said, drawing back from the parapet, "what can I do for you?"

Hester said something about looking for Charlie Smeeth who, as she had half-expected, was not there: then herself turning to look at the churning water, she said, "Jonathan — there was something I wanted to ask you — do you mind?"

"What is it?" Jonathan said, folding his arms across his chest.

She rested her hands on the rough brick of the parapet, having taken off her gloves first: Lyle had got her into the habit of wearing them when she went out, telling her she wasn't a servant any more and should remember her position, but she didn't like them — you couldn't feel the textures of things — it was like being half-blind. "It's just something I heard," she said, "a sort of rumour — you know how you do; and I wondered if perhaps you could tell me the truth of it."

"Well, go on," said he.

"I should think you know Ly — my husband went down the Labour In Vain the other night in a soldier's coat — he'd got hold of this coat and he thought it would be fun to see if anybody recognised him in it . . . " How foolish it sounded, put like that!

"Yes: I was there that night," said Jonathan.

"Were you?" Hester said, turning to him. "What happened, Jonathan? I don't want to — to bother my husband about it, he's very busy," she added lamely. "Only — was there something to do with Chad Langtoft?"

444

After a moment's silence, Jonathan said yes, and told her in a few plain words of the trick Lyle had played on Chad. As she listened she stared into the evanescent rainbow that the sun drew around the water-wheel, and her heart sank.

"Well — of course, he didn't mean no harm, but — tell me," she said, conscious that she had come here seeking truth, and was now seeking advice, "you were there — do you think I ought to apologise to Chad?"

Jonathan, with folded arms, as straight and unmoving as the engine chimney-stack behind him, said promptly: "No, missus. I think the whole thing's best forgot. Folk do worse things every day; and Chad's pickled half the time lately anyway." Then, as she was feeling a touch of guilty relief, he added in a sharper tone: "Besides that, if it's a matter of apologising, I don't reckon it's your job: your husband should do it."

She glared at him: she remembered that tone of lofty arrogance. "Well — that ain't none of your business," she said — needled because deep down she had felt the same thing herself. "Thass between me and him."

"So it is," Jonathan said without heat, "and none of this is my business, but you asked me."

"Well — what I mean is, you shouldn't speak against him to me — I won't hear it," she said, further irritated. She might have added that she would not hear herself speak against Lyle either: her loyal reaction to the slightest imputation against him was so excessive because she feared it might put the spark to the tindery doubts in her own heart.

"All right then: but besides that, I still think it'd be better if you didn't speak to Chad."

"Why?"

"Because I understand he once had a taking for you," Jonathan said with great, though quiet, distinctness, "and that complicates things: so it's best left alone."

He seemed set on articulating all the things she did not want to think of; and in a sort of provoked flurry she replied airily, "Oh, pooh — why — that's a long time ago — and I'm married, and so is Chad, and — well, after all, you had a taking for me once, or you thought you did: but you don't mind me."

It was the first mention of it between them, and only her confusedly fluttered state could have brought her to allude to it; but Jonathan said readily, "Yes: so I did, or I thought I did, as you say: and I don't mind you. But I'm not Chad Langtoft."

This cool echo of her words afflicted Hester with a peculiar bleakness but, already troubled as she was, the feeling had no clearer identity than a darker patch in a clouded sky. "Oh! I don't know what to do for the best," said she, giving way to her vexation, then recovering herself and adding, "I mean — it's such a trifling thing, it hardly seems worth all this trouble . . ."

"Leave it alone, then," said Jonathan. "It'll be soon forgot."

"Even by Chad?" she said, raising her eyes to him.

"Well, I can't answer for him; but he's such a thin-skinned article, always fancying an insult, and teks you up on the slightest thing — so he's always got some grievance or other. I've no love for the man at all; but I still think it was a poor trick your husband played — a poor trick."

"Well — I never asked your opinion about that," said Hester, her defences going up again.

"Thass nonsense," said Jonathan bluntly. "You asked me what I thought, and I'm told you. Now, like you say, it's a trifling thing, and if you'll pardon me, Mrs Saunders, I'm got work to do."

He left her, and went into the mill. Hester lingered irresolutely by the mill-drain, half-inclined to ask Jonathan something more, but feeling that she had already gone too far in revealing her private troubles to him, and chafed besides by some indefinable resentment of him; and at last she turned and set out for home.

All day she was gnawed at by indecision. She knew Jonathan's advice was sound — she knew, in spite of her annoyance, that he gave it disinterestedly, and was not a man to simply tell you what you wanted to hear: she knew indeed that he was right. And yet it was impossible that he should fully understand her own case. She had once done wrong by Chad Langtoft, even if the moral colour of that episode had been far more pepper-and-salt than black and white; and though she had never considered that she owed Chad anything, lately a new, half-superstitious feeling had begun to assert itself within her. It was a feeling that something had gone wrong in her life (much had gone wrong, said a desolate heart-whisper, much had gone terribly wrong) — and that somehow she must make atonement. She could not trace any logical path that led from her own unhappiness to her sensation of guilt towards Chad — only felt, with an intuitive conviction, that she must apologise to him. Of course, it would appear to Jonathan that she had acted contrary to his advice from mere perversity — but she did not propose that Jonathan, or Lyle, or anybody, should know about it. She would see Chad alone, apologise to him for what her husband had done, and thus in some way propitiate the gods.

The problem of how to see Chad alone was easily solved: the turf-digging season had begun, and she knew that Chad had begun digging a plot in the turf-fen. He went there at dawn, to get in a morning's digging before working the rest of the day on his father's farm; and Hester was always up at first light, three or sometimes four hours before Lyle. She did not delay once her mind was made up; and so the next morning she set out, whilst Edie was still yawning over the range in the kitchen and Lyle was buried beneath the blankets as oblivious as a winter root.

It was a morning of thick mist, which lay low across the fields, thinning to a dank white sky above and resolving to a heavy dew underfoot, so that the whole world seemed to be made of varying compounds of moisture, and the very shapes of the trees appeared as denser patches in a general texture of fog. The newly risen sun was a circular blob of filmy, clammy yellow, like an uncooked egg, and gave off no more heat than a live coal wrapped in a fleece. The sound of a horse-keeper calling to his team afield came to Hester's ears through the inspissated air like a spirit voice; and in keeping with this suspended, uncanny atmosphere, blackbirds and thrushes ran across Hester's path within inches of her skirts, pausing with the suddenness of enchanted things, and exhibiting that mixture of boldness and wary attention indicative of young in the nest.

Hester arrived at the drove leading to the turf-fen, which she could distinguish by the long walls of stacked cesses, like the uncovered ruins of an ancient town. There was no movement there, and she elected to wait for Chad up on the high road: she turned her face away from the turf-pit, more disturbed by the memories it raised than she had anticipated. Time seemed to be swallowed up too in the featurelessness of the mist, and she did not know how long she waited there, though her hair and dress were soon as wet as if she stood in a rainstorm. When a figure, bearing a spade and shovel at the slope, at last materialised, Hester started forward and began walking towards it, with a sudden idea that it would be better if it seemed a chance meeting in passing.

"Morning, Chad," she called as they approached each other. "You're at work early."

Chad, after a silent moment of recognition, grunted and said, "Have to be."

449

"This fog's a nuisance, ain't it?"

"I don't mind it," he said in his colourless way. He had slowed his pace momentarily, but now seemed about to proceed past her, and she was forced to stop and say, "Chad — I'm glad I saw you, there's — there's something I wanted to say."

Chad hesitated, and regarded her with a sort of half-averted face, like a dog pulling at the leash. His pale hair was flat and dun-coloured with the moisture. "Whass that then?"

"Well — it's silly, really, but — " No, no, that was wrong, it wasn't silly. "It's just that I heard about my husband playing one of his jokes the other night and, well, some people don't like that sort of thing, and I quite understand that, and so I wanted to say sorry to you — for what happened."

Chad still did not look straight at her. The drink he was putting away had not fattened him: he seemed slighter and more angular than ever, his pinched mouth and nostrils like slashes in the taut skin of his face.

"It didn't bother me," he said at last, with a boy's casualness.

"No . . . well, any road — he didn't mean no harm, but I wanted to say sorry."

Chad shrugged, a sharp neural twitch of the shoulders. "Didn't bother me," he said.

It was a mistake, she thought, to meet him so near to the turf-fen: the air teemed with unspoken recollection. Uncomfortably she said: "Well — if you say so . . . thass all right then. I just thought — "

450

"I don't care about him anyway," said Chad. "I couldn't give a tinker's damn for your husband." His voice was flat, but his breast rose and fell with the swift palpitation of an injured animal. "He thinks he's so clever, but it don't bother me."

"All right then," she said, beginning to move past him. She had done what she set out to do: she wanted no quarrel. But Chad had not finished. Pointing a stiff finger as she passed him he said, "I don't care — I could tell you a thing or two about *him* if I wanted."

She hurried on: she would not rise to that: it was a little flourish of vengeful bravado, that was all. You could only apologise to people — you couldn't make them accept your apology. She got home, boiled up a copper of taters for the pigs, cleaned out the hen-coop, and swilled out the dairy-shed, singing as she did so. When she came in to find Lyle sitting at the breakfast-table blearily studying a letter, she flung her arms round his neck and covered him with kisses.

"By the left, this is a bit much for a Thursday morning, isn't it?" he said in surprise. He put his hand to her cheek, looking into her eyes. "Hes? What's up?"

"Oh! nothing," she said, hiding her face in his neck with a broken laugh. "Just glad to see you — thass all."

★ ★ ★

On the first of May Jonathan had his quarterly appointment with the Drainage Commissioners

451

in Stokeley, at which he told them of any problems at the mill, rendered his accounts for coal, oil and other necessaries, and received his wage. Having prepared himself for the formality of the occasion by putting on a clean neckerchief and combing out his hair after his bath till it shone the colour of a conker, he set out to walk to the town with ample time, vaguely wondering whether to indulge himself with a visit to the bookstall in Infirmarer's Street. He could not dwell on this with complete satisfaction, however, for he was troubled in his mind by the meeting with Hester the other day. Had he, he asked himself, said the wrong thing after all? He had tried to be honest. He had no time for Chad Langtoft, as he had said: in his stern way he thought him a self-pitying fellow, with something covert about him that he could never trust. It had been handsome of Hester to think of apologising to him; and in his disapproval of her husband, Jonathan had perhaps not conveyed that. Had he not, rather, seemed to put the blame on her side? He didn't know: he wished he had never allowed himself to get involved in the business. Never get involved, that was the golden rule: he must stick by it.

Passing by the Langtofts' farm, he saw Wag Langtoft, Chad, and the two younger boys at work digging out a black oak from the field by the high road. As he was in no hurry, he went down to see if he could help.

"I'm been putting off gitting this beggaring ole root out for years, Jonathan bor," Mr Langtoft said. "I dunno why, 'cos it's broke ploughs

452

enough, and wishing wun't mek it disappear."

The black oaks, or bog-oaks, which lay buried under the fen fields were the remains of giant trees, felled by some natural catastrophe thousands of years ago, and preserved in the peat; the shrinkage of which brought them gradually nearer the cultivated surface, to the despair of farmers. Jonathan, in whose soul practicality and romanticism were intertwined like the red and white of a barber's-shop pole, took up a spade to help dig round the 'beggaring ole root', at the same time marvelling at the sight of the great black trunk with all its gnarled grooves and vermiculations as clear to the eye as when the tree had stood flourishing in the sunlight an inconceivable age ago. Acorns were sometimes found alongside these venerable hulks, perfectly formed and soft as putty until they were dried: Andrew Surfleet had a tinful of them at home, and whenever Jonathan took them on his palm he always thought with excitement of the moment when those acorns had pattered to the ground, when the fen had been a forest roamed by strange beasts. Jonathan was like that: he had never forgotten once setting his foot upon a Roman causeway that had been unearthed in a potato-field, and how the sheer thought of it had made his heart race — though he would have been embarrassed to tell anyone of this. The black trunk that was protruding from Mr Langtoft's field was more than fifty feet long: one end had been dug completely clear of the peat, and Mr Langtoft and Chad, by means of great labour with axes, wedges and sledgehammers, at last succeeded in cutting off a ten-foot length and hitching it up with rope to the waiting plough-team to be dragged off to the yard and there broken up or burned. "Twouldn't be so bad if there were some use to the awkud ole stuff," Mr Langtoft said, before leading the horses away. "Must be the only thing as comes out of the ground thass no use to anybody — but there, I suppose the Almighty must ha' known what he was doing, though I'm beggared if I can see it."

Jonathan, with the Langtoft sons, continued digging round the remainder of the black oak, and became absorbed with speculations on what primeval disaster of climate, wind or wave could have felled all the trees. He was roused by the sound of swift wheels, and looked up to see Lyle Saunders pulling up his pony-and-trap on the high-road above. He was dressed for leisure, in a Norfolk jacket with a light bowler: he raised his gloved hand to them affably and said, "Morning, morning, how's everybody? Chad, about that business at the Labour In Vain. I hope we're still friends. No hard feelings — eh?"

Chad, suspending his spade, looked at Lyle for some time before answering, "Your wife's already said sorry about that, as it happens."

"Did she?" Lyle said. "Well, anyway, accept my apologies too."

"I wun't tek nothing from you," Chad said.

Lyle's eyebrows lifted a little. "Please yourself."

"And here — I'll tell you another thing," Chad said cumbrously. Jonathan wished he would stop; it was folly: to see him glowering up at Lyle Saunders was like seeing some dull and sullen dog barking at a canny cat high on a fence. "I tell you — you don't deserve the wife you're got."

"Ha, ha! Well, Chad," Lyle said lightly, "I dare say you deserve *yours*."

The flush on Chad's face was terrible to see. "You want to watch it," he cried, lifting his spade slightly, "you'll be just a bit too clever one of these days!"

"Well, there's no danger of that in your case," Lyle said, laughing and flicking the reins.

"You watch it!" Chad called as the trap rattled away, brandishing the spade. Jonathan put a restraining hand on his arm. "Steady," Jonathan said. "No call for that."

Chad shook him off with a resentful stare. "It's nowt to do with you," he said. "It ain't your business." He turned and resumed his digging, energetically, with tight mouth and blank eyes.

Jonathan shrugged, said good-day to the two boys and continued on his way to Stokeley: it was, as Chad had said, none of his business. In the town, after meeting the Drainage Commissioners, he hurried down Infirmarer's Street with his wages dancing in his pocket — telling himself that one second-hand book wouldn't break him, and that his patched shirt would last a while yet. After a long combing of the bookstall he settled on Kingsley's *Hereward the Wake*; and he was looking into it as he took a short cut down a narrow alley that led to the High Street. The alley, bounded by fragments of ancient wall, opened at one point to a double yard: on one side belonging to the Hand and Heart public house, on the other to a firm dealing in agricultural implements. There was no fence or wall dividing the two premises, and the ploughs and harrows seemed to defend their half of the yard with a display of bared iron teeth. On the pub side there were several carts and light carriages; and Jonathan, looking up from his book, caught sight of Lyle Saunders, beside his pony and trap. He was with a girl — they were both patting the pony, and smiling — and the girl was not Hester.

Jonathan was past the mouth of the yard almost before this had sunk in. He wavered — he experienced a moment of hatred for himself, but it was no good — he had to step back, and look again. Lyle was helping the girl up into the trap. She was young, pretty, smartly dressed in a tailor-made costume with broad lapels and flared skirts. As she climbed up Lyle darted a kiss at her hand: she drew it back with mock reproach, and they both laughed.

Jonathan went quickly on his way, fumbling his book into his pocket, and bumping into several people in his haste. Not until he was past the Abbey ruins, and striking the high-road out to Hinching Fen, did he slow his pace: and then he sternly tackled himself for his reaction. He had seen Lyle, at the least, flirting: what then? Wasn't that, too, none of his business? But he could not dismiss it: he felt sick and shaken as if he had seen someone run down in the street.

Lyle hadn't seemed to care — somehow that

was the awful thing. It wasn't furtive — there they were in broad daylight in the little town of Stokeley, where anyone might see. Had others seen such things, and told them? Rumour blew about the fen like dandelion-seed.

Jonathan felt himself to be up against something for which he had no ready responses. Perhaps he was a prig — perhaps other folk would laugh. And part of him went down like a bull's horns, saying: reject it; forget it; live to yourself, and let these people get all mired and entangled if they want, and thank the stars you're out of it — it just shows what a fool's game it all is. Yet what he had seen demanded more of him — his heart demanded more of him than this.

"She must never hear of it," he said to himself with decision; "and she shall never hear it from me." For there was the memory of a treasured vision to which he still owed a loyal duty, if nothing more.

2

IT was so unusual for Hester and Lyle to do anything together nowadays that when he came shopping with her in St Ives one May afternoon the occasion seemed to her to wear something of the aspect of a holiday. Once in the town, he left her to go and see a man who had a pony for sale — though there was one in the stables at home that he had bought to train and still not sold; but she would not allow herself to protest. It had dawned on her the other day that she might be worsening the strain between them by becoming a nag: moreover those stupid parting words of Chad's — *I could tell you a thing or two about* him — had stayed with her, and she felt that she must not give in to the malicious poison of them by seeming to reproach or mistrust her husband in any way. It was a sadly subdued and chastened condition that Hester thus found herself in, and she could not help but be conscious of the change in herself, from the carefree girl who had gaily gone away to the sea with her new husband last year: but the weather was warm, Lyle was in a good mood, and she was managing to shoe-horn her mind into a moderately cheerful groove as she returned down the High Street to meet Lyle with the trap, when she saw Westerby, the seedsman, hailing her from the door of his shop.

"Quite unseasonably warm, ain't it, Mrs

Saunders?" Mr Westerby said, scooping a fat finger under his stiff collar. "I'm glad I happened to catch you — I wouldn't dream of mentioning it under normal circumstances, but if I might just draw your attention to something — my bill, in short."

"Oh!" Hester said.

"As I say, I wouldn't normally mention it — not so public-like — only it's outstanding, you see — it's outstanding something alarming; and Mr Saunders wrote me some time ago that he'd be coming to see me about it."

"And hasn't he?" Hester said.

" . . . No, Mrs Saunders," the seedsman said, after a painful pause, in which he seemed to search desperately for some gentler word. "I'm afraid not — and I'm really going to have to insist, you know. I'm got four mouths to feed, and they don't get any smaller, or less liable to munching; and I just can't afford to give unlimited credit. Would you be so good as to mention it to Mr Saunders — and say I shall be sending another bill directly? The fifth, I'm afraid — " he winced delicately — "the fifth, Mrs Saunders."

Hester said she would see to it that the bill was paid: and went on to find Lyle waiting for her with the trap in Spread Eagle Yard, quaffing a glass of beer. "Devil of a thirst," he said. "All done?"

They set out for home, Hester taking the reins. It was still and humid, and the sunlight, though bright, had a tarnished look about it; and there was a sullen haziness about the horizons which seemed to presage an unsettled end to the long fine spell. Hester waited until they were out on the high-road, and then told Lyle what the seedsman had said.

"That was a bit of a cheek, catching you in the street like that," Lyle said.

"Is he right, though, Lyle?"

"Eh? Oh! he might be — to be honest, I thought I'd paid that bill. We'll have to look when we get home. It won't hurt him to wait a bit longer, anyhow — he's not short of a few bob."

"But — " Hester bit her tongue, and applied herself to her driving. Lyle enjoyed having his own coachwoman, he said, but as usual when they came to the main drain he took over the reins. The sleeper-bridge over the main drain, which was wide and deep as a small river, was narrow and unfenced, and though Hester had been over it umpteen times on her own, Lyle never quite trusted her steering just here.

"Those huge Belgian horses would never do in these parts," Lyle said as they rumbled across. "I reckon they'd go through these little bridges like matchwood." His mind had been running on Belgium lately; and when they got home she had to remind him about the seedsman's bills.

"Oh! yes," he said, and extricated a wad of unsorted papers from the old roll-top desk in the parlour. Humming a waltz, he went through them. "Ta-da, ta-da, ta-yom-pom-pom — what is that one? Is it 'Wine, Women and Song', or 'Vienna Blood'? Ah, my apologies to Westerby — here it is. Well, I could have sworn I'd paid

460

that in. Oh! well, I'll pay it next week."

"He did say it was urgent," Hester said timidly.

"They always do, my dear. Ah, there's that letter from Mr Dielman. Wants to know when he'll see me in Brussels again. God! it would be good to have a holiday. I don't see why I can't manage it . . . You'd love Brussels, Hes."

"Yes," she murmured; but at that moment she felt anything but yes. Who said she would love Brussels? She hated being simply told she would love something like that. She retrieved the seedsman's bill from where he had pushed it aside. It was more than she thought.

Lyle was absently arranging the papers into a fan shape. "I don't see why we shouldn't go after the harvest. And Ostend, it's very smart there . . . "

Suddenly Hester had a terrible dizzying feeling of looking down a precipice. Her husband was an arm's length away, and yet a chasm lay between them. Here they were with not even the seedsman's bills from months ago paid — and, she guessed, without the wherewithal to pay them — and Lyle was talking about jaunts to Belgium! The realisation entered her, like a burning lance, that she and the man she loved, in that sun-smelling wainscoted room, were dwellers in two different worlds: that while she stood close enough to him to feel the emanated warmth of his flesh, his mind and hers were moving in such widely separated orbits that it seemed impossible they should ever touch. She recoiled from the horror of it; and in recoiling grew angry.

"And there's Ghent — absolute fairy-tale of a place — God! it'll be good to get away," Lyle was saying dreamily. Hester snatched up the bills, and carrying them away said curtly: "Perhaps you should take Mr Westerby with you — in lieu of paying his bill."

As she stalked away there was a moment of surprised silence behind her, followed by a gust of laughter.

Later that evening she saw Lyle looking at the latest letter from the bank, and presently he said, impatiently crumpling it up, "Well, it doesn't look as if there's any chance of a holiday this year, anyhow."

Repenting a little of her sharpness, she said, "We could manage a break nearer home perhaps, Lyle: down to Bournemouth again — or the east coast, Cromer or somewhere — "

He gave a loud mirthless chuckle. "Hardly worth it. From one cage to another." He glanced at his watch. "Think I'll go over to the Labour In Vain for a spell." He had slipped out, in his limber way, before she could answer.

He was not yet back when she went to bed and lay, with the covers thrown back for coolness, staring at the dormer-slope above her. While she felt still her severance from Lyle, and bleakly contemplated the way their inclinations seemed to face away from each other like two plants opening to two different suns, yet as she stretched out in the sultry darkness she longed, almost with an ache of amputation, to have him beside her. She could no more cease to give

462

love than a spring cease to give water; and a single gesture of love from him would have been like a word spoken in a canyon, echoing back manifold in a joyous shout. She had sunk into a doze when she heard the iron bed creak and felt Lyle climbing in beside her: stirring, she turned over and put her arms round him, fitting herself to his slender, hipless body.

After a few moments he twitched, and said over his shoulder: "Hes, I can't sleep when you maul me about like that."

She disengaged herself, and resumed her staring at the lowering roof above.

★ ★ ★

The next morning Lyle was away early with the trap, taking the new pony he had bought and groomed: there was a possible buyer for it in Huntingdon, he told her. Something about his manner suggested that he was going to see his mother; but the morning was so airless and oppressive, with May-time thunderiness, that Hester had not the spirit to challenge him. Listlessly she went about her tasks, baking a batch of bread, feeding the hens and the pigs, mucking out the stables; and when she was returning to the house across the yard she saw the first stroke of lightning arc across the swollen sky above her head, clear as a vein in a clenched arm. Within the house it was as dark as dusk. Hester swept the hearth and tidied the parlour, listening to the thunder rolling around the horizons. Carefully she dusted the china cat

463

which stood on the mantelpiece. It was a thing she loved: Lyle had bought it for her on their honeymoon, when it had seemed to catch her eye through the shop window with its artful expression; something about it always made her feel happy and amused. As she was gathering up her brushes and dusters Edie Smeeth came bouncing in and said in her best parlour-maid voice: "Here's some chap to see you, missus — I dunno who."

It was a little stout stooped man with a few strands of hair scraped over a liver-spotted scalp. "How do, missus," he said, briefly showing tobacco-brown teeth. "Cresswell's the name. It's Mr Lyle Saunders I'm after — is he about?"

"No, he's out," Hester said. "Can I help?"

"Know when he'll be back?"

"No."

"Well, I'll have to wait, then — I'll not be put off now," grunted the man, glancing around the parlour.

"What's it about?"

"It's about a bay pony — thass what. A bay pony what I sold to Mr Lyle Saunders."

"Oh! that one. But that was a long while ago — Lyle sold it to someone in Stokeley."

"Did he indeed! Well he'd no right, missus: he still ain't paid me for it — thass what."

"I don't understand — "

"It's plain enough," the man said, breathing stertorously through his nose, and continuing to look all round him. "Mr Lyle Saunders paid a deposit down, with an engagement to pay the rest later. Which he ain't done — and

464

I'm been trying to track him down for long enough — thass what. I ain't going to be put off now — I want my money, and I shan't go away without it. I'll wait here while he turns up, if it's all the same to you."

"No, it ain't all the same to me," Hester said, more disquieted than she cared to show. "I don't know when he'll be back — and I'm got work to do — "

"I can't help that, missus," said Cresswell. "I'll not be diddled any more. Your husband's got to come home some time, and I'll wait while bull's noon if I have to — I reckon it's the only way I'll get hold of him. He's a slippery one — it's like trying to git hold of a Eel — thass what!"

"It must be a mistake. I can't believe Lyle didn't mean to pay you the money," Hester said; but she knew she was lying.

"I don't know nothink about that. All I know is my money's in his pocket, and I ain't going home till I'm seen him. I'm sorry, missus: you needn't think of fetching somebody to put me out, as I ain't in the mood to be put out. I shan't git in your way, but I shan't go neither."

Hester stared at him a moment. There was no doubting he meant it. "You'd better sit down then," she faintly said.

"Shall I tek your 'at?" said Edie; but Cresswell tucked his bowler carefully under his arm. "No, ta, gel," he said, lowering himself on to the edge of a chair. "I'll keep it by me: it ain't that I don't trust you, but I'm been robbed enough — thass what."

Hester answered Edie's questioning gaze with a slight shrug. "You'd best start dinner, Edie," she said. "I'll be along to help you soon. If our visitor don't object."

Thunder sounded above the house, like a hammering at awful gates, and almost immediately following it came the lightning, filling the parlour with an instant of unhealthy light and throwing a spindly black shadow behind every stick of furniture. The sky at the window was the colour of a damson, but there was no sign of rain yet, and the low-ceilinged house was so stifling that even the carved settles and Windsor-chairs seemed to exhibit a sheen of sweat. Cresswell sat stolidly, nursing his bowler hat, and trying to ignore the perspiration that trickled down his temples, as if even that might be a ruse to deflect him from his purpose.

"Mr Saunders never owes him money like he says — never!" hissed Edie in the kitchen, her crisp curls, in the electrified atmosphere, seeming to bristle with indignation.

Hester glanced down the passage at Cresswell. "Well, I don't know him — but I dare say there's — I dare say there's some explanation." She felt like a traitor, for instinctively she believed the man: instinctively she knew Lyle owed him money; and though she hated him for coming here like this, it was mainly because he had thus revealed to her what she tried to deny — that she could not and did not trust Lyle.

The sky palpitated with hot thunder. The heavy charged air lay like a suffocating sheepskin across the fen. Hester went outside to shut away

466

the agitated hens, and found Cresswell following her. "No offence, missus," he said. "But I can't let you out of my sight. You're my only link to that there Eel." He flinched as there was a crack overhead as if a giant vault had been blasted open, and a sulphurous flourish of lightning seemed to scrawl down from the highest heavens to within an inch of the stable roof. "I'd advise you to go in, missus, any road."

"Well, I don't know — I'm got work to do out here," said Hester, with devilment, seeing he was frightened. But a moment later the first raindrops, fat as falling fruit, hit the cobbles of the yard, and she was forced to run in.

Dinner was on, and the house sweltered. In the parlour Hester tried to settle to some mending, whilst Cresswell perspired and fidgeted on the chair opposite her. The pounding of the rain drowned out the heavy tick of the old Dutch clock, and at the window nothing could be seen but a glistening screen of water, as if it must be descending in some more voluminous form than mere raindrops. The air had scarcely cooled, and Hester's sensation of oppression, of being hardly able to breathe, mounted into a more specific feeling of resentment. Trapped — that was what she was — trapped here, watched over as if by a policeman, whilst Lyle — well, what was Lyle doing? Dancing attendance on his mother, trying to wheedle his way back into her good books, the very thing he had said he wouldn't do? Furiously she flung down the sewing and went to throw open the window, not caring whether the rain came in, desperate for a breath of air. As she did so she saw the trap coming up the drive.

"That's him, is it?" Cresswell said, and hurried to meet him in the hall.

Hester stayed where she was. She heard them arguing for some time, Lyle's voice at first light and cordial and evasive, until it sharpened at last. "All right . . . damn it, you'll get it, I tell you, you'll get it!" There was the sound of the door being opened, Cresswell shouting "Ten days, mind! Else I'll tek it to law — " and then a slam. It was faintly echoed by a last dying growl of thunder in the distance. A few minutes later Lyle came in, having run upstairs to change out of his wet clothes, rubbing his hair with a towel.

"That's all I need," he said, "that silly old fool dunning me just when I get home soaked to the skin. Why didn't you get rid of him?"

"I couldn't," she said.

"You shouldn't let these people in — that's the trick of it. It's when you let 'em past the door that the trouble starts. If — "

"You do owe him that money then?"

He looked at her for the first time, alerted by her tone: then resumed his towelling. "He's a daft old beggar. He'll get it eventually. He's not a professional, that's his trouble — just does a bit of horse-dealing on the side — "

"Unlike you," Hester said, "who do a bit of farming on the side."

Lyle's eyebrows went up. "Who rattled your cage this morning, Hes?"

"Nobody. I just don't like feeling like a prisoner in my own home." She was going

468

to cause a scene: she couldn't help it; she was smarting so, with frustration and indignation and sheer weariness at the way their life was going. "And finding out from a stranger how much we're in debt. While you're out as usual doing God knows what — while you just let the farm and everything we planned for go to pot, never thinking of how we're going to manage . . . I want this place to work, but I can't do it all on my own — it just seems you don't even want to try, your mind's never here at all — "

"Leave off, for God's sake, Hes," Lyle said, "I've had enough damn discouragement for one day."

He began violently to brush his hair, tugging at the tangles.

"You're been to your mother's, haven't you?" she said quietly.

"Oh! if you say so. You seem to know so much about me."

"You have, Lyle — haven't you?"

"All right," he snapped. "I've been to my mother's. Not a crime, is it?"

"You didn't tell me," she said. Her heart, racing a moment ago, seemed to have slowed to a sluggish labouring. "Did you see her?"

"No, I didn't, as a matter of fact," Lyle said, with a sort of stubborn neutrality. "She wouldn't see me."

"When you married me," Hester said carefully, "you said it didn't matter about your mother — it was me you wanted and it didn't matter if she cut you off. And now you wear yourself thin trying week after week to win her round, while

I keep this place going . . . And she *still* won't see you. Don't you see, Lyle — you'll never do it! You can't beat her — she meant what she said. You burnt your bridges. Why won't you accept that?"

"Well, by God, you needn't sound so pleased about it," said Lyle in a pinched voice. "I swear you're glad you separated me from my own family!"

"I did?" she breathed.

"Yes, who else?" With a chill briskness Lyle marched over to examine his reflection in the mirror over the mantelpiece. "You're always going on at me not to go there. You seem to get some odd pleasure out of splitting us up. It was you who rushed things — pestering me to marry you before I could work Mother round to the idea. You were determined to drive a wedge between us. Well, I hope you're satisfied, my dear, because it's your doing. If I'm in a mess, it's your doing."

A quiver ran through her: she felt the injustice like a physical assault; but more horribly and profoundly, in that moment, she had seemed to see the image of Gideon in the figure of Lyle standing stiffly before the mirror — had seemed to see, in a ghastly flash like the lightning that had passed, an incarnation of self looking at self, obsessed with self, able to see nothing but endless self. She felt paralysed; and all the words she could pronounce were those that flared like a firework in her mind: "It's almost as if you wish you'd never married me!"

Lyle gave her a sardonic glance. "Never mind

470

the *almost*, my dear," he said.

Hester fled. She ran from the parlour, but still the walls of the Crooked House seemed to crowd in on her, like a tightening ring of hostile presences; and, gasping with distress, she flung open the door and ran out into the rain.

The storm was over, and the weird coppery light had been replaced by a uniform murk of sombre cloud fitted over the fen like an upturned bowl. The drove down which Hester ran was pitted with wheel-ruts, and was turning momently to a cocoa-coloured ooze. On all sides the further fields could barely be seen for the rippling distortion of the rain, which fell bouncing in the dyke like coins dropped on a table-top, and formed before Hester's eyes a shimmering mass, shaken here and there by stirring currents of breeze, so that serpentine shapes seemed to writhe for an instant through the corridors of water. Hester had run out just as she was in her day-dress and apron; as she came to the end of the drove and splashed out on to the high-road her mud-soaked skirts were as heavy as mail, and her hair was clinging in thick tendrils to her face. She was crying without being properly aware of it — crying as though she would never know content again; and just as the tears were indistinguishable from the rain on her cheeks, she could scarcely tell what it was she was feeling. She stumbled along the road in a sort of trance, in which existence and wretchedness seemed conterminous, and her body had detached itself from her will.

At last a pothole tripped her, and she nearly

fell, just saving herself with her hands: the jolt awakened her a little, and though the thought of returning to the Crooked House was unbearable, some renascent voice of rationality protested at the miserable drenching, and urged her to shelter. The prospect was bare but for a large, solitary elm tree beside the road up ahead, and ducking her head she began to run to it.

A tree in the fens, often standing utterly single and alone in a low flat expanse, its outline sharply delineated, retains thus something of the primal potency it bore for our ancestors, for whom its shape might express a giant, a transformed mortal, or a god. To Hester's eyes, streaming and half-blinded, the spreading branches of the tree gave a strong impression of generous, protective arms waiting to receive her: sobbing violently, and at the end of her breath, she staggered beneath the dripping canopy of leaves and flung herself against the thick trunk, half embracing it, feeling the ridged bark like a great hide beneath her hands. Looking up, she found herself completely roofed-in by foliage which, immature as it was, kept the ground immediately at her feet as dry as a sanded floor. As she gazed higher, her distress was riven for a moment by the sight of those leaves, bright spring green and tender, springing forth from the aged tree: in the bole and limbs was all the gnarled solidity of age, with great lumps and knots that on a human body would have appeared as the most hideous abscesses — yet this ugliness, every year through long lifetimes, yielded at its finger-ends the feathery freshness of a sapling. She was momentarily transfixed by a disconnected and childlike sense of wonder; and then she heard for the first time her own stuttering sobs, again like a child, that grows weary of crying. She tried to wipe her eyes on her sleeve, and through blurred lashes saw all at once that she was not alone.

On the other side of the tree-bole stood Jonathan, sheltering from the rain: that she had not seen him was accounted for not only by her blinding distress but by his extreme stillness, a stillness scarcely less deep and rooted than that of the ancient tree. There was a reason for it: for as Hester met his gaze, he said quietly, "Don't move," and signalled with his eyes to a spot a few feet away.

"Oh!" she said, involuntarily drawing back her skirts — for an adder was moving noiselessly through the grass, a spade's-length from her feet.

"Keep still — it's all right," Jonathan said in the same calm and soothing voice. Adders were quite common in the fens, turf-diggers coming across them daily, but Hester greatly feared them, and her breath died in her throat. Jonathan, seeming to sense this, reached out and gently gripped her upper arm, which his large hand entirely enclosed so that middle finger and thumb touched, holding her still until the snake had slipped away into the field below.

Jonathan's hand left her arm, and then was back again, proffering a handkerchief. He was silent while Hester wiped her face: she could not look at him. The rain fell in a steady hiss, deepening to a papery, drumming sound on the layers of leaves above them.

"Is there something I can do?" Jonathan said at length.

Hester shook her head, and her sobs burst out afresh. She didn't know what sort of spectacle she must present, or what Jonathan must be thinking; but obviously he could see much was amiss.

"It isn't anything," she stammered, muffled in his handkerchief. "It's just — it's just sometimes . . . "

"Yes, I know," said he gravely, as if she had said something eminently coherent and reasonable.

"I — must seem — a terrible fool," she gasped, trying to control herself.

"No."

"I don't know — what it is. Sometimes — things . . . " But she did know what it was: she felt at that moment as if innocence had died from the world for ever.

"It's all right," Jonathan said; and again his voice, deep as a cello, seemed to instil a great calm. All at once she abandoned trying to explain things away: she felt with relief that he did not demand it, any more than the great unquestioning presence of the tree did.

"It's clearing," he said. "Look."

He pointed to where a corner of the sky was pierced by a diagonal rod of pale light, like a ray through a chink in curtains. Just then such a naked emblem of hope seemed more mocking than genuine, but she nodded, and forced herself to take a deep breath, inhaling the bracing scent of earth quickened by rain. "Yes," she said, leaning against the bole of the tree, "it's clearing."

Jonathan looked at her and hesitated. "Shall I leave you?" he said.

She nodded, her lips pressed together. "I — I'll stay out here a while."

"All right." He paused. "You're soaked. Don't take cold — go in soon."

"I will . . . Jonathan!" she cried as he started to go.

"Yes?"

"You won't tell anyone you — saw me like this — will you?" Pride was all that remained to her: somehow he was the only person she could bear having been a witness to her distress. "Please — I don't want anyone to . . . "

"I won't say a word," Jonathan said. "On my honour." This strange phrase seemed natural coming from his lips. "I'll leave you now."

She stayed for some time after he had gone, her face against the bark of the tree, until the rain had stopped, and the sun, gilding the dispersing clouds, threw brilliant reflections of its handiwork into the broad puddles on the high-road. When at last she pushed back her wet hair and began the walk back to the Crooked House, it seemed to her like a new journey to a strange place — for she could not think of it as a return to home.

★ ★ ★

Half an hour after he had left her, Jonathan went back to the elm tree by the roadside: he had a misgiving, having seen the state she was in, that she might still be there in those drenched clothes, and he was relieved to find she had gone. He paused a while to contemplate the site of that meeting: for here he had felt a great temptation. As he beheld Hester's tear-stained face, and her throat pulsing like that of a singing bird, he had suddenly thought of asking her: was it worth it? It was plain whence her unhappiness came: did she know what her husband was up to? He had seemed to see in her the first painful tearing of the veil of illusion, and a savage wish had gone through him to rip it apart completely.

Jonathan had scaled down his own hopes and desires, which had been as strong as unexpressed, and this violent impulse had alarmed him — it threatened the temperate detachment which he had made his refuge. Fortunately, his sense of honour towards Hester had prevented him speaking out; fortunately, he had felt the influence of nothing more than that: and the thing he did not want reawakened slept on, a sleep indistinguishable from death.

★ ★ ★

In the Crooked House Hester knew how it felt to be a ghost — to haunt with longing frustration the scenes of former happiness.

Superficially there was no need for this. In the aftermath of their quarrel she and Lyle settled down to normal life together just as they had done before. He was not cruel to her — not even unpleasant: he was not short or snide with her, or continually harking back to what had been said. He was airily casual and easy as ever. There was nothing to mark this off from any other passage in their married life, except for the kernel of conviction, at the centre of Hester's consciousness, that her husband hated her.

His resentment seemed to her to fill the rooms like a noxious vapour, which she inhaled on first waking, and which lingered in her nostrils even as she drifted into sleep at night. There was nothing she could do to dispel it; nothing she could say to him that would not come out as reproaches, and provoke in its turn the utterly unjust and yet utterly unanswerable reproach that she had trapped him into a life he found insupportable.

Nothing to be done here; but in Stokeley, it seemed to her, there was something she could do — one lone and difficult chance that, after three intolerable days of terrible, seething calm, she knew she must take. She would go and see Mrs Saunders, whose long shadow fell blightingly on their marriage — see her, and set things straight once and for all. She would confront her with a choice — forgive Lyle and make it up with him, or signal to him as she had yet failed to do that he had nothing to hope from her. The cat-and-mouse game she was playing was futile: it was doing nothing but poisoning their marriage at its roots; and Hester could still not believe — refused to believe — that such was what Mrs Saunders single-mindedly and maliciously sought.

She walked across the fields to Stokeley at mid-morning. Looking up at the Saunders house before she knocked, she remembered her days here as a companion-help — remote as schooldays they seemed now — and she wondered that it had never occurred to her then just how grim and aloof this house was, with its louring eaves, massive stanchions, and high narrow windows, so heavily curtained they gave an impression of eyes blindfolded for some sinister purpose.

"OH dear," Judy exclaimed on seeing Hester, "I'm not sure as the mistress can SEE you I'm sure but I'll INQUIRE if you'd be so GOOD as to wait, ahem!"

There was a smell of paint in the hall, and dust-covers on the furniture. Judy returning led Hester through to the dining-room, where she found decorators at work, and Mrs Saunders hovering watchfully about their stepladders, as if even the painting of picture-rails could not go forward without some subtle plan to cheat her manifesting itself sooner or later.

"What do you want here, gel?" Mrs Saunders said, betraying no surprise even if she felt it.

"I want to speak to you, please, Mrs Saunders," Hester said. Mrs Saunders — her own name — how mad it was!

"Do you!" Mrs Saunders glanced round at the decorators. "Oh, well. Judy, you keep an eye on 'em. I shan't be long. Come in here."

Mrs Saunders led Hester through to the

adjoining room — the winter parlour, a small room that was seldom used. This too was all emptied, sheeted and stripped for redecoration: and Hester remembered long afterwards the way her mother-in-law had received her in a blank room, without so much as a chair.

"High time we had this place redecorated," Mrs Saunders said. "Not that I shall pay what these chaps are asking — they needn't think I will. Well, what is it?"

Hester looked at the long sallow mask of a face. Had the lines grown deeper and harsher, or was that her own doubts deceiving her?

"I don't rightly know how to say it — straight out," Hester began.

"Can't be worth saying, then, I reckon," snapped Mrs Saunders. "Something to do with Lyle, is it? Here — " suddenly there was a flash of vulnerability — "there's nothing up with him, is there?"

"No — well, yes, there is. That's what I come to see you about. Lyle ain't right, he ain't right at all, because of the way things are — between us and you, Mrs Saunders."

"Us?" she said heavily, sour again now.

"The way things are," Hester said, trying to stay composed. "He ain't right because of — well, because of falling out with you."

"I told him," Mrs Saunders said with contempt. "I told him what would happen — he wouldn't listen. That's all."

Hester ignored this. "He wants to make it up with you, Mrs Saunders. He wants it more than anything, I know. I want that too, because

479

. . . Mrs Saunders, I'm come to ask you — look, I'm begging you — make it up with Lyle, please. All right, he went against your will, and he's suffered for it — we both have — so please, forgive and forget. Be friends again, for God's sake."

"That's what you've come to ask, is it?" Mrs Saunders said.

"Not just that. Something else. If you can't forgive and forget, then say so. Finish it, and let us lead our own lives. Don't keep him hanging on all the time — forever looking for a way back that ain't there. I know you can't like me — but you must love Lyle — and he ain't happy, and surely, surely, that's not what you want."

Her words had the curious distinct flatness of wrenchingly deep feeling: they seemed to exhaust her.

"That's it, is it?" Mrs Saunders said crisply. "Well, you've got sense, gel, because, like you say, there's no way back for that boy of mine. And if he doesn't know that — if he doesn't know me well enough by now — then it's no good me telling him. You tell him, gel." Her eyes had the bright pitiless gleam of broken glass. "He's yours now. It's your job to tell him he's got nothing to hope for but that piddling farm and your face looking at him over the bread-and-seam. Tell him, and see how he likes it. See who he blames."

"You don't love him," breathed Hester. "You really don't love your son at all, do you?"

"Love, love, that's all you folk ever think about, spooning and slobbering and canoodling!"

480

cried Mrs Saunders, flaring up for the first time. "It doesn't mean a thing! I always thought Lyle realised that — till you came along, spoiling it all! And see what it's got you!"

Hester turned away; and found herself saying, as if the protest was torn from her not against the stubborn old woman but against the tyranny of fate: "I always meant well — always!"

Mrs Saunders opened the door. "You needn't bother coming again," she said. "You know your way out."

Hester stared into her mother-in-law's face: stared, in the last hope of detecting some flicker of hesitation, of doubt, of remorse. But she was the first to drop her eyes — it was like staring at a portrait. She opened her mouth to speak, then closed it with a snap and swept past her.

She was walking blind when she wrenched open the front door, and in the porch she collided with Gideon, just coming in.

"What the devil are you doing here?" he said, patting down his cravat as if she had spoiled it.

"God knows," she said. He smelt of whisky, and his eyes were bloodshot. He looked drawn and irritable — more ground-down than ever, in fact — and it struck Hester that since Lyle's leaving, Gideon had probably come in for much of Mrs Saunders' resentment and bitterness. His next remark confirmed that.

"Well, don't expect me to give you a welcome," he said. "You've caused enough trouble here already."

She brushed past him. His little eyes followed

481

her, and as she reached the gate he said, "Didn't last long anyway, did it? — I suppose you know Lyle's been carrying on with any little piece that catches his eye. I saw him in Huntingdon with a girl just the other day — he didn't even bother to hide it."

"Well, they're in no danger from *you*, that's for sure," she said venomously, and stalked away down the street without looking back.

The answer seemed to have risen to her lips quite independently of her mind, which was reeling groggily back from the blow. Her body too was working like an automaton, and it had taken her briskly across the fields half-way home before she came to herself.

She stood still a moment on the field-path. On all sides the green fen was empty. The wind boomed and mumbled in her ears, the wind that blew from a far continent across great tracts of naked land and yet seemed to bring its muttered secrets to her solitary consciousness alone. As she recovered from the shock, a little faint-heart voice within her was advising: forget it — ignore it. Just Gideon's spite. And what Chad had hinted too — coincidence. Pretend you never heard it, and stay sane.

But she would not be convinced, for the plain reason that as soon as Gideon had spoken, she had believed, and though her heart cried out in anguish at her mind's betrayal, she believed still. She could not deny the truthfulness of her own nature though she wanted to, and in the same way she could not deny that her trust in Lyle was gone. And yet in the same instant she knew

482

— with a sort of despair in the knowledge — that her love for Lyle persisted, not one whit the less: indeed the terrible insinuation seemed to drive her love for him deeper into the aching vitals of her self, like a dagger thrust deeper into flesh.

"Oh Lyle!" Involuntarily she spoke aloud. She looked up, and was almost tempted to cry her pain to the skies; but instead she breathed deeply and carried on walking. In Hester a seam of adamant existed deep beneath the layers of easy pliability; and she had struck its tough face now, in a conscious refusal to bow to fate. The faint-heart voice had told her to be passive, to hide, to go under, but Hester walked hardily on to the Crooked House, nourished by a determination to do none of those things, and to save her marriage. Lyle, she knew now, was the sort to yield when things did not go well: all right, she accepted that; she would have to do it alone.

And she would have to confront him. She dreaded it, but she dreaded delay even more, and she hardly knew what to do with herself when she found he was not home. At last she made herself sit, quite still, in the parlour, with her hands in her lap, and thus she waited until in the late afternoon she heard the sound of the trap in the yard, and Lyle came in.

"Hullo, love. Wait till you see what I've got. Picked it up for a song," he said. He had a parcel under his arm, which he unwrapped before her, revealing a framed print — a Regency horse-rider taking a fence. "Nice thing, isn't it? Worth what I paid just for the frame." He began holding it up at various places around the parlour and examining the effect. "How about here?"

"Yes."

He glanced round at her. "You're quiet," he said. "Had a hard day?"

"Yes, in a way." She clenched her hands together. "I went to see your mother this morning."

He froze: with his back to her he said, "You did what?"

"I went to Stokeley to see your mother."

He turned round: his cheeks had gone pink. "What the hell did you do that for?"

"I went to try and sort things out," she said, forcing herself to look him full in the face. "Because we can't go on the way things are, with you and her. It's ruining everything — "

"You bloody little fool!" stormed Lyle, putting the print down with shaking hands: Hester flinched. "How dare you go interfering between me and my mother!"

"You're married to me — not her," she said, keeping her voice level. "And as long as you're being pulled both ways there's no hope for us. That's why I went to see her — to ask her to settle it one way or the other."

Lyle put his knuckles on his hips and stared down at her. "So, you've finally done your best to turn my mother against me, have you, Hes? Get what you've always wanted."

"That ain't fair — "

"Don't you ever go there again, do you hear me? Not ever." Lyle's voice had gone as thin

484

and tindery as the crackling of brushwood.

"I won't," she said, her breast heaving even as she gripped the arms of the chair and tried to hold on to the calm she had instilled in herself. "Not because you say so — because she treated me like muck."

"What did you expect?" Lyle snapped. He paced over to the mirror, glared a moment at his burning reflection, then turned edgily round to her, punching his clenched hands into his pockets. "Well, that little contribution of yours must have just about finished my prospects. You've pretty well wrecked my life, you know, Hes," he said, in a ghastly echo of a conversational tone. "This marriage. Oh, I'm not saying it wouldn't have been a viable proposition, later on, if we'd waited. But you wouldn't wait, you pushed me into it. I had smart prospects, I had a future — but you pushed me into losing the lot."

Even at this she somehow clung on to her calm, and her voice was as steady as her gaze into his smoke-blue eyes as she said, "I never pushed you into meeting other girls, though."

Lyle was still, his head on one side like a listening cat. "What's that supposed to mean?"

"Gideon told me. Something about you and a girl, in Huntingdon." She swallowed down a monstrous indignation that rose in her throat like acid. "Is it true?"

"So you believe Gideon's word rather than mine, is that it?" Lyle said.

"I just want to know the truth."

Lyle shrugged and moved restively away.

485

"What shall I say? I dare say he did see me with a girl. I'm trying to sell her that pony I bought. She rides, she's got money. She needs buttering up a bit. It doesn't mean anything. It's nothing serious. I'm not a serious person, Hes. That's the way it is. You knew that when you married me. You just have to take me as I am. You didn't suppose you were getting some hymn-singing model of virtue, did you? Isn't it enough that you've got me here in this damn cage? My God, I need to break out of it sometimes, and remember what it's like to enjoy myself."

Hester stared at her husband, with the hallucinatory feeling that he was simply not seeing her — that she was really not there at all — that she was melting into vapour. Struggling still to be practical, to outface the crisis, she said: "Tell me you won't see that girl again."

Lyle did not answer: he walked to the door.

"Where are you going?" she said.

"Out."

"Lyle — tell me you won't see her!"

"Eh? Don't be ridiculous," he said casually.

"Please — Lyle, don't go like that — wait," she cried, springing up and running to him. Tears were trickling down her face: for all at once poor Hester had lost the fight with herself. The pride that had sustained her had crumbled in a terrible instant of dread at the idea of Lyle's withdrawing his love: she had seen all that she cherished, all that she valued about to disappear into the abyss; and her dignity and self-respect were simply torn away by the passionate desperation that whipped through her, so that she found herself clinging to Lyle's arm and sobbing out: "Wait, Lyle — just say you love me best — please, Lyle, say you love me best!" At that moment she could no more feel shame at this abasement than a tree broken and humbled in the blast of a gale.

Lyle's face expressed the mild distaste he reserved for the display of strong emotions. "Don't start the water-works, Hes," he said. "Now I'm going out."

"Where?" she said, her hands still on his arm.

"Huntingdon maybe. Or St Ives, or Stokeley. Anywhere I can have a little fun. Remember that? It's what we don't have any more."

He disengaged himself from her hands, and opened the door. Gasping and paralysed, she watched him walk out into the hall.

"You're hateful," she said in a choked, mechanical voice to his back. "You're hateful."

He went out. Leaning her forearm on the door-jamb, covering her eyes, she heard him talking to one of the ponies as he harnessed up the trap: then at last the clatter of hooves and the rattling away of wheels. Stiffly, like a person rising from a fever-bed, she turned back into the parlour. The friendly eyes of the china cat on the mantelpiece met hers. She picked it up, with an instinctive, child-like groping for comfort. But the comfort the child within her sought, the china cat could not supply to the adult woman. She did not know whether it was because of this that she suddenly drew back her arm and, hurling the ornament against the wall, smashed it to fragments. It seemed some deeper response prompted her to thus destroy by her own hand what she loved — as if defiantly to rob the fates of their power to hurt her more, by doing it herself.

The crash brought Edie running from the kitchen. "Oh, missus — thass that sweet little cat all broke!" she cried, flinging herself down on her knees amid the pieces. "Can we glue it together?"

"I don't think so, Edie," Hester said. "I don't think it can be mended."

★ ★ ★

The recent rain had left the turf-fen as wet as a marsh, and Chad Langtoft had had a wretched muddy time of it digging in his pit early that morning. It started the day off badly. The cesses would take longer to dry now; but what chiefly irritated Chad was the fact that it made the stacks all messy, for he was a man who liked things neat. His white duck trousers were caked in slub when he went out to his father's fields for the rest of the day, and he did not like that either. Then when his dinner was barely settled in his belly he had to go out again to help with digging out the last of that stubborn bog-oak. The end of the trunk seemed to go right down to the level of the buttery clay, which made him more of a muck than ever; and it was early dusk before they had freed the oak sufficiently to begin hauling it away. It was about then that Chad looked up at the high-road above the field to see Lyle Saunders go speeding by in his pony-and-trap, all dashing and dandy in his sporty bowler and jacket, with his characteristic air of knowing not a care in the world.

"Ah! Off on the skylark again," grunted Mr Langtoft, in his mild way, watching Lyle whisk by.

"All right for some," said Chad, for whom the sight was like a final emphatic underlining of all his reasons for discontent. It was dark when at last they trudged back to the house, where Mary-Ann welcomed him by shooing him out of the kitchen.

"Git away wi' them boots — gret lumps of mud dropping all over the floor — I'm been on my knees scrubbing that this morning! Honestly, Chad, what shall I do wi' you — you are a yawnucks sometimes!" she said, bundling him away. There was more of affection in this than Chad was prepared in his present mood to see: perhaps too there was a certain insecurity in Mary-Ann's insistence on the floor that she had cleaned, for she was seldom allowed to feel she had any stake in a household of which Mrs Langtoft remained firmly the mistress. All Chad saw at that moment was his young wife giving him a dressing-down again; and the evening seemed to hold out no other prospect than more of the same, with Mary-Ann pecking on at him about when they were going to get a place of their own. Her argument was that they could afford to do so sooner if he spent less money at the Labour In Vain: but if she didn't

489

go on at him so, he wouldn't need to, was his obscurely felt rejoinder; and nothing would stop him getting his beer tonight, after the day he had had. He told her if he couldn't come into his own home in his boots, he'd go elsewhere; and set out for Milney St Mary with a growl in his stomach at having had no supper.

The Labour In Vain beamed its welcome to him as ever: though he could not get a corner seat, and this further annoyed him. A steady succession of tankards of beer, which Jass Phelps kept strong, dark and heady, did their accustomed work on Chad, floating his mind away like a boat lifted from a strand by incoming tide; and bringing him to a secure conviction, which always seemed darkly to elude him in sobriety, that he was in the right, and misunderstood. He was just about to order another pint when he heard the sound of wheels outside, and a moment later Lyle Saunders came in, cheerfully calling out greetings, and declaring his mouth felt like burnt paper.

Chad got up and slipped out, the blood thumping in his head. He refused to stay with Saunders there: that was that. Outside he saw Saunders' trap, the pony tied to the railings beside the pub, which indicated that he would probably not be staying long. But still, Chad would not go back. It ruined his drinking when Saunders was around. It ruined everything.

Chad swore — an unusual thing for him — and began to walk unsteadily down the village street. It was a deep blue starlit night,

490

the cool air laced with fresh and sappy scents of spring which under darkness seemed more potent and more acidic. As he walked Chad's resentment mounted. He had just fancied one more pint, and being robbed of that one seemed to him to cancel out the effect of all the others. His day had finished as badly as it had begun, thanks to Saunders.

He struck the empty high-road. He began to gnaw on an idea that Saunders, seeing him slinking away when he arrived, must think him a weakling. He had after all let Saunders insult him and make a fool of him, and never shown any fight at all. Fenmen were supposed to have a reputation for standing up for themselves; and Chad laboured under a smarting feeling that Saunders must be laughing up his sleeve, and thinking he was a poor sort of fenman, with no guts at all. He swore again.

He came in sight of the sleeper-bridge that crossed the main drain. This was where he normally turned to take the field-paths over to his father's farm, but instead he stopped. An accumulation of frustration throbbed at his temples. When he got home there would be the usual wigging from Mary-Ann, and meanwhile Lyle Saunders would be confirmed in his opinion of him. He resolved, or the liquor in his veins resolved, that he would salvage something out of his miserable day, and teach Mr Lyle Saunders not to laugh at him. He would wait for him, and give him what for — it was high time. He had never in his life felt so utterly ready for a scrap — it seemed the only possible thing that could equal in satisfaction that last pint he had missed.

Whenever Saunders came, he would have to cross the bridge over the drain, and there, on the far side, Chad composed himself to wait for him. Not that he reckoned Saunders knew how to use his fists, anyway — it was him who was the weakling, leaving his own wife to go and apologise for that trick he had played. Chad began to brood on that; and finding himself more weary than he thought, sat himself down on the edge of the sleeper-bridge. He stared woozily at the stars reflected in the brimming drain below, and lost track of time; and came to himself with a start, gripping the beams of the bridge with his hands as he saw how close he had come to nodding over the edge — and a fuddled moment later realising that the sound of hooves and wheels in his ears was what had roused him.

He saw the white blaze on the approaching pony's face, and the white too of Saunders' dandy collar: typically, confidently, Saunders was coming at the bridge at quite a lick — it would be just like him to speed by and frustrate him again, thought Chad; and as the hooves and wheels came with a hollow thundering on to the bridge, Chad leapt up and forward shouting: "Hoy, you — stop, I want you, you bastard — "

With a whinny so shrill it was almost a shriek, the pony shied at the yelling figure springing up in its path: iron-shod hooves hammering on the wooden bridge, it reared and side-stepped in a dainty dance of alarm. "What the hell — ?" Lyle cried, standing up in the trap and wrestling with the reins: his exclamation was cut short by a fearful grinding squeal — the backward thrusts of the pony in the shafts had driven the right-side wheel over the edge of the narrow bridge; and before Chad's eyes the trap tilted, overbalanced, and plunged down into the drain, hitting the water with Lyle underneath it, and dragging the screaming and plunging pony after.

A spray of cold dyke-water covered Chad's face, blinding him for a moment: he blinked and wiped it away, but when he opened his eyes again the scene was unchanged — the pony bucking and struggling in the water below, and the sinking shafts of the overturned trap, and the thrashing spume sparkling in the starlight. He stared, hardly able to connect what he saw with the normal world of a handful of moments ago: his legs would not move — seemed indeed barely able to hold him up, as if there were no bone within the flesh. All at once his mind broke free of the numb clutch of shock, was lucid for a moment, and then careered into a blank wall of panic. With a rambling cry he turned and ran. He ran with his soft, low, furtive gait, across the field-paths towards his home; and he did not slow his pace until he had left the scene far behind him, and could begin the task, necessary and terrible, of persuading himself that he never saw it at all.

★ ★ ★

493

Jonathan had been over to the adjoining fen, to consult with the old miller there about a problem he was having with the boiler-engine, and on the way home he dropped in late at the Labour In Vain for a half. When he left, in company with Henry Wake and Artie Gill, it was a clear still night the beauty of which all three men fell silent to appreciate.

"Is that a voice I hear?" Henry Wake said at last.

They stopped and listened. The sound came again, carrying far over the flat, empty distances.

"A hoss," Jonathan said.

"That must be a hoss gone in the dyke somewheres," Artie Gill said. "That way — hark at it!"

Without another word they began to run: all were accustomed to dropping everything and running across the fields to help when a neighbour's plough-team or carthorse went into the dyke. Jonathan's long stride soon left the other two behind; and when Henry and Artie came to the bridge over the main drain, Jonathan was already slithering down the bank where the pony, half-drowned, had somehow — with that invincible will to survive — dragged its front legs out of the water and was feebly struggling there like a great eel, covered in mud.

"Have a care, Jonathan — it's deep — she'll thrash you down with her!" cried Henry from the bridge; but Jonathan had already plunged into the chill dark water and was sawing at the leather traces with his clasp-knife to free the pony from the shafts.

"Dear God, thass Mr Saunders' rig," Henry breathed, as Jonathan came clambering back up the bank.

"She can't get to the top — need a rope — shift the trap — at the mill," Jonathan gasped; and set off immediately at a run, following the bank of the drain, which would take him directly to the mill. He had the ability to still completely the workings of his mind at moments when critical action was called for, and he had never been so grateful for it as now. He did not know how many minutes elapsed in his furious sprint to the mill, where he grabbed a coil of rope and a storm-lamp: that was one of the things he did not think of. When he came pounding back to the bridge he found someone else there — a young farmhand passing along the road — who had thrown off his jacket and was swimming along the reedy edge of the drain, sweeping and feeling with his hands.

It was a long business, nightmarishly long and laborious and nightmarishly lit by the swaying beams of the lamp — hauling the pony out of the way and tying the rope to the shafts of the overturned trap and dragging it round and across to the bank. The leather seat came heeling up, puffed and glistening in the lamplight, like some robust and grotesque water-creature.

"He mebbe got out — further down — mebbe he crawled out further down," Henry Wake was saying, over and over, as he held the head of the shivering pony.

It was the young farmhand, tirelessly swimming, who found him. Jonathan joined him, and together they dragged the slight and water-logged form on to the bank, where Artie Gill straddled it and began to thump with his huge thick hands.

Jonathan stood back, reeling a little: for the first time in his life he felt himself near the end of his strength. The young farmhand was stretched out on the grass, exhausted. Jonathan watched the hunchings of Artie Gill's square shoulders: he could not bring himself to look down at the pale face, with the weed intricately tangled in its crown of curly hair.

Artie stopped: sat slowly back on his haunches, and rubbed his hand across his face.

"Artie," Jonathan said, "what's — Try again, Artie!" His voice rose. "Damn it, try again!"

Artie got to his feet, shaking his head. "No, no," he said softly, patting Jonathan's arm and turning away. "No, no."

3

SUMMER came like the unfurling of a banner after a chequered spring. On Hinching Fen, where folk lived in as close relation to the sun as pears on a wall, there was a swift ripening of complexions in the ever-lengthening days — the light of evening persisting so long and the light of morning appearing so early that they seemed almost to meet, leaving only the thinnest sliver of true night between them. In the fields bare arms and throats grew ruddy, moderately fair men turned Viking blond, and young girls pulled their sunbonnets low, and despaired of their pink noses being put right even by buttermilk. And yet Hester was as pale as any duchess in a closed carriage: she saw no more of the sun than a grub under a stone, and as little sought it.

She remembered as a girl hearing stories of the old queen as the Widow of Windsor, and how silly she had thought her, shutting herself away like that. Now in her own widowhood she embraced a similar seclusion — insofar as conscious will could be said to be involved, for she shrank from the world as a wound closes against infection. For the first time in her life, Hester failed in courage — an attribute she had not even known she possessed until it deserted her.

Lizzie Gosling had come to stay with her for

the first week after Lyle's death, unasked, in an instinctive movement of solidarity. Her sturdy capable presence had shown itself indispensable at that time: quietly doing things that had to be done, quietly rousing Hester to do the things only she could do. Lizzie offered to stay longer, but with the same instinct perceived that she was not wanted — that beyond a certain point her bluff practicality was no more effective than a candle-flame in a cavern. Hester struggled to express both her gratitude and her need to be left alone — struggled, for all the channels of feeling within her seemed to be dammed, choked, and locked to an everlasting confinement — and she could only hope that Lizzie understood.

The Crooked House was her keep and fastness, guarded by Edie Smeeth, who alone could Hester bear to have continually by her. Young Edie protected Hester from the world's incursions with the doughty resource of a mother bird guarding a nest of young. She revealed a great deal of tact along the way: for Hester, desolately imprisoned within herself, could not convey, and the neighbours could not at first understand, that their kindly attentions seemed like invasions of a last redoubt of selfhood remaining to her. And the people of the fen, though they would have rejected as self-admiring and sentimental any Cockneyish claims to a familial community, had a ready sympathy with loneliness. They came one by one to the Crooked House to offer whatever help they could. Peggy Chettle brought a tonic wine, which she admitted was more wine than tonic, but if it made you feel better then God meant you to have it was her motto; Andrew Surfleet, looking about as brawny as an ancient pixie, came to say if there was any heavy work wanted doing, he was the man. Most distressing of all to Hester were the frequent visits of Henry Wake — distressing because she hated to seem ungrateful to a man who had shown her the most delicate kindness. It was Henry who had taken on himself the job, that night in May, of bringing her the news of Lyle's fatal accident; Henry who had shown, in the way he broke that news to her, that a sometimes conceited and absurd little man bore within him a selfless gentleness and grace. She longed to let him know how profoundly she appreciated that, but could not; longed to see a time, however distant, when she would be heart-whole enough to say it — but could not. Impenetrable shades had closed in upon her view, beyond which the most familiar and comforting figures were the merest wraiths, and the future a dark vale of doubtful contours. She could only listlessly register the names of callers that Edie brought her — Jonathan Eastholm's was the only one that did not occur — and hope that they would not think badly of her for withdrawing from a sympathy that would flay what it meant tenderly to touch.

From one potential source of commiseration — and that surely the most natural — she had nothing to fear: her late husband's family. No gesture in recognition of common suffering came her way from Mrs Saunders; there was to be none of the union in grief that Hester had

499

heard about in stories. At the funeral, which had taken place in Stokeley, Mrs Saunders had not spoken one word to her: none, Hester supposed, had been needed; eloquently enough came the message that if Lyle had not married her, he would still be alive. She remembered very little of the funeral except that Phoebe Purefoy had been extremely kind to her, and that when the coffin was lowered there had been a brilliant flash from the brass plate in the sunlight, as if Lyle's own mercurial gaiety had sparked out for the last time. There had been no more communication between her and Mrs Saunders, and the extent of the old woman's jealous resentment, thus revealed, only failed to wound Hester because she was already numbed beyond the power of further pain. No help was forthcoming with the legal matters consequent on Lyle's death, except when Gideon accompanied her once to the solicitor's in Huntingdon — and this, Hester guessed, because Phoebe had made him do so.

The dealings with the solicitor were the only ventures Hester made outside her self-enclosure. The property which devolved on her from her late husband was encumbered with debts, some of which she knew about, others of which were new to her; and the solicitor was at pains to point out to her, as discreetly as possible, that material stresses were soon likely to be added to the sorrows of widowhood, unless she applied herself to her affairs. This had no closer effect on Hester than if he had informed her that the sun would cool down in a million years' time.

While the busiest season of the year for the farm approached, Hester scarcely glanced at the grain ripening in the fields, and the eggs and the milk went off, or were given away. When old Walt the horsekeeper, or Billy Onyett the daysman came to her to ask for instructions, she could only tell them to do as they thought best; and if she was not properly aware that young Edie Smeeth was not only keeping the house but seeing to the pigs and fowls and the two milch-cows and dealing with tradesmen as well, it was because Edie kept it hidden from her: the young girl proving thus, unwitnessed, that the greatest acts of heroism are not necessarily performed with swords and standards, nor recorded on any monument.

Immured in the Crooked House, Hester ignored the broadening, flourishing summer outside: indeed she obscurely felt it all to be an illusion; for she was still mentally stuck fast in that cool spring night when Lyle had walked out of the house and out of life, and she could not move forward from it. His death had been no more nor less than a tragic accident: certainly he had been at the Labour In Vain and had a drink or two, very probably he had been driving too fast as usual, but the dykes and drains had been the scene of so many drownings, and so many vehicles had come to grief by not getting their wheels straight on the sleeper-bridges, that there was nothing unusual to protest about in this random stroke of fate. The trap that had pinned him underneath it had been taken away and broken up, the pony sold at market — Lizzie Gosling had quietly seen to those things; and Hester's inevitable self-reproaches that she should have somehow stopped him driving so fast and drinking so freely did not last long — Lyle would not have been Lyle without those ways. No, she felt that she might eventually reconcile herself to the fact of his death, were it not for another, more elusive fact that made it unbearable: a fact that only she could appreciate as such — that there had been a death twice over. Something had died between them before that night, and it was because of that knowledge that Hester was trapped within a dry stony vault of grief, and breathed its vitiated air in a suffocation of self-loathing. The hideous, insuperable obstacle cutting her off from consolation — cutting her off even from ordinary healing tears — was the image of Lyle walking out of the house to his death with words of hate ringing between them. *You're hateful*, she had said to him; and, worst of all, she knew that at that moment she had meant it. Worst of all? — was there not a further refinement of torture: the knowledge at last that Lyle had simply ceased to care whether she loved or hated him anyhow? No: there was no worst of all, for all was tangled in an agonising knot of sorrow and guilt and regret, like some convolution of throbbing veins at her heart, and it seemed she could not unravel it without tearing herself in twain.

Much as she had always disliked mourning-weeds, she wore her black — she would scarcely have noticed if she had been clad in rags, and a mute obedience to the conventions helped her efface herself from the world. The colour did not suit her: her whole situation, viewed from an exterior perspective, did not suit her. Trial had given to Hester's young, truthful-natured womanhood a distinctive dignity, but it was not of a tragic sort, any more than a meadow-flower resembles an orchid; and there was no nobly elevated beauty in the pale face she saw in the glass. It was a measure of how deeply Hester was suffering that she looked drawn, shapeless, and plain — and not a trivial measure: for Hester the soul and body could no more be disjoined than the power of vision and the eyes. When Edie Smeeth sometimes helped her to put up her hair, the two reflected faces in the mirror might have been separated by fifteen years instead of half a dozen. Equally new to her, though not so much foreign to her nature as a forced development of it, was the deep introspection in which she passed her days. Hester felt that she had never till now known what silence was: how it was not mere absence of sound but had a positive quality of its own, like heat or light; how silence, through the long waning of an afternoon, could seem in its accumulated weight and profundity to be on the verge of an utterance. Never before had she spoken so little: when she did speak her voice came hoarse and hesitant, as if she hardly knew how to frame her words. And never before had she truly known what thought was — how it could be as absorbing, exacting and exhausting as labour. It was not really a matter of thinking *about* anything: her mind simply had locked horns with the awesome thing that happened to her, in a static grappling. Memories of Lyle, memories of that last night, speculations about what he was thinking or feeling as he left her, who he had gone to see when he left her, longings to undo what had been done, suspicions that nothing could have been done — these were but recurrent motifs in a ceaseless mental jangling. While Hester sat in motionless silence, there was a deafening cacophony in her head, a rough-music that came to no resolution — as utterly fragmented as the beautiful dream of love that had begun a year ago, which was now in so many jagged pieces that nothing, not even the merest consoling memento, could be salvaged from it.

Just occasionally she forced herself to go out of the house for air: she slipped out at night when there would be no one around. In the lingering dusks of midsummer she walked briefly about the field-paths, a gliding black figure as insubstantial as the stretched shadows: whilst all about her the flat world brimmed with light like honey in a comb. For the first time in her life, Hester felt herself dissociated from her environment. The fields, waters and skies of her Anglian homeland, which had always borne as personal and intimate a relation to her consciousness as the shape of her own hands, blankly met her gaze as if they had no more to do with her than polar ice or alpine steeps. The power of the landscape to interact with human feeling seemed lost: there was nothing of hope or even mocking irony in the growing richness of the season; it all seemed to her to be going on behind a thick pane of glass. Returning home, she saw the trees that surrounded the Crooked House, their twisted roots exposed by the shrunken soil, with an unutterable sensation of strangeness; and looking up at the roosting birds, which formed soft blots among the leaves, she had the impression that if she were to shout and clap at them or even pelt them with stones they would not be disturbed, or acknowledge her existence by so much as the stir of a feather.

She knew what it was that made her think, dimly, that she ought to begin to break this sterile circle — it was the sight of Edie one morning, through the kitchen window, crossing the yard with an empty pail and breaking into a skip as she did so. Edie had doted on Lyle — girls did, Hester was able to say to herself without bitterness — and had mourned him deeply, but in that unconscious skip was revealed the unconquerable urge towards happiness, the assertiveness of life, as uncompromising in its way as death. Hester perceived this too at one remove, as if through glass — it was apt that she saw it as a tableau through a window; but she strained to apply it to herself. "I ought to be glad I'm alive," she murmured. "I ought to feel — feel *something*." All her human faculties seemed to have shrunk inward, as if she were undergoing a slow turning to stone: she saw at that moment that she was *willing* the process; and feebly, without conviction, she sought to wrest her will another way. "I must do something," she told herself; and an opportunity seemed to present itself very soon.

Henry Wake, making one of his regular calls to ask after her, mentioned that he was going in his dog-cart to Peterborough — "Mrs Wake requiring sundry purchases not to be got at in the immediate vicinity" — said what a treat the weather was, and invited Hester, without much hope of success, to accompany him. Hester flinched at the prospect: but, desperately grasping at that resolve she had formed before it withered away completely, she forced herself to accept. While Henry waited in the yard, urbanely chaffing Edie, she dressed herself to go out — this feeling as bizarre to her as putting on armour. Pinning on her straw hat, she suddenly noticed the trimming of little crêpe flowers circling the crown — she had always liked them: now they struck her as an emblem of innocence lost, of a vanished gaiety and freedom from care as irrecoverable as Eden: all at once she convulsively clawed at them, whimpering like a creature in pain as she plucked them off and threw them to the floor.

"I can't go — I can't," cried she, standing amidst the torn petals, and covering her face with her hands. For some minutes she remained thus, staring into the dancing blackness of her closed lids; until, the sound of Henry Wake's voice filtering through to her from the yard below, she wrenched her hands away, took a deep breath, and went downstairs.

"Morning — morning — glad you could come — splendid day for it," Henry Wake said, nodding approval as she came out, and exhibiting a cheerful determination not to notice anything at all about her appearance. "I said to Mrs Wake this morning, I must ask Mrs Saunders if she'd care to accompany me, seeing as I'm got the conveyance out, and it's so fine — not a chance of rain — no clouds anywhere — there'll be no rain."

As they set out Henry repeated several times his assurances that it would not rain; and indeed the sky was that piercing and rarefied blue that makes all other colours seem drab, while the warm air was like an exhalation from the sweetened summer earth. Henry beamed so appreciatively at the unrolling scene, as if with perfect confidence in its recuperative powers upon Hester, that she found herself consciously turning her head about and looking at everything — the green crops, the trees with their deep furbelows of shade, the sheep in the rich wash-meadows, even the cow-parsley along the roadside — her motions, in their absence of spontaneity, sadly resembling those of a clockwork toy. "Lovely day," Henry said several times, "splendid day," and finally, glancing at her sitting stiffly beside him: "Any little purchases you'd like to make in Peterborough, I wonder?"

Numbly she tried to think of something they needed at the Crooked House. She had no idea: she had left it all to Edie; she struggled as if she had been asked some teasingly difficult question. "No — I don't know — I don't think so . . ."

"Oh! not to worry — just wondered. The ride will do you good, any road." As if this were too naked a reference to her situation, he went on hurriedly: "Mrs Wake's very particular about who she buys from — very loyal in her custom is Mrs Wake. I remember we bought our tea from a different supplier once, and we'll never do that again. It turned the teacups green. Which *can't* be right."

In Peterborough they left the dog-cart at one of the many old inns which still gave the cathedral city, girded with railways and brickyards, a Pickwickian air at its gabled core; and Henry Wake gave her his arm with his peculiar bowler-hatted chivalry. It was very long since she had been amongst so many people: she found herself staring into their faces — rudely, she supposed, but she could not rid herself of a feeling that she was somehow invisible to them. "Tell me if you're tired, now," Henry said as they went about the shops, "just say the word, and we'll have a rest." But she was not tired: she was trying to somehow bring into focus the busy scene, the golden stone of old buildings, the bright colours of market awnings, the sight of a little dog tied to a lamppost — to convert her random thoughts about these things — 'That's nice — that's interesting — that's sad' — into some genuine currency of feeling. This effort continued when, shopping done, they took a walk through the cathedral close, through the brilliant flower-beds of the Bishop's Garden, and then down to the river-embankment. Everything seemed to be striving to charm her eye: the running sparkle on the water, the massy trees bending to wash their gorgeous reflections, the

508

sails of little pleasure-craft flinging back tenfold the white rays of the sun. And her eye was charmed — dazzled — whilst her mind stood back from it, like a patient parent to whom the things that are enrapturing its child have long been commonplace.

"Ah, that's a handsome sight — I never git tired of that," Henry said, turning to look at the long profile of the cathedral, rising like a walled city in itself above the trees. "That reminds me — Milney St Mary church is to be closed — did you know? Oh! not permanent. It's all to be restored — practically rebuilt from inside out, Sunny Daintree says. Not that that will greatly concern us chapel folk, but it'll mean no place in the parish licensed for christenings and weddings, and such, which is a bit awk'ud."

He had nearly said *and funerals*, Hester perceived, but had adroitly covered it up. She wished she could tell him that she didn't mind if he mentioned the funeral, Lyle, any of it: at least that seemed to have some reality. For the worst part of her failure to respond to the pageant of sublime and homely sights that he had prepared for her was just that: it seemed simply a pageant — as flat as a stage set, with nothing behind it.

They rode back to Hinching Fen. Hester felt tired — not from the unaccustomed exercise, but from the continual effort to convince Henry, with a show of animation, that his kindly plan to take her out of herself had been effective. It appeared she succeeded: he nodded with satisfaction at her very weariness, and said

509

there was nothing like fresh air; and when he dropped her at the Crooked House, he genially shook her hand and said, "Well, now — that was a rare nice day. Next time I mek that trip I shall tek the liberty of calling again — no, it's no trouble to me — not a bit of it."

She thanked him as warmly as she could; and fled into the house with a sort of smothered horror at the thought of doing it again. She hid in her room, burying her face in the bed-clothes. She seemed to have come to a new and terrible knowledge, which her young frame could hardly bear to have thrust upon it — that the human capacity for pleasure was finite, while its capacity for suffering was limitless.

Edie did not disturb her; and at long last she raised her head to look at the tin clock by the bedside, and then at the window, where the sky was suffused with a subdued radiance, like light seen through fine china. She went to throw back the curtains, and looked out at a landscape still at eleven o'clock seething with rose-pink shadows; and for the first time she remembered that today was the longest day of the year.

★ ★ ★

It was a couple of weeks after her outing with Henry Wake, and Hester was taking one of her evening walks about the farm. She was dully watching the turning sails of the mill in the distance when Edie Smeeth came calling for her in distress.

510

"Missus! Oh, missus, come quick — in the yard — it's old Rusty — he's gone funny, I dunno what to do!"

Hester hurried after her to the yard, where she found Rusty, the oldest and most reliable of the two farm-horses, lying on his side outside the stables. His belly was swollen, and his great chestnut flank heaved like a bellows.

"Oh! whatever happened to him?" cried Hester.

"I dunno, missus — I come out here and found him just like that. Walt's gone home, missus — who shall I run for? Mr Wake, mebbe?"

"Wait a moment," Hester said: she had just noticed that the barn door was standing open. With a heavy heart she went in to find her fears realised. Rusty, being the most docile of horses, was often left to amble at will about the yard, which was bounded by the house, the stable-block and the barn, with a stout gate leading to the stack-yard beyond: on this occasion the barn door had been left open, the corn-bin left uncovered, and Rusty had obviously wandered in and helped himself. "He's got at the wheat," Hester said to Edie, who had followed her. "It'll kill him if he's drunk water on top of it."

They ran across the yard to the water-butt; and looking into it Edie moaned and clutched her pinafore to her lips. "Oh! missus," she said, her round black eyes liquid, "that were near full this afternoon — I know it."

A deep groan from the prostrate horse confirmed the grim diagnosis. Hester knelt down beside him and gently touched her hand to his heaving, hardened side.

"Can't we do nothing?" said Edie in a hushed voice.

"No, Edie," Hester said. She had lived long enough on farms to know that nothing could be done for a wheat-blown horse once it had drunk. All at once the tears that had been aridly sealed within her for so long sprang to her eyes: her heart seemed to unlock at last — through pity for something other than herself. "Oh! the poor thing," she cried, as her tears dropped on to the chestnut coat, "poor thing — suffering so," and she continued tenderly to stroke the old horse, until within a mercifully few moments he stretched out his neck and died.

Hester rose to her feet, wiping her face; and became aware that somewhere in the trees a blackbird was singing, in pellucid, endless roulades, as if there were nothing but joy in the world.

"Thass my fault," said Edie, bleakly. "I should ha' seen the barn door was open — I'll bet it was me who left it like that — "

"No, no," Hester said. "It's not your fault, Edie. It's my fault. You and Walt can't be expected to do everything: it's not fair on either on you. It wouldn't have happened if I'd been doing my share — if I'd stopped feeling sorry for myself and — and got up out of my bloody pit before now."

She spoke harshly: Edie gazing at her said, "Oh, missus!" in mingled reproach and surprise.

"It's true, Edie: it's true. And the knacker

512

shan't have poor old Rusty: it was my fault, and it'd be an even worse shame if I got so much as a penny from it; we shall bury him tomorrow, over in the paddock corner," said Hester. "I want you to wake me very early tomorrow, Edie — I mustn't lie abed in the mornings any more: I'm got to — to change my ways."

Hester shed more tears when she went to bed that night: but, wretched and self-accusing as she felt, there was tremendous relief too, relief from the long barren ache that had threatened to become a permanent paralysis of the senses. She did wonder whether the morning might see her sunk once again in a slough of apathy, but she woke in the same freshened mood: poor Rusty's death had effected what summer flowers had failed to do, forcibly wrenching her from an inward absorption that had become a sheer self-embrace. Compelled thus to sympathy with something outside herself, she swiftly advanced to the logical next step — realising how much she owed to the loyalty of Edie and Walt who had kept the farm going while she languished: and it was the first thing she said to Edie when she came down next morning.

"I'm never given you a word of thanks for all the extra things you're had to do, Edie," she said. "I'm not sure how to say it even now — I should probably start roaring again: and I'm done enough of that. I reckon the best way for me to show how much I appreciate everything you're done is to start doing a few things for myself, and take the weight off your

513

shoulders: and I'm starting now."

After she had done the morning chores, and sadly watched Billy Onyett and Walt digging a grave for faithful old Rusty, Hester told Edie to come upstairs with her and help sort out the master's things. In the bedroom she flung open the closet and the drawers, and stood contemplating Lyle's many clothes — untouched since his death, and seeming still to await his return.

"What you going to do with 'em all, missus?" Edie said from the doorway.

"I don't know — I don't know what to do," Hester said, touching with a tremor the empty sleeve of a jacket. "I'm been trying not to think about these. I can't just hang on to them for ever while the moths get them — but it seems so hard to throw them out . . . " Impetuously she seized an armful of the hanging clothes and piled them on the bed. "No — I'm got to do it now, else I never shall — I can't hide any more. There's poor folk on the fen desperate for warm clothes come winter — they'll be glad of 'em — and they're doing no good hanging here. I know the vicar's wife distributes such things — I shall pass them on to her."

The only way to perform such a painful task was to do it quickly, and within minutes she had filled several boxes. Suddenly she hesitated and looked up at Edie.

"You don't think I'm hard, do you, Edie?" she said plaintively.

"I think you're right brave, missus," Edie said.

"No . . . I ain't brave . . . But I'm going to

514

have to be. It's the only way."

Somehow she got through the sorting of Lyle's possessions. Refusing to allow herself to dwell on what she had done, she next addressed herself to the state of the farm, and made a tour of the fields. Being on the edge of the upland, they had hay-fields, which she saw were late in being cut: the wheat looked well but the root crops needed thinning. The dykes were in a terrible condition and could hardly be draining at all: how had they ever got like that? Returning to the house, she got out the accounts — telling the tale, in their scrappy disorder, of Lyle's loss of interest — and presently called Edie and asked her to fetch old Walt and Billy Onyett.

It was wages day: Lyle had used to pay the workpeople through the open window, but Hester brought them in to the parlour, and after she had given them their money asked if they would stay a moment.

"I wanted to say thank you for all the work you're been doing these past weeks," she said, standing by the bureau with the accounts, and feeling highly self-conscious in this role of chatelaine. "And I'm sorry I'm not been more help, and you're hardly known where you are or what you're meant to be doing — thass done with now, I promise you. That is, if you still want to go on working for me."

"Ah, we ain't gooing anywhere, are we, Walt?" said Billy Onyett, a long-shanked stork of a man with a wry comic mouth and a complaisant temper.

"Not I," Walt said.

"Well, I'm glad," Hester said. "I'm got to — I'm got to make a fist at working this farm on my own, and keeping it going somehow. You may as well know that my — my husband left a few debts: and now with poor Rusty gone we shall need another draught-horse . . . So all in all it ain't going to be easy to manage, and I can't offer you no more than the standard wage you're been getting, even with the busy time coming up — but I hope you'll each take this extra five shilling now, just as a thank-you from me for keeping the farm going. Now the next thing," she hurried on before they could embarrass her with thanks, "is to see about getting more labour. We're late starting on the hay — I know you couldn't help that — and there's corn-harvest and root-lifting not far off, and even with me pulling my weight again, we shall want more workers. Do you know of anybody who's available straight away?"

"There's most folk been took on while harvest already, missus," Billy Onyett said. "At Farmer Mather's and such. I tell you what though — there's Jonathan-up-at-the-mill. Summer months he has buckets of time, and does all manner of casual work, where it's wanted, and you wun't find more brawn on a ox."

"Ah — he's the very man," said old Walt, who never advanced an independent opinion, but functioned as a comfortable echo to whatever was proposed.

"Oh! yes — Jonathan-up-at-the-mill," said Edie, "ask him, missus."

"Well — I don't know — he's never come

516

near me all this time," Hester said in a small voice. "He's perhaps busy . . . "

"Jonathan never turns down wukk," said Billy Onyett, "and there's no one sets in more willing, missus."

Hester's thoughts had, indeed, instinctively turned to Jonathan; but he had always held himself aloof from the farm, more so since her widowhood it seemed, and she felt timid of asking him. Seeing her hesitation, Edie said: "My brother Charlie sees him every day at the mill, missus — how about if Charlie was to ask him?"

Hester agreed readily to that: and she concluded her first day out of the pit with a concentrated assault on the backlog of letters, bills and invoices that Lyle had dealt with by stuffing them behind the clock on the mantel-shelf. The resulting piles of paid and unpaid bills showed an unpromising disproportion, and it was as much as Hester could do to let them lie and tentatively plan a trip to market, bank and solicitor's in one go. There was nothing so calm as acceptance in this new mood of hers: it was the fruit of a decision made against despair rather than for anything positive, and it required a constant effort of grim application to maintain it. She was trying to render herself as impervious to thought or feeling as a labouring ant; but still when she went to bed that night, the emptied cupboards seemed to reproach her for seeking to live on.

★ ★ ★

The coal-dray was making a delivery to the mill when Charlie Smeeth arrived. Jonathan, hoisting a sack of coal on to his back, gave Charlie a cheery greeting, but was firm when Charlie proposed shouldering a sack of his own — it would be like a grasshopper trying to lift a brick. "Go in and open the coal-hole for me, Charlie, if you will," he said, "and then we'll have a pinch of tea."

That young Charlie had something of moment to communicate to him was obvious from the way the boy twined himself into knots, and did everything with his cap but put it on his head before finally bursting out: "I'm got a message for you, sir — from Edie — not from Edie though — from the missus at the Crooked House."

"Ah?" said Jonathan, pausing in brushing off the coal dust from his shirt.

"Mrs Saunders has got to see to the running of the farm herself — she ain't been up to it, Edie says, but now she's setting her mind to it proper," Charlie said. "And seeing as she wants a good worker, Edie said you're the man — was that all right, sir?"

"Eh? Oh! yes . . . that was very good of Edie."

"And so the missus says to ask you whether you're very busy at the moment, and would you think about going to work at the farm if you're not. Thass the message, sir."

"I see." Jonathan, after unsuccessfully craning round to get the dust off his back, pulled off his shirt and shook it at the door; then stood in thought, forgetful of his uncovered state, whilst Charlie suffered a lowering of spirits, and sorrowfully counted his own ribs. "How are things there, Charlie?" Jonathan said at last. "Difficult?"

"Missus ain't got much money, Edie says, and she'll have her work cut out to manage, all on her own. Except she ain't quite, because Edie's sticking by her."

Jonathan had fallen into his peculiar poised stillness, the light falling through the open door making of him a parti-coloured creature, with cream breast and copper back. All at once he threw on his shirt and declared: "I'm afraid I can't tek that work, Charlie: will you pass the message on, and say thank you for the offer, but — but I'm afraid I can't. Will you do that for me?"

Charlie, about to protest something, stopped at the sight of Jonathan's deep inward frown, which was like the pulling down of a vizor. "All right, sir," he said. "I'll tell Edie."

Jonathan had lately moved out of the Surfleets', where space had been so restricted, and moved into a rented cottage of his own: it was part of an old T-shaped stone house at the end of Milney St Mary, which Farmer Mather had divided into three small dwellings. Thither Jonathan returned that night, and in his lamplit house-place, amongst oak furniture as smooth as glass with age, applied himself to mending his shirts and stockings — his long-established solitariness making him as adept at this as a seaman, and as little self-conscious about it.

But he was far from at peace with himself, as an observer looking in at the domestic vignette through the latticed window might have supposed. It was foreign to him to dwell on a decision once it was made — but he could not simply dismiss the one he had made today. Ever since he had seen Lyle Saunders' drowned body stretched out on the drain bank, the stout keystone of Jonathan's life had been a determination not to intrude on the widow's grief. Even before the fruitless visits of Henry Wake and others had revealed that Hester needed to be left alone, an instinctive feeling, a fundamental identification with the needs of the embattled soul, had kept Jonathan at a discreet distance. He had called at the Crooked House often — daily at first — but always very early in the morning, asking Edie if there was anything he might do, and extracting a promise from Edie that she would not bother her mistress by telling her of his visits. Just as Jonathan for all his physical size and strength was very light on his feet, so the large blunt profile of his emotions was offset by a peculiar refinement. His own jealously guarded individuality had given him a horror of crudely imposing on that of others. The effect of his pity and sympathy for Hester, profound as they were, was to make him draw a large ring around her, beyond which he did not wish to trespass, especially as her widowed position was so fraught with delicacy. It was because of this that he had made that unhesitating refusal today.

He was so accustomed to referring to his sense

of honour as the supreme tribunal that he did not know why he should be aware of a small pocket of dissatisfaction within him. He went to bed convinced that he had made the honourable choice; and so he could not place the demurring voice that disturbed his rest — could not tell whether it was his conscience, or his inmost heart, that accused him of cloaking craven self-preservation with the name of honour, and pretending not to hear a call for help.

★ ★ ★

It had been a July day of brazen heat, and an exhausting one for Hester, who had been to the bank and the solicitor's in Huntingdon and then to see a farmer on Tick Fen who had a carthorse for sale. With the trap gone she had to make these trips in an old farm wagon, which she supposed made her seem even more eccentric: already she was a conspicuous figure, a lone young woman going about business in those unwelcoming panelled offices, which were as dourly masculine as pipe-smoke. The necessary expense of the horse had been grudgingly conceded by the bank, and Hester's nerve was feeling fragile again when she got home; Jonathan Eastholm's cool refusal to take a job with her had dismayed her and was preying on her mind; but she resisted the temptation to hide, snail-like, inside the house. Billy Onyett had begun the delayed cutting of the hay, and she took him out a jar of home-brewed ale. Her skirts trailed a long train of shadow as she crossed the field in the bright afternoon: the upright figure of Billy, standing in his cleared swathe, cast a shade as clear as a sun-dial.

"Ah! thass a good drop of ale out your cellar, missus," Billy Onyett said. "Reckon I could drink enough of that to be sorry for it. Now who's that coming over from Will's mother's? There's only Jonathan-up-at-the-mill I know as sits atop a pair o' legs like that."

Hester shaded her eyes with her hand. With the sun behind him, crowning his head with a ruddy aureole, Jonathan was striding towards them, ploughing like a wader through the uncut hay. "Yes — it's Jonathan," she murmured — startled: there was something larger than life in the way he had suddenly appeared out of the sun, and at that moment his onward progress through the waist-high grass seemed somehow to suggest the advance of an irresistible force.

"Day to you, miller," Billy called.

"How do, Billy." Jonathan came right up to where Hester stood clasping the empty jar, and put up a hand to push back his sweat-damp hair, with a vestige of doffing of the hat in the gesture.

"Mrs Saunders," he said. "I'm come to work for you, if you still want me."

She was glad to be called Mrs Saunders — so many people went out of their way not to say it, as if Lyle had never existed at all; but her chief emotion was a relief overpowering in its intensity. To her burdened mind, Jonathan's great-shouldered figure seemed an incarnate challenge to all the difficulties that beset her;

and for a moment she could not speak.

"I'm sorry I haven't come before," Jonathan said.

"No, no," said she. "You're here now, and — well — when can you start?"

"This very moment," Jonathan said promptly. "I'll set in with Billy here, if you've another scythe."

"Come up to the farm," she said, "there's one in the tool-shed."

He walked beside her, across the fields to the Crooked House.

"I can pay you the going rate," she said. "Of course there's the mill — I mustn't take you from that — "

"Don't worry about that — this is the slack time, I'm hardly having to pump at all. I can be here morning to dusk: every day, if you want."

As he said this the melting relief within her almost reached the point of tears; and stopping in her tracks she said reproachfully, unable to meet his eyes: "Oh, Jonathan — I thought you were ignoring me or something — when you turned the work down, I didn't know what to think . . . "

"I'm sorry, Mrs Saunders," said he. "That must have seemed churlish of me."

"Perhaps I should have come to see you myself — instead of sending a message by Charlie Smeeth — but — "

"No, no." He seemed to wish to close the subject, and walking on said, "They're a nice pair, them young Smeeths."

"Oh, I couldn't do without Edie," Hester said.

"Charlie's a big help to me at the mill. I give him a few bob, though I have a job to make him take it. I just hope that uncle of his don't git his hands on it."

"You've heard about Uncle too," Hester said. "Have you ever seen him?"

"No — he lives over on New Fen. I wouldn't mind seeing him, though," he added grimly.

"Well, if you ever do, send him on to me when you're finished with him," she said, and they exchanged a smile.

"Your crops look well," Jonathan said as they came to the yard. "It should be a good harvest this year."

"I don't know . . . I'm afraid the fields haven't been — well, properly attended to," she said, opening the tool-shed. "Billy Onyett's done his best, but it's been too much work for him really."

Jonathan surprised her by breaking into a broad smile. "Don't you worry," he said, shouldering a scythe, and seeming to radiate strength at every pore. "It'll all be safely gathered in."

★ ★ ★

Jonathan threw himself into the work of the farm. He was afield before the sun had cleared the horizon, and even on wages day he was late in coming to the house for his money, arriving at last from the hay-meadows when Hester was

524

despondently looking over the accounts once more.

"Should have it all cut by Monday," Jonathan said, pocketing his money.

"I wish I could have all these debts paid by then," Hester said, adding an unpleasant letter from the draper to the pile.

Jonathan hesitated, then said: "Bad?"

"Oh! just a lot of little things — but they all add up. I suppose lots of people run up these bills, but . . . "

"I hate being in debt myself, no matter how much," Jonathan said. "You never feel easy."

"Thass just it," she said gratefully: she was glad he did not think her priggish — it was simply that her honesty chafed at these things which Lyle had always shrugged off. "When I go into Stokeley I feel like I ought to go creeping down the back alleys . . . Silly, ain't it?"

"Not really. You know, Mrs Saunders, if it would help, you could pay my wage at the end of the month — or even when the harvest's in."

"Oh, I couldn't do that!" she said, looking up at him in surprise.

"Well, I get my pay for minding the mill, you know; and if you're struggling — "

"Well, it's just a few bills . . . "

"But you hate having them outstanding. I understand that. Now what would make you feel easier in your mind? — I mean, what's your first priority?"

"Well . . . " She nodded. "To get these bills paid off."

"Then thass what you should do. Instead of

paying me by the week, put that money to settling the bills: and then when the harvest's in we can see where we stand."

The prospect of being free of these oppressive debts, which were undermining her still frail resolve, was very attractive; but she did not want to seem to be taking advantage of her own vulnerability, playing on folk's sympathy to get concessions. Yet Jonathan spoke straightforwardly, with no pitying overtones.

"It's a very kind offer, Jonathan," she said. "But I don't think these bills will break me, you know — and I'd have to be absolutely sure you can manage."

"I reckon I can manage — if I don't, I shall have to ask you for a little sub," he said with a slight smile, "but I reckon it'll work. Suppose you draw up an account each wage day, putting my wage into the bill fund, like this — " She passed him a blank sheet of paper. "Pardon me — " he wiped his hands — "I'm all of a sweat from the field — now suppose you draw up a plan, setting all these little bills in order, and giving yourself a particular target every week or fortnight, say, so you can cross 'em off one by one. You'll feel better seeing the list gitting less and less."

"Yes — thass what I need — to feel I'm getting somewhere — at the moment I just seem to be banging my head against a wall," she said. "Well, I'll do it this way, then, Jonathan: it's very generous of you."

"Practical, thass all," he said, with the slight smile again.

"I ought to make some sacrifices of my own — I ought to start thinking of some little economies — "

"Write them down too," he said. "Then you can see 'em add up. Sort of make a challenge of it. You can work it, Mrs Saunders: I'm sure of it." He took the money she had given him from his pocket and placed it on the bureau. "And there's a start. See you tomorrer."

He was gone, leaving behind a faint odour of sun-soaked labour, and seeming too to leave with her a little of his overflowing strength.

It stayed with her, indeed, for a couple of days in which she was refreshed and heartened, and set about her work with a will; but then she was cruelly set back by a visit from Cresswell, the ugly little man who had virtually imprisoned her in the house that stormy day when he had come dunning for the money Lyle owed him. To have those memories revived was bad enough: worse was Cresswell's cold-blooded insistence that he didn't give a fig whether her husband was alive or dead — he was still owed money. Her self-command was barely intact by the time she had got rid of him, promising him a banker's draft on the first of next month. She had not the heart to get out the accounts and place another figure on the debit side; nor at that moment could she bear to be in the house. Though she had given his clothes to the needy and put away his small personal effects, there were still times when Lyle's presence seemed intensely, intolerably strong in the Crooked House, and this was one of them. Hester's spirits were dangerously low, and she had to force herself with a grim effort of will to go out to the hayfields, the last of which was being cut by Jonathan, and do the raking.

Jonathan just paused in his mowing, holding his scythe in the back-stroke a moment to nod a greeting to her, and then sweeping it forward again with his long easy motion. His swing was as fluid as a dance, seeming to have nothing strenuous about it at all, as if he could go on mowing for ever. About half the field was already cut. Hester picked up the hay-rake and began to turn the bleaching rows of cut grass with their little wreaths of wild flowers. The heat of the afternoon pressed down on the field, shadeless but for a couple of pollard willows in one corner. Sharp flecks of light flew from Jonathan's swinging scythe, leaving a jagged dazzle on her retinas whenever she looked up. On all sides the horizons simmered, and there was no sound but the rustling of her rake and the soft swish of Jonathan's scythe as he advanced through the hay, leaving behind him a neat wake of symmetrical swathes.

The idleness of those long weeks when she had shut herself away had caught up with her: she felt exhausted. As she straightened up and wiped her brow the field seemed to swim dizzily around her. It was as if all the vitality which she had once had in such abundance had come to an end, for ever. Jonathan, pausing to take his whetstone from his belt, saw her wilting.

"You'd best stop a minute," he said, coming over.

"Oh, I can't," she said. "We're late as it is."

"Just for a minute," he said.

She had brought out a basket with some ale and buttermilk and a few girdle-scones. They stood in the shade of the willows and drank, and Jonathan urged her to eat.

"You'll feel better," he said.

"Oh, I don't see how I can feel better just now," she said, sounding peevish, for her heart was in blackest shadow. "I may as well just work — at least then I can't think."

"Is there something new?" he said after a moment. "To do with money, I mean?"

She nodded. "Not much — just one more . . . Oh, I can't manage it," she said, feeling herself yielding to despair, letting go, unable to control herself. "I can't manage this place alone, I know I can't. I just ain't got the heart." Strangely, it was the first real mention of her situation that there had been between them. She had not meant to say it to him: the words burst from her. "I don't know what to do. I just don't see how I can go on."

"You can," Jonathan said, calmly tilting the jar of ale on his forearm and taking a long drink. "I'm not just saying that to be comforting or anything like that. What I mean is, you're got an established farm, planted, working. You know farming. I know it don't seem like it, but thass a head start. It won't go under unless you do. I suppose it's odd me saying this, when I lost my own little place — but thass the point. I was starting from scratch when I had that little farm, I hadn't even thought properly about it, just jumped into it — I was tekking a big risk and it didn't come off — "

"Oh! Jonathan — don't reproach me," she said, with fresh distress at this reminder of how he had once overturned his life because of her. "I can't bear it if you reproach me."

"I'm not," said he, "truly: thass not what I meant. The thing is, I lost that farm because of bad luck — a fen-blow. I used to think it was somehow my fault, that I'd failed because I hadn't tried enough. I thought that for a long time. But now I know it was just bad luck: I'm stopped accusing myself. I worked at that place as hard as I could, and thass a satisfaction in itself. Believe me, it is."

"I'm not afraid of the work," she said, though feebly. "It's just — it's just that I can't see any point in it."

"Well, I know the farm mebbe doesn't seem worth much at the moment — mebbe seems nothing more than a pile of bricks, a few fields of black muck. But even if you can't think of it as anything more than that, still it's worth working. There's salvation in work, Mrs Saunders — making that earth yield — making your own *self* yield."

"Is there really, Jonathan?" she said. She longed to be convinced, though the demon of doubt held her fast.

"I know it. And I'm not just handing you second-hand saws from the old grannies." With his eyes fixed on the quivering hot distance, Jonathan went on: "When I was a lad my

530

father died and my mother married again. My stepfather didn't want a boy into the bargain and he — well, he let me know it. There's more than one way of being cruel . . . Anyway he got me out, and so I was on my own. I felt the world hated me. Folk talk a lot of blather about being carefree when you're young, being able to bounce back . . . all I know is I never want to know such darkness as that again. I was down at the bottom of the well and I couldn't see any way out. But it was work that got me out, in the end. Not quickly; and I don't reckon I was even aware of the moment when I got into the light again. But work did it: it made me whole again."

The singing stillness of summer flowed back as Jonathan paused. Hester became aware of the hum of bees, like a furry tingle in the warm air, passing among the grass-twined flowers. Something in the way Jonathan spoke, both tentative and distinct, gave her the feeling that he was telling something long hidden, telling it perhaps for the first time.

"You're got the farm," he said. "Work at it. Mebbe there'll be no satisfaction in it at first, but it'll stop you going mad — I swear to that. There's enough waste in the world already, Mrs Saunders, enough cruel waste to make a man shake his fist at the heavens for pity — you know that too well, I'm afraid. It'd be a shame to see this farm thrown in the dust: I don't want to see that."

"Neither do I, I suppose," said she listlessly. "I just wish I could *care* more."

Jonathan fixed her with a hard attentive look. "You can't love life now," he said. "I know that. I dare say you can't see a time when you ever will love life again. All right: but you can fight it instead. Fight it, and throw it. With hate, if you like."

"Was that how it was for you?" she said. His tale of his youth had called forth a glint of curiosity, at least: she stepped outside her brooding self for a moment.

"Yes," he said; and added after a hesitation, "Too much hate perhaps." He stoppered the jar of ale and picked up his scythe. "You look worn out," he said in quite a different voice. "I can manage here. You mustn't go making yourself ill."

He returned to his mowing. Hester lingered beneath the willows, watching him, sipping the last of the buttermilk, and scarcely seeming to have the energy to brush away the teasing flies. At last she picked up the rake and, half sulkily, but with a sort of subdued determination like a reef beneath still water, resumed her work.

★ ★ ★

Hester kept on: somehow, as the summer deepened, she made herself go on. If there was no alteration within her, there was a visible difference to her appearance; the long days she spent at hay-turning swiftly brought colour back to her skin, and she no longer looked like the papery and bloodless ghost that had haunted the field-paths at eventide.

She adhered to the plan she had formed with Jonathan of paying off the backlog of bills, and the fact that he was prepared to postpone his wages to help the farm put a little iron into her own soul. She set her mind dourly to the task of economy, yoked it and drove it, permitting herself to think of nothing but survival: she was as narrowly absorbed as the most obsessive old miser. She so forced herself to think of this as an end in itself that she was unprepared for the sense of satisfaction when, on successive wages days, she found herself crossing off the debts one by one.

Jonathan always came to the house last on wages day — they had agreed on this lest the others find out he was receiving no money and think it might be expected of them; and she took a pleasure in showing him the diminishing pile of bills. Always she sought a definite assurance that he was managing: always he told her, "I'm gitting by, Mrs Saunders — don't worry about that." Always, too, he was quick to be away once he had congratulated her on the latest little success and she had noted down his week's work; he never lingered to chew the fat as did Walt or Billy Onyett. Indeed it was notable that he always placed himself carefully on the opposite side of the table on which she wrote, as if to emphasise the distance between them. This perplexed her — perplexed her more as the little triumphs gradually put to flight the worst shadows of despair, and enabled her to appreciate his efforts. The very perplexity was an indication that she was beginning, however painfully and gradually, to lift her head and raise her eyes from the earth. Another indication was her noticing for the first time that Edie Smeeth had an admirer.

Rob Risby, the tallyman, had recently taken on a boy to help him with his rounds: a stocky youth of peeled and gingery aspect, with a sprouting growth of hair in the middle of his chin like the base of an onion. Though they never bought anything from the tallyman, Risby's boy habitually got down from the cart at the end of the drove and came up to the Crooked House, and hanging his face and hands over the top bar of the yard gate like a man in the stocks, inquired, "Anythink today?"

Edie was always quick to reply: "No thank you very much!", with shrill emphasis, but Risby's boy lingered at the gate, wrinkling his brows and following Edie with his eyes, like a recumbent dog that hopes against hope for a walk. All the time Edie marched briskly about, her face as serene as a madonna, and expressed by means of severe sweepings and pumpings and pig-feedings, her utter unawareness that any such a thing as a tallyman's boy existed anywhere under the sun; occasionally stopping short, and noticing the mournful face with a tremendous start of surprise, and an exclamation of "Not today thank you!" It was notable, however, that she always found something to do in the yard when Risby's boy was there; and when the moony face disappeared at last, she always ran to the gate and watched the youth's departure as attentively as she had ignored his presence.

One hot morning Hester was witness to a startling development in this intrigue. She returned from the hay-field, where the carting had just finished, to find Risby's boy in his usual place, and to hear him solemnly declare to Edie: "I like yer 'air."

Edie, fastening the barn door, stopped and looked all the way around her. "Are you addressing me?"

"I like yer 'air," said Risby's boy again, as if this were a gambit compelling enough to bear repetition.

"Git away wi' you!" cried Edie, giving her curls an unconscious shake. "Passing remarks on a person's Hair indeed!"

"Well," said the youth, after an enormous pause, during which Edie locked and unlocked the barn door numerous times, "I do."

"Oh! can't a person git no peace!" said Edie. "Ain't you got no work to do, 'stead of bothering a person to distraction?" And she sailed into the house, examining the bunch of keys as if keys were the one thing she found most fascinating in all the world.

"Well, Edie," Hester said soon afterwards, as together they lifted the heavy iron tray of new bread out of the range, "it looks like you're made a conquest."

"Oh him!" said Edie, with the greatest unconcern, as they set the tray down: then covered her mouth with her apron and gave a shriek of laughter. "The gret yawnucks!"

"Don't you like him?" Hester said smiling.

"Him! huh!" Edie said with another shriek, and then, "He's all right."

"You weren't very nice to him."

"Pooh — show 'em any encouragement and they start sticking to you tight as the miller's shirt when he's mowing. *I'll* manage that 'un, missus." Edie gave a little chuckle to herself, then looked up at Hester with a sudden apprehension. "Oh! you don't mind him hanging around like that, do you, missus? It's only fun, but — I mean, I just thought, if it meks you feel sad about things, seeing us — oh! I'll send him away, missus. I feel awful now — I never thought — "

"No, no, Edie," said Hester, quieting her with a gentle hand on her shoulder. "I don't mind a bit; it don't make me feel sad. I know life's got to go on. I can't expect nobody ever to have any fun because of me — and I don't want that now, though a while ago I'm afraid I probably did. I was selfish then; I suppose I didn't think it right that life should go on, and young folk fall in love, and flirt and have fun — but of course it's right."

"Well, you're young yourself, missus," said Edie earnestly.

"I suppose so," Hester said, kneeling down to rake out the oven. "I suppose I am . . . But not in that way, Edie. All that's finished for me, now. I shan't ever have them young feelings. It's a pity, but I don't regret it really — I don't want that back again. I'd rather just look on. That's the best way."

* * *

Harvest began a fortnight into August. On the land of larger proprietors like Farmer Mather the horse-drawn reaping-machine could be seen whirling its spindly arms, but around the Crooked House (which was now slowly becoming known as Mrs Saunders' Farm) the work went ahead with scythe and rake just as it had when villeins had tilled the estates of Stokeley Abbey. Harvest was when every hand was needed and every hand did all it could, and the work of Jonathan, Billy Onyett and Walt was supplemented on a casual basis by many of Hester's old friends on Hinching Fen. Sunny Daintree, his bald head the colour of a flower-pot beneath the hot sun, came from time to time; so did Artie Gill, who, singularly, declined the ale that Hester supplied to the reapers, saying it made him heady, and refreshing himself instead with frogskin-wine — dyke-water — which he scooped up in his hat. Even old Andrew Surfleet, who was past wielding a scythe, did a little raking, whilst Hester herself and sometimes Edie followed behind, making the bonds and tying the sheaves. In their manner towards Hester there was a quiet curiosity, veiled by respect. She could understand that; for here at last in full view was the hermit-like widow of the Crooked House, who had hidden herself away from their solicitude. Often, indeed, when she looked up from gathering in her arms a spiky, lolloping sheaf, and saw the people working around her, their movements conforming to immemorial patterns, yet each stamped with the idiosyncrasy of the individual, she was

537

moved by an extraordinary gratitude for their presence, which even as she felt it she saw no way of expressing.

Resting a moment in the shade beside Andrew Surfleet, she remarked how hale and brown he was looking.

"Well, thass funny, gel," Andrew said — using a local mode of address, perfectly polite, for any female under sixty, "I'm not got no browner, the last ten years, I reckon; just git topped up to the same level of brownness every summer, like." He contemplated his forearms, on which the walnut-coloured skin appeared as loose as a cat's nape. "And yet you'd think you'd goo on gitting browner all the time, and be dark as a black-bloke by the time you git to my age. I can tek any amount of sun, meself — not like my ole missus. The sun meks her sneeze, you know, and thass another thing I'm never understood, how the sunlight can git up your nose and mek it sneeze."

"Is Mrs Surfleet's rheumatiz better, Andrew? — I'm not seen her for ages."

"Ah, she's diddling, gel, she's diddling: excepting when this sun meks her sneeze, as it happens — not that there'd be any hurt in that, but she wun't let a sneeze come out, my ole missus — she's such a tidy body: 'I wun't have no splashing, Dad,' says she, and she holds 'em in so, I'm afraid sometimes she's gooing to go pop like a bottle of beer."

It was then that Hester wanted to say something in acknowledgement of Mrs Surfleet's kindness in sending her some tender beans from their garden, in those weeks when she had been shut away; but she found she could not. Somehow it seemed inadequate, nothing more than a belated and dutiful thank-you note.

It was Jonathan at last whom she asked about this: it was Jonathan who drove the harvest forward like a great untiring engine, and in whom the springs of resilient life, towards which she was slowly groping, flowed most forcefully. They were reaping one day in the Popple Field, so named for the magnificent row of poplars, regular as street-lamps, that bounded it on one side, and when Jonathan sat down in the shade to eat his dockey she took her question to him.

"Folk were so kind to me — and I couldn't properly appreciate it at the time," she said. "And now I can appreciate it, but I can't say it properly."

"They'll not be offended — they understand," said Jonathan. "You're showing your appreciation just by the way you are. I felt something similar, you know, when I lost my own place, and folk pulled round to help me stay on my feet. I felt uncomfortable about it — like they were putting me under an obligation. It took me a while to realise it weren't like that — and that they don't offer help expecting anything back. I don't think fen-folk like a lot of fuss and ompolodge. They're reserved. Like when they meet they never say 'How are you?' and all that — but it don't mean they're not interested if you're sick or sorry."

"I remember when I worked for old Mrs

539

Saunders, and the posh customers used to come in for tea, and it was all 'How are you?' 'How are *you*?', and I used to think how daft it was," she said smiling: and suddenly realising that she had calmly brought out, without pain, this reference to a time she had hitherto found unbearable to recollect. If Jonathan recognised this he made no sign; only smiled too and, finishing his dockey, took an ear of wheat and threshed it in his cupped hands, blowing out the chaff and showing her the ripe grains on his palms.

"That's good wheat," he said. "Your own crop. That's fine, isn't it?"

She nodded; it did feel fine: fine, too, was the sight of the line of poplars like stiff torches against the sky. The green beauty of them touched Hester a fraction before the guilt. The old guilt, the feeling that she was being a traitor to the dead by finding things to enjoy in life — would it ever leave her? But the guilt had come tardily: for a moment her soul had responded like a sun-opened flower to the beauty of the trees. She felt torn: it was sweet to rediscover the desire for life, even fleetingly, but should she not crush it and deny it?

"Jonathan," she said suddenly, "that was a sad story you told me a while ago. About when you were a boy, and your stepfather. Did you — were you never friends?"

"Never," Jonathan said. "He tried to make it up once, but I wouldn't have it."

"Do you ever wish that you had, after all?" she said; and as he was silent she added, "I'm sorry — I'm being nosy."

540

"No, no," he said. "I'm trying to think of an honest answer. I was very bitter for a long time: mebbe that weren't a good thing."

"You're not bitter any more?"

Stretching out his great legs, Jonathan said, "It's funny — I suppose I'm not, now, but I couldn't have told you when it stopped — it's like when you're got a headache, and suddenly you realise it's gone, but you couldn't have pinned down the moment when it left you."

"Just time, I suppose."

"Just time."

Time, and work: they formed the medium in which the shape of Hester's grief and shock was gradually moulded, until presently that grief and shock coexisted with normal life instead of monstrously displacing it. In the harvest fields the sun blazed, the wheat toppled, thick and dark as reeds, and Hester, stretching her arms around the sheaves, felt the old give and bend in her young body like the flex of a sapling, and undressing at night saw the familiar dimplings and cross-hatchings on her bare forearms where the ears of wheat had scratched her. These things, true and valid in themselves, could exist alongside the terrible thing that had happened: accepting them for the good in them did not mean accepting or forgetting the other. Instead of a uniform grey there was light against a background of dark. And a day of bright light came at the end of August, when after paying her workers their wage she reckoned up her accounts, and was able to cross off the last of the bills left behind by Lyle.

She was just solvent for now — no more; but a good harvest should see her able in the next quarter to meet the long-term advance from the bank, and breathe freely. It was an achievement; her undeniable pleasure in it was fused with gratitude to Jonathan for his help both in setting it before her and in reaching it, and when he came in from the field she had a tankard of ale waiting for him.

"Here, Jonathan," she said. "Drink a toast to debts paid off."

"That I will!" he said. "Thass fine news, Mrs Saunders. I knew you could do it."

He drained the tankard, and seemed about to take his leave when she said: "And now, now I'm out of the wood — won't you take this?" taking a pile of shillings from the table.

"Well, I reckon we might as well go on as we started, and settle up when the harvest's in," Jonathan said. "Oh — unless it's more convenient for you like this."

"Well . . . no, I suppose." She had meant him to take a gift, as a mark of friendship; but his punctiliousness was discouraging.

"Right then. Now I'd best be off, Mrs Saunders."

Instinctively she had wanted to share her feeling of mild celebration, and his coolness dismayed her. "You're always running away from me, Jonathan," she said, half laughing. "I feel as if I'm got something catching."

"I'm sorry, Mrs Saunders," he said. "I didn't mean to seem rude."

"No — it's me who's been rude," she said,

regretting the way she had spoken, and yet feeling she must be frank. "It's just — I wanted to say how I appreciated the way you've helped keep the farm going. You're done so much — so generously — I can't just speak to you like boss to workman after all you're done. And yet at first you wouldn't come to work for me at all . . . I don't understand."

Jonathan frowned and licked his lips. "Well, Mrs Saunders, I'll tell you," he said. He glanced into the passage: Edie was singing in the kitchen. "Come outside, if you will."

Mystified, Hester followed him out, and they walked round the south side of the house, where the skewed trees threw their addled shadows, towards the paddock.

"Have I seemed distant with you?" he said.

"Well . . . sometimes."

He bent his gaze to the ground, and spoke carefully. "After your husband died, I didn't want to intrude. That was my first thought. And then there was your reputation. It's best that we be business-like, because people will talk. A widow's in a vulnerable position, and it don't take much malice — it don't take much more than curiosity — for people to start saying how Miller Eastholm's taking advantage, and trading on your situation. Just gossip," he hurried on, as she was about to speak, "and ridiculous, I know: but there it is. I wanted to spare you all that — you're got quite enough on your plate without that sort of nonsense coming to your ears. I don't know whether you're gitting any peace of mind yet — if you are, it's been hard-won, and it's too precious to spoil. Thass what it is, Mrs Saunders: I never meant to offend."

"Oh, no, you didn't offend, Jonathan — and I do understand," she said earnestly. Her surprise was great, for she had not even thought of such things; and momentarily she was profoundly touched by this disinterested protectiveness which she had not guessed at. She shook the moment away, however, for a bewildered indignation rose up as she said: "But can't folk ever think of anything else? Don't they realise that that's all over for me?" She stopped beneath the apple trees, where a cloud of gnats hung like a thick mesh stirring in the sulky air. "Yes, I'm got a little peace of mind, Jonathan: not much, not all the time, but it's there, and you helped me to it . . . But that don't mean I can — I can ever be like I was before. Or ever want to be — thass the thing. I'm learnt my lesson — with love you think you'll get the moon and stars in a basket, but really there's nothing but pain and heartache to be got."

"I understand why you feel like that," he said. "When such a terrible thing happens — "

"No," she said, "no, I don't just mean — I don't just mean Lyle's death. Oh, that sounds awful — I know there *couldn't* be anything more terrible — what I'm trying to say is, it all comes to heartache one way or another — whichever way it ends . . . " She looked at him very soberly. "I can say this to you because — well, you remember that day of the storm, when you saw me under the tree?"

544

He nodded.

"That's what I mean. You couldn't help but see the way I was. The way Lyle and me were — there's no point in hiding it, I suppose it was common knowledge on the fen. That's what makes it all seem so fiendish and empty. It wouldn't be so bad, maybe, if you felt that you'd at least made that person happy — "

"Mrs Saunders, you don't have to say this — "

"No," she insisted, "I need to say it — I'm so needed to say it to someone who understands. Because I couldn't feel I'd made that person happy: that was the worst part. That it had all been a waste, a waste of life and heart. And that's why it seems almost like a sickness, what I'm had, and won't have again."

Jonathan had leaned his arm against the tree-bole and was gazing concentratedly upon her; but when he spoke it was in an abstracted tone, as if to himself. "A fool's game," he said softly. "All a fool's game."

"Yes," she said. "I knew you'd understand."

Stirring, he looked up into the foliage, sticky-green as if varnished. "No fruiting on this one?" he said.

"No, it's sterile," she said. "Jonathan — it's very good of you to be — well, to think of my reputation like that. But I don't want to see a good friendship spoiled by talk. Like you say, there's some things too precious. One thing I'm learnt now is to value what's true and real and honest. I didn't think I would be able to care about the farm, and working at it to make it pay — but it has been worth it, just like you

545

said. When you told me there was salvation in work I must admit I only half believed you."

"But you stuck at it," he said smiling. "And the credit's yourn."

"Well. If you say so." They walked on, round to the rear of the house. "And you really won't take that money, Jonathan — as a friend?"

"As a friend," he said, "I can say no. We'll stick to our plan, eh? And wait till this stack-yard's all brimming with wheat ready for the threshing. And now I really must be going." Just as he was about to turn, however, they saw Edie Smeeth go bouncing across the yard, skirts flapping, clucking in imitation of the hens. They both smiled at the sight, and Jonathan said: "Charlie tells me Edie's got a beau."

"Rob Risby's boy," Hester said. "She's as sharp as glissy-needles with him — I don't know how he puts up with it — but he moons after her all the more. And he can't bring himself to say he likes her, and if she likes him, she don't give none of it away."

"Aye," Jonathan said, shaking his head, and then lifting his hand in farewell. "A fool's game."

★ ★ ★

Jonathan woke suddenly in his cottage bedroom some hours before dawn. Since he had become a miller his sleep had grown as light as a wild animal's, and the slightest shift in wind or weather would interrupt it. He lay for a few moments staring into the darkness, his senses bristling. The air that touched his face was cool. The broad backdrop of sustained sound behind the silence of the room was not the wind, as he had first thought: it was raining in a steady torrent.

Jonathan slipped into corduroy trousers and a shirt and padded downstairs. Lighting a lamp, he swallowed a mouthful of cold tea and pulled on his boots, whilst the stray kitten that had lately adopted him blinked crossly at him from his chair. Jonathan remembered that the kitten had been repeatedly washing behind its ears last night, which was supposed to presage heavy rain; and recalled too the arrow-wiggles that had invaded the house-place from cracks in the walls. All this past week August had been dying in humid fits of thunder, interspersed with downpours which cleared to freshness only to cloud over again; but he had thought yesterday that they were entering a fine and settled spell. Now when he threw open the door his lamp cast its light upon a glistening barrier of rain, which beat down upon the wide village street in a furious drumming, and chattered in piccolo tricklings from every sill and roof-eave.

Putting on his cap and throwing an old oilcloth over his shoulders, Jonathan set out for the mill. Milney St Mary's street was awash, and he was soaked up to the knees in a few moments. As he struck the plashy path alongside the main drain, he could hear the pounding hiss of the rain upon the drain-water, which was already high from those summer storms, and when he got to the mill he was drenched by the solid

547

spouts that were coursing off the motionless sails. He paused only to light a lamp before plunging into the stoke-hole to fire the boilers; and within a few minutes of waking, with not a crumb of breakfast inside him, Jonathan was working like a galley-slave.

By the time the boilers were fired, and the pump working, the light of the oil-lamp had died in the light of dawn like a spent moon. The noise of the engine-beam and the water-wheel had obscured any sound outside, and for a moment Jonathan thought the rain had stopped, but a glance out at the mill-drain showed that it was still descending in a breezeless deluge from a stone-coloured sky: the underbelly of cloud seemed no higher than the cap of the mill or the sodden tops of the trees. Jonathan watched the water-wheel doing its work, and thought of the harvest still half-gathered in the fields.

Old Andrew Surfleet came pottering along the high-road, and passed the time of day with Jonathan as was his custom.

"Reckon this'll clear today, Andrew?"

"I wouldn't wait for it 'less I was sitting comfy," Andrew said, with water pouring from the brim of his hat all the way round so that he seemed to be wearing a bee-keeper's veil. "It must have come down in pails and tubs last night. Stokeley Drain's all full to the lip, they reckon. The corn'll want fetching in quick if it keeps up. I'm glad we're got you manning the pump, Jonathan bor."

"I'd best git back to it then, Andrew."

He stoked the boilers till dinner-time, stripping

off his shirt in the heat of them, and emerging with his skin coated in oil and coal-dust, so that Charlie Smeeth, running over to see him from Henry Wake's, was startled by his swarthy appearance and flashing eyes.

"Coh, sir, you'll be worn to a shade at this rate!" cried Charlie.

"Got to keep the pump going, Charlie — never git much wind with heavy rain like this."

"Let me do a bit o' stoking, sir — I can manage it."

"No, boy: you'll bust a gut with willingness one of these days . . . I tell you what though — it'd help if you could step down Mrs Saunders' drove on your way back. You know I'm been harvesting for her, but I can't leave the mill while the dykes are filling like this. Give her my apologies, will you — and tell her I shall try and come afield later — just as soon as I can."

"I'll do it, sir!" said Charlie, setting off like a hare, and unerringly succeeding in treading in all the deepest puddles as he went, with a groan of surprise at each one.

The weather did not clear that afternoon: it was like a detached piece of greyest November thrust into the hot summer. The pumping-engine throbbed, the water-wheel thrashed, and Jonathan shovelled coal until the sooty sweat ran down his wrists; whilst all the time his mind dwelt on Hester's nearly-reaped fields. The wheat would need cutting, carting and stacking as soon as possible, unless the weather improved dramatically: wet wheat might grow in the ear, and roots might soon be drowned. He remembered tales of wet years when the harvest had to be gathered in by boat. It wasn't that bad . . . but still he was haunted by images of those fine crisp sheaves which Hester had tied, standing inch-deep in muddy water. It seemed to him that a failed harvest now would cost her more than just financial security: it was plain that making a success of the farm had done much to lift her from the stagnation of despair, and it would be the cruellest blow to her delicately poised equilibrium — a waste doubly destructive. Too much waste in the world, as he had said to her.

Late in the afternoon Jonathan stoked up as high as she would go, touched the feed-pipe to make sure she wasn't overheating, and set out across the waterlogged fields to Mrs Saunders' farm. He had had nothing to eat all day but some hard-tack and bungo — ship's biscuit and rock-like cheese that he kept in a tin in the mill for just such an emergency — and he had to rely on the still torrential rain to give him an impromptu wash, which it did very imperfectly, so that he arrived at Hester's harvest-fields resembling a half-drowned chimney-sweep.

Billy Onyett was there, still mowing: and there was Hester, in the old fen-woman's padded bonnet and a dripping shawl, raking the heavy damp wheat. She looked up in astonishment at the great blackened figure jogging up to her, and then gave a cry of relief.

"Oh! Jonathan, it is you — Charlie gave me your message. What a sight I must look!"

"No picture myself, I'm afraid, Mrs Saunders," Jonathan said, roping back his hair, which was as wet as a swimmer's.

"Folk must think we're mad reaping in this weather," Hester said, "but if it's going to keep up, I thought we ought to get on with it and not waste a minute."

"You did right," Jonathan said, picking up a scythe. "I'm sorry I couldn't come before — but I can put in a couple of hours now."

"Jonathan, have you been running the engine all day?" Hester said. "You must be so tired already — haven't you had any dinner?"

"I'm had a bite," Jonathan said. "Let's git this wheat finished, eh?" He was swinging the scythe before he had finished speaking.

At supper-time Billy Onyett, looking more than ever like a bedraggled wading-bird, took himself off home; but Jonathan and Hester laboured on, the only moving things beneath the tent of cloud, with all about them the vivid percussive sound of rain on standing wheat, like the endless applause of a vast crowd. They did not speak: they did not even look up until Edie Smeeth came out to them from the house with an umbrella.

"Ain't you coming in, missus? It'll be dark any minute," she said — holding the umbrella over Hester, as if she were not already so drenched that she inhabited a pool of water within her clothes. "I'm put some good soup on — you could smell it from here if the rain weren't in the way."

Hester pressed her hands to the small of

her back as she straightened. "Ow! I suppose I'd better come in. Jonathan, won't you have some soup? — I'm sure you could do with something."

"Much obliged, Mrs Saunders," Jonathan said, "but I'm got to git back to the mill — the engine'll want firing."

"Shall you have to be there all night?" Hester said. "How will you sleep?"

"I'll tek a cat-nap once she's all stoked up," said Jonathan. He looked about him, where a corner of the field like the hem of a handkerchief remained to be mown. "I'll be here as soon as I can tomorrer."

"Make sure you get some sleep," she said. "And Jonathan — thank you — " but already he was jogging back in the direction of the mill.

The rain did not stop that night. Jonathan ran the pump continually, until the mill-house sweltered and the steam ran down the walls, but still the water in the drain, bearing the burden of the Hinching Fen dykes, brimmed at the banks. Some time before dawn he snatched a doze on his mattress on the floor, but anxiety about the pump kept starting him awake with galvanic jerks, and always in his mind he was either shovelling coal or scything wheat. In the morning he dipped his head in a bowl of cold water to freshen him, swallowed some tea and hard-tack, and after stoking again ran over to put in a couple of hours' work on the harvest. He succeeded in getting the last of the wheat cut, and before he had to go back to the mill he stood a minute with Hester looking at the fields under

552

their curtain of steady rain. Already the heads of the stooks, which had stood up like golden shaving-brushes, were draggled and drooping.

"It's like the summer's gone all wrong," Hester said, leaning on her rake.

"I remember a downpour like this in '80," said Jonathan. "Best get the wheat carted as soon as you can."

He meant to get back to the farm late that afternoon, but he was delayed when he found a boiler overheating: the feed-pipe was blocked and he had to dismantle it and clean it before he felt the engine was safe to leave for a while. It was early evening when he finally got over to the fields, and after a short remission it was raining again. Old Walt, after a day's carting, was getting ready to go home: his joints played him up in the wet. Billy Onyett stayed until it began to fall dark, but after that there was only Jonathan and Hester.

"Do you want to go in, Mrs Saunders?" Jonathan said.

"No — if you can stay a bit longer, Jonathan, I'll carry on," she said. "I'll fetch a storm-lamp: and I can go up on the cart."

He hesitated. "It's heavy work — are you sure . . . ?"

"I reckon I'm as strong as old Walt, and I can handle a hoss. Give me a budge up."

Jonathan lifted her on to the cart; and they worked on into darkness. At last, returning to the stack-yard with the laden cart, Jonathan walking beside the horse's head saw Hester slumping over the reins.

"You're half asleep," he said as she got down. "This had better be the lot. Throw a rick-cloth over the load for tonight."

"I am weary now," she said, wiping an open hand across her face, child-like as one is when deeply tired. "We're done well, though, haven't we?"

"Safely gathered in," he said with a smile. "Git going again early tomorrow. Shall I see to the hoss for you?"

"No, I can do that, Jonathan — you're done enough, you'll want your sleep. You will be able to get home for a proper rest tonight, won't you?"

"I should think so," he said. "Good night."

But there was little chance of that. There was still scarcely a breath of wind to ripple the unrelenting rain, and he had to run the pump at the mill all night. Once, sitting down for a moment to rest, he fell asleep in the chair with his head against the wall, and woke sweating from a dream in which the boiler was about to explode and he was locked in the mill. He went outside to clear his head, and found that the rain had stopped. A few stars were reflected in the swollen drain.

"Now stay like that," Jonathan said.

He went in, slept a good sleep on his mattress, and rose to find battalions of cloud re-forming, and the rain coming down.

All morning as he fed the boilers he chafed at the thought of the wet stooks in Hester's fields. If only Charlie Smeeth could mind the mill for him — but the boy would have his

554

hands full at Henry Wake's, getting in the harvest there . . . At three o'clock he piled on coal, then flung on his jacket and left the pump working. The mill would have to manage by itself for a while — that was all there was to it.

Again he worked at carting till it was dark, and again he and Hester were the last, labouring on by lamplight. Once she raised her face to the sky and shook her fist. "Oh, stop your damn everlasting rain!" she cried. "Why d'you have to be so cruel?"

"I'm often done that myself," Jonathan said. "But I'm never got an answer."

"D'you believe there's anyone up there to hear, Jonathan?" she asked him.

"I don't know. Sometimes I do. But whoever it is, I don't reckon he's the listening sort."

"Neither do I," said she. "I'm glad I'm not the only one. And folk think you're wicked for that, don't they? As if you can choose not to believe."

"You can choose not to give in," Jonathan said. "Thass what we're doing."

"Yes." She mopped back her dripping hair, then bent again to lift the unwieldy sheaves. "I shan't give in."

When he got back to the mill at ten, not having seen his home for three days, he was startled to find a light within. Charlie Smeeth appeared, black with coal-dust.

"There you are, sir — hope you didn't mind — I come to see you and I lifted the latch and found the mill empty and the boilers had

555

nearly gone out, so I stoked up — was that all right, sir?"

"Gone out?" said Jonathan with alarm.

"All but cold, sir — I got 'em going again."

"You're a fine fellow, Charlie — you'll make a better miller than I some day," Jonathan said. "Run home to your bed now — you're earned it."

When Charlie had gone Jonathan set about replenishing the boilers with an agitated mind. The consciousness of having neglected his duty, even briefly, was bitterest gall to him: the knowledge that most millers had their lax moments was no consolation to a nature which was both exacting and tinged with arrogance — that was well enough for *them*, but *he* should have known better. He set his face against any sleep that night. He was down beneath the floorboards oiling the pumps when there was a great hammering at the mill-house door, and he opened it to find Chad Langtoft there.

"Come quick, Miller," Chad said. "Milney Bank's busted — a gret crack big as a field-gate — Sunny Daintree and Henry Wake and me were bank-watching when we saw it. There's folk there trying to stem it but we s'll have a job."

"I'll come," Jonathan said, throwing on his jacket. "God above, Milney Bank? The whole fen'll be drowned."

"We're been watching it every night — Milney Drain's been full to the brim these three days. You got anything here we can tek to put in the breach?"

"Damn, not a thing," Jonathan said. "And raining still."

They spoke little as they hurried along the path by the drain. Chad Langtoft seemed to have been trying to change his ways, and not drink so much: the change was since about the time of Lyle Saunders' death, and perhaps that was what had made him stop feeling sorry for himself and pull himself together, folk said — but instead he drank deeply of an intolerant brew of religion, which caused sudden outbursts about sin, and he took you up sharper than ever; so Jonathan had as few words with him as possible. His mind, moreover, was caught up at that moment with troubled thoughts of the harvest, and the precious root crops still unlifted.

He found a swarm of people at the breach in the drain bank, all talking at once — cursing, lamenting, suggesting, and arguing with each other in their alarm. A couple of horses and carts had been brought up, and all manner of miscellaneous material was being heaped into the breach like a barricade. Jonathan found himself shifting bags of cement, gate-posts, an old mattress, a gunning-boat, and numerous iron hurdles with which to shore the whole mess up, whilst Henry Wake ran round and round on his short legs, telling everybody to put everything everywhere else. But when someone finally illumined the shadowy scene, by lighting paraffin in a brazier so that a great white flare went up, Jonathan saw how feeble and how pathetic had been their efforts — the sad pile of homely goods from house and yard looking so childish, and presenting an eloquent image of the puniness of man's efforts against nature, once she decided to flex even indolently her muscles. Whilst the rain still poured from the sky, it was difficult to tell where the general wetness ended and the flow of flood-water began; but old Andrew Surfleet, standing beside Jonathan as he rested a moment, lifted the end of his stick with a fragment of weed sticking to it. "No," he said, shaking his head with the resignation of a lifelong war with flood, "there wun't be a happy end to this one, Jonathan bor. You'd best jack your furniture up on bricks, and lay a plank for the puss-cat."

★ ★ ★

Hester heard that Milney Bank had blown some time before dawn, when Billy Onyett called at the Crooked House on his way to the breach to pass on the news. Within a few minutes she was dressed and hurrying over there to see if there was anything to be done. There was a greyness in the sky, more like a weakening of darkness than the positive coming of light, when she arrived at the scene. A few people were still there, struggling to shore up the barricade in the crumbling bank-earth, but most had gone home to look to their own affairs as the water crept up. "We shall be awash, missus," Artie Gill said, at her inquiring look, "thass the breadth of it — awash."

Hester's mind flew to her hard-won harvest,

558

with an almost maternal intensity of feeling. All that work gone to waste? All that labour, in which she had invested her bruised self and found some redemption, come to nothing? Suddenly she saw Jonathan, still striving to heap up the motley barrier, and called his name.

"Ain't there nothing to be done, Jonathan?"

"Not now she's blown," Jonathan said. "I reckon that late frost we had must have cracked the bank-earth. Well, no point in worrying about the mill now. I'll just have to shut down the engine till we get word from the Drainage Commissioners — can't pump into a breached drain — you're just pumping straight on to the fields." He presented to her a grim smile. "He didn't listen, did he? We were right."

"At least we're got most of the wheat in," Hester said. "Oh, but all the taters, all the roots — " Potatoes were an increasingly precious fenland crop, and the loss of hers would be the most telling blow to her precarious solvency.

"Only one thing to do," Jonathan said. "Lift 'em all now, before they're quite ruined."

She looked solemnly at him: she saw how his eyes had the raw stare of fatigue. "Can we do it?" she said.

"I'm ready," he said. "I'm ready now."

He walked back to the farm with her. He trudged slowly and, concerned at his tiredness, she suggested he go home and get some sleep first; but he would not hear of it, and by the time they reached the Crooked House, his stride had lengthened again, as if he had somehow tapped a fresh vein of vitality within him.

Walt, Billy Onyett, and a couple of day-men got on with the carting of the remainder of the wheat, and the mounting of the stacks on high staddles out of the wet, whilst Jonathan and Hester repaired to the root-fields.

The potato-fields, which had been a mass of purple flower in early summer, presented a bleak sight. The flooding of the fen was both dramatic and coolly impersonal. In the creeping up of the dun waters there was a dreadful and soul-blighting reversal, for those who had tilled the drowning fields with hope and sinew — but it was also, with harsh irony, a reversal to normality: the water was simply claiming its own. Across this colourless wash of landscape Hester and Jonathan moved with bent backs, grubbing up the cold potatoes from the mud, urgent and unthinking — fighting the hostile earth for food quite as elementally as if their sodden clothes were skins and furs, and their tools of bone and horn.

Hester learnt that day that discomfort, whilst never becoming anything more than discomfort, could yet be as afflicting as actual pain. She was up to her ankles in water; water still drizzled from the sky, running down her neck and back and breast and trickling from her very eyebrows; water chapped her hands, so that she could barely feel the haft of her fork. Whenever she straightened up to look round at the drear scene about her, with the water steadily rising to the tops of the rows, there was a feeling in her lower back of taut threads being terribly tightened; and when she trudged back to the

560

house for something to eat, the mud pulled at her boots with grotesque suckings, as if the earth begrudged her even the facility of walking.

Jonathan stayed out in the field, working on. She took him out a pork dumpling and new bread and hot tea and made him eat.

"You can't go on without food," she said, finding what shelter there was under a thorn bush. "Rest a while."

Jonathan ate mechanically, occasionally putting out an upturned hand to feel the rain. "Fighting on two fronts, thass the trouble," he said. "I reckon we'll git most of 'em up, though — if we just stick at it."

"The house is all right, any road," Hester said. "That's one good thing about it standing up proud of the peat — the floors are higher than the flood. Oh! Jonathan — your cottage — won't the water come in?"

"A bit, mebbe," he said. "It won't hurt — the floor's loose brick, just made for floods, and there's no furniture that ain't got its feet wet before." He bolted the last of his food. "Thank you for that, Mrs Saunders. I'll set in again now."

Back at the house Hester sat down for a few moments, pulling off her boots and stockings. Her feet and calves were as cold, wet and white as the new-dug potatoes. She leaned back, closed her eyes, and felt soft plumes of indifference caressing her and cajoling her to let go and give in. Her life, since her resolution to go on, had been a series of stepping-stones — each day of work, of managing and striving and succeeding,

561

leading on to the next; but now as she stretched out her aching limbs, it seemed to her that she had come to the end of the stepping-stones, and the end of her capacity to care.

"Coh! missus, you look right trampled," said Edie coming in. "I'll fetch you some clean stockings. Walt says they'll git the last cart of corn in and stacked before sundown, don't you worry . . . Is the miller still in the tater-field, missus?"

"Yes, Edie." Against her will, the vision of Jonathan's long-backed figure stooping along the flooded rows appeared on her closed lids. It was he who had roused her to wrestle with the farm, and set out a plan of salvation: was it up to him alone to carry it through to the end?

She sat up, put on the stockings that Edie brought her, and pulled on her boots. "Back to work, Edie," she said.

Billy Onyett joined them in the potato-field that afternoon, carting away the lifted roots to clamp, and later Edie came too, hopping along the rows in her white apron like a bright wagtail. Just before dusk the rain stopped, quite suddenly, and the day ended with a brief coda of streaky sunshine.

"It's a bit late for that, you ole beggar," Hester said to the sky. "Jonathan, you're done wonders, but you ought to go home. You can only do so much — we're got a fair few up."

Jonathan glanced blankly round at her. His fatigue made him look bleached, as if he had been bled. "I'll carry on a while," he said.

"Water's still rising — these'll be drowned soon."

He stayed out there after darkness fell, working by lamplight. Hester, after a bite of supper, sent Edie to bed — even her energy was exhausted — and then went round the stack-yard and looked at the tall covered ricks, the mound of roots. It was true: he had done wonders. The harvest, scrambled and part-spoiled as it was, had been got in, as much as was humanly possible. He could do no more.

She found him in the mangold-field. He did not know she was there until she touched his shoulder, and he started.

"Enough, Jonathan," she said. "Please. You're only flesh and blood — " As she said the word *blood* she looked down at his hands. The days of stoking the engines and labouring in the waterlogged field had left them rubbed raw. "Oh! Jonathan — your hands — I didn't know . . . Come on. You must put something on them. I'm got some goose-grease in the house."

Still crouched over the rows, Jonathan said, "But these mangolds — and there's the turnips — "

"The stack-yard's nearly full," Hester said. "We're done it — I'll survive — truly. Come on . . . What is it?"

Jonathan winced and shook his head. "I can't straighten up," he said. "Dear God — I shall be walking about like poor ole Andrew Surfleet."

"It's the wet that's done it," she said. Wet-harvesting, stooping for hours at a time in cold water, could send crippling pains shooting through the back and loins: she remembered Mr Langtoft saying he had once wept like a child with it. "You must get dry. Come on — lean on me. Lean on my shoulder."

He hesitated. "I'm no feather, Mrs Saunders — "

"Well, I'm no weakling neither," said she smiling. "You're got to lean on someone every now and then, Jonathan — you can't always stand alone."

Slowly they made their way back to the house, Jonathan hunched and hobbling, and in spite of his protests that he'd be off home in a minute she made him sit in the kitchen before the range, which was still hot, while she smeared the goose-grease on to his large cracked hands.

"First time I'm ever been waited on," he said.

"It won't hurt you for once . . . Is it very bad — your back?" she said anxiously, seeing the sharp line between his brows.

"It — I'm known nicer feelings," he said through clenched teeth.

"Mr Langtoft reckoned horse-oils made him feel easier. I know Walt keeps some. Could you bear to be treated like a hoss, d'you think?"

"Nay," he said. He was in that gripping, startling pain which somehow squeezes the mind into a feeble flippancy. "Well — if you don't mind . . . "

She found the horse-oils and, peeling up his shirt, rubbed the glistening stuff with her fingers into the skin of Jonathan's lower back. To

564

the eye this smooth and well-shaped physique seemed scarcely susceptible to pain, and only the way the muscles twanged beneath her hands like tortured wires showed what he was suffering. The sight of him, so indomitably strong, reduced like this, and the knowledge that it was on her behalf, touched her with almost unbearable keenness; and she wished that her soul might speak out at her fingertips and soothe as deeply as she felt.

"Any better?" she said at length.

He nodded. "Thank you . . . You're very kind."

"It's me who should be thanking you, Jonathan — but it's like we were saying the other week: I just can't say my thanks any way equal to what I feel . . . As long as you know it. Now, drink this," she said, mixing him a hot toddy of rum. "I shan't forgive myself if you're gone and ruined yourself clawing up my harvest."

"Right as rain in a while," he said, swallowing the drink. "Well — not rain."

"No — definitely not rain," she laughed. "What an end to the summer . . . There'll be lots of crops spoiled on the fen, won't there? What will the Drainage Commissioners do?"

"They'll have to get some contractors to repair the breach in the bank properly. No good pumping till then — just have to wait for the water to go down." Jonathan consulted his turnip watch. "I'd better be moving." He levered himself out of the chair, and by a great effort of will stood almost upright.

"Jonathan, are you sure? I mean — will you be all right?"

"I reckon so, Mrs Saunders. The horse-oils worked a treat. I ought to git home for once — my poor ole cat'll be hungry — 'less he's caught a fish in the street."

She smiled. "Well, don't come early tomorrow — d'you hear? This is me being sharp with you. And when you do come, I shall give you them wages at last — and you shan't turn 'em down this time. And if there should be a bonus there you'll take it — as a friend — like we said. D'you hear?"

"Right you are." He walked stiffly to the door, then on the threshold turned, with a smile that was for the moment clear of pain. "All safely gathered in, eh? Good night, Mrs Saunders."

4

WITHIN the barn behind the Crooked House, above a dozen people were gathering in a kindly October dusk. On the lintel above the door were fixed sheaves of wheat, signifying the harvest supper, or as it was known in the fens, the horkey.

This was a special horkey. The idea for it had grown in Hester's mind out of her increasing desire to do something to say thank you to all the people who had helped her in the first stricken months of her widowhood; and the generally gloomy state of Hinching Fen following the flood offered another motive. If it had been a bad year, then she reasoned — with an echo of her old gaiety of spirit — that there was all the more need for a little junketing; and her harvest had been better than most. And so all the friends who had worked for her or helped or offered to help or had simply been consoling landmarks in a waste of despair were invited to the farm to eat and drink as hugely as they might at the long trestle tables in the lamplit barn, which was the only place big enough to hold them.

Hester and Edie had been busy all day preparing the feast, and Lizzie Gosling had come over in the afternoon to lend a hand. Working beside her in the kitchen, Lizzie had paused and taken Hester by the elbow and held her at arm's length.

"Let's have a look at you, then," Lizzie said. "Let's see how the land lies."

Hester smiled at Lizzie's dark, clever, tolerant face. "What d'you see then?"

"Well, I see a human — thass summat," said Lizzie.

"Didn't you before, then?" Hester said, smiling, but soberly.

Lizzie shook her head. "Not really. Midsummer I was frit to see you . . . You was like a shadow what had been torn away from the person it belonged to."

"Was I? I suppose that's how I felt," Hester said. "I didn't think I'd ever climb up. I did — but not on my own . . . I'm not frit any more, Lizzie — not always sort of flinching at life. It's like a skin's grown back somewhere. There's still a sort of hollow feeling, right deep inside, and I don't reckon that can ever change. But I know I'm going to go on — and that there's years ahead, waiting to be dealt with, and I'm not afraid of 'em."

So it was: she had climbed up, most of all out of the clinging entrapment of self, and it was a great satisfaction to her to see the company sit down at the trestle tables, and attack the eatables with a flattering lack of ceremony. The food was all set out along the centre, between vases of flowers sprigged with corn-ears, and the idea was that if there was something you could not reach, you hollered for it to be passed down to you: thus Hester and Edie could sit down with the rest, and did not have to wait on them. Hams and legs of cold roast pork formed the mainstay of the supper, but there were pork pies, bowls of boiled eggs, pickled onions jostling to the lip of the jar, potatoes speckled with mint, new bread and new butter like two extremes of gold, apple and plum pies and tarts as deep as tubs, and an abundance of ale still with the cold sweat of the Crooked House's peaty cellar on the jars. Hester sat at the head, with Edie and Charlie Smeeth on either side; Henry Wake had characteristically appropriated the other end of the table (Mrs Wake remaining as usual incommunicado) and was ostentatiously carving for Peggy Chettle, who had left her bicycle in the stable just as if it were a beast of the manger, and whose great teeth crunched upon onions with a noise like breaking brushwood. Artie Gill had brought his fiddle, but was not drunk enough yet to play it, and was grumpily denying to Sunny Daintree that he was going to play at all; Andrew Surfleet and Mrs Surfleet gnawed diminutively, like two hoary squirrels, and reminisced with old Walt through a long backward succession of horkeys; Lizzie Gosling and her brother Jack came in for all Billy Onyett's broadest, cheesiest jokes.

Only Jonathan was not there. He had sent word that he might be delayed, having been called to a special meeting of the Drainage Commissioners in Stokeley. Since the repair of Milney Bank he had been almost continually occupied at the mill, running the pump to clear the last of the flood waters. His absence could not be helped; yet it seemed to Hester that a harvest supper at the Crooked House — after

569

those labours of his for which the word heroic was alone appropriate — was sadly incomplete without him.

"How did Jonathan go to Stokeley, do you know, Charlie — on the carrier?" Hester asked Charlie Smeeth.

"I dunno, missus — I doubt it — anythink less'n ten mile he goes on his legs. He had his best clo'es on the smorning, any road — I went to show him mine — and he said my blue gansy was an out-and-outer, he did!" concluded Charlie, with a modest reference to his neckerchief.

"Best blue gansy and a hole in his trews," Edie said, with sisterly disesteem. "Honestly, Charlie Smeeth, what an item you are wi' that gret tater sticking out your knee."

"I couldn't help it — I tunnied over on the way here."

"I dunno," Edie said. "Only you could fall over on a flat road in broad daylight. I dunno what you'd do if you lived where there was hills!"

"I should think I should fall over like fun," said Charlie, with equal humility and logic.

"You were hurrying to get here, I should think, Charlie," Hester said. "And I take that as a very nice compliment."

"Thass a pity the lad's so awk'ud in his limbs, though," Sunny Daintree said. "Ooh! dear. I wouldn't be a bit surprised if he's outgrowing his strength. I knew a lad like that once, as had to tek to his bed when he turned sixteen, and lay there like a gret daddy-long-legs for a whull year, waiting for his strength to catch up, and tekking his meals through a straw."

"I'm strong — I am," said Charlie. "It's just me feet go on too long."

"And one's bigger than tother," Edie said.

"That wun't hurt," said Andrew Surfleet. "It gives a body a bit o' character. 'Fearfully and wonderfully made', thass what the psalm says we are — fearfully and wonderfully made. Why, one of my legs goes up higher than tother, at the top: I can't recall which one it is, just on the tip o' the moment, but I know it's one on 'em — and it don't seem to go no further down, but it surely goes up higher than tother one at the top — don't it, gel?" he said to his wife.

"Andrew," Mrs Surfleet said, affrontedly, "don't talk Sauce."

"They're mebbe giving Miller a bonus, for all the work he's put in," said Billy Onyett.

"Ah! he belongs to git a bit of recognition," Andrew Surfleet said. "A boon — thass what he's been. Not as I weren't a bit frit of him at fust — the way he used to frown down at you from atop o' them gret shoulders; but thass more manner than meaning."

"Well, I'm a married woman," Peggy Chettle said, "and I'd not trade Chettle, even with his little trouble: but if I was a few dark hairs younger, and bare-fingered, and forward with it — why, wouldn't I give that miller a buss! — and never mind cheeks neither!"

The barn was, at least in part, considerably older than the Crooked House itself. The far stone wall was pierced by high narrow ogive

571

windows, through which the late sunlight was syringed in honey-coloured concentration, revealing lofty and massive roof-beams hung with immemorial cobwebs as heavy as tapestry. The great door stood open to the quiet evening, and from time to time a sparrow would flit in and out, as casually as if it were passing beneath a canopy of trees. The smooth floor of the barn standing well proud of the earth, the feasters within bore an air of being slightly larger than life, and uplifted above the mortal — an impression reinforced by a general haze and bloom of straw-dust which, teeming in the orange light, seemed to make their every gesture magnified and deliberate, as in a half-way house between men and gods. There was no doubt that, after the ache and fret of the wet harvest, and with the pinch of winter lying ahead, all felt their present situation at the convivial table could scarcely be more desirable; and Billy Onyett declared that if he didn't eat his length in rashers, he'd never trust his teeth more.

"A sad sight to see, Milney St Mary church all closed and boarded as it is," Sunny Daintree said. "It's all to be turned innards-out, vicar says: restoration they call it. I know the screen were like a lace-hankercher wi' worm."

"It's hard for church-folk," said Henry Wake, resplendent in a high and roomy starched collar into which his head periodically sank up to the eyebrows. "Us chapel-folk can go to church if we will, but church-folk can't be doing with chapel — rather like a cat can't follow a mouse through a mousehole, though the mouse can go through the cat-flap. Thass what you call a similitude, you know."

"I call it stuff," grunted Artie Gill. "Cats and mice, indeed!" He was tetchy because no one had asked him to play his fiddle lately, and given him the pleasure of refusing.

"Ah, thass a heathenish thing to lack a church, even if you don't go to it," Sunny Daintree said. "What we could do with is that there floating church coming down our river."

"Why, whass that then?" said Andrew Surfleet, open-mouthed.

"Thass a barge, bor, all roofed over like, where they hold church services," Sunny said, forking up a vast slice of ham and chewing it in like a goat eating a newspaper. "Vicar over Ely way had it built, reckoning as a lot of folk out on the lone fen weren't gitting benefit of clergy; and he sails it from place to place, and fetches folk aboard, to top 'em up wi' religion. I'm seen it moored at Pondersbridge — the Fenland Ark they call it. Pews and all, and a little organ sounding off the note, just like a real one."

"Well, I don't know about that," said Andrew, with a glance of wonderment at his wife. "That can't be right. A church has got to be on consecrated ground, don't it? Thass not on any ground!"

"Well, there's pews," Sunny said. "I can answer for the pews; and thass church enough for me."

"The water's consecrated, I dare say," said Henry Wake comfortably. "I think you'll find thass what they'd do — consecrate the waters."

"Why, holy water's Popish, ain't it?" said Andrew, alarmed. "Chaps in night-shirts, sprinkling it out of salt-cellars — I'm seen it in a book. No, no — none of that for me: old Oliver Grumble'd squirm in his casket."

"I should like to see that there Ark," Charlie Smeeth said with energy. "I never do see things somehow — like when a balloon went over, from Pete'borough Fair, and I missed it on account of just when I were looking up, a little fly flew right in my eye, and the balloon had gone over by the time I come un-blind again."

"Ah — it's wicked when a fly goes in your eye like that," said Andrew. "You just see it coming before it plunges in — and it's almost like it's aiming for you!"

"Terrible queer case for the fly, an' all," Sunny said. "Meeting its end in a gret eye. Ooh! dear — just think on it — with the gret lashes flapping round you . . . I shall likely have a bad dream about that tonight," he added to himself, "I wouldn't be a bit surprised."

"Well, now, neighbours," Henry Wake said, loudly clearing his throat and getting to his feet, which brought him about level with Peggy Chettle sitting down, "I hope you're all got a drop in your mugs: I reckon a toast's in order. I'm not a man of many words meself, but if I might just say a very few — "

"You might," said Artie Gill in an undertone, "but I bet you won't."

"I'm sure we'd all like to raise our sups to Mrs Saunders, for laying on such a do," Henry continued, "all the better for coming after a

574

poor ole time what we'll none of us be sorry to see the tail of, not to mention a particular sad time for one among us, which we won't allude to, which is to say except with sincerest respect, which we all feel, which I'm sure of." Becoming rather entangled in whiches, Henry coughed and disappeared into his collar for a moment. Surfacing again, he went on: "And I'm sure there's a lesson to us all, laid out in this here tasteful spread, and the hospitality of neighbours, what we'll all lay to our souls . . . " Billy Onyett chose this moment to launch a sulphurous belch, as a suave hint that Henry was somewhat losing his audience; and Henry concluded at the gallop: "Which I mean to convey as it were, a toast to Mrs Hester Saunders, and good health to her!"

They cheered and drank. Hester, profoundly moved, found herself rigid with unaccustomed shyness; and at last was only able to stammer out, half laughing, "Oh — you're very kind, and thank you — and I can't think what to say except thank you again — and have another drink, do — and — won't you play your fiddle when you're ready, Artie?"

Amid the general laughter and the commotion as Artie Gill at last struck up a tune, Hester was able surreptitiously to wipe her eyes — she still had a strange dread of being seen in tears — and to present a tolerably composed face when Edie asked her in a whisper, "Shall I clear all these here broken meats, missus?"

"No, leave them, Edie," Hester said. "Folk'll mebbe get a second appetite after a few dances.

You can fetch some more ale, though: it'll all soon get sweated out, and we want plenty for Jonathan when he comes."

There was space at the end of the barn for dancing, on what had been the threshing-floor, and here Artie Gill mounted on an upturned bran-tub and poured forth jigs and reels. Lizzie Gosling, laughing with her eyes though not her lips, footed it with Billy Onyett, in his tipsiness as limber as an eel; Lizzie's brother Jack danced with Edie, who seemed to be on springs; the ancient Surfleets slowly trod some decorous measure of their own, which might have been danced in powdered perukes and face-patches, and which gave the venerable couple the appearance of the little mechanical figures that come beetling out of twin doors on clock-faces to strike the hour; whilst Peggy Chettle and Henry Wake stood up together, after a brief discussion as to its propriety. "Bless you, dear man, two old married bodies like us, who're known each other practically since Ballyclava," said Mrs Chettle, "not to mention my trade, where I'm seen more britches down than up, and it don't mean no more to me than the sight of a dabbling duck — why, it's as innocent as lambs," and she proceeded to engulf Henry's hands in her own, and fling him about like someone shaking out a feather pillow. Charlie Smeeth, with the uneasy aloofness of his years at such an occasion, looked on at a distance; and perceiving this, Hester engaged him in conversation, accepting that her own place now was as an onlooker, with quietude, and with a certain wistfulness that she was glad to find was not bitter.

At length Artie Gill paused in his fiddling to take a long pull of ale. "A pity Miller's not here with his squeeze-box," said Andrew Surfleet. "He used to be shy as a man having his teeth drawn about it, but he'll play now, if you ask him."

Hester consulted the watch at her waistband. Where was Jonathan? It wasn't fair if those old buffers were keeping him at the Commissioners' meeting all this time.

All at once there was a cheer as Billy Onyett appeared holding aloft a broomstick he had fetched from the yard. "Show us, Sunny," he said, handing the broomstick to Sunny Daintree, who shook his head and groaned from the very depths of his soul, "give us the broomstick dance!"

"Ooh! I don't know," Sunny sighed, as the others joined their voices in calling for the broomstick dance. "I ain't done that since the ole Queen's last jubilee, and I swore then I wouldn't never do it again, not if she asked me herself with her crown on."

"Goo on, Mr Daintree," Charlie Smeeth said, "I'm never seen it — I missed the jubilee being laid up wi' the chicken-pox and all I had was a paper flag on the bed-post — goo on, do."

"Well, if I'm got to," said Sunny, ambling with the broomstick on to the threshing-floor, as Artie Gill struck up a fast jig. "Ooh! I'm too old for this game — I shall rue it — I shall never bend to me mole-traps in the morning — "

Abruptly Sunny ceased his moans, and sprang into an astonishing dance: grasping the handle of the broomstick with the besom resting on the floor before him, and executing a series of hops, throwing first one leg and then the other over the broom, and going faster and faster as the onlookers clapped in time, until his capering legs were almost a blur — all the time wearing the expression of a man performing some humdrum and slightly distasteful task which he will be glad to get over with. It was doubtful who would weaken first, Artie fiddling or Sunny dancing, but at the last it was Artie, breaking off the music with a despairing cadence, whilst Sunny went on to execute a few final unaccompanied leaps before dropping the broomstick and retiring with gloomy head-shakings to his seat amid the applause.

"No," he said, sipping his ale, "I tole you I couldn't do it."

While the others resumed the dancing, Hester looked at her watch again and spoke to Edie. "It's funny Jonathan not being here yet," she said: happy as she was that the horkey was going so well, she missed his presence sharply. "I wonder if he's all right."

"D'you want me to run and see if he's home yet, missus?" said Edie. "I can be there and back in two shakes."

"No — it's all right, Edie — I reckon I'll slip down to the village myself. I'm got an idea he might not like to turn up so late — you know how particular he can be about such things. Everything's all right here," she said, looking at the pounding dancers. "Make sure everyone's got enough to drink, Edie — I won't be long."

Hester stepped into the house to put on her hat, and walked across the stubble-fields, soaked in the autumn afterglow, to Milney St Mary. At Jonathan's cottage, before knocking, she glanced in at the window. He was there; seated in his hard chair before the cold hearth, staring intently into the middle distance, with his shirt-sleeved elbows upon his knees, and his pipe loosely held in his cupped hands. Immediately she had a sensation of being flung back in time — the scene reminded her so forcibly of the very first time she had ever seen Jonathan, through the smoke of that waterside inn to which her wanderings had brought her. What a strange, foolish, long-ago creature she saw in herself then! Hard on the heels of this impression came another — that Jonathan had been home some time, and had ignored her invitation to the horkey. This idea hurt her, and she stood in hesitation a moment immobilised by the pain of it, undecided whether to knock after all. But something odd about the way he was sitting there by the ashes turned the question for her. He answered her knock after a few moments: he looked more preoccupied than surprised.

"Mrs Saunders."

"Hullo, Jonathan. I — we wondered where you were."

"Ah. Of course. Will you come in?"

She entered the spartan house-place, all softened with dusky shadows. A kitten came to her, and she picked it up and gave it her finger to bite.

"Will you have a seat?" Jonathan said.

"It's all right, Jonathan — I'm just come to ask if you won't come along to the horkey. I know it's a bit late, but it don't matter — everybody's still kicking up their heels, and there's lots of ale — "

"I'm sorry, Mrs Saunders — I should have sent a message." Jonathan drew away from her and leaned his arm on the mantelshelf. "I'm had a bit of a day of it, to tell the truth."

"Oh, did you have a long meeting with the Commissioners? We were just saying, at the horkey, how you might be getting a bonus for all your extra work — "

"Nothing like that," he said, with a twitch of a smile. "I'm afraid I shan't be miller for Hinching Fen no more: they give me the sack."

For a second she thought he must be joking. "Jonathan . . . No! Why? How can they?"

"Oh . . . " Jonathan worked his hand through his hair, shrugged, and seemed about to dismiss it. "Something and nothing."

"But they must have a reason!"

Frowning down at the floor, Jonathan said: "Failing in your duty's what they call it. It was the time of that downpour — before the bank broke. Somebody came to the mill when I weren't there — when I'd left it unattended: whether it was one of the Commissioners, or just a busybody, I don't know. It don't matter: it got back to 'em that I were neglecting the mill just at the worst time, with the drain filling — and so I'm to be dismissed."

"Thass ridiculous. You all but broke your back keeping that mill going — anybody round here'll say so — " She stopped and bit her lip. "Oh! Jonathan — it was when you were helping me. It was when you were getting my harvest in — that must have been it — oh, I feel awful . . . Jonathan, I'm so sorry . . . "

"No, no," said he shortly, shaking his head, avoiding her eyes. "It don't matter — it can't be helped."

"But your job . . . Anybody on Hinching Fen'll vouch for you: I will. Yes, can't I go to the Commissioners — ?"

"It's no good, Mrs Saunders. Fact is, I reckon the whole situation was ripe for a scapegoat. Milney Bank should never have bust like it did: it seems likely the Commissioners weren't seeing to the upkeep of the banks like they should have, and I reckon they knew it. Just bad luck my head has to roll. In any case, once they had me up on the carpet like that . . . well, let's just say I was damned if I were going to beg and plead at 'em for the job," he said with harsh pride.

"Quite right too!" Hester said. "It's a terrible pity — I know how you liked that job . . . but any road, it's their loss. You know you don't have to worry about a living while I'm got the farm — at least I know a good man when I see one: and now I'm got set on my feet, we can think about you being a proper farm bailiff, and — "

"No, Mrs Saunders, I'm sorry," Jonathan said quickly. "I can't do that. I was going to tell you

— I can't work for you any more."

"Have you got another job?" she said, putting down the kitten.

"No, not yet, but I'll find one of some sort." He took a spill from the mantelshelf and toyed with it.

Hester regarded him steadily: still he would not look at her. "It's because you lost your miller's job on my account," she said. "I see that — I feel terrible about it, Jonathan, really — "

"No, it ain't that," he said. "Honestly, it ain't that at all."

"Then what is it?" she said, taking a step closer to him.

"I just think it's best I don't go on working for you, Mrs Saunders," Jonathan said, drawing himself up stiffly. "I'm glad the farm's all secure now — and I was glad to do what I could to help set it up. And now you're all right, I reckon I'll look for work elsewhere."

His coolness was utterly dismaying to her. It seemed to thrust her backwards — back towards the dry, empty, self-imprisoned days which she thought she had left behind; and all the small, healing triumphs she had made appeared suddenly hollow. She could hardly believe that the man who had shown such a discreet and delicate touch upon her flinchingly sore feelings should now turn about and hurt her in this way. She struggled to speak.

"Jonathan, I don't understand — I thought you were my friend . . . I really thought you were my friend."

Jonathan snapped the spill between his fingers.

582

"No offence, Mrs Saunders," he said, speaking briskly and yet looking everywhere but at her. "I'm grateful for all the work you give me, and truly there's no bad feeling towards you over me losing the mill job — I would have done exactly the same if I'd known that was going to happen. But I really think it's best for all concerned if I git work elsewhere from now on. I'm happy you're got things on an even keel, and I hope they stay so — I'm sure they will. Sorry about the horkey, but I'm a bit weary-limbed." The frown and the lowering of his heavy lids seemed to make his eyes physically withdraw, as if in token of his greater withdrawal from her.

She did not understand; and the coldness seemed all the sharper after the warm and genial feelings of that day. "Well," she said quietly. "If you say so." Her dismay was too great even to allow her to challenge him, and something — perhaps maturity — inhibited her from wantonly throwing back the darts of pain from her own breast. The room had passed from dusk to darkness as they talked, and she fumbled blind for the door-latch. "Goodbye, then," she said, and stumbled out before she could hear his reply.

★ ★ ★

Gentle autumn gave birth to a stern, gaunt, thrustful winter, who howled in chill winds through the broken slates and decayed window-frames of the Crooked House, and reminded Hester that she must begin to turn her mind

583

to the state of the buildings, now that the farm as an economic concern was moderately secure. She was far from approaching a condition of luxury — there were no fortunes to be made with wheat twenty-six shillings a quarter — but neither was she in debt; and at the banker's and solicitor's she noted some raising of grizzled eyebrows at the way she had put through a programme of retrenchment and brought the farm round to solvency so smartly. What, she wondered, had these men expected? Did they suppose she would squander herself bankrupt on frocks and hats as soon as she was out of six months' mourning? It was a pleasure to feel the rebirth of this feisty scepticism within her: she found that, imperceptibly, she had ceased to be intimidated by the panelled offices and wing-collars — and it must have shown, for now a clerk was always despatched respectfully to conduct her out to the little spring-cart in which she had invested.

She had bought that for a song, too, having successfully beaten down the farmer who sold it to her; the thriftiness which had been a life-sustaining challenge was now a habit. Unhappily, she no longer found the same satisfaction in it. She had left behind the dark valleys of bereaved and helpless grief, and now found herself on a plateau of neutral acceptance, featureless to the view, and leading nowhere in particular — a prospect comfortably without threat, but seeming to offer nothing to engage the powers of her reviving soul. The work of the farm went on in the cold and overcast days — ploughing and drilling, all the potatoes to be riddled and the wheat threshed — there was always enough to do to keep her busy twenty hours a day if she chose; and at first she thought the tang of weariness was nothing new. Only gradually did she come to see that this sensation of being utterly alone, of forever feeling the yoke of life pressing down on her sole shoulders, was not a continuation of the helplessness of her bereavement: that had been left behind, and this was something new. Only gradually did she come to realise how acutely the loss of Jonathan's friendship affected her, and in the process to perceive the strengths of that friendship, which at the time had been as the stout unseen keel of a buoyant ship.

And it was in working the farm that she missed it most: in work — demanding, satisfying, undertaken side by side — their friendship had struck roots. On Jonathan she had relied without depending; in him she had confided, with no furtive feeling of thrusting secrets on an unwilling ear, and she had been rewarded with a reciprocal confidence, as natural as the earth they tilled together. It was this unforced and organic quality about their friendship that made the absence of it so disorientating, and caused her mind to worry at it like a tongue probing the gap of a missing tooth; and left her pensively puzzling over Jonathan's decision, and how it was that he so coolly accepted a withdrawal which was to her a disabling wrench.

The explanation that occurred most insistently to her was Jonathan's pride. If she was to believe his assertion that he did not blame her for the loss of his miller's job — and to imagine Jonathan lying was like imagining the stars being made of tinsel — then the most plausible reason for his refusing to work for her was that he was simply too proud; that to continue taking work from her, once the crisis was over, would seem to him like taking charity — and their friendship would make the situation all the more uncomfortable. This accorded well with what she knew was a sternly, sometimes bleakly honourable nature; and yet it did not quite fit. He must know that she needed labour, that Billy Onyett was more well-meaning than reliable, and that there would be quite as much commonsense as gratitude in her employing the man who had almost single-handedly saved her harvest. Surely he must see that.

She was troubled too by thoughts of how Jonathan was managing without his steady miller's wage. There was much sympathy and good feeling towards him on Hinching Fen, and the new miller, a droopy object who had come over from Norfolk where they all had chalk for brains, was poorly thought of; but it was the lean season, and work was thin on the ground. In December Sunny Daintree, who acted as the local rat-catcher, came to rat the stack-yard at the Crooked House, and Hester took the opportunity to ask him what Jonathan was doing.

"Turns his hand to whatever's going, I reckon, missus," said Sunny. "A while ago he did blackbelly-picking for that chap as comes down from Wisbech wi' the baskets and pays you by the pound — starve-gut sort of work: but he's been on the land as well, stone-picking here, digging gault there. Ooh! they're narrow sort of times, these, missus: I'm not sure as we shall ever squeeze through 'em. And now chaps going off to fight these here Boo-ers over tother side of the world — don't ask me why — there's enough battles near at hand without going looking for 'em. Old Gladstone would never have allowed it. Ooh! dear. If there's better coming, it's on tother side of a pile of worst."

Even allowing for Sunny's habit of looking on the dark side, this was a discouraging report of Jonathan. Its shadow touched an otherwise convivial Christmas that Hester kept at the Crooked House with Lizzie and Jack Gosling, and it lingered into a freezing, flint-hearted new year, until a chance remark one day galvanised her, and set her quiescent emotions on end like hackles.

The steam threshing-tackle was making its tour of the farms, and benevolently signalling its progress by flattening out the rutted, ankle-turning surface of the winter droves. While the machine was at Henry Wake's, Hester went over to see the engineer and fix the date when he should come to the Crooked House for the threshing of her wheat. This engineer was a coaly, sinewy, taciturn man, who worked as hard as he drank; and Edie Smeeth informed Hester later that day that he had been thrown out of the Labour In Vain the other night.

"Too drunk, was he?" Hester said.

"Oh! no," Edie said, "he couldn't git drunk

enough — thass what it was — he reckoned Jass Phelps were watering the beer, 'cause he'd had six pints and he couldn't feel no difference — so there was a bit of name-calling, and he were turfed out. I don't know whether it's true about the beer, but they reckon Jass Phelps can't afford to lose custom like that, what wi' Chad Langtoft mending his ways and going all funny and religious instead of supping, and then the miller-as-was refusing to set foot in the place any more."

"Jonathan? Why's that, Edie?"

"Oh!" Edie suddenly flushed from nape to scalp. "It were — it were just a quarrel — I dunno."

"Jonathan quarrelling?" Hester said. "No, I don't believe it. Edie . . . come on, tell me."

"Oh — I don't like to say, missus." Edie swallowed, as visibly as a frog. "It was just . . . well, they reckon Jass Phelps — you know what he's like — said summat about how Jonathan seemed to be keeping his distance nowadays from — from that pretty widow at the Crooked House, and how it was about time too, and it looked like he wasn't going to get his legs under her table after all. Thass Jass Phelps saying it, not me, missus! And they reckon Jonathan didn't say nothing, just got hold of Jass Phelps by his neckercher, and picked him right up till his boots weren't touching the floor — and then it was as though he thought better of it, and let him go like a sack of taters, and he walked out and won't go back there no more . . . I'm sorry, I didn't want to say it, missus . . . "

"Well, I did ask you, Edie," Hester said gently.

But she wished she had not: or at least, wished that she had not heard, or . . . She did not know what to think. How mean and stupid people could be! She remembered how careful Jonathan had been of her reputation before. No wonder he had half throttled Jass Phelps: she felt like it herself. The tale certainly threw some light on why Jonathan had elected not to work for her any more . . . but the substance of her reaction to it was a sad disgust at the friendship she had valued being chewed and mangled in gossiping mouths. It seemed more than ever a pitiable waste of what was good and true.

It was the chill middle of February, the time of the year that most closely corresponds to the small hours of the night, when all the faculties of life are at their lowest ebb, and the merest pulsebeat differentiates the sleeper in darkness from death: thus it was with the earth, frozen beneath an overpowering leaden sky. This sky, plainly stored with snow, yet remained obstinately dry, as if even to release the flakes would be a relenting — an adulteration of pure winter. In the stack-yard of the Crooked House the steam-engine that ran the thresher throbbed and rumbled, throwing out sparks that hissed upon the frosted cobblestones, and Hester, pulling on her gloves and pinning a muffler round her throat preparatory to going out, watched Billy Onyett and Walt begin feeding the first sheaves into the machine. Billy, looking unsteady on the vibrating platform, did not care for this work: what a pity Jonathan was not here — how he would sail through it as if it were nothing! Yet she had resolved that her feeling of loyalty towards Jonathan would not be wasted in regrets: if he would not work for her, then she would help him to other work — extend to him a supporting hand, as he had disinterestedly done to her, even if she could only do so by proxy. She had recently learned that Lyle could have served as a Drainage Commissioner for Hinching Fen, as the farm was of the required acreage. Characteristically, he had not bothered; but as the property was now hers, she had a right to attend the Commissioners' meetings (even though there would surely be resistance to a woman being actually sworn in as a Commissioner) and take part in their decisions. And amongst those decisions was who should run the Hinching Fen mill.

So she drove the little spring-cart to Stokeley, and sat down with the Commissioners in a private room at the Spread Eagle; and in spite of their efforts to asphyxiate her with pipe-smoke, and drown her out with jingling watch-chains, and generally put paid to her with a great parade of velvet-waistcoated, round-bellied, patronising masculinity, she patiently persisted in raising the matter of Jonathan Eastholm's dismissal from the post of miller, and stating why she believed it to be a mistake. She referred for testimony to the many small proprietors of Hinching Fen, and drew attention to the deficiencies of the new miller; and she found an ally in Farmer Mather, who said he had always opposed the decision. An old buffer who sported a huge bristly moustache, as if he were inhaling a hedgehog, began to come round to her way of thinking, though it seemed he was impressed more by her pretty ankles than her arguments; and the meeting adjourned with an agreement to inspect thoroughly the work of the new miller, and if he was found to be unsatisfactory, to consider reinstating Jonathan Eastholm in the post.

This was vague enough, but solid enough too: Hester had regained enough of her old self-belief to be convinced that she could completely settle the matter at the next meeting, with a combination of advocacy and ankle-work; and she was so pleased with her success that she decided to take the news at once to Jonathan herself. She knew that he was currently doing casual labour for the masons who were restoring Milney St Mary church, and so from Stokeley she drove straight to the village, descending from the spring-cart at the churchyard gate, and hitching the pony to the yew-tree fence.

She saw Jonathan at once on entering the churchyard. He was engaged in sawing up into disposable pieces a section of the old removed screen, which he had propped upon two ancient gravestones a few feet apart, as if on a workbench. Other broken and disjointed fragments of the church interior littered the churchyard: in this energetic destruction of ecclesiastical ornament there would have been much to please the eye of Cromwell's soldiers, who in this very corner of Anglia had done the very same thing for different reasons, two hundred and fifty years since. Everything around Jonathan was bleached and colourless — the white splintered heart of the timber he sawed, the weathered tombstones, the gravel and grass all gripped by profound frost, even his own soda-white shirt; yet the tan of summer harvesting seemed scarcely to have faded from him at all, and the skin of his bare forearms was as smooth and brown as a hen's egg. So pleased was she to see him in that so typical posture of tensile yet graceful labour — the freshness of his colour like a memory of summer made fresh — that she called out "Jonathan!", suddenly and involuntarily, making him start.

"Oh! I'm sorry," she said, drawing near, "what a fool — I might have made you cut your finger off."

"How do, Mrs Saunders," he said, suspending the saw. "Were you looking for someone?"

"Yes, you," she said.

"Ah?"

She scarcely noticed his wary tone. "Jonathan, I'm got some good news for you — any road, I think it's good news, though perhaps I shouldn't count my chickens . . . " She told him of her meeting with the Drainage Commissioners, and her efforts to get the miller's job back for him. "Of course, they're got to stroke their whiskers and hum and haw about it for a while, because they don't like to admit they were wrong. But I reckon the ole beggars have learnt their lesson — and come the next meeting I wouldn't be a bit surprised, as Sunny says, if they made a decision to ask you to be miller again."

Jonathan was silent for some moments, brushing sawdust from his hands. "Well, it's very good of you, I'm sure," he said at last.

He did not sound glad: he sounded almost surly. "Don't you — don't you want your old job back?" she said.

"Oh! I dare say."

His face was dark and set. Surprised, she said, "I thought you'd be pleased."

"Like I say, it's very good of you . . . I'm sure you meant well," Jonathan said curtly. He picked up the saw again, as if to resume his work — as if to dismiss her. For a moment, crestfallen and bewildered as she was, she was speechless.

"What am I done wrong?" she said finally. "Jonathan — " All at once the sight of his broad back made her angry. "Jonathan, will you please stop ignoring me? I just don't understand you. Tell me, if I'm done the wrong thing. I only meant to — "

"Don't you see?" he said, turning on her. "Don't you see how this will seem? Don't you realise what folk are going to say about me taking favours from you? Think how folk will talk about you. Think, Mrs Saunders."

"I don't care what folk say," she said quite calmly. "That don't matter a bean to me, Jonathan. I told you before." As he made a brusque gesture she went on: "Why should it matter? There's things that are so much more important. Like being true to a true friend. Jonathan, you half crippled yourself helping me get my harvest in — you did everything for me so selflessly — how can I just forget that? I wanted to help you in return and now I'm found a way. How can there be anything wrong with that?"

Jonathan did not speak, but leaned his arms upon the broken screen, his eyes lowered.

Hester's disappointment was complete; but now she was determined to speak out. The chill of these long months since he had so bafflingly withdrawn from her — she could bear it no longer. "I know you're a proud sort of man," she said. "But this ain't a question of favours. I felt so glad about maybe getting you your old job back. Same as I did about you carrying on working at the farm. I still don't understand the way you — well, the way you turned so cold and hard on me. All this time I'm thought about that. It was almost as if you wanted to hurt me."

"No, no," he said quickly. "No, not that."

"Well, I'm glad," she said. "But it seemed that way . . . It still does. Why?"

All at once Jonathan gave a deep bass sigh, and surprised her with a gentle smile. "Life can be a wry business sometimes," he said. "The very person you don't want to hurt is the one you end up hurting . . . I'm sorry if that's the impression I gave you: though in a way I'm not, because that's the impression I wanted to give, I suppose . . . but I shall have to say it now. The thing is, you see — all that time when I helped you at the farm, I wanted it to be absolutely plain that this was a practical arrangement — no strings, like. I couldn't bear it to seem like I was — well, taking advantage. Looking out for

594

what I could get . . . It didn't seem that way, did it?" he said with sudden appeal, his brows puckered.

"Why, no," she said earnestly. "Never."

"Well, that's it, you see," Jonathan said. "I had to stop working for you — being with you — when I realised I couldn't be disinterested any more. You said about me acting selflessly; but I knew I weren't being selfless any more. It couldn't be a matter of business because — because I'd started to feel more. Much more. I never meant it to happen: I tried to deny it to myself; but there was no help for it. That night of the horkey when you came to my house, and you said you thought I was your friend . . . Friend!" he said fiercely. "As if that were all I felt for you! As if I wouldn't roll up this whole fen like a carpet, or catch the east wind in a net, if you asked me to!"

The white steam of his breath whirled about in the bitter air as he spoke these words, whilst Hester's mind whirled too: giddily she snatched at a multitude of fugitive emotions that flew upon her like dead leaves before the blast.

"I'm sorry," he said, dully. "That's why, you see. That's why I had to keep away. There was you being so kind to me, confiding, trusting — I felt like a traitor, feeling for you the way I do."

Unsteadily she put out a hand to touch the mossy marble of a headstone. It was as cold as ice. "Oh, Jonathan — why didn't you tell me this before?" she said. Light was breaking in: much of the recent past was swiftly becoming

595

clear. "I didn't know — that night of the horkey
. . . Why didn't you say?"

"How could I?" said he softly. "How could I
do that — when there was you, just beginning
to get a grip on life — just beginning to smile
a little again? I loved to see your smile coming
back, like seeing the first buds on the trees
. . . How could I go and destroy that smile,
by telling you something that — well, that
could only be unwelcome to you? You'd had
burdens enough. It's not that I don't cherish
your friendship. God, no. Nothing on earth
could have made me break that — except
one thing: knowing that what I felt wasn't
just friendship . . . that it had gone beyond
that . . . Well! like I say, I'm sorry. I'm had
to say it in the end. So you won't think I'm
cold and ungrateful. That's the last thing I am
— the very last."

Hester turned her face from him, trying
to think clearly; but she groped in mists of
astonishment and self-reproach. Of course she
should have seen: but how could she have
seen what he had so scrupulously guarded
against her seeing? For the moment her own
predicament presented itself less vividly to her
than Jonathan's, which her heart ached to
behold. What a torment it must have been to
him! A momentary recollection of that night of
the wet-harvesting — her hands massaging his
naked back — made her cheeks sting, and she
hurriedly thrust it away. She must say something
to him. He was looking steadily at her, as if
readying himself for some harsh response, and

she owed it to him to show the same respect for his feelings that he had shown for hers. But she struggled in vain to speak.

"There," he said. "It's happened — just what I was afraid of. That shadow's come back to your face. Look, try and forget what I said — "

"I can't do that," she said. "How can I?"

"No . . . " He was sombre. "I suppose not."

"But it's not that I — I mean, I can't blame you for saying it, Jonathan — it's right that you did. I'm only sorry you're had to bottle it up so long. Now that I see, now that I see how blundering I'm been, I feel awful about it — "

"Don't," he said emphatically. "Don't feel awful. You did nothing wrong: you couldn't have been expected to know."

The truth of these words seemed to her an incomplete truth: she still felt herself impaled on a sharp point of conscience. "I should have known," she murmured. "But I never imagined . . . Whatever you once felt for me, I thought that was long, long dead."

Jonathan seemed to weigh his thoughts carefully, his chin lowered, his hands thrust in his pockets. "So did I," he said at length. "And in truth I think it was. The man I was then and the man I am now seem to me like two different people — made of the same clay, mebbe, but no more. When I came to work at your farm I thought I came heart-whole — I would never have come otherwise. I didn't want none of them tangling feelings that break your rest and turn you into a fool. But they came in

597

spite of me. When I looked in your face for that smile, I found it wasn't just that I wanted you to be happy: I wanted that smile for myself. So the game was up. I'm sorry."

"I'm sorry, too, Jonathan," she said. There were tears on her lashes which she wished he might not see — she did not want him to reproach himself with having made her unhappy. "Sorry because — it seems so cruel and wicked that what you feel for me should be wasted . . . It's a bitter world where something as true and good as that can go to waste . . . But you know that's all over for me, Jonathan: you know I'm finished with all that." These words had become so automatic with her that she spoke them without thinking, her mind moving ahead of them.

"Aye, I know," he said.

"But even though I haven't got a heart to give, I'm got a heart to feel grateful — flattered — oh, everything except hurt by what you've said. Truly, Jonathan. Do you believe me?"

"Yes," he said, straightening with a smile. "I believe you."

"I'm got to go away now — but I can't go if you're believing, deep down, that I think badly of you — promise, now, that that's not what you believe," she said, with a desperate sort of lightness.

"I promise," he said.

"And there was me going on about your mill job . . . I feel a fool about that — yet I don't, because you deserve it, and I shall always want the best for you. I just wish . . . Oh! goodbye," she said brokenly, unable to restrain her tears any longer. She turned and picked a path through the gravestones, her boots imprinting crisp dimples in the frosted grass.

* * *

Jonathan went on with his work. He was supposed to have all this timber disposed of today, and the master-mason was a bit of a tartar. It went hard with him to yes-sir and no-sir for the few shillings this job paid, but there was no help for it — it was the only practical course. It was perhaps odd that Jonathan could feel he was being practical when he shunned good work and struggled to get by on bad, simply because of the unruly longings of the heart; but Jonathan's practicality was another man's romanticism. He laboured on now, in flat contradiction of an opposite urge, very powerful within him, to give it up and hide his head in a dark place.

He had told her: in a way he still wished he hadn't, but it was done now. Yes, love was a fool's game, but he was a fool and that was all there was to it. On the night of the horkey he had known he must break away from Hester or he was lost, but in truth he had been lost some time before that. Stealthily and relentlessly had the infection taken hold: the blind god needed no ambience of candlelight and silk — in harvest-fields, quiet comradeship, labour, even pain, he could work his disturbing magic. A number of layers had covered Jonathan's feeling: a chivalrous protectiveness; a growing admiration for the way Hester's spirit rose to grapple with adversity; a friendship characterised by unhurried confidence. Each was true in its way, but his heart's-truth pierced them all.

And he had seen the tears, just now, that she had tried to conceal — seen the tears he had caused! A wry world, as he had said: a wry world, and a dark. Not even the Old Goblin, it turned out, had known how dark.

★ ★ ★

Hester reached home in the early afternoon. The steam-thresher was still there, and the first stack had diminished. Billy Onyett was complaining of frost-bite in his hands: he couldn't untie the sheaves wearing gloves, he said. Mechanically Hester told Edie to make him some beef-tea: mechanically, still in her veil-tied hat and cape, she wandered out to the paddock, where they had recently begun clearing the great tangle of thorn and elderberry that bounded it. The dry, black and knotted growth, scarred by fagging-hook and mattock, looked in the wintry light as lifeless as wire, and no more liable to leaf and flower than an iron railing.

She found herself walking away from the farm, taking the field-paths on to the upland, where the ploughed clay stood forth in jagged clots. The cold intensified momently, a congealing cold, as if the world were slowly setting like starch. She did not notice it: the brisk rhythm of walking not only warmed her but soothed the jangling perplexity of her mind, and she wanted just to go on, away from everyone, the earth her only companion.

A wry world, Jonathan had said: that it was! Had her sense of humour been working, she might have laughed at the memory of her old vain self, and how she would have relished men falling in love with her. But there was no place for humour here: it was fearfully serious. Jonathan's revelation had thrown everything out of joint — there was not a corner or crevice of her life that was unaltered by it. Her peace of mind was cleft to its foundations. (But had it really been peace of mind? Or a dull, cottony muffling of the emotions?) And protest as she might about the disruption, she could not wish his declaration unsaid; for in that there would be a hiding, a retreat, as life-destroying in its way as her grieving self-imprisonment in the Crooked House last year.

Ahead of her rose that most unusual sight in this part of Anglia — a hill. It was Oxey Hill, an ancient earthwork, the ramparts of which still appeared in sinuous contour in spite of the smoothings of grass and time, like the muscles of some half-tamed but powerful creature. Love had suddenly bulked too into the flat terrain of her life, but not tempered and softened as was this work of perished hands: it pressed urgently, dismayingly upon her. She had not sought Jonathan's love: she could not have wished it upon him, for love was pain — did she not know that? — and she could not wish such pain upon anyone, least of all Jonathan,

601

for whom she deeply cared. This whole winter had been a lesson in how deeply she did care for him. And now he had walked into that dark thicket of pain, of poison and thorns!

She climbed a footworn track up the slope of Oxey Hill: silent starlings waddled and hopped out of her path, as if they had no more power of flight than chickens. She passionately wished there was something she might have said to Jonathan today, something that would have helped him — something that would not have left him stricken, hopeless, and surely regretting that he had ever spoken at all. It seemed to her that as it was, she would never know a moment's rest again after that meeting.

Of course there was something she could have said. Something which was as simple as earth or air — and yet which to her mind was a treacherously complex labyrinth, which even to think of was to shun. No, no: as she had told him before, that was all over, that was not for her, not any more — that part of her self was consigned to as permanent an oblivion as the dark side of the moon. She knew it to be so, and was glad of it. The kernel of dissent within her, which murmured that it was a pity, was not to be trusted.

From the summit of the earthwork she looked out across the fens. The sun, which had been no more than a faintly shining mark like the trail of a slug upon the surface of smothering snow-cloud, had drawn clear as it neared the horizon, and now the red disc scattered the embers of the short day over the western fields, whilst to the east the land died into smoke-coloured shadow, traced with a cobweb pattern of dykes. Hester, standing with tingling cheeks and steaming breath on the top of the hill, was the sole human being within sight: the high-road that crossed the landscape was deserted, the nearest cottage as insubstantial as a relic in the consuming dusk. She saw it all, the miles of encircling space, with a keen eye — turning herself slowly about so as to take in the whole panorama — while yet her mind's eye conned the expanse of her past life, and beheld a wasteland strewn with wrong decisions. She gave a sort of groaning sigh: the great stretch of ancient and indifferent fen seemed to thrust upon her small figure the whole burden of consciousness. How much easier to be like the unfeeling earth! Wasn't that the best way to live?

Yet as she thought of Jonathan, and cast her mind back over the past year, a sort of tender wonder stole over her as his every action fell into place. In everything he had done he had thought solely of her — sought her good but sought no return. His rugged devotion he had refined to a delicacy of conduct which she had only just begun tremulously to grasp. It was true that she had been shut up within herself . . . it was not true, after all, that she had been alone.

The sun was on the horizon: Hester began to descend the slope. Somewhere out there was Jonathan — just such a vital pinprick of identity as she. She wondered what he was doing at this moment. Out of the blur of her confusion and perplexity, one hard fact appeared to her. If she were to be consistent with what she had said today, then she ought not to see him any more: that was only fair to him, for anything else would be to torment him.

Yet that was a hard fact indeed: it gripped her bleakly, more bleakly than was in the power of the cruellest winter that ever denied the inevitable spring.

★ ★ ★

For a couple of days the cold loosened its bonds sufficiently to allow a few sporadic showers of snow to fall, settling in powdery fichus on the dykeside only to freeze again. The steam threshing-tackle had developed a fault in the boiler, and had only just begun working again on the day Charlie Smeeth came to the Crooked House: it was Edie's half-day, and they were going together to Stokeley. Hester met him in the kitchen, where he greeted her with a paroxysm of coughing.

"That sounds like a bad chill, Charlie," she said.

"Oh! it's about the usual for this time o' year, missus," Charlie said. "I reckon me tubes git froz, and won't shift — like the shutters of the mill-sails in the frost. They're stuck fast now."

"I didn't know you still went to the mill, Charlie," Hester said.

"Not usually — but Mr Eastholm's there this morning, so I went to see him."

"Mr Eastholm?" she said in surprise.

"Yis — oh, he's just giving a word of advice to that poor ole Norfolk dumpling they're got wukking there now, who ain't got no more brains than a pig's got pockets. Mr Eastholm's finished his job at the church, and I suppose you're got to tek pity on this new miller. Not that *I'd* call him a miller," Charlie said loftily.

Hardly knowing what she did, Hester gave Edie and Charlie a baked apple and a pastry each, and stood at the window staring out. Abruptly she said: "Charlie — Edie — on your way, would you stop off at the mill and ask Jonathan if he'll step over here when he's got a minute? I'm got some news for him — business."

"All right missus — cheer-oo."

After the Smeeths had gone, Hester remained where she was, repeatedly smoothing her apron and gazing out at the threshing going on in the yard. Still she had the curious feeling of hardly knowing what she was doing: something had impelled her to summon Jonathan, something demanded that she must see him, but beyond that she came up against a blank wall within herself. At length she returned to the parlour, where she had begun her campaign of renovation by tearing down the worm-eaten panelling that she disliked; but she had scarcely mounted the rickety stepladder before there was a knock at the back door. She went to open it.

"Jonathan," she said, "I'm glad you could come — I hope I'm not took you away from anything, only I'm got some news, from the Commissioners . . . Come in."

There was a fresh smell of outdoors about him as he stepped into the kitchen. He looked both puzzled and guarded, as if he were determined to betray no expression.

"Charlie tells me you're finished at the church," she said, folding and refolding some linen.

"Yes, it was only temporary work," he said.

"Oh — well — what I wanted to tell you was, Farmer Mather called the other day, and — he thinks the Commissioners might soon come round to our way of thinking — and if not, he's heard that the miller over on New Fen might soon be retiring — and so there's another possibility for you there. I thought you'd — I thought you'd like to know."

"Thank you," he said. "Matter of fact, I'm got a proper job lined up. I went over yesterday to a small brickyard over Yaxley way to see if there was owt going: I start next week."

"Oh! that's good. At least . . . Is it? I mean, is it what you want?"

"It'll pay the rent for the time being," he said.

She folded the linen again. This was madness. An impulse had told her, with the force of a command, that she must speak to him, that all was dangerously incomplete between them and she must face him again, but the impulse had not told her what to say. God knew what he must think of her.

He rescued her: glancing out of the window at the yard he said, "Why, what a cobble Billy's making of feeding that thresher!"

"Oh, I know," she said joining him. "I have a job to get him to do it. He don't trust the machine at all — he says it makes his teeth rattle." She laughed nervously.

"You want another man feeding," Jonathan said, in his slightly arrogant way, "thass what. And have Billy taking the sheaves down. It'll take for ever at this rate."

Hester hesitated, not looking at him. "I hardly dare ask," she said.

"What — if I'll do it?"

"Oh, I do understand if you don't want to, Jonathan: I would have asked you before, but — "

"Do you want me to do it?" said he plainly.

She nodded. A smile came and went on his face.

"I will, then," he said.

Within minutes Jonathan was in place on the platform of the thresher, and the work was going on apace: the very engine seemed to throb with new vigour. Later Hester herself joined the team, untying the bonds of the sheaves to hand them to Jonathan: the rhythm was swift, and the stack was soon down to the staddles; she felt once more the satisfaction of the old companionable toil of the harvest-field. Harmony succeeded to the nagging discord of her thoughts. Whatever it was she had meant to say to him, she simply let it go like the chaff on the breeze: an enigma that had been compelling became, in his presence, merely dispensable. It was just so good to have him at the farm again: there was a sense of rightness that extinguished the

607

haggard questionings and ambiguities as the sun extinguishes the moon.

"Tomorrow?" he said to her when the day's work was done.

"If you could . . . we've got on so much better," she said. "But have you things to do . . . ?"

"Job doesn't start for a week," he said. "This work'll fill in nicely."

She could not tell what he was thinking; but she found she could not reproach herself for irresponsibility, for selfishness, for allowing things to go on unresolved. It was as if a moral shutter had come down. She slept well that night, and woke in the morning feeling more alive than she had done for months. She worked on the thresher beside Jonathan until dinner-time, and in the afternoon attacked the parlour panelling again with cheerful gusto: when she went out to see the men on the thresher, she was covered in dust and flakes of plaster.

"You needn't have got yourself all dressed up," said Jonathan from the platform.

She grinned up at him and blew a smut from the tip of her nose. "Now you can tell folk what Mrs Saunders does in the afternoon," she said. "She gets plastered."

That evening she found her nerves all a-jangle: she could not sit down. She went on tearing at the panelling until bedtime, and even when she lay in bed her fingers seemed to itch to attack it again. At last she uneasily slept, and dreamt that someone had replaced all the panelling just as it was. This ghostly, formless figure stood admiring its handiwork, while she shouted at it: "You can't put the past back, you know! You can't — it's done with!"

The next morning she did not join the men on the threshing-machine: she went feverishly back to the panelling as if it were the most important thing in the world. She was still absorbed in this at noon when Edie called, "Here's Mr Eastholm, missus."

Jonathan stood in the parlour doorway. "We're all finished, Mrs Saunders — it's all threshed."

"Already?" she cried — in such a strange, plaintive tone that she startled herself, and Jonathan gave her a quizzical look.

"The engineer's getting ready to go," he said.

"I'd best settle up with him then." She dusted her hands, and looked at the chaos of the parlour. "Oh! damn. It seemed like a good idea at the time."

"Are you leaving that side intact?"

"No — I can't prise it off — I feel like setting light to it!"

"Let me have a go," he said, taking up the crowbar. "It'll make a change from bashing churches."

She went out to pay the engineer, and when she came back into the house a great ripping and screeching noise confirmed that Jonathan was doughtily at work. There was a great crash and a cloud of plaster as she entered the parlour: Jonathan smiled out at her from the choking midst of it, coated in dust.

"That's shifted it!" he said.

"Oh, Jonathan," she laughed, "you're always getting in a mess for me. Here — " She handed him a clothes-brush.

"I shall be in a worse muck than this at the brickyard, I should think," he said.

"Of course, the brickyard . . . I can't imagine you there somehow."

"I shall get along. I'm done so many jobs. Milling, digging, building . . . " He tilted his head forward and ran his hand rapidly through his hair to get the dust off: Hester stared, transfixed by a sharply revived memory that for a moment she could not place. Then it came to her — the day she had left his lighters, on the towpath below Saunders' horse-yard; blossoms had fallen on to his hair and he had shaken them off with just that gesture. Something about it made her heart seem to expand to the tips of her breasts.

"And boating," she said.

"And boating." He smiled, but without ease.

"D'you ever think about the old lighters?" she said.

"Oh, often." Jonathan studied the splintered panelling still intact above the cornice: as he lifted his head she saw there was a little dust on the bare skin of his throat where it emerged, smooth and rounded as a column, from the collar of his striped shirt. "I think about it . . . but it's all in the past. Gone. You know."

"Yes," she said. "I know."

Jonathan stretched up, long-bodied as a cat, to touch the cornice. "No," he said, "need the stepladder — even I can't reach that."

"It must be lovely to be that tall," she said.

He looked at her in surprise as he opened out the stepladder. "D'you think so? It's funny, you know — when I was a lad I hated it, I thought I was too tall — I wanted to be like everyone else."

"Oh! but it looks right on you," she said. "You wouldn't be you without your height. It's part of you . . ."

All at once Hester found she could not look at him. She was crushed by a sense of her self of the last couple of days as an alien, unfathomable being. When did the change begin — was it when she had stood in the graveyard with Jonathan? And who was she now? What was she doing?

"Jonathan," she said huskily. "I . . . I don't know what you must think of me . . ."

He was silent, his long brown hand poised on the stepladder.

"I'm been meaning to — to say something, truly, after — after the other day . . ."

"That's forgotten," he said quickly. "Don't think of it."

"But it was awful the way I sort of ran away," she said, "I didn't answer you properly, and now it must seem like I — like I'm ignoring it . . ."

"Hush," he said. "That's best."

She shook her head in distress. "No, it isn't."

"Yes it is." He smiled faintly. "You always were a contrary one . . . I wouldn't have stayed if I thought that — well, it was upsetting you

— and I'll be off now, if it is. Is it?"

"No," she said, smiling in return.

He turned his face quickly from her. "Let's finish this job," he said, pounding up the creaking stepladder, which swayed perilously.

"Oh dear, be careful!" she said, gripping the stepladder and wedging her foot against it. "I don't trust this thing — it squeals like an old sow in farrow. How much do you weigh?"

"I'm got no idea," he said, ripping at the panelling.

"How tall are you?"

"I don't know that either," he said, and suddenly they were both laughing.

"You gret yawnucks!" she said. "We shall have to measure you. You'll be saying next you don't know how old you are — except I do — you must be near twenty-seven, because I remember you telling me — except you were twenty-five then — so I'm added it on, you see."

"Oh, I see," Jonathan said, mockingly grave; then gave a great wrench at the last panel, almost losing his balance. "Look out below!"

The panel crashed down. Jonathan came pounding back down the ladder, no-hands. "Mind!" Hester said, holding on to the wobbling structure. "Honestly, Jonathan, you ain't safe . . . " As his waist came level with her eyes she had a sickly feeling as if a heavy plumb-line had dropped from her throat right down through her body. Jonathan stepped down to the floor, and without a word Hester put her arms around him and with closed eyes pressed her face against his chest. She inhaled the scent of him for the space of two deep heartbeats, throbbing at her ear, before his own arms encircled her, and they clung together, entwined like one creature, amidst the broken timber, plaster and dust.

"This is why I wished I was a bit taller," she whispered, reaching up to kiss him.

Releasing her lips at last, he shook his head, studying her so intently that she seemed to feel the focus of his brown eyes like a palpable caress about the curves of her face. "No," he said, "don't change a thing — not a thing."

She smiled, and moved her arms to clasp him more closely: her fingertips meeting between his shoulder-blades, her whole body was as tightly moulded to his as the rind upon a fruit. But suddenly she could not look at him, for she remembered the untruth that had led to this wonderful moment, and a bat's-wing of superstition brushed her. She buried her face in his neck, and said, half sobbing: "Oh, Jonathan, I lied . . . when I asked you here the other day, and said I had news for you, about the Commissioners and everything — I didn't have any news at all really, I just pretended because — I wanted so to see you . . . and so I'm started off with a lie . . . I'm sorry . . . "

Slowly she became aware of a sort of tremor, passing from his body directly to hers. He was tenderly laughing, deep in his chest.

"That's a white lie, my dear," he said, turning her face to his with one firm finger. "If ever I heard one — that's a white one."

613

Snow had begun falling: the large slow flakes spoke softly at the parlour window. With the imperviousness of lovers to discomfort, Hester and Jonathan had only slowly disengaged themselves from their embrace in the centre of the littered room, and now he was sitting on the oak settle and she upon his knee. Her arm was around his shoulders, which felt as warm as a sunned wall, and her other hand was engaged in a long tactile examination of the contours of his face, which now and then she interrupted to convulsively press her lips to it, with a feeling as if her heart were being pulled up at the roots.

The prospect of Edie coming in was one of the many things which did not seem to matter.

"Are you — " said Jonathan, "did you — "

"What?"

His teeth playfully closed on her thumb for a moment. "I forgot what I was going to say," he said. "I was just trying to work it out . . . It's a mystery, ain't it? Here, I mean — " pointing to his heart.

"It is," said she. "I'll never understand it." Their mood, mutually reflected, was curiously both light and solemn. "Let me feel that heart," she said, placing her hand on his chest.

"Is it going?"

She nodded. "Nineteen to the dozen."

He laughed, a boy's laugh, slightly hushed. "That's how I feel," he said. As her hand still rested on his heart he said, "It's yours. Will you have it?"

"Yes. Yes, please." She ran her fingers across his chest and round his neck. "Fearfully and wonderfully made — that's from a psalm, ole Andrew says. That's what you are, Jonathan — fearfully and wonderfully made . . . Oh! dear — I should have thought you'd have hated me, instead of loving me."

"Now how d'you work that out?"

"Well — I don't know . . . When you told me the other day — I just ran away; ran away inside my head as well. I wouldn't face it. A coward. All this time I'm been so cold and closed-up and afraid — "

"You're just going to have to get used to being loved," he said, "because I'm not going to stop it."

"How much do you love me, then?" she said, with an air of curiosity.

For answer he made a huge expansive gesture with his arms, before enfolding her in them again.

"It's the same for me," she said. "More. From here to the sea — from here to the stars — that's how much I love you, Jonathan."

He gazed raptly on her, like a knight before the grail, as if his very soul would brim out at his eyes; and for a moment neither was able to speak.

"If only — " she said.

"What?"

She looked down at his hand upon her hip, which seemed to fit together like lock and key. "I was just thinking — that time at the Spread Eagle yard, long ago, when you proposed to me

. . . if only I'd said yes then — if only an angel or something could have come down and told me what to do!"

"Ah, who knows?" he said. "I wonder if it would have been right then, somehow: I don't know whether I could have given you all the love you deserve — all the love I want to give you now." He breathed out a long breath and shook his head. "And that's all I can give you, Hester! Then I had a farm of my own — and now I'm got nothing. Can you take me as I am?"

"I'll take you as you are, Jonathan," she said. "Nothing else will do. I seem to have been running in the wrong direction for half my life — I shall make sure I go the right way, this time." She buried her lips in his hair, and her glance fell for the first time on the window, which was framed like a cameo with white. "Oh, look — it's snowing!"

"Drifting, too, by the look of it," he said.

"Oh, well — we're safe here, ain't we?"

He wrapped his arms around her. "Yes," he said. "Safely gathered in."

5

THE end of February, the shortest and longest month of the year, brought not gleams of spring but snow. The sky imprisoning the fen was a sombre steel-grey, darkening almost to black in places, so that it seemed impossible that such whiteness should fall from it, and the spiralling flakes might have been plausibly expected to be the colour of soot. On the flat fields the layer of snow was as smooth as linen, folded into blue shadow only on the marge of dyke and hedge, and frozen and re-frozen to a crystalline consistency, so that the spiky footprints of birds were preserved on its spangled surface like etchings of beautiful delicacy. Within the dykes and drains the crust of ice thickened nightly, with strange, creaking, protesting sounds in the emptiness, as if the water were not merely freezing but undergoing an agonising and irreversible transformation into solid. The snowfalls gave place only to a bitter north-easter, which scourged the fettered landscape as if with an almighty Cossack whip: its pagan whoops resounded between the high drain banks, and the snow upon every rush and reed was frozen as it blew, so that each assumed the appearance of a tiny white pennant forever fixed in the instant of its unfurling.

On just such a bleakly sparkling evening, Hester and Lizzie Gosling walked together down the wide street of Milney St Mary, which the cold moon illumined like a streetlamp to the tip of every last pendant icicle. Their caped and gloved forms had a large bloom-like softness in this angular world of ice, and they were laughing.

"They got Artie Gill to do it last year," Lizzie said, "and he got so drunk he fell asleep with his costume still on, and woke up in the morning all covered with weals like he'd been horsewhipped."

"Well, I'm never seen Jonathan drunk," Hester said. "He seems to swallow it down without it hurting him."

"Ah! you wait till you're wed — you'll mebbe learn all sorts about him."

"Lizzie Gosling," Hester said, "I swear you're getting more cynical than ever!"

Lizzie grinned sidelong at her. "You don't want to tek no notice of me," she said, "and I know you ain't anyway — you're got such a shine in your eyes as I never saw."

"Am I really?" said Hester. "I know that's how I feel — except it's more like a sort of shine all over. Daft, ain't it!"

"Dear oh lor — you *have* got it bad," said Lizzie. She gave Hester a devilishly searching look. "A shine all over, eh? Whatever are you pair gitting up to — and with the banns not even called yet!"

"Git away with you," Hester said, aware of a blush conveniently hidden by the general tingle of her cheeks in the cold air, and unable to repress a secret and involuntary smile. "Lizzie

— serious, though — you do think it's a good thing, don't you? Me and Jonathan?"

"Why, what's it matter what anyone thinks?" Lizzie said.

"You're not just anyone — you're my friend," said Hester.

Lizzie gave her one of her brisk, abrupt squeezes. "If your looks are anything to go by, it's the best thing as ever happened," she said. "And the miller's looks too — he seems two inches taller, if thass possible. Oh! I shall have to get used to not thinking of him as the miller — unless he's taking that job back, is he?"

"It might well be offered to him," Hester said, "but I don't think he'll do it. We'll have the farm, you know — and I want him with me: if he was milling I shouldn't hardly see him from one day to the next!"

"Or one night to the next," Lizzie said. "No, you don't want a husband who's always off to oil the luffing-gear . . . you want him at home oiling yours."

"Lizzie!" reproached Hester, choking on her laughter.

"And stoking your boiler . . . Well, it's good to see you laugh," Lizzie said, with one of her sudden swerves from saltiness to affection. "That does my heart good. And Jonathan too — you seem to have brought that out in him. Softened the edges a bit. And in turn I reckon he'll just steady you — you always did need a bit of ballast. There, I'm sounding like a regular old gipsy-granny!"

"That's all right," Hester said. "A gipsy once told me something true — he said I'd wait for gold; and I have, and now it's come. I thought I knew what love was like before . . . but I dunno. I didn't know this was love until I found I was deep in — over my head. It wasn't really a question of will. I'm joined to Jonathan, fixed — like a magnet to north."

To forestall the inevitable gossip, Hester and Jonathan had swiftly decided to let it be known, informally to their friends on Hinching Fen, that they were engaged, and planned to be married some time in the spring. Hester's feelings were such that she would have been happy to shout it from the rooftops, but a word to Peggy Chettle performed the same function. In the meantime Jonathan came every day to work at the farm, though she was afraid very little got done . . . How could you spend a whole morning just gazing at someone? Quite easily, was the answer. Even as she talked and laughed with Lizzie, she kept falling into deep pockets of abstraction in which the memory of the touch of his fingers upon her cheek was so vividly present to her that she had to give it her whole attention, and she came to herself with a sensation of waking from a doze.

They reached their destination at the end of the village — Jonathan's cottage, which was brightly lit within, and full of people. They knocked, and Charlie Smeeth flung open the door with an excited greeting. "He's ready!" Charlie cried. "It took us ages, though — I reckon we'll pick somebody shorter next year

— we must have used a barnful of straw!"

In the house-place, and filling it to the sills, were Billy Onyett, Lizzie's brother Jack Gosling, and Artie Gill; and a strange apparition, a towering creature seemingly made entirely of oat-straw — Jonathan, dressed in the traditional costume of the Straw Bear. He came forward and gravely kissed Hester's hand.

"Evening, my dear," he said. "You're just caught me trying on my wedding clothes."

"Oh, Jonathan, we'll clash — there was me going to wear a grass skirt and a hay-bale on my head," she said, going off into a scream of laughter.

"Took us ages, but he looks a treat, don't he?" Billy Onyett said proudly. "Thass summat *like* a bear. I remember the year Henry Wake did it — more like a straw cub, that was — we had to keep him out the way of the cows, in case they took him for a snack."

"I don't know how I'm going to manage if nature calls," Jonathan said, looking critically down at himself.

"You'd best bring along a pair o' scissors, Hester," Lizzie said, to shouts of laughter. "You know the spot!"

The Straw Bear was an ancient fen custom, possibly widespread once but now surviving only in Stokeley and, obstinately, in a few surrounding districts like Hinching Fen. Each year one of the menfolk of the fen was chosen by his fellows to represent the Straw Bear: the choice perhaps falling on Jonathan this year as a tribute to his engagement, with an element of

621

the mock-ordeal that has always been inflicted on men soon to be married. On the appointed day the man chosen was dressed by the others from head to foot in clean straight lengths of oat-straw, which was plaited and bound to him with lengths of twine, and brought to a peak above his brow, so that only his face showed. Come nightfall this 'bear' was then led on a rope by his friends around the farms and cottages and pubs, garnering largesse with mock-threats and capers. The men had decided on this occasion that all offerings in the form of drink and eatables would go down their throats, whilst any money obtained would go towards the Gooding, the traditional winter collection made for the elderly poor women of the parish. Jonathan, who claimed that his dancing resembled a real bear's too closely, had rehearsed a song to the accompaniment of Artie Gill's fiddle. What might be the origins of the custom of the Straw Bear it was impossible to say: certainly it bore no relation to the Christian festivals of the agricultural year, and a darker world of propitiation and sacrifice might have been glimpsed behind its present jokey manifestation. Hester laughed to see her lover dressed in the quaint costume, but when at last they all set out from the cottage to begin the ritual tour, it struck her that Jonathan with his breadth and stature made an alarming figure to anyone not in the know; and when he turned to give her a peck on the cheek she said, "Oo-er — I'm a bit frit of you like that."

"Grr," Jonathan said, in a tiny voice, with a grin.

People turned out at their cottage doors as the procession passed down the street, and children craned from upstairs windows to see: tumblers of hot sugared beer and toddy and trays of girdle-scones and baked apples and chestnuts were brought out, and one old woman produced some of the local home-made elderberry wine which, hot and spiced, hit the stomach and then the head like a firecracker. It all made a pleasant interruption to the dead season between Christmas and Easter, and presently a large knot of people were out in the street, wrapped up in mufflers, laughing and blowing on their hands and stamping on the frozen snow, which was barred with orange where the open cottage doors sent forth the glow of fire and lamp from within.

"Shall we be gooing to the Labour In Vain, sir?" Charlie Smeeth earnestly inquired of Jonathan. "There'll be a lot of folk there, and they always expect the Straw Bear, you know." There was doubt on this point, of course, because of Jonathan's quarrel with Jass Phelps the landlord, over those insinuations he had made. Privately, however, Jonathan had already agreed with Hester that they should let bygones be bygones; after all, as Hester remarked, Jass Phelps was only prophesying what was to come, if you looked at in a charitable light — and they were both in greatly charitable mood.

"Yes, Charlie — the Labour In Vain it shall be," Jonathan said. "And if ole Jass Phelps don't give us all drinks on the house, I shall sing at him, so help me!"

★ ★ ★

At the Labour In Vain old Andrew Surfleet had just arrived, and was lowering himself with infinite slowness into a seat beside Sunny Daintree. "A bitter night — bitter! That wind blows right through you and buttons up at the back," Andrew said. "I wouldn't have ventured, meself, only I like to see Straw Bear Night: I could hear the procession up tother end of the village — they'll doubtless be here soon."

"Well, now — unless the miller-as-was decides he don't care to come in here, where there was certain aspersions cast, and who could blame him," said Henry Wake with measured severity.

"Don't look at me!" said Jass Phelps, his arms daintily folded atop his great balloon of a body. "I'm sure I never meant no harm — not a grain of it. I were wishing the miller and Mrs Saunders well — thass what it was — not my fault if I git took up wrong."

"I remember the year they picked me for the Straw Bear," Sunny Daintree said. "Ooh! dear. The straw brought me up in a red rash, and I had to lay in a salt bath, and Peggy Chettle made a joke about how in a week I'd be Cured, which I weren't in a way to appreciate."

"I think you'll find Jonathan'll bear no grudge, you know," Henry Wake said, "and the procession'll come here. As for me, I was like a dog with two tails when I heard that news about Mrs Saunders and Jonathan's engagement — the best thing that could happen: me being one of the first to be told, as it happens, being a particular friend to those parties."

"Ah! Cured — I see it," said Andrew Surfleet with a chuckle. "Thass a good one, that."

In his habitual corner, Chad Langtoft slowly sipped his half-pint. He didn't intend staying for that Straw Bear business. It was heathen, he considered; and he was a God-fearing man. It was a pity, because he could just fancy another half — no more, he knew how to keep it within limits: but no, he was to be denied that simple pleasure, because of this heathen tomfoolery! It contributed in his mind to a general sense of unfairness, which proceeded from this engagement they were all talking about.

Chad had a vague but powerful feeling that that engagement was not right. After a long period of refusing to believe that there could possibly be any real blame attaching to him for Lyle Saunders' death nearly a year ago — a period in which he had hungrily embraced the religion which seemed to offer the self-vindication he craved — Chad had at last come round, with a sort of serenity, to a conviction that he had, in some measure, freed Hester from that Saunders one. It was as if Providence had worked through him — and Providence, after all, could not be guilty, could not be right or wrong: it just was. And yet here Hester was, enjoying the fruits of that Providence — deciding to marry

625

again — whilst he was still stuck with the same grinding, put-upon life with Mary-Ann. It was a grim confirmation — not that he needed one — of the injustice of life towards him. And there was the miller worming his way into Hester Saunders' favour — what had he ever done for her? If anyone, it should have been he, Chad, moving in there, but the world had thwarted him at every turn: not that he wanted anything to do with her anyhow — there was nothing but trouble to be got from women; he should know, for one of them had trapped him good and proper. But it irked him to hear them all talking on as if everything were satisfactory; and when Henry Wake said something about wishing them happiness Chad burst out, with an irritable twitch of his shoulders, "Why, who says they deserve to be happy? You can't just expect happiness to be given you on a plate — thass for the Almighty to decide."

"I take your meaning, Chad," Henry Wake said. "But you wouldn't wish them unhappiness, would you? There's sufficient of that knocking about the place."

"Man was born to suffer," Chad said. "Besides, who's to say they'll be any good for each other? Everybody knows what a disaster her and that Saunders one were. Who's to say this'll be any different? It's all a rum business, if you ask me."

Henry Wake sighed. In the small fenland communities there was a great tolerance, even appreciation, of idiosyncrasy, but they were all rather weary of Chad's monotonous mistrust, interspersed with poison darts of scripture. "Charity, Chad, remember charity," Henry said.

"It's a funny thing — there's always somebody who can't bear other bodies to have a mite of happiness," said Andrew Surfleet.

Chad subsided, hunched down in his seat, with a dully smouldering outrage. He couldn't even speak his mind, it seemed — they were all against him! Though he had always known that.

Henry Wake had opened the door. "Ah! here they come," he said. "Watch this here bear don't get you, Jass."

"The miller'll tek a drink on me, I hope," Jass Phelps said, perspiring rather. "We're good friends really, you know."

Chad finished his half and was ready to go — he wanted none of it, it would make him sick to see them — but just as he stood up, in came the Straw Bear party, with Artie Gill playing his fiddle, Lizzie and Hester jigging — what right had she to jig? — and a whole crowd of folk from the village pouring in after, laughing and cheering at the tops of their voices. The crush was such that Chad could not get to the door: they treated him, he thought, as if he didn't exist!

"Evening, Mrs Saunders — evening, Miller," Jass Phelps was saying, with a fixed and sweaty smile. "A very fine Straw Bear you make, Miller — quite the best I'm seen; and congratulations on your engagement, by the by, and have a drink on it — have two drinks — "

"Oh! that'll do, Jass," Jonathan said, laughing. "Here, shake hands with a happy man."

While Sunny Daintree was tossing some coppers into the hat, Chad began to edge his way round to the door — as best he could, with everyone trying to trap him in with this heathen rubbish. It was just typical of his luck that Billy Onyett should turn and see him at that moment.

"Here, Chad — no sneaking out without coughing up fust," Billy said. "C'mon — ha'penny'll do."

Chad froze, the backs of his thighs jammed against a table. Jonathan loomed towards him, smiling and shaking the hat. She was there, smiling too, holding on to the rope: yes, she had roped him in good and proper, Chad thought blackly — soon be leading him a real dance. Such filth.

"Aye, come on, Chad — else I'll sing at you," Jonathan said to a general laugh, waving the hat.

"You needn't come near me wi' that heathen muck," Chad said, his eyes flicking from Jonathan to Hester and back again.

"Well — never mind that," Jonathan said. "A copper for the poor widows, eh?"

"You'd know all about helping widows!" Chad cried: they were all pressing round him and staring — with a sudden clawing movement he struck out at Jonathan. His fist glancingly connected. There was a gasp; but Jonathan scarcely flinched.

"Make it a shilling," he said, with a deep

fierce frown upon Chad, "and I'll forget about that blow."

Chad threw a wild glance round at the ring of faces. "You're all agin me!" he burst out; and with a sudden twist of his body, seized the oil-lamp from the table behind him and dashed it with a sweeping movement against Jonathan's body. The glass globe smashed upon the floor, and the straw costume caught fire with an upward flourish of flame.

Hester could never remember whether her own voice figured amongst the screams that followed; she remembered only a series of bright, disjointed images — the blood dripping from her own pricked finger as she tore the brooch from her cape and flung the cape around Jonathan's legs to smother the flames; Chad hurling himself out at the door just as Billy Onyett made a grab at his collar; Henry Wake ineffectually throwing water from a jug on the bar on to the burning straw — before Sunny Daintree, moving with astonishing speed, came cannoning into Jonathan and bodily drove him outside, shouting, "In the snow! Douse it in the snow!"

By the time she had fought her way outside with the rest — seconds that seemed like hours — Sunny had thrust Jonathan down upon the ground and was rolling him in the drifted snow before the door. Steam was hissing and rising in the bitter air. Hester flung herself down upon her knees beside Sunny, heaping snow with her hands on to Jonathan's body, little animal gasps coming from her throat. Sunny put his hand on her arm. "It's all right, missus," he said, "it's out."

Jonathan sat up, his eyes bleary with smoke and smuts. "The damn fool," he said. "The poor damn fool."

"Any hurts, bor?" Sunny said.

Jonathan shook his head and got to his feet, his hand on Sunny's shoulder. "No harm done," he said shakily. "Don't ask me to be Straw Bear again, though, will you, neighbours?"

Hester gripped his hand and pressed it against her face, her eyes closed.

"A terrible thing nearly — terrible!" Henry Wake said. "Where did Chad go?"

"Took to his heels," Billy Onyett said. "I tried to git a hold on him — he was away like an eel."

"He mustn't get away with this — he ought to go before the law!" Henry Wake said. "We all on us saw what he was about."

"Come on, we'll catch him — he can't have got far," said Billy Onyett. "Who's wi' me?"

"I'll come!" cried Charlie Smeeth, in a voice of unaccustomed force.

In a moment Billy was off on his long legs, with Charlie Smeeth and Jack Gosling and Artie Gill following, and Henry Wake pattering along behind. Hester, with Sunny's help, began stripping off the damp, blackened straw. Jass Phelps, elbowing aside the clucking onlookers, handed Jonathan a large tot of rum. "Get that down you quick," he said.

"Gladly," Jonathan said, draining it in one go

and coughing. Presently the last of the straw was peeled off him, and he stood shivering slightly: the costume had been warm and he had worn no jacket underneath.

"You're damp," Hester said, putting a hand to his shirt. "Come in and get warm."

"No," he said. "I reckon I ought to go after them fellows — Billy and Artie are hot-headed sorts — no knowing what they'll do."

She regarded him steadily a moment. "All right," she said. "I'll come too."

They set out after the others, with Sunny Daintree carrying a storm-lamp from the pub, though there was a broad light from the moon. At the end of the village the tracks in the crusted snow led them on to the field-paths, and out into white sparkling openness that extended for miles on either hand.

"There — that long streak's Billy Onyett, I know," cried Sunny, pointing. "And Charlie along of him." They ran along the dyke-side where the snow was thin, and drew level with Billy and Charlie close to the main drain.

"Lost him," Billy said, clutching a stitch in his side and panting out white vapour. "Artie and Jack went across the bridge to head him off — "

"Ahoy!" came a shout from the further extremity of the field behind them. Hester, whirling round, saw three figures — Chad Langtoft racing across the field, and Artie Gill and Jack Gosling advancing on him from opposite points of the compass. There was something weird and deliberate about all their movements that for a moment she could not understand: they seemed to be running as one runs in a dream, laboriously, with balletic slowness. Then she realised — with each step they were sinking almost up to their knees in the pure untouched snow that covered the field.

"We're got him — head him off," Billy said. As he started to move Chad saw him, made a sudden hare-like swerve, and headed straight for the drain bank. He lurched clear of the deep snow a few yards ahead of his pursuers, scrambled up the bank like a spider, and tore away from them — running on the smooth frozen surface of the drain, which aimed at the horizon like a straight glassy road.

"That bastard!" Artie Gill grunted, struggling exhausted to the top of the bank. "We shall never catch him now." But within an instant of his speaking, there was a curious noise like the dropping of a load of slates, and a flat cry; and the stubby figure of Henry Wake, who had got himself lost, appeared in silhouette on the crest of the opposite bank, fifty yards further along, calling for help.

"Here — he's gone through the ice!"

Jonathan was the first to reach the spot along the bank opposite Henry. "There!" Henry cried. "See — where the reeds are . . . "

Close to the bank someone had made a dipping-hole in the ice to get water, which had then thinly frozen over again to a treacherous cat-ice, barely discernible but for a faint sugary glitter; and here a splintered hole gaped, the water beneath tilting and rippling and stippled with moonlight.

Hester clutched at Jonathan. "Don't go down there, Jonathan," she cried vehemently, and held him back, "don't!"

The men formed a chain down the bank, gripping each other's belts, with Charlie Smeeth, the lightest, tentatively inching out on to the cracking ice. He groped an arm up to the shoulder into the water, but all was still and silent there.

"There ain't nothing," Charlie said, shuddering at the numbing clutch of the water. "He ain't here."

"He's underneath the ice," Artie said quietly.

More people had arrived from the village, some with lamps. All began to roam up and down the banks of the drain, throwing the lamplight down upon the grooved and glinting sheet of ice below, shouting and pointing at every shadow and clump of reeds. Hester and Jonathan worked their way downstream, not speaking, until they were in sight of the mill, when there was another shout from Henry Wake on the other side of the drain. He had mounted the brick parapet surrounding the mill-pool, into which the drain led, and was pointing downward.

Hester ran up to the mill ahead of Jonathan. She peered sickly over the wall into the mill-pool. The great water-wheel was still, with a neat pan-pipe of icicles hanging from each paddle, but the water in the pool was only partly frozen, with clear patches that shone like black oil. Chad's drowned body lay amongst weed and slivers of ice, face down, his head buried in the crook of his left arm, as if he had sulkily turned his back on life.

6

A LIGHT two-wheeled cart came rattling into the yard of the Crooked House on a gusty morning in late May. Walt came out to hold the pony's head, and Henry Wake stepped down from the cart with a certain dash, short legs notwithstanding, that would have done credit to a silk-hatted gent in Rotten Row. He stopped to rearrange the flower in his buttonhole before glancing up and urbanely waving to Hester, who saw him from her bedroom window.

"Henry Wake's here," she said, waving back. "Go down and let him in, Edie. No — wait — are you sure I look all right?"

"Bless you, missus, of course you do!" said Edie. Taking Hester by the elbows, she guided her to the mirror. "There," she said looking over Hester's shoulder, "not much wrong with *that* face!"

Hester gazed into her own brightly reflected eyes, and found herself smiling. "You know, I reckon I *do* look all right," she said gaily. "Jonathan's a lucky fellow, really, ain't he? I hope he knows it."

"He knows it, missus," Edie said. "Oh! 'ell, I'm just thought — what am I to call him when he comes back here — I mean, when he's here to live, like? Should I say mairster?"

"Oh, I think Jonathan wouldn't know where to

635

look if you called him mairster!" Hester laughed. "Anyway — don't count your chickens — he might have done a bunk at the altar."

"Never!" Edie said with huge emphasis.

"Yes, he's a lucky man," Hester said, smoothing the high-necked bodice of the pearl-grey frock, and regarding herself in the mirror, while Edie ran downstairs. "And I'm a lucky woman . . . " She smiled again, gently. What else was there to say? She remembered Mrs Dawsmere, the housekeeper at the Saunders' yard, and how she would have crossed her fingers forebodingly to hear her say that. But you couldn't question your luck when it came to you, Hester thought: you just had to seize it and rejoice in it. Take the light: push back the dark. And, by God, so she would. Her luck was waiting for her now at the church: she must go and get him. She glanced round at the bedroom, to which she and her luck would be returning later. She had a suspicion that he might knock his head on that low beam . . . Oh, well, he wouldn't be walking about too much anyway — she'd see to that . . . She forced herself to stop smiling, and picked up her bouquet.

"I'm ready," she said to her reflection.

Henry Wake was waiting for her in the parlour. His trousers fitted his legs like gloves, and there was so much mascassar oil on his hair that his bowler hat kept sliding off. "Well, now," he said admiringly, on greeting Hester, "I don't know as I'm ever seen anything finer in the illustrated papers — no, not in the *Sixpenny Gallery of the Fashionable Fair*

— that's a monthly publication, you know, taken occasionally by Mrs Wake — who's indisposed today, I'm afraid, but sends her best. Now, shall we depart? You might not believe it, but I'm never been called upon to give a bride away before, though I'm performed quite a few responsible functions in my time, no good pretending I haven't . . . "

They climbed into the dog-cart and set off at an appropriately ceremonial pace, Hester seated beside Henry, with Edie sitting on the backboard with her legs swinging. The west wind was bowling the white clouds swiftly across the sky, so that giant stretches of shadow and sunlight continually alternated across the level fields, with an effect like the rolling and unrolling of vast carpets. They did not take the road to the village, for Milney St Mary church was still closed for restoration. They took the Stokeley road, which ran directly alongside the green river; and then followed a short turning, which led to the river itself, and a small landing-place for boats amongst a few hoary willows. Here a peculiar vessel was tied up at the bank: a long barge, roofed-over with timber and iron, from which, through the open doorway, came the reedy sound of a harmonium. It was the Fenland Ark — the floating church, which had come to Hinching Fen to serve the bereft parishioners.

Henry Wake hitched the pony to a tree, and very carefully handed Hester on to the boarding-plank. She was all right, though — she knew all about boarding barges . . . How strange, and appropriate, she thought, that she should be marrying Jonathan on a boat! Who could have foreseen it? The only certain thing about the future, it seemed, was that it was uncertain . . . The gipsy had said she'd wear an eelskin wedding-ring, and that was wrong — but also that she'd wait for gold, and that was right . . . The barge was swaying very gently as she advanced down the narrow planked aisle. Met on a boat — married on a boat: perhaps it was a good omen. Then she saw a large shoulder jutting out ahead of her — Jonathan's dark head turned, and he smiled at her, and somehow she knew that he had been thinking exactly the same thing. She smiled too as she drew level with him. That was the only omen she cared about . . .

"Oh! 'ell — thass Mr Wake's Chloe tied up there," said Charlie Smeeth, as he, Sunny Daintree and the Surfleets turned off the high-road and approached the river. "We're late for the wedding — we'll miss it — everybody else must be there — I told you!" All the way from the village he had been trying to get the other three to hurry, which was rather like attempting to hurl a feather.

"Calm yourself, bor," said Sunny, "the bride's likely only just this minute arrived, and the parson'll still be on about the brute beasts wi' no understanding, and the prosecution o' children. Ooh! it goes on for yards, that service. You could grow a beard before they git to the joining-together and putting-asunder, and whiskers to suit."

"I ain't much of a boater — I hope I shan't git sea-sick," Charlie said.

"Well, like I say, I'm never held with this idea of a floating church," said Andrew Surfleet, stepping gingerly on to the boarding-plank. "I still say it ain't on consecrated ground; and though Henry Wake explained it to me tother night, with a stack o' tall words, and made it sound straight enough, I'm still got me misdoubts. It meks you wonder if it's a bad omen for the pair, gitting wed this funny way: what do you reckon, Sunny?"

"Ooh! I don't know," Sunny said, as they entered the church. "I reckon they might be all right together, you know, this pair — I wouldn't be a bit surprised."

THE END

Other titles in the Charnwood Library Series:

PAY ANY PRICE
Ted Allbeury

After the Kennedy killings the heat was on — on the Mafia, the KGB, the Cubans, and the FBI . . .

MY SWEET AUDRINA
Virginia Andrews

She wanted to be loved as much as the first Audrina, the sister who was perfect and beautiful — and dead.

PRIDE AND PREJUDICE
Jane Austen

Mr. Bennet's five eligible daughters will never inherit their father's money. The family fortunes are destined to pass to a cousin. Should one of the daughters marry him?

THE GLASS BLOWERS
Daphne Du Maurier

A novel about the author's forebears, the Bussons, which gives an unusual glimpse of the events that led up to the French Revolution, and of the Revolution itself.

BERLIN GAME
Len Deighton

Bernard Samson had been behind a desk in Whitehall for five years when his bosses decided that he was the right man to slip into East Berlin.

HARD TIMES
Charles Dickens

Conveys with realism the repulsive aspect of a Lancashire manufacturing town during the 1850s.

THE RICE DRAGON
Emma Drummond

The story of Rupert Torrington and his bride Harriet, against a background of Hong Kong and Canton during the 1850s.

FIREFOX DOWN
Craig Thomas

The stolen Firefox — Russia's most advanced and deadly aircraft is crippled, but Gant is determined not to abandon it.

CHINESE ALICE
Pat Barr

The story of Alice Greenwood gives a complete picture of late 19th century China.

UNCUT JADE
Pat Barr

In this sequel to CHINESE ALICE, Alice Greenwood finds herself widowed and alone in a turbulent China.

THE GRAND BABYLON HOTEL
Arnold Bennett

A romantic thriller set in an exclusive London Hotel at the turn of the century.

SINGING SPEARS
E. V. Thompson

Daniel Retallick, son of Josh and Miriam (from CHASE THE WIND) was growing up to manhood. This novel portrays his prime in Central Africa.

THE RIDDLE OF THE SANDS
Erskine Childers

First published in 1903 this thriller, deals with the discovery of a threatened invasion of England by a Continental power.

WHERE ARE THE CHILDREN?
Mary Higgins Clark

A novel of suspense set in peaceful Cape Cod.

KING RAT
James Clavell

Set in Changi, the most notorious Japanese POW camp in Asia.

THE BLACK VELVET GOWN
Catherine Cookson

There would be times when Riah Millican would regret that her late miner husband had learned to read and then shared his knowledge with his family.

THE WHIP
Catherine Cookson

Emma Molinero's dying father, a circus performer, sends her to live with an unknown English grandmother on a farm in Victorian Durham and to a life of misery.

SHANNON'S WAY
A. J. Cronin

Robert Shannon, a devoted scientist had no time for anything outside his laboratory. But Jean Law had other plans for him.

THE JADE ALLIANCE
Elizabeth Darrell

The story opens in 1905 in St. Petersburg with the Brusilov family swept up in the chaos of revolution.

THE DREAM TRADERS
E. V. Thompson

This saga, is set against the background of intrigue, greed and misery surrounding the Chinese opium trade in the late 1830s.

THE DOGS OF WAR
Frederic Forsyth

The discovery of the existence of a mountain of platinum in a remote African republic causes Sir James Manson to hire an army of trained mercenaries to topple the government of Zangaro.

THE DAYS OF WINTER
Cynthia Freeman

The story of a family caught between two world wars — a saga of pride and regret, of tears and joy.

REGENESIS
Alexander Fullerton

It's 1990. The crew of the US submarine ARKANSAS appear to be the only survivors of a nuclear holocaust.

SEA LEOPARD
Craig Thomas

HMS 'Proteus', the latest British nuclear submarine, is lured to a sinister rendezvous in the Barents Sea.

A HERITAGE OF SHADOWS
Madeleine Brent

This romantic novel, set in the 1890's, follows the fortunes of eighteen-year-old Hannah McLeod.

BARRINGTON'S WOMEN
Steven Cade

In order to prevent Norway's gold reserves falling into German hands in 1940, Charles Barrington was forced to hide them in Borgas, a remote mountain village.

THE PLAGUE
Albert Camus

The plague in question afflicted Oran in the 1940's.

THE RESTLESS SEA
E. V. Thompson

A tale of love and adventure set against a panorama of Cornwall in the early 1800's.

Lindis-Chloe Guinness

AN INFAMOUS ARMY

BY THE SAME AUTHOR

Historical Romances

THESE OLD SHADES
BEAUVALLET
POWDER AND PATCH
THE BLACK MOTH
THE CONVENIENT MARRIAGE
DEVIL'S CUB
THE MASQUERADERS
REGENCY BUCK
THE TALISMAN RING
THE CONQUEROR
AN INFAMOUS ARMY
ROYAL ESCAPE
THE SPANISH BRIDE
THE CORINTHIAN
FARO'S DAUGHTER
FRIDAY'S CHILD
THE RELUCTANT WIDOW
THE FOUNDLING
ARABELLA
THE GRAND SOPHY
THE QUIET GENTLEMAN
COTILLION
THE TOLL-GATE
BATH TANGLE
SPRING MUSLIN
APRIL LADY
SYLVESTER: OR THE WICKED UNCLE
VENETIA
THE UNKNOWN AJAX
A CIVIL CONTRACT
THE NONESUCH
FALSE COLOURS

Short Stories

PISTOLS FOR TWO

Thrillers

DEATH IN THE STOCKS
THE UNFINISHED CLUE
WHY SHOOT A BUTLER?
BEHOLD HERE'S POISON
THEY FOUND HIM DEAD
NO WIND OF BLAME
A BLUNT INSTRUMENT
PENHALLOW
ENVIOUS CASCA
DUPLICATE DEATH
DETECTION UNLIMITED

C. 7

AN INFAMOUS ARMY

Georgette Heyer

NEW YORK
E. P. DUTTON & CO., INC.
1965

"I have got an infamous army; very weak and ill-equipped, and a very inexperienced Staff."

Wellington to Lieut.-Gen. Lord Stewart, G.C.B.
8th May, 1815.

AUTHOR'S NOTE

In writing this story I have realized an ambition which, though I fear it may have been presumptuous, I could not resist attempting. Apart from the epic nature of the subject, the spectre of Thackeray must loom over anyone wishing to tackle the battle of Waterloo. It would not allow me to set pen to paper until I banished it, at last, with the reflection that no one, after all, would judge a minor poet by Shakespeare's standard of excellence. I should add, perhaps, that it is many years since I read *Vanity Fair*; and although I have encroached on Thackeray's preserves, at least I have stolen nothing from him.

With regard to the Bibliography published at the end of this book, to obviate the necessity of appending a somewhat tedious list of Authorities, I have limited it to those works which, in writing a Novel, and not a History, I have found most useful. Works dealing with the purely tactical aspect of the Campaign have been omitted; so too have many minor accounts; and a host of Biographies, Memoirs, and Periodicals which, though not primarily concerned with any of the personages figuring in this story, contained, here and there, stray items of information about them. It will further be seen that, with the exception of Houssaye, no French Authorities have been given: the French point of view was not relevant to my purpose. On the other hand, certain works have been included which, though they do not deal with the Waterloo Campaign, were invaluable for the light they throw on Wellington's character, and the customs obtaining in his army.

Wherever possible, I have allowed the Duke to speak for himself, borrowing freely from the twelve volumes of his Despatches. If it should be objected that I should not have made him say in 1815 what he wrote in 1808, or said many years after Waterloo, I can only hope that, since his own words, whether spoken or written, were so infinitely superior to any which I could have put into his mouth, I may be pardoned for the occasional chronological inexactitudes thus entailed.

GEORGETTE HEYER.

CHAPTER I

THE youthful gentleman in the scarlet coat with blue facings and gold lace, who was seated in the window of Lady Worth's drawing-room, idly looking down into the street, ceased for a moment to pay any attention to the conversation that was in progress. Amongst the passers-by, a Bruxelloise in a black mantilla had caught his eye. She was lovely enough to be watched the whole way down the street. Besides, the conversation in the salon was very dull: just the same stuff that was being said all over Brussels.

"I own, one can be more comfortable now that Lord Hill is here, but I wish the Duke would come!"

The Bruxelloise had cast a roguish dark eye up at the window as she passed; the gentleman in scarlet did not even hear this remark, delivered by Lady Worth in an anxious tone which made her morning visitors look grave for a minute.

The Earl of Worth said dryly: "To be sure, my love: so do we all."

Georgiana Lennox, who was seated on the sofa with her hands clasped on top of her muff, subscribed to her hostess's sentiments with a sigh, but smiled at the Earl's words, and reminded him that there was one person at least in Brussels who did not wish for the Duke's arrival. "My dear sir, the Prince is in the most dreadful huff! No other word for it! Only fancy! he scolded me for wanting the Duke to make haste—as though I could not trust *him* to account for Bonaparte, if you please!"

"How awkward for you!" said Lady Worth. "What did you say?"

"Oh, I said nothing that was not true, I assure you! I like the Prince very well, but it is a little too much to suppose that a mere boy is capable of taking the field against Bonaparte. Why, what experience has he had? I might as well consider my brother March a fit commander. Indeed, he was on the Duke's Staff for longer than the Prince."

"Is it true that the Prince and his father don't agree?" asked Sir Peregrine Taverner, a fair young man in a blue coat with very large silver buttons. "I heard——"

A plump gentleman of cheerful and inquisitive mien broke into the conversation with all the air of an incorrigible gossip-monger. "Quite true! The Prince is all for the English, of course, and that don't suit Frog's notions at all. Frog, you know, is what I call the King. I believe it to be a fact that the Prince is much easier in English or French than he is in Dutch! I heard that there was a capital quarrel the other day, which ended with the Prince telling Frog in good round terms that if he hadn't wished him to make his friends amongst the English he shouldn't have had him reared in England, or have sent him out to learn his soldiering in the Peninsula. Off he went, leaving Papa and Brother Fred without a word to say, and of course poured out the whole story to Colborne. I daresay Colborne don't care how soon he goes back to his Regiment. I would not be Orange's Military Secretary for something!"

The Bruxelloise had passed from Lord Hay's range of vision; there was nothing left to look at but the pointed gables and nankeen-yellow front of a house on the opposite side of the street. Lord Hay, overhearing the last remark, turned his head, and asked innocently: "Oh, did Sir John tell you so, Mr. Creevey?"

An involuntary smile flickered on Judith Worth's lips; the curled ostrich plumes in Lady Georgiana's hat quivered; she raised her muff to her face. The company was allowed a moment to reflect upon the imaginary spectacle of more than six feet of taciturnity in the handsome shape of Sir John Colborne, Colonel of the Fighting 52nd, unburdening his soul to Mr. Creevey.

Mr. Creevey was not in the least abashed. He shook a finger at the young Guardsman, and replied with a knowing look: "Oh, you must not think I am going to divulge *all* the sources of my information, Lord Hay!"

"I like the Prince of Orange," declared Hay. "He's a rattling good fellow."

"Oh, as to that——!"

Lady Worth, aware that Mr. Creevey's opinion of the Prince would hardly please Lord Hay, intervened with the observation that his brother, Prince Frederick, seemed to be a fine young man.

"Stiff as a poker," said Hay. "Prussian style. They call him the Stabs-Captain."

"He's nice enough to look at," conceded Lady Georgiana, adjusting the folds of her olive-brown pelisse. "But he's only eighteen, and can't signify."

"Georgy!" protested Hay.

She laughed. "Well, but you don't signify either, Hay: you know you don't! You are just a boy."

"Wait until we go into action!"

"Certainly, yes! You will perform prodigies, and be mentioned in despatches, I have no doubt at all. I daresay the Duke will write of you in the most glowing terms. 'General Maitland's A.D.C., Ensign Lord Hay——' "

There was a general laugh.

" 'I have every reason to be satisfied with the conduct of Ensign Lord Hay,' " said Hay in a prim voice. "Old Hookey writing in glowing terms! That's good!"

"Hush, now! I won't hear a word against the Duke. He is quite the greatest man in the world."

It was not to be expected that Mr. Creevey, a confirmed Whig, could allow this generous estimate to pass unchallenged. Under cover of the noise of cheerful argument, Sir Peregrine Taverner moved to where his brother-in-law stood in front of the fire, and said in a low voice: "I suppose you don't know when the Duke is expected in Brussels, Worth?"

"No, how should I?" replied Worth in his cool way.

"I thought you might have heard from your brother."

"Your sister had a letter from him about a week ago, but he did not know when he wrote when the Duke would be free to leave Vienna."

"He ought to be here. However, I'm told that since

3

Lord Hill came out the Prince has not been talking any more of invading France. I suppose it's true he was sent to keep the Prince quiet?"

"I expect your information is quite as good as mine, my dear Peregrine."

Sir Peregrine Taverner had attained the mature age of twenty-three, had been three years married, and two years out of the Earl of Worth's guardianship, and was, besides, the father of a pair of hopeful children, but he still stood a little in awe of his brother-in-law. He accepted the snub with a sigh, and merely said: "One can't help feeling anxious, you know. After all, Worth, I'm a family man now."

The Earl smiled. "Very true."

"I don't think, if I had known Boney would get away from Elba, I should have taken a house in Brussels at all. You must admit it is not a comfortable situation for a civilian to be in." He ended on a slightly disconsolate note, his gaze wandering to the scarlet splendour of Lord Hay.

"In fact," said the Earl, "you would like very much to buy yourself a pair of colours."

Sir Peregrine grinned sheepishly. "Well, yes, I would. One feels confoundedly out of it. At least, I daresay you don't, because you are a military man yourself."

"My dear Perry, I sold out years ago!" The Earl turned away from his young relative as he spoke, for Lady Georgiana had got up to take her leave.

Beside Judith Worth's golden magnificence, Lady Georgiana seemed very tiny. She submitted to having her pelisse buttoned close to her throat by her tall friend, for even on this 4th day of April the weather still remained chilly; stood on tiptoe to kiss Judith's cheek; promised herself the pleasure of meeting her at Lady Charlotte Greville's that evening; and went off under Hay's escort to join her mother, the Duchess of Richmond, at the Marquis d'Assche's house at the corner of the Park.

Since Mr. Creevey showed no immediate disposition to go away, Lady Worth sat down again, and made kind

4

enquiries after his wife and stepdaughters. One of the Misses Ord, he confided, had become engaged to be married. Lady Worth exclaimed suitably, and Mr. Creevey, beaming all over his kindly face, disclosed the name of the fortunate man. It was Hamilton; yes, Major Andrew Hamilton, of the Adjutant-General's Staff: an excellent fellow! Between themselves, Hamilton kept him pretty well informed of what was going on. He got all the news from France, but under pledge of strict secrecy. Lady Worth would understand that his lips were sealed. "And you too," he added, fixing his penetrating gaze upon her, "I daresay *you* have information for your private ear, eh?"

"I?" said Lady Worth. "My dear Mr. Creevey, none in the world! What can you be thinking of?"

He looked arch. "Come, come, isn't Colonel Audley with the Great Man?"

"My brother-in-law! Yes, certainly he is in Vienna, but I assure you he doesn't tell me any secrets. We don't even know when we may expect to see him here."

He was disappointed, for news, tit-bits of scandal, interesting confidences whispered behind sheltering hands, were the breath of life to him. However, since there was nothing to be learned from his hostess, he had to content himself with settling down to what he called a comfortable prose with her. He had already told her, upon his first coming into her salon, of a singular occurrence, but he could not resist adverting to it again: it was so very remarkable. Sir Peregrine had not been present when he had first related the circumstance, so he nodded to him and said: "You will have heard of the new arrivals, I daresay. I was telling your good sister about them."

"The King?" said Peregrine. "The French King, I mean? Is he really coming to Brussels? I did hear a rumour, but someone said it was no such thing."

"Oh, the King!" Mr. Creevey waved his Sacred Majesty aside with one plump hand. "I was not referring to him —though I have reason to believe he will remain in Ghent for the present. Paltry fellow, ain't he? No, no, some-

5

thing a little more singular—or so it seemed to me. Three of Boney's old Marshals, no less! I had the good fortune to see them all arrive, not ten days ago. There was Marmont, who went to the Hôtel d'Angleterre; Berthier, to the Duc d'Aremberg's; and Victor—now where do you suppose? Why, to the Hôtel Wellington, of all places in the world!"

"How ironic!" remarked Worth, who had come back into the room from seeing his other guests off. "Is it true, or just one of your stories, Creevey?"

"No, no, I promise you it's quite true! I knew you would enjoy the joke."

Lady Worth, who had accorded the tale at this second hearing no more than a polite smile, said in a reflective tone: "It is certainly very odd to think of Marmont in particular being in the English camp."

"The Allied camp, my love," corrected the Earl, with a sardonic smile.

"Well, yes," she admitted, "but you know I can't bring myself to believe that the Dutch-Belgian troops count for much, while as for the Prussians, the only one I have laid eyes on is General Röder, and—well——!" She made an expressive gesture. "He is always so stiff, and takes such stupid offence at trifles, that it puts me out of all patience with him."

"Yes, *he* will never do for the Duke," agreed Mr. Creevey. "Hamilton was telling me there is no dealing with him at all. He thinks himself insulted if any of our officers remain seated in his presence. Such stuff! A man who sets so much store by all that ceremonious nonsense won't do for the Duke's Headquarters. They couldn't have made a worse choice of Commissioner. There's another man, too, who they say will never do for the Duke." He nodded, and pronounced: "Our respected Quarter-master-General!"

"Oh, poor Sir Hudson Lowe! He is very stiff also," said Lady Worth. "People say he is an efficient officer, however."

"I daresay he may be, but you know how it is with these

6

fellows who have served with the Prussians: there's no doing anything with them. Well, no doubt we shall see some changes when the Beau arrives from Vienna."

"If only he would arrive! It is very uncomfortable with him so far away. One cannot help feeling uneasy. Now that all communication with Paris has been stopped, war seems so very close. Then Lord Fitzroy Somerset and all the Embassy people being refused passports to come across the frontier, and having to embark from Dieppe! When our Chargé d'Affaires is treated like that it is very bad, you must allow."

"Yes," interjected Peregrine, "and the best of our troops being in America! That is what is so shocking! I don't see how any of them can be brought back in time to be of the least use. When I saw the Prince he was in expectation of war breaking out at any moment."

"No chance of that, I assure you. Young Frog don't know what he's talking about. Meanwhile, we have some very fine regiments quartered here, you know."

"We have some very young and inexperienced troops," said Worth. "Happily, the cavalry did not go to America."

"Of course, you were a Hussar yourself, but you must know very well there's no sense in cavalry without infantry," replied Peregrine knowledgeably. "Only to think of all the Peninsular veterans shipped off to that curst American war! Nothing was ever so badly contrived."

"It is easy to be wise after the event, my dear Perry."

Lady Worth, who had listened to many such discussions, interposed to give the conversation a turn towards less controversial subjects. She was assisted very readily by Mr. Creevey, who had some entertaining scandal to relate, and for the remainder of his visit nothing was talked of but social topics.

Of these there were many, since Brussels overflowed with English visitors. The English had been confined to their own island for so long that upon the Emperor Napoleon's abdication and retirement to Elba they had flocked abroad. The presence of an Army of Occupation in the Low Countries made Brussels a desirable goal.

7

Several provident Mamas conveyed marriageable daughters across the Channel in the wake of the Guards, while pleasure-seeking ladies such as Caroline Lamb and Lady Vidal packed up their most daring gauzes and established their courts in houses hired for an indefinite term in the best part of Brussels.

The presence of the Guards was not, of course, the only attraction offered by Brussels. Mr. Creevey, for instance, had brought his good lady to a snug little apartment in the Rue du Musée for her health's sake. Others had come to take part in the festivities attendant upon the long-exiled William of Orange's instatement as King of the Netherlands.

This gentleman, whom Mr. Creevey and his friends called the Frog, had been well known in London; and his elder son, the Hereditary Prince of Orange, was a hopeful young man of engaging manners, and a reputation for dashing gallantry in the field, who had lately enjoyed a brief engagement to the Princess Charlotte of Wales. The breaking-off of the engagement by that strong-minded damsel, though it had made his Highness appear a trifle ridiculous in English eyes, and had afforded huge gratification to Mr. Creevey and his friends, did not seem to have cast any sort of cloud over the Prince's spirits. It was felt that gaiety would attend his footsteps; nor were the seekers after pleasure destined to be disappointed. Within its old ramparts, Brussels became the centre of all that was fashionable and light-hearted. King William, a somewhat uninspiring figure, was proclaimed with due pomp at Brussels, and if his new subjects, who had been quite content under the Bonapartist régime, regarded with misgiving their fusion with their Dutch neighbours, this was not allowed to appear upon the surface. The Hereditary Prince, who spoke English and French better than his native tongue, and who announced himself quite incapable of supporting the rigours of life at The Hague, achieved a certain amount of popularity which might have been more lasting had he not let it plainly be seen that although he liked his father's Belgian subjects better than his Dutch ones, he preferred the English to them all. The truth was, he was never seen but in the society of his English friends, a circumstance which had caused so much annoyance to be felt that the one man who was known to have influence over him was petitioned to write exhorting him to more diplomatic behaviour. It was a chill December day when M. Fagel brought his Highness a letter from the English Ambassador in Paris, and there was nothing in the austere contents of the missive to make the day seem warmer. A letter of reproof from his Grace the Duke of Wellington, however politely worded it might be, was never likely to produce in the recipient any other sensation than that of having been plunged into unpleasantly cold water. The Prince, with some bitter animadversions upon tale-bearers in general, and his father in particular, sat down to write a promise to his mentor of exemplary conduct, and proceeded thereafter to fulfil it by entering heart and soul into the social life of Brussels.

But except for a strong Bonapartist faction the Bruxellois also liked the English. Gold flowed from careless English fingers into Belgian pockets; English visitors were making Brussels the gayest town in Europe, and the Bruxellois welcomed them with open arms. They would welcome the Duke of Wellington too when at last he should arrive. He had been received with enormous enthusiasm a year before, when he had visited Belgium on his way to Paris. He was Europe's great man, and the Bruxellois had accorded him an almost hysterical reception, even cheering two very youthful and self-conscious Aides-de-Camp of his who had occupied his box at the opera one evening. That had been a mistake, of course, but it showed the good-will of the Bruxellois. The Bonapartists naturally could not be expected to share in these transports, but it was decidedly not the moment for a Bonapartist to proclaim himself, and these gentry had to be content with holding aloof from the many fêtes, and pinning their secret faith to the Emperor's star.

The news of Napoleon's landing in the south of France had had a momentarily sobering effect upon the merry-

9

makers, but in spite of rumours and alarms the theatre-parties, the concerts, and the balls had still gone on, and only a few prudent souls had left Brussels.

There was, however, a general feeling of uneasiness. Vienna, where the Duke of Wellington was attending the Congress, was a long way from Brussels, and whatever the Prince of Orange's personal daring might be it was not felt that two years spent in the Peninsula as one of the Duke's Aides-de-Camp were enough to qualify a young gentleman not yet twenty-four for the command of an army to be pitted against Napoleon Bonaparte. Indeed, the Prince's first impetuous actions, and the somewhat indiscreet language he held, alarmed serious people not a little. The Prince entertained no doubt of being able to account for Bonaparte; he talked of invading France at the head of the Allied troops; wrote imperative demands to England for more men and more munitions; invited General Kleist to march his Prussians along the Meuse to effect a junction with him; and showed himself in general to be so magnificently oblivious of the fact that England was not at war with France, that the embarrassed Government in some haste despatched Lieutenant-General Lord Hill to explain the peculiar delicacy of the situation to him.

The choice of mentor was a happy one. A trifle elated, the Prince of Orange was in a brittle mood, ready to resent the least interference in his authority. General Clinton, whom he disliked, and Sir Hudson Lowe, whom he thought a Prussianized martinent, found themselves unable to influence his judgment, and succeeded only in offending. But no one had ever been known to take offence at Daddy Hill. He arrived in Brussels looking more like a country squire than a distinguished general, and took the jealous young commander gently in hand. The anxious breathed again; the Prince of Orange might be in a little huff at the prospect of being soon relieved of his command, but he was no longer refractory, and was soon able to write to Lord Bathurst, in London, announcing the gratifying intelligence that although it would have been mortifying to him to give up his command to anyone else, to the Duke he could do it with pleasure; and could even engage to serve him with as great a zeal as when he had been his Aide-de-Camp.

"*I shall never forget that period of my life,*" wrote the Prince, forgetting his injuries in a burst of enthusiasm. "*I owe everything to it; and if I now may hope to be of use to my country it is to the experience I acquired under him that I have to attribute it.*"

Such a frame of mind augured well for the future; but the task of controlling the Prince's martial activities continued to be a difficult one. The British Ambassador to The Hague transferred his establishment to Brussels with the principal motive of assisting Lord Hill in his duty, and found it so arduous that he more than once wrote to the Duke to tell him how necessary was his presence in Brussels. "*You will see that I have spared no efforts to keep the Prince quiet,*" wrote Sir Charles Stuart in his plain style. . . . "*Under these circumstances I leave you to judge of the extreme importance we all attach to your early arrival.*"

Meanwhile, though the Congress at Vienna might declare. Napoleon to be *hors la loi,* every day saw French Royalists hurrying a little ignominiously over the frontier. Louis XVIII, yet another of Europe's uninspiring monarchs, removed his Court from Paris to Ghent, and placidly explained that he had been all the while impelled, in France, to employ untrustworthy persons because none whom he could trust were fit to be employed. Certainly it did not seem as though anyone except his nephew, the Duc d'Angoulême, had made the least push to be of use in the late crisis. That gentleman had raised a mixed force at Nîmes, and was skirmishing in the south of France, egged on by a masterful wife. His brother, the Duc de Berri, who had accompanied his uncle into Belgium, found less dangerous employment in holding slightly farcical reviews of the handful of Royalist troops under his command at Alost.

These proceedings were not comforting to the anxious, but the proximity of the Prussian Army was more reassuring. But as General Kleist's notions of feeding this Army consisted very simply of causing it to subsist upon the country in which it was quartered, the King of the Netherlands, who held quite different views on the subject, and was besides on bad terms with his wife's Prussian relatives, refused to permit of its crossing the Meuse. This not unnaturally led to a good deal of bad feeling.

"Your Lordship's presence is extremely necessary to combine the measures of the heterogeneous force which is destined to defend this country," wrote Sir Charles Stuart to the Duke, with diplomatic restraint.

Everyone agreed that the Duke's presence was necessary; everyone was sure that once he was in command all the disputes and the difficulties would be immediately settled, even Mr. Creevey, who had not been used to set much store by any of "those damned Wellesleys".

It was wonderful what a change was gradually coming over Mr. Creevey's opinions; extraordinary to hear him adverting to the Duke's past victories in Spain, just as though he had never declared them to have been grossly exaggerated. He was still a little patronising about the Duke, but he was going to feel very much safer, tied as he was to Brussels by an ailing wife, when the Duke was at the head of the Army.

But he thought it very strange that Worth should have had no news from his brother in Vienna. Probe as he might, nothing could be elicited. Colonel Audley had not mentioned the subject of his Chief's coming.

Mr. Creevey was forced to go away unsatisfied. Sir Peregrine lingered. "I must say, I agree with him, that it's odd of Charles not to have told you when he expects to be here," he complained.

"My dear Perry, I daresay he might not know," said Lady Worth.

"Well, when one considers that he has been on the Duke's personal Staff since he went back to the Peninsula after your marriage in August of 1812 it seems quite extraordinary he should be so little in Wellington's confidence," said Sir Peregrine.

His sister drew her work-table towards her, and began

to occupy herself with a piece of embroidery. "Perhaps the Duke himself is uncertain. Depend upon it, he will be here soon enough. It is very worrying, but he must know what he is about."

He took a turn about the room. "I wish I knew what I should do!" he exclaimed presently. "It's all very well for you to laugh, Judith, but it's curst awkward! Of course, if I were a single man I should join as a volunteer. However, that won't do."

"No, indeed!" said Judith, rather startled.

"Worth, what do you mean to do? Do you stay?"

"Oh, I think so!" replied the Earl.

Sir Peregrine's brow lightened. "Oh! Well, if you judge it to be safe—I don't suppose you would keep Judith and the child here if you did not?"

"I don't suppose I should," agreed the Earl.

"What does Harriet wish to do?" inquired Lady Worth.

"Oh, if it can be considered safe for the children, she don't wish to go!" Sir Peregrine caught sight of his reflection in the mirror over the fireplace, and gave the starched folds of his cravat a dissatisfied twitch. Before his marriage he had aspired to dizzy heights of dandyism, and although he now lived for the greater part of the year on his estates in Yorkshire, he was still inclined to spend much thought and time on his dress. "This new man of mine is no good at all!" he said, with some annoyance. "Just look at my cravat!"

"Is that really necessary!" said the Earl. "For the past hour I have been at considerable pains not to look at it."

A grin dispersed Sir Peregrine's worried frown. "Oh, be damned to you, Worth! I'll tell you what it is, you did a great deal for me when I was your ward, but if you had taught me the way you have of tying your cravats I should have been more grateful than ever I was for any of the rest of the curst interfering things you did."

"Very handsomely put, Perry. But the art is inborn, and can't be taught."

Sir Peregrine made a derisive sound, and, abandoning the attempt to improve the set of his cravat, turned from the mirror. He glanced down at his sister, tranquilly sewing, and said in a burst of confidence: "You know, I can't help being worried. *I* don't want to run home, but the thing is that Harriet is in a delicate situation again."

"Good God, already?" exclaimed Judith.

"Yes, and you see what an anxious position it puts me in. I would not have her upset for the world. However, it seems certain Boney can't move against us yet. I shall wait until the Duke comes before I decide. That will be best."

The Earl agreed to it with a solemnity only belied by the quivering of a muscle at the corner of his mouth. Sir Peregrine adjured him to let him have any reliable news he might chance to hear and took himself off, his mind apparently relieved of its care.

His sister was left to enjoy a laugh at his expense. "Julian, I think you must have taken leave of your senses when you permitted Perry to marry Harriet! Two children, and another expected! It is quite absurd! He is only a child himself."

"Very true, but you should consider that if he were not married we should have him enlisting as a volunteer."

The thought sobered her. She put down her embroidery. "I suppose we should." She hesitated, her fine blue eyes raised to Worth's face. "Well, Julian, our morning visitors have all talked a great deal, but you have said nothing."

"I was under the impression that I said everything that was civil."

"Just so, and nothing to the point. I wish you will tell me what you think. Do we stay?"

"Not if you wish to go home, my dear."

She shook her head. "You are to be the judge. I don't care for myself, but there is little Julian to be recollected, you know."

"I don't forget him. Antwerp is, after all, comfortably close. But if you choose I will convey you both to England."

She cast him a shrewd look. "You are extremely obliging, sir! Thank you, I know you a little too well to accept that offer. You would no sooner have set me down in England than you would return here, odious wretch!"

He laughed. "To tell you the truth, Judith, I think it will be interesting to be in Brussels this spring."

"Yes," she agreed. "But what will happen?"

"I know no more than the next man."

"I suppose war is certain? Will the Duke be a match for Bonaparte, do you think?"

"That is what we are going to see, my dear."

"Everyone speaks as though his arrival will make all quite safe—indeed, I do myself—but though he was so successful in Spain he has never fought against Bonaparte himself, has he?"

"A circumstance which makes the situation of even more interest," said Worth.

"Well!" She resumed her stitching. "You are very cool. We shall stay then. Indeed, I should be very sorry to go just when Charles is to join us."

The Earl put up his quizzing-glass. "Ah! May I inquire, my love, whether you are making plans for Charles's future welfare?"

Down went the embroidery; her ladyship raised an indignant rueful pair of eyes to his face. "You are the most odious man that I have ever met!" she declared. "Of course I don't make plans for Charles! It sounds like some horrid, match-making Mama. How in the world did you guess?"

"Some explanation of your extreme kindness towards Miss Devenish seemed to be called for. That was the likeliest that presented itself to me."

"Well, but don't you think her a charming girl, Julian?"

"I daresay. You know my taste runs to Amazons."

Her ladyship ignored this with obvious dignity. "She is extremely pretty, with such obliging manners, and a general sweetness of disposition which makes me feel her to be so very eligible."

"I will allow all that to be true."

"You are thinking of Mr. Fisher. I know the evils of her situation, but recollect that Mr. Fisher is her uncle only by marriage! He is a little vulgar perhaps—well, very vulgar, if you like!—but I am sure a kind, worthy man who has treated her quite as though she were his own daughter, and will leave the whole of his fortune to her."

"That certainly is a consideration," said Worth.

"Her own birth, though not noble, is perfectly respectable, you know. Her family is an old one—but it does not signify talking, after all! Charles will make his own choice."

"Just what I was about to remark, my dear."

"Don't alarm yourself! I have no notion of throwing poor Lucy at his head, I assure you. But I shall own myself surprised if he does not take a liking to her."

"I perceive," said the Earl, faintly amused, "that life in Brussels is going to be even more interesting than I had expected."

CHAPTER II

WHEN Judith, on setting out for Lady Charlotte Greville's evening party, desired Worth to direct the coachman to call at Mr. Fisher's for the purpose of picking up Miss Devenish, she could not help looking a little conscious. She avoided his ironic gaze, but when he settled himself beside her, and the carriage moved forward over the pavé, said defensively: "Really, it is not remarkable that I should take Lucy with me."

"Certainly not," agreed Worth. "I made no remark."

"Mrs. Fisher does not like to go into company, you know, and the poor child would be very dull if no one offered to escort her."

"Very true."

Judith cast a smouldering glance at his profile. "I do not think," she said, "that I have ever met so provoking a person as you."

He smiled, but said nothing, and upon the carriage's drawing up presently in front of a respectable-looking house in one of the quiet streets off the Place Royale, got down to hand his wife's protégée into the carriage.

She did not keep him waiting for many seconds, but came out of the house, escorted by her uncle, a little stout man of cheerful vulgarity who bowed very low to the Earl, and uttered profuse thanks and protestations. He was answered with the cool civility of a stranger, but Lady Worth, leaning forward, said everything that was kind, enquired after Mrs. Fisher, who had lately been confined to the house by a feverish cold, and engaged herself to take good care of Miss Devenish.

"Your ladyship is never backward in any attention—most flattering distinction! I am all obligation!" he said, bowing to her. "It is just as it should be, for I'm sure Lucy is fit to move in the first circles—ay, and to make a good match into the bargain, eh, Lucy? Ah, she don't like me to quiz her about it: she is blushing, I daresay, only it is too dark to see."

Judith could not but feel a little vexation that he should expose himself so to Worth, but she passed it off with tact. Miss Devenish was handed into the carriage, the Earl followed her, and in a moment they were off, leaving Mr. Fisher bowing farewell upon the pavement.

"Dear Lady Worth, this is very kind of you!" said Miss Devenish, in a pretty, low voice. "My aunt desired her compliments. I did not keep you waiting, I hope?"

"No, indeed. I only hope it won't prove an insipid evening. I believe there may be dancing, and I suppose all the world and his wife will be there."

It certainly seemed so. When they arrived, Lady Charlotte's salons were already crowded. The English predominated, but there were any number of distinguished foreigners present. Here and there were to be seen the blue of a Dutch uniform, and the smart rifle-green of a Belgian dragoon; and everywhere you should chance to look you might be sure of encountering the sight of scarlet: vivid splashes of scarlet, throwing into insignificance all the ladies' pale muslins, and every civilian gentleman's more sober coat. Civilian gentlemen were plainly at a discount, and the young lady who could not show at least one scarlet uniform enslaved was unhappy indeed. Wits and savants went by the board; the crowd was thickest about Lord Hill, who had dropped in for half an hour. His round face wore its usual placid smile; he was replying with inexhaustible patience and good-humour to the anxious inquiries of the females clustering round him. Dear Lord Hill! So kind, so dependable! He was not like the Duke, of course, but one need not pack one's trunks and order the horses to be put to for an instant flight to Antwerp while he was there to pledge one his word the Corsican Monster was still in Paris.

He had just reassured the Annesley sisters, two ethereal blondes, whose very ringlets were appealing. When Worth's party came into the room, they had moved away from Lord Hill, and were standing near the door, a lovely fragile pair, so like, so dotingly fond!

They were both married, the younger, Catharine, being one of the season's brides, with a most unexceptionable young husband to her credit, Lord John Somerset, temporarily attached to the Prince of Orange's personal Staff. It was strange that Catharine, decidedly her sister's inferior in beauty and brain, should have done so much better for herself in the marriage-market. Poor Frances, with her infinite capacity for hero-worship, had made but a sad business of it after all, for a less inspiring figure than her tow-headed, chattering, awkward Mr. Webster would have been hard to find. You could hardly blame her for having fallen so deeply in love with Lord Byron. Quite an *affaire* that had been, while it lasted. Happily that had not been for very long—though long enough, if Catharine's indiscreet tongue were to be trusted, to enable her to secure one of the poet's precious locks of hair. That was more than Caro Lamb could boast of, poor soul.

She too was in Brussels, quite scandalizing the old-fashioned with her gossamer gauzes, always damped to make them cling close to her limbs, generally dropping off one thin shoulder, and allowing the interested an intimate view of her shape. Old Lady Mount Norris was ready to stake her reputation on Caroline's wearing under her gauze dresses not a stitch of clothing beyond an Invisible

Petticoat. Well, her own daughter might possess a lock of Byron's hair, but one was able to thank God she did not flaunt herself abroad next door to naked.

Lord Byron was not in Brussels. Perhaps he was too taken up with that queer, serious bride of his; perhaps he knew that even a poet as beautiful and as sinister as himself would not make much of a mark in Brussels on the eve of war.

His marriage had been a great shock to Caro Lamb, said the gossipers. Poor thing, one was truly sorry for her, however ridiculous she might have made herself. It was quite her own fault that she now looked so haggard. She was unbecomingly thin too; every lady was agreed on that. Sprite? Ariel? Well, one had always thought such nicknames absurd; one really never had admired her. Only gentlemen were sometimes so silly!

There were quite a number of gentlemen round Lady Caroline, all being regrettably silly. A murmur from Miss Devenish reached Lady Worth's ears: "Oh! she's so lovely! I like just to look at her!"

Judith hoped that she was not uncharitable, but had no wish to exchange more than a smile and a bow with Lady Caroline. One was not a prude, but really that lilac gauze was perfectly transparent! And if it came to loveliness, Judith considered her protégée quite as well worth looking at as any lady in the room. If her eyelashes were not as long and curling as Lady Frances Webster's the eyes themselves were decidedly more brilliant, and of such a dove-like softness! Her shape, though she might conceal it with discretion, was quite as good as Caro Lamb's; and her glossy brown curls were certainly thicker than Caroline's short feathery ringlets. Above all, her expression was charming, her smile so spontaneous, the look of grave reflection in her eye so particularly becoming! She dressed, moreover, with great propriety of taste, expensively but never extravagantly. Any man might congratulate himself on acquiring such a bride.

These reflections were interrupted by the necessity of exchanging civilities with the Marquise d'Assche. Judith turned from her presently to find Miss Devenish waiting to engage her attention.

"Dear Lady Worth," said Miss Devenish, "you know everyone, I believe. Only tell me who is that beautiful creature come into the room with Lady Vidal. Is it very wrong?—I could not but gasp and think to myself: 'Oh, if I had but that hair!' Everyone is cast into the shade!"

"Good gracious, whom in the world can you have seen?" said Judith, smiling with a little amusement. However, when her eyes followed the direction of Miss Devenish's worshipful gaze, the smile quickly faded. "Good God!" she said. "I had no idea that she was back in Brussels! Well, Lucy, if you are looking at the lady with the head of hair like my best copper coal-scuttle, let me tell you that she is none other than Barbara Childe."

"Lady Barbara!" breathed Miss Devenish. "I wondered—— You must know that I never till now set eyes on her. Yes, one can see the likeness: she is a little like her brother, Lord Vidal, is she not?"

"More like Lord George, I should say. You do not know him: a wild young man, I am afraid; very like his sister."

Miss Devenish made no reply to this observation, her attention remaining fixed upon the two ladies who had come into the salon.

The elder, Lady Vidal, was a handsome brunette, whose air, dress, and deportment all proclaimed the lady of fashion. She was accompanied by her husband, the Marquis of Vidal, a fleshy man, with a shock of reddish hair, a permanent crease between thick, sandy brows, and a rather pouting mouth.

Beside Lady Vidal, and with her hand lightly resting on the arm of an officer in Dutch-Belgian uniform, stood the object of Miss Devenish's eager scrutiny.

Lady Barbara Childe was no longer in the first flush of her youth. She was twenty-five years old, and had been three years a widow. Having married to oblige her family at the age of seventeen, she had had the good fortune to lose a husband three times as old as herself within five years of having married him. Her mourning had been of the most perfunctory: indeed, she was thought to have grieved more over the death of her father, an expensive nobleman of selfish habits, and an unsavoury reputation. But the truth was she did not grieve much over anyone. She was heartless.

It was the decision of all who knew her, and of many who did not. No one could deny her beauty, or her charm, but both were acknowledged to be deadly. Her conquests were innumerable; men fell so desperately in love with her that they became wan with desire, and very often did extremely foolish things when they discovered that she did not care the snap of her fingers for them. Young Mr. Vane had actually drunk himself to death; and poor Sir Henry Drew had bought himself a pair of Colours and gone off to the Peninsula with the declared intention of being killed, which he very soon was; while, more shocking than all the rest, Bab had allowed her destructive green eyes to drift towards Philip Darcy, with the result that poor dear Marianne, who had been his faithful wife for ten years, now sat weeping at home, quite neglected.

It was a mystery to the ladies what the gentlemen found so alluring in those green eyes, with their deceptive look of candour. For green they were, let who would call them blue. Bab had only to put on a green dress for there to be no doubt at all about it. They were set under most delicately arched brows, and were fringed by lashes which had obviously been darkened. That outrageously burnished head of hair might be natural, but those black lashes undoubtedly were not. Nor, agreed the waspish, was that lovely complexion. In fact, the Lady Barbara Childe, beyond all other iniquities, painted her face.

It became apparent to those who were gazing at her that the Lady Barbara had not, on this night of April, stopped at that. One foot was thrust a little forward from under the frills of a yellow-spangled gown, and it was seen that the Lady Barbara, wearing Grecian sandals, had painted her toe-nails gold.

Miss Devenish was heard to give a gasp. Lady Sarah Lennox, on the arm of General Maitland, said: "Gracious, only look at Bab's feet! She learned that trick in Paris, of course."

"Dashing, by Jove!" said the General appreciatively.

"Very, very fast!" said Lady Sarah. "Shocking!"

It was not the least part of Barbara's charm that having arrayed herself in a startling costume she contrived thereafter to seem wholly unconscious of the appearance she presented. She was never seen to pat her curls into place, or to cast an anxious glance towards the mirror. No less a personage than Mr. Brummell had taught her this magnificent unconcern. "Once having assured yourself that your dress is perfect in every detail," had pronounced that oracle, "you must not give it another thought. No one, I fancy, has ever seen me finger my cravat, twitch at the lapels of my coat, or smooth creases from my sleeve."

So the Lady Barbara, in a shimmering golden gown of spangles which clung to her tall shape as though it had been moulded to it, with her gold toe-nails, and her cluster of red curls threaded with a golden fillet, was apparently quite oblivious of being the most daringly dressed lady in the room. Fifty pairs of eyes were fixed upon her, some in patent disapproval, some in equally patent admiration, and she did not betray by as much as a flicker of an eyelid that she was aware of being a cynosure. That dreadfully disarming smile of hers swept across her face, and she moved towards Lady Worth, and held out her hand, saying in her oddly boyish voice: "How do you do? Is your little boy well?"

In spite of the fact that Judith had been by no means pleased, three months before, to see her infant son entranced by the Lady Barbara's charms, this speech could not but gratify her. "Very well, thank you," she replied. "Have you been back in Brussels long?"

"No, two days only."

"I did not know you had the intention of returning."

"Oh——! London was confoundedly flat," said Bab carelessly.

Miss Devenish, who had never before heard such a mannish expression on a lady's lips, stared. Lady Barbara glanced down at her from her graceful height, and then looked at Judith, her brows asking a question. A little unwillingly—but, after all, it was not likely that Bab would waste more than two minutes of her time on little Lucy Devenish—Judith made the necessary introduction. The smile and the hand were bestowed; Barbara made a movement with her fan, including in the group the officer on whose arm she had entered the salon. "Lady Worth, do you know M. le Capitaine Comte de Lavisse?"

"I believe we have met," acknowledged Judith, devoutly hoping that Brussels' most notorious rake would not take one of his dangerous fancies to the damsel in her charge.

However, the Captain Count's dark eyes betrayed no more than a fleeting interest in Miss Devenish, and before any introduction could be made a young gentleman with embryonic whiskers, and a sandy head at lamentable difference with his scarlet dress-coat, joined them.

"Hallo, Bab!" said Lord Harry Alastair. "Servant, Lady Worth! Miss Devenish, do you know they are dancing in the other room? May I have the honour?"

Judith, smiling a gracious permission, could not but feel that the path of a chaperon was a hard one. The reputation of the Alastairs, from Dominic, Duke of Avon, down to his granddaughter, Barbara, was not such as to lead a conscientious duenna to observe with pleasure her charge being borne off by any one of them. She comforted herself with the reflection that Lord Harry, an eighteen-year-old Ensign, could hardly be considered dangerous. Had it been Lord George, now! But Lord George, happily, was not in Belgium.

By the time Lord Harry had escorted Miss Devenish to the ballroom, the inevitable crowd had gathered round his sister. Lady Worth escaped from it, but not before she had been asked (inevitably, she thought) for news from Vienna.

Rumours and counter-rumours were as usual being circulated; the English in Brussels seemed to be poised for flight; and the only thing that would infallibly reassure the timorous was the certain news of the Duke's arrival.

It was easy to see what Brussels would make of him

23

when he did come. "The pedestal is ready for the hero," said Judith, with rather a provocative smile. "And *we* are all ready to kneel and worship at the base. I hope he may be worthy of our admiration."

General Maitland, to whom she had addressed this remark, said: "Do you know him, Lady Worth?"

"I have not that pleasure. Pray do not mention it, but I have never so much as laid eyes on him. Is it not shocking?"

"Oh!" said the General.

She raised her brows. "What am I to understand by that, if you please? Shall I be disappointed? I warn you, I expect a demi-god!"

"Demi-god," repeated the General, stroking one beautiful whisker. "Well, I don't know. Shouldn't have called him so myself."

"Ah, I am to be disappointed! I feared as much."

"No—no," said the General. "Not disappointed. He is a very able Commander."

"That sounds a little flat, I confess. Is it only the ladies who worship him? Do not his soldiers?"

"Oh no, nothing like that!" said the General, relieved to be able to answer a plain question. "I believe they rather like him than not: they like to see his hook-nose amongst them at any rate; but they don't worship him. Don't think he'd care for it if they did."

She was interested. "You present me with a new picture, General. My brother-in-law is quite devoted to him, I believe."

"Audley? Well, he's one of his family, you see." He observed a bewildered look on her face, and added: "On his Staff, I should say. That's another matter altogether. His Staff know him better than the rest of us."

"This is more promising. He is unapproachable. A demi-god should certainly be so."

He laughed suddenly. "No, no, *you* won't find him unapproachable, Lady Worth, I pledge you my word!"

Their conversation was interrupted by Sarah and Georgiana Lennox, who came up to them with their arms entwined. The General greeted the elder sister with such a warm smile that Lady Worth was satisfied that rumour had not lied about his purpose of re-marriage. Lady Sarah went off on his arm; Georgiana remained beside Judith, watching the shifting crowd for a few moments. She presently said in rather a thoughtful voice: "Do you see that Bab Childe is back?"

"Yes, I have been speaking to her."

"I must say, I wish she had stayed away," confided Georgiana. "It is the oddest thing, because, for myself, I don't dislike her, but wherever she is there is always some horrid trouble, or unhappiness. Even Mama, who is never silly, is a little afraid she may cast her eyes in March's direction. Of course, we don't breathe a word of such a thing at home, but it's perfectly true."

"What, that your brother——"

"Oh no, no, but that Mama fears he *might!* One can't blame her. There does seem to be something about Bab which drives quite sensible men distracted. Dreadful, isn't it?"

"I think it is."

"Yes, so do I," said Georgiana regretfully. "I wish I had it."

Judith could not help laughing, but she assured her vivacious young friend that she was very well as she was. "All the nicest men pay their court to Georgy," she said. "It is men like the Comte de Lavisse who run after Lady Barbara."

"Yes," sighed Georgiana, looking pensively in the direction of the Count. "Very true. Of course one would not wish to be admired by such a person."

This sentiment was echoed by the Lady Barbara's brother, much later in the evening. As his carriage conveyed him and his ladies home to the Rue Ducale he said in a peevish tone that he wondered Bab could bear to have that foreign fellow for ever at her elbow.

She only laughed, but his wife, who had been yawning in her corner of the carriage, said sharply: "If you mean Lavisse, I am sure I don't know why you should. I only

25

wish Bab may not play fast and loose with him. I believe he is extremely rich."

This argument was one that could not but appeal to the Marquis. He was silent for a few moments, but presently said: "I don't know about that, but I can tell you his reputation doesn't bear looking into."

"If it comes to that, Bab's own reputation is not above reproach!"

Another gurgle of laughter came from the opposite corner of the carriage. The Marquis said severely: "It's all very well to laugh. No doubt it amuses you to make your name a byword. For my part, I have had enough of your scandals."

"Oh, pray spare us a homily!" said his wife, yawning again.

"Don't be anxious, Vidal! They're laying odds against Lavisse's staying the course for more than a month."

The carriage passed over an uneven stretch of pavé. Unpleasantly jolted, the Marquis said angrily: "Upon my word! Do you like to have your name bandied about? your affairs made the subject of bets?"

"I don't care," replied Barbara indifferently. "No, I think I like it."

"You're shameless! Who told you this?"

"Harry."

"I might have known it! Pretty news to recount to his sister!"

"Oh lord, why shouldn't he?" said Lady Vidal. "You'll be a bigger fool than I take you for, Bab, if you let Lavisse slip through your fingers."

"I don't let them slip," retorted Barbara. "I drop them. I daresay I shall drop him too."

"Be careful he doesn't drop you!" said her ladyship.

The carriage had drawn up before one of the large houses in the Rue Ducale, facing the Park. As the footman opened the door, Barbara murmured: "Oh no, do you think he will? That would be interesting."

Her sister-in-law forbore to answer this, but, alighting from the carriage, passed into the house. Barbara followed

26

her, but paused only to say good-night before picking up her candle and going upstairs to her bedroom.

She had not, however, seen the last of Lady Vidal, who came tapping on her door half an hour later, and entered with the air of one who proposed to remain some while. Barbara was seated before the mirror, her flaming head rising out of the foam of sea-green gauze which constituted her dressing-gown. "Oh, what the deuce, Gussie?" she said.

"Send your girl away: I want to talk to you," commanded Augusta, settling herself in the most comfortable chair in the room.

Barbara gave an impatient sigh, but obeyed. As the door closed behind the maid, she said: "Well, what is it? Are you going to urge me to marry Etienne? I wish you may not put yourself to so much trouble."

"You might do worse," said Augusta.

"To be sure I might. We are agreed, then."

"You know, you should be thinking seriously of marriage. You're twenty-five, my dear."

"Ah, marriage is a bore!"

"If you mean husbands are bores, I'm sure I heartily agree with you," responded Augusta. "They have to be endured for the sake of the blessings attached to them. Single, one has neither standing nor consequence."

"I'll tell you what, Gussie: the best is to be a widow—a dashing widow!"

"So you may think while you still possess pretensions to beauty. No longer, I assure you. As for 'dashing', that brings me to another thing I had to say. I believe I'm no prude, but those gilded toe-nails of yours are the outside of enough, Bab."

Barbara lifted a fold of the gauze to observe her bare feet. "Pretty, aren't they?"

"Vidal informs me he has seen none but French women (and those of a certain class) with painted nails."

"Oh, famous!"

Barbara seemed to be so genuinely delighted by this piece of news that Lady Vidal thought it wiser to leave the subject. "That's as may be. What is more important is what you mean to do with your future. If you take my advice, you'll marry Lavisse."

"No, he would be the devil of a husband."

"And you the devil of a wife, my dear."

"True. I will live and die a widow."

"Pray don't talk such stuff to me!" said Augusta tartly. "If you let slip all your opportunities of getting a husband I shall think you are a great fool."

Barbara laughed, and getting up from the stool before her dressing-table, strolled across the room to a small cupboard and opened it. "Very well! Let us look about us! Shall I set my cap at dear Gordon? I could fancy him, I believe."

"Sir Alexander? Don't be absurd! A boy!"

Barbara had taken a medicine bottle from the cupboard and was measuring some of its contents into a glass. She paused, and wrinkled her brow. "General Maitland? That would be suitable: he is a widower."

"He is as good as promised to Sarah Lennox."

"That's no objection—if I want him. No, I don't think I do. I'll tell you what, Gussie, I'll have the Adjutant-General!"

"Good God, that would not last long! They call him the Fire-eater. You would be for ever quarrelling. I wish you would be serious! You need not marry a soldier, after all."

"Yes, yes, if I marry it must be a soldier. I am quite determined. The Army is all the rage. And when have I ever been behind the mode? Consider, too, the range of possibilities! Only think of the Guards positively massed in the neighbourhood. I have only to drive to Enghien to find an eligible *parti*. The Cavalry, too! All the Household Troops are under orders to sail, and I had always a liking for a well set-up Life Guardsman."

"That means we shall have George here, I suppose," said Augustua, without any appearance of gratification.

"Yes, but never mind that! What do you say to a gallant Hussar? The 10th are coming out and they wear

28

such charming clothes! I have had a riding dress made à la Hussar, in the palest green, all frogged and laced with silver. Ravishing!"

"You will set the town by the ears!"

"Who cares?"

"*You* may not, but it is not very agreeable for us. I wish you would consider me a little before you put Vidal out of temper."

Barbara came back into the middle of the room, holding the glass containing her potion. "Where's the use? If I don't, George will. Vidal is such a dull dog!"

Augusta gave a laugh. "I had rather have him than George, at all events. What are you taking there?"

"Only my laudanum drops," replied Barbara, tossing off the mixture.

"Well, I take them myself, but I have the excuse of nervous headaches. *You* never had such a thing in your life. If you would be less restless——"

"Well, I won't, I can't! This is nothing: it helps me to sleep. Who was the demure lass dancing with Harry? She came with Lady Worth, I think."

"Oh, that chit! She's of no account; I can't conceive what should possess Lady Worth to take her under her wing. There is an uncle, or some such thing. A very vulgar person, connected with Trade. Of course, if Harry is to lose his head in that direction it will be only what one might have expected, but I must say I think we might be spared that at least. I can tell you this, if you and your brothers create any odious scandals, Vidal will insist on returning to England. He is of two minds now."

"Why? Is he afraid of me, or only of Boncy?"

"Both, I daresay. I have no notion of staying here if Bonaparte does march on Brussels, as they all say he will. And if I go you must also."

Barbara shed her sea-green wrap and got into bed. The light of the candles beside her had the effect of making her eyes and hair glow vividly. "Don't think it! I shall stay. A war will be exciting. I like that!"

"You can scarcely remain alone in Brussels!"

Barbara snuggled down amongst a superfluity of pillows. "Who lives will see."

"*I* should not care to do so in your situation."

A gleam shot into the half-closed eyes; they looked sideways at Augusta. "Dearest Gussie! So respectable!" Barbara murmured.

CHAPTER III

LADY WORTH walked into her breakfast-parlour on the morning of the 5th April, to find that she was not, as she had supposed, the first to enter it. A cocked-hat had been tossed on to a chair, and a gentleman in the white net pantaloons and blue frock-coat of a Staff officer was sitting on the floor, busily engaged in making paper-boats for Lord Temperley. Lord Temperley was standing beside him, a stern frown on his countenance betokening the rapt interest of a young gentleman just two years old.

"Well!" cried Judith.

The Staff officer looked quickly up, and jumped to his feet. He was a man in the mid-thirties, with smiling grey eyes, and a mobile, well-shaped mouth.

Lady Worth seized him by both hands. "My dear Charles! of all the delightful surprises! But when did you arrive? How pleased I am to see you! Have you breakfasted? Where is your baggage?"

Colonel Audley responded to this welcome by putting an arm round his sister-in-law's waist and kissing her cheek. "No need to ask you how you do: you look famous! I got in last night, too late to knock you up."

"How can you be so absurd? Don't tell me you put up at an hôtel!"

"No, at the Duke's."

"He is here too? Really in Brussels at last?"

"Why certainly! We are all of us here—the Duke, Fremantle, young Lennox, and your humble servant." A tug at his sash recalled his attention to his nephew. "Sir! I beg pardon! The boat—of course!"

The boat was soon finished, and put into his lordship's fat little hand. Prompted by his Mama, he uttered a laconic word of thanks, and was borne off by his nurse.

Colonel Audley readjusted his sash. "I must tell you that I find my nephew improved out of all recognition, Judith. When I last had the pleasure of meeting him, he covered me with confusion by bursting into a howl of dismay. But nothing could have been more gentlemanlike than his reception of me to-day."

She smiled. "I hope it may be true. He is not always so, I confess. To my mind he is excessively like his father in his dislike of strangers. Worth, of course, would have you believe quite otherwise. Sit down, and let me give you some coffee. Have you seen Worth yet?"

"Not a sign of him. Tell me all the news! What has been happening here? How do you go on?"

"But my dear Charles, *I* have no news! It is to you that we look for that. Don't you know that for weeks past we have been positively hanging upon your arrival, eagerly searching your wretchedly brief letters for the least grain of interesting intelligence?"

He looked surprised, and a little amused. "What in the world would you have me tell you? I had thought the deliberations of the Congress were pretty well known."

"Charles!" said her ladyship, in a despairing voice, "you have been at the very hub of the world, surrounded by Emperors and Statesmen, and you ask me what I would have you tell me!"

"Oh, I can tell you a deal about the Emperors," offered the Colonel. "Alexander, now, is—let us say—a trifle difficult."

He was interrupted. "Tell me immediately what you have been doing!" commanded Judith.

"Dancing," he replied.

"Dancing!"

"And dining."

"You are most provoking. Are you pledged to secrecy?

If so, of course I won't ask you any awkward questions."

"Not in the least," said the Colonel cheerfully. "Life in Vienna was one long ball. I have been devoting a great part of my time to the quadrille. *L'Eté, la Poule, la grande ronde*—I have all the steps, I assure you."

"You must be a very odd sort of an Aide-de-Camp!" she remarked. "Does not the Duke object?"

"Object?" said the Colonel. "Of course not! He likes it. William Lennox would tell you that the excellence of his *pas de zéphyr* is the only thing that has more than once saved him from reprimand."

"But seriously, Charles——?"

"On my honour!"

She was quite dumbfounded by this unexpected light cast upon the proceedings at Vienna, but before she could express her astonishment her husband came into the room, and the subject was forgotten in the greeting between the brothers, and the exchange of questions.

"You have been travelling fast," the Earl said, as he presently took his seat at the table. "Stuart spoke of the Duke's still being in Vienna only the other day."

"Yes, shockingly fast. We even had to stop for lard to grease the wheels. But with such a shriek going up for the Beau from here, what did you expect?" said the Colonel, with a twinkle. "Anyone would imagine Boney to be only a day's march off from the noise you have been making."

The Earl smiled, but merely said: "Are you rejoining the Regiment, or do you remain on the Staff?"

"Oh, all of us old hands remain, except perhaps March, who will probably stay with the Prince of Orange. Lennox goes back to his regiment, of course. He is only a youngster, and the Beau wants his old officers with him. What about my horses, Worth? You had my letter?"

"Yes, and wrote immediately to England. Jackson has procured you three good hunters, and there is a bay mare I bought for you last week."

"Good!" said the Colonel. "I shall probably get forage allowance for four horses. Tell me how you have been going on here! Who's this fellow, Hudson Lowe, who

32

knows all there is to be known about handling armies?"

"Oh, you've seen him already, have you? I suppose you know he is your Quartermaster-General? Whether he will deal with the Duke is a question yet to be decided."

"My dear fellow, it was decided within five minutes of his presenting himself this morning," said the Colonel, passing his cup-and-saucer to Lady Worth. "I left him instructing the Beau, and talking about his experience. Old Hookey as stiff as a poker, and glaring at him, with one of his crashing snubs just ripe to be delivered. I slipped away. Fremantle's on duty, poor devil!"

"Crashing snubs? Is the Duke a bad-tempered man?" enquired Judith. "That must be a sad blow to us all!"

"Oh no, I wouldn't call him *bad*-tempered!" replied the Colonel. "He gets peevish, you know—a trifle crusty, when things don't go just as he wishes. I wish they may get Murray back from America in time to take this fellow Lowe's place: we can't have him putting old Hookey out every day of the week: comes too hard on the wretched Staff."

Judith gave him back his cup-and-saucer. "But, Charles, this is shocking! You depict a cross, querulous person, and we have been expecting a demi-god."

"Demi-god! Well, so he is, the instant he goes into action," said the Colonel. He drank his coffee, and said: "Who is here, Worth? Any troops arrived yet from England?"

"Very few. We have really only the remains of Graham's detachment still, the same that Orange has had under his command the whole winter. There are the 1st Guards, the Coldstream, and the 3rd Scots; all 2nd battalions. The 52nd is here, a part of the 95th—but you must know the regiments as well as I do! There's no English cavalry at all, only that of the German Legion."

The Colonel nodded. "They'll come."

"Under Combermere?"

"Oh, surely! We can't do without old Stapleton Cotton's long face amongst us. But tell me! who are all these school-boys on the Staff, and where did they spring from? Scarcely

33

a name one knows on the Quartermaster-General's Staff, or the Adjutant-General's either, for that matter!"

"I thought myself there were a number of remarkably inexperienced young gentlemen calling themselves Deputy-Assistants—but when the Duke takes a lad of fifteen into his family one is left to suppose he likes a Staff just out of the nursery. By the by, I suppose you know you have arrived in time to assist at festivities at the Hôtel de Ville to-night? There's to be a fête in honour of the King and Queen of the Netherlands. Does the Duke go?"

"Oh yes, we always go to fêtes!" replied the Colonel. "What is it to be? Dancing, supper—the usual thing? That reminds me: I must have some new boots. Is there anyone in the town who can be trusted to make me a pair of Hessians?"

This question led to a discussion of the shops in Brussels, and the more pressing needs of an officer on the Duke of Wellington's Staff. These seemed to consist mostly of articles of wearing apparel suitable for galas, and Lady Worth was left presently to reflect on the incomprehensibility of the male sex, which, upon the eve of war, was apparently concerned solely with the price of silver lace, and the cut of a Hessian boot.

The Colonel had declared his dress-clothes to be worn to rags, but when he presented himself in readiness to set forth to the Hôtel de Ville that evening his sister-in-law had no fault to find with his appearance beyond regretting, with a sigh, that his present occupation made the wearing of his Hussar uniform ineligible. Nothing could have been better than the set of his coat across his shoulders, nothing more resplendent than his fringed sash, nothing more effulgent than his Hessians with their swinging tassels. The Colonel was blessed with a good leg, and had nothing to fear from sheathing it in a skin-tight net pantaloon. His curling brown locks had been brushed into a state of pleasing disorder, known as the style *au coup de vent*; his whiskers were neatly trimmed; he carried his cocked-hat under one arm; and altogether presented to his sister-in-law's critical gaze a very handsome picture.

34

That he was quite unaware of it naturally did not detract from his charm. Judith, observing him with a little complacency, decided that if Miss Devenish failed to succumb to the twinkle in the Colonel's open grey eyes, or to the attraction of his easy, frank manners, she must be hard indeed to please.

Miss Devenish would be present this evening, Judith having been at considerable pains to procure invitation tickets for her and for Mrs. Fisher.

The Earl of Worth's small party arrived at the Hôtel de Ville shortly after eight o'clock, to find a long line of carriages setting down their burdens one after another, and the interior of the building already teeming with guests. The ante-rooms were crowded, and (said Colonel Audley) as hot as any in Vienna; and her ladyship, having had her train of lilac crape twice trodden on, was very glad to pass into the ballroom. Here matters were a little better, the room being of huge proportions. Down one side of it were tall windows, with statues on pedestals set in each, while on the opposite side were corresponding embrasures, each one curtained, and emblazoned with the letter W in a scroll.

A great many of the guests were of Belgian or of Dutch nationality, but Lady Worth soon discovered English acquaintances amongst them, and was presently busy presenting Colonel Audley to those who had not yet met him, or recalling him to the remembrances of those who had. She did not perceive Miss Devenish in the room, but since she had taken up a position near the main entrance, she had little doubt of observing her arrival. Meanwhile, Colonel Audley remained beside her, and might have continued shaking hands, greeting old friends, and being made known to smiling strangers for any length of time, had not an interruption occurred which immediately attracted the attention of everyone present.

A pronounced stir was taking place in the ante-room; a loud, whooping laugh was heard, and the next moment a well-made gentleman in a plain evening dress embellished with a number of Orders walked into the ballroom, escorted

35

by the Mayor of Brussels, and a suite composed of senior officers in various glittering dress uniforms. The ribbon of the Garter relieved the severity of the gentleman's dress, but except for his carriage there was little to proclaim the military man. Beside the gilded splendour of a German Hussar, and the scarlet brilliance of an English Guardsman, he looked almost out of place. He had rather sparse mouse-coloured hair, a little grizzled at the temples; a mouth pursed slightly in repose, but just now open in laughter; and a pair of chilly blue eyes set under strongly marked brows. The eyes must have immediately attracted attention had this not been inevitably claimed by his incredible nose. That high-bridged bony feature dominated his face and made it at once remarkable. It lent majesty to the countenance and terror to its owner's frown. It was a proud, masterful nose, the nose of one who would brook no interference, and permit few liberties. It was also a famous nose, and anyone beholding it would have had to be very dull-witted not to have realized at once that it belonged to the Duke of Wellington.

Lady Worth grasped its significance, but could scarcely believe that quite the most soberly-dressed gentleman in the room (if you left out of account that casual sprinkling of Orders) could really be the Field-Marshal himself. Even Lord Hill, at his elbow, was more resplendent, while any Cornet of Hussars would have cast him in the shade.

That was Lady Worth's first impression, but a second, following it swiftly, at once corrected it. The Duke had no need of silver lace or a scarlet-and-gold coat to attract the eye. He had a presence which made itself felt the instant he entered the room. He stood surrounded by his General Staff, and they became no more than a splendid background for his trim figure. It was very odd, reflected Lady Worth, watching him, for his height was no more than average, and he did not bear himself with any extraordinary dignity. Indeed, there seemed to be very little pomp about him. He was shaking hands briskly with the Belgian notables presented by the Mayor; he was laughing again, and really, his laugh was over-loud, not unlike the neighing of a horse.

He came farther into the ballroom, pausing to greet individuals, and, catching sight of Colonel Audley, said in a quick, resonant voice: "Ah, there you are, Audley! One of my family, Baron—Colonel Audley, who has been with me in Vienna, and will show us all how they perform the *grande ronde* there."

"Why, Charles, how do you do?" exclaimed the Duchess of Richmond, giving him her hand. "And Lady Worth! My dear Duke, I think you have not met Charles's sister-in-law. Lady Worth, the Duke of Wellington!"

Judith found herself under the piercing scrutiny of the Duke's deep-set eyes, which surveyed her with an expression of decided approbation. She would have bowed merely, but he took her hand in a firm grasp, and shook it, saying: "Delighted! You must let me tell you how delighted I am to meet Audley's sister. Do you make a long stay in Brussels? Eh? Yes? That's capital! I shall hope for a better acquaintance."

Judith said something graceful, and as his Grace seemed inclined to linger, presented her husband. A brief How-de-do? was exchanged; other people pressed forward to claim the Duke's attention; and he passed on, bowing to one person, shaking hands with another, calling out: "Hallo, how are you? Glad to see you!" to a third. Unlike the figure of her imagination, he seemed very much at home in a ballroom, quite accessible, cheerful to the verge of jocularity, and ready to be pleased. Such remarks of his as reached Lady Worth's ears were none of them profound, and when the anxious besought his opinion of the political situation he replied with a joviality which had almost the effect of making him appear to be a little stupid.

Lady Worth was still looking after the Duke when she caught sight of Miss Devenish, standing not many paces distant, beside her aunt. Judith noticed with satisfaction that she was in her best looks, her hair very prettily dressed, her cheeks faintly flushed, and her large eyes glowing.

She had just decided not to seem to be in too great a hurry to introduce Charles, when his voice said in her ear: "Who is that?"

Nothing, thought Judith, could have been more opportune! Lucy was far too unaffected to have purposely placed herself beside a plain young female in a dress of particularly harsh puce, but the effect could not have been more advantageous to her. How right she had been to advise the child to wear her white satin! It was no wonder that she had caught Charles's eye. She replied in a careless tone: "Oh, that is a young friend of mine, a Miss Devenish."

"Will you present me?"

"Why, certainly! She is pretty, is she not?"

"Pretty!" repeated the Colonel. "She is the loveliest creature I ever beheld in my life!"

Prejudiced as Judith was in Miss Devenish's favour, this encomium seemed to be to her somewhat exaggerated. Charles sounded quite serious too: in fact, oddly serious. She turned her head, and found to her surprise that he was not looking in Miss Devenish's direction, but towards the big double doorway.

"Why, Charles, whom can you be staring at?" she began, but broke off as her gaze followed his. It was quite obvious whom Colonel Audley was staring at. He was staring at a vision in palest green satin draped in a cloud of silver net. The Lady Barbara Childe had arrived, and was standing directly beneath a huge chandelier, just inside the ballroom. The candlelight touched her hair with fire, and made the emerald spray she wore in it gleam vividly. The heavy folds of satin clung to her form, and clearly revealed the long, lovely line of a leg, a little advanced beyond its fellow. Shoulders and breast were bare, if you ignored a scarf of silver net, which (thought Lady Worth) was easily done. Any woman would have agreed that the bodice of the wretched creature's gown was cut indecently low, while as for petticoats, Lady Worth for one would have owned herself surprised to learn that Barbara was wearing as much as a stitch beneath her satin and her net.

A glance at Colonel Audley's face was enough to inform

38

her that this disgraceful circumstance was not likely to weigh with him as it should.

His hand came up to grasp her elbow, not ungently, but with a certain urgency. "Miss Devenish, did you say?"

"No, I did not!" replied Judith crossly. She recollected herself, and added with an attempt to conceal her annoyance: "You are looking at the wrong lady. That is Barbara Childe. I daresay you may have heard of her."

"So that is Barbara Childe!" he said. "Are you acquainted with her? Will you present me?"

"Well, really, Charles, my acquaintance with her is of the slightest. You know, she is not quite the thing. I will allow her to be excessively handsome, but I believe you would be disappointed if you knew her."

"Impossible!" he replied.

Judith looked wildly round in search of inspiration, and encountered only the mocking eyes of her lord. She met that quizzical glance with one of entreaty not unmixed with indignation. The Earl took snuff with a wonderful air of abstraction.

Help came from an unexpected quarter. Those standing by the door fell back; the orchestra struck up *William of Nassau*; the King and Queen of the Netherlands had arrived.

There could be no question of performing introductions at such a moment. As the ushers came in, the crowd parted, till an avenue was formed; their Majesties were announced; every lady sank in a deep curtsy; and in walked King William, a stout gentleman, with his stout Queen beside him, and behind him his two sons.

Majesty was in an affable mood, smiling broadly, ready to have any number of presentations made, and to be extremely gracious to everyone; but the Princes attracted more attention. The younger, Frederick, was a fine young man, with not inconsiderable pretensions to good looks. He bore himself stiffly, and favoured his acquaintances with an inclination of the head, accompanied by a small, regal smile.

His brother, the Prince of Orange, though arrayed in

39

all the magnificence of a General's dress-uniform, was a much less impressive figure. He was very thin and held himself badly, and his good-humoured countenance bore a slight resemblance to that of a startled faun. His smile, however, was disarming, and a marked tendency to wink at cronies whom he observed in the crowd could not but endear him to his more unceremonious friends. When he caught sight of Colonel Audley, an expression of delight leapt to his rather prominent eyes, and he waved to him; and when the Duke of Wellington, having bowed punctiliously over the King's hand, turned to pay his respects to him, he frustrated any attempt at formality by starting forward, and taking the Duke's hand with all the reverence of a junior officer honoured by a great man.

"I hope I see your Royal Highness in good health?" said the Duke.

"I am so glad to see you, sir," stammered his Royal Highness. "I would have reported at your house this morning, but I did not know—I was at Braine-le-Comte —you must forgive me!"

The Duke's face relaxed. "I shall be happy to see your Highness to-morrow, if that should be convenient to you."

"Yes, of course, sir!" his Highness assured him.

Majesty, listening indulgently to this interchange, intervened to draw the Duke's attention to his younger son. The Prince of Orange seized the opportunity to efface himself, and would have slipped away in search of more congenial companionship had not the signal for the dancing to begin been given at that moment. He was obliged to lead the opening quadrille with the Duchesse de Beaufort, and to dance a couple of waltzes with Madame d'Ursel and Madame d'Assche. After that, he considered his duty conscientiously performed, and disappeared from the ballroom into one of the adjoining rooms where refreshment and kindred spirits were to be found.

He entered between looped curtains to find a small but convivial party assembled there. Lord March, a fresh-faced young man with grave eyes and a quick smile, was leaning on a chair-back, adjuring Colonel Audley, seated on the edge of the table, and Colonel Fremantle, lounging against the wall, to make a clean breast of their doings in Vienna. The fourth member of the group was Sir Alexander Gordon, a young man with a winning personality, who was engaged in filling his glass from a decanter.

"Charles!" cried the Prince, coming forward in his impetuous style. "My dear fellow, how are you?"

Colonel Audley stood up. "Sir!" he said.

The Prince wrung his hand. "Now, don't, I beg you! I am so pleased you are here! Do not let us have any ceremony! This is like Spain: we need only Canning, and Fitzroy to walk in asking, 'Where's Slender Billy?' and we are again the old family."

"That's all very well, but you've become a great man since I saw you last," objected Colonel Audley. "I think —yes, I think a Royal Tiger."

A general laugh greeted this old Headquarters' joke. The Prince said: "You can't call *me* a Tiger: I am not a visitor to the camp! But have you seen the real Tigers? *Mon Dieu*, do you remember we called the Duc d'Angoulême a Royal Tiger? But, my dear Charles—my dear Fremantle—the Duc de Berri! No, really, you would not believe! You must see him drilling his men to appreciate him. He flies into a passion and almost falls off his horse. But on my honour!"

"*No*, sir!" protested March.

"I swear it!" He accepted a glass of wine from Gordon, and perched himself on the arm of a chair. "Confusion to Boney!" he said, and drank. "And General Röder!" he resumed.

"Confusion to him too, sir?" murmured Gordon.

"No—yes! The worst of our Tigers! Have you met General Röder, Charles? He doesn't like the British, he doesn't like the Dutch, he doesn't like the Belgians, he doesn't like the French, he doesn't even like your humble servant. So here is confusion to General Röder!"

While this toast was being drunk, a pleasant-faced officer in Dutch uniform had peeped round the curtain and then come into the room. He was considerably older than any of the young men drinking confusion to the unfortunate Prussian Commissioner, but was hailed by them with cheerful affection.

"Hallo, Baron! Come in!" said Audley. "How are you?"

"Glass of wine with you, Baron?" Fremantle held up the decanter invitingly.

"Constant! We are drinking confusion to General von Röder. Join us immediately!" commanded his Royal master.

The Baron Constant de Rebecque glanced swiftly over his shoulder. He accepted a glass of wine, but said in very good English: "I beg of you, sir——! Consider where you are, and who you are, and—very well, very well, here is confusion to him, then! And now will you recollect, sir, that this is a fête for their Majesties, and it is expected that you will conduct yourself *en prince!* Your absence will be noticed: his Majesty will be displeased."

The Prince shrugged his shoulders. "It is absurd. I will not spend all the evening being civil to the Tigers, and I will not conduct myself *en prince* if that means I must not drink a glass of wine with my friends."

"Sir, you are also the General in Command of the Army, and not any more a junior Aide-de-Camp."

The Prince patted his arm. "Constant, *mon pauvre*, you have not seen—you have not heard! You are dreaming, in fact. Go and look who is here to-night. My poor command is quite at an end."

"*Mon prince*, you are still in command, and you must mingle with your guests."

"That's quite true, sir," said Fremantle. "The Duke hasn't taken over the command yet. Duty calls you, General!"

At this moment, and while the Prince still looked recalcitrant, a very tall man with the buff collar and silver lace of the 52nd Regiment appeared between the curtains, and stood silently surveying the group. He was Saxon-fair, with ice-blue eyes, a high-bridged nose, and a fighting

42

chin, and was built on splendid lines that were marred only by the droop of his right shoulder, the joint of which had become anchylosed, from a wound incurred in the Peninsula. At sight of him, Lord March straightened himself instinctively, and Colonel Fremantle jumped up from his chair.

The Prince turned his head, and pulled a grimace. "You need not tell me! You are looking for me. First my Quartermaster-General, and now my Military Secretary. Your health, Sir John!"

"Thank you, sir," said Colonel Colborne in his slow deep voice. A smile crept into his eyes. "I thought I should find you with the riff-raff of the Staff," he remarked. "If I were your Highness, I would return to the ballroom."

"Because my father will be displeased," said the Prince. "I have that by heart."

"No," replied Sir John. "Because his Majesty is more than likely to request the Duke to speak to you, sir."

"Oh, *mon Dieu!*" exclaimed the Prince, preparing for instant flight. "You are entirely right! Charles, my hôtel is in the Rue de Brabant! I charge you, don't forget! I will go and do my duty, and dance with all the ugly old women. Would you like to be presented to a fat *Frau?* No? Well, then, *au revoir!*"

"Stay a moment!" said Colonel Audley suddenly. "Do that for me, sir, will you?"

The Prince paused in the doorway, looking back with a laugh in his eyes. "What, present you to a fat *Frau?*"

"No, to the Lady Barbara Childe."

The Prince's brow shot up; a low whistle broke from Lord March; Colonel Fremantle said solicitously: "My poor fellow, you are not yourself. Take my advice and go quietly home to bed."

Audley reddened, but only said: "I am perfectly serious. I have been trying for the past hour to get an introduction, but there's no coming near her for the crowd round her. *You* could present me, sir, if you would."

"Steal into the supper-room and change the tickets on the tables," suggested March flippantly.

43

"Don't do it, sir!" recommended Fremantle.

The Prince laughed. "But Charles, this is the road to ruin! Really, you wish it?"

"Most earnestly, sir."

"Come, then, but mind, I am not to be blamed for the consequences!"

Colonel Audley had not exaggerated the difficulty of approaching Barbara Childe. When she left the dancing-floor on the arm of her partner she became engulfed in a crowd of impatient supplicants who would scarcely give place to any under the rank of a General. All had, however, to fall back before the Prince of Orange, who led Colonel Audley up to her ladyship, and said with his appealing smile: "Lady Barbara, I want to present to you a friend of mine who desires beyond anything this introduction. Colonel Audley—Lady Barbara Childe!"

Colonel Audley bowed, and looked up to find the Lady Barbara's brilliant gaze upon him. There was candid speculation in it, a tolerant smile just parted the lady's lips. The Colonel returned the look, smiled, and said in his pleasant voice: "How do you do?"

"How do you do?" responded Barbara slowly, still looking at him.

CHAPTER IV

THE Colonel, finding a gloved hand held out to him, took it in his, and bent his head to kiss it. Barbara looked down at it with a little bewilderment, as though she wondered why she had extended it.

"Do please grant the Colonel one waltz!" said the Prince, amusement quivering in his voice.

He moved away. The Comte de Lavisse said in English: "But how should that be possible, one asks oneself?"

"May I have the honour?" said the Colonel.

"But no!" objected the Count. "This leads to an affair

of the most sanguinary! I shall immediately send my friends to call upon you!"

"We shall all send our friends to call upon you!" declared an officer of the 1st Guards. "Audley, this is piracy! Those wishing to dance with Lady Bab must present their credentials a full week beforehand!"

Captain Chalmers, of the 52nd, said: "Send him about his business, Bab! These Staff officers are not at all the thing. Stick to the Light Division!"

"These Light Division men, Lady Barbara," said Colonel Audley, "fancy themselves more important than the rest of the Army put together. I tell you in confidence, but you know it is a fact that they brag shockingly."

"An insult!" declared Chalmers. "An insult from a Staff officer! Bab, I appeal to your sense of justice!"

Barbara laughed, and, laying her hand on Colonel Audley's arm, said: "Oh, the wishes of Royalty are tantamount to commands, gentlemen." She kissed her hand to her court, and walked back on to the floor with Colonel Audley.

He danced well, and she as though by instinct. Neither spoke for one or two turns, but presently Barbara raised her eyes to his face, and asked abruptly: "Why did you look at me *so*?"

He smiled down at her. "I don't know how I looked. I have been wanting to dance with you all the evening. Does every man say that to you?"

"Yes," she replied nonchalantly.

"I was afraid it must be so. I wish I might think of something to say to you which would interest you by its novelty."

"Oh! . . . Can you not?"

"No. If I said the only thing I can think of to say you would find it abominably commonplace."

"Should I? What is it?"

"I love you," replied the Colonel.

Momentary surprise, which caused her wonderful eyes to fly upwards to his again, gave place immediately to frank amusement. Her enchanting gurgle of laughter

45

escaped her; she said: "You are wrong. The unexpected cannot be commonplace."

"Was it unexpected? I had not thought that possible."

"Certainly. At the end of a week I might expect you to say just that, but you have said it within ten minutes of making my acquaintance, and so have taken my breath away. Go on: I like to be surprised."

"That is all," said the Colonel.

Again she cast him that considering glance. "You are very clever, or very simple. Which is it?"

"I haven't a notion," replied the Colonel.

"Ah! Is this strategy—from a Staff officer?"

"No, it is the truth."

"But, my friend, you are fantastic! You will next be making me an offer!"

He nodded. She saw the twinkle in his eye and responded to it. "Let us sit down. I don't care to dance any more. Who are you?"

He compelled her to continue dancing the length of the room, and then led her off the floor to the entrance doors, and through them into the first antechamber.

"My name is Charles Audley; my Army rank Lieutenant-Colonel; my Regimental rank, Major. What else shall I tell you?"

She interrupted him. "Audley . . . Oh, I have it! You are Worth's brother. Why did the Prince present you to me?"

"Because I asked him to. That was my only strategy."

She sat down upon a couch against the wall, and with a movement of her hand invited him to take his place beside her. He did so, and after a moment she said with her odd, boyish curtness: "I think I never saw you before to-night, did I?"

"Never. I have been employed in the Peninsula, and later in Paris and Vienna. But I have a little the advantage of you. *You*, I daresay, had never heard of me before, but *I* had heard of you."

"That's horrid!" she said quickly.

"Why?"

46

"Oh! People never say nice things about me. What have you been told?"

"That you were beautiful."

"And?"

"And disastrous."

"I don't mind that, but should not you take care?"

"You are forgetting that I am a soldier, and therefore inured to risks."

She laughed. "You've a confoundedly ready tongue! Come, take me back into the ballroom: my reputation won't stand all this sitting about in antechambers, I can tell you."

He rose at once, but said: "I wonder why you chose to tell me that?"

She too was on her feet; she had to look up to meet his eyes, but only a little. "You don't like it, do you?"

"No. I don't."

"Nevertheless, it is the truth. I play fair, you see."

He looked at her for a moment, half smiling, then raised his head, and held up a finger. "Listen! Do you know that waltz they are playing? It has been the rage in Vienna. Will you dance with me again?"

A shade of admiration came into her eyes; she said appreciatively: "The deuce take it! I believe—yes, I believe that was a snub! But you must not snub me!"

He turned towards her, and took both her hands in a strong clasp. "Don't speak ill of yourself, and I won't. There!" He raised her hands one after another to his lips, and lightly kissed them. "My dance, I think, Lady Barbara?"

They went back into the ballroom; the Colonel's arm encircled that supple waist; a gloved hand lay light as a feather on his shoulder; Barbara murmured: "You waltz charmingly, Colonel."

"So do you, Lady Barbara."

She stole a mischievous glance up at his face. "That was to be expected. It is still thought a trifle *fast* in England, you know."

From a little distance, Georgiana Lennox, circling

47

round very dashingly with Lord Hay, caught sight of them, and promptly exclaimed: "Oh, how infamous!"

"Where? Who?" demanded Hay.

"Over there, stupid! Don't you see? Bab Childe has seized on one of the nicest men in Brussels! Of all the wretched pieces of work! I do think she might be content with her odious Lavisse, and not steal Charles Audley as well!"

"Lucky devil!" said Hay.

"Sir!" said Georgiana in outraged accents. "Take me back to Mama this instant, if you please!"

"Oh lord!" gasped Hay ruefully. "I didn't mean it, Georgy, really, I didn't!"

She allowed herself to be mollified, but remarked sagely: "You may think him lucky, but I expect Lady Worth won't."

She was quite right. From the harbour of Sir Henry Clinton's gallant arm, Judith too had perceived her brother-in-law and his partner. That the couple could waltz better than any other in the room, and were attracting some attention, afforded her not the slightest gratification. She had observed the look on Colonel Audley's face, and although she had never before seen him wear that particular expression she had not the least doubt of its significance.

Sir Henry, noticing the direction of her troubled gaze, manœuvred that he too might see what had caught her eye. He said: "Your brother-in-law, is it not, Lady Worth?"

"Yes," she acknowledged.

"Dances very well, I see. All the Duke's family do, of course. But he will be making enemies if he monopolizes Bab Childe."

"Monopolizes her?" faltered Judith. "Is not this the first time he has danced with her?"

"Oh no! He was dancing with her the last waltz. My wife tells me the young fellows form up in column for the honour of obtaining the lady's hand."

"Charles is fortunate, then," said Judith.

48

"If you choose to call it fortunate," said Sir Henry, giving her a somewhat shrewd look. "I don't want to see any of my Staff entangled in that direction. She has a very unsettling effect, from what I can discover. One of Barnes's boys lost his head badly over her, and is now of about as much use to Barnes as my wife's little spaniel would be."

"I wonder who introduced Charles to her?"

Sir Henry laughed shortly. "I can tell you that, dear lady. The Prince of Orange."

Judith pursued the subject no further. Sir Henry's differences with the Prince made it tactless to introduce that ebullient young gentleman's name into any conversation with his Second-in-Command.

Colonel Audley relinquished Barbara presently, and, discovering a disinclination in himself to dance with anyone else, went away in search of other amusement. This was not hard to find, for he had many friends present, and was able to spend a pleasant hour wandering about the ballroom and the adjoining salons, exchanging greetings and news with his acquaintances.

Two suppers were being served at midnight, the one a select affair given by the King to his more distinguished guests; the other a less select and more informal entertainment held in an adjoining salon. The Earl and Countess of Worth were of the first party; so, too, was Colonel Audley, in his character of Aide-de-Camp. He was about to join the stream of people passing through the ballroom to the King's supper-parlour, and was standing by the entrance to one of the apartments leading out of the main antechamber, when the curtains obscuring the room behind him were thrust back, and Miss Devenish came out, almost running, her cheeks flushed, and one hand clasping to her shoulder a torn frill of lace.

So precipitate was her arrival in the antechamber that she nearly collided with Colonel Audley and recoiled with an exclamation on her lips and an appearance of great confusion.

Colonel Audley had turned, with a word of apology for

49

obstructing the way. Miss Devenish, still clutching her torn frill, said in a breathless voice: "It is of no consequence. It was quite my fault. I beg your pardon—I was going in search of my aunt!"

Colonel Audley glanced from this agitated little lady towards the room from which she had fled in such haste, and took a step towards the entrance. Miss Devenish put out her hand quickly to stop him: "Oh, please!" she said. "I don't wish—I am being very stupid. So vexing! I have had the misfortune to tear my lace, and must get it pinned up."

Colonel Audley took her trembling hand in his, and held it in a comfortingly firm clasp. "My dear ma'am, what has happened to distress you?" he asked. "Is there anything I can do?"

"Oh no, indeed! You are very kind, but it was nothing —really nothing at all! If I could find my aunt—it is time to be going in to supper, I believe."

Colonel Audley glanced towards the ballroom. "We will do our best to discover her, but I am afraid it will be a difficult task," he said. "Does she expect you to join her in the supper-room?"

"Oh yes! That is, nothing was said, but of course she would expect me. I was to have gone in with a—a gentleman, only . . ." She broke off, blushing more furiously than ever.

"Only that perhaps the gentleman had had a trifle too much to drink, and so forgot himself," finished the Colonel in a matter-of-fact voice.

Miss Devenish gave a gasp, and looked quickly up into his face. The smile in his eyes seemed to reassure her. She said: "Yes, that was it. Oh, how singular it must appear to you! But indeed——"

"It doesn't appear in the least singular to me," he interrupted. "But your lace! That is a more serious matter. If you had a pin—or even two pins—in your reticule, and could trust to my bungling fingers, I believe I could set it to rights."

The fright had by this time quite died out of her eyes.

50

A smile quivered on her lips. She replied: "I have a pin —two pins—but are you sure you can?"

"No," said the Colonel. "But I am sure I can try. Give me your pins."

She glanced round, but they were alone in the ante-chamber. "Thank you: you are very obliging!" she said and opened her reticule.

The pins once discovered, it was a matter of a minute or two only before the frills were in place again. Miss Devenish was quite astonished by the Colonel's deediness. "I made sure you would prick me at least!" she said merrily. "But I am quite in your debt! Thank you!"

He offered his arm. "May I take you to your aunt, if we can find her?"

"Oh——! I should be very happy: but am I not trespassing on your time?"

"How should you be? Perhaps your aunt may be waiting for you in the ballroom. "

No trace, however, of Mrs. Fisher was to be found there, nor was she discovered in the corridor leading to the second supper-room.

"I am afraid there is nothing for it but for you to accept me in place of your other supper partner," said the Colonel. "Your aunt must have gone in already, and from what I have seen of the crowd there you will be lucky indeed if you contrive to find her. Shall we go in?"

She looked doubtfully at him. "But are you sure you are not expected in the other room? I thought—someone told me—that nearly all the Staff officers were invited, and you are one, are you not?"

"I am, but no one will care a button whether I sup in the other room or not, I assure you," replied the Colonel. "It will be very dull, if I know these state functions."

"Will it?"

"Oh, I give you my word! It will last an interminable time, and a great many people will make interminable speeches. I should infinitely prefer to sup with you."

Miss Devenish smiled. "I shall be very happy to go with you," she said. "Indeed, I think I should feel wretchedly lost by myself. There are so many people!"

They fell in with the slow-moving stream of guests, and presently found themselves in a large, brilliantly-lit room set out with any number of tables, and already bewilderingly full of people. As they paused within the room, looking about them for a couple of vacant places, Miss Devenish exclaimed: "Oh, there she is!" and started towards a table near the door, at which was seated a stout, good-humoured-looking lady in purple sarsnet and a turban.

"There you are, my love!" said Mrs. Fisher. "I came in early to be sure of obtaining a good place. Well, and are you enjoying yourself? For my part I find the rooms very hot, but I daresay young people don't notice such things. You had better sit down while you may. I assure you I have been quite put to it to keep these seats for you."

Miss Devenish turned to Colonel Audley. "Thank you so very much! You need not miss your engagement in the other room after all, you see."

Mrs. Fisher, having favoured the Colonel with a sleepy yet shrewd scrutiny, interposed to invite him most hospitably to join her at the table. "I would not go into the other room if I were you," she told him. "I daresay they will be making speeches for as much as a couple of hours."

"Just what I have been saying to your niece, ma'am," he replied, pulling out a chair for Miss Devenish.

As he did so a hand smote him on the shoulder. "Hallo, Charles! How are you? What are you doing here? I thought you were supping in state! Judith and Worth are."

The Colonel turned. "Hallo, Perry!" he said, shaking hands. "How do you do, Lady Taverner? Yes, I ought to be in the other room, but I missed Worth, and so came here instead. Are you staying long in Brussels? Do you like it?"

"Oh, pretty fair! 'Evening, ma'am—'evening, Miss Devenish. Look, Harriet, there's Dawson waving to us: he has secured a table. Charles, are you staying with Worth? Oh then, I shall see you!"

He passed on, and the Colonel turned back to Miss Devenish to find her staring at him in the liveliest surprise. He could not help laughing. "But what have I done? What have I said?" he asked.

"Oh! nothing, of course! But I had no idea you were Colonel Audley until Sir Peregrine spoke to you. Lady Worth is such a particular friend of mine!"

Mrs. Fisher interposed to say in rather a bewildered voice: "My love, what is all this? Surely you have been introduced!"

"No," admitted Miss Devenish. "I came upon Colonel Audley quite by accident."

"But we were as good as introduced, ma'am," said the Colonel, "for I distinctly remember my sister telling me that she would present me to Miss Devenish. But just then the King and Queen arrived, and the opporunity was lost."

Mrs. Fisher smiled indulgently, but remarked that she had never known her niece to be so shatter-brained.

A couple of hours later Lady Worth, coming back into the ballroom on her husband's arm, was dumbfounded by the sight of Colonel Audley waltzing with Miss Devenish.

"Oh, so you contrived it, did you?" said Worth, also observing this circumstance.

"I did no such thing!" replied Judith. "In fact, I had quite made up my mind it would be useless to present him to poor Lucy, straight from Bab Childe's clutches! But was there ever such a provoking man? Not but what I am very glad to see him with Lucy. Even you will admit that *that* would be preferable to an entanglement with Lady Barbara! I wonder who introduced him to her?"

She was soon to learn from the lady herself in what manner the Colonel had become acquainted with Miss Devenish, for Lucy joined her presently and confided the story to her sympathetic ear.

"Very disagreeable for you," said Judith. "I am glad Charles was at hand to be of assistance."

"He was so very kind! But I am afraid you must have been wondering what had become of him. Was it very wrong of me to let him have supper with us?"

53

Judith started. "So that was where he was! To be sure, I could not see him at any of the tables, but there was such a crowd I might easily miss him. I make no doubt he had a much more agreeable time of it with you."

"We had a very cosy party," replied Miss Devenish, "if only my aunt had not found the heat so oppressive! Colonel Audley has such pleasant, open manners that he makes one feel one has known him all one's life."

Lady Worth agreed to it, and had the satisfaction, during their drive home, of hearing Colonel Audley comment favourably on Miss Devenish. "A very charming, unaffected girl," he said.

"I am glad you were able to be of service to her."

"Pinning up her lace? No very great matter," replied the Colonel.

"I understood she had a disagreeable adventure: some young man (she would not tell me his name) was ungentlemanly enough to force his attentions upon her, surely?"

"Oh, I had nothing to do with that!" said the Colonel. "He was probably in his cups, and meant no serious harm."

"She is unfortunately situated in having an aunt too indolent to chaperon her as she should, and an uncle whose birth and manners cannot add to her consequence. The fact of her being an heiress makes her very generally sought after."

"An enviable position!" said the Colonel.

"Ah, you do not know! But I was an heiress myself, and I can tell you it was sometimes a very unenviable position."

Worth said, with a note of amusement in his voice: "*My* position was certainly so, but that *you* experienced anything but the most profound enjoyment comes as news to me."

She was betrayed into a laugh, but said: "Well, perhaps I did enjoy teasing you at least, but recollect that I was never a shy creature like Lucy."

"I recollect that perfectly," said the Earl.

"Is Miss Devenish shy? I did not find her so," said the Colonel. "Shy girls are the devil, for they won't talk, and have such a habit of blushing that one is for ever

54

thinking one has said something shocking. I found Miss Devenish perfectly conversable."

Judith was satisfied. The Colonel, though ready to discuss the fête, had apparently forgotten Barbara Childe's existence. Not one word of admiration for her crossed his lips; her name was not mentioned.

"Julian, what a mercy! I don't believe he can have liked her after all!" confided her ladyship later, in the privacy of her own bedroom. "Indeed, I might have trusted to his excellent good sense. Did you notice that he did not once speak of her?"

"I did," replied the Earl somewhat grimly.

"Well?"

He looked at her, smiling, and took her chin in his hand. "You are an ever-constant source of delight to me, my love. Did you know?" he said, kissing her.

Judith returned this embrace with great readiness, but asked: "Why? Have I said something silly?"

"Very silly," Worth assured her tenderly.

"How horrid you are! Tell me at once!"

"My adorable simpleton, Charles induced no less a personage than the Prince of Orange to present him to the most striking woman in the room, seized not one but two waltzes which I have not the least doubt were bespoken days ago by less fortunate suitors, and comes away at the end of the evening with apparently not one word to say of a lady whom even you will admit to be of quite extraordinary beauty."

"Oh!" she said. "Is that a bad sign, do you think?"

"The worst!" he answered.

She was shaken, but said stoutly: "Well, I don't believe it. Charles has great good sense. I am perfectly at ease."

Had she been privileged to observe Colonel Audley's actions not very many hours later her faith in his good sense might have suffered a shock. The Colonel's Staff training had made him expert in obtaining desired information, and he had not wasted his time at the fête. While his sister-in-law still lay sleeping, he was up, and in the Earl's stables. Seven o'clock saw him cantering gently

55

down the Allée Verte, beyond the walls of the town, mounted on a blood-mare reserved for his brother's exclusive use.

Nor was this energy wasted. The edge had scarcely gone from the mare's morning freshness before the Colonel was rewarded by the sight of a slim figure, in a habit of cerulean blue, cantering ahead of him, unattended by any groom, and mounted on a raking grey hunter.

The Colonel gave the mare her head, and in two minutes was abreast of the grey. Lady Barbara, hearing the flying hooves, had turned her head, and immediately urged the grey to a gallop. Down the deserted Allée raced the horses, between two rows of thick lime-trees, and with the still waters of the canal shining on their left.

"To the bridge!" called Barbara.

The Colonel held the mare in a little. "Done! What will you wager?"

"Anything you please!" she said recklessly.

"Too rash! I might take an unfair advantage!"

"Pooh!" she returned.

They flew on, side by side, until in the distance the bridge leading over the canal to the Laekon road came into sight. Then the Colonel relaxed his grip and allowed the Doll to lengthen her stride. For a moment or two the grey kept abreast, but the pace was too swift for her to hold. The mare pulled ahead, flashed on up the avenue, was checked just short of the bridge, and reached it, dancing on her hooves and snatching a little at the bit.

Barbara came up like a thunderbolt, and reined in, panting. "Oh, by God! Three lengths!" she called out. "What do I lose?"

The Colonel leaned forward in the saddle to pat the Doll's neck. Under the brim of his low-cocked hat his eyes laughed into Barbara's. "I wish it might be your heart!"

"My dear sir, don't you know I haven't one? Come now! In all seriousness?"

He looked at her thoughtfully. She had had the audacity to cram over her flaming curls a hat like an English officer's

56

forage cap. She wore it at a raffish angle, the leathern peak almost obscuring the vision of one merry eye. Her habit was severely plain, with no more than two rows of silver buttons adorning it, but the cravat round her throat was deeply edged with lace, its ends thrust through a button-hole.

"One of your gloves," said the Colonel, and held out his hand.

She pulled it off at once, and tossed it to him. He caught it, and tucked it into the breast of his coat.

She wheeled her mount, and prepared to retrace her steps. The Colonel fell in beside her at a walking pace.

"Do you collect gloves, Colonel?"

"I have not up till now," he replied. "But a glove is a satisfactory keepsake, you know. Something of the wearer always remains with it."

"Let me tell you that a gallant man would have let me win!" she said, with a touch of raillery.

He turned his head. "Are you in general so spoilt?"

"Of course! I'm Bab Childe!" she replied, opening her eyes at him.

"And challenged me to a race in the expectation of being permitted to win?"

Her mouth lifted a little at the corners; the one eye he could see glinted provocatively. "What do you think?"

"I think you are too good a sportsman, Lady Barbara."

"Am I? I wonder?" Her gaze flitted to the Doll; she said appreciatively: "I like a man to be a judge of horse-flesh. What's her breeding?"

"I haven't a notion," replied the Colonel. "To tell you the truth, she is out of my brother's stable."

"I thought I knew her. But this is abominable! How was I to guess you would steal one of Worth's horses? I consider you to have won almost by a trick! She's the devil to go, isn't she? Does he know you have her out?"

"Not yet," admitted the Colonel. "My dependence is all on his being still too delighted at having me restored to him to object."

She laughed. "You deserve to be thrown out of doors!

57

I believe that to be the mare he habitually rides himself!"

"Oh, it won't come to that!" said the Colonel. "I shall implore my sister-in-law's intercession. That is a nice fellow you have there."

She passed her hand over the grey's neck. "Yes, this is Coup de Grâce. We are in the same case, only that while you stole your lady, I have been lent this gentleman."

"Whom does he belong to?" asked the Colonel, running an eye over his points. "He may have a French name, but I'll swear he's of English breeding."

"Captain de Lavisse bought him in England last year," she replied with one of her sidelong looks.

"Did he?" said the Colonel. "Captain de Lavisse—is he the man who was standing beside you last night, when I first met you?"

"I don't recollect, but it is very probable. He is in the 5th National Militia: Count Bylandt's brigade, stationed somewhere near Nivelles—Buzet, I think. He has estates north of Ghent, and a truly delightful house in the Rue d'Aremberg, here in Brussels."

"A gentleman of consequence, evidently."

"Fabulously rich!" said Barbara with an ecstatic sigh, and touching the grey's flank with her heel, went ahead with a brisk trot.

He rode after; both horses broke into a canter, and their riders covered some distance under the limes without speaking. Barbara presently turned her head and asked bluntly: "Did you ride this way, and at this hour, to meet me?"

"Yes, of course."

She looked a little amused. "How did you know I rode here before breakfast?"

"Something you said last night gave me the clue, and I discovered the rest."

"The deuce you did! I had thought very few people knew of this habit of mine. Don't betray me, if you please I don't want an escort."

"Shall I go?" inquired the Colonel with uplifted brows.

She reined in again to a walk. "No. You have had the

luck to encounter me in a charming mood, which is not a thing that happens every day of the week. I warn you, I have the most damnable temper, and it is generally at its worst before breakfast."

"Oh, that is capital!" declared the Colonel. "You show me how I can be of real service to you. I will engage to be here to quarrel with you any morning you may wish for a sparring partner."

"I think," she said quite seriously, "that you would not make a good sparring partner. You would spare me too much."

"Not I!"

She did not answer. A solitary horseman, cantering down the avenue towards them, had caught her attention. As he drew nearer, she turned to the Colonel with one of her wicked looks, and said: "You are about to meet the Captain Count de Lavisse. Shall you like that? He is quite charming!"

"Then obviously I shall," he answered. "But I thought you said he was stationed at Nivelles?"

"Oh, he has leave, I suppose!" she said carelessly.

The Captain Count, very smart in a blue uniform with a scarlet-and-white collar, and a broad-topped shako, set at an angle on his handsome head, drew rein before them, and saluted with a flourish. "Well met, Bab! Your servant, *mon Colonel!*"

The Colonel just touched his hat in acknowledgment of this magnificent salute, but the lady blew a kiss from the tips of her fingers. "Let me make you known to each other," she offered.

The Count flung up a hand. "Unnecessary! We have met already, and there is between us an unpaid score. I accuse you of *volerie*, Colonel, and demand instant reparation!"

"Your waltzes, were they?" said the Colonel. "My sympathy is unbounded, believe me, but what can I do? The Duke is devilish down on duelling, or I should be happy to oblige. You will have to accept my profound apologies."

59

"This is dissimulation of the most base! I am assured that you would serve me again the same *tour*—if you could!" said the Count gaily. His eyes rested for an instant on Barbara's ungloved right hand. He made no comment, but there was a gleam of understanding in the glance he flashed at the Colonel. He wheeled his horse, and fell in beside Barbara. Across her, he addressed Colonel Audley: "Your first visit to Brussels?"

"No; I was here last year for a short space. A delightful town, Count."

The Count bowed. "A compliment indeed—from one who has known Vienna! Our endeavours must be united to preserve it from the Corsican *maraudeur.*"

"*Your* endeavours may be," remarked Barbara, "but I have met some who wish quite otherwise."

He stiffened. "Persons of no consequence, I assure you!"

"By no means!"

"Madame, when the time comes you shall see how the suspected Belgians shall comport themselves!" He threw a somewhat darkling look at Colonel Audley, and added: "Rest assured, we are aware what *malveillants* reports have been spread of us in England, and by whom! Is it not so, *mon Colonel?* Have you not been warned that our sympathies are with Bonaparte, that we are, in effect, *indignes de confiance?*"

The Colonel responded with easy tact, but lost no time in turning the conversation into less dangerous channels. A civil interchange was maintained throughout the remainder of the ride, but the Lady Barbara, suddenly capricious, was silent. Only when they arrived at Vidal's house in the Rue Ducale did she seem to recover from her mood of abstraction. She gave the Colonel her hand then, and the shadow of a tantalizing smile. "Do you really care to quarrel with me, Colonel?"

"Above all things!"

"You have not met my brother and his wife, I think? They are holding a soirée here to-morrow evening. It will be confoundedly boring, but come!"

"Thank you: I shall not fail."

A few minutes later, Barbara dropped into a chair at her brother's breakfast-table, and tossed her forage cap on to another. Vidal said peevishly: "I suppose you have been making yourself remarkable. If you choose to ride out before breakfast, you may for all I care, but I wish you will not go unescorted!"

"No such thing! I was escorted—I was doubly escorted! Tell me all you know of Charles Audley, Robert."

"I don't know anything of him. How should I?"

"A younger son, with no prospects," said Augusta trenchantly.

"But with such charm of manner, Gussie!"

"I daresay."

"And such delightful smiling eyes!"

"Good God, Bab, what is all this?"

"Oh, I have had the most enchanting morning!" Barbara sighed. "They rode on either side of me, Etienne, and this new suitor of mine, and how they disliked one another! I have invited Charles Audley to your party, by the way."

"Oh, very well! But what is the matter with you? What is there in all this to put you in such spirits?"

"I have lost my heart—to a younger son!"

"Now you are being absurd. You will be tired of him in a week," said Augusta with a shrug.

CHAPTER V

FROM the Rue Ducale, with its houses facing the Park and backing on to the ramparts of the town, to Worth's residence off the Rue de Bellevue, was not far. Colonel Audley arrived in good time for breakfast, laughed off his sister-in-law's demand to know what could have possessed him to ride out so early after a late night, listened meekly to some pithy comments from his brother on his appropriation of the Doll, swallowed his breakfast, and made off on foot to the Duke of Wellington's Headquarters in the Rue

Royale. This broad street lay on the opposite side of the Park to the Rue Ducale, its houses overlooking it. Two of these made up the British Headquarters, but the Guard posted outside consisted merely of Belgian gendarmerie, the Duke, whose tact in handling foreigners rarely deserted him, having professed himself perfectly satisfied with such an arrangement.

The Duke, when Colonel Audley arrived, was closeted with the Prince of Orange, who had brought with him a welter of reports, letters for his Grace from Lord Bathurst, the English Secretary for War, and his own instructions from the British Commander-in-Chief, his Royal Highness the Duke of York. Colonel Audley, learning of this circumstance from Lord March, whom he met in the hall, ran upstairs to a large apartment on the first floor overlooking the Park, where he found two of his fellow Aides-de-Camp, in curiously informal attire, kicking their heels.

A stranger, unaware of the Duke of Wellington's indifference to the manner in which his officers chose to dress themselves, might have found it difficult to believe that either of the two gentlemen in the outer office could be an Aide-de-Camp on duty. Fremantle, lounging in a chair with his legs thrust out before him, was certainly wearing a frock-coat, but had no sash; while Colonel the Honourable Sir Alexander Gordon, who was seated in the window, engaged in waving to acquaintances passing in the street below, was frankly civilian in appearance, his frock-coat being (he said) quite unfit for further service.

Fremantle was looking harassed, but Gordon's sunny temper seemed to be unimpaired.

"In the immortal words of our colleague, Colin Campbell," he was saying, as Colonel Audley strolled in, " '*Je voudrais si je coudrais mais je ne cannais pas!*' "

"Don't be so damned cheerful!" begged Fremantle. His jaundiced eye alighted on Colonel Audley's immaculate Staff dress. "Lord, aren't we military this morning!" he remarked. "That ought to please the Beau: we have had one snap already about officers presenting themselves for duty in improper dress."

"Oh!" said Audley. "Crusty, is he?"

"Yes, and he'll be worse by the time he's done with all Slender Billy's lists and requisitions and morning-states," replied Fremantle, with a jerk of his head towards the door leading to the Duke's office.

Gordon, who was looking down into the street, announced: "Here comes old Lowe. I wonder whether he's realized yet that the Duke doesn't like being told how he ought to equip his army? Someone ought to drop him a hint."

"Fidgety old fool!" said Fremantle. "There'll be an explosion if he cites the Prussians to the Beau again. I'm glad *I'm* not going to Ghent."

"Ghent? Who is going to Ghent?" asked Audley.

"You are, my boy," replied Fremantle comfortably.

"When?"

"To-night or to-morrow. Don't know for certain. The news is that Harrowby and Torrens are arriving from London to-day for a conference with the Duke. He is going with them to Ghent, to pay his respects to the French king."

"Damnation!" exclaimed Audley. "Why the devil must it be me?"

"Ask his lordship. Daresay he noticed your fine new dress-uniform last night. He must know mine ain't fit to be taken into Court circles. Why shouldn't you want to go to Ghent, anyway? Very nice place, so I'm told."

"He's got an assignation with the Fatal Widow!" said Gordon. "That's why he's so beautifully dressed! New boots too. And just look at our elegant sash!"

Colonel Audley was saved from further ribaldry by the sudden opening of the door into the inner sanctum. The Duke came out, escorting the Prince of Orange. He did not, at first glance, appear to be out of humour, nor did the Prince bear the pallid look of one who had had the ill-luck to find his Grace in a bad temper.

However, when the Duke returned from seeing his youthful visitor off, there was a frosty look in his eye, and no trace of the joviality which had surprised Lady Worth

63

at the Hôtel de Ville. He had, at the fête, given everyone to understand that he was entirely care-free, and perfectly satisfied with all the preparations for war which had been made.

But the Duke at a ball and the Duke in his office were two very different persons. Lord Bathurst, in London, had been quite as anxious to see him at the head of the Army as any in Brussels, but Lord Bathurst was shortly going to be made to realize that his Grace's arrival in Belgium was not to be a matter of unmixed joy for officials at home.

For the Duke was not in the least satisfied with the preparations he found, and did not hesitate to inform Lord Bathurst that he considered the Army to be in a bad way. He had received disquieting accounts of the Belgian troops, thought the English not what they ought to be, and expressed a wish to have forty thousand good British infantry sent him, with not less than a hundred and fifty pieces of field artillery, fully horsed. It did not appear to his Grace that a clear view of the situation was being taken in England. "*You have not called out the militia, or announced such an intention in your message to Parliament,*" he complained. "*. . . and how we are to make out 150,000 men, or even the 60,000 of the defensive part of the treaty of Chaumont, appears not to have been considered.*" His boldly-flowing pen travelled on faster. He wanted, besides good British infantry, spring-wagons, musket-ball cartridge carts, entrenching-tool carts, the whole Corps of Sappers and Miners, all the Staff Corps, and forty pontoons, immediately, fully horsed. "*Without these equipments,*" he concluded bluntly, "*military operations are out of the question.*"

Yes, the Duke might not yet have taken over the command of the Army, but he was already making his presence felt. General Count von Gneisenau, the Prussian Chief-of-Staff, whom his Grace had visited at Aix-la-Chapelle on his journey from Vienna, also had a letter, written in firm French, to digest. General Gneisenau had proposed a plan, in the event of an attack by the French, of which the Duke flatly disapproved. Nothing could have been more civil than the letter the Duke wrote from Brussels on the 5th day of April, presenting a counter-plan for the General's consideration, but if his Excellency, reading those polite phrases, imagined that a request to him to "*take these reasons into consideration, and to let me know your determination,*" meant that his lordship was prepared to follow any other military determination than his own, he had a great deal yet to learn of the Duke's character.

A copy of this suave missive was enclosed in the despatch to Bathurst, a formal note sent off to the Duke of Brunswick, and the returns presented by the Prince spread out on the table.

The Duke's Aides-de-Camp might groan at his crustiness, but no one could deny that there was enough to try the patience of even the sweetest-tempered General.

Of his Peninsular veterans only a small percentage was to be found in Belgium, the rest being still in America. His Quartermaster-General was also in America, and in his place he found Sir Hudson Lowe, who was a stranger to him, and, however able an officer, not in the least the sort of man he wanted to have under him. The Prussians were going to be difficult too; General Gneisenau, a person of somewhat rough manners, evidently mistrusted him; and the Commissioner, General von Röder, was doing nothing to promote a good understanding between the two Headquarters. That would have to be attended to: probably matters would go more smoothly now that old Blücher was to take over the command from Kleist; but the hostility of the King of the Netherlands towards his Prussian allies meant that his lordship would have the devil of a task to keep the peace between them. He suspected that King William was going to prove himself an impossible fellow to deal with, while as for the Dutch-Belgic troops, a more disaffected set he hoped never to see. The only hope of making something of them would be to mix them with his own men, but it was plain that that suggestion had not been liked. Then there was the Prince of Orange, a nice enough boy, and with a good understanding, but quite inexperienced. He would have to be

65

given a command, of course: that was inevitable, but damned unfortunate. It was a maxim of the Duke's that an army of stags commanded by a lion was better than an army of lions commanded by a stag. The Prince would have to be kept as much under his own eye as possible. He must be warned, moreover, to be on his guard with several of his Generals. But he had a good man in Constant de Rebecque, and another in General Perponcher, who had seen service with the British in the Peninsula, and had done well with the Portuguese Legion formed at Oporto in 1808.

"Your Lordship's presence is extremely necessary to combine the measures of the heterogeneous force which is destined to defend this country," had written Sir Charles Stuart, and it did not seem that he had exaggered the difficulties of the situation. When the Anglo-Allied Army was at last brought together it would be found to be heterogeneous enough to daunt any Commander with less cool confidence than the Duke. A large proportion of the force would consist of Dutch-Belgic troops, many of them veterans who had fought under the Eagles, and as many more young soldiers never before under fire. In addition, a contingent from Nassau had been promised; and the Duke of Brunswick, the Princess of Wales's brother, was to place himself and his Black Brunswickers at the Duke's orders. There was to be a Hanoverian contingent also, tolerably good troops: but his lordship had found in Spain that the Germans had a shockingly bad habit of deserting, which made them troublesome. That did not apply so much to the King's German Legion, of course: those stout soldiers were as good as any English ones; and they had good commanders too: Count Alten; old Arendtschildt, the model of a Hussar leader; Ompteda, with his large dreamy eyes at such odd variance with his soldierly ability; Du Plat, always to be relied on to keep his head. His lordship was not so sure of this new fellow, Major-General Dörnberg, commanding a brigade of Light Dragoons; his lordship was not acquainted with him, and in his present mood his lordship was not inclined to look favourably upon strangers.

Besides all these foreign troops, there were the British, who must be used as a stiffening to the whole. The devil of it was there were not enough of them, and too many of the regiments now in Belgium were composed of young and untried soldiers. If he only had his old Peninsular Army he would have nothing to complain of. He could have gone anywhere, done anything with those fellows. His lordship had not been accustomed, in Spain, to such flattering language about his troops, but the truth was his lordship was always more apt to condemn faults than to praise excellence. He had said some pretty harsh things of his Peninsular veterans in his time, but in his grudging way he valued them, and wished he had them in Belgium now. His lordship, in one of his bitter moods, might say that they had all enlisted for drink, but anyone else rash enough to speak disparagingly of them would very soon learn his mistake. Acrid disparagement of his troops was his lordship's sole prerogative.

Well, such Peninsular regiments as were available would have to be sent out. In the force at present under Orange's command were only the second battalions of three of these, and a detachment of the 95th Rifles. There were the Guards, of course, who would certainly maintain their high reputation, but his lordship's mouth turned down at the corners as he ran over the lists of the remaining regiments. Young troops for the most part, inexperienced except for their brief campaign under Graham in Holland. He would have to get good officers into them, and hope for the best, but the fact was he had under his hand the nucleus of what bade fair to be, in his estimation, an infamous army.

There were other, minor vexations to try his patience, notably the absence of his Military Secretary. When he left Paris for Vienna, Lord Fitzroy Somerset had remained there as Chargé d'Affaires, and was now in Ghent. He missed his quiet competence damnably; he must have him back: someone must be chosen to assist Stuart with the King of France in his stead; Colonel Hervey's brother Lionel, perhaps. He must have Colin Campbell too, and

67

must prevail upon Colquhoun Grant to come out as Head of the Intelligence Department. With him and Waters he should do very well in that direction, but from the look of it he would be obliged to make a clean sweep of all these youngsters at present filling Staff appointments, and, in his opinion, quite unfit for such duties. He must come to a plain understanding, also, with King William, on the question of the troops to be employed on garrison duty. All the chief posts would have to be held by the British: his instructions from London were perfectly precise on that point, and he agreed with them, though it was already evident that King William did not.

Taking one thing with another, his present position was unenviable, and the future dark with difficulties. A super-human task lay before him, as bad as any he had ever tackled, but although he might complain peevishly of lack of support from England, of wretched troops in Belgium, of the impossibility of dealing with King William, of the damned folly of that fellow Lowe, no real doubts of his ability to deal with the situation assailed him.

"I never in my life gave up anything that I once undertook," said his lordship, in one of his rare moments of expansiveness.

Fremantle came into the room with some papers for him to look over. He took them, and remembered that he had been devilish short with Fremantle this morning, for some slight fault. He had not meant to be, but it was unthinkable that he should say so; he could not do it: to admit that he had been in the wrong was totally against his principles. The nearest he could ever bring himself to it was to invite the unfortunate to dinner, or, if that were ineligible (as in Fremantle's case it was, since he would dine with him in the ordinary way), to say something pleasant to him, to show that the whole affair was forgotten.

"I'll tell you what, Fremantle!" he remarked in his incisive way. "We must give a ball. Find out what days are left free. It will have to be towards the end of the month, for it won't do if I clash with anyone else."

"They say that the Catalani is coming to Brussels, sir," suggested Fremantle.

"That's capital: we'll have a concert as well, and engage her to sing at it. But, mind, fix the figure before you settle with the woman; I hear she's as mercenary as the devil." He picked up his pen again, and bent over his table, but added as Fremantle was leaving the room: "You can have my box, if you mean to go to the theatre to-night: I shan't be using it. Take the curricle."

So Colonel Fremantle was able to report in the outer office that his lordship's temper was on the mend. But within half an hour, his lordship, glaring at his Quarter-master-General, was snapping out one of his hasty snubs. "Sir Hudson, I have commanded a far larger army in the field than any Prussian General, and I am not to learn from their service how to equip an army!"

One would have thought this would have stopped the damned fellow, but no! in a few moments he was at it again.

"*Sir Hudson Lowe will not do for the Duke,*" wrote Major-General Torrens next day, to London, with diplomatic restraint.

Lord Harrowby, and Major-General Torrens, arriving on the 6th April to confer with him, found that there was much that would not do for the Duke, and much that he required from England with the greatest possible despatch. His lordship—it was strange how that title stuck to him—might be uncomfortably blunt in his manner, but the very fact of his knowing so positively what he wanted, showed how sure was his grasp on the situation. And, after all, General Torrens had dealt with him for long enough to know, before ever he reached Brussels, that he was going to hear some very plain truths from him.

But his criticisms were not merely destructive: what he said to the delegates from London left them in no doubt of his energetic competence. The news he brought from Vienna was quite as good as could have been expected. The treaty between Great Britain, Austria, Russia, and Prussia had been signed; there had been a little trouble over the question of subsidies; but his lordship was able to report that the Russians and Austrians were mobilizing in large numbers; and even that the Emperor of Russia had expressed a wish (though not a very strong one) to have him with him. "But I should prefer to carry a musket!" said his lordship, with a neigh of sardonic laughter.

For their part, Lord Harrowby and Sir Henry Torrens had brought soothing intelligence from home. All the available cavalry were under orders, and some already marching for embarkation to Ostend; of the infantry, in addition to the corps and detachments already despatched, and now in Belgium, about two thousand effectives were to proceed from a rendezvous in the Downs to Ostend. The Government was willing, and indeed anxious, to meet his lordship's requirements in every possible way.

His lordship stated these with disconcerting alacrity. He wanted equipment, and ammunition; he wanted field artillery, and horses; he wanted the militia called out: "Nothing can be done with a small and inefficient force," said his lordship uncompromisingly. "The war will linger on, and will end to our disadvantage."

Harrowby began to explain the constitutional difficulties attached to calling out the militia. It was plain that his lordship made very little of these, but he was not one to waste his time in fruitless argument. He had another scheme, already proposed by him in a despatch to Lord Castlereagh. He thought it would be advisable to try to get twelve or fourteen thousand Portuguese troops into the Netherlands. "We can mix them with ours, and do what we please with them," he said. "They become very nearly as good as our own."

Upon the following day, a third visitor from London appeared in the person of the Duke's brother, the Marquis Wellesley. The Marquis was fifty-five years old, and nine years senior to the Duke. There was not much resemblance between the brothers, but strong ties of affection had survived the strain put on them by the younger man's rise to heights beyond the elder's reach. It had been Richard, not Arthur, who was to have been the great man of the family; it was Richard who had set Arthur's feet on the ladder of his career, and had fostered his early progress from rung to rung. But Arthur, his feet once firmly planted, had climbed the ladder so fast that Richard had been left far behind him. It was only twenty-eight years since Richard had written to remind the Duke of Rutland of a younger brother of his, whom his Grace had been so kind as to take into his consideration for a commission in the Army. *"He is here at this moment, and perfectly idle,"* Richard had written. *"It is a matter of indifference to me what commission he gets, providing he gets it soon."* Richard, with his brilliant mind and scholarship, had been a coming man in those days, Arthur a youth of no more than ordinary promise. Seventeen years later, a Major-General, he had been made a Knight Companion of the Bath, and after that the honours had fallen so thick upon him that it had been difficult to keep count of them. He had been created in swift succession Viscount Wellington of Talavera, Earl of Wellington, then Marquis, and lastly Duke; he was a Spanish Grandee of the First Class, Duke of Ciudad Rodrigo, Duke of Victoria, a Knight of the Garter, of the Golden Fleece, of the Order of Maria Theresa, of the Russian Order of Saint George, of the Prussian Order of the Black Eagle, of the Swedish Order of the Sword. An Emperor had lately clapped him on the shoulder, saying: *"C'est pour vous encore sauver le monde!"* and yet he remained, reflected Richard, with a faint, whimsical smile, the same unaffected creature he had ever been. Nor had he outgrown his boyhood's admiration of Richard. "A wonderful man," he called him, and honestly believed it.

The Marquis was a wonderfully handsome man, at all events, with large, far-sighted eyes under heavily-marked dark brows, an aquiline nose, with delicate, up-cut nostrils, a fine, rather thin-lipped mouth, and a lacquered skin of alabaster. He had beautiful manners too, a natural stateliness tempered by charm, and an instinct for ceremonial. No sudden cracks of loud laughter broke from him; he had never been known to utter hasty, harshly-worded snubs; and his stateliness never became mere stiffness. The Duke, on the other hand, could be absurdly stiff, and painfully rude, while his ungraciousness towards those whom he disliked was proverbial. He had no taste for pomp, very little for creature comforts, and although he had been christened Beau Douro in the Peninsula on account of a certain neatness and propriety of dress, he set no store by personal adornment. He was outspoken to a fault; his mind ran between straight and clearly defined lines; and he knew nothing of dissimulation. Ask him a question, and you might be sure of receiving an honest answer—though perhaps not the one you had hoped to hear, for his lordship, unconcerned with considerations of personal popularity, was rigorously concerned with the truth, and with what he saw to be his clear duty. Tact, such as his brother possessed, he did not employ; and when the members of His Majesty's Government acted, in his judgment, foolishly, he told them so with very little more ceremony than he would have used with one of his own officers.

He met his elder brother with frank delight, gave his hand a quick shake, and said briskly: "Glad to see you, Wellesley! How d'ye do?"

"How do *you* do?" returned the Marquis, holding his hand a moment longer.

"We are in a damned bad case," replied the Duke bluntly.

The Marquis did not make the mistake of taking this to mean that his brother envisaged defeat at Bonaparte's hands; he knew that it was merely the prelude to one of Arthur's trenchant and comprehensive complaints of the Government's supine behaviour. Already, and though he had not been in his presence above a minute, he was aware of Arthur's driving will. Arthur's terrible energy made him feel suddenly old. Presently, seated with Harrowby and Torrens at a table covered with papers, and listening to the Duke's voice, he found that, well as he knew him, he could still be surprised by Arthur's amazing capacity for detail. For Arthur had rolled up his

72

maps and was being extremely definite on the subject of the ideal size and nature of camp-kettles.

An extraordinary fellow, dear Arthur: really, a most bewildering fellow!

CHAPTER VI

THE information imparted to Colonel Audley by Fremantle turned out to be correct, and not, as Audley had more than half suspected, a mild attempt to hoax him. He was to accompany the Duke to Ghent, but not, providentially, until the 8th June. He was free therefore to present himself at Lady Vidal's party on the 7th.

The fact of his being engaged to dine at the Duke's table made it unnecessary for him to tell his sister-in-law where he meant to spend the rest of the evening. The Worths were bound for the Opera, where Judith hoped he might perhaps be able to join them.

Lady Barbara, wise in the ways of suitors, expected to see him amongst the first arrivals, and was piqued when he did not appear until late in the evening. He found her in a maddening mood, flirting with one civilian and two soldiers. She had nothing but a careless wave of the hand for him, and the Colonel, who had no intention of forming one of a court, paused only to exchange a word of greeting with her before passing on to pay his respects to Lady Frances Webster.

That inveterate hero-worshipper had found a new object for her affections, a very different personage from Lord Byron, less dangerous but quite as glorious. At the fête at the Hôtel de Ville her eyes had dwelled soulfully upon the Duke of Wellington, and the Duke had lost very little time in becoming acquainted with her. When the Lady Frances discovered from Colonel Audley that there was no likelihood of his Grace's putting in an appearance that evening, she sighed, and seemed to lose interest in the world.

So that's Hookey's latest, is it? thought the Colonel. Too angelic for my taste!

Caro Lamb recognized him, and summoned him to her side. He went at once, and was soon engaged in a light, swift give and take of badinage with her. His manners were too good to allow of his attention wandering, his gaze did not stray from the changeful little face before him; nor, when Caro presently flitted from him to another, did he do more than glance in Barbara's direction. She was lying back in her chair, laughing up into Lavisse's face, bent a little over her. There was a suggestion of possessiveness in Lavisse's pose, and his left hand was resting on Barbara's bare shoulder. Repressing a strong inclination to seize the slim Belgian by the collar and the seat of his elegant knee-breeches and throw him out, the Colonel turned away, and found himself confronting a sandy-haired Ensign, who smiled and offered him a glass of wine. "You're Colonel Audley, aren't you, sir?" he said. "Bab said you were coming. I'm Harry Alastair."

"How do you do?" said the Colonel, accepting the glass of wine. "I believe I once met your brother George."

"Oh, did you? George is a Bad Man," said Harry cheerfully. "I heard to-day that the Life Guards are under marching orders, so he'll be here pretty soon, I expect. But I say, what's the news, sir? We are going to war, aren't we?"

Colonel Audley did not think there was much doubt of that.

"Well, I'm very glad to hear you say so," remarked his youthful interlocutor with simple pleasure. "Only, people talk such stuff that one doesn't know what to believe. I thought you would probably know." He added in a burst of confidence: "It's a great thing for me: I've never been in action, you know."

Colonel Audley expressed a gratifying surprise. "I had thought you must have been with Graham," he said.

"No," confessed Lord Harry. "As a matter of fact, I was still at Oxford then. Well, to tell you the truth, I only joined in December."

"How do you like it?" asked the Colonel. "You're with General Maitland, aren't you?"

"Yes. Oh, it's famous sport! I like it above anything!" said Lord Harry. "And if only we have the luck to come to grips with Boney himself—all our fellows are mad for the chance of a brush with him, I can tell you! Hallo, what's Bab at now? She's as wild as fire to-night! When George arrives they'll set the whole town in a bustle between them, I daresay."

A hot rivalry appeared to have sprung up between the men surrounding Barbara for possession of the flower she had been wearing tucked into her corsage. It was in her hand now, and as the Colonel glanced towards her she sprang lightly upon a stool, and held it high above her head.

"No quarrelling, gentlemen!" she called out. "He who can reach it may take it. Oh, Jack, my poor darling, you will never do it!"

Half a dozen arms reached up; the Lady Barbara, from the advantage of her stool, laughed down into the faces upturned to her. Colonel Audley, taller than any of that striving court, set down his wine-glass and walked up behind her, and nipped the flower from her hand.

She turned quickly; a wave of colour rushed into her cheeks. "Oh! You! Infamous! I did not bargain for a man of your inches!" she said.

"A cheat! Fudged, by Jove!" cried Captain Chalmers. "Give it up, Audley, you dog!"

"Not a bit of it," responded the Colonel, fitting it in his buttonhole. "He who could reach it might take it. I abode most strictly by the rules." He held out his hands to Barbara. "Come down from your perch! You invited me here to-night and have not vouchsafed me one word."

She laid her hands in his, but drew them away as soon as she stood on the floor again. "Oh, you must be content with having won your prize!" she said carelessly. "I warn you, it came from a hot-house and will soon fade. Dear Jack, I'm devilish thirsty!"

The young man addressed offered his arm; she was

75

borne away by him into an adjoining saloon. With a shade of malice in his voice the Comte de Lavisse said: "*Hélas!* You are set down, *mon Colonel!*"

"I am indeed," replied Audley, and went off to flirt with one of the Misses Arden.

He was presently singled out by his host, who wanted his opinion on the military situation. Lord Vidal was suffering from what his irreverent younger brother described as a fit of the sullens, but he was pleasant enough to Audley. His wife, her hard sense bent on promoting a match between an improvident sister-in-law and a wealthy (though foreign) nobleman, seized the opportunity to inform the Colonel that her family expected hourly to receive the tidings of Bab's engagement to the Comte de Lavisse. The desired effect of this confidence was a little spoiled by her husband's saying hastily: "Pooh! nonsense! I don't more than half like it."

Augusta said with a tinkle of laughter: "I doubt of Bab's considering that, my dear Vidal, once her affections have been engaged."

The Marquis reddened, but said: "The old man wouldn't countenance it. I wish you will not talk such rubbish! Come now, Audley! In my place, would you remove to England?"

"On my honour, no!" said the Colonel. He correctly guessed "the old man" to be the Duke of Avon, a gentleman of reputedly fiery temper, who was the Lady Barbara's grandfather, and lost very little time in finding Lord Harry Alastair again.

There was no more friendly youth to be found than Lord Harry. He was perfectly ready to tell the Colonel anything the Colonel wanted to know, and it needed only a casual question to set his tongue gaily wagging.

"Devil of a tartar, my grandfather," said Lord Harry. "Used to be a dead shot—daresay he still is, but he don't go about picking quarrels with people these days, of course. Killed his man in three duels before he met my grandmother. Those must have been good times to have lived in! But I believe he settled down more or less when he married. George is the living spit of what he used to be, if you can trust the portraits. Bab and Vidal take after my *great*-grandmother. She was red-haired, too, and French into the bargain. And *her* husband—my great-grandfather, that is—was the devil of a fellow!" He tossed off a glass of wine, and added, not without pride: "We're a shocking bad set, you know. All ride to the devil one way or another. As for Bab, she's as bad as any of us."

The Lady Barbara seemed, that evening, to be determined to prove the truth of this assertion. No folly was too extravagant for her to throw herself into; her flirtations shocked the respectable; the language she used gave offence to the pure-tongued; and when she crowned an evening of indiscretions by organizing a table of hazard, and becoming, as she herself announced, badly dipped at it, it was felt that she had left nothing undone to set the town by the ears.

She was too busy at her hazard-table to notice Colonel Audley's departure, nor did he attempt to interrupt her play to take his leave. But seven o'clock next morning found him cantering down the Allée Verte to meet a solitary horsewoman mounted on a grey hunter.

She saw him approaching, and reined in. When he reached her she was seated motionless in the saddle, awaiting him. He raised two fingers to his cocked-hat. "Good morning! Are you in a quarrelsome humour to-day?" he asked.

She replied abruptly: "I did not expect to see you."

"We don't start for Ghent until noon."

"Ghent?"

"Yes, Ghent," he repeated, not quite understanding her blank stare.

"Oh, the devil! What are you talking about?" she demanded with a touch of petulance. "Are you going to Ghent? I did not know it."

"Didn't you? Then I don't know what the devil I'm talking about," he said.

A laugh flashed in her eyes. "I wish I didn't like you,

but I do—I do!" she said. "Do you wonder that I didn't expect to see you here this morning?"

"If it was not because you thought me already on my way to Ghent I most certainly do."

"Odd creature!" She gave him one of her direct looks, and said: "I behaved very shabbily to you last night."

"You did indeed. What had I done? Or were you merely cross?"

"Nothing. Was I cross? I don't know. I think I wanted to show you how damnably I can conduct myself."

"Thank you," said the Colonel, bowing in some amusement. "What will you show me next? How well you can conduct yourself?"

"I never conduct myself well. Don't laugh! I am in earnest. I am odious, do you understand? If you will persist in liking me, I shall make you unhappy."

"I don't like you," said the Colonel. "It was true what I told you the first time I set eyes on you. I love you."

She looked at him with sombre eyes. "How can you do so? If you were in a way to loving me did not that turn to dislike when you saw me at my worst?"

"Not a bit!" he replied. "I will own to a strong inclination to have boxed your ears, but I could not cease to love you, I think, for any imaginable folly on your part." He swung himself out of the saddle, and let the bridle hang over his horse's head. "May I lift you down? There is a seat under the trees where we can have our talk out undisturbed."

She set her hand on his shoulder, but said, half-mournfully: "*This* is the greatest imaginable folly, poor soldier."

"I love you most of all when you are absurd," said the Colonel, lifting her down from the saddle.

He set her on her feet, but held her for an instant longer, his eyes smiling into hers; then his hands released her waist, and he gathered up both the horses' bridles, and said: "Let me take you to the secluded nook I have discovered."

"Innocent!" she said mockingly, falling into step beside him. "I know all the secluded nooks."

He laughed. "You are shameless."

She looked sideways at him. "A baggage?"

"Yes, a baggage," he agreed, lifting her hand to his lips a moment.

"If you know that, I consider you fairly warned, and shall let you run on your fate as fast as you please."

"*Faute de mieux*," he remarked. "Here is my nook. Let me beg your ladyship to be seated!"

"Oh, call me Bab! Everyone does." She sat down, and began to strip off her gloves. "Have you still my rose?" she enquired.

He laid his hand upon his heart. "Can you ask?"

"I begin to think you an accomplished flirt. I hope the thorns may not prick you."

"To be honest with you," confessed the Colonel, "the gesture was metaphorical."

She burst out laughing. "Your trick! Tell me what it is you want! To flirt with me? I am perfectly willing. To kiss me? You may if you choose."

"To marry you," he said.

"Ah, now you are talking nonsense! Has no one warned you what bad blood there is in my family?"

"Yes, your brother Harry. I am much obliged to him, and to you, and must warn you, in my turn, that I had an uncle once who was so much addicted to the bottle that he died of it. Furthermore, my grandfather——"

She put up her hands. "Stop, stop! Abominable to laugh when I am in earnest! If I married you we should certainly fight."

"Not a doubt of it," he agreed.

"You would wish to make me sober and well-behaved, and I——"

"Never! To shake you, perhaps, but I am persuaded your sense of justice would pardon that."

"My sense of justice might, but not my temper. I should flirt with other men: you would not like that."

"No, not permit it."

"My poor Charles! How would you stop me?"

"By flirting with you myself," he replied.

"It would lack spice in a husband. I don't care for marriage. It is curst flat. *You* do not know that; but *I* have reason to. Did Gussie tell you I was going to marry Lavisse?"

"Most pointedly. But I think you are not."

"You may be right," she said coolly. "It is more than I can bargain for, though. He is extremely wealthy. I should enjoy the comfort of a large fortune. My debts would ruin you in a year. Have you thought of that?"

"No, but I will, if you like, and devise some means of meeting the difficulty when it arises. Should you object very much to living in a debtors' prison?"

"It might be amusing," she admitted. "But it would become tiresome in time. Things do, you know." She began to play with her riding-whip, twisting the lash round her fingers. Watching her, he saw that her eyes had grown dark again, and that she had gripped her lips together in a mulish fashion. He was content to look at her, and presently she glanced up, and said brusquely: "To be plain with you, Charles, you are a fool! Am I your first love?"

"My dear! No!"

"The more shame to you. Don't you know—— Good God, can you not see that we should never deal together? We are not suited!"

"No, we are not suited, but I think we might deal together," he answered.

"I have been spoilt from my cradle!" she flung at him. "You know nothing of me! You have fallen in love with my face. In fact, you are ridiculous!"

He said rather ruefully: "Do you think I don't know it? I can discover no reason why you should look with anything but amusement upon my suit. I am a younger son, with no prospects beyond the Army——"

"Gussie said that," she interrupted, her lip lifting a little.

"She was right."

She put her whip down; something glowed in her eyes. "Have you nothing to recommend you to me, then?"

"Nothing at all," he replied, with a faint smile.

She leaned towards him; sudden tears sparkled on her lashes; her hands went out to him impulsively "Nothing at all! Charles, dear fool! Oh, the devil! I'm crying!"

She was in his arms, and raised her face for his kiss. Her hands gripped his shoulders; her mouth was eager, and clung to his for a moment. Then she put her head back, and felt him kiss her wet eyelids.

"Oh, rash," she murmured. "I darken 'em Charles— my eyelashes! Does it come off?"

He said a little unsteadily: "I don't think so. What odds?"

She disengaged herself. "My dear, you are certainly mad! Confound it, I never cry! How dared you look at me just so? Charles, if I have black streaks on my face, I swear I'll never forgive you!"

"But you have not, on my honour!" he assured her. He found his handkerchief, and put his hand under her chin. "Keep still: I will engage to dry them without the least damage being done." He performed this office for her, and held her chin for an instant longer, looking down into her face.

She let him kiss her again, but when he raised his head, flung off his arms, and sprang up. "Of all the absurd situations I ever was in! To be made love to before breakfast! Abominable!"

He too rose, and caught and grasped her hands, holding them in a grip that made her grimace. "Will you marry me?"

"I don't know, I don't know! Go to Ghent: I won't be swept off my feet!" She gave a gurgle of laughter, and burlesqued herself: "You must give me time to consider, Colonel Audley! Lord, did you ever hear anything so Bath-missish? Let me go: you don't possess me, you know."

"Give me an answer!" he said.

"No, and no! Do you think I must marry where I kiss? They don't mean anything, my kisses."

His grip tightened on her hands. "Be quiet! You shall not talk so!"

Her mouth mocked him bitterly. "You've drawn such a pretty picture of me for yourself, and the truth is I'm a rake."

He turned from her in silence to lead up her horse. With the knowledge that she had hurt him an unaccustomed pain seized her. "Now you see how odious I can be!" she said in a shaking voice.

He glanced over his shoulder, and said gently: "My poor dear!"

She gave a twisted smile, but said nothing until he had brought her horse to her. He put her into the saddle, and she bent towards him, and touched his cheek with her gloved hand. "Go to Ghent. Dear Charles!"

For a moment her eyes were soft with tenderness. He caught her hand and kissed it. "I must go, of course. I shall be back in a day or two and I shall want my answer."

She gathered up the bridle. "I shall give it you— perhaps!" she said, and rode off, leaving him still standing under the elm-trees.

He made no attempt to overtake her, but rode back to the town at a sober pace, arriving at his brother's house rather late for breakfast. His sister-in-law, regarding him with a little curiosity, asked him where he had been, and upon his answering briefly, in the Allée Verte, rallied him on such a display of matutinal energy.

"Confess, Charles! You had an assignation with an unknown charmer!"

He smiled, but shook his head. "Not precisely—no!"

"Don't tell me you rode out for your health's sake! You have not been alone!"

"No," he replied, "I had the good fortune to meet Lady Barbara."

She concealed the dismay she felt, but was for the moment too much nonplussed to say anything. The Earl filled what might have been felt to have been an awkward pause by enquiring in his languid way: "Is an early morning ride one of her practices? She is an unexpected creature!"

"She is a splendid horsewoman," said the Colonel evasively.

"Certainly. I have very often seen her at the stag-hunting during the winter."

"Perry calls her a bruising rider!" remarked Judith, with a slight laugh. She poured herself out some coffee, and added in a casual tone: "Is it true that she is about to become engaged to the Comte de Lavisse?"

The Colonel raised his brows. "What, does gossip say so?"

"Oh yes! That is, his attentions have been so very particular that it is regarded as quite certain. I suppose it would be a good match. He is very wealthy."

"Very, I believe."

This response was too unencouraging to allow of Judith's pursuing the subject any further. The Colonel started to talk of something else, and as soon as he had finished his breakfast, went away to order his servant to pack his valise. He was soon gone from the house, and although Judith was sorry he was obliged to accompany the Duke to Ghent, she was able to console herself with the reflection that at least he would be out of Barbara Childe's reach.

She might be a little uneasy about his evident admiration for Barbara, but as she had no suspicion of how far matters between them had already gone, she felt no very acute anxiety, and was able to welcome the Colonel home on the following evening without misgiving.

The Earl having an engagement to dine with some officers at the Hôtel d'Angleterre, Judith had invited Miss Devenish to keep her company, and was seated with her in the salon when Colonel Audley walked in.

Both ladies looked up; Judith exclaimed: "Why, Charles, are you back so soon? This is delightful! I believe I need not introduce you to Miss Devenish."

"No, indeed: I had the pleasure of meeting Miss Devenish the other evening," he replied, shaking hands, and drawing up a chair. "Is Worth out?"

"Yes, at the Hôtel d'Angleterre. Is the Duke back in Brussels? Lord Harrowby and Sir Henry too?"

"No, the visitors are all on their way home to England.

The Duke is here, however, but I am afraid you will be obliged to make up your mind to exist without him for a little while," he said, with a droll look. "Are you like my sister, Miss Devenish? Do you suffer from nightmares when the Duke is not here to protect you from Boney?"

She smiled, but shook her head. "Oh no! I am too stupid to understand wars and politics, but I feel sure the Duke would never leave Brussels if there were any danger to be apprehended in his doing so."

He seemed amused; Judith enquired why she must do without the Duke, and upon being informed of his intention to visit the Army, professed herself very well satisfied with such an arrangement.

The tea-tray was brought in a few moments later, and Judith had the satisfaction of hearing her protégée and Colonel Audley chatting with all the ease of old acquaintances over her very choice Orange Pekoe. Nothing could have been more comfortable! she thought. Charles, she knew well, had a sweetness of disposition which made him appear to be pleased with whatever society he found himself in, but she fancied there was more warmth in his manner than was dictated by civility. He was looking at Lucy with interest, taking pains to draw her out; and presently, when the carriage was bespoken to convey her to her uncle's lodging, he insisted on escorting her.

When he returned he found his sister-in-law still sitting in the salon with her embroidery, and the Earl not yet come home from his dinner engagement. He took a seat opposite to Judith, and glanced idly through the pages of the *Cosmopolite*.

"No news more of the Duc d'Angoulême, I see," he remarked.

"No. There was something in the *Moniteur*, some few days ago, about his having had a success near Montéli-mart. I believe he has advanced into Valence."

"I doubt of his enjoying much success. If he favours his brother, I should judge his venture to have been hope-less from the start. You never saw such a set of fellows as the French at Ghent! The worst is that they, most of them, seem to think the war lost before ever it is begun."

She lowered her embroidery. "What, even now that the Duke is here?"

"Oh yes! They are quite ready to admit that he did very well in Spain, but now that he is to meet Boney in person they think the result a foregone conclusion."

"And the King?"

"There's no telling. But whether we can succeed in putting him back on the Throne—— However, that's none of my business."

"What an odd creature he must be! What does he feel about it all, I wonder?"

"I haven't a notion. He seems to care for nothing in the world but comfort and a quiet life. Poor devil! Fitzroy has been making us laugh with some of his tales of what goes on at the Court."

"Oh, has Lord Fitzroy come back with you? I am glad."

"So are we all," said the Colonel, his eyes twinkling. "Headquarters without Fitzroy are apt to become a trifle sultry. By the by, how in the name of all that's wonderful did that Devenish child come to have such a queer stick of an uncle?"

"He is only her uncle by marriage," Judith answered. "Her aunt is perfectly ladylike, you know. And *she*——"

"My dear Judith, I meant nothing against her! I daresay she will make some fortunate fellow a capital wife. An heiress, isn't she?"

She said archly: "Yes, a considerable heiress. And yet she doesn't squint like a bag of nails!"

He put the *Cosmopolite* down, wrinkling his bow in perplexity. "Squint like a bag of nails? You're quizzing me, Judith! What is the joke?"

"Have you forgotten my first meeting with you?"

"Good God, I never can have said such a thing of you!"

"Very nearly, I assure you! You came into the room where I was standing with your brother, and demanded: 'Where is the heiress? Does she squint like a bag of nails? Is she hideous? They always are!' "

He burst out laughing. "Did I indeed? No, I will admit

85

that Miss Devenish doesn't squint like a bag of nails. She is a very pretty girl—but I wonder what troubles her?"

"Troubles her?" she repeated in accents of surprise. "Why, what should trouble her?"

"How should I know? I thought perhaps you might."

"No, indeed! You have certainly imagined it. She is reserved, I know, and I could wish that that were not so, but I believe it to be due to a shyness very understandable in a girl living in her circumstances. Do you find it objectionable?"

"Not in the least. I merely feel a little curiosity to know what causes it. There is a look in the eye—but you will say I am indulging my fancy!"

"But, Charles, what can you mean? There is a *gravity*, I own. I have found it particularly pleasing in this age of volatile young females."

"Oh, more than that!" he said. "I had almost called it a guarded look. I am sure she is not quite happy. But it is infamous of me to be discussing her in this way, after all! It is nothing but nonsense, of course."

"I hope it may be found so," replied Judith. "*I* have been told nothing of any secret sorrow, I assure you."

She said no more, but she was not ill-pleased. Charles seemed to have been studying Lucy closely, and although she could not but be amused at the romantic trend of his reflections, she was glad to find that she had found her young friend of so much interest.

But at seven o'clock next morning Charles was riding down the Allée Verte, no thought of Lucy Devenish in his head. He cantered to the bridge at the end of the Allée without encountering Barbara, and dismounted there to watch the painted barges drifting up the canal. Fashionable people were not yet abroad, but a couple of Flemish wagons, drawn by teams of fat horses, passed over the bridge. The drivers walked beside him, guiding the horses by means of cord-reins passed through haims studded with brass nails. Bright tassels and fringes decorated the horses' harness, and the blue smocks worn by the drivers were embroidered with worsted. They wore red night-caps on their heads, and wooden sabots on their feet, over striped stockings. The horses, like all Colonel Audley had seen in the Netherlands, were huge beasts, and very fat. Good forage to be had, he reflected, thinking of the English cavalry and horse artillery on the way to Ostend. From what he had seen of the country it was rich enough to supply forage for several armies. Wherever one rode one found richly cultivated fields, with crops of flax and wheat growing in almost fabulous luxuriance. The Flemish farmers manured their land lavishly; very malodorous it could be, he thought, remembering his journey through the Netherlands the previous year. Except for the woods and copses dotted over the land the whole country seemed to be under cultivation. There should be no difficulty in feeding the Allied Army: but the Flemish were a grasping race, he had been told.

A gendarme in a blue uniform, with white grenades, and high, gleaming boots, rode over the bridge, glancing curiously at the Colonel, who was still leaning his elbows on the parapet and watching the slow canal traffic. He passed on, riding towards Brussels, and for some little time the Colonel's solitude was undisturbed. But presently, glancing down the Allée, he saw a horse approaching in the distance, and caught the flutter of a pale blue skirt. He swung himself into the saddle, and rode to meet the Lady Barbara.

She came galloping towards him and reined in. Cheeks and eyes were glowing; she stretched out her hand, and exclaimed: "I thought you still in Ghent! This is famous!"

He leaned forward in the saddle to take her hand; it grasped his strongly. "I have been bored to death!" Barbara said. "Confound you, I have missed you damnably!"

"Excellent! There is only one remedy," he said.

"To marry you?"

He nodded, still holding her hand.

She said candidly: "So I feel to-day. You are haunting me, do you know? But in a week, who knows but that I may have changed my mind?"

"I'll take that risk."

"Will you?" She considered him, a rather mischievous smile hovering on her lips. "You have not kissed me, Charles," she murmured.

He caught the gleam under her long lashes, and laughed. "No."

"Don't you want to—dear Charles?"

"Yes, very much."

"Oh, this is a pistol held to my head! If I want to be kissed I must also be married. Is that it?" she asked outrageously.

"That is it, in a nutshell."

Her eyes began to dance. "Kiss me, Charles: I'll marry you," she said.

CHAPTER VII

COLONEL AUDLEY was very late for breakfast. He came into the parlour to find his brother standing by the window, glancing through the *Gazette de Bruxelles*, and his sister-in-law with her chair already pushed back from the table. She looked searchingly at him as he entered, for she had heard the front door slam a minute earlier and knew that he had been out riding again. Her heart sank; she had never seen quite that radiant look on his face before. "Well, Charles," she said. "You've been out already?"

"Yes." He held out his hands to her. "Wish me joy!" he said.

She let him take her hands, but faltered: "Wish you joy? What can you mean?"

"Lady Barbara has promised to be my wife," he answered.

She snatched her hands away. "Impossible! No, no you're joking!"

He looked down at her, half-laughing, half-surprised. "I assure you I am not!"

"You scarcely know her! You cannot mean it!"

"But, my dear Judith, I do mean it! I am the happiest man on earth!"

The dismay she felt was plainly to be read in her face. He drew back. "Don't you intend to wish me joy?" he asked.

"Oh, Charles, how could you? She will never make you happy! You don't know——"

"She has made me happy," he interrupted.

"She is fast—a flirt!"

"You must not say that to me, you know," he said, quite gently, but with a note in his voice that warned her of danger.

The Earl, who had lowered his paper at the Colonel's first announcement, now laid it down, and said in his calm way: "This is very sudden, Charles."

"Yes."

Judith would have spoken again, but Worth engaged her silence by the flicker of a glance in her direction. "Your mind is, in fact, quite made up?" he said.

"Quite!"

"Then of course I wish you joy," said Worth. "When do you mean to be married?"

"Nothing is decided yet. I must see her grandfather. She is her own mistress, but I don't want to—— It is not as though I were a very eligible *parti*, you know."

"You are a great deal too good for her!" exclaimed Judith.

He turned his head, and said with a smile: "Oh no, Judith! It is she who is a great deal too good for me. When you know her better you will agree."

She replied as cheerfully as she was able: "I do wish you very happy, Charles. I will try to know Lady Barbara better."

He looked at her in rather a troubled way as she went out of the room. But when he had closed the door behind her the trouble vanished from his eyes, and he walked back to the table, and sat down at it, and began to eat his breakfast.

The Earl watched him for some moments in silence.

Presently he said: "Is your engagement to be publicly announced, Charles?"

"Why, I suppose so! There is no secret about it, you know."

"It is very wonderful," Worth observed. "What did she find in you to like so well?"

The Colonel grinned. "I don't know."

"You would not, of course," Worth said dryly. "Forgive my curiosity, but does Lady Barbara mean to follow the drum?"

"She would, I think, and like it very well. Women do, you know—have you ever met Juana, Harry Smith's wife?"

"I have not met Juana, nor have I met Harry Smith."

"He's a Rifleman: a rattling good fellow, mad as a coot! He went out to America with Pakenham, more's the pity! He married a Spanish child after Badajos: it's too long a story to tell you now, but you never saw such a little heroine in your life! I believe she would go with Harry into action if he would let her. I have seen her fording a river with the water right up to her horse's girths. She will sleep out in the open by a camp-fire, wrapped up in a blanket, and never utter a word of complaint. Bab is made of just that high-spirited stuff."

"I hope you may be right," said Worth, unable to picture the Lady Barbara in any such situations.

Not very far away, in the Rue Ducale, Lady Vidal shared this mental inability and did not scruple to say so. She had looked narrowly at her sister-in-law when she had come in to breakfast, and had not failed to notice the flame in Barbara's eyes and the colour in her cheeks. "What have you been doing?" she asked. "You look quite wild, let me tell you!"

"Oh yes! I am quite wild!" Barbara answered. "I have taken your advice, Gussie! There! Aren't you pleased?"

"I wish I knew what you meant!"

"Why, that I am engaged to be married, to be sure!"

Her brother's attention was caught by these words. "What's that? Engaged? Nonsense!"

Lady Vidal exclaimed: "Bab! Are you serious? It is Lavisse?"

"Lavisse?" repeated Barbara, as though dragging the name up from the recesses of her memory. "No! Oh no! My Staff officer!"

"Are you mad? Charles Audley? You cannot mean it!"

"Yes, I do—to-day, at least!"

Augusta said bitterly: "I never reckoned stupidity amongst your faults. Good God, Bab, how can you be such a fool? With your looks and birth you may marry whom you please: the lord knows you've had chances enough! and you choose a penniless soldier! I will not believe it of you!"

"Charles Audley?" said Vidal. He looked his sister over frowningly, but not displeased. "Well, I must say I am surprised. A very good family—perfectly eligible!"

Augusta broke in angrily: "Eligible! A penniless younger son with no chance of inheriting the title! Pray, how do you propose to live, Bab? Do you see yourself in the tail of an army, sharing all the discomforts of a campaign with your Charles?"

"I might, I think," said Barbara, considering it. "It would be something new—exciting!"

"I have no patience with such folly!"

Vidal interposed to say in his heavy fashion: "It is not a brilliant match—by no means brilliant! I could wish him wealthier, but as for his being penniless—pooh! I daresay he has a very respectable competence."

"Then Bab will have to learn to live upon a competence," said Augusta. "I hope, my dear love, that you have not forgotten the terms of your late husband's Will?"

"Oh, who cares! With a handsome fortune I had never enough money, so I may as happily live in debt on a mere competence."

This ingenious way of looking at the matter had the effect of pulling down the corners of Vidal's mouth. He began to read his sister a homily, but she interrupted him with a little show of temper, and ran out of the room, slamming the door behind her.

Lady Vidal remarked that if one thing were more certain than another it was that the engagement would be of short duration.

"I hope not," replied Vidal. "Audley is a very good sort of fellow, very well-liked. If she throws *him* over it will go hard with her in the eyes of the world. What I fear is that a sensible man will never bear with her tantrums. I wish to God she had stayed in England!" He added with an inconsequence Augusta found irritating: "We must ask him to dine with us. I wish you will write him a civil note."

"By all means!" she returned. "The more Bab sees of him the sooner she'll be bored by him. He may dine with us to-night, if he chooses, and accompany us to Madame van der Capellan's party afterwards."

The civil note was, accordingly, sent round by hand to the British Headquarters, where it found Colonel Audley in the company of the Prince of Orange and Lord Fitzroy Somerset.

The Colonel took the note, and tore it open with an eagerness which did not escape the Prince. That young gentleman, observing the elegance of the hot-pressed paper and the unmistakably feminine character of the hand-writing, winked at Lord Fitzroy, and said: "Aha! The affair progresses!"

The Colonel ignored this sally, and moved across to a desk and sat down at it to write an acceptance of the invitation. The Prince strolled after him, and perched on the opposite side of the desk, swinging his thin legs. "It is certainly an assignation," he said.

"It is. An invitation to dinner," replied the Colonel, rejecting one quill and choosing another.

"And it was I who set your feet on the road to ruin! Fitzroy, Charles is in love!"

Lord Fitzroy's small, firm mouth remained grave, but a smile twinkled in his eyes. "I thought he seemed a little elated. Who is she?"

"The Widow!" answered the Prince.

"What widow?"

The Prince flung up his hands. "He asks me what widow! *Mon Dieu*, Fitzroy, don't you know there is only one? The Incomparable, the Dashing, the Fatal Barbara!"

"I am not a penny the wiser," said Lord Fitzroy, his quiet, slightly drawling voice in as great a contrast to the Prince's vivacity as were his fair locks and square, handsome countenance to the Prince's dark hair and erratic features. "You forget how long it is since I was in England. Charles, that's my pen, and it suits me very well without your mending it. What's more, it's my desk, and I've work to do."

"I shan't be more than a minute," replied the Colonel. "Have you noticed how devilish official he's become lately, Billy? It's from standing in the Great Man's shoes, I suppose."

"You shall not divert me," said the Prince. "I observe the attempt, but it is useless. When do you announce your approaching marriage?"

"Now, if you like," said the Colonel, dipping his pen in the ink, and drawing a sheet of paper towards him.

The Prince's jaw dropped. He stared at Colonel Audley, and then laughed. "Oh yes, I am very stupid! I shall certainly swallow that *canard!*"

"If he's going to conduct his flirtations on Government paper, I demand to know the identity of the Fatal—— what did you say her name was, Billy?"

"Barbara! The disastrous Lady Barbara Childe!" answered the Prince dramatically.

"Barbara Childe? Oh, I know! Bab Alastair that was. Is she accounted fatal?"

"But entirely, Fitzroy! A veritable Circe—and *I* delivered Charles into her power!"

The Colonel looked up. "Yes, you did, so you shall be the first to know that she is going to become my wife."

The Prince blinked at him. "*Plaît-il?*"

Colonel Audley sealed his letter, wrote the direction, and got up. "Quite true," he assured the Prince, and went out to deliver his note to the waiting servant.

The Prince turned an astonished countenance towards

Lord Fitzroy, and said, stammering a little, as he always did when excited. "B—but it's—it's n—not possible! Scores of men have offered for Lady Bab, and she refused them all!"

"Well, she's chosen a very good man in the end," responded Fitzroy, seating himself at the desk.

"My poor Fitzroy, you do not understand! It is most remarkable—*éclatant!*"

"I see nothing very remarkable in two persons falling in love," said Fitzroy with unaltered calm. "Did I happen to mention that I was busy?"

"I am your superior officer," declared the Prince. "I command that you attend to me, and immediately treat me with respect."

Lord Fitzroy promptly stood up, and clicked his heels together. "I *beg* your Royal Highness's pardon!"

His Royal Highness made a grab at a heavy paper-weight on the desk, but Lord Fitzroy was quicker. The entrance into the room of a very junior member of the Staff put an end to what promised to be a most undignified scene. Lord Fitzroy at once released the paper-weight, and the Prince, acknowledging the newcomer's salute, departed in search of a more appreciative audience.

By the end of the day the news of the engagement had spread all over Brussels. Both parties to it had had to endure congratulation, incredulity, and much raillery. The Colonel bore it with his usual good-humour, but he was not surprised, on his arrival in the Rue Ducale, to find his betrothed in a stormy mood. Neither his host nor his hostess was in the salon when he entered it; there was only Lady Barbara, standing by the fireplace with her elbow on the mantelshelf, and one sandalled foot angrily tapping the floor.

The servant announced Colonel Audley, and he walked in to encounter a flashing glance from Barbara's eyes. Her lips parted, not smiling, and he saw her teeth gritted together. He laughed, and went up to her, and took her hands. "My dear, has it been very bad?" he asked. "Do you think you can bear it?"

94

She looked at him; her teeth unclenched: she said: "Can you?"

"Why yes, but my case is not so hard. They all envy me, of course."

The white, angry look left her face. She pulled one of his hands up to her mouth, and softly kissed it. "You're a dear, Charles."

He took her in his arms. "You mustn't do that," he said.

"I wanted to," she replied, turning her face up to his. "I always do what I want. Oh, but Charles, how odiously commonplace it is! I wish we had eloped instead!"

"That would have been worse—vulgar!"

"What I do is not vulgar!" she said snappishly.

"Exactly. So you didn't elope."

She moved away from him to cast herself into a chair by the fire. She thrust one bare foot in its golden sandal forward, and demanded: "How do you like my gilded toenails?"

"Very well indeed," he answered. "Is it a notion of your own?"

"Oh no! It's a trick Parisian harlots have!" she flung at him.

Contrary to her expectation, this made him laugh. She stiffened in her chair. "Don't you care, then?"

"Not a bit! It's a charming fashion."

"You will hear it very badly spoken of to-night, I warn you!"

"Oh no, I shan't!" said the Colonel cheerfully. "Whatever criticisms may be made of you will certainly not be made to me."

"Do you mean to fight my battles? You will be kept busy!" She opened her reticule, and drew a letter from it and handed it to him. "Your sister-in-law sent me these felicitations. She doesn't like me, does she?"

"No, I don't think she does," responded the Colonel, glancing through Judith's civil letter.

An impish look came into her eye. "I wonder whether she meant you to fall in love with that insipid protégée of

95

hers?" she said. "I can't recall her name. But an heiress, I believe. Oh, famous! I am sure that was it!"

"But who?" he demanded. "You do not mean Miss Devenish?"

"Yes, that was the name! Lord, to think I've lost you a fortune, Charles!"

"You must be crazy! I am persuaded Judith could never have entertained such an absurd notion!"

"Flirt with the chit, and see how your sister likes it!"

"No, no, I leave all that sort of thing to you, my sweet!"

"Wretch! Good God, how has this come about? I have talked myself into a good humour. I swear I meant to quarrel with you!" A doubt assailed her; she said challengingly: "Charles! Was it your doing?"

"Strategy of a Staff officer? On my honour, no!"

She jumped up, and almost flung herself into his arms. There was an urgency in the face upturned to his; she said: "Marry me! Marry me soon—at once—before I change my mind!"

He took her face between his hands, staring down at her. She felt his fingers tremble slightly, and wondered what thoughts chased one another behind the trouble in his eyes. Suddenly his hands dropped to her shoulders, and thrust her away from him. "No!" he said curtly.

"No?" she repeated. "Don't you want to, Charles?"

"Want to!" He broke off, and turned from her to the fireplace, and stood looking down at the smouldering logs.

She gave a little laugh. "This is certainly intriguing. I am rejected, then?"

He looked up. "Do you think you don't tempt me? To marry you out of hand—to possess you before you had had time to regret! Oh, my love, don't speak of this again! You spoke of changing your mind. If that is to come, you shall not be tied to me."

"You gave me time to consider? Strange! I had never a suitor like you, Charles!"

"I love you too much to snatch you before you know me, before you know your own heart!"

"Ah! You are wiser than I am," she said, with a faint smile.

They were interrupted by Lady Vidal, who came into the room, followed by her husband. She greeted Colonel Audley with cold civility, but her lack of warmth was atoned for by Vidal's marked display of friendliness. He was able to wish the Colonel joy with blunt cordiality, and even to crack a jest at his sister's expense.

They were soon joined by Lord Harry, who had ridden in from Enghien to attend the evening's party. He seemed to be delighted by the news of the betrothal. He wrung the Colonel's hand with great fervour, prophesied a devilish future for him at Bab's hands, and expressed a strong wish to see how Lavisse would receive the tidings.

"M. de Lavisse, my dear Harry, is quite a matrimonial prize," said Augusta. "I fancy your sister cannot boast of an offer from him. He is adroit in flirtation, but it will be a clever woman who persuades him to propose marriage."

"Dear Gussie! How vulgar!" said Barbara.

"Possibly, but I believe it to be true."

"Stuff!" said Lord Harry. "I can tell you this, Gussie, it will be a pretty fool of a woman who lets that fellow persuade her into marrying him!"

"You are a schoolboy, and know nothing of the matter," responded Augusta coldly.

"Oh, don't I, by Gad?" Lord Harry gave a crack of laughter. "Don't be such a simpleton!"

Barbara interrupted this dialogue with a good deal of impatience. "Do not expose yourselves more than you are obliged!" she begged. "Charles is as yet unacquainted with my family. If he must discover how odious we are, pray let him do so gradually!"

"Very true," said Augusta. "We are all of us strangers to him, and he to us. How odd it seems, to be sure!"

Her husband moved restlessly, and said something under his breath. Colonel Audley, however, replied without an instant's hesitation: "Odd, indeed, but you set me perfectly at my ease, ma'am. You are in a cross humour, and do not scruple to show it. I feel myself one of the family already."

Barbara's gurgle of laughter broke the astonished silence that followed these words. "Charles! Superb! Confess, Gussie, you are done-up!"

Augusta's stiffened countenance relaxed into a reluctant smile. "I am certainly taken aback, and must accord Colonel Audley the honours of *that* bout. Come, let us go in to dinner!"

She led the way into the dining-parlour, indicated to the Colonel that he should sit at her right hand, and behaved towards him throughout the meal, if not with cordiality, at least with civility.

There was no lack of conversation, the Colonel being too used to maintaining a flow of talk at Headquarters' parties ever to be at a loss, and Lord Harry having an inexhaustible supply of chit-chat at his tongue's end. Barbara said little. An attempt by Lord Harry to twit her on her engagement brought the stormy look back into her face. The Colonel intervened swiftly, turning aside the shaft, but not before Barbara had snapped out a snub. Augusta said with a titter: "I have often thought the betrothed state to be wretchedly commonplace."

"Very true," agreed the Colonel. "Like birth and death."

She was silenced. Vidal seized the opportunity to advert to the political situation, inaugurating a discussion which lasted until the ladies rose from the table. The gentlemen did not linger for many minutes, and the whole party was soon on its way to Madame van der Capellan's house.

It was an evening of music and dancing, attended by the usual crowd of fashionables. More congratulations had to be endured, until Barbara said savagely under her breath that she felt like a performing animal. Lady Worth, arriving with the Earl and her brother and sister-in-law, was reminded of a captive panther, and though understanding only in part the fret and tangle of Barbara's nerves, felt a good deal of sympathy for her. She presently moved over to her side, saying with a smile: "I think you dislike all this, so I shall add nothing to what I wrote you this morning."

"Thank you," Barbara said. "The insipidity—the inanity! I could curse with vexation!"

"Indeed, an engagement does draw a disagreeably particular attention to one."

"Oh the devil! I don't care a fig for that! But this is a milk-and-water affair!" She broke off, as Worth strolled up to them, and extended a careless hand to him. "How do you do? If you have come to talk to me, let it be of horses, and by no means of my confounded engagement. I think of setting up a phaeton: will you sell me your bays?"

"No," said Worth. "I will not."

"Good! You don't mince matters. I like that. Your wife is a famous whip, I believe. For the sake of our approaching kinship, find me a pair such as you would drive yourself, and I will challenge her to a race."

"I have yet to see a pair in this town I would drive myself," replied the Earl.

"Ah! And if you had? I suppose you would not permit Lady Worth to accept my challenge?"

"I am sure he would not," said Judith. "I did once engage in something of that nature—in my wild salad days, you know—and fell under his gravest displeasure. I must decline, therefore, for all I should like to accept your challenge."

"Conciliating!" Barbara said with a harsh little laugh. She saw Judith's eyes kindle, and said impulsively: "Now I've made you angry! I am glad! You look splendid just so! I could like you very well, I think."

"I hope you may," Judith replied formally.

"I will; but you must not be forbearing with me, if you please. There! I am behaving abominably, and I meant to be so good!"

She clasped Judith's hand briefly, allowed her a glimpse of her frank smile, and turned from her to greet Lavisse, who was coming towards her across the room.

He looked pale. He came stalking up to Barbara, and stood over her, not offering to take her hand, not even

99

according her a bow. Their eyes were nearly on a level, hers full of mockery, his blazing with anger. He said under his breath: "Is it true, then?"

She chuckled. "This is in the style of a hero of romance, Etienne. It is true!"

"You have engaged yourself to this Colonel Audley? I would not believe!"

"Felicitate me!"

"Never! I do not wish you happy, I! I wish you only regret."

"That's refreshing, at all events."

He saw several pairs of eyes fixed upon him, and with a muttered exclamation clasped Barbara round the waist and swept her into the waltz. His left hand gripped her right one; his arm was hard about her, holding her too close for decorum. "*Je t'aime; entendstu, je t'aime!*"

"You are out of time," she replied.

"Ah, *qu'importe?*" he exclaimed. He moderated his steps, however, and said in a quieter tone: "You knew I loved you! This Colonel, what can he be to you?"

"Why, don't you know? A husband!"

"And it is I who love you—yes, *en désespère!*"

"But I do not remember that you ever offered for this hand of mine, Etienne." She tilted her head back to look at him under the sweep of her lashes. "That gives you to think, eh, my friend? Terrible, that word *marriage!*"

"*Effroyant!* Yet I offer it!"

"Too late!"

"I do not believe! What has he, this Colonel, that I have not? It is not money! A great position?"

"No."

"Expectations, perhaps?"

"Not even expectations!"

"In the name of God, what then?"

"Nothing!" she answered.

"You do it to tease me! You are not serious, in fact. Listen, little angel, little fool! I will give you a proud name, I will give you wealth, everything that you desire! I will adore you—ah, but worship you!"

She said judicially: "A proud name Charles will give me—if I cared for such stuff! Wealth? Yes, I should like that. Worship! So boring, Etienne, so damnably boring!"

"I could break your neck!" he said.

"Fustian!"

He drew in his breath, but did not speak for several turns. When he unclosed his lips again it was to say in a tone of careful nonchalance: "One becomes dramatic: A pity! *Essayons encore!* When is it to be, this marriage?"

"Oh, confound you, is not a betrothal enough for one day? Are we not agreed that there is something terrible about that word marriage?"

His brows rose. "So! I am well content. Play the game out, amuse yourself with this so gallant Colonel; in the end you will marry me."

A gleam shot into her eyes "A bet! What will you stake —gamester?"

"Nothing! It is sure, and there is no sport in it, therefore."

The music came to an end; Barbara stood free, smiling and dangerous. "I thank you, Etienne! If you knew the cross humour I was in! Now! Oh, it is entirely finished!" She turned upon her heel; her gaze swept the room, and found Colonel Audley. She crossed the floor towards him, her draperies hushing about her feet as she walked.

"That's a grand creature!" suddenly remarked Wellington, his attention caught. "Who is she, Duchess?"

The Duchess of Richmond glanced over her shoulder. "Barbara Childe," she answered. "She is a granddaughter of the Duke of Avon."

"Barbara Childe, is she? So that's the prize that lucky young dog of mine has won! I must be off to offer my congratulations!" He left her side as he spoke, and made his way to where Colonel Audley and Barbara were standing.

His congratulations, delivered with blunt heartiness, were perfectly well received by the lady. She shook hands, and met that piercing eagle-stare with a look of candour, and her most enchanting smile. The Duke stayed talking to her until the quadrille was forming, but as soon as he saw the couples taking up their positions, he said briskly: "You must take your places, or you will be too late. No need to ask whether you dance the quadrille, Lady Barbara! As for this fellow, Audley, I'll engage for it he won't disgrace you."

He waved them on to the floor, called a chaffing word to young Lennox on the subject of his celebrated *pas de zéphyr*, and stood back to watch the dance for a few minutes. Lady Worth, only a few paces distant, thought it must surely be impossible for anyone to look more care-free than his lordship. He was smiling, nodding to acquaint-ances, evidently enjoying himself. She watched him, wondering at him a little, and presently, as though aware of her gaze, he turned his head, recognized her, and said: "Oh, how d'ye do? A pretty sight, isn't it?"

She agreed to it. "Yes, indeed. Do all your Staff officers perform so creditably, Duke? They put the rest quite in the shade."

"Yes, I often wonder where would Society be without my boys?" he replied. "Your brother acquits himself very well, but I believe that young scamp, Lennox, is the best of them. There he goes—but his partner is too heavy on her feet! Audley has the advantage of him in that respect."

"Yes," she acknowledged. "Lady Barbara dances very well."

"Audley's a fortunate fellow," said the Duke decidedly. "Won't thank me for taking him away from Brussels, I daresay. Don't blame him! But it can't be helped."

"You are leaving us, then?"

"Oh yes—yes! for a few days. No secret about it: I have to visit the Army."

"Of course. We shall await your return with impatience, I assure you, praying the Ogre may not descend upon us while you are absent!"

He gave one of his sudden whoops of laughter. "No fear of that! It's all nonsense, this talk about Bonaparte! Ogre! Pooh! Jonathan Wild, that's my name for him!"

He saw her look of astonishment, and laughed again, apparently much amused, either by her surprise or by his own words.

She was conscious of disappointment. He had been described to her as unaffected: he seemed to her almost inane.

CHAPTER VIII

UPON the following day was published a General Order, directing officers in future to make their reports to the Duke of Wellington. Upon the same day, a noble-browed gentleman with a suave address and great tact, was sent from Brussels to the Prussian Head-quarters, there to assume the somewhat arduous duties of Military Commissioner to the Prussian Army. Sir Henry Hardinge had lately been employed by the Duke in watching Napoleon's movements in France. He accepted his new rôle with his usual equanimity, and, commiserated with by his friends on the particularly trying nature of his commission, merely smiled, and said that General von Gneisenau was not likely to be as tiresome as he was painted.

The *Moniteur* of this 11th day of April published gloomy tidings. In the south of France, the Duc d'Angoulême's enterprise had failed. Angoulême had led his mixed force on Lyons, but the arrival from Paris of a competent person of the name of Grouchy had ended Royalist hopes in the south. Angoulême and his masterful wife had both set sail from France, and his army was fast dwindling away.

It was not known what King Louis, in Ghent, made of these tidings, but those who were acquainted with his character doubted whether his nephew's failure would much perturb him. Never was there so lethargic a monarch: one could hardly blame France for welcoming Napoleon back.

The news disturbed others, however. It seemed as

though it were all going to start again: victory upon victory for Napoleon; France overrunning Europe. Shocking to think of the Emperor's progress through France, of the men who flocked to join his little force, of the crowds who welcomed him, hysterical with joy! Shocking to think of Marshal Ney, with his oath to King Louis on his conscience, deserting with his whole force to the Emperor's side! There must be some wizardry in the man, for in all France there had not been found sufficient loyal men to stand by the King and make it possible for him to hold his Capital in Napoleon's teeth. He had fled, with his little Court, and his few troops, and if ever he found himself on his throne again it would be once more because foreign soldiers had placed him there.

But how unlikely it seemed that he would find himself there! With Napoleon at large, summoning his Champ de Mai assemblies, issuing his dramatic proclamations, gathering together his colossal armies, only the very optimistic could feel that there was any hope for King Louis.

Even Wellington doubted the ability of the Allies to put King Louis back on the throne, but this doubt sprang more from a just appreciation of the King's character than from any fear of Napoleon. Sceptical people might ascribe the Duke's attitude to the fact of his never having met Napoleon in the field, but the fact remained that his lordship was one of the few generals in Europe who did not prepare to meet Napoleon in a mood of spiritual defeat.

He accorded the news of Angoulême's failure a sardonic laugh, and laid the *Moniteur* aside. He was too busy to waste time over that.

He kept his Staff busy too, a circumstance which displeased Barbara Childe. To be loved by a man who sent her brief notes announcing his inability to accompany her on expeditions of her planning was a new experience. When she saw him at the end of a tiring day, she rallied him on his choice of profession. "For the future I shall be betrothed only to civilians."

He laughed. He had been all the way to Audenarde

and back, with a message for General Colville, commanding the 4th Division, but he had found time to buy a ring
of emeralds and diamonds for Barbara, and although
there was a suggestion of weariness about his eyelids, he
seemed to desire nothing as much as to dance with her the
night through.

Waltzing with him, she said abruptly: "Are you tired?"

"Tired! Do I dance as though I were tired?"

"No, but you've been in the saddle nearly all day."

"Oh, that's nothing! In Spain I have been used to ride
fifteen or twenty miles to a ball, and be at work again by
ten o'clock the next day."

"Wellington trains admirable suitors," she remarked.
"How fortunate it is that you dance so well, Charles!"

"I know. You would not otherwise have accepted me."

"Yes, I think perhaps I should. But I should not dance
with you so much. I wish you need not leave Brussels just
now."

"So do I. What will you do while I am away? Flirt
with your Belgian admirer?"

She looked up at him. "Don't go!"

He smiled, but shook his head.

"Apply to the Duke for leave, Charles!"

He looked startled. As his imagination played with the
scene her words evoked, his eyes began to dance. "Unthinkable!"

"Why? You might well ask the Duke!"

"Believe me, I might not!"

She jerked up a shoulder. "Perhaps you don't wish for
leave?"

"I don't," he said frankly. "Why, what a fellow I should
be if I did!"

"Don't I come first with you?"

He glanced down at her. "You don't understand, Bab."

"Oh, you mean to talk to me of your duty!" she said
impatiently. "Tedious stuff!"

"Very. Tell me what you will do while I am away."

"Flirt with Etienne. You have already said so. Have
I your permission?"

"If you need it. It's very lucky: I leave Brussels on the 16th, and Lavisse will surely arrive on the 15th for the dinner in honour of the Prince of Orange. I daresay he'll remain a day or two, and so be at your disposal."

"Not jealous, Charles?"

"How should I be? You wear my ring, not his."

His guess was correct. The Comte de Lavisse appeared in Brussels four days later to attend the Belgian dinner at the Hôtel d'Angleterre. He lost no time in calling in the Rue Ducale, and on learning that Lady Barbara was out, betook himself to the Park, and very soon came upon her ladyship, in company with Colonel Audley, Lady Worth and her offspring, Sir Peregrine Taverner, and Miss Devenish.

The party seemed to be a merry one, Judith being in spirits and Barbara in a melting mood. It was she who held Lord Temperley's leading strings, and directed his attention to a bed of flowers. "Pretty lady!" Lord Temperley called her, with weighty approval.

"Famous!" she said. She glanced up at Judith, and said with a touch of archness: "I count your son one of my admirers, you see!"

"You are so kind to him I am sure it is no wonder," Judith responded, liking her in this humour.

"Thank you! Charles, set him on your shoulder, and let us take him to see the swans on the water. Lady Worth, you permit?"

"Yes indeed, but I don't wish you to be teased by him!"

"No such thing!" She swooped upon the child, and lifted him up in her arms. "There! I declare I could carry you myself!"

"He's too heavy for you!"

"He will crush your pelisse!"

She shrugged as these objections were uttered, and relinquished the child. Colonel Audley tossed him up on to his shoulder, and the whole party was about to walk in the direction of the pavilion when Lavisse, who had been watching from a little distance, came forward, and clicked his heels together in one of his flourishing salutes.

Lady Worth bowed with distant civility; Barbara looked as though she did not care to be discovered in such a situation; only the Colonel said with easy good humour: "Hallo! You know my sister, I believe. And Miss Devenish—Sir Peregrine Taverner?"

"Ah, I have not previously had the honour! Mademoiselle! Monsieur!" Two bows were executed; the Count looked slyly towards Barbara, and waved a hand to include the whole group. "You must permit me to compliment you upon the pretty *tableau* you make; I am perhaps *de trop*, but shall beg leave to join the party."

"By all means," said the Colonel. "We are taking my nephew to see the swans."

"You cannot want to carry him, Charles," said Judith in a low voice.

"Fiddle!" he replied. "Why should I not want to carry him?"

She thought that the picture he made with the child on his shoulder was too domestic to be romantic, but could scarcely say so. He set off towards the pavilion with Miss Devenish beside him; Barbara imperiously demanded Sir Peregrine's arm; and as the path was not broad enough to allow of four persons walking abreast, Judith was left to bring up the rear with Lavisse.

This arrangement was accepted by the Count with all the outward complaisance of good manners. Though his eyes might follow Barbara, his tongue uttered every civil inanity required of him. He was ready to discuss the political situation, the weather, or mutual acquaintances, and, in fact, touched upon all these topics with the easy address of a fashionable man.

Upon their arrival at the sheet of water by the pavilion his air of fashion left him. Judith was convinced that nothing could have been further from his inclination than to throw bread to a pair of swans, but he clapped his hands together, declaring that the swans must and should be fed, and ran off to the pavilion to procure crumbs for the purpose.

He came back presently with some cakes, a circumstance

which shocked Miss Devenish into exclaiming against such extravagance.

"Oh, such delicious little cakes, and all for the swans! Some stale bread would have been better!"

The Count said gaily: "They have no stale bread, mademoiselle; they were offended at the very suggestion. So what would you?"

"I am sure the swans will much prefer your cakes, Etienne," said Barbara, smiling at him for the first time.

"If only you may not corrupt their tastes!" remarked Audley, holding on to his nephew's skirts.

"Ah, true! A swan with an unalterable *penchant* for cake: I fear he would inevitably starve!"

"He might certainly despair of finding another patron with your lavish notions of largess," observed Barbara.

She stepped away from the group, in the endeavour to coax one of the swans to feed from her hand; after a few moments the Count joined her, while Colonel Audley still knelt, holding his nephew on the brink of the lake, and directing his erratic aim in crumb-throwing.

Judith made haste to relieve him of his charge, saying in an undervoice as she bent over her son: "Pray let me take Julian. You do not want to be engaged with him."

"Don't disturb yourself, my dear sister. Julian and I are doing very well, I assure you."

She replied with some tartness: "I hope you will not be stupid enough to allow that man to take your place beside Barbara! There, get up! I have Julian fast."

He rose, but said with a smile: "Do you think me a great fool? Now *I* was preening myself on being a wise man!"

He moved away before she could answer him, and joined Miss Devenish, who was sitting on a rustic bench, drawing diagrams in the gravel with the ferrule of her sunshade. In repose her face had a wistful look, but at the Colonel's approach she raised her eyes, and smiled, making room for him to sit beside her.

"Of all the questions in the world I believe *What are you thinking about?* to be the most impertinent," he said lightly.

She laughed, but with a touch of constraint. "Oh—I don't know what I was thinking about! The swans—the dear little boy—Lady Worth—how I envy her!"

These last words were uttered almost involuntarily. The Colonel said: "Envy her? Why should you do so?"

She coloured, and looked down. "I don't know how I came to say that. Pray do not regard it!" She added in a stumbling way: "One does take such fancies! It is only that she is so happy, and good . . ."

"Are you not happy?" he asked. "I am sure you are good."

She gave her head a quick shake. "Oh no! At least, I mean, of course I am happy. Please do not heed me! I am in a nonsensical mood to-day. How beautiful Lady Barbara looks in her bronze bonnet and pelisse." She glanced shyly at him. "You must be very proud. I hope you will be very happy too."

"Thank you. I wonder how long it will be before I shall be wishing you happy in the same style?" he said, with a quizzical smile.

She looked startled. A blush suffused her cheeks, and her eyes brightened all at once with a spring of tears. "Oh no! Impossible! Please do not speak of it!"

He said in a tone of concern: "My dear Miss Devenish, forgive me! I had no notion of distressing you, upon my honour!"

"You must think me very foolish!"

"Well," he said, in a rallying tone, "do you know, I do think you a little foolish to speak of your marriage as impossible! Now you will write me down a very saucy fellow!"

"Oh no! But you don't understand! Here is Lady Barbara coming towards you: please forget this folly!"

She got up, still in some agitation of spirit, and walked quickly away to Judith's side.

"Good God! did my approach frighten the heiress away?" asked Barbara, in a tone of lively amusement. "Or was it your gallantry, Charles? Confess! You have been trifling with her!"

"What, in such a public place as this?" protested the Colonel. "You wrong me, Bab!"

She said with a gleam of fun: "I thought you liked public places, indeed I did! Parks—or Allées!"

"Allées!" ejaculated Lavisse. "Do not mention that word, I beg! I shall not easily forgive Colonel Audley for discovering, with the guile of all Staff officers (an accursed race!), that you ride there every morning."

The Colonel laughed. Barbara took his arm, saying: "I have made such a delightful plan, Charles. I am quite tired of the Allée Verte. I am going further afield, with Etienne."

"Are you?" said the Colonel. "A picnic? I don't advise it in this changeable weather, but you won't care for that. Where do you go?"

It was Lavisse who answered. "Do you know the Château de Hougoumont, Colonel? Ah, no! How should you, in effect? It is a little country seat which belongs to a relative of mine, a M. de Lunéville."

"I know the Château," interrupted the Colonel. "It is near the village of Merbe Braine, is it not, on the Nivelles road?"

The Count's brows rose. "You are exact! One would say you knew it well."

"I had occasion to travel over that country last year," the Colonel responded briefly. "Do you mean to make your expedition there? It must be quite twelve or thirteen miles away."

"What of that?" said Barbara. "You don't know me if you think I am so soon tired. We shall ride through the Forest, and take luncheon at the Château. It will be capital sport!"

"Of whom is this party to consist?" he enquired.

"Of Etienne and myself, to be sure."

He returned no answer, but she saw a grave look in his face, which provoked her into saying: "I assure you Etienne is very well able to take care of me."

"I don't doubt it," he replied.

Lady Worth had joined them by this time, and was,

listening to the interchange in silence, but with a puckered brow. The whole party began to walk away from the lake, and Judith, resigning her son into Peregrine's charge, caught up with Barbara, and said in a low voice: "Forgive me, but you are not in earnest?"

"Very seldom, I believe."

"This expedition with the Count: you cannot have considered what a singular appearance it will give you!"

"On the contrary: I delight in singularity."

Judith felt her temper rising; she managed to control it, and to say in a quiet tone: "You will think me impertinent, I daresay, but I do most earnestly counsel you to give up the scheme. I can have no expectation of *my* words weighing with you, but I cannot suppose you to be equally indifferent to my brother's wishes. He must dislike this scheme excessively."

"Indeed! Are you his envoy, Lady Worth?"

Judith was obliged to deny it. She was spared having to listen to the mocking rejoinder, which, she was sure, hovered on the tip of Barbara's tongue, by Colonel Audley's coming up to them at that moment. He stepped between them, offering each an arm, and having glanced at both their faces, said: "I conclude that I have interrupted a duel. My guess is that Judith has been preaching propriety, and Bab announcing herself a confirmed rake."

"I have certainly been preaching propriety," replied Judith. "It sounds odious, and I fear Lady Barbara has found it so."

"No! Confoundedly boring!" said Barbara. "I am informed, Charles, that you will dislike my picnic scheme excessively. Shall you?"

"Good God, no! Go, by all means, if you wish to—and can stand the gossip."

"I am quite accustomed to it," she said indifferently.

Judith felt so much indignation at the lack of feeling shown by this remark that she drew her hand away from the Colonel's arm, and dropped behind to walk with her brother. This left Miss Devenish to the Count's escort, an arrangement which continued until Barbara left the party.

The Count then requested the honour of being allowed to conduct her home; Colonel Audley, who was obliged to call at Headquarters, made no objection, and Miss Devenish found herself once more in the company of Sir Peregrine, Lady Worth and Colonel Audley walking ahead of them.

After a few moments, Judith said in a vexed tone: "You will surely not permit her to behave with such impropriety!"

"I see no impropriety," he replied.

"To be alone with that man the whole day!"

"An indiscretion, certainly."

She walked on beside him in silence for some way, but presently said: "Why do you permit it?"

"I have no power to stop her even if I would."

"Even if you would? What can you mean?"

"She must be the only judge of her own actions. I won't become a mentor."

"Charles, how nonsensical! Do you mean to let yourself be ridden over roughshod?"

"Neither to be ridden over nor to ride roughshod," he answered. "To manage my own affairs in my own way, however."

"I beg your pardon," she said, in a mortified voice.

He pressed her hand, but after a slight pause began to talk of something else. She attempted no further discussion with him on the subject of the picnic, but to Worth, later, spoke her mind with great freedom. He listened calmly to all she had to say, but when she demanded to know his opinion, replied that he thought her intervention to have been ill-judged.

"I had no notion of vexing her! I tried only to advise her!"

"You made a great mistake in doing so. Advice is seldom palatable."

"I think she is perfectly heartless!"

"I hope you may be found to be wrong."

"And, what is more, she is a flirt. I am sure there can be nothing more odious!" She paused, but as Worth showed no sign of wishing to avail himself of the opportunity of answering her, continued: "Nothing could be more unfortunate than such an entanglement! I wonder you can sit there so placidly while Charles goes the quickest way to work to ruin his life! She has nothing to recommend her. She has not even the advantages of fortune; she is wild to a fault; indulges every extravagant folly; and in general shows such a want of delicacy that it quite sinks my spirits to think of Charles forming such a connection!" She again paused, and as Worth remained silent, said: "Well? Can you find anything to admire in her, beyond a beautiful face and a well-turned ankle?"

"Certainly," he replied. "She has a great deal of natural quickness, and although her vivacity often betrays her into unbecoming behaviour, I believe she wants neither sense nor feeling."

"You will tell me next that you are pleased with the engagement!"

"On the contrary, I am sorry for it. But depend upon it, a man of thirty-five is capable of judging for himself what will best suit him."

"Oh, Julian, I know she will make him unhappy!"

"I think it extremely probable," he replied. "But as neither of us has the power to prevent such a contingency we should be extremely foolish to interfere in the matter."

She sighed, and picked up her embroidery. After a period of reflection, she said in a mollified tone: "I don't wish to be censorious, and I must say she is extremely kind to little Julian."

The entrance of the Colonel put an end to the conversation. He had been dining at the Duke's table, and seemed to be more concerned with the difficulties of the military situation than with Barbara's volatility. He sat down with a sigh of relief before the fire, and said: "Well! we depart (I need hardly say) at daybreak. It will be a relief to leave these Headquarters behind us. If his temper is to survive this campaign Old Hookey must have a respite from the letters they keep sending from the Horse Guards."

"Crusty, is he?" said Worth.

"Damned crusty. I don't blame him: I wouldn't be in

his shoes for a thousand pounds. What is needed is good troops, and all we hear of is General Officers. Added to that, the Staff which has been employed here is preposterous. One is for ever tumbling over Deputy-Assistants who are nothing more than subaltern officers, and no more fit for Staff duty than your son would be. They are all being turned off, of course, but even so we shall have too many novices still left on the Staff."

"If I know anything of the matter, you will have more —if Wellington pays any heed to the recommendations he will receive," remarked Worth.

"He don't, thank the lord! Though, between ourselves, some of those recommendations come from very exalted quarters." He stood up. "I am off to bed. Have you made up your mind whether you come along with us, or not, Worth?"

"Yes, as far as to Ghent. Where do you go from there?"

"Oh, Tournay—Mons! All the fortifications. We shall be away for about a week, I suppose."

Both men had left the house when Judith came down to breakfast next morning. She sat down at the table, with only *The British and Continental Herald* to bear her company, and was engaged in perusing the columns of Births, Marriages and Deaths, when the butler came in to announce the Lady Barbara Childe.

Judith looked up in surprise; she supposed Lady Barbara to be in the salon, but before she could speak that tempestuous beauty had brushed past the butler into the room.

She was dressed in a walking costume, and carried a huge chinchilla muff. She looked pale, and her eyes seemed overbright to Judith. She glanced round the room, and said abruptly: "Charles! I want to see him!"

Judith rose, and came forward. "How do you do?" she said. "I am sorry, but my brother has already left for Ghent. I hope it is nothing urgent?"

Barbara exclaimed: "Oh, confound it! I wanted to see him! I overslept—it's those curst drops!"

Her petulance, the violence of the language she used,

did nothing to advance her claims to Judith's kindness. "I am sorry. Pray will you not be seated?"

"Oh no! There's no use in my staying!" Barbara replied dejectedly. Her mouth drooped; her eyes were emptied of light; she stood swinging her muff, apparently lost in her own brooding thoughts. Suddenly she looked at Judith, and laughed. "Oh, heavens! what did I say? You are certainly offended!"

Judith at once disclaimed. Barbara said, with her air of disarming candour: "I am sorry! Only I did wish to see Charles before he left, and I am always cross when I don't get what I want."

"I hope it was not a matter of great importance."

"No. That is, I behaved odiously to him yesterday—oh, to you, too, but I don't care for that! Oh, the devil, *now* what have I said?"

She looked so rueful, yet had such an imp of mischief dancing behind her solemnity that Judith was obliged to laugh. "I wish you will sit down! Have you breakfasted?"

Barbara dropped into a chair. "No. I don't, you know." She sighed. "Life is using me very hardly to-day. You will say that that is my own fault, but it is nevertheless monstrous that when I do mean to be good, to make amends, I must needs oversleep."

After a moment's hesitation, Judith said: "You refer, I collect, to your picnic scheme?"

"Of course. I wanted to tell Charles I was only funning."

"You do not mean to go, then!"

"No."

"I am so glad! I was completely taken in, I confess."

"Oh no! I did mean to go—yesterday! But Gussie——" She broke off, grinding her teeth together.

"Your sister-in-law advised you against the scheme?"

"On the contrary!" said Barbara, with an angry little laugh.

"I don't think I quite understand?"

"I daresay you might not. She had the infernal impudence to approve of it. She will be a famous match-making mama for her daughters one of these days."

115

"Can you mean that she wishes you to marry the Comte de Lavisse?" gasped Judith.

"Most earnestly. Ah, you are astonished. You are not acquainted with my family."

"But your engagement to my brother! She could not wish to see that broken!"

"Why not?"

"A solemn promise—the scandal!"

Barbara burst out laughing. "Oh, you're enchanting when you're shocked! An outraged goddess, no less! But you must learn to know my family better. We don't care for scandal."

"Then why do you forgo your picnic?" demanded Judith.

"I don't know. To spite Gussie—to please Charles! Both, perhaps."

This answer was not encouraging. Judith was silent for a moment. She stole a glance at Barbara's face, and of impulse said: "Do you love him?" The words were no sooner uttered than regretted. Such a question was an impertinence; she was not on terms of sufficient intimacy with Barbara to allow of its having been asked.

Flushing, she awaited the snub she felt herself to have earned. But Barbara replied merely: "Yes."

"I should not have asked you," Judith apologized.

"It's of no consequence. I daresay you wish that Charles had never met me. I should, in your place. I'm horrid, you know. I told him so, but he wouldn't listen to me. I never loved anyone before, I think."

This remark accorded so ill with her reputation that Judith looked rather taken aback.

Barbara gave a gurgle of irrepressible amusement. "Are you recalling my flirtations? They don't signify, you know. I flirt to amuse myself, but the truth is that I never fancied myself in love with anyone but Charles."

"I beg your pardon, but to fancy yourself in love could surely be the only justification for flirting!"

"Oh, stuff!" Barbara said. "Flirtation is delightful; being in love, quite disagreeable."

"*I* never found it so!"

"Truly?"

Judith considered for a moment. "No. At least—yes, I suppose sometimes it can be disagreeable. There is a certain pain—for foolish causes."

"Ah, you are not so stupid after all! I hate pain. Yes, and I hate to submit, as I am doing now, over this tiresome picnic!"

"That I understand perfectly!" Judith said. "But you do not submit to Charles; *he* made no such demand! Your submission is to your own judgment."

"Oh no! I don't go because Charles does not wish it. How tame! Don't talk of it! It makes me cross! I want to go. I am bored to death!"

"Well, why should you not?" Judith said, as an idea presented itself to her. "A party of pleasure—there could be no objection! If you will accept of my company, I will go with you."

"Go with me?" said Barbara. "In Lavisse's place?"

"No such thing! *You* may ride with the Count; *I* shall drive with my sister, Lady Taverner. I am persuaded she would delight in the expedition. I daresay my brother will join us as well."

The green eyes looked blankly for a moment, then grew vivid with laughter. "Thus turning a *tête-à-tête* into the most sedate of family parties! Oh, I must do it, if only for the fun of seeing Etienne's dismay!"

"Would you not care for it?" asked Judith, a little dashed.

"Of all things!" Barbara sprang up. "It's for to-morrow. We start early, and lunch at this Château Etienne talks of. It will be charming! Thank you a thousand times!"

CHAPTER IX

THE weather remaining fine, and the Taverners declaring themselves to be very ready to join the picnic, the whole party assembled in the Rue Ducale the next morning. As Lady Taverner's situation made riding ineligible for her, Judith, who would have preferred to have gone on horseback, was obliged to drive with her in an open barouche. Sir Peregrine bestrode a showy chestnut, and Barbara, as usual, rode the Count's Coup de Grâce.

Upon her first setting out Judith had felt perfectly satisfied with her own appearance. She was wearing a round robe, under a velvet pelisse of Sardinian blue. A high-crowned bonnet, lined with silk and ornamented with a frilled border of lace, gloves of French kid, a seal-skin muff, and half-boots of jean, completed a very becoming toilet. Beside her sister-in-law, who had chosen to wear drab merino cloth over olive-brown muslin, she looked elegant indeed, but from the moment of Barbara's descending the steps of the house in the Rue Ducale she felt herself to have been cast quite in the shade.

Barbara was wearing a habit of pale green, resembling the dress of a Hussar. Her coat was ornamented with row upon row of frogs and braiding; silver epaulettes set off her shoulders; and silver braiding stretched half-way up her arms. Under the habit, she wore a cambric shirt with a high-standing collar trimmed with lace; a cravat of worked muslin was tied round her throat; and there were narrow ruffles at her wrists. Set jauntily on her flaming head was a tall hat, like a shako, with a plume of feathers adding the final touch of audacity to a preposterous but undeniably striking costume.

Lady Taverner was shocked; Judith, who considered the dress too daring for propriety, yet could not suppress a slight feeling of envy. She could fancy herself in just such a habit.

"How can she? Such a quiz of a hat!" whispered Lady Taverner.

However much she might agree with these sentiments, Judith had no notion of spoiling the day's pleasure by letting her disapproval appear. She leaned out of the carriage to shake hands with Barbara, saying with the utmost amiability: "How delightfully you look! You put me quite out of conceit with myself."

"Yes, I'm setting a fashion," replied Barbara. "You will see: it will be the established mode in a month's time."

Lady Vidal, who had come out of the house with her husband, merely bowed to Judith from the top of the stone steps, but Vidal put himself to the trouble of coming up to the barouche to thank Judith for her kindness in joining the expedition. He said in a low voice: "Bab is a sad romp! One of these days her crotchets will be the ruin of her. But *your* presence makes everything as it should be! I shan't conceal from you that I don't above half like that fellow Lavisse."

Not wishing to join in any animadversions on one who was for this day in some sort her host, Judith passed it off with a smile and a trivial remark. Her dislike of Lavisse was as great as Vidal's, but she was forced to acknowledge the very gentlemanlike way in which he had received the news of the augmentation of his party. Not by as much as the flicker of an eyelid did he betray the mortification he must feel. His civility towards the ladies in the barouche was most flattering; he was all smiles and complaisance, prophesying fine weather, and displaying a proper solicitude for their comfort.

"Don't you wish you were coming, Gussie?" Barbara called.

"My dear Bab, you must know that of all insipidities I most detest a family party," returned Augusta.

Barbara bit her lip, glancing towards the barouche as though she saw it with new eyes. Suddenly impatient, she said: "Well, why do we wait? Let us, for God's sake, start!"

The Count, who was giving some directions to Judith's coachman, looked over his shoulder with a smile of perfect comprehension. "*En avant*, then!" he said, reining his horse back to allow the barouche to pass. When it had moved forward, with Peregrine riding close behind it, he fell in beside Barbara, and said with some amusement: "You repent already, and are asking yourself what you do in this *galère.*"

"Oh, by God, I must have been mad!" she said.

"Little fool! I admire the guard set about you by your Staff Officer. It is most formidable!"

"It was not his doing. The notion was Lady Worth's, and I fell in with it."

"*Impayable!* Why, for example?"

She laughed. "Oh, to make you angry, of course!"

"But I am not at all angry; I am entirely amused," he said.

They were making their way down the Rue de la Pépinière in the direction of the Namur Gate. Once outside the walls of the town, the road led through some neat suburbs to the Forest of Soignes, a huge beechwood stretching for some miles to the south of Brussels, and intersected by the main Charleroi Chaussée. The Forest was almost entirely composed of beech trees, their massive trunks rising up out of the ground with scarcely any underwood to hide their smooth, silvery outlines.

Judith had often ridden in this direction, but this was her first visit to the Forest in springtime. She was enchanted with it, and even Lady Taverner, whose spirits were always low during the first months of pregnancy, was moved to exclaim at the grandeur of the scene. Sir Peregrine, in spite of already having got his uppers splashed by the mud of the unpaved portion of the road, seemed pleased also, though he would not allow the vista to be comparable to an English scene.

For the first mile or two the party remained together, Barbara and Lavisse riding at a little distance behind the barouche, but from time to time pressing forward to exchange remarks with its occupants. Shortly after the Forest had been entered, however, Barbara announced herself to be tired of riding tamely along the road. She waved her whip in a rather naughty gesture of farewell, and set her horse scrambling up the bank of the wood. The Count lingered only to assure Judith of the impossibility of her coachman's missing the way, saluted, and followed Barbara.

"I do think her the most unaccountable creature!" exclaimed Lady Taverner. "It is very uncivil of her to make off like that, besides being so indiscreet!"

Judith, herself disappointed in this fresh evidence of flightiness in Barbara, endeavoured to give her sister-in-law's thoughts another direction.

It was inconceivable to Lady Taverner that any female who was betrothed to one gentleman could desire a *tête-à-tête* with another, and for some time she continued to marvel at Barbara's conduct. Judith did not attend very closely to her remarks; she was lost in her own reflections. She could appreciate the cause of Barbara's perversity, but although she might sympathize with that wildness of disposition which made convention abhorrent to Barbara, she could not but be sorry for it. She was more than ever convinced that this spoiled, fashionable beauty would make Colonel Audley a wretched wife. Her imagination dwelled pitifully upon his future, which must of necessity be a stormy affair, made up of whims and tantrums and debts; and she could not forbear to contrast this melancholy prospect with the less exciting but infinitely more comfortable life he would enjoy if he would but change Barbara for Lucy.

She was roused from these musings by hearing Peregrine announce a village to have come into view. She looked up; the trees flanking the road dwindled ahead in perspective to the village of Waterloo. A round building, standing on the edge of the Forest, half-bathed in sunlight, presented a picture charming enough to make her long for her sketch-book and water-colours.

They had by this time covered some nine and a half miles, and were glad to be leaving the shade of the Forest, In a few minutes the village was reached, and Lady Taverner was exclaiming at the size and style of the church, a strange edifice with a domed roof, standing on one side

121

of the chaussée. Opposite, amongst a huddle of brick and stone-built cottages, was a small inn, with a painted sign-board bearing the legend, Jean de Nivelles. There was little to detain sightseers, and after pausing for a short while to look at the church, they drove on, up a gentle acclivity leading to the village of Mont St. Jean, three miles farther on.

Here the chaussée diverged, one fork continuing over the brow of a hill, and crossing, a little over half a mile beyond Mont St. Jean, an unpaved hollow-road running from Wavre to Braine l'Alleud, towards Charleroi; and the other running in a south-westerly direction towards Nivelles. The Nivelles road, which the coachman had been instructed to follow, was straight and uninteresting, bordered by straggling hedges, and proceeding over undulating ground until it descended presently between high banks into a ravine extending from the village of Merbe Braine to Hougoumont.

The Château was situated to the south of the hollow-road from Wavre, which here, having taken a turn to the south-west, crossed the Nivelles chaussée; and to the east of the chaussée, from which it was approached by an avenue of fine elm trees. The Count's directions had been exact; the coachman turned into the avenue without hesitation; and the carriage bowled along under the spreading branches, and soon passed through the northern gate-way of the Château. The travellers found themselves in a paved courtyard, surrounded by a motley collection of buildings.

The Château was one of the many such residences to be found in the Netherlands, a semi-fortified house, half manor, half farm. The Château itself, built of stone and brick, was a pretty house, with shuttered windows; there was a small chapel at the southern end of the courtyard; and opposite the Château, on the western side, were some picturesque barns. A gardener's cottage and a cowshed made up the rest of the buildings, which were all clustered together in a friendly fashion, and bathed, at this moment, in pale spring sunlight.

As the barouche drew up outside the door of the Château, Barbara strolled out, with the tail of her habit caught up over one arm, and a glass of wine in her hand. She had taken off her hat, and her short red curls were clustering over her head in not unpleasing disorder. She looked rather mannish, and neither her eyes nor her glancing smile held a hint of the softness which Judith had seen in both the day before.

"Have you had a pleasant drive?" she called out. "We beat you, you observe."

"Yes, a delightful drive," replied Judith, stepping out of the carriage. "And I have now fallen quite in love with this pretty little Château! How cosy it is! There is nothing stiff, nothing at all formal about these Flemish country-houses."

Lavisse came out of the house at this moment, and while he welcomed the ladies, and directed the coachman where to stable his horses, Barbara stood leaning negligently against the door-post, sipping her wine and blinking, cat-like, at the sunshine.

The owner of the house was away, but Lavisse, who appeared to be quite at home, had advised the house-keeper of his advent, and a light luncheon had been prepared for the party. A *fille de chambre* conducted the ladies upstairs to a bedroom where they could leave their pelisses and bonnets, and when they were ready led them down again to a parlour overlooking a walled garden with an orchard beyond.

A table had been laid in the middle of the room, and a fire burned in the hearth. Barbara was lounging in the window, leaning her shoulders against the lintel. As Judith and Harriet came in, a burst of laughter from the two men indicated that she was in funning humour.

The Count at once came forward. He drew Harriet to a chair by the fire, declaring that she must be chilled from the long drive, and insisted on her taking a glass of wine. She accepted, and he stayed by her, engaging her in conversation, while Judith went to the window to admire the garden.

It was laid out in neat walks, much of it under cultivation for vegetables, but there were some flower-beds as well, and the tops of the fruit-trees beyond the mellow brick wall were heavy with blossom. From the window could be seen rose-bushes, some fine fig trees, and several orange trees. Judith thought the garden must be enchanting in summer.

"I daresay it is," agreed Barbara. "We might arrange another expedition here, perhaps in June."

"June! Who knows what may have happened by then?"

"Oh, you are thinking of the war, are you? I am tired of it: we have heard too much of it, and nothing ever happens."

"It certainly seems out of place in this peaceful little Château," Judith remarked. "You must have had a delightful ride through the Forest. Such noble trees! I do not think there can be any tree to compare with the beech."

"Beech trees, are they? To tell you the truth, I did not notice them particularly," said Barbara. "Etienne, fill my glass, if you please!"

"Ah, allow *me!*" Peregrine said, hurrying to the table for the decanter that stood on it.

She held out her glass, smiling at him. He filled it, and his own, saying audaciously: "To your green eyes, Lady Bab!"

She laughed. "To your blue ones, Sir Peregrine!"

Luncheon was brought in at this moment, and soon the whole party was seated round the table, partaking of minced chicken and scalloped oysters.

Lady Barbara was in spirits, the Count scarcely less so, and everything might have gone off merrily enough had not Lady Taverner taken one of her rare dislikes to Barbara. Like many shy women, she had some strong prejudices. She had never liked Barbara. Until to-day, she had known her merely by sight and by repute, and, being a just little creature, had refused to condemn her. But from the moment of seeing Barbara come down the steps of her home in her Hussar dress she had felt that gossip had not lied. Barbara was fast, and, since she chose deliberately to ride off alone with a dreadful rake, unprincipled into the bargain. She offended every canon of good taste: lounged like a man, tossed off her wine like a man, and (thought Harriet, in her innocence) swore like a trooper. Listening to her conversation at the luncheon table, Harriet decided that some of her sallies were a trifle warm. Shocked, and with a very prim expression on her face, she tried to give the conversation a more decorous turn. It was too pointed an attempt; Barbara looked at her, blankly at first, and then in frank amusement. She addressed an idle remark to Harriet, received the chilliest of monosyllables in reply, and openly laughed.

Judith intervened, and the awkward moment passed. But as Harriet, mortified by the laugh, remained for the rest of the meal apparently oblivious of Barbara's presence, she began to wish that she had never hit upon the idea of arranging this pleasure-party. The task of talking to Harriet without ignoring Barbara taxed her powers to the utmost, and by the time they rose from the table she would have been hard put to it to say which of the two ladies she most blamed.

Luncheon at an end, a walk in the orchard and wood was proposed. Harriet declined it, but when she had been comfortably settled with a book by the fire, the rest of the party strolled out into the garden, and after wandering about its paths for a little while, made their way into the orchard. Daffodils were growing under the fruit trees in great profusion. Judith could not resist the temptation of picking some. The Count gave instant permission: his cousin would be only too happy! had, in fact, written to beg that the visitors would consider the Château their own. She soon had an armful; he very considerately ran back to the house with them, to save her the trouble of carrying them; and returned to find her waiting for him under a gnarled old apple tree, Barbara having gone off to explore the wood with Peregrine.

Judith believed Peregrine to be too devoted to his Harriet to be in danger of succumbing to Barbara's charms, but the light raillery that had been going on between them made her feel a little uneasy. Courtesy had obliged her to wait for Lavisse's return, but when he joined her it was she, and not he, who suggested catching up with the others.

They made their way into the wood, but after they had been walking about for a time without seeing anything of the truants, the Count suggested that they should follow the track which led from the Château, through the wood, and over a slight hill to the Charleroi road.

"I mentioned to Bab that there is a view to be obtained from the top of the hill. Without doubt they have gone there," he said. "You will not be too tired? It is perhaps a kilometre's distance."

"I should enjoy it of all things. This spring weather is invigorating, don't you agree?"

"Certainly. But I fear my poor country must disappoint one accustomed to the varied scene in England."

"By no means. Perhaps there is a variety in England not elsewhere to be found: I myself am a native of Yorkshire, where, we flatter ourselves, we have unsurpassed grandeur. But there is something very taking about this country of yours. If you have none of the rugged beauty I could show you in Yorkshire, you have instead a homely, thriving scene which must inevitably please. So many rivers, so many neat farmsteads, shady copses, and rich fields!"

"This is unexpected praise, madame. Bab declares my country to be too tame. Nothing can happen here, she says."

"She speaks lightly," Judith replied. "*My* knowledge of history, though not at all profound, reminds me that, in spite of every appearance to the contrary, stirring events have happened here."

"You are thinking of your Duke of Marlborough. It is true: this poor land of mine has been often the battle-field of Europe, and may be so yet again—perhaps many times: who knows?"

"Oh, do not think of such a thing! There must be no

more wars: we seem to have been fighting ever since I can remember! We shall defeat Bonaparte, and win a lasting peace. Can you doubt it?"

"Be sure I do not desire to doubt it, madame," he replied.

They were climbing a slight hill, and were soon rewarded by the sight of Barbara and Peregrine, resting at the top. Barbara had found shelter from the wind in the lee of a hedge, and was sitting on the bank. She waved, and called out: "It is all a hum! Nothing to be seen but a plain sprinkled with hillocks, and a great many fields of green corn."

Country-bred Peregrine corrected her. "No, no, you understate, Lady Bab! There are fields of rye as well, and at least two of clover. What a height the crops must grow to here! I never saw anything to equal it, so early in the year!"

"Oh, now you go beyond me! I find myself at one with Dr. Johnson, who declared—did he not?—that one green field was just like another!"

"Horrid old man!" said Judith, who had come up to them by this time. She looked around her. "Why, how could you libel the view so perversely? How pretty the grey stone walls look through the trees! Is that the Charleroi road?"

"Yes, madame," said Lavisse. "The little farm you are looking at is La Belle Alliance."

"Delightful!" said Judith. "So many of the villages and the farms here have pretty names, I find. Can we see the place where you are quartered from here?"

"No, it is too far. I ride to it by the Nivelles road, until I am tired of that way, which is, in effect, quite straight and not very amusing. If you should ever honour Nivelles with a visit, I recommend you to come by the Charleroi road. It is a little longer, but you would be pleased, I think, with the village of Vieux-Genappe which one passes through. There is an old stone bridge, and many of the quaint cottages you admire."

"I know the way you mean," said Peregrine. "I went to Nivelles one day last autumn, with a party of friends, and I believe we turned off the chaussée at a cross-road about four miles beyond Genappe."

"That would be Quatre-Bras," said the Count.

"Another pretty name for you, Lady Worth," said Barbara. "What is that monument I can see in the distance, Etienne?"

He glanced southwards, following the direction of her pointing finger. "Merely the Observatory. There is nothing here of interest, no monuments, no famous scenes."

"Very true; it is infamously tame!" she said, with one of her flickering smiles. "And yet I don't know! Had you taken us to Malplaquet, or Audenarde, you would have dragged us through hedges and over muddy fields to look at an old battlefield, I daresay. Nothing is more tedious, for there is never anything to be seen but what you may as well look at anywhere else! My late husband plagued my life out with such expeditions. I have seen Sedgemoor, and Naseby, and Newbury—*two* battlefields there, as I remember—and I give you my word there was nothing to choose between any of them, except that one was not so far from the road as another."

Peregrine, who had been gazing abstractedly to the south, said: "Well, I suppose for all we know there might be a battle fought hereabouts, might there not? Isn't the Charleroi road one of the main ways into France?"

"Oh, don't, Perry!" said his sister. "This is too peaceful a spot for battles. There are other ways into France, are there not, Count?"

"Assuredly, madame. There is, for instance, the road through Mons. But Sir Peregrine has reason. It is to guard this highway that my division is quartered about Nivelles."

"Oh, you don't frighten us, Etienne!" said Barbara. "When Boney comes—*if* he comes, which I am beginning to doubt—you will meet him at the frontier, and send him about his business. Or he may send you about yours. I shall certainly remain in Brussels. How exciting to be besieged!"

"How can you talk so?" Judith said, vexed at the

flippancy of these remarks. "You do not know what you are saying! Come, it is time we were returning to the Château!"

But at this Barbara began to take a perverse interest in her surroundings, desiring Lavisse to name all the hamlets she could perceive, and wishing that she could explore the dark belt of woods some miles to the east of them. From where they stood, half a mile to the west of La Belle Alliance, a good view of the undulating country towards Brussels could be obtained, and not until Lavisse had pointed out insignificant farmsteads such as La Hay Sainte, north of La Belle Alliance, on the chaussée; and obscure villages such as Papelotte, and Smohain, away to the east, could she be induced to quit the spot. But at last, when she had satisfied herself that the rising ground beyond the hollow cross-road that intersected the chaussée made it impossible for her to see Mont St. Jean, and that the wood she wished to explore was quite three miles away, she consented to go back to the Château.

Lady Taverner had been dozing by the fire, and woke with a guilty start when the others rejoined her. A glance at the clock on the mantelpiece made her exclaim that she had no notion that the afternoon could be so far advanced. She began to think of her children, of course inconsolable without her, and begged Judith to order the horses to be put to.

This was soon done, and in a very short time Harriet was seated in the barouche, warmly tucked up in a rug, with her hands buried deep in her muff.

Barbara was standing in the doorway when Judith came out of the house, and said: "I wonder where Charles is now?"

"In Ghent, I suppose," Judith replied.

"I wish he had been with us," Barbara said, with a faint sigh.

"I wish it too."

"Oh! you are disliking me again? Well, I am sorry for it, but the truth is that respectable females and I don't deal together. I should be grateful to you for getting this party together. Shall I thank you? Confess that it has been an odious day!"

"Yes, odious," Judith said.

She directed a somewhat chilly look at Barbara as she spoke, and for an instant thought that she saw the glitter of tears on the ends of her lashes. But before she could be sure of it Barbara had turned from her, and was preparing to mount her horse. The next glimpse she had of her face made the very idea of tears seem absurd. She was laughing, exchanging jests with Peregrine, once more in reckless spirits.

Any plan that Peregrine might have formed of deserting the barouche was nipped in the bud by his sister, who said so pointedly that she was glad to have the escort of one gentleman at least that there was nothing for him to do but jog along beside the carriage with the best grace he could muster.

Lavisse and Barbara soon allowed their horses to drop into a walk; the barouche outstripped them, and was presently lost to sight over the brow of a slight hill. Lavisse studied Barbara's profile with a faint smile, and said softly: "Little fool! Little adorable fool!"

"Don't tease me! I could weep with vexation!"

"I know well that you could. But why?"

"Oh, because I'm bored—tired—anything that you please!"

"It does not please me that you should be bored or tired. I do not wonder at it, however. For me, these saintly Englishwomen are the devil."

"I don't dislike Lady Worth, if only she would not look so disapproving."

"Consider, my Bab, she will do so all your life."

"Oh, confound her, I'll take care she don't get the chance!"

"*Ma pauvre*, I see you surrounded by prim relatives, growing staid—or mad!"

"Wretch! Be quiet!"

"But no, I will not be quiet. Figure to yourself the difference were you to marry me!"

An irrepressible laugh broke from her. "I do. I should then be surrounded by your light-o'-loves. I have seen enough of that in my own family to be cured of wanting to marry a rake."

"You have in England a saying that a reformed rake——"

"My dear Etienne, if you were reformed you would be as dull as the next man. You are wasting your eloquence. I do not love you more than a very little. You are an admirable flirt, I grant, and I find you capital company."

"Do you find your Colonel—capital company?"

She turned her head, regarding him with one of her clear looks. "Do you know, I have never thought of that: it has not occurred to me. It is the oddest thing, but if you were to ask me, what does he look like? how does he speak? I couldn't tell you. I think he is handsome; I suppose him to be good company, because it doesn't bore me to be with him. But I can't particularize him. I can't say, he is handsome, he is witty, or he is clever. I can only say, he is Charles."

The smile had quite faded from his face; his horse leapt suddenly under a spur driven cruelly home: "Ah, *parbleu*, you are serious then!" he exclaimed. "You are love-sick —besotted! I wish you a speedy recovery, *ma belle!*"

CHAPTER X

JUDITH saw nothing of Barbara on the following day, but heard of her having gone to a fête at Enghien, given by the Guards. She was present in the evening at a small party at Lady John Somerset's, surrounded by her usual court, and had nothing more than a nod and a wave of the hand to bestow upon Judith. The Comte de Lavisse had returned to his cantonments, but his place seemed to be admirably filled by Prince Pierre d'Aremberg, whose attentions, though possibly not serious, were extremely marked.

If Barbara missed Colonel Audley during the five days

131

of his absence, she gave no sign of it. She seemed to plunge into a whirl of enjoyment; flitted from party to party; put in an appearance at the Opera; left before the end to attend a ball; danced into the small hours; rode out before breakfast with a party of young officers; was off directly after to go to the races at Grammont; reappeared in Brussels in time to grace her sister-in-law's soirée; and enchanted the company by singing *O Lady, twine no wreath for me*, which had just been sent to her from London, along with a setting of Lord Byron's famous lyric, *Farewell, Farewell!*

"How can she do it?" marvelled the Lennox girls. "*We* should be dead with fatigue!"

On the 20th April Brussels was fluttered by the arrival of a celebrated personage, none other than Madame Catalani, a cantatrice who had charmed all Europe with her trills and her quavers. Accompanied by her husband, M. de Valbrèque, she descended upon Brussels for the purpose of consenting graciously (and for quite extortionate fees) to sing at a few select parties.

On the same evening Wellington drove into Brussels with his suite, and Colonel Audley, instead of ending a long day by drinking tea quietly at home and going to bed, arrayed himself in his dress uniform and went off to put in a tardy appearance at Sir Charles Stuart's evening-party. He found his betrothed in an alcove, having each finger kissed by an adoring young Belgian, and waited perfectly patiently for this ceremony to come to an end. But Barbara saw him before her admirer had got beyond the fourth finger, and pulled her hands away, not in any confusion, but merely to hold them out to the Colonel. "Oh, Charles! You have come back!" she cried gladly.

The Belgian, very red in the face, and inwardly quaking, stayed just long enough for Colonel Audley to challenge him to a duel if he wished to, but when he found that the Colonel was really paying no attention to him, he discreetly withdrew, thanking his gods that the English were a phlegmatic race.

The Colonel took both Barbara's hands in his. Mischief

132

gleamed in her eyes. She said: "Would you like to finish René's work, dear Charles?"

"No, not at all," he answered, drawing her closer.

She held up her face. "Very well! Oh, but I am glad to see you again!"

They sat down together on a small sofa. "You did not appear to be missing me very much!" said the Colonel.

"Don't be stupid! Tell me what you have been doing!"

"There's nothing to tell. What have *you* been doing? Or daren't you tell me?"

"That's impertinent. I have been forgetting Charles in a whirl of gaiety."

"Faithless one!"

"I have been to the Races, and was quite out of luck; I went to the Opera, but it was Gluck and detestable; I have danced endless waltzes and cotillions, but no one could dance as well as you; I went to a macao-party, and was dipped; to Enghien, and was kissed——"

"What?"

He had been listening with a smile in his eyes, but this vanished, and he interrupted with enough sharpness in his voice to arrest her attention and make her put up her chin a little.

"Well?"

"Did you mean that?"

"What, that I was kissed at Enghien? My dear Charles!"

"It's no answer to say 'My dear Charles', Bab."

"But can you doubt it? Don't you think I am very kissable?"

"I do, but I prefer that others should not."

"Oh no! how dull that would be!" she said, sparkling with laughter.

"Don't you agree that there is something a trifle vulgar in permitting Tom, Dick and Harry to kiss you?"

"That's to say *I'm* vulgar, Charles. Am I, do you think?"

"The wonder is that you are not."

"The wonder?"

"Yes, since you do vulgar things."

She flushed, and looking directly into his eyes, said: "You are not wise to talk like that to me, my friend."

"My dear, did you suppose I should be so complaisant as to allow other men to kiss you? What an odd notion you must have of me!"

"I warned you I should flirt?"

"And I warned you it would only be with me. To be plain with you, I expect you not to kiss any but myself."

"Tom, Dick and Harry!" she flashed, betraying a wound.

"Yes—or, for instance, the Comte de Lavisse."

There was an edge to the words; she glanced swiftly at him, understanding all at once that he was actuated as much by jealousy as by prudery. The anger left her face; she exclaimed: "Charles! Dear fool! You're quite out: it wasn't Etienne!"

He said ruefully: "Wasn't it? Yes, I did think so."

"And were longing to call him out!"

"Nothing so romantic. Merely to plant him a facer."

She was amused. "What the devil's that?"

"Boxing cant. Forget it! If you were to add that to your vocabulary it would be beyond everything!"

"Oh, but I know a deal of boxing cant! My brother George is much addicted to the Fancy—himself *displays to advantage*, so I'm told! No *shifting*, not at all *shy*; in fact *rattles in full of gaiety!*"

"Bab, you incorrigible hussy!"

Their disagreement was forgotten; she began to talk to him of George, who was already on his passage to the Netherlands.

It was evident that George, a year older than his sister, was very near her heart. Colonel Audley was barely acquainted with him, but no one who had once met Lord George could fail to recognize him again. When he arrived in Brussels some days later it was from Liedekerke, in the vicinity of Ninove, where he was quartered. He rode into Brussels with the intention of surprising his family at dinner, but happening to encounter a friend on his way up the Montagne de la Cour, went off instead to join a riotous party at the Hôtel d'Angleterre. When he presented himself in the Rue Ducale some hours later it was to learn from the butler that Lord and Lady Vidal were at the Opera, and his sister at a soirée.

"Well, I won't go to the Opera, that's certain," said his lordship. "What's this soirée you talk of?"

"I understand, my lord, a gathering of polite persons, with a little music, a——"

"Sounds devilish," remarked his lordship. "Who's holding it?"

"Lord and Lady Worth, my lord."

"Lady Worth, eh?" His lordship pricked up his ears. "Oh! Ah! I'll go there. Won't throw me out, will they?"

The butler looked horrified. "Throw you out, my lord?"

"Haven't been invited: don't know the Worths," explained George. "I'll risk it. Where do they live?"

Judith's salons were crowded when he arrived, and since the evening was too far advanced for her to expect any more guests, she had left her station by the door and was standing at the other end of the long room, talking to two Belgian ladies. The footman's voice, announcing Lord George, was not audible above the clatter of conversation, and Judith remained unaware of his entrance until Madame van der Capellan directed her attention towards him, desiring to know who *ce beau géant* might be.

She turned her head, and saw his lordship standing on the threshold, looking round him with an air of perfect sang-froid. A handsome giant was a description which exactly hit him off. He stood over six foot, in all the magnificence of a Life Guardsman's dress uniform. He was a blaze of scarlet and gold; a very dark young man with curling black hair, and dashing whiskers, gleaming white teeth, and a pair of bold, fiery eyes.

"It is Lord George Alastair," said Judith. She moved towards him, by no means pleased at the advent of this uninvited guest.

He came at once to meet her. His bow was perfection; the look that went with it was that of a schoolboy detected in crime. "Lady Worth?"

"Yes," she acknowledged. "You——"

"I know! I know! You're not acquainted with me—don't know me from Adam—wonder how the deuce I got in!"

She was obliged to smile. "Indeed, I do know you. You are Lord George Alastair."

"Oh, come now, that's famous! I daresay you won't have me thrown out after all."

"I am sure it would be a very difficult task," she said. "You have come in search of your sister, I expect? She is here, and your brother too. I think they must both be in the further salon. Shall we go and find them?"

"Devilish good of you, Lady Worth. But don't put yourself out on my account: I'll find 'em."

She saw that he was looking beyond her, at someone at the other end of the room. She glanced in the same direction, and discovered that the object of his gaze was none other than Miss Devenish. It was plain that Lucy was aware of being stared at; she was blushing uncomfortably, and had cast down her eyes.

"I will show you the way to your sister," said Judith firmly.

"Thank you—in a moment!" said his lordship, with cool impudence. "I have seen a lady I know. Must pay my respects!"

He left her side as he spoke, and bore ruthlessly down upon Miss Devenish. She was seated on a sofa, and cast such a scared look up at George that Judith felt impelled to go to her rescue. George was towering over her— enough to frighten any girl! thought Judith indignantly —and Lucy had half-risen from the sofa, and then sunk back again.

By the time Judith, delayed by Mr. Creevey in the middle of the room, reached her, George had not only shaken hands, but had seated himself beside her. His eyes were fixed on her downcast face with an ardent expression Judith much disliked, and a teasing smile, as impish as his sister's, curled his lips. When Judith came up he rose. "I am recalling myself to Miss Devenish's memory," he said. "It's my belief she had forgotten me."

136

"I was not aware that you were acquainted with Lord George, my dear?" Judith said, a question in her voice.

"Oh!" faltered Lucy. "We met once—at a ball!"

"If that is all, it is no wonder that you were forgotten, Lord George!" Judith said.

"All! No such thing! Miss Devenish, can you look me in the face and say we met only once, at a ball?"

She did look him in the face, but with such an expression of reproach in her eyes as must have abashed any but an Alastair. She replied in a low voice, and with a good deal of dignity: "It is true that we have several times met: I do not forget it."

She got up as she spoke, and with a slight inclination of her head moved away to where her aunt was seated. Lord George looked after her for a moment, and then turned to his hostess, saying briskly: "Where's Bab? In the other salon? I'll go and find her. Now, don't bother your head about me, Lady Worth, I beg! I shall do very well."

She was perfectly willing to let him go, and with a nod and a smile he was off, making his way across the crowded room through the double-doors leading into the further salon. These had been thrown open, and as he approached them George saw his brother Harry standing between them in conversation with Lord Hay. He waved casually, but Harry, as soon as he caught sight of him, left Hay and surged forward.

"Hallo, George! When did you arrive? Where are you quartered? I am devilish glad to see you!"

George answered these questions rather in a manner of a man receiving a welcome of a boisterous puppy; twitted Harry on the glory of his brand-new regimentals; and demanded: "Where's Bab?"

"Oh, with Audley somewhere, I daresay! But what a hand you are, not to have written to tell us you were coming!"

"Who's Audley?" interrupted George, looking over the heads of several people in an attempt to see his sister.

"Why, Worth's brother, to be sure! Lord, don't you know? Bab's going to marry him—or so she says."

This piece of intelligence seemed to amuse George. "Poor devil! No, I didn't know. New, is it?"

"Oh, they've been engaged for a fortnight or more! Look, there they both are!"

A moment later Barbara was startled by an arm being put familiarly round her waist. "Hallo, Bab, my girl!" said his lordship.

She turned quickly in his embrace, an exclamation on her lips. "George! You wretch, to creep up behind me like that!"

He kissed her cheek, and continued to hold her round the waist. "What's all this I hear about your engagement?" He glanced at Colonel Audley, and held out his free hand. "You're Audley, aren't you? How d'ye do? Think we've met before, but can't recall where. What the devil do you mean by getting engaged to my sister? You'll regret it, you know!"

"But you must see that I can't, in honour, draw back now," returned the Colonel, shaking hands. "When did you arrive? At Liedekerke, aren't you? We're deuced glad to see you fellows, I can tell you. How strong are you?"

"Two squadrons. What are these Dutchmen like, hey? Saw some of them on our way up from Ostend. They're not so badly mounted, but they can't ride."

"That's the trouble," admitted the Colonel. "A great many of them are shocking bad riders. You know we are not getting Combermere to command the cavalry after all? The Horse Guards are sending Lord Uxbridge out to us."

"Oh, he's a good fellow! You'll like him. But you've served under him, of course. You were with Moore, weren't you? I say, Audley, you Peninsular fellows have the advantage of us—and by Jove, don't you mean to let us know it! A damned Rifleman I met to-night called *my* lot Hyde Park soldiers!"

"So you knocked him down, and poor Vidal will be faced with another scandal!" remarked Barbara.

"No, I didn't. Fellow was my host. But when it

138

comes to fighting we'll show you what Hyde Park soldiers can do!"

Barbara, who was tired of a purely military conversation, changed the subject by asking him how her grandfather did. He confessed that he had not seen that irascible gentleman quite lately, but thought—from the energetic tone of his correspondence—that he was enjoying his customary vigorous health.

"In debt again?" asked Barbara. "Would he not come to the rescue?"

"Oh lord, no! Wrote that he'd see me to the devil first!" replied George. "But I daresay if I come out of this little war alive he'll pay up."

"Return of a hero?" enquired the Colonel. "You'd better get wounded."

"Devilish good notion," agreed his lordship. "Of course if I'm killed it won't matter to me how many debts I've got. Either way I'm bound to win. What are the Prussians like, Audley?"

"I haven't seen much of them, so far. Old Blücher has arrived at Liége, and says he can put 80,000 men in the field. Some of them pretty raw, of course—like our own."

"Queer old boy, Blücher," remarked George. "Saw him last year, when he was in London with the Emperors and all that crowd. Seemed to take very well—people used to cheer him whenever he showed his face out of doors."

Lady Barbara moved away; Lord George wandered off, and presently discovered Miss Devenish again. He apparently prevailed upon her to present him to her aunt, for when Judith caught sight of him an hour later he was sitting beside Mrs. Fisher, making himself agreeable. Judith could see that Mrs. Fisher was pleased with him, and hoped that she would not allow herself to be carried away by a title and a handsome face. She had little dependence, however, on that amiable lady's judgment, and was not much surprised to see her beckon to her niece to come and join in her chat with Lord George. Miss Devenish obeyed the summons, but reluctantly. Lord George jumped up as she approached, and in a few minutes succeeded in detaching her from her aunt and bearing her off in the direction of the parlour, where the refreshments were laid out.

It was not until the end of the evening, when her guests were beginning to disperse, that Judith found an opportunity to speak to Lucy. She said then: "I hope Lord George did not tease you? He is rather a bold young man, I am afraid."

Lucy coloured, but replied quietly: "Oh no! I knew him before, in England."

"Yes, so you told me. I was surprised: I don't think you ever mentioned the circumstance to me?"

There was a little hesitation, a faltering for words. "I daresay I might not. The occasion did not arise, our acquaintance was not of such a nature——"

"My dear, why should you? I implied no blame! But I was sorry to see him single you out with such particularity. I could see you were a little discomposed, and did not wonder at it. His manners are a great deal too familiar."

Miss Devenish opened and shut her fan once or twice, and replied: "I was discomposed, I own. The surprise of seeing him here—and his singling me out, as you describe, put me out of countenance."

"The attentions of men of his type are apt to be very disagreeable," said Judith. "Happily, the violent fancies they take do not last long. I believe Lord George to be a shocking flirt. You, however, have too much common sense to take him seriously."

"Oh yes! That is, I know what people say of him. Forgive me, but there are circumstances which make it painful for me to discuss—but it is not in my power to explain."

"Why, Lucy, what is this?" Judith exclaimed. "I had not thought your acquaintance to be more than a chance meeting at a ball!"

"It was a little more than that. I became acquainted with him when I was staying in Brighton with my cousins last year. There was a degree of intimacy which—which I could not avoid."

140

Her voice failed. Judith suspected that the attentions of a dashing young officer had not been wholly unwelcome. She had no doubt that Lord George had speedily over-stepped the bounds of propriety, and understood, with ready sympathy, Lucy's feelings upon being confronted with him again. She said kindly: "I perfectly understand, and beg you won't think yourself bound to confide in me. There is not the least necessity!"

She was obliged to turn away directly after, to shake hands with a departing guest. Lucy rejoined her aunt, who was making signs to her that it was time to go, and no further talk was held on the subject. Lord George, who was engaged with a dazzling brunette, did not observe her departure. Judith, who knew that at least two other ladies had been the objects of his gallantry that evening, was encouraged to hope that his persecution of Lucy had been nothing more than a piece of Alastair devilry, designed merely to make the poor child uncomfortable.

He soon came up to take his leave. He was escorting his sister, whose head just topped his broad shoulder. In spite of the difference in colouring there was a remarkable like-ness between them. Spiritually, too, they seemed to be akin; they delighted in the same mischief, used the same careless, engaging manners, shocked the world like children anxious to attract attention to themselves. Judith, con-fronting them, admitted their charm, and looked indulgently on such a handsome couple.

"I have spent a capital evening, Lady Worth," said George. "When you give your next party I hope you may send me a card. I shall certainly come."

"Of course," she replied. "I am glad you took your courage in your hands and came to-night. It would have been a sad thing not to have seen your sister after riding all that way for the purpose."

"Did he tell you he had come expressly to see me?" said Barbara. "George, what a liar you are! Depend upon it, Lady Worth, he had quite another quarry in mind. Shall I see you at the Review to-morrow?"

"At Nivelles? Oh no! It is too far—and only a Review

141

of Belgian troops. I shall wait to see our own troops reviewed, I believe."

"Then we shall not meet. But you will be at the Duke's party, I daresay, on Friday. Oh, where is Charles? He must procure an invitation for George!"

She drew her hand from her brother's arm as she spoke, and darted off to find the Colonel. She soon came back with him; he promised that a card should be sent to George, and accompanied them both to the door of the carriage. George shook hands at parting, and said warmly: "You're a good fellow: I wish you happy—though I don't above half like to find Bab engaged to a damned Staff Officer, I can tell you!"

"We all have our crosses!" retorted the Colonel. "Mine is to be saddled with a Hyde Park soldier for a brother-in-law."

"Oh, the devil! You know, you're so puffed up, you Peninsular men, that there's no bearing with you! Good-night: I shall see you on Friday, I suppose?"

He got into the carriage beside his sister and settled himself in one corner. "Well, that makes the tenth since Childe died," he remarked.

"No! I was only once engaged before!"

"Twice."

"Oh, you are thinking of Ralph Dashwood! *That* was never announced, and can't signify. I am serious now."

He gave a hoot of laughter. "Until the next man drifts by! Has he any money?"

"I suppose him to have a younger son's portion. He is not rich."

"Well, what the devil made you choose him?" demanded George. "I see no sense in it!"

"I don't care for money," she replied pettishly.

"More fool you, then. I never knew you when you weren't dipped. Besides, this fellow Audley: I like him, he's a good man—but he ain't your sort, Bab."

"True, but I loved him from the first. I don't know how it came about. Isn't it odd that one should keep one's heart intact so many years, only to have it crack for a man no more handsome or wealthy than a hundred others? I can find no reason for it, unless it be the trick his eyes have of smiling while his mouth is grave—and that's nonsensical"

He said rather gloomily: "I know what you mean. Take it from me, it's the devil."

"It *is* the devil. I wish to be good, to behave as I should —and yet I don't! If I had never been married to Childe it would be so different! Damnable to have done that to me! I believe it ruined me."

He yawned. "Where's the use in worrying? You were willing, weren't you?"

"At eighteen, and the hoyden that I was! What could I know of the matter? Papa made the match; I married to oblige my family, and wretched work I made of it! Jasper—oh, don't let us talk of him: how I grew to loathe him! I was never more glad of anything than his death, and I swore then that no one—*no one* should ever possess me again! Even though I love Charles, even when I desire most earnestly to please him, there is something in me that revolts—yes, revolts, George! It drives me to commit such acts of folly! I use him damnably, I suppose, and shall end by making us both wretched."

"Shouldn't be surprised," said George, with brotherly unconcern. "I know *I* wouldn't be in his shoes for a thousand pounds."

She underwent one of her lightning changes of mood, breaking into a gurgle of laughter. "You, without a feather to fly with! You'd sell your soul for half the sum!"

CHAPTER XI

THE Review of the Dutch-Belgian Army at Nivelles, by King William and the Duke of Wellington, passed off creditably. The Duke found the Nassau troops excellent; the Dutch Militia good, but young; and the Cavalry, though bad riders, remarkably well-mounted.

Prince Frederick impressed him as being a fine lad, and he wrote as much to Earl Bathurst, in a private letter.

The pity was that his lordship was not similarly pleased with Prince Frederick's father. He was the most difficult person to deal with his lordship had ever met. "*With professions in his mouth of a desire to do everything I can suggest, he objects to everything I propose; it then comes to be a matter of negotiation for a week, and at last is settled by my desiring him to arrange it as he pleases, and telling him that I will have nothing to say to him.*"

Bathurst, who was well acquainted with the Duke's temper, might smile a little over this letter, but there was no doubt that his lordship was being harassed on all sides. He was hampered by possessing no command over the King's Army; and he was receiving complaints of the conduct of his engineers at Ypres, who were accused of cutting his Majesty's timber for palisades. He believed the complaints to be groundless, and was not quite pleased with the way in which they were made.

But the jealousies of the Dutch and the Belgians were small matters compared with the behaviour of the Horse Guards in London. He was accustomed to meet with annoying hindrances in foreign countries, and could deal with them. The powers at the Horse Guards were irritating him far more, with their mania for sending him out bevies of ineligible young gentlemen to fill Staff posts. No sooner had he turned off eight officers from the Adjutant-General's Staff than he received an official letter from Sir Henry Torrens appointing eight others. He had written pretty sharply to Sir Henry on the subject. They talked glibly at the Horse Guards of all such appointments resting at his nomination, but, in actual fact, this was far from being true. His lordship complained of being wholly without power to name any of the officers recommended by his generals, because every place was filled from London. "*Of the list you and Colonel Shawe have sent, there are only three who have any experience at all,*" wrote his lordship acidly. "*Of those there are two, Colonel Elley and Lord Greenock, who are most fit for their situations, and I am most happy they are selected.*

. . . As for the others, if they had been proposed to me I should have rejected them all."

The very same day he was sending off another despatch to Torrens, begging him to let him see more troops before sending any more General officers. *"I have no objection; on the contrary, I wish for Cole and Picton to command divisions,"* wrote his lordship, with every intention of seeming gracious. *"I shall be very happy to have Kempt and Pack, and will do the best I can for them . . ."* Quite an affable despatch, this one, much more conciliatory than the one that was on its way to Lord Bathurst. His lordship was not getting the artillery he had demanded; instead of 150 pieces he was to have only eighty-four, including German artillery. He considered his demand to have been excessively small, and he told Bathurst so. *"You will see by reference to Prince Hardenberg's return of the Prussian Army that they take into the field nearly 80 batteries, manned by 10,000 artillery. Their batteries are of eight guns each, so that they will have about 600 pieces. They do not take this number for show or amusement,"* continued his lordship sardonically, *"and although it is impossible to grant my demand, I hope it will be admitted to be small."*

But in spite of the querulous tone of his despatches to London he was not so ill-pleased, after all. He might complain that in England they were doing nothing, and were unable to send him anything, but before April was out he was writing quite cheerfully to Hardinge, English Commissioner to the Prussians, that he was getting on in strength, and had now 60,000 men in their shoes, of whom at least 10,000 were cavalry.

He was glad when Prince Blücher arrived at the Prussian Headquarters. He liked old Marshal "Forwards", but he wished he would not write to him in German.

But Blücher, with his dozen words of English, and his execrable French, was a better man to deal with than his Chief-of-Staff. A jealous fellow, Gneisenau, always making difficulties and suspecting him of duplicity.

However, that was a minor annoyance; on the whole, his lordship was satisfied with his Prussian allies, though the circumstance of their being continually at loggerheads with King William gave him a good deal of trouble. Poor old Blücher was quite lacking in polish; nor could he be made to realize the value of tact in dealing with a fellow like King William. He was for ever omitting to make just those courteous gestures which would have cost him so little and soothed the King's dignity so much. Rather a difficult yoke-fellow, Blücher, apt to get the bit between his teeth, and, unfortunately, imbued with such a dislike of the French that he could not be brought to tolerate even the Royalists amongst them. But he was not afraid of meeting Bonaparte in the field, and he was a likeable old man, with his fierce, rosy face and fine white whiskers, his spluttering enthusiasm, and his beaming smile.

His lordship was much more comfortable at Headquarters now, for he had got his Miliary Secretary back, and Sir Colin Campbell too. His lordship was fond of Lord Fitzroy Somerset, who had lately married his niece, and had so become his nephew by marriage. Lord Fitzroy exactly suited him; for he did what he was told, never committing the appalling offence of setting up ideas of his own and acting on them. His lordship detested independently-minded subordinates. It was not the business of his officers to think for themselves. "Have my orders for whatever you do!" he said. It was an inflexible rule; nothing made him angrier than to have it broken.

Lord Fitzroy never broke it. He could be trusted to obey every order punctiliously. He got through an amazing amount of work, too, often in the most unsuitable surroundings, and always with a quiet competence that seemed to make little of the mass of correspondence on his hands. He was not one of those troublesome officers, either, who were for ever wanting to go home on leave to attend to urgent private affairs—which his lordship was convinced could be quite as well settled by correspondence. Nor had he ever discovered (just when he was most needed) that the climate in Spain disagreed with his constitution. You could always be sure of Fitzroy.

His lordship was sure of Colin Campbell, too, who had

been with him so many years, and managed his household so admirably, in spite of his inability to speak intelligibly any foreign language.

In fact, his lordship was perfectly happy in his Personal Staff. As for his General Staff, though he complained peevishly of having strangers foisted on to him, and of being unable to entrust the details of the departments to any of the young gentlemen on the Staff, he was not (if the truth were told) so very badly off there either. He might write to Torrens that he had no means of naming any of the officers he would prefer to all others, but somehow they began to appear on the General Staff: seasoned men like Elley, and Waters, Felton Hervey, Greenock, Woodford, Gomm, Shaw, and any number of others. He had Barnes for his Adjutant-General; and was getting De Lancey sent out as Quartermaster-General in place of Sir Hudson Lowe. He wanted Murray, of course: De Lancey was only a Deputy: but Murray was still in America, and he could not really blame Torrens for being unable to spirit him back to Europe.

To read his lordship's despatches you might think he had no power at all over the appointments in the Army. In one of his irritable moods, he wrote another barbed letter to Bathurst. "*I might have expected that the Generals and Staff formed by me in the last war would have been allowed to come to me again,*" he complained, and continued in a sweeping style which made Lord Bathurst grin appreciatively: "*But instead of that, I am overloaded with people I have never seen before; and it appears to be purposely intended to keep those out of my way whom I wished to have.*" His lordship felt much better after that explosion of wrath, and added: "*However, I'll do the best I can with the instruments which have been sent to assist me.*"

But gentlemen applying for Staff appointments in the Duke's army were told at the Horse Guards that the selection of officers to fill these was left to the Duke; and occasionally his lordship seemed to forget that he had no power to employ gentlemen of his own choosing. He might complain of having his hands tied, but when it came to the point his lordship seemed to do very much what he liked. When he wanted Lieutenant-Colonel Grant to come out to him to be at the head of the Intelligence Department, and Lieutenant-Colonel Scovell to take charge of the Department of Military Communications, he told Lord Fitzroy to write offering the posts to both these gentlemen, and only afterwards informed Torrens of having done so. He hoped, coolly, that it would be approved of, and, in point of fact, had not the least doubt that it would be approved of.

But you could not be surprised at his lordship's being a little testy. He was not a pessimistic man, but he rather liked to have a grievance, and was very apt to grumble that he was obliged to do everyone's work in addition to his own. He had, moreover, an overwhelming amount of work of his own to do, and endless annoyances to deal with. The wonder was not that he was peevish in his office but that he was so cheerful out of it. Quite apart from the all-important task of putting the country and the Army in a state of readiness for war, he was obliged to tackle such problems as the amounts of the subsidies to be granted to the various countries engaged in the campaign. First it was Hanover (a complicated business, that); then Austria; then Russia (shocking people to deal with, the Russians); and next it would be the Duke of Brunswick, already on the march with his troops to join the Army.

Subsidies one moment, wagons for the Hanoverians the next; then some quite trivial matter, such as old Arendts-childt's request for permission for certain of his officers to receive a Russian decoration: there was no end to the business requiring his lordship's attention; yet in the midst of it all he could find time to review troops, pay flying visits to garrisons, attend parties, and even to give a large party himself, and appear as light-hearted at it as though he had not a care in the world.

His lordship had a natural taste for festivities, and during his late spell of office as Ambassador to King Louis, had acquired the habit of planning his own parties on a lavish scale. His first in Brussels was a brilliant affair, comprising a dinner at the Hôtel de Belle Vue to his more important guests, including the King and Queen of the Netherlands, followed by a concert, ball, and supper at the Salle du Grand Concert, in the Rue Ducale.

It quite eclipsed the Court party, held some days previously. Everything went off without the smallest hitch; the Catalani was in her best voice; the Duke was the most affable of hosts; his Staff seconded him ably; and the Salle was so crowded with distinguished persons that it became at times quite difficult to move about.

The invitation list was indeed enormous, and had cost the Staff many a headache, for besides the English in Brussels all the Belgian and Dutch notables had received elegant, cream-laid, gilt-edged cards requesting the honour of their presence. Nearly all of them had accepted, too: the Duc d'Ursel, with his big nose and tiny chin; cheerful little Baron Hoogvorst, and Madame; competent M. van der Capellan, the Secretary of State; the Duc and Duchesse de Beaufort, and Mademoiselle; bevies of Counts and Countesses and Dowager Countesses, all with their blushing daughters and hopeful sons; and of course the Royals: King William, and his lethargic spouse, with their splendid young son, Frederick, and an extensive suite. The Prince of Orange was present as well, but could hardly be included in the Royal party, since he arrived separately, was dressed in the uniform of the Prince of Wales's Own, talked nothing but English, and consorted almost exclusively with his English friends and fellow-Generals. He had quite forgotten his huff at being superseded in the command of the Army. He was going to be given the 1st Corps, Lord Hill having the 2nd; and his dread mentor was treating him with so much confidence that he had nothing left to wish for. "*For ever your most truly devoted and affectionate William, Prince of Orange,*" was how the Prince subscribed himself exuberantly in his letters to the Duke. All he ever received in return was: "*Believe me, & etc., Wellington.*" His lordship was never fulsome. "*Je supplie Votre Altesse d'agréer en bonté les sentiments respectueux avec lesquels j'ai l'honneur d'être,*

Monseigneur, de Votre Altesse le très humble et très obéissant serviteur," would write some Prussian General painstakingly. *"Write him that I am very much obliged to him,"* scrawled the Duke at the foot of such despatches.

But the Prince of Orange was too well acquainted with his lordship to be cast down by his chilly letters. In fact, the Prince was in high fettle. His Personal Staff was composed of just the men he liked best: all English, and including his dear friend the Earl of March. He was very happy, sparkling with gaiety, looking absurdly young, and just a little conscious of the dizzy military heights to which he had risen. Sometimes he felt intoxicatingly important, and was a trifle imperious with the Generals under his command; but when he found himself in Lord Hill's presence, and looked into that kindly face, with its twinkling eyes and fatherly smile, his importance fell away from him, and he was all eager deference, just as he was with the Duke, or with the veteran Count Alten of the German Legion, whose bright, stern gaze could always disconcert him. Sir Charles Count von Alten was under the Prince, in command of the 3rd Division, which was formed of one British brigade, under Sir Colin Halkett; one brigade of the German Legion, under Baron Ompteda; and one Hanoverian brigade, under Count Kielmansegg. Count Alten was fifty-one years of age, seasoned in war, and rather grim-faced. He was an extremely competent General—so competent that even the men of the Light Division had approved of him when he had commanded them—and a somewhat alarming person for a young gentleman only twenty-four years old to have under him. He was very polite to the Prince, and they got on really very well together, but his Royal Highness was glad that the rest of the 1st Corps, with the exception of the Guards, was composed of Dutch-Belgian troops under two Generals who, though experienced soldiers, naturally had a respect for their Hereditary Prince which the English and the Germans could not be expected to share. His *bête noire*, and late Second-in-Command, Sir Henry Clinton, was commanding a division in Hill's Corps; and that much more alarming person even than Count Alten, Sir Thomas Picton, was destined for the Reserve.

Sir Thomas was not expected to arrive in the Netherlands for quite some time, but it was certain that he was coming sooner or later, for the Duke, although he did not much care for him in a personal way, had made a point of asking for him.

The latest important arrival was Lord Uxbridge. A General Order instructing Brigade Commanders of Cavalry to report in future to him had been issued from the Adjutant-General's printing office on the day of the Duke's ball. He was to have command of all the British and German cavalry, and was reputed to be a very dashing leader.

He had arrived in the Netherlands in time to attend the Duke's party, and was present at the preceding dinner. When he appeared in the Salle du Concert he attracted a great deal of attention, for the men were anxious to see what sort of a fellow he was, and the ladies could hardly drag their eyes from his resplendent person.

The Peninsula Army had been accustomed to Stapleton Cotton, now Lord Combermere, but the Earl of Uxbridge was the better cavalry General. He had served with distinction under Sir John Moore, but two circumstances had prevented his being employed under Wellington. He had been senior to the Duke, and had further complicated the situation by absconding with the wife of Wellington's brother Henry. This unfortunate affair put the Pagets and the Wellesleys on the worst of bad terms. Henry had been obliged to divorce Lady Charlotte, and any scheme of sending Lord Uxbridge out to Spain had naturally been felt to have been out of the question. Five years later, in 1815, it was an understood thing that Combermere would again command the Cavalry: the Army wanted him, and it was certain that the Duke had applied for him. But to everyone's surprise the Horse Guards sent Uxbridge instead. It was said they had done so at the instigation of that meddlesome person, the Prince Regent, and it was generally felt that the appointment would not only cause grave scandal in England but must also offend the Duke. But the Duke, like the Regent, was not remarkable for holding the marriage tie in any peculiar degree of sanctity, and upon a friend's saying to him that Lord Uxbridge's appointment would give rise to much scandal, replied, with one of his high-nosed stares: "Why?"

A little disconcerted, his well-meaning friend stammered: "Well, but—but your **Grace** cannot have forgotten the affair of Lady Charlotte!"

"No! I haven't forgotten that."

"Oh! Well—well, that's not all, you know. They say Uxbridge runs away with everyone he can."

"I'll take damned good care he don't run away with me!" replied the Duke caustically. "I don't care about anyone else."

The Army, like the Duke, did not care a button for Lord Uxbridge's amatory adventures: it merely wanted a good cavalry leader. Lord Uxbridge was said to be a veritable Murat: it remained to be seen whether this was true. He was also said to be very haughty. He did not seem so, at first glance: his manners were most polished, his smile ready, and his handshake freely given. His mouth had, indeed, a slightly disdainful curve, and his brilliant dark eyes were rather heavy-lidded, which made them look a little contemptuous, but he showed no signs of snubbing junior officers (which rumour accused him of doing frequently), and seemed, without being over-conciliatory, or in any way affected, to be bent on getting on good terms with his people.

Like the Prince of Orange, he wore full-dress Hussar uniform, but with what a difference! No amount of silver lace, swinging tassels, rich fur, or shining buttons could invest the Prince's meagre form with dignity. In that most splendid of uniforms he looked over-dressed, and rather ridiculous. But Lord Uxbridge, tall and most beautifully proportioned, carried it off to perfection. He was forty-seven years old, but looked younger, and was obviously something of a dandy. His white net pantaloons showed not a single crease; over a jacket fitting tightly to the body and almost obscured by the frogs that adorned it, he wore a furred and braided pelisse, caught round his neck with tasselled cords and flung back to hang negligently over his left shoulder. Under the stiff, silver-encrusted collar of his jacket, a black cravat was knotted, with the points of his shirt collar just protruding above it. Several glittering orders, very neat side-whiskers, and fashionably arranged hair completed his appearance. He had not brought his lady out from England, but whether he had left her behind out of tact or from the circumstance of her being in the expectation of a Happy Event was a matter for conjecture. Two of his Aides-de-Camp were with him: Major Thornhill, of his own Regiment, the 7th Hussars; and Captain Seymour, supposed to be the strongest man in the British Army. He was certainly the largest: he topped even the Life Guardsmen, and had such a gigantic frame that he was a butt to his friends and an object of considerable respect to everyone else.

As usual, the military predominated at the ball. Lord Hill was present, with all three of his brothers; Generals Maitland and Byng; old Sir John Vandeleur, very bluff and affable; General Adam; Sir Henry Clinton, with Lady Susan on his arm; General Colville, who had come all the way from Audenarde to attend the function; Sir Hussey Vivian, with his shattered hand in a sling, but still perfectly capable of leading his Hussar brigade in any charge; Sir William Ponsonby, newly arrived from England with the Union Brigade of Heavy Dragoons; handsome Colonel Sir Frederick Ponsonby, of another branch of the family, with his sister, Lady Caroline Lamb; both the gallant Halketts, Sir Colin and his brother Hew; the Adjutant-General, sharp-faced and fiery-spirited; Colonel Arendtschildt, talking to everyone in his incorrigibly bad English; General Perponcher; and genial Baron Chassé, whom the French, under whom he had served, called Captain Bayonette; Baron Constant de Rebecque, a favourite with the Peninsula officers; Count Bylandt, from Nivelles; and a cluster of Dutch and Belgian cavalry leaders: Baron Ghigny, a little assertive; Baron van Merlen, a little melancholy; General Trip, a heavy man, like his own Carabiniers.

Besides these distinguished personages, there were any number of young officers, all very smart and gallant, and acquitting themselves nobly on the floor of the ballroom under the Duke's indulgent eye. Provided there was no question of neglected duty involved, his lordship liked to see his boys dancing the night through, and always made a point of inviting young officers (of the best families, of course) to his balls. They made a good impression on foreigners: such a nice-looking, well-set-up lot as they were! But besides that, his lordship liked the younger men; he kept his eye on the promising ones amongst them, and would very often single them out above their elders. Colborne had been one of his favoured young men; Harry Smith, that mad boy with the Spanish child-wife; and poor Somers Cocks, who had ended a brilliant career at Burgos. "The young ones will always beat the old ones," said his lordship, and those he chose for his patronage certainly seemed to prove the truth of his dictum.

As for his Personal Staff, he was really fond of those youngsters. The oldest of them was Audley at thirty-five, and the rest were mere lads in their twenties, even Lord Fitzroy, at present engaged in shepherding two Belgian ladies to a couple of seats in the front row.

The Duke's eagle eye swept the concert hall, noting with satisfaction that his family were all present, and all performing their duties as hosts to the throng of guests. A good deal of surprise had been felt in Paris at the youthful aspect of his Staff, but his lordship knew what he was about when he chose these young scions of noble houses to live with him. He did not want middle-aged men with distinguished records with him: they could be better employed elsewhere, and would, moreover, have bored him. He wanted polished young men of good families, who were of his own world, who knew how to make themselves pleasant in exalted circles, and could amuse his leisure moments with their adventures, and their fun, and their bubbling energy. On an occasion such as this they were invaluable: nothing awkward about any of them; all well-bred boys who had come to him from Oxford or Cambridge (and not from any new-fangled Military College), accustomed all their lives to moving in the first circles, and consequently assured in their manners, graceful in the ballroom, conversable in the salon.

When he came in with his Royal guests, the rest of the party was already assembled. Everyone stood up, the soldiers to attention, civilian gentlemen deeply bowing, and all the ladies swaying into curtsies like lilies in a high wind. The King and Queen acknowledged their reception, the Duke gave a quick look round, saw that everything was just as it should be, nodded his satisfaction to Colonel Audley, who happened to be standing near him, and escorted the Royals to their places.

The concert began with a Haydn Symphony, but although his lordship, who had a great appreciation of good music, enjoyed it, the *pièce de résistance* for most of his guests was the appearance of La Catalani. His lordship described her as being as sharp as a Jew, and Colonel Fremantle had certainly found her so. Nothing could induce her to sing more than two songs, and she had haggled over them. However, when she mounted the platform, she looked as lovely as any angel, and when she opened her mouth and let the golden notes soar heaven-wards, even Fremantle felt that he must have misjudged her. She favoured the company first with an aria from Porto-Gullo, and then with an allegro, which showed off the flexibility of her voice to admiration. She was cheered, and encored, but there was no getting another song out of her. She curtsied again and again, blew kisses to the audience, and finally withdrew, apparently exhausted.

The dancing began soon afterwards. The Duke, finding himself standing beside Barbara Childe, said: "Lovely voice that Catalani woman has, don't you agree?"

"Yes, she sings like an angel, or a nightingale, or what-ever the creature is that sings better than all others. She has put me quite out of temper, I can tell you, for *I* had a song for you, Duke, and flattered myself I should have made a hit!"

"What? Are you going to sing to me?" he asked, delighted. "Capital! I shall enjoy *that*, I assure you! What is your voice? Why have I not heard it before?"

"Oh," she said saucily, "it is not my voice which I depended on to make the hit with you, but the song!"

"Ah, now I believe you are quizzing me, Lady Bab! What song is this?"

She looked demurely, under her lashes, and replied: "I am sure you would have been pleased! I should have sung for you *Ahé Marmont, onde vai, Marmont!*"

He gave his neigh of sudden laughter. "Oh, that's very good! That's famous! But, hush! Can't have that song nowadays, you know. Who told you about it? That rascal Audley, was it? They used to sing it a lot in Spain. Pretty tune!"

"Charming! Where was he going, poor Marmont?"

"Back to France, of course," said his lordship. "Chased out of Spain: rompéd: that's what the song's about."

"Oh, I see! He was in Brussels last month, I believe. Did you reckon him a great General, Duke?"

"Oh no, no!" he said, shaking his head. "Masséna was the best man they ever sent against me. I always found him where I least wanted him to be. Marmont used to manœuvre about in the usual French style, nobody knew with what object."

He caught sight of his niece, and beckoned to her, and patted her hand when she came up to him. "Not tired, Emily? That's right! Lady Bab, you must let me present my niece, Lady Fitzroy Somerset. But you must not be standing about, my dear!" he added, in a solicitous undervoice. Lady Fitzroy flushed faintly, but replied in her gentle way that she was not at all tired, had no wish to sit down, and was, in point of fact, looking for her mother and sister. The Duke reminded her bluffly that she must take care of herself, and went off to exchange a few words with Sir Charles Stuart. Lady Frances Webster, who had been watching him, was very glad to see him go. She profoundly mistrusted Barbara Childe, and had suffered quite an agonizing pang at the sight of his lordship whooping with laughter at what Barbara had said to him.

Barbara, however, had no desire to steal his lordship's affection. She had begun to waltz with Colonel Ponsonby; passed from his arms to those of Major Thornhill; and found herself at the end of the dance standing close to Lord Uxbridge, who immediately stepped up to her, exclaiming: "Why, Bab, my lovely one! How do you do? They tell me you're engaged to be married! How has that come about? I thought you were a hardened case!"

She gave him her hand. "Oh, so did I, but you know how it is! Besides, Gussie tells me I shall soon be quite *passée*. Have you seen her? She is here somewhere."

"I caught a glimpse, but to tell you the truth I have been the whole evening shaking hands with strangers. Who is the lucky man? I hope he is one of my fellows?"

"In a way I suppose you may say that he is. He's on the Duke's Staff, however—Charles Audley. But tell me, Harry: are you glad to be here?"

"Yes," he replied instantly. "Oh, I know what you are thinking, but that's old history now!"

She laughed. "It is an enchanting situation! Do you find it awkward?"

"Not a bit!" he said, with cheerful unconcern. "I go on very well with Wellington, and shall do the same with the fellows under me, when they get to know me—and I them. What's forming? A quadrille! Now, Bab, you must and you shall dance with me—for old time's sake!"

"How melancholy that sounds! You must settle it with Colonel Audley, who is coming to claim it. I daresay he won't give it up, for I told him that you were my first love, you know. Charles, I must make you known to Lord Uxbridge."

"How do you do? Bab tells me you should by rights be one of my people. By the by, you must let me congratulate you: you are a fortunate fellow! I have been Bab's servant any time these ten years—knew her when she had her hair all down her back, and wouldn't sew her sampler. You are to be envied."

"I envy you, sir. I would give much to have known her then."

"She was a bad child. Now, if you please, you are to fancy yourself back in your Regiment, and under my command. I have to request you, Colonel Audley (but I own it to be a dastardly trick!), to relinquish this dance to me."

The Colonel smiled. "You put me in an awkward position, sir. My duty, and all the Service Regulations, oblige me to obey you with alacrity; but how am I to do so without offending Bab?"

"I will make your peace with her, I promise you," replied Uxbridge.

"Very well, sir: I obey under strong protest."

"Quite irregular! But I don't blame you! Come, you witch, or it will be too late."

He led Barbara into the set that was forming. A hand clapped Colonel Audley on the shoulder. "Hallo, Charles! Slighted, my boy?"

The Colonel turned to confront Lord Robert Manners. "You, is it? How are you, Bob?"

"Oh, toll-loll!" said Manners, giving his pelisse a hitch. "I have just been telling Worth all the latest London scandal. You know, you're a paltry fellow to be enjoying yourself on the Staff in stirring times like these, upon my word you are! I wish you were back with us."

"Enjoying myself! You'd better try being one of the Beau's A.D.C.s, my boy! You don't know when you're well-off, all snug and comfortable with the Regiment!"

"Pho! A precious lot of comfort we shall have when we go into action. When you trot off in your smart cocked-hat, with a message in your pocket, think of us, charging to death or glory!"

"I will," promised the Colonel. "And when you're enjoying your nice, packed charge, spare a thought for the lonely, and damnably distinctive figure galloping hell for leather with his message, wishing to God every French sharpshooter didn't know by his cocked-hat he was a Staff officer, and wondering whether his horse is going to hold up under him or come down within easy reach of the French lines: he will very likely be me!"

"Oh, well!" said Lord Robert, abandoning the argument. "Come and have a drink, anyway. I have a good story to tell you about Brummell!"

The story was told, others followed it; but presently Lord Robert turned to more serious matters, and said, over a glass of champagne: "But that's enough of London! Between friends, Charles, what's happening here?"

"It's pretty difficult to say. We get intelligence from Paris, of course, and what we don't hear Clarke does: but one's never too sure of one's sources. By what we can discover, the French aren't by any means unanimous over Boney's return. All this enthusiasm you hear of belongs to the Army. It wouldn't surprise me if Boney finds himself with internal troubles brewing. Angoulême failed, of course; but we've heard rumours of something afoot in La Vendée. One thing seems certain: Boney's in no case yet to march on us. We hear of him leaving Paris, and of his troops marching to this frontier—they *are* marching, but he's not with them."

"What about ourselves? How do we go on?"

"Well, we can put 70,000 men into the field now, which is something."

"Too many 2nd Battalions," said Lord Robert. "Under strength, aren't they?"

"Some of them. You know how it is. We're hoping to get some of the toops back from America. But God knows whether they'll arrive in time! We miss Murray badly—but we hear we're to have De Lancey in his place, which will answer pretty well. By the by, he's married now, isn't he?"

"Yes: charming girl, I believe. What are the Dutch and Belgian troops like? We don't hear very comfortable reports of them. Disaffected, are they?"

"They're thought to be. It wouldn't be surprising: half of them have fought under the Eagles. I suppose the Duke will try to mix them with our own people as much as possible, as he did with the Portuguese. Then there will be the Brunswick Oels Jägers: they ought to do well, though they aren't what they were when we first had them with us."

"Well, no more is the Legion," said Lord Robert.

"No: they began to recruit too many foreigners. But they're good troops, for all that, and they've good Generals. I don't know what the other Hanoverians are like: there's a large contingent of them, but mostly Landwehr battalions."

"It sounds to me," said Lord Robert, draining his glass, "like a devilish mixed-bag. What are the Prussians like?"

"We don't see much of them. Hardinge's with them: says they're a queer set, according to our notions. When Blücher has a plan of campaign, he holds conferences with all his Generals, and they discuss it, and argue over it, under his very nose. I should like to see old Hookey inviting Hill, and Alten, and Picton, and the rest, to discuss his plans with him!"

Lord Robert laughed; Mr. Creevey peeped into the room, and seeing the two officers, came in, rubbing his hands together, and smiling like one who was sure of his welcome. There might be news to be gleaned from Audley, not the news that was being bandied from lip to lip, but tit-bits of private information, such as an officer on the Duke's Staff would be bound to hear. He had buttonholed the Duke a little earlier in the evening, but had not been able to get anything out of him but nonsense. He talked the same stuff as ever, laughing a great deal, pooh-poohing the gravity of the political situation, giving it as his opinion that Boney's return would come to nothing. Carnot and Lucien Bonaparte would get up a Republic in Paris; there would never be any fighting with the Allies; the Republicans would beat Bonaparte in a very few months. He was in a joking mood, and Mr. Creevey had met jest with jest, but thought his lordship cut a sorry figure. He allowed him to be very natural and good-humoured, but could not perceive the least indication in him of superior talents. He was not reserved; quite the reverse: he was communicative; but his conversation was not that of a sensible man.

"Well? What's the news?" asked Mr. Creevey cheerily. "How d'ye do, Lord Robert?"

"Oh, come, sir! It's you who always have the latest news," said Colonel Audley. "Will you drink a glass of champagne with us?"

"Oho, so that's what you are up to! You're a most complete hand, Colonel! Well, just one then. What's the latest intelligence from France, eh?"

"Why, that Boney's summoning everyone to an assembly, or some such thing, in the Champ du Mars."

"I know *that*," said Mr. Creevey. "I have been talking about it to the Duke. We have had quite a chat together, I can tell you, and some capital jokes too. *He* believes it won't answer, this Champ de Mai affair; that there will be an explosion; and the whole house of cards will come tumbling about Boney's ears."

"Ah, I daresay," responded the Colonel vaguely. "Don't know much about these matters, myself."

Mr. Creevey drank up his wine, and went away in search of better company. He found it presently in the group about Barbara Childe. She had gathered a number of distinguished persons about her, just the sort of people Mr. Creevey liked to be with. He joined the group, noticing with satisfaction that it included General Don Miguel de Alava, a short, sallow-faced Spaniard, with a rather simian cast of countenance, quick-glancing eyes, and a tongue for ever on the wag. Alava had lately become the Spanish Ambassador at The Hague, but was at present acting as Military Commissioner to the Allied Army. He had been Commissar at Wellington's Headquarters in Spain, and was known to be on intimate terms with the Duke. Mr. Creevey edged nearer to him, his ears on the prick.

"But your wife, Alava! Is she not with you?" Sir William Ponsonby was demanding.

Up went the expressive hands; a droll look came into Alava's face. "*Ah non, par exemple!*" he exclaimed. "She

stays in Spain. *Excellente femme!—mais forte ennuyeuse!"*
Caroline Lamb's voice broke through the shout of
laughter. "General Alava, what's the news? You know
it all! Now tell us! Do tell us!"
"Mais, madame, je n'en sais rien! Rien, rien, rien!"
Decidedly, Mr. Creevey was out of luck to-night.

CHAPTER XII

MAY came in, bringing trouble. There seemed to be
no end to the difficulties for ever springing up round
his lordship. Now it was Major-General Hinüber,
querulously demanding leave to resign his Staff, and to
retire to some German spa, because he was not to command the Legion as a separate Division: he might go with
the Duke's good-will, but it meant more letter-writing,
more trouble; now it was news from his brother William,
in London: the Peace party was attacking his lordship in
Parliament, accusing him of being little better than a
murderer, because he had set his name to the declaration
that made Napoleon *hors la loi:* he did not really care, he
had never cared for public opinion, but it annoyed him.
To attack a public servant absent on public service seemed
to him "extraordinary and unprecedented". Then there
was the constant fret of being obliged to deal with the
Dutch King, a jealous man, continually raising difficulties,
or turning obstinate over petty issues. He could be
managed, in the end he would generally give way, but it
took time to handle him, and time was what his lordship
could least spare.

The question of the Hanoverian subsidy had become
acute; King William should have shared the payment
with Great Britain, but he was wriggling out of that
obligation, on the score that he had only been bound to
pay it while he had no troops of his own. His lordship
had had an interview with M. de Nagel over the business,
but in the end he supposed the whole charge of the

Hanoverian subsidy would fall upon Great Britain.

Trouble sprang up in the Prussian camp. The Saxon troops at Liége mutinied over some question of an oath of allegiance to the King of Prussia, and poor old Blücher was obliged to quit the town. The Saxons would have been willing enough to have come over to the British camp, but his lordship did not want such fellows, and knew that the Prussians would never agree to his having them if he did. They would have to be got rid of before they spread disaffection through the Army, but the question was how to get them out of the country. Blücher wanted them to be embarked on British ships, but his lordship had no transports; his troops were sent out to him on hired vessels, which returned to England as soon as their cargoes were landed. If they were to be escorted through the Netherlands, King William's permission must be obtained, but there was no inducing Blücher to realize the propriety of referring to the King. It would fall on his lordship's shoulders to arrange matters, writing to Hardinge, to Blücher, to King William.

And, like a running accompaniment to the rest, the bickering correspondence with Torrens over Staff appointments dragged on, until his lordship dashed off one of his hasty, biting notes, requesting that it should cease. "*The Commander-in-Chief has a right to appoint whom he chooses, and those whom he appoints shall be employed,*" he wrote in a stiff rage. "*It cannot be expected that I should declare myself satisfied with these appointments till I shall find the persons as fit for their situations as those whom I should have recommended to his Royal Highness.*"

On the 6th May his lordship was able to tell Lord Bathurst that King William had placed the Dutch-Belgian Army under his command. The appointment had been delayed on various unconvincing pretexts, but at last, and when his lordship had reached the end of his patience, it had been made. Things should go better now; he could begin to pull the whole Allied Army into shape, drafting the troops where he thought proper without the hindrance of having to make formal application for permission to His Majesty.

The month wore on; the weather grew warmer; no more friendly log-fires in the grates, no more fur-lined pelisses for the ladies. Out came the cambrics and the muslins: lilac, pomona-green, and pale puce, made into wispy round-dresses figured with rose-buds, with row upon row of frills round the ankles. Knots of jaunty ribbons adorned low corsages, and gauze scarves floated from plump shoulders in a light breeze. The feathered velvet bonnets and the sealskin caps were put up in camphor. Hats were the rage; chip-hats, hats of satin-straw, of silk, of leghorn, and of willow: high-crowned, flat-crowned, with full-poke fronts, and with curtailed poke-fronts: hats trimmed with clusters of flowers, or bunches of bobbing cherries, with puffs of satin ribbon, drapings of thread-net, and frills of lace. Winter half-boots of orange jean or sober black kid were discarded: the ladies tripped over cobbled streets in sandals and slippers. Red morocco twinkled under ruched skirts; Villager hats and Angoulême bonnets framed faces old or young, pretty or plain; silk open-work mittens covered rounded arms; frivolous little parasols on long beribboned handles shaded delicate complexions from the sun's glare. Denmark Lotion was in constant demand, and Distilled Water of Pineapples; strawberries were wanted for sunburnt cheeks; Chervil Water, for bathing a freckled skin.

The balls, the concerts, the theatres continued, but picnics were added to the gaieties now, charming expeditions, with flowery muslins squired by hot scarlet uniforms; the ladies in open carriages; the gentlemen riding gallantly beside; hampers of cold chicken and champagne on the boxes; everyone light-hearted; flirtation the order of the day. There were Reviews to watch, fêtes to attend; day after day slid by in the pursuit of pleasure; days that were not quite real, but belonged to some half-realized dream. Somewhere to the south was a Corsican ogre, who might at any moment break into the dream and shatter it, but distance shrouded him; and, meanwhile, into the Netherlands was streaming an endless procession of British troops, changing the whole face of the country, swarming in every village; lounging outside estaminets, in forage caps, with their jackets unbuttoned; trotting down the rough, dusty roads with plumes flying and accoutrements jingling; haggling with shrewd Flemish farmers in their broken French; making love to giggling girls in starched white caps and huge voluminous skirts; spreading their Flanders tents over the meadows; striding through the streets with clanking spurs and swinging sabretaches. Here might be seen a looped and tasselled infantry shako, narrow-topped and leathern-peaked; there the bell-topped shako of a Light Dragoon, with its short plume and ornamental cord; or the fur cap of a Hussar; or the glitter of sunlight on a Heavy Dragoon's brass helmet, with its jutting crest and waving plume.

Like bright colours in a kaleidoscope, merging into ever-changing patterns, the troops were being drafted over the countryside. Life Guardsmen in scarlet and gold, mounted on great black chargers, sleek as satin and splendid with polished trappings, woke dozing villages on the Dender; Liedekerke gaped at the Blues, swaggering up the street as though they owned it; Schendelbeke girls came running to see the Hussars ride past with tossing pelisses, and crusted jackets; Castre and Lerbeke billeted Light Dragoons in blue with silver lace, and facings of every colour: crimson, yellow, buff, scarlet; Brussels fell in love with Highland kilts and jaunty bonnets, and blinked at trim Riflemen in their Jack-a-Dandy green uniforms; Enghien and Gram-mont swarmed with the Footguards, the Gentlemen's Sons, with their hosts of dashing young Ensigns and Captains, all so smart and gay, riding in point-to-point races, hurry-ing off to Brussels in their best clothes to dance the night through, or entertaining bevies of lovely ladies at fêtes and picnics. But thundering and clattering along the roads that led from Ostend came the Artillery, grim troops in sombre uniforms and big black helmets, scaring the light-hearted into momentary silence as they passed, for though the Guards danced, and the Cavalry made love, and Line Regiments scattered far and near swarmed over the country like noisy red ants, it was the sight of the guns that made the merry-makers realize how close they stood to war. All through April and the early weeks in May they landed one after another in the Netherlands: Ross, with his Chestnut Troop of 9-pounders; bearded Major Bull, with heavy howitzers; Mercer, with his artist's eye for landscape and his crack Troop; Whinyates, with his cherished Rockets; Beane; Gardiner; Webber-Smith; and the beau ideal of every Artillery officer, Norman Ramsay, of Fuentes de Oñoro fame. After the Troops came the Field Brigades: Sandham's, Bolton's, Lloyd's, Sinclair's, Rogers's; all armed with five gleaming 9-pounders and one howitzer. They were an imposing sight; ominous enough to give a pause to gaiety.

But the merry-making went on, uneasy under the surface, sometimes a little hectic, as though while the sun continued to shine and the Ogre to remain in his den, the civilians and the soldiers and the lovely ladies were being driven on to cram into every cloudless day all the fun and the gaiety it could hold. The Duke gave ball after ball; there were Court parties at Laeken; Reviews at Vilvorde; excursions to Ath, and Enghien, and Ghent; picnics in the cool Forest of Soignes.

There was a rumour of movement on the frontier; a tremor of fear ran through Brussels. Count d'Erlon was marching on Valenciennes with his whole Corps; the French were massing on the Allied front, a hundred thousand strong; the Emperor had left Paris: he was at Condé; he was about to launch an attack. It was false: the Emperor was still in Paris, and had postponed his meeting of the Champ de Mai until the end of the month. The ladies and the civilians, poised for flight, could relax again: there was nothing to fear: the Duke had told Mr. Creevey that it would never come to blows; and was holding another ball.

"Pooh! Nonsense!" said the Duke. "Nothing to be afraid of yet!"

"I never saw a man so unaffected in my life!" said Mr. Creevey. "He is as cheerful as a schoolboy, and talks as though there were no possibility of war!"

"Then he is damned different with you from what he is with me," said Sir Charles Stuart bluntly.

"*I have got an infamous Army, very weak, and ill-equipped, and a very inexperienced Staff,*" wrote the Duke, in the midst of his balls, and his Reviews, his visits to Ghent, and his latest charming flirtation.

"Pooh! Nonsense," said the Duke, but wrote to Hill at Grammont: "*Matters look a little serious on the frontier.*"

The Duke knew as well as any man what was stirring beyond the frontier, for he had got Colonel Grant out in charge of the Intelligence, and no one knew better than Grant how to obtain desired information. More reliable than the data collected by Clarke and his French spies were Grant's brief reports sent in to General Dörnberg at Mons, and forwarded on by him to Brussels. Grant told of bridges and roads being broken up in the Sambre district, as though for defence; of Count d'Erlon's Corps lying between Valenciennes and Maubeuge in four divisions of Infantry; of Reille at Avesnes, with five Infantry divisions and three Cavalry; of Vandamme between Mézières and Rocroi; and of Count Lobau, at Laon. His information was precise and always to be trusted: no flights into the realms of conjecture for Colonel Grant, a dry Scot, dealing only in facts and figures. Oh yes! matters certainly looked serious on the frontier; and his lordship had received, besides, disquieting intelligence of a huge body of cavalry forming. Sixteen thousand Heavy Cavalry were in readiness to take the field, and all over France horses were being bought, to bring the total up to forty thousand or more. A report was spread of Murat's having fled by sea from Italy; it was supposed that he would be put in command of this mass of cavalry, for who so brilliant as Murat in cavalry manœuvres? More serious still was the news that Soult had accepted the office of Major-General under the Emperor. That would bring many wavering men over to Napoleon, for Soult's was a name that carried weight.

The Duke of Brunswick arrived, with his Black Brunswickers: men in sable uniforms, with a skull and cross-bones on their shakos, and the death of the Duke's father at Jéna to avenge. A handsome man, the Duke, gallant in the field and stately in the ballroom, with gentle manners and a grave, sweet smile. His men were quartered at Vilvorde, north of Brussels, but he himself was continually at Headquarters, troubled over the eternal question of subsidies

The Nassauers were on the way, led by General Kruse, and a hopeful young Prince, whom his lordship had promised to take into his family. Rather an anxiety, these hereditary princelings, but they were all of them agog to fight under his lordship, flatteringly deferential and eager to be of use.

Blücher moved his Headquarters from Liége to Hannut, drawing closer to the Anglo-Allied Army; De Lancey arrived from England with his young bride, taking Sir Hudson Lowe's place. With a Deputy-Quartermaster-General he knew, and could trust to do his work without for ever wishing to copy Prussian methods, his lordship found his path smoother. He still had General Röder with him, but meant to drop a word in Blücher's ear when he next saw him. The fellow would have to be removed: he could not learn to fit into the pattern, or to get over his anti-British prejudice. The other Commissioners gave his lordship no trouble: Alava was an old friend; he had a real value for clever Pozzo di Borgo from Russia; liked Baron Vincent from Austria; and was on pretty good terms with Netherlandish Count van Reede.

He had been shifting his troops about all the month, skilfully concentrating them, forming new brigades, extending here, drawing his regiments in there, until he felt himself to be in a position to withstand any attack. The Prince of Orange's Headquarters were fixed at Braine-le-Comte, but his lordship placed Lord Hill, wise in war, farther west, at Grammont, because to the west lay his communication lines, and the great Mons and Tournay roads from France. In addition to Clinton's and Colville's divisions, forming the Second Corps under Hill, his lordship transferred Prince Frederick's Corps to him, moving it north-west from Soignes and Braine-le-Comte, by way of Hal and Grammont, to Sotteghem, like a piece on a chess-board. Prince Frederick, surviving an interview with his lordship, betrayed a flash of unsuspected humour. "*Il ne m'a ni grondé, ni mis aux arrêts,*" he wrote to his brother.

On the 29th May, a day of blazing sunshine, the Duke reviewed the British Cavalry in a natural theatre of ground on the banks of the Dender, not far from Grammont. It was an event that drew the fashionables from Brussels and Ghent on horseback and in carriages: ladies in their newest gauzes, gentlemen very natty in polished topboots, long-tailed blue coats, and skin-tight pantaloons. Worth drove his Judith there in a curricle; Lady Barbara drove herself in a phaeton, with a tiger perched up behind; the Vidals came sedately in their carriage; the amazing Sir Sydney Smith, newly arrived from Vienna, and looking so like a mountebank that it was almost impossible to see in him the hero of Acre, sat beside his lady in an open barouche; Sir Peregrine Taverner rode out on a mettlesome bay, like a score of others; and a host of French Royalists flocked out from Ghent to gaze, gasp, fling up their hands, and exclaim to see such magnificent troops, such noble horses, such glittering accoutrements!

But the Cavalry paid no heed to the early French arrivals. The roads were thick with dust, and as each squadron, each Troop, came on to the ground, off went belts, haversacks, and coats, and out came brushes and wisps of hay, and a regular scrubbing and dusting and polishing began, for the Duke was coming, with a galaxy of foreign visitors, headed by Marshal Blücher, and not one speck of dust must dull a shining boot or spoil the smartness of a scarlet coat, and not one hair of a charger's tail or mane must be out of place.

The arena lay on the opposite side of the river from the village of Schendelbeke, whence the Duke's cortège was expected to arrive, and a temporary bridge had been thrown across the Dender. Many were the anxious glances cast towards the rising ground over the river, as the men rubbed down their horses, spat on silver buttons, and polished them till the sweat ran off their bodies; and once an alarm was raised, an agonized cry of: "The Duke! the Duke!"

It was a full hour before he was expected to arrive, but a group of richly-dressed horsemen with waving plumes could clearly be seen coming down the hill from the village. Brushes and rags were thrust into haversacks, coats were flung on and belts buckled, but it turned out to be a false alarm. It was not Wellington after all, but the Duc de Berri, and what did the Iron Duke's troops care for him? The brushing and the polishing were renewed, and the Duc, after riding slowly down to the bridge, suddenly set off at a gallop towards the saluting-point, and halted there, glaring at the serried ranks before him. A few cursory glances were cast at him, and one or two coarse jokes cut at his expense, but no further notice was paid him, until he sent one of his suite forward to confer with Lord Uxbridge. A short colloquy took place; the word spread through the ranks that his Highness was claiming the reception due to a Prince of the Blood-Royal, and loud guffaws greeted this jest. The troops knew Mounseer; they had seen him drilling them French fellows; proper bully-ragger he was!

Back went the envoy, and off galloped his Royal Highness in a rage, his suite labouring behind him up the slope to Schendelbeke. Lord Uxbridge had evidently refused the required salute: that was the way! hurrah for his lordship!

Not until two o'clock did the Duke arrive, and by that time all the polishing was done, and the Cavalry was drawn up in three imposing lines, facing the bridge. Lining the bank of the river were the Hussars, in squadrons, widely spaced, and with batteries of Horse Artillery on each flank; behind them stood the Heavy Dragoons in compact order, with four batteries; and behind them, in the same close formation, the Light Dragoons, flanked by Troops of 9-pounders. There were six thousand men drawn up, and it was small matter for wonder that Marshal Blücher was impressed by the sight. He rode beside the Duke, his blue eyes staring under bushy white brows, and a beaming smile under his long moustache. *"Mein Gott, mein Gott!"* he said. *"Ja, ja,* it is goot—it is fery goot, mein frient!"

The troops, sweating under a scorching sun, choked by their high, tight collars, sat their chargers like statues, gazing rigidly before them, while the cortège passed slowly along the ranks. They knew the Duke's hook-nose and low cocked-hat right enough; they knew Lord Uxbridge, in his Hussar dress; and Sir George Wood, who commanded the Artillery; they even knew the Duke of Brunswick, and guessed that the stout old gentleman with the white whiskers was Marshal Blücher; but who the rest of the fine gentlemen might be, in their plumed hats and fancy foreign uniforms, they neither knew nor cared. One or two old soldiers recognized General Alava, but Generals Gneisenau, Kleist, and Ziethen, Pozzo di Borgo, and Baron Vincent, Counts van Reede, and d'Aglié, exclaiming in outlandish tongues amongst themselves, did not concern them. They thought the Marshal Prince von Blücher a rum touch if ever there was one, opening his bone-box to splutter out his *Achs,* and his *Mein Gotts,* and his *Fery Goots!*

But the Marshal Prince was enjoying himself. He had come over from Tirlemont with his Chief-of-Staff, and several of his Generals, for this occasion, and his friend and colleague had given them a very good luncheon, sent on their horses to Ninove and driven them out from Brussels in comfortable carriages. He was on the best of terms with his colleague, and although he spoke very little English, and very bad French, they had a great deal of conversation together, and found themselves perfectly in accord. A Hussar himself, he was loud in his praise of the Hussars drawn up before him; as for the Heavy Dragoons, *quels physiques, quels beaux chevaux!* Indeed, the horses impressed him more than anything. When he came to Mercer's Troop, there seemed to be no getting him past it; each subdivision was inspected, every horse exclaimed at. *"Mein Gott,* dere is not von vich is not goot for Veldt-Marshal!" he declared.

171

The Duke acknowledged it. It was not to be expected that he would share in the Marshal's rapture, but he asked Sir George Wood whose Troop it was, and seemed to approve of it. It did not occur to him to speak to Captain Mercer, following him as he made the inspection. He paid no heed to him, but Mercer was not surprised: it was just like the Duke; he had never a good word for the unfortunate Artillery.

The inspection took a long time; some of the spectators grew rather bored with looking at the motionless ranks, and several ladies complained of the heat. Sir Peregrine Taverner, whose Harriet was in low spirits and had refused to attend the Review, edged his way to Barbara's phaeton; and Lady Worth, her head aching a little from the glare of the sun, closed her eyes, with a request to her lord to inform her if anything should begin to happen.

The Duke and the Marshal at last returned to the saluting-point; Lord Uxbridge marched the troops past; Judith woke up; and all the wilting ladies revived at the near prospect of being able to move out of the sun and partake of refreshments.

The military cortège began to move about amongst the civilians before riding back to Ninove. Various persons were presented to the Marshal Prince; and Colonel Audley was able to seize the opportunity of exchanging a few words with Lady Barbara.

"How do you contrive to look so cool?" he asked ruefully.

"I can't think. I'm bored to tears, Charles!"

"I know. Devilish tedious, isn't it?"

"I only came to see George, and I couldn't even pick him out in that dreadful scarlet mass!" she said pettishly.

"He looked very handsome, I assure you."

She yawned. "I'll swear he was cursing the heat! I wish you will drive home with me. We will dine outside the town in one of those charmingly vulgar places in the suburbs, and drink our wine at a table by the roadside, just as the burghers do. It will be so amusing!"

"Oh, don't!" he begged. "It sounds delightful, and I can't do it!"

"Why can't you?" she demanded, lifting her eyebrows. "Is it beneath the dignity of a Staff Officer?"

"You know very well it's not beneath my dignity. But I'm dining at Ninove."

"That stupid Cavalry party of Uxbridge's! Oh, nonsense! it can't signify. No one will give a fig for your absence: you won't even be missed, I daresay."

He laughed, but shook his head. "My darling, I daren't!"

She hunched a shoulder. "I am tired of your duty, Charles. It is so tedious!"

"It is indeed."

"I see nothing of you. George and Harry can get leave when they want it; why should not you?"

"George and Harry are not on the Staff," he replied. "I'd get leave if I could, but it's impossible."

"Well!" She closed her parasol with a snap, and laid it on the seat beside her. "If it is impossible for you I must find someone else to go with me. Ah, the very man! Sir Peregrine, come here!"

A little startled, the Colonel turned to see Peregrine hurriedly obeying the summons. A bewitching smile was bestowed upon him. "Sir Peregrine, I want to dine in the suburbs, and Charles won't take me! Will you go with me?"

"Oh, by Jove, Lady Bab, I should think I will—anywhere!" replied Peregrine.

"Good. No dressing-up, mind! I intend to go just as I am. You may call for me in the Rue Ducale: is it agreed?"

"Lord, yes, a thousand times! It will be capital fun!" A doubt struck him; he looked at the Colonel, and added: "That is—you don't mind, Audley, do you?"

"My dear Perry, why should I mind? Go by all means: I wish I might join you."

"Oh, devilish good of you! At about six, then, Lady Bab: I'll be there!"

He raised his hat to her and walked away; the Colonel said: "What's your game, Bab?"

"I don't understand you. I had thought the fact of Sir Peregrine's being a connexion of yours must have made him unexceptionable. Besides, I like him: have you any objection?"

"I'm not jealous of him, if that is what you mean, but I've a strong notion that it would be better for him not to be liked by you."

"Ah, perhaps you are right!" she said. Her voice was saintly, but two demons danced in her eyes. "Lavisse comes to Brussels this evening: I will engage him instead."

"You're a devil in attack, Bab," he said appreciatively. "That's a pistol held to my head, and, being a prudent man, I capitulate."

"Oh, Charles! Craven! And you a soldier!"

"True: but a good soldier knows when to retreat!"

"Shall you come about again?"

"Yes, but I shall be more careful of my ground. To-day I rashly left my flank exposed."

She smiled. "And I rolled it up! Well, I will be good! Sir Peregrine shall take me, because it would be stupid to cry off now, but I will be very sisterly, I promise you."

He held up his hand to her. "Defeat without dishonour! Thank you!"

She leaned down from her high perch, putting her hand in his. His face was upturned; she said, with her gurgle of laughter: "Don't smile at me, Charles! If you do I must kiss you just *there!*" She drew her hand away, and laid a finger between his brows.

"Do!"

"No, this place is confoundedly public: I should put you to shame. By the by, Charles, that chit whose name I never can remember—the heiress whom your sister-in-law meant you to marry—you know whom I mean?"

"I do, but it's nonsense that Judith intended her for me."

"Oh no, I'm sure it's not! But it doesn't signify, only that I thought you would like to know that I rather fancy George to be a little *épris* in that direction."

"I hope he will not give her a heartache!"

174

"I expect he will, however. The odd thing is that she is not at all the sort of young woman he has been in the habit of deceiving." She added thoughtfully: "One comfort is that he is more likely to make a fool of her than she of him."

"Really, Bab!" he protested.

"Now, don't be shocked! It would never do for George to marry her. He won't, of course. He depends too much upon my grandfather, and wouldn't dare. *She* may be perfectly ladylike, but her connection with that horrid little Cit of an uncle makes her quite ineligible. My grandfather was himself held to have married beneath him, but that does not make him indulgent towards any mésalliance *we* might wish to make! He is pleased, by the way, with my engagement. I have had letters from him and my grandmother by to-day's post. You never told me you had written to him, Charles!"

"Of course I wrote to him. Have we his blessing?"

"Decidedly! You are unexceptionable. He did not suppose me to have so much good sense. My grandmother, who is quite the most delightful creature imaginable, writes that she is in doubt of her felicitations being still acceptable by the time they reach me. You observe, Charles, you have broken all records!" She gathered up the reins, and signed to her tiger to jump up behind. "There seems to be nothing to stay for: I shall go. Who is invited to this dinner of Uxbridge's?"

"All commanding Cavalry Officers, and of course the foreign visitors."

"Ah, a horrid male party! You will enjoy it excessively, I daresay, get abominably foxed, and come reeling back to Brussels with the dawn."

"Well! You have drawn no rose-coloured picture of my character, at all events! There can be no disillusionment for you to fear!"

"No, none for *me*," she said.

He saw that she was ready to give her horses the office to start, but detained her. "Do you mean to drive alone? Is not Harry with you?"

"Certainly I mean to drive alone. Harry is not here."

"Don't tell me there are no young gentlemen eager for the chance to escort you?"

"I have sometimes a strong liking for my own company," she replied. "But as for being alone, pray observe Matthew, my tiger."

"Let someone ride back with you, Bab."

"Are you afraid I may be molested by the brutal soldiery? I don't fear it!"

"You might well meet with unpleasantness. Is not Vidal here?"

"Yes, driving with Gussie. You will not expect me to curb my horses to keep pace with a sober barouche. I shall spring 'em, you know."

He stepped back. She said saucily: "Retiring again, Charles? You're the wisest man of my acquaintance. Good-bye! Don't be anxious: I am a famous whip."

She began to make her way out of the ranks of carriages; the Colonel mounted his horse again, and rode off to his brother's curricle. He saluted Judith, but without attending to what she had to say of the Review, addressed Worth. "Julian, be a good fellow, will you, and follow Bab? She's alone, and I don't care for her to be driving all that distance without an escort. You need not so proclaim yourself, by the way, but I should be glad if you would keep her in sight."

"Certainly," said Worth.

"Thank you: I knew I might depend on you."

He raised two fingers to his hat, and rode off. Judith said: "Well, if she's alone it must be for the first time. Poor Charles! I daresay she has done it simply to vex him."

"Very possibly," Worth agreed. "There is a bad streak in the Alastairs."

"Yes. Lord George, in particular, is not at all the thing. I am so disturbed to see him making Lucy the object of his attentions! It was most marked last night: he danced with her three times."

"She did not appear to mind."

"You are wrong: I saw her look distressed when he came up to her the third time. She is not the girl to have her head turned by a handsome Life Guardsman."

"She is singular, then," he said in his driest tone.

CHAPTER XIII

MAY had worn itself out; and looking back over four weeks of pleasure-seeking, Judith could not feel that there had been unalloyed gaiety. She was aware of tension; she had herself been carried into the swirl. No one could foretell what the future held; but everyone knew that these weeks might be the last of happiness. Except when news crept through of movement on the frontier, war was not much talked of. Talking of it could not stop its coming; it was better to put the thought of it behind one, and to be merry while the sun still shone.

But Judith had good sense to guide her, nor was she any longer a single beauty with scores of admirers clamouring for her favours. If she grew tired, she could rest; but Barbara, it seemed, could not rest, and appeared not to wish even to draw breath. She was beginning to look a little haggard; that she took laudanum was an open secret. What caprice it was that drove her on Judith could not imagine. The very fact of her being betrothed to Charles should have made it possible for her to have lived more quietly; she ought not to want to be for ever at parties. When he could he accompanied her, but he had very little leisure for picnics, or for spending days at the races. Often he came off duty looking so tired that it put his sister-in-law out of all patience to find him bent on attending some ball or reception. He denied that he felt tired, and the harassed little frown between his eyes would vanish as he laughed at her solicitude. She was not deceived; she could have shaken Barbara for her selfishness.

But Charles, keeping pace with his betrothed, never allowed a hint of languor to appear in his face or manner.

Once Barbara said to him: "Is it wrong of me not to give up the parties and all the fun? I love it so! And when I am married I shall have to be so sober!"

"No, no, never think that!" he said quickly.

"Gussie says it must be so."

"It shall not be so! Don't listen to Augusta, I beg of you! Do you think I have not known from the start how little she likes our engagement?"

"Gussie!" she said scornfully. "I never listened to her in my life!"

But even though she scoffed at Augusta she did listen to her, with an unconscious ear.

"Make the most of your freedom, my dear," said Augusta. "You won't have the chance when you've married your Staff Officer. Will you miss your court, do you think? Shall you mind not being crowded round at every ball you go to? And oh, Bab, do you mean to wear a matronly cap, and bear your Charles a quiverful of stout children? How I shall laugh to see you!"

No, one did not set any store by what Gussie said, but nevertheless those barbs found their mark. Gallant young gentlemen, too, would cry imploringly: "Oh, don't turn into a sober matron, Bab! Only conceive of a world without Bad Bab to set everyone by the ears!"

They all drew the same picture of her, grown grave, and thinking not of her conquests but of her household; perhaps being obliged to languish in some dull garrison town, with nothing to do but visit other officers' wives, and be civil to Charles.

She would see herself like that, and would thrust the picture behind her, and hurry away to be gay while she could. When Charles was with her, the picture faded, for Charles swore he wanted no such wife. Yet some sobriety Charles did want. There had been an incident in May which he had not laughed at. Some of the officers of Lord Edward Somerset's brigade had given one of the moonlight picnics of which the old-fashioned people so much disapproved. Lord George had been at the root of it; he had engaged Miss Devenish to go to it with his sister, laying

178

his careless command upon Barbara to bring the chit with her. The wonder was that Miss Devenish had liked to go, *And* but she did go, and had managed to get lost with Lord George in a coppice for over an hour. It was no concern of Barbara's. "Good God, Charles, if a chaperon had been wanted *I* was not the one to choose for the part! Everyone contrived to lose themselves. Why, I had the most absurd half-hour myself, with an engaging child from George's regiment on one side of me and Captain Clayton of the Blues on the other."

"It sounds safe and rather stupid," he said. "But Miss Devenish's prolonged absence with George has caused a little talk. I can't but blame you, Bab. You should not have allowed it."

"My dear Charles, I suppose her to know her own business. The truth is that you are like your sister, and disapprove of moonlight picnics."

He was silent. She thought he looked displeased, and said with a light laugh: "Do you wish me to give up such frivolous amusements?"

"I shan't ask you to give them up, Bab."

"Do you think I would not?"

"I don't know," he replied. "I only know that if you did so at my request it would be against your will. If you did not care to go without me, well, that would be different."

Her eyes danced; she looked half-roguish, half-rueful, and murmured coaxingly: "Oh, confound you, Charles, you make me seem the veriest wretch! Don't look so gravely at me! I swear I would rather stay at home with you than go to the most romantic of picnics. But when you can't be with me, what the devil *am* I to do?"

She peeped at him under her lashes; he was obliged to laugh, even though there was very little laughter in his heart.

Judith, when she heard of the famous picnic, was aghast. She could not understand how Mrs. Fisher could have permitted her niece to take part in such an expedition. The reason was not far to seek: Mrs. Fisher was dreaming of bridals. Young people, she said, often behaved foolishly, and indeed she had scolded Lucy for her thoughtlessness, but she dared say there was no harm done, after all.

Judith blamed Barbara for the whole, and wondered how long Charles would bear with her capriciousness.

"I have always felt a little sorry for Bab Alastair," said the Duchess of Richmond once, in her quiet way. "Her mama died when Harry was born, and that is a very sad thing for a girl, you know. I am afraid the late Lord Vidal was rather dissolute, and Bab grew up without that refining influence which her mama must have exercised. She has never been in the way of being checked, and was unfortunate in being made a pet of by her papa."

"Oh!" exclaimed Judith. "Could that have done harm to a daughter's character?"

"The melancholy truth was, my dear, that Lord Vidal's principles were not high, and he did not scruple to instil into Bab his own cynical notions. You will not repeat it, but Lord Vidal's household was apt to include females of whose very existence young girls should be unaware."

"But her grandparents!"

"Oh yes, but, you see, Lord Vidal was not always upon terms with his father," said her Grace. "And the Duchess was not of an age to dance attendance upon a flighty granddaughter. She was most distressed at that wretched marriage, I know. There can never have been a more shocking business! Childe was a man whose reputation, whose whole manner of life——but I am talking of the dead, and indeed have said too much already."

"I am glad you have told me as much; it may help me to be patient. I own, I cannot like Barbara."

"I am sorry for it. Yet she is not heartless, as so many people say. I could tell you of a hundred generous actions. She is accounted perfectly selfish, but I have been a good deal touched by her kindness to my boy during his long, painful convalescence. I believe no one is aware how often she has forgone some pleasure party merely to sit with poor William for a little while, quite taking him out of himself."

"Ah, that was kind indeed! You are right: it warms

one's heart towards her to hear of such conduct. How does poor William go on? He has not left his room?"

"Oh no! It must be weeks yet before he will be able to stand upon his feet. It was a dreadful accident—he was thrown in such a way! But I don't care to think of it, and can only thank God he has been spared to me."

Nothing more was said of Barbara, but the conversation remained in Judith's memory. She was able to meet Barbara with more cordiality, and even to pardon some of her wildness; and for a little while could almost hope that she might make Charles happy.

The incident of the moonlight picnic, however, brought back all the old disgust; she could hardly forgive Barbara for having lent herself to what she believed to have been nothing less than a trap laid for Lucy Devenish.

Lucy's own distress was evident. She looked so pale and wretched that Judith began to fear that her affections had been seriously engaged. Lord George was as brazen as might have been expected. He had made Lucy the subject of the latest scandal, but when taxed with it by his elder brother, would do nothing but laugh.

"I wish you will consider me!" complained Vidal.

"Consider you? Why the devil should I?" demanded George.

"It is no very pleasant thing for me, I can tell you, to have my brother pointed out as a rake and a libertine on the one hand, and my sister on the other as——"

"Keep your damned tongue off Bab, unless you want your teeth knocked down your throat, Vidal!" said George, looking ugly.

"Pray do not bring your ringside manners into my drawing-room, George," said Augusta sharply. "I find your championing of Bab more than a little absurd, let me tell you!"

He turned, looking down at her from his great height with an expression of mocking indifference. "You do, do you? And what the devil do you think I care for your opinion?"

"Thank you, I am well aware of your habit of disregarding everyone's opinion but your own. However, Bab's conduct has nothing to do with your folly in entangling yourself with that Devenish chit. Depend upon it, her uncle is merely awaiting his opportunity to force you into marrying her. I know what men of his stamp are like, if you do not."

"Oho, do you really, Gussie? Where did you come by your knowledge, I should like to know?"

She replied coldly: "Laugh, if you choose, but do not look to me for help when you find yourself trapped. I suppose you have thought how you will break the news to your grandfather. I don't envy you that task!"

He flushed, seemed about to retort, and then turned on his heel and walked away.

Whatever Mr. Fisher's plans might be, Miss Devenish at least did not appear to be desirous of encouraging George's attentions. Judith was a witness of a decided rebuff to his lordship, and could only be glad of it, although she felt sorry for the pain it seemed to cause Lucy. Lucy's wan looks began to make Judith feel anxious, and she even cast about in her mind for some eligible young man to take Lord George's place in the girl's affections.

At the Review of the Cavalry, she thought she had found a gentleman who might answer the purpose, but before she could put into execution her amiable plan of inviting him and Lucy to dine one evening her anxieties were diverted in quite another direction.

Sir Peregrine, either from a slight feeling of guilt or from mere thoughtlessness, did not inform his Harriet of his assignation in the suburbs. Upon his return to Brussels he had found Harriet far from well, and quite in the dumps. He bounced in, ready to recount all the day's happenings, but she had the headache, was sipping hartshorn and water, and announced her intention of going to bed and having her dinner sent up to her on a tray.

"Well, I am sorry you have the headache, Harry. Shall you mind if I dine from home? If you would like me to stay with you——"

"Oh no! I shall be better to-morrow, I daresay, but

my head aches too much to make me pleasant company to-night. Go out, by all means. I am only sorry to be such a stupid creature!"

So Peregrine had sallied forth to call for Barbara, and had spent an entertaining evening with her in one of the cafés beyond the ramparts.

Had Colonel Audley been able to see them he must have acquitted Barbara of any desire to flirt, but he could scarcely have been pleased with the result of her sisterly behaviour. When she chose to treat a man *en camarade*, she was at her most enchanting. She had not the smallest intention of captivating Peregrine, but her candid way of looking at him, her rippling laugh, her boyish speech, and her sense of fun charmed him irresistibly. He was not in love with her, but he had never in his life encountered so dazzling a creature.

Barbara said frankly at the outset: "This is capital! I shall pretend you are my young brother. I, if you please, am your elder sister—though I fear I am not quite like Lady Worth."

Peregrine did not think that she was in the least like Judith, except in being able to talk sensibly of horses. He soon found himself describing his yacht to her; discovered that she also was fond of sailing; and from that moment became her slave. Sailing, riding, cocking, prize-fighting: they talked of them all. No squeamish nonsense about Lady Bab! Why, it was like talking to a man, only much more exciting.

It was all quite innocent, but as ill-luck would have it they were seen by some people who were driving back to Brussels from Nivelles, and in less time than might have been thought possible the news that Sir Peregrine was Bab's latest victim was not only current but had reached Harriet's ears.

She was thunderstruck, and, in her nervous condition, easily convinced that the woman whom she had detested ever since the fatal expedition to Hougoumont was stealing from her Peregrine's affections. No doubt he was tired of such a dull, ailing wife: she did not blame him—or, at any rate, not very much—but no words were bad enough to describe Barbara's wicked malice.

She carried the story to Judith, casting herself upon her bosom and sobbing out her woes. Judith heard her with incredulity. She insisted upon her calming herself, obliged her to drink a glass of wine, and to sit down on the sofa, and said with brisk good sense: "I don't believe a word of it! What has Perry to say for himself?"

Oh, Harriet might be a fool, but she was not such a fool as to attack Perry with his infidelity!

"Infidelity!" said Judith. "Stuff and nonsense! What a piece of work about nothing! I daresay he may admire Barbara: who does not? But as for the rest of it—why, Harriet, it is the merest irritation of nerves! If you take my advice you'll think no more of it!"

"How can you be so heartless?" wept Harriet. "I might have guessed this would happen! I mistrusted her from the start. Perry is tired of me, and she has stolen him from me."

"I have a great affection for Perry," responded Judith tartly, "but I doubt very much his having the power to engage Lady Barbara's interest. Depend upon it, you are making a mountain out of a molehill."

"Oh no! I have been so poorly of late that I have had no spirits to go into society, and so he has looked elsewhere for amusement. I see it all!"

"Well, Harriet, if he had looked elsewhere it would not be surprising. You know how much I have always deprecated your giving way to lowness as you do. If you have a particle of sense you will abandon your sofa and your everlasting hartshorn, give up maudling your inside with tea, and go about a little, and forget your delicate situation. There! That is plain speaking, but good advice. Dry your tears, and do not waste another thought on the matter. You must have forgotten that Lady Barbara is betrothed to Charles. How could she possibly flirt with Perry?"

"There is nothing too base for that creature to do!" Harriet said, roused to a ferocity surprising in one ordinarily

184

so gentle. "I pity Charles Audley! He may be deceived, but I am not."

"That must be considered an advantage. With your eyes open to a possible danger you may act with tact and prudence."

"It is very easy for you to talk in that careless way! Your husband has not been stealing away from you to flirt with a fast, unprincipled female!"

"Come! This is much better," said Judith, with a smile. "If flirtation is all you have to worry about, there can be no occasion for such heat. Lady Bab flirts with everyone, but I believe it to be no more than a fashionable diversion, signifying precisely nothing."

Harriet burst into tears, and while Judith was endeavouring to give her thoughts a more cheerful direction, Colonel Audley strolled into the room with his nephew on his shoulder. He stopped dead on the threshold when he saw what lay before him, hastily begged pardon, and retreated with all a man's horror of becoming mixed up in a scene of feminine vapours. But before he could make good his escape Judith had called to him to stay.

"Charles, for goodness' sake come here and tell Harriet what a goose she is!"

"Oh!" gasped the afflicted lady. "*He* must not know!"

"Fiddle!" said Judith. "If the tale is all over town, as you say it is, he will know soon enough. Charles, Harriet has taken a notion into her head that Perry has fallen in love with Lady Barbara, and has been seen dining with her in the suburbs. Now, is there one word of truth in it?"

"I hope he has not fallen in love with her, but it is quite true that they dined together in the suburbs," replied the Colonel. He set his nephew down, and sent him back to his nurse with a friendly pat. "Off with you, monkey! I am afraid you must blame me, Lady Taverner: it was entirely my fault."

"Oh no, no!"

"On the contrary, it is oh yes, yes!" he said, smiling. "The case was, that Bab took a fancy into her head to dine by the roadside at one of those cafés outside the Porte de Namur. I could not escort her, and so Perry became my deputy. That is the whole truth in a nutshell."

"I knew there must be some very ordinary explanation," exclaimed Judith. "Now, Harriet, you can be satisfied, I hope. If Charles sees no harm I am sure you need not."

But Harriet was far from being satisfied. If the affair had been innocent, why had Perry kept it a secret?

"What! did he forget to tell you?" said the Colonel, exchanging a startled glance with his sister-in-law. "Stupid young rascal! I advise you to take him severely to task: he's a great deal too forgetful!"

It would not do. Harriet dried her tears, but a score of incidents had been recalled to her mind, and she could not convince herself that Peregrine had not from the outset been attracted by Barbara's wiles. The Colonel's presence made it impossible for her to say that it was all Barbara's fault, which she was sure it was, and so she was silent, allowing Judith to talk, but too busy with her own thoughts to lend more than half an ear to all the sensible things that were being said to her.

She presently went away, leaving Judith and Audley to look at one another in some consternation.

"My dear Charles, nothing could be more unfortunate!" Judith said, with a rueful laugh. "I acquit Lady Barbara of wishing to enslave poor Perry, but I am afraid there may be a grain of truth in Harriet's suspicions. It has sometimes seemed to me that Perry was a trifle smitten with Lady Barbara."

"Yes, I think he is," admitted the Colonel. "But really, Judith, I believe it to be Harriet's own fault!"

"Oh, undoubtedly, and so I have told her! It all arose out of that wretched expedition to Hougoumont! I wish I had not meddled!"

He looked at her with an arrested expression in his eyes. "Why?" he asked. "What occurred at Hougoumont to give rise to this piece of nonsense?"

The colour rushed into her face. Vexed with herself for having allowed such unguarded words to escape her, she said: "Oh, nothing, nothing! It was only that Harriet took a dislike to Lady Barbara!"

"Indeed! Why should she do that?"

She found herself unable to meet his gaze with composure, and turned away on the pretext of shaking up the sofa cushions. "Oh! You know what a country-mouse Harriet is! She has not been in the way of meeting fashionable people, and is easily shocked. Lady Barbara was in one of her capricious moods, and I daresay that may have set Harriet against her."

"You may as well tell me the truth, Judith. Did Bab's caprice lead her to flirt with Perry, or what?"

"No, certainly not. Perry was with us the whole time," she said involuntarily.

"Perry was with you! Where, then, was Bab?"

"She was with us too, of course. But Harriet and I drove in a barouche, the others rode. I only meant that Perry rode beside us, while Lady Barbara and the Count were not unnaturally tempted to leave the road for the Forest. I am sure they were not to be blamed for that: I should have liked to have done so myself."

"I see," he replied.

An uncomfortable silence fell; the Colonel was looking abstractedly out of the window, one hand fiddling with the blind-cord. Judith felt herself impelled to say presently: "There was nothing more, I assure you. Do not be imagining anything foolish!"

He turned and smiled at her. "My dear Judith, you are looking quite anxious! There is really not the least cause, I promise you. As for this affair of Perry's, I'll speak to Bab."

"Don't if you had rather not!" she said. "I daresay it is all nonsense."

"The scandal, if there is one, had better be scotched, however."

But Barbara, when she heard of Harriet's suspicions, exclaimed indignantly: "Oh, that's a great deal too bad! Of all the injustices in this wicked world! I treated him as I treat Harry—I did really, Charles!"

187

"I don't doubt it," he said. "The truth is, I suspect, that you were much more enchanting than you knew. Is Perry in danger of losing his heart to you, do you think?"

"I think he might be made to lose it," she replied candidly. "But what a fool his wife must be!"

"I believe she is in a delicate situation just at present."

"Oh, poor creature! Very well, I will make everything right with her. Then she may be comfortable again."

The occasion offered itself that same day. Walking in the Park with a party of friends, Barbara saw Lady Taverner approaching with her sister-in-law. She left her friends, and went forward to meet Harriet, holding up a frilled parasol in one hand and extending the other in a friendly fashion. "I have been wanting to meet you, Lady Taverner," she said, with one of her swift smiles. "I believe there is a nonsensical story current, and though I have no doubt of your laughing at it, I daresay it may have vexed you a little."

The hand was ignored. Lady Taverner turned scarlet and, with a glance of contempt, whisked round on her heel and walked away.

Judith, sensible of the generosity that had prompted Barbara to approach Harriet, stood rooted to the ground in dismay. What could possess Harriet to behave with such rudeness? The folly of it passed her comprehension; she could only gaze after her in amazement. The path was full of people; twenty or thirty pairs of eyes must have witnessed the snub. She said in a deeply mortified voice: "I beg your pardon! My sister-in-law is not quite herself. I do not know what she could be thinking of!"

She glanced at Barbara, and was not surprised to see her green eyes as hard as two bits of glass. A little colour had stolen into her cheeks; her lips were just parted over her clenched teeth. If ever anyone was in a rage she was in one now, thought Judith. She looked ripe for murder, and really one could not blame her.

"That," said Barbara, "was neither wise nor well-bred of Lady Taverner. Convey my compliments to her,

188

if you please, and inform her that I shall endeavour not to disappoint her very evident expectations."

"She is extremely foolish, and I beg you will not notice her rudeness!" said Judith. "No one regards what you so rightly call the nonsensical story which is current."

"How simple of you to think so! The story must *now* be implicitly believed. By to-morrow I shall be credited with a sin I haven't committed, which touches my pride, you know. I always give the scandal-mongers food for their gossip."

"To give them food in this case would be to behave as foolishly as my sister-in law," said Judith, trying to speak pleasantly.

"Oh, I have my reputation to consider!" Barbara retorted. "I make trouble wherever I go: haven't you been told so?"

"I have tried not to believe it."

"A mistake! I am quite as black as I am painted, I assure you. But I am keeping you from Lady Taverner. Go after her—and don't forget my message!"

CHAPTER XIV

JUDITH did not go after her sister-in-law. She had very little hope of inducing Harriet to apologize, nor, upon reflection, did she feel inclined to make the attempt. She could not think Barbara blameless in the affair. However well she might have behaved in extending an olive-branch, the original fault was one for which Judith could find little excuse. If Barbara wanted to dine in the suburbs (which, in itself, was a foolish whim) she might as well have chosen an evening when Charles would have been free to have escorted her.

Judith acquitted her of wanting to make mischief. It had all been the result of thoughtlessness, and had Harriet behaved like a sensible woman nothing more need have come of it. But Harriet had chosen to do the one thing that would lend colour to whatever gossip was afoot, and had besides made an enemy of a dangerous young woman. It still made Judith blush to think of the scene. In Barbara's place she would, she acknowledged, have been angry enough to have boxed Harriet's ears. But such sudden anger was usually short-lived. She hoped that a period of calm reflection would give Barbara's thoughts a more proper direction, and determined to say nothing of the occurrence to Charles.

She heard her name spoken, and came out of her reverie to find herself confronting Lord Fitzroy Somerset, who, with his elder brother, Lord Edward, and their nephew, Henry Somerset, was strolling along the path down which her unconscious footsteps had taken her.

Greetings and handshakes followed. Judith was acquainted with Lord Edward, but Lieutenant Somerset, who was acting as his uncle's Aide-de-Camp, had to be presented to her. Lord Edward had only lately arrived from England, to command the brigade of Household Cavalry. He was twelve years Lord Fitzroy's senior, and did not much resemble him. Fitzroy was fair, with an open brow, and very regular features. Lord Edward was harsh-featured and dark, with deep lines running down from the corners of his jutting nose and his close-lipped mouth, and two clefts between his brows. His eyes were rather hard, and he did not look to have that sweetness of disposition which made his brother universally beloved; but he was quite unaffected, laughed and talked a great deal, and seemed perfectly ready to be agreeable. Judith enquired after his wife; he had not brought her to the Netherlands; he thought—saving Lady Worth's presence! —that the seat of an approaching war was not the place for females.

"Your husband is not engaged in the operations, and so the case is different," he said. "But I assure you, the women who would persist in following the Army in Spain were at times a real hindrance to us. Nothing would stop them! Very courageous, you will say, and I won't deny it, but they were the devil to deal with on the march, choking the roads with their gear!"

She smiled, and agreed that it must have been so. She had turned to retrace her steps with the Somersets, and as the path was not broad enough to allow of their walking abreast, Lord Fitzroy and his nephew had gone ahead. She indicated Fitzroy with a nod, and remarked that his brother must not speak so in his hearing.

"Oh, Fitzroy knows what I think!" replied Lord Edward. "However, he is not an old married man like me, so he must be pardoned. Not but what I think it a great piece of folly on his part. Of course, you know Lady Fitzroy has lately been confined?"

"Indeed I do, and I am one of her daughter's chief admirers!"

"I daresay. A nice thing it would have been had she been obliged to remove in a hurry!"

"Depend upon it, had there been any fear of that her uncle must have known of it, and she could have retired without the least hurry to Antwerp. *He* does not appear to share your prejudice against us poor females!"

"The Duke! No, that he does not!" replied Lord Edward, laughing. "But, come, enough of the whole subject, or I can see I shall be quite out of favour with you! I understand I have to congratulate Audley upon his engagement?"

She acknowledged it, but briefly. He said in his downright way: "I don't know how you may regard the matter, but I should have said Audley was too good a man for Bab Childe."

She found herself so much in accordance with this opinion that she was unable to forbear giving him a very speaking glance.

"Just so," he said, with a nod. "I have known the whole family for years—got one of them in my brigade now: handsome young devil, up to no good—and I shouldn't care to be connected with any of them. As for Audley, he's the last man in the world I should have expected to be caught by Bab's tricks. Great pity, though I shouldn't say so to you, I suppose."

"Lady Barbara is very beautiful," Judith replied, with a certain amount of reserve.

He gave a somewhat scornful grunt, and said no more. They had reached one of the gates opening on to the Rue Royale by this time, and Lord Edward, who was on his way to Headquarters, took his leave of Judith, and strode off up the road with his nephew.

Lord Fitzroy gave Judith his arm. He had to pay a call at the Hôtel de Belle Vue, and was thus able to accompany her to her door. They walked in that direction through the Park, talking companionably of Lady Fitzroy's progress, of the infant daughter's first airing, and other such mild topics, until presently they were joined by Sir Alexander Gordon, very smart in a new coat and sash, on which Lord Fitzroy immediately quizzed him.

Judith listened, smiling, to the interchange of friendly raillery, occasionally being appealed to by one of them, to give her support to some outrageous libel on the other.

"Gordon," Fitzroy informed her, "is one of our dressier colleagues. He has seventeen pairs of boots. That's called upholding the honour of the family."

"One of Fitzroy's grosser lies, Lady Worth. Now, the really dressy member of the family is Charles."

"He has the excuse of being a Hussar. They can't help being dressy, Lady Worth. However, the strain of trying to procure a sufficiency of silver lace in Spain wore the poor fellow out, and in the end he was quite thankful to be taken into the family. I say, Gordon, why didn't you join a Hussar Regiment? Was it because you were too fat?"

"A dignified silence," Gordon told Judith, "is the only weapon to use against vulgar persons."

"Very true. It is all jealousy, I daresay. I feel sure you would set off a Hussar uniform to admiration."

"Fill it out, don't you mean?" enquired Fitzroy.

Sir Alexander was diverted from his purpose of retaliating in kind by catching sight of Barbara Childe between two Riflemen. "When does that marriage take place, Lady Worth?" he asked.

"The date is not fixed."

"There's hope yet, then. That's Johnny Kincaid with her—the tall lanky one on her right. Perhaps he'll cut Charles out. Very charming fellow, Kincaid."

Fitzroy shook his head. "No chance of that. Kincaid loves Juana Smith—or so I've always fancied."

Judith said: "Is that how you feel, Sir Alexander? About Charles's engagement, I mean?"

"I beg pardon! I shouldn't have said it."

"You may say what you please. I am forced in general to be very discreet, but you are both such particular friends of Charles's that I may be allowed to speak my mind—which is that it would be better if the marriage never took place."

"Of course it would be better! There was never anything more unfortunate! We laughed at Charles when it began, but it has turned out to be no laughing matter. It was all the Prince's fault for making the introduction in the first place."

"Nonsense, Gordon! If he had not someone else would have done it. I am afraid Charles is pretty hard hit, Lady Worth."

"I am afraid so, too. I wish he were not, but what can one do?"

"One can't do anything," said Gordon. "That's the sad part of it: to be obliged to watch one of your best friends making a fool of himself."

"Do you dislike Lady Barbara?"

"No. I like her, but the thing is that I like Charles much more, and I can't see him tied to her for the rest of his life."

"It may yet come to nothing."

"That's what I say, but Fitzroy will have it that if Bab throws him over it will be the end of him."

"No, I didn't say that," interposed Lord Fitzroy. "But you can't live with a man for as long as I've lived with Charles, and come through tight places with him, and work with him day in, day out, without getting to know him pretty well, and I do say that I believe him to be in earnest over this. I expect he knows his own business best —only I do wish he would stop burning the candle at both ends!"

"He can't," said Gordon. "You have to run fast if you mean to keep pace with Bab."

They had reached the Rue du Belle Vue by this time, and no more was said. Lord Fitzroy took his leave, Sir Alexander escorted Lady Worth to her own door, and she went in, feeling despondent and quite out of spirits.

The Duchess of Richmond held an informal party that evening, at her house off the Rue de la Blanchisserie, which was situated in the northern quarter of the town, not far from the Allée Verte. The Duke of Wellington had, from its locality, irreverently named it the Wash-house, but it was, in fact, a charming abode, placed in a large garden extending to the ramparts, and with a smaller house, or cottage, in the grounds which was occupied, whenever he was in Brussels, by Lord March.

The Duchess's parties were always popular. She had a great gift for entertaining, knew everyone, and had such a numerous family of sons and daughters that her house was quite a rendezvous for the younger set. Besides the nursery party, which consisted of several lusty children who did not appear in the drawing-room unless they had prevailed upon some indulgent friend, like the Duke of Wellington, to beg for them to come downstairs, there was a cluster of pretty daughters, and three fine sons: Lord March, Lord George Lennox, and Lord William.

Lord March was not present at the party, being at Braine-le-Comte with the Prince of Orange; and Lord William, who had had such a shocking fall from his horse, was still confined to his room; but Lord George, one of Wellington's Aides-de-Camp, was there; and of course the four daughters of the house: Lady Mary, Lady Sarah, Lady Jane, and Lady Georgiana.

The Duke of Wellington did not gratify the company by putting in an appearance. The redoubtable Duchesse d'Angoulême had lately arrived in Ghent, and he had gone there to pay his respects to her, taking Colonel Audley with him. But although the party was composed mostly of young people, several Major-Generals were present with their wives, quite a number of distinguished civilians, and of course Sir Sydney Smith, working his startling brows up and down, flashing his eyes about the room, and drawing a great deal of attention to himself with his theatrical eccentricities.

Lady Worth, who arrived rather late with her husband, was glad to see that Harriet had torn herself from her couch and had come with Peregrine. It was evident that she had entered the lists against Barbara, for she was wearing one of her best gowns, had had her hair dressed in a new style, and had even improved her complexion with a dash of rouge. She seemed to be in spirits, and Judith was just reflecting on the beneficial results of a spasm of jealousy when in walked Barbara, ravishing in a white satin slip under a robe of celestial blue crape, caught together down the front with clasps of flowers. Judith's complacency was ended. Peregrine, like nearly everyone else, was gazing at the vision. Who, Judith wondered despairingly, would look twice at Harriet in her figured muslin and her amethysts, when Barbara stood laughing under the great chandelier, flirting a fan of frosted crape which twinkled in the candlelight, the brilliants round her neck no more sparkling than her eyes?

She glanced round the room, blew a kiss to Georgiana, nodded at Judith. Her gaze swept past Peregrine, and Judith found herself heaving a sigh of relief: she was going to be good, then! The next instant her spirit quailed again, for she caught sight of Harriet's face, set in rigid lines of disdain, and heard her say in a clear, hard little voice to the lady standing beside her: "My dear ma'am, of course it is dyed! I should not have thought it could have deceived a child. Perry, let us remove into the salon: I find this place a little too *hot* for me."

That her words had reached Barbara's ears was evident to Judith. The green eyes rested enigmatically on Harriet's face for a moment, and then travelled on to Peregrine. A little tantalizing smile hovered on the lovely mouth; the eyes unmistakably beckoned.

"In a minute!" said Peregrine. "I must say how do you do to Lady Bab first."

He left Harriet's side as he spoke, and walked right across the room to where Barbara stood, waiting for him to come to her. She held out her hand to him; he kissed it; she murmured something, and he laughed, very gallantly offered his arm, and went off with her towards the glass doors thrown open into the garden.

"But what finesse!" said Worth's languid voice, immediately behind Judith. "I make her my compliments. In its way, perfect!"

"I should like to box her ears, and Harriet's, and Peregrine's, and yours too!" replied Judith in a wrathful whisper.

"In that case, my love, I will remove one temptation at least out of your way."

She detained him. "Worth, you must speak to Perry!"

"I shall do no such thing."

"It is your duty: after all, he is your ward!"

"Oh no, he is not! He *was* my ward. That is a very different matter. Moreover, my heart wouldn't be in it: Harriet offered battle, and has been defeated in one brilliant engagement. I cannot consider it to be any concern of mine—though I shall be interested to see the outcome."

"If you have taken it into your head to save your brother at the expense of mine, Julian, I tell you now that I won't have it!" said Judith.

He smiled, but returned no answer, merely moving away to join a group of men by the stairs.

The rest of the evening passed wretchedly enough for Judith. It was some time before Peregrine reappeared, and when he did at last come back from the garden he was in high fettle. Harriet, employing new tactics, had joined the younger guests in the ballroom, and was behaving in a manner quite unlike herself, chattering and laughing, and promising more dances than the night could possibly hold. Never remarkable for his perception, Peregrine beamed with pleasure, and told her that he had known all along that she would enjoy herself.

"I am afraid you have come too late, Peregrine!" she said, very bright-eyed. "Every dance is booked!"

"Oh, that's capital!" he replied. "Don't bother your head over me: I shall do famously!"

After this well-meaning piece of tactlessness, he withdrew from the ballroom, and was next seen in the salon, turning over the leaves of her music for Barbara, who had been persuaded to sing Mr. Guest's latest ballad, *The Farewell*.

On the following morning, while she sat at breakfast, a note was brought round to Judith by hand. It was directed in a fist that showed unmistakable signs of agitation, and sealed with a lilac wafer set hopelessly askew.

"Harriet!" said Judith in long-suffering accents. She tore the sheet open, and remarked: "Blotched with tears! She wants me to go to her immediately."

"Will you have the carriage ordered at once, or will you delay your departure long enough to pour me out some more coffee?" enquired the Earl.

"I haven't the least intention of going until I have finished my breakfast, spoken with my housekeeper, and seen my son," replied Judith, stretching out her hand for his cup. "If Harriet imagines I shall sympathize with her she very much mistakes the matter. Her behaviour was odiously rude, and I am out of all patience with her. Depend upon it, she has crowned her folly by quarrelling with Perry. Well, I wash my hands of it! Do you think Perry is really in love with that horrid creature?"

"Certainly not," he answered. "Perry is a trifle intoxicated, and extremely callow. His present conduct reminds me irresistibly of his behaviour when he first discovered in himself an aptitude for sailing. He has not altered in the smallest degree."

"Oh, Worth, it would be a dreadful thing if this wretched affair were to come between him and Harriet!"

"Very dreadful," he agreed, picking up the *Gazette*.

"It is all very well for you to say 'Very dreadful' in that hateful voice, just as if it didn't signify an atom, but I am extremely anxious! I wonder why Harriet wants me so urgently?"

It appeared, when Judith saw her an hour later, that Harriet wanted to announce the tidings of her imminent demise. "I wish I were dead!" she moaned, from behind a positive rampart of bottles of smelling-salts, hartshorn, and lavender-drops. "I shall die, for Perry has been so wickedly cruel, and my heart is broken, and I feel quite shattered! I hope I never set eyes on either of them again, and if Perry means to dine at home I shall lock myself in my room, and go home to Mama!"

"You might, if you were silly enough, perform one of those actions," said Judith reasonably, "but I do not see how you can accomplish both. For heaven's sake, stop crying, and tell me what is the matter."

"Perry has been out riding before breakfast with That Woman!" announced Harriet in tragic accents.

Judith could not help laughing. "Dear me, is that all, you goose?"

"In the Allée Verte!"

"Shocking!"

"By appointment with her!"

"No!"

"And alone!"

"My dear, if there is more to come I shall be obliged to borrow your smelling-salts, I fear."

"How can you laugh? Have you no sensibility? He actually told me of it! He was brazen, Judith! He said she was the most stunning creature he had ever laid eyes on! He said that to *me!*"

"If he said it to you it is a sure sign that his affections are not seriously engaged. If I were you I would take him back to Yorkshire, and forget the whole affair."

"He won't go!" said Harriet, burying her face in her handkerchief. "He said so. We have had a terrible quarrel! I told him——"

Judith flung up her hands. "I can readily imagine what you told him! Perry is nothing but a heedless boy! I daresay he never dreamed of being in love with Lady Barbara. He thought of her as Charles's fiancée, he found her good company, he admired her beauty. And what must you do but put it into his head to fall in love with her! Oh, Harriet, Harriet, what a piece of work you have made of it!"

This was poor comfort for an afflicted lady, and provoked Harriet to renewed floods of tears. It was some time before she was able to regain any degree of calm, and even when her tears were dried Judith saw that no advice would be attended to until she had had time to recover from the ill-effects of her first quarrel with Peregrine. She persuaded her to take the air in an open carriage, and sat beside her during the drive, endeavouring to engage her interest in everyday topics. Nothing would do, however. Harriet sat with her veil down; declined noticing the flowers in the Park, the barges on the canal, or the pigeons on the steps of St. Gudule; and was morbidly convinced that she was an object of pity and amusement to every passer-by who bowed a civil greeting. Judith was out of all patience long before the drive came to an end, and when she at last set Harriet down at the door of her lodging her sympathies lay so much with Peregrine that she was able to wave to him, when she caught sight of him presently, with a perfectly good will.

Such feelings were not of long duration. A second note from Harriet, received during the evening, informed her that Peregrine had returned home only to change his dress, and had gone out again without having made the least attempt to see his wife. Harriet declared herself to be in no doubt of his destination, and ended an incoherent and blistered letter by the expression of a strong wish to go home to her mama.

By the following day every suspicion had been confirmed: Peregrine had indeed been in Barbara's company. He had made one of a party bound for the neighbourhood of Hal, and had picnicked there on the banks of the Senne, returning home only with the dawn. To make matters worse, it had been he whom Barbara had chosen to escort her in her phaeton. Every gossiping tongue in Brussels was wagging; Harriet had received no less than five morning calls from thoughtful acquaintances who feared she might not have heard the news; and more than one matron had felt it to be her duty to warn Judith of her young brother's infatuation. Loyalty compelled Judith to make light of the affair, but by noon her patience had become so worn-down that the only person towards whom her sympathy continued to be extended was Charles Audley.

He had not made one of the picnic party, and from the circumstance of his being employed by the Duke all the following morning it was some time before any echo of the gossip came to his ears. It reached him in the end through the agency of Sir Colin Campbell, the Commandant, who, not supposing him to be within earshot, said in his terse fashion to Gordon: "The news is all over town that that young woman of Audley's is breaking up the Taverner household."

"Good God, sir, you don't mean it? Confound her, why can't she give Charles a little peace?"

Sir Colin grunted. "He'll be well rid of her," he said dourly. He turned, and saw Colonel Audley standing perfectly still in the doorway. "The devil!" he ejaculated. "Well, you were not meant to hear, but since you have heard there's no helping it now. I'm away to see the Mayor."

Colonel Audley stood aside to allow him to pass out of the room, and then shut the door, and said quietly: "What's all this nonsense, Gordon?"

"My dear fellow, I don't know! Some cock-and-bull story old Campbell has picked up—probably from a Belgian, which would account for its being thoroughly garbled. Did I tell you that I found him bewildering the *maître d'hôtel* the other day over the correct way to lay a table? He kept on saying: '*Beefsteak, venez ici! Pettypatties, allez là!*' till the poor man thought he was quite mad."

"Yes, you told me," replied Audley. "What is the news that is all over town?"

A glance at his face convinced Sir Alexander that evasion would not answer. He said, therefore, in a perfectly natural tone: "Well, you came in before I had time to ask any questions, but according to Campbell there's a rumour afloat that Taverner is making a fool of himself over Lady Bab."

"That doesn't seem to me any reason for accusing Bab of breaking up his household."

"None at all. But you know what people are."

"There's not a word of truth in it, Gordon."

"No."

There was a note of constraint in Gordon's voice which Audley was quick to hear. He looked sharply across at his friend, and read concern in his face, and suddenly said: "Oh, for God's sake——! You needn't look like that! The very notion of such a thing is absurd!"

"Steady!" Gordon said. "It isn't my scandal."

"I know. I'm sorry. But I am sick to death of this town, and the gossip that goes on in it!" He sighed, and walked over to the desk, and laid some papers down on it. "You had much better tell me, Gordon. What is it now? I suppose you've heard talk?"

"Charles, dear boy, if I had I wouldn't bring it to you," replied Gordon. "I don't know what's being said, or care."

Colonel Audley glanced up and suddenly laughed. "Damn you, don't look so sorry for me! What a set you are! I'm the happiest man on earth!"

"Famous! If you are, stop wearing a worried frown, and try going to bed at night for a change." He lounged over to where Audley was standing, and gripped his shoulder, slightly shaking him. "Damned fool! Oh, you damned fool!"

"I daresay. Thank God, I'm not a fat fool, however!" He drove a friendly punch at Gordon's ribs. "Layers of it! What you need is a nice, hard campaign, my boy, to take some of it off."

"Not a chance of it! We'll be in Paris a month from now. I'll give you a dinner at a little restaurant I know where they have the best Chambertin in the whole city."

"I shall hold you to that. Where is it? I thought I knew all the restaurants in Paris."

"Ah, you don't know this one! It's in the Rue de— Rue de——confound it, I forget the name of the street, but I shall find it quick enough. Hallo, here's the Green Baby!"

Lieutenant the Honourable George Cathcart, lately enrolled as an Extra Aide-de-Camp, had come into the room. He owed his appointment to the Duke's friendship with his father, the British Ambassador at St. Petersburg. He was only twenty-one years old, but during the period of Lord Cathcart's office as Military Commissioner to the Russian Army, he had acted as his Aide-de-Camp, and was able to reply now with dignity: "I am *not* a green baby. I have seen eight general actions. And what's more," he added, as the two elder men laughed, "Naploeon commanded in them all!"

"One to you, infant," said Audley. "You have us on the hip."

"Do you think Boney knows he's with us?" said Gordon anxiously.

"Oh, not a doubt of it! He has his spies everywhere."

"Ah, then, that accounts for him holding off so long! He's frightened."

"Oh, you—you——!" Cathcart sought for a word sufficiently opprobrious to describe Sir Alexander, and could find none.

"Never mind!" said Gordon. "You won't be the baby much longer. We shall have his Royal Highness the Hereditary Prince of Nassau-Usingen with us soon, and we understand he's only nineteen."

"He can't be of any use. What the devil do we want him for?"

"We don't want him. We're just having him to lend tone to the family. Charles, are you going to Braine-le-Comte?"

"Yes, I'm waiting for the letters now. Any messages?"

"No. Such is my nobility of character that I'll go in your stead. Now, don't overwhelm me with thanks! Sacrifice is a pleasure to me."

"I shan't. Pure self-interest gleams in your eye. Give my compliments to Slender Billy, and don't outstay your welcome. Is he giving a dinner-party?"

"This ingratitude! How can you, Charles?" Gordon said.

"Easily. I shall laugh if you find the Duke has labelled the despatch 'Quick'."

"If there's any 'Quick' about it, you shall take it," promised Gordon.

"Not I! You offered to go, and you shall go. Young Mr. Cathcart will enlarge his military experience by kicking his heels here; and Colonel Audley will seize a well-earned rest from his arduous duties." He picked up his hat from a chair as he spoke, and with a wave to Gordon and an encouraging nod to Cathcart, made for the door. There he collided with a very burly young man, whose bulk almost filled the aperture. He recoiled, and said promptly: "In the very nick of time! Captain Lord Arthur Hill will be in reserve. Don't be shy, Hill! Come in! You know Gordon likes to have you near him: it's the only time he looks thin."

Lord Arthur, who enjoyed the reputation of being the fattest officer in the Army, received this welcome with his usual placid grin, and remarked as the Colonel disappeared down the stairs: "You fellows are always funning. What's happened to put Audley in such spirits? I suppose he hasn't heard the latest scandal? They tell me——"

"Oh, never mind what they tell you!" Gordon said, with such unaccustomed sharpness that Lord Arthur blinked in surprise. He added more gently: "I'm sorry, but Audley's a friend of mine, and I don't propose to discuss his affairs or to listen to the latest scandal about his fiancée. It's probably grossly exaggerated in any case."

"Oh, quite so!" said Lord Arthur hastily. "I daresay there's nothing in it at all."

CHAPTER XV

LEAVING Wellington's Headquarters, Colonel Audley made his way across the Park to Vidal's house. Barbara was not in, and as the butler was unable to tell Colonel Audley where she was to be found, he went back into the Park, and walked slowly through it in the direction of the Rue de Belle Vue. He was not rewarded by any glimpse of Barbara, but on reaching his brother's house he found Lady Taverner sitting with Judith, and indulging in a fit of weeping. He withdrew, nor did Judith try to detain him. But when Harriet had left the house he went back to the salon, and demanded an explanation of her grief.

Judith was reluctant to tell him the whole, but after listening for some moments to her glib account of nervous spasms, ridiculous fancies, and depression of spirits, he interrupted her with a request to be told the truth. She was obliged to confess that Peregrine's infatuation with Barbara was the cause of Harriet's tears. She described first the incident in the Park, feeling that it was only fair that he should know what had prompted Barbara's outrageous conduct.

He listened to her with a gradually darkening brow. "Do you expect me to believe that Bab is encouraging Peregrine's advances out of spite?" he asked.

"*I* should not have used that word. Revenge, let us say."

"Revenge! We need not employ the language of the theatre, I suppose! What more have you to tell me? I imagine there must be more, since I understand that the whole town is talking of the affair."

"It is very unfortunate. I blame Harriet for the rest. She quarrelled with Perry, and I have no doubt made him angry and defiant. You know what a boy he is!"

He replied sternly: "He is not such a boy but that he knew very well what he was about when he made advances to my promised wife!"

"It was very bad," she acknowledged. "But, though I do not like to say this to you, Charles, I believe it was not all his fault."

"No! That is evident!" he returned. He walked over to the window and stood staring out. After a slight pause, he said in a quieter voice: "Well, now for the rest, if you please."

"I do not like the office of tale-bearer."

He gave a short laugh. "You need not be squeamish, Judith. I suppose I have only to listen to what the gossips are saying to learn the whole of it."

"You would hear a garbled version, I assure you."

"Then you had better let me hear the true version."

"I only know what Harriet has told me. I am persuaded that had it not been for *her* conduct, which, you know, was very bad, the affair would never have gone beyond that one unfortunate evening in the suburbs. But she cut Lady Barbara in the rudest way! That began it. I could see how angry Lady Barbara was: indeed, I didn't blame her. I hoped her anger would cool. I think it might have—I think, in fact, it had cooled. Then came the Duchess of Richmond's party. I saw Lady Barbara look round the hall when she arrived, and I can vouch for her having made no sign to Perry. I don't think she gave him as much as a civil bow. There was a lull in the conversation; everyone was staring at Lady Barbara—you know how they do! —and Harriet made a remark there could be no misunderstanding. It was stupid and ill-bred: I know I felt ready to sink. She then told Perry that she wished to remove into the salon, saying that the hall was too *hot* for her. Lady Barbara could not but hear. It was said, moreover, in such a tone as to leave no room for anyone to mistake its meaning."

She paused. The Colonel had turned away from the window, and was attending to her with a look of interest. He was still frowning, but not so heavily, and at the back of his eyes she fancied she could perceive the suspicion of a smile. "Go on!" he said.

She laughed. "Worth said that in its way it was perfect. I suppose it was."

"He did, did he? What happened?"

"Well, Lady Barbara just took Perry away from Harriet.

It is of no use to ask me how, for I don't know. It may sound absurd, but I saw it with my own eyes, and I am ready to swear she neither moved nor spoke. She looked at him, and smiled, and he walked right across the room to her side."

He was now openly laughing. "Is that all? Of course, it was very bad of Bab, but I think Harriet deserved it. It must have been sublime!"

"Yes," she agreed, but with rather a sober face.

He regarded her intently. "Is there more, Judith?"

"I am afraid there is. As I told you, Harriet quarrelled with Perry. You remember, Charles, that you were in Ghent. It seems that Perry rode out with Lady Barbara before breakfast next morning. I believe she is in the habit of riding in the Allée Verte every morning."

"You need not tell me that," he interrupted. "I know. She appointed Perry to ride with her?"

"So I understand. He made no secret of it, which makes me feel that he cannot have intended the least harm. But Harriet was suffering from such an irritation of nerves that she allowed her jealousy to overcome her good sense; they quarrelled; Perry left the house in anger; and, I daresay out of sheer defiance, joined a party Lady Barbara had got together to picnic in the country that evening. The gossip arose out of his being the one chosen to drive with her in her phaeton. I am afraid he has done little to allay suspicion since. It is all such a stupid piece of nonsense, but oh, Charles, if you would but use your influence with Lady Barbara! Harriet is in despair, and indeed it is very disagreeable, to say the least of it, to have such a scandal in our midst!"

"Disagreeable!" he exclaimed. "It is a damnable piece of work!" He checked himself, and continued in a more moderate tone: "I beg your pardon, but you will agree that I have reason to feel this strongly. Is Peregrine with Bab now?"

"I do not know, but I judge it to be very probable." She saw him compress his lips, and added: "I think if you were to speak to Lady Barbara——"

"I shall speak to Barbara in good time, but my present business is with Peregrine."

She could not help feeling a little alarmed. He spoke in a grim voice which she had never heard before, and when she stole a glance at his face there was nothing in its expression to reassure her. She said falteringly: "You will do what is right, I am sure."

He glanced down at her, and seeing how anxiously she was looking at him, said with a faint smile, but with a touch of impatience: "My dear Judith, do you suppose I am going to run Peregrine through, or what?"

She lowered her eyes in a little confusion. "Oh! of course not! What an absurd notion! But what do you mean to do?"

"Put an end to this nauseating business," he replied.

"Oh, if you could! Such affairs may so easily lead to disaster!"

"Very easily."

She sighed, and said rather doubtfully: "Do you think that it will answer? I would have spoken to Perry myself, only that I feared to do more harm than good. When he gets these headstrong fits the least hint of opposition seems to make him worse. I begged Worth to intervene, but he declined doing it, and I daresay he was right."

"Worth!" he said. "No, it is not for him to speak to Peregrine. I am the one who is concerned in this, and what I have to say to Peregrine I can assure you he will pay heed to!" He glanced at the clock over the fireplace, and added: "I am going to call at his house now. Don't look so anxious, there is not the least need."

She stretched out her hand to him. "If I look anxious it is on your account. Dear Charles, I am so sorry this should have happened! Don't let it vex you: it was all mischief, nothing else!"

He grasped her hand for a moment, and said in a low voice: "Unpleasant mischief! It is the fault of that wretched upbringing! Sometimes I fear—— But the *heart* is unspoiled Try to believe that: I know it."

She could only press his fingers understandingly. He

held her hand an instant longer, then, with a brief smile, let it go and walked out of the room.

Peregrine was not to be found at his house, but Colonel Audley sent up his card to Lady Taverner, and was presently admitted into her salon.

She received him with evident agitation. She looked frightened, and greeted him with nervous breathlessness, trying to seem at ease, but failing miserably.

He shook hands with her, and put her out of her agony of uncertainty by coming straight to the point. "Lady Taverner, we are old friends," he said in his pleasant way. "You need not be afraid to trust me, and I need not, I know, fear to be frank with you. I have come about this nonsensical affair of Peregrine's. Shall we sit down and talk it over sensibly together?"

She said faintly: "Oh! how can I—— You—I do not know how to——"

"You will agree that I am concerned in it as much as you are," he said. "Judith has been telling me the whole. What a tangle it is! And all arising out of my stupidity in allowing Peregrine to be my deputy that evening! Can you forgive me?"

She sank down upon the sofa, averting her face. "I am sure you never dreamed—Judith says it is my own fault, that I brought it on myself by my folly!"

"I think the hardest thing of all is to be wise in our dealings with the people we love," he said. "I know I have found it so."

She ventured to turn her head towards him. "Perhaps I was a fool. Judith will have told you that I was rude and ill-bred. It is true! I do not know what can have possessed me, only when she came up to me, so beautiful, and—oh, I cannot explain! I am sorry: this is very uncomfortable for you!"

Her utterance became choked by tears; she groped for her handkerchief amongst the sofa cushions, and was startled by finding a large one put into her hand. Her drenched eyes flew upwards to the Colonel's face; a sound between a sob and a laugh escaped her, and she said unsteadily: "Thank you! You are very obliging! Oh dear, how can you be so—so—I am sure I don't know why I am laughing when my heart is broken!"

Colonel Audley watched her dry her cheeks, and said: "But your heart isn't broken."

Harriet emerged from his handkerchief to say with a good deal of indignation: "I don't see how you can know whether my heart is broken or not!"

"Of course I can know, for I know mine is not."

This seemed unanswerable. Harriet could only look helplessly at him, and wait for more.

He smiled at her, and took his handkerchief back. "Crying won't mend matters. I rely on you to help me in this business."

The idea was so novel that she blinked at him in surprise. "How can I?"

"By behaving like the sensible woman I know you to be. Confess! didn't you mishandle Peregrine shockingly?"

"Yes, perhaps I did, but how could he be so faithless? I thought he loved me!"

"So he does. But he is very young. In general, a boy goes through a number of calf-loves before he marries, but in your case it was different. I expect you were his first love."

"Yes," whispered Harriet.

"Well, that was charming," he said cheerfully. "Only, you see, this was bound to happen."

"Bound to happen?"

"Yes, certainly. *You* have not been very well; *he* has been left to his own devices, and in circumstances where it would have been wonderful indeed if, at twenty-three, he had kept his head. This life we are all leading in Brussels is ruinous. Are you not conscious of it?"

"Oh yes, a thousand times yes! I wish I were safely at home!"

"I am glad to hear you say so, for that is what, if you will let me, I am going to advise you to do. Go home, and forget all this."

"He won't go home!"

209

"Yes, he will. Only you mustn't reproach him just yet. Later, if you like, and still want to, but not now. He will be very much ashamed of himself presently, and wonder how he can have been such a fool."

"How can you know all this?"

He smiled. "I have been twenty-three myself. Of course I know. You may believe me when I tell you that this doesn't signify. No, I know you cannot quite see how that may be true, but I pledge you my word it is."

She sighed. "How kind you are! You make me feel such a goose! How shall I prevail upon Perry to take me home? What shall I say to him?"

"Nothing. I am going to have a talk with him, and I think you will find him only too ready to take you home." He rose, and took out his card-case, and, extracting a card, wrote something on the back of it with a pencil picked up from Harriet's escritoire. "I'll leave this with your butler," he said. "It is just to inform Peregrine that I am coming to call on him after dinner to-night. You need not mention that you have seen me."

"Oh no! But he is sure to be going out," she said mournfully.

"Don't worry! He won't go out," replied the Colonel.

She looked doubtful, but it seemed that the Colonel knew what he was talking about, for Peregrine, the card with its curt message in his waistcoat-pocket, retired after dinner to his study on the ground-floor. Dinner had been an uncomfortable meal. When the servants were in the room a civil interchange of conversation had to be maintained; when they left it, Harriet sat with downcast eyes and a heavy heart, while Peregrine, making a pretence of eating what had been put before him, wondered what Colonel Audley was going to say to him, and what he was to reply.

The Colonel, who had dined at the Duke's table, did not arrive until after nine o'clock, and by that time Peregrine had reached a state of acute discomfort. When the knock at last fell on the front-door, he got up out of his chair and nervously straightened his cravat. When the Colonel was shown into the room, he was standing with his back to the empty fireplace, looking rather pale and feeling a trifle sick.

One glance at his visitor's face was enough to confirm his worst fears. This was going to be an extremely unpleasant interview. He wondered whether Audley would insist on satisfaction. He was not a coward, but the knowledge of having behaved very shabbily towards Audley set him at a disadvantage, and made him hope very much that the affair was not going to culminate in a meeting outside the ramparts in the chill dawn.

He tried, from sheer nervousness, to carry the thing off with a high hand, advancing with a smile, and saying with as much heartiness as he could muster: "Well, Charles! How do you do?"

The Colonel ignored both the greeting and the outstretched hand. He laid his hat and gloves down on the table, saying in a voice that reminded Peregrine unpleasantly of Worth's: "What I have to say to you, Peregrine, will not take me long. I imagine you have a pretty fair notion why I am here."

"I——" Peregrine stopped, and then said defiantly: "I suppose I have. Well, say it, then!"

"I'm going to," said the Colonel grimly.

Peregrine squared his shoulders and set his teeth. At the end of three minutes he was bitterly regretting having invited the Colonel to speak his mind, and at the end of ten he would have been very glad if the ground had miraculously opened and swallowed him. The Colonel spoke with appalling fluency, and in the most biting of voices. What he said was so entirely unanswerable that after two stumbling attempts to defend himself Peregrine relapsed into silence, and listened with a white face to an exposition of his character which robbed him of every ounce of self-esteem.

When the Colonel at last stopped, Peregrine, who for some time had been standing by the window, with his back to him, cleared his throat, and said: "I am aware how my conduct must strike you. If you want satisfaction, of course I am ready to meet you."

This handsome offer was not received quite as Peregrine

had expected. "Don't talk to me in that nonsensical fashion!" said the Colonel scathingly. "Do you imagine that you're a rival of mine?"

Peregrine winced, and muttered: "No. It isn't—I didn't——"

"You are not," said the Colonel. "You are merely an unconditioned cub in need of kicking, and the only satisfaction I could enjoy would be to have you under me for just one month!"

Peregrine resumed his study of the window-blinds. It seemed that Colonel Audley had not yet finished. He spoke of Harriet, and Peregrine flushed scarlet, and presently blurted out: "I know, I know! Oh, damn you, that will do! It's all true—every word of it! But I couldn't help it! I——" He stopped, and sank into a chair by the table, and covered his face with his hands.

Audley said nothing, but walked over to the fireplace, and stood there, leaning his arms on the mantelpiece, and looking down at the fire-irons.

After a few minutes, Peregrine raised his head, and said haltingly: "You think me a low, despicable fellow, and I daresay I am, but on my honour I never meant to—— Oh, what's the use of trying to explain?"

"It is quite unnecessary."

"Yes, but you don't understand! I never realized till it was too late, and even then I didn't think—I mean, I knew it was you she cared for, only when I'm with her I forget everything else! She's so beautiful, Audley!"

"Yes," said the Colonel. "I understand all that. The remedy is not to see any more of her."

"But I shall see her! I must!"

"Oh no, you must not! I imagine you do not expect her to elope with you?"

"No, no! Good God, such an idea never——"

"Very well then. The only thing you can do, Peregrine, since the sight of her is so disastrous, is to leave Brussels."

A long silence fell. Peregrine said at last, in a dejected tone: "I suppose it is. But how can I? There's Stuart's ball to-morrow, and the Duke's on the 7th, and——"

"A civil note to Stuart will answer the purpose," replied the Colonel, with the tremor of a smile. "Your wife's indisposition is sufficiently well known to provide you with a reasonable excuse. If you need more, you can inform your friends that the recent activities on the frontier have made you realize the propriety of conveying your family back to England."

"Yes, but—damn it, Charles, I won't dash off at a moment's notice like that!"

"A packet leaves Ostend on Monday," said the Colonel. "You may easily settle your affairs here to-morrow, and be off to Ghent on Sunday. That will enable you to reach Ostend in good time on Monday."

Peregrine looked at him. "You mean that I'm not to go to Stuart's to-morrow?"

"Yes, I do."

"I ought at least to take my leave of Lady Barbara."

"I will convey your apologies to her."

Another silence fell. Peregrine got up. "Very well. You are right, of course. I have been a fool. Only—*you* must know—how it is when she smiles at one. It—I never—oh, well!"

The Colonel walked over to the table, and picked up his hat and gloves. "Yes, I know. But don't begin to think yourself in love with her, Perry. You're not."

"No. Of course not," said Peregrine, trying to speak cheerfully.

The Colonel held out his hand. "I daresay I shan't see you to-morrow, so I'll say good-bye now."

Peregrine gripped his hand. "Good-bye. You're a damned good fellow, Charles, and I'm devilish sorry! I—I wish you very happy. She never thought of me, you know."

"Thank you! Very handsome of you," said the Colonel, with a smile. "My compliments to Lady Taverner, by the way. Don't forget to make my excuses for not going up to take leave of her!"

"No. I'll tell her," said Peregrine, opening the door, and escorting him out into the hall. "Good-bye! Come safely through the war, won't you?"

"No fear of that! I always take good care of my skin!" replied the Colonel, and raised his hand in a friendly salute, and ran down the steps into the street.

Peregrine went slowly upstairs to the salon. He had probably never been so unhappy in his life. Harriet was seated by the window, with some sewing in her hands. They looked at one another. Peregrine's lip quivered. He did not know what to say to her, or how to reassure her when his own heart felt like lead in his chest. All that came into his head to say was her name, spoken in an uncertain voice.

She saw suddenly that he was looking ashamed and miserable. The cause receded in her mind; it was not forgotten, it would never, perhaps, be forgotten, but it became a thing of secondary importance before the more pressing need to comfort him. She perceived that he was no older than his own son, as much in need of her reassurance as that younger Perry, when he had been naughty, and was sorry. She got up, throwing her stitchery aside, and went to Peregrine, and put her arms round him. "Yes, Perry. It's no matter. It doesn't signify. I was silly."

He clasped her to him; his head went down on her shoulder; he whispered: "I'm sorry, Harry. I don't know what——"

"Yes, dear: never mind! It was the fault of this horrid place. Don't speak of it any more!"

"We'll go home."

"Yes." She stroked his hair caressingly. The thought of Barbara no longer troubled her. A deeper grief, which she would never speak of, was the discovery that Peregrine was not a rock of strength for her to lean on, not a hero to be worshipped, but only a handsome, beloved boy who went swaggering bravely forth, but needed her to pick him up when he fell and hurt himself. She put the knowledge away from her. His abasement made her uncomfortable; even though she knew it to be make-believe he must be set on his pedestal again. She said: "Yes, we'll go home. But how shall we settle our affairs here? Will it not take some time?"

He raised his head. "No, I'll see to everything. You have only to pack your trunks. There is a packet leaving Ostend on Monday."

"This house! Our passages! How shall we manage?"

"Don't worry: I'll do it all."

He was climbing back on to the pedestal; they would not speak of this incident again; they would pretend, each one of them, that it had not happened. In the end, Peregrine would believe that it had not, and Harriet would pretend, even to herself, because there were some truths it was better not to face.

Judith, anxiously awaiting the result of the Colonel's interview with her brother, could scarcely believe him when he told her curtly that the Taverners were leaving Brussels. She exclaimed: "You don't mean it! I had not thought it to be possible! What can you have said to constrain him?"

"There was no other course to follow. He was fully sensible of it."

He spoke rather harshly. She said in a pleading tone: "Do not be too angry with him, Charles! He is so young."

"You are mistaken: I am not angry with him. I am excessively sorry for him, poor devil!"

"I am persuaded he will soon recover."

"Oh yes! But that one so near to me should have caused this unhappiness——" He checked himself.

"If it had not been Lady Barbara it would have been another, I daresay."

He was silent, and she did not like to pursue the topic. Worth presently came in, followed by the butler with the tea-tray, and Judith was glad to see the Colonel rouse himself from a mood of abstraction, and join with all his usual cheerfulness in the ordinary commonplace talk of every day.

He did not go out again that evening, nor, next morning, was his horse saddled for an early ride. The sky was overcast, and a thin rain was falling. It stopped later, and by noon the sun was shining, but a press of work at Headquarters kept the Colonel busy all the morning.

In the afternoon there was a Review in the Allée Verte of the English, Scottish, and Hanoverian troops quartered in and about Brussels. These constituted the Reserve of the Army, and included the 5th Division, destined for the command of Sir Thomas Picton. They were crack troops, and the crowd of onlookers, watching them march past, felt that with such men as these to defend them there could be no need for even the most timorous to fly for safety to the coast.

"Some of our best regiments," said the Duke, as they went past him.

There was good Sir James Kempt's brigade, four proud regiments: the Slashers, the 32nd, the Cameron Highlanders, and the 1st battalion of the 95th Riflemen, in their dark green uniforms and their jaunty caps.

There was fiery Sir Denis Pack, with his choleric eye, and his heavily arched brows, at the head of the Highland brigade. The Belgians began to cheer, for the kilt never lost its fascination for them, and in this 9th brigade was only one English regiment. The Royal Scots went by with pipes playing, followed by Macara, with his 42nd Royal Highlanders, and by handsome John Cameron of Fassiefern, with the 92nd: the Gay Gordons. The cheering broke out again and again; small boys, clinging to their fathers' hands, shouted: "*Jupes! Jupes! Jupes!*" in an ecstasy of delight; hats were waved, handkerchiefs fluttered; and when the last of the kilts and the tall hats with their nodding plumes had gone by, it was felt that the best of the Review was over. Colonel von Vincke's Hanoverians excited little enthusiasm, but the Duke, as he watched them march past, said in his terse fashion: "Those are good troops, too—or they will be, when I get good officers into them."

The British Ambassador's ball had been fixed to take place in the evening, and the Duke was entertaining a party at dinner before attending it. The Prince of Orange rode in from his Headquarters at Braine-le-Comte in high spirits, and full of news from the frontier; several Divisional Commanders were present, and the usual corps of foreign diplomats attached to the Anglo-Allied Army. The conversation related almost entirely to the approaching war, and was conducted, out of deference to the foreigners, in firm British-French by everyone but Sir Colin Campbell, who, having, to the Duke's unconcealed amusement, made three *gaffes*, relapsed into defiant English, and relied on Colonel Audley to translate such of his remarks as he wished to be made public.

The evening was considerably advanced when the dinner-party broke up, and the Duke and his guests were almost the last to arrive at Sir Charles Stuart's house. A cotillion was being danced; Colonel Audley saw Barbara, partnered by the Comte de Lavisse; and her two brothers: Harry with one of the Lennox girls, and George with Miss Elizabeth Conynghame. Miss Devenish was not dancing, but stood a little way away, beside Lady Worth. The Colonel soon went to them, claimed both their hands for dances, and stood with them for some moments, watching the progress of the cotillion. Catching sight of him, Barbara kissed her fan to him. He responded with a smile, and a wave of the hand, and without any appearance of constraint. Judith could not but wonder at it, and was reflecting upon the unfairness of its having been Peregrine who had borne all the blame, when the Duke's voice, speaking directly behind her, made her turn her head involuntarily.

"Oh yes!" he was saying, in his decided way. "The French Army is without doubt a wonderful machine. Now, I make my campaigns with ropes. If anything goes wrong, I tie a knot, and go on."

"What is the most difficult thing in war, Duke?" someone asked him idly.

"To know when to retreat, and to dare to do it!" he replied, without hesitation. He saw Judith looking at him, and stepped up to her. "How d'ye do? I'm very glad to see you. But you are not dancing! That won't do!"

"No, for I arrived when the cotillion was already formed. May I present to your Grace one who had long desired that honour?—Miss Devenish!"

217

Blushing, and torn between delight and confusion, Lucy made her curtsy. The Duke shook hands with her, saying with a laugh: "It's a fine thing to be a great man, is it not? Very happy to make Miss Devenish's acquaintance. But what is all this standing-about? Don't tell me that there is no young fellow wishing to lead you out, for I shan't believe you!"

"No indeed, there are a great many!" replied Judith, smiling. "But the thing is that Miss Devenish, like me, arrived too late to take part in this set. You will not see her standing-about again to-night, I assure you."

"That's right! Always dance while you may."

"How long will that be, Duke?" enquired Judith.

"Oh, now you are asking me more than I can tell you! For as long as you please, I daresay."

He nodded, and passed on. The cotillion came to an end soon after, and as Barbara walked off the floor Colonel Audley went forward to meet her.

She held out her hand to him. "Wretch! Do you know how confoundedly late you are?"

"Yes. Have you kept my waltzes?"

"Oh, I am in a charming humour! You may have as many as you please."

"All, then. How do you do, Lavisse? How do you go on in your neighbourhood?"

The Count shrugged. "Oh, *parbleu!* We watch the frontier, and grow excited at the mere changing of an advance guard. And you? What news have you?"

"Very little. We hear of the Russians approaching Frankfort, and of General Kruse being at Maestricht. Hallo, Harry! *More* leave?"

Lord Harry Alastair had come up to them, and replied to this quizzing remark with a grin and a wink. Having decided upon first meeting him that Audley was a very good sort of a fellow, he had lost no time in making him feel one of the family. He had several times borrowed money from him, which, however, he generally remembered to pay back, soon treated him with affectionate respect, and had even asked his advice on the conduct of an alarming affair with a Belgian lady of easy virtue. The Colonel's advice had been so sound that his lordship declared he owed his preservation to it, and opined darkly that Audley must have learned a thing or two worth knowing in Spain.

Barbara coolly referred to this affair, enquiring: "How is the opulent Julie, Harry?"

"Lord, didn't I tell you? I got clear away. It was a near thing, I can tell you. All Charles's doing. He's a man of wide experience, Bab, I warn you!"

"Charles, how shocking! Spanish beauties?"

"Dozens of them!" said the Colonel.

"Depraved! What is this they are striking up? A waltz! I am yours, then."

He led her on to the floor. She gave a sigh as his arm encircled her waist. He heard it, and glanced down at her. "Why the sigh, Bab?"

"I don't know. I think it was voluptuous."

He laughed. "Abominable word!"

"You dance so delightfully!" she murmured. "Where have you been hiding these last days?"

"At Headquarters, when I was not laming my horses on these shocking roads, By the by, *had* you to create a scandal in my family?"

"It seemed as though I had to," she admitted. "Did it come to your ears?"

"Every word of it. You stirred up a great deal of unhappiness, Bab."

"What, by permitting poor bored Perry to gain a little experience? Nonsense! I behaved charmingly to him. Oh, you are recalling that I said I would be a sister to him! Well, so I was, until his ridiculous wife chose to challenge me. I won that encounter, however, and will sheathe my sword now, if you like."

"I wish you had never drawn it, Bab. Lady Taverner wasn't a worthy foe."

"Ah, that's charming of you! Well, I will engage to let him out of my clutches. I don't see him to-night: is he not coming?"

"No. He is going back to England."

"Going back to England? He told me nothing of this!"

"It has only quite lately been decided. Brussels does not agree with Lady Taverner. I am charged with a message from Peregrine: his apologies for not being able to take his leave of you in person."

She was staring at him. "It is your doing, in fact!" He nodded. Her breast heaved. "Insufferable!" The word burst from her. "My God, I could hit you!"

"Why, certainly, if you like, but I don't recommend you to do so in such a public place as this."

She wrenched herself out of his hold, and walked swiftly off the dancing-floor. He followed her, and took her hand, and drawing it through his arm held it there firmly. "Calm yourself, Bab. If you want to quarrel with me you shall. I daresay Sir Charles would be pleased to lend us his morning-room for the purpose."

"You are right!" she said, in a low, furious voice. "This quarrel will not keep!"

He led her out of the ballroom and across the hall to a small parlour. There was no one in it, but the candles had been lit in the wall-sconces. The Colonel shut the door, and remained with his back to it, watching Barbara with a grave look in his eyes.

She went with long, hasty steps to the table in the centre of the room, and there faced him. When she spoke it was plain that she was making an effort to control her voice. "I desire to understand you. Did you think I had fallen in love with that youth?"

"Of course not. It was he who fell in love with you."

She made a contemptuous gesture. "An affair of great moment, that!"

"It was an affair of very great moment to him, and to his wife."

"What are either of them to you?"

"Not very much, perhaps. That does not signify. I wouldn't let you come between any husband and his wife."

"Unfortunate! It is one of my pastimes!"

He was silent, his mouth shut hard, his arms folded

across his chest. She said angrily: "You have made me ridiculous! You dared—you *dared* to bundle Peregrine out of the country without a word to me! Do you wish me to confess myself in the wrong? Very well, I behaved after the fashion of my family, badly! But not so badly that it was necessary to set the Channel between Peregrine and my charms! As though I would not have given him up at a word from you!"

"You are unreasonable," he replied. "Was there not a word from me? I seem to remember that you promised to set all to rights. I trusted you, but you broke your word to me. Is it for you to reproach me now? You took Perry from his wife out of spite. That makes me feel sick, do you know? If I thought that you knew what unhappiness—but you didn't! It was mischief—thoughtlessness! But, Bab, you cannot undo that kind of mischief merely by growing cool toward the poor devil you've made to fall in love with you! To see you, to hear your voice, is enough to keep that passion alive! The only course for Peregrine to follow was to go away."

Her lip curled. "This is decidedly in the tragic manner! Well! It is at least comforting to know that the scandal Peregrine's flight will create will be of your making. But I have an odd liking for creating my own scandals. You will agree that I am sufficiently adept to require no assistance."

He moved away from the door, and came towards her. "My God, where are we drifting? Is that the sum of your ambition, to create a scandal?"

"Oh, certainly! Did I not inform you of it, two months ago?"

"You don't mean what you say. Don't try to make me angry too! This wretched business is over. There is no need to discuss it, believe me!"

"You know very well that there is. You have given me a taste of high-handedness which I don't care for. I dare-say you would like me to cry meekly on your shoulder, and promise not to offend again."

"I would like to believe that you had a heart!"

"Oh, I have, and bestow little bits of it here and there in a most generous fashion."

"Was *I* the recipient of one of those little bits?"

She grew white, and said abruptly: "There has been enough of this. I warned you—did I not?—that you were making a mistake when you chose to invest me with all the virtues. Let me advise you to try your fortune with Miss Devenish. She would make you an admirable wife. You might be as possessive as you pleased, and she would love you for it. You can no longer persist in thinking me a suitable bride!"

"Every word you say seems designed to convince me that you are not!"

"Capital!" She did not speak quite steadily, but the smile still curled her lips. "The truth is, my dear Charles, that we have both of us been fools. I at least should have known better, for I had the advantage of you in having been married before. I admit that I was a little carried away. But I am bored now, confoundedly bored!"

"I envy you!" he said harshly. "Boredom seems a little thing compared with what I have had to suffer at your hands!"

"Your mistake! Boredom is the most damnable of all sufferings!"

"No! The most damnable suffering is to have your faith in one you love slowly killed. But what should you know of that? You don't deal in love!"

"On the contrary, I deal in it most artistically!"

"I have another word for it," he said.

"The devil you have! There, it is off at last! You may have perceived that I have been tugging at your ring for the last ten minutes. It should, of course, have been cast at your feet some time ago, but the confounded thing was always too tight. Take it!"

He looked at her for a moment, then held out his hand without a word. She dropped the ring into it, turned sharply on her heel, and went out of the room.

It was some time before the Colonel followed her, but he went back into the ballroom presently, and sought out

222

Miss Devenish. "Forgive me!" he said. "I have kept you waiting."

She looked up with a start. "Oh! I beg your pardon, I was not attending! What did you say?"

"Isn't this our dance?" he asked.

"Our dance—oh yes, of course! How stupid of me!"

She got up, resolutely smiling, but he made no movement to lead her on to the floor. "What is it?" he said quietly.

She gave a gasp, and pressed her handkerchief to her lips. "Nothing! nothing!"

He took her arm. "Come into the garden. You must not cry here."

She allowed herself to be propelled towards the long, open window, but when they stood on the terrace she said in a trembling voice: "You must think me mad! It is the heat: my head aches with it!"

"What is it?" he repeated. "You are very unhappy, are you not? Can I do anything to help you?"

A deep sob shook her. "No one can help me! Yes, I am unhappy. Oh, leave me, please leave me!"

"I can't leave you like this. Won't you tell me what the trouble is?"

"Oh no, how could I?"

"If you are unhappy I am in the same case. Does that make a bond?"

She looked up, trying to see his face in the dusk. "You? No, that cannot be true! You are engaged to the woman you love, you——"

"No, not now."

She was startled. "Oh, hush, hush! What can you possibly mean?"

"My engagement is at an end. Never mind that: it is your unhappiness, not mine, that we are concerned with."

She clasped his hand impulsively. "I am so sorry! I do not know what to say! If there were anything I could do——"

"There is nothing to be done, or said. Lady Barbara and I are agreed that we should not suit, after all. I have told you my trouble: will you not trust me with yours?"

"If I dared, you would think me—you would turn from me in disgust!"

"I can safely promise that I should not do anything of the sort. Come, let us sit down on this uncomfortably rustic bench! . . . Now, what is it, my poor child?"

CHAPTER XVI

THE news that Colonel Audley's engagement was at an end afforded curiously little satisfaction to his friends. They had all wanted to see it broken, and the crease smoothed from between the Colonel's brows, but the crease grew deeper, and a hard look seemed to have settled about his mouth. Occasionally the old, charming smile flashed out, but although he would talk lightly enough, laugh at the Headquarters' jokes, spar sometimes with his fellow-officers, and dance at the balls as willingly as he had ever done, those who knew him found his cheerfulness forced, and realized sadly that the gay Hussar had vanished, leaving in his place an older man, who was rather aloof, often abstracted, and had no confidences to make. The young Prince of Nassau, entering shyly upon his very nominal duties on the Duke's Staff, was even a little nervous of him, a circumstance which at first astonished Colonel Gordon. "Stern?" he repeated. "Audley? I think your Highness has perhaps mistaken the word?"

"*Un peu sévère,*" said the Prince.

"It's quite true," said Fremantle. "Damn the wench!" he added, giving his sash a vicious hitch. "I wish to God she would go back to England and give the poor devil a chance to forget her! If she had a spark of sensibility she would!"

"Perhaps she doesn't want him to forget her," suggested Gordon. "Do you think she means to get him back?"

"If she does she ain't going the right way to work.

They're saying she'll have that Belgian fellow—what's his name? Bylandt's brigade: all teeth and eyes and black whiskers. Ugh!"

"Lavisse," said Gordon, apparently recognizing the Count from this description without any difficulty.

"That's it. Such a dog with the ladies! Well, they'll make a nicely-matched pair, and I wish them joy of one another."

"It must hit Charles pretty badly."

"Of course it does! Look at him! The Prince here says he looks stern. I daresay that's how it would strike anyone who didn't know him. He looks to me as if he were enjoying a taste of hell."

He had gauged the matter exactly. Colonel Audley, who had known that Peregrine Taverner's only hope of overcoming his infatuation lay in removing immediately from Barbara's neighbourhood, was tied to Brussels, and was obliged, day after day, to endure tantalizing glimpses of Barbara, and night after night to see her waltzing with the Comte de Lavisse, looking up into his face with a smile on her lips and a provocative gleam in her eyes.

There were those who said that if Barbara had been quick to find consolation, so too had Audley. Neither was showing a bruised heart to the world. She had her handsome Belgian always at her side, and the Colonel seemed to have turned to little Miss Devenish. Well, said the interested, she would probably make him a very good wife.

Judith, wishing to believe that Charles, freed from his siren, had become sensible of Lucy's worth, still could not quite convince herself that it was so. "Do you think," she asked her husband hopefully, "that a man who had fancied himself in love with Lady Barbara might perhaps suffer from a revulsion of feeling, and so turn to her very opposite?"

"I really have no idea," replied Worth.

"It is quite true that he has been very much in her company since the engagement was broken off. He dances with her frequently, and seems to look at her with a great deal of kindness. Only——"

She broke off. Worth regarded her with a faint smile. "What profound observation are you about to make?" he enquired.

"I can't believe that if he were falling in love with Lucy he would be so unhappy. For he is, Worth: you can't deny it! There is an expression in his face when he thinks one is not looking at him—I would like to kill that wicked creature! *She* to jilt Charles!"

"This is all very bewildering," complained Worth. "I thought your hopes had been centred on her eventually doing so?"

"Yes, I did hope it, but I didn't know it had gone so deep with him. How wretched everything is! Even my spirits are quite oppressed. Lucy, too! She has no appearance of happiness, which makes me fear that Charles only feels towards her as a brother might."

He raised his brows. "Is she in love with him?"

"I very much fear it."

"Now you have gone quite beyond me," he said. "I was under the impression that you had made up your mind that she should fall in love with him?"

"So I had, but I never dreamed then that he would become entangled with the horridest woman in Brussels. If he could requite Lucy's love it would be the most delightful thing imaginable, but I don't believe he does."

"You will admit it to be early days yet for him to be bestowing his affections a second time."

"Lady Barbara does not seem to find it too early! But Lucy!" She paused, frowning. "I was afraid that the child was losing her prettiness over Lord George, but nothing could be more resolute than her shunning of his society. It has seemed to me that since Charles has been free, she has been regaining some of her spirits. But I would not for the world encourage *that* attachment, if there is no hope of Charles's affections becoming animated towards her."

"May I make a suggestion?"

"Of course: what is it?"

"That you cease to worry your head over either of

them," said Worth. "You will do no good by it, and if you begin to lose *your* prettiness you will find you have me to reckon with."

She smiled, but shook her head. "I cannot help but worry over them. If only Lady Barbara had had enough good feeling to go away from here! It must be painful beyond words for Charles to find himself continually in her company. My only dependence is on his being at last disgusted by her conduct."

"We will hope for that agreeable end. Meanwhile, Charles can at least consider himself fortunate in being kept busy by the Duke."

"I suppose so. What does he think of it? Has he made any comment?"

"None to me."

"I daresay he might not care. I do not consider him a man of much sensibility. He is very amiable and unaffected, but there is a coldness, a lack of feeling for others, which, I confess, repels me at times."

"He's a hard man, no doubt, but it is just possible, my dear, that he has matters of more moment to occupy him than the love-affairs of his Staff," said Worth, somewhat ironically.

The Duke, however, did comment on the broken engagement, though not perhaps in a manner which would have raised Judith's opinion of his character, had she been able to hear him. "By the by, Fitzroy," he said, looking up from the latest missive from General Decken on the vexed question of the Hanoverian subsidy, "what's this I hear about Audley?"

"The engagement is at an end, sir, that's all I've been told."

"By God, I'm very glad to hear it!" said his lordship, dipping his pen in the standish. "She was doing him no good, and I'm damned if I'll have my officers ruined for their duties by her tricks!"

That was all his lordship had to say about it, but, as Worth had correctly surmised, he was too busy to have any time to waste on the love-affairs of his Staff.

He had got his Army together, but spoke of it in the most disparaging terms, and was continually being chafed by the want of horses and equipment. General Decken's demands were rapacious: he could do nothing with the fellow, and would be obliged to refer the whole question of the Hanoverian subsidy to the Government. King William had taken some nonsense into his head over the junction of the Nassau contingent, under General Kruse, with the Dutch-Belgian troops, and was in one of his huffs. It was very difficult to know what went on in that froggish head, but his lordship believed the trouble to have arisen largely out of the Duke of Nassau's failure to write formally to his Majesty on the subject of these troops. Well, if the King would not have them his lordship would be obliged to make some other arrangement.

He had had an exasperating letter from his Royal Highness the Duke of Cambridge, putting a scheme before him for the augmentation of the German Legion by volunteers from the Hanoverian Line regiments. If the Royal Dukes would be a little less busy his lordship would be the better pleased. A nice feeling of dissatisfaction there would be if any such measures were put into action!

"Both the Legion and the line would be disorganized exactly at the moment I should require their services," he wrote, and enclosed for his Royal Highness's digestion a copy of the objections to the precious scheme which he had sent to Lord Bathurst.

In polite circles he was still being flippant about the chances of war, but occasionally he dropped the pretence now. When Georgiana Lennox mentioned a pleasure party to Lille, or Tournay, which some officers had projected, he said decidedly: "No, better let that drop."

He gratified Mr. Creevey by talking to him in the most natural way, joining him in the Park one day, where Mr. Creevey was walking with his stepdaughters. He spoke quite frankly of the debates in Parliament on the war, and Mr. Creevey, finding him so accessible, asked with one of his twinkling, penetrating glances: "Now then, will you let me ask you, Duke, what you think you will make of it?"

"By God!" said his lordship, standing still. "I think Blücher and myself can do the thing!"

"Do you calculate upon any desertion in Bonaparte's army?" enquired Creevey.

No, his lordship did not reckon upon a man. "We may pick up a Marshal or two," he added, "but not worth a damn."

Mr. Creevey mentioned the French King's troops at Alost, but that made his lordship give one of his whoops of laughter. "Oh! don't mention such fellows!" he said. "No, no! I think Blücher and I can do the business!" He saw a British soldier strolling along at some little distance, and pointed to him. "There," he said. "It all depends on that article whether we do the business or not. Give me enough of it, and I am sure."

This was good news to take home to Mrs. Creevey. It gave Creevey a better opinion of the Duke's understanding, too, and made him feel that in spite of every disquieting rumour from the frontier there was no need to fly for safety yet.

There were plenty of rumours, of course, but people had been alarmed so many times to no purpose that they were beginning to take only a fleeting interest in the news that came from France. It was said that everywhere on the road from Paris to the frontier preparations were being made for the movements of troops in carriages. It was said that Bonaparte was expected to be at Laon on the 6th June; on the 10th June report placed him at Maubeuge, but the Duke had certain intelligence of his being still in Paris, and issued invitations for a ball he was giving later in the month.

He was always giving balls, informal little affairs got up on the spur of the moment, but this was to be a splendid function, outdoing all the others which had been held in Brussels. There would be so many Royalties present that the Duchess of Richmond declared that there would be no room for a mere commoner. The Dutch King and Queen were coming; the Prince of Orange, and Prince Frederick; the Duke of Brunswick; the Prince of Nassau; Prince

229

Bernhard of Saxe-Weimar, who commanded the 2nd Dutch-Belgic brigade under General Perponcher; and of course the Duc de Berri, with his entourage of exalted personages.

There was much laughing rivalry between his lordship and the Duchess of Richmond over this question of balls. The best hostess in Brussels was not to be outdone by his lordship, and whipped in before him with her gilt-edged invitations for the night of the 15th June. His lordship acknowledged himself to have been outmanœuvred, and was obliged to postpone his own ball until later in the month. "Honours are even, however," said Georgiana. "For though Mama has the better date, the Duke has the King and Queen!"

"Pooh!" said her Grace. "They will make the party very stiff and stupid. It will be all pretension, Duke! I promise you, my ball will be the success of the season!"

"No such thing! It will be forgotten in the success of mine."

"It will be too hot for dancing by that time. Have you thought of that?"

"We will take this young woman's ruling on that point. Is it ever too hot for dancing, Georgy?" demanded his lordship, pinching her chin.

"No, never!" responded Georgiana. "Mama, consider! If you provoke the Duke, perhaps he won't come to our party, and then we shall be undone!"

"That would be too infamous!" said the Duchess. "I will not believe him capable of such dastardly behaviour."

"No, no, I shall be there!" promised his lordship.

It was hard to believe that in the midst of these light-hearted schemes, other and much grimmer plans were revolving in his lordship's head. Foreigners, coming to Brussels, found the Duke's Headquarters a perplexing place, and his Staff incurably flippant. No one seemed to take the approaching war seriously; young officers lounged in and out, talking to one another in a careless drawl that had so much annoyed General Röder; Lord Fitzroy could pause in the writing of important letters to exchange a joke with some friend who apparently thought nothing of interrupting his work; in the Adjutant-General's teeming office, Assistants and Deputy-Assistants demanded the names of bootmakers, or discussed the chances of competitors in the horse races at Grammont. It had never seemed to poor General Röder that anyone did any work, for work was mentioned in the most off-hand fashion; yet the work was done, and the lounging young officers who looked so sleepy, and dressed so carelessly, carried the Duke's messages to the Army at a speed which made the Prussian General blink. They would drag themselves out of their chairs, groaning, twitting each other on the need for exertion, and stroll out with yawns, and lazy demands for their horses. You would see them mount their English hunters: "Well, if I don't come back you'll know I've lost myself—— Where *is* the damned place?" they would say. But long before you would have believed it possible they could have reached their destination, let alone have returned from it, there they were again, with nothing but the dust on their boots to betray that they had ever left Brussels. General Röder, accustomed to officers bustling about their business, clicking their heels together smartly in salute, discussing military matters with zest and enthusiasm, would never be able to understand these English, who, incomprehensibly, considered it bad *ton* to talk about anything but quite childish trivialities.

But General Röder had been relieved at last, thanking God to be going away from such Headquarters, and in his place a very different officer had come to Brussels. General Baron von Müffling brought no prejudices with him, or, if he did, he concealed them. Gneisenau had warned him to be very much on his guard in the English camp, but General Müffling had dealt with Gneisenau for many years, and knew him to be a prey to preconceived ideas. The General came to Brussels with an open mind, and immediately endeared himself to his hosts by confessing with a disarming smile that in his early studies of the English language he had never got beyond *The Vicar of Wakefield* and Thomson's *Seasons*. He made it his business to try to understand the English character, and to earn the Duke's confidence, and succeeded in both aims to admiration. The Duke found him to be a sensible man, given to speaking the plain truth; and the Staff, accustomed to the glaring disapproval of General Röder declared him to be a very good sort of a fellow, and made him welcome in their own easy, unceremonious fashion.

He was soon on good terms with everyone. His manners were polished, his address a mixture of tact and dignity. He did not snort at graceless lieutenants, and he never committed the solecism of introducing grim topics of conversation at festive gatherings. He seemed, in fact, to enjoy life in Brussels, and to be amused by the Headquarters' jokes.

"I think you are something of a wizard, Baron," said Judith. "Your predecessor was never on such terms with us all, though he had been in Brussels for so long."

"That is true," he replied. "But General Röder's irritability carried him too far. It is unfair for anyone in the midst of a foreign nation to frame his expectations on the ideas he brings with him. He should instead study the habits and customs of his hosts."

"Do you find our customs very different from your own?"

"Oh yes, certainly! In your Army, for instance, I find some customs better than ours; others perhaps not so good. There is much to bewilder the poor foreigner, I assure you, madame. There are the Duke's Aides-de-Camp and *galopins*, for example. One is at first astonished to find that these gentlemen are of the best families, and count it an honour to serve the Duke in this manner. Then one is astonished to see them so nonchalant." A smile crept into his eyes; he said: "One finds it hard to believe them to be *des hommes sérieux!* But I discover that these so languid young officers make it a point of honour to ride four of your English miles in eighteen minutes, whenever the Duke adds the word *Quick* to his despatch. So then I perceive that I have been misjudging them, and I must reassemble my ideas."

"How do you go on with the Duke?" asked Worth.

"Very well, I believe. He is agreeable, and in matters of service very short and decided."

"Excessively short, I understand!" said Judith, with a laugh.

"Perhaps, yes," he acknowledged. "He exercises far greater power in the Army he commands than Prince von Blücher does in ours. It is not the custom, I find, to criticize or control your Commander-in-Chief. With us it is different. On our Staff everything is discussed openly, in the hearing of all the officers, which is, I find, not so good, for time is wasted, and there are always what the Marshal calls *Trübsals-Spritzen*—I think you say, *trouble-squirts?*"

"No, you won't find the Duke discussing his plans with his officers," said Worth. "He is not held to be over-and-above fond of being asked questions, either."

The Baron replied in a thoughtful tone: "He *allows* questions. It would be more correct to say that he dismisses all such as are unnecessary. There is certainly an inpatience to be observed sometimes, but his character is distinguished by its openness and rectitude, and must make him universally respected. There should be the utmost harmony between him and the Marshal, and the exertions of myself and of your estimable Colonel Hardinge must be alike directed towards this end."

"Yes, indeed," said Judith faintly. "I am sure—— And how do you like being in Brussels, Baron? I hope you do not agree with General von Röder in thinking us very frivolous!"

"Madame, it is not possible!" he said, with a gallant bow. "Everyone is most amiable! One envies the English officers the beautiful wives who follow them so intrepidly to the seat of war."

She could not help laughing. "Oh! Are you married, Baron?"

"Yes," he replied. "I am the possessor of a noble-minded wife and three hopeful children."

"How—how delightful!" said Judith, avoiding her husband's eye.

But in spite of the occasionally paralysing remarks he made, Baron Müffling was a man of considerable shrewdness, and he soon learned not only to adapt himself to his company but to induce the Duke to trust him. He was perfectly frank with his lordship. "Prince Blücher will never make difficulties when the talk is of advancing and attacking. In retrograde movements his vexation sometimes overpowers him, but he soon recovers himself," he told the Duke. "General Gneisenau is chivalrous and strictly just, but he believes that you should always require from men more than they can perform, which is a principle which I consider as dangerous as it is incorrect. As for our Infantry, it does not possess the same bodily strength or powers of endurance as yours. The greater mass of our troops are young and inexperienced. We cannot reckon on them obstinately continuing a fight from morning till evening. They will not do it."

"Oh! I think very little of soldiers running away at times," said his lordship. "The steadiest troops will occasionally do so—but it is a serious matter if they do not come back."

"You may depend upon one thing," Müffling assured him. "When the Prince has agreed to any operation in common, he will keep his word."

Yes, the Duke could be more than ever sure that he and old Blücher would be able to do the business, in spite of his infamous Army, his inexperienced Staff, and every obstacle put in his way by the people at home. His personal Staff had been augmented by Lieutenant-Colonel Canning, who had served him in the Peninsula, and had had the temerity to beg to be employed again as an Aide-de-Camp; and by Major the Honourable Henry Percy, whom he had enrolled as an Extra. He had nothing to complain of in his own family at least, though he was inclined to think it a great pity that Audley should not have recovered from his affair with Barbara Childe. However, it did not seem to be interfering with his work, which was all that signified.

Colonel Audley had, in fact, flung himself into his work

with an energy that must have pleased General Röder, had he been there to see it. It did not help him to forget Barbara, but while he was busy he could not be thinking of her, picturing the glimmer of her eyes, the lustre of her hair, the lovely smile that lifted the corners of her mouth; or torturing himself with wondering what she was doing, whether she was happy, or perhaps secretly sad, and, most of all, who was with her.

There was very little room for doubt about that, he knew. She would be with Lavisse, riding with him, or waltzing with him, held too close in his arms for propriety, his black head close to her flaming one, his lips almost brushing her ear as he murmured his expert love-making into it. She was behaving outrageously; even those who had grown accustomed to her odd flights were shocked. She had borrowed Harry's clothes, and had gone swaggering through the streets with George for a vulgar bet; she had won a race in her phaeton against a wild young ne'er-do-weel in whose company no lady of breeding would have permitted herself to have been seen. She had appeared at the Opera in a classical robe which left one shoulder bare and revealed beneath its diaphanous folds more than even the most daring creature would have cared to show; she had set a roomful of gentlemen in a roar by singing in the demurest way a couple of the most shocking French ballads. The ladies present had been unable to follow the words of the songs, which were extremely idiomatic, but they knew when their husbands were laughing at improper jokes, and there was not a married man there who had not to endure a curtain-lecture that night.

Lord Vidal was furious. He threatened to turn his sister out-of-doors, which made her laugh. He could not do it, of course, for ten to one she would simply install herself at one of the hôtels, and a pretty scandal that would create. There was only one person to whom she might possibly attend, and that was her grandmother. Vidal had written to that wise old lady the very night the engagement was broken off, begging her to exert her influence, but apparently she did not choose to do so, for she had neither answered his letter nor written one to Barbara.

Even Augusta was taken aback by Barbara's behaviour, and remonstrated with her. Barbara turned on her with a white face and blazing eyes. "Leave me alone!" she said. "I'll do what I choose, and if I choose to go to the devil it is my business, and not yours!"

"Oh, agreed!" said Augusta, shrugging bored shoulders. "But I find your conduct very odd, I must say. If you are hankering after your Staff Officer——"

A harsh little laugh cut her short. "Pray do not be ridiculous, Gussie! I had almost forgotten his existence!"

"I am happy to hear you say so, but I fail to see the purpose of all this running about. Why can you not be still?"

"Because I can't, because I won't!"

"Do you mean to have Lavisse?"

"Oh, don't talk to me of more engagements. I have had enough of being tied, I can assure you."

"Take care he does not grow tired of your tricks. In my opinion you are playing a dangerous game." She added maliciously: "You are not irresistible, you know. Colonel Audley seems to have had no difficulty in consoling himself elsewhere. How do you like to be supplanted by a little nobody like Lucy Devenish?"

She had the satisfaction of seeing a quiver run over Barbara's face. Barbara replied, however, without hesitation: "Oh, she'll make him a capital wife! I told him so."

Lord George received the news of the broken engagement with careless unconcern. "I daresay you know your own business best," he said. "I never thought him our sort."

But Lord Harry nearly wept over it. "The nicest fellow that ever was in love with you, and you jilt him for a damned frog!" he exclaimed.

"If you mean Lavisse, he is a Belgian, and not a Frenchman, and I did not jilt Charles Audley. He was perfectly ready to let me go, you know," replied Barbara candidly.

"I don't believe it! The truth is you played off your tricks till no man worth his salt would stand it! I know you!"

She twisted her hands in her lap, gripping her fingers together. "If you know me you must admit that we were not suited."

"No!" he said hotly. "You are only suited to a fellow like Lavisse! He will do very well for you, and I wish you joy of him!"

"Thank you," she said, with a crooked smile. "I have not yet accepted him, however."

"Why not? He's as rich as Crœsus, and he won't care how you behave as long as you don't interfere with his little pleasures. You'll make a famous pair!"

He slammed out of her presence, and sought Colonel Audley. The interview was rather a trying one for the Colonel, for there was no curbing Harry's impetuous tongue. "Oh, I say, sir, don't give her up!" he begged. "She'll marry that Belgian fellow if you do, sure as fate!"

"My dear boy, you don't——"

"No, but only listen, sir! It ain't vice with Bab—really it ain't. She's spoilt, but she don't mean the things she says, and I'm ready to swear she's never gone beyond flirtation. I daresay you're thinking of that Darcy affair, but——"

"I am not thinking of any affair, Harry."

"Of course I know she has the devil's own temper— gets it from my grandfather: George has it too—but perhaps you don't understand that the things they do when they are in their rages don't mean anything. Of course, George is a shocking fellow, but Bab isn't. People say she's heartless, but myself I'm devilish fond of her, and if she marries a damned rake like Lavisse it'll be just too much to bear!"

"I'm sorry, Harry, but you have it wrong. It wasn't I who broke the engagement."

"But, Charles, if you would only see her!"

"Do you imagine that I am going to crawl to your sister, begging to be taken on the strength again?"

Harry sighed. "No. No, of course you wouldn't do that."

"You say that she is going to marry Lavisse. If that is so, there is no possibility of our engagement's being renewed. In any case—— No! it will not do. I have been brought to realize that, and upon reflection I think you must realize it too."

"It's such a damned shame!" Harry burst out. "I don't want Lavisse for a brother-in-law! I never liked any of the others half as well as you!"

He sounded so disconsolate that in a mood less bleak the Colonel must have been amused. His spirits were too much oppressed, however, for him to be able to bear such a discussion with equanimity. He was glad when Harry at last took himself off.

Harry's artless disclosures left a painful impression: an unacknowledged hope had lingered in the Colonel's mind that Barbara's encouragement of Lavisse might have been the outcome merely of pique. But Harry's words seemed to show that she was indeed serious. Her family looked upon the match as certain; Colonel Audley was forced to recall the many occasions during their engagement when she had seemed to feel a decided partiality for the Count. He had believed her careless flirtations to be only the expression of a certain volatility of mind, which stronger ties of affection would put an end to. It had not been so. The mischief of her upbringing, the hardening effect of a distasteful marriage, had vitiated a character of whose underlying worth he could still entertain no doubt. That the heart was unspoiled, he was sure: could he but have possessed himself of it he was persuaded all would have been different. Her conduct had convinced him that he had failed, and although, even through the anger that had welled up in him at their last meeting, he had been conscious of an almost overpowering impulse to keep her upon any terms, a deeper instinct had held him silent.

He had passed since then through every phase of doubt, sometimes driven so nearly mad by the desire to hold her in his arms that he had fallen asleep at night with the fixed intention of imploring her to let everything be as it had been before their quarrel, only to wake in the morning to a realization of the impossibility of building happiness upon such foundations. Arguments clashed, and nagged in his brain. He blamed himself for lack of tact, for having been too easy, for having been too harsh. Sometimes he was sure that he had handled her wrongly from the start; then a profounder knowledge would possess him, and he would recognize with regret the folly of all such arguments. There could be no question of tact or mishandling where the affections were engaged. He came back wearily to the only thing he knew to be certain: that since the love she had felt for him had been a light emotion, as fleeting as her smile, nothing but misery could attend their marriage.

After prolonged strife the mind becomes a little numb, repeating dully the old arguments, but ceasing to attach a meaning to them. It was so with Colonel Audley. His brain continued to revolve every argument, but he seemed no longer capable of drawing any conclusions from them. He could neither convince himself that the rift was final nor comfort himself with the hope of renewing the engagement. He was aware, chiefly, of an immense lassitude, but beneath it, and underlying his every word and thought, was a pain that had turned from a sharp agony into an ache which was always present, yet often ignored, because familiarity had inured him to it.

The unfortunate circumstance of his being obliged to remain in Brussels, where he must not only see Barbara continually but was forced to live under the eyes of scores of people whom he knew to be watching him, imposed a strain upon him that began very soon to appear in his face. Judith, obliged to respect his evident wish that the affair should be forgotten, was goaded into exclaiming to Worth: "I could even wish the war would break out, if only it would take Charles away from this place!"

Upon the following day, the 14th June, it seemed as though her wish would be granted. She was at Lady Conynghame's in the evening, congratulating Lord Hay

239

upon his win at the races at Grammont upon the previous day, when Colonel Audley came in with news of serious movement on the frontier. On the 13th June, Sir Hussey Vivian, whose Hussar brigade was stationed to the south of Tournay, had discovered that he had opposite him not a cavalry picket, as had previously been the case, but a mere collection of *douaniers*, who, upon being questioned, had readily disclosed the fact of the French army's concentration about Maubeuge. Shortly after the Colonel's entrance some other guests came in with a rumour that the French had actually crossed the frontier. All disbelief was presently put an end to by the Duke's arrival. He was calm, and in good spirits, but replied to the eager questions put to him that he believed the rumour to be true.

CHAPTER XVII

ON the following morning the only news was of Sir Thomas Picton's arrival in Brussels. He was putting up at the Hôtel d'Angleterre with two of his Aides-de-Camp, Chaptain Chambers of the 1st Footguards, and an audacious young gentleman who ought to have been in London with the 1st battalion of that regiment, but who had procured leave, and contrived to get himself enrolled on Sir Thomas Picton's Staff as Honorary Aide-de-Camp. It seemed reasonable to Mr. Gronow to suppose that he could quite well take part in a battle in Belgium and be back again in London in time to resume his duties at the expiration of his leave.

While Sir Thomas, a burly figure in plain clothes—for the trunks containing his uniforms had not yet arrived in Brussels—was seated at breakfast, Colonel Canning came in to say that the Duke wished to see him immediately. He finished his breakfast, and went off to Headquarters. He met Wellington in the Park, walking with the Duke of Richmond and Lord Fitzroy Somerset. All three were deep in conversation. Sir Thomas strode up to them, accosting his chief with his usual lack of ceremony, and received a chilling welcome.

"I am glad you are come, Sir Thomas," said his lordship stiffly. He looked down his nose at the coarse, square-jowled face in front of him. He valued old Picton for his qualities as a soldier, but he had never been able to like him. "As foul-mouthed an old devil as ever lived," he had once said of him. Picton's familiarity annoyed him; he delivered one of his painful snubs. "The sooner you get on horseback the better," he said. "No time is to be lost. You will take the command of the troops in advance. The Prince of Orange knows by this time that you will go to his assistance."

A slight bow, and it was plain that his lordship considered the interview at an end. Picton was red-faced, and glaring. Richmond, sorry for the rough old man's humiliation, said something civil, but Picton was too hurt and angry to respond. He moved away, muttering under his breath, and his lordship resumed his conversation.

No further news having arrived from the frontier, Brussels continued its normal life. It was generally supposed that the previous night's report had been another false alarm. The usual crowd of fashionables promenaded in the Park; ladies looked over their gowns for the Duchess of Richmond's ball; gentlemen hurried off to the market to order posies for their inamoratas.

Colonel Audley had left his brother's house before Judith was up, but he came in about midday for a few minutes. There was no news; he told her briefly that the chances were that the concentration on Maubeuge was the prelude to a feint; and was able to assure her that no alarm was felt at Headquarters. The Duchess of Richmond's ball would certainly take place; the Prince of Orange was coming in from Braine-le-Comte to dine with the Duke about three; Lord Hill was already in Brussels; and Uxbridge and a host of Divisional and Brigade Commanders were expected to arrive during the course of the afternoon, for the purpose of attending the ball. This certainly did not seem as though an outbreak of hostilities was expected; and further confirmation was later received from Georgiana Lennox, who, meeting Judith on a shopping errand during the afternoon, was able to report that Lord Hill had called in the Rue de la Blanchisserie, and had disclaimed any knowledge of movement on the frontier.

The Prince of Orange arrived in Brussels shortly after two o'clock, in his usual spirits, and after changing his dress in his house in the Rue de Brabant, went round to Headquarters. He had heard no further news, set very little store by the previous night's report, and had ridden in light-heartedly to take part in the evening's festivities, leaving Constant de Rebecque in charge at Braine-le-Comte.

"Well, well!" drawled Fremantle, when his Highness had gone off upstairs to pay his respects to the Duke. "Our Corps Commander! One comfort is that old Constant will do much better without him. Think there's anything brewing, Canning?"

"I don't know. Another hum, I daresay. Müffling has heard nothing: he was in here a few minutes ago."

The Duke dined early, sitting down to table with the Prince of Orange and the various members of his Staff. At three o'clock a despatch was brought in for the Prince, from Braine-le-Comte. It was from Constant, containing a report received from General Behr at Mons, just after the Prince's departure from his headquarters. The 2nd Prussian Brigade of Ziethen's 1st Corps had been attacked early that morning, and alarm guns fired all along the line. The attack seemed to be directed on Charleroi.

The Duke ran his eye over the despatch. "H'm! Sent off at 9.30, I see. Doesn't tell us much."

"Behr had it from General Steinmetz, through Van Merlen," said the Prince. "That would put the attack in the small hours, for Steinmetz's despatch, you see, was sent off from Fontaine-l'Evêque. Sir, do you think——?"

"Don't think anything," said his lordship. "I shall hear from Grant presently."

At four o'clock Müffling came in with a despatch from General Ziethen, which was dated 9.0 a.m. from Charleroi. It contained the brief information that the Prussians had been engaged since 4.0 a.m. Thuin had been captured by the French, and the Prussian outposts driven back. General Ziethen hoped the Duke would concentrate his army on Nivelles, seven miles to the west of the main Charleroi-Brussels chaussée.

The Duke remained for some moments deep in thought. Müffling presently said: "How will you assemble your army, sir?"

The Duke replied in his decided way: "I will order all to be ready for instant march, but I must wait for advice from Mons before fixing a rendezvous."

"Prince Blücher will concentrate on Ligny, if he has not already done so."

"If all is as General Ziethen supposes," said the Duke, "I will concentrate on my left wing the Corps of the Prince of Orange. I shall then be *à portée* to fight in conjunction with the Prussian Army."

He gave back Ziethen's despatch and turned away. It was evident to Müffling that he had no more to say, but he detained him for a moment with the question, *When* would he concentrate his army? The Duke repeated: "I must wait for advice from Mons."

He spoke in a calm voice, but a little while after Müffling had left the house he showed signs of some inward fret, snapping at Canning for not having immediately understood a trivial order. Canning came away with a rueful face, and enquired of Lord Fitzroy what had gone wrong.

"No word from Grant," replied Fitzroy. "It's very odd: he's never failed us yet."

"Looks as though the whole thing's nothing but a feint," remarked Fremantle. "Trust Grant to send word if there were anything serious on hand!"

This belief began to spread through the various offices: if Colonel Grant, who was the cleverest Intelligence Officer the Army had ever had, had not communicated with Headquarters, it could only be because he had nothing of sufficient importance to report.

The afternoon wore on, with everyone kept at his post in case of emergency, but a general feeling over all that the affair would turn out to be a false alarm. Previous scares were recalled; someone argued that if Bonaparte had been in Paris on the 10th June with the Imperial Guard, it was impossible for him yet to have reached the frontier.

At five o'clock a dragoon arrived from Braine-le-Comte with despatches for Lord Fitzroy. The Duke was in his office with Colonel de Lancey, but he broke off his conversation as Fitzroy came in, and barked out: "Well?"

"Despatches from Sir George Berkeley, sir, enclosing reports from General Dörnberg, Baron Chassé, and Baron van Merlen."

"Dörnberg, eh?" His lordship's eye brightened. "Has he heard from Grant?"

"No, sir," replied Fitzroy, laying the papers before him. "General Dörnberg's letter, as your lordship will see, is dated only 9.30 a.m."

"Nine-thirty!" An explosion seemed imminent; his lordship picked up the letters and read them with a cold eye and peevishly pursed lips. Dörnberg, at Mons, merely stated that he had found a picket of French Lancers on the Bavay road, and that the troops at Quivrain had been replaced by a handful of National Guards and Gendarmes. All the French troops appeared to be marching towards Beaumont and Philippeville.

The Duke gave the despatch to De Lancey without comment, and picked up Chassé's and Van Merlen's reports. Van Merlen, writing at an early hour of the morning from Saint Symphorien, stated that the Prussians under General Steinmetz were retiring from Binche to Gosselies, and that if pressed the I Corps would concentrate at Fleurus.

De Lancey looked up with a worried frown from the despatch in his hand. He was finding the post of Quartermaster-General arduous; he had brought a young bride with him to Brussels, too, and was beginning to look rather careworn. "Then it comes to this, sir, that we have no intelligence later than nine this morning."

"No. All we know is that there has been an attack on the Prussian outposts and that the French have taken Thuin. I can't move on that information."

His lordship said no more, but both De Lancey and Fitzroy knew what was in his mind. He had always been jealous of his right, for in that direction lay his communication lines. It was his opinion that the French would try to cut him off from the seaports; he was suspicious of the attack on the Prussians: it looked to him like a feint. He would do nothing until he received more certain information.

Between six and seven o'clock he issued his first orders. The Quartermaster-General's Staff woke to sudden activity. Twelve messages had to be written and carried to their various destinations. The whole of the English cavalry was to collect at Ninove that night; General Dörnberg's brigade of Light Dragoons of the Legion to march on Vilvorde; the Reserve Artillery to be ready to move at daybreak; General Colville's 4th Infantry Division, except the troops beyond the Scheldt, to march eastward on Grammont; the 10th Brigade, just arrived from America under General Lambert and stationed at Ghent, to move on Brussels; the 2nd and 5th Divisions to be at Ath in readiness to move at a moment's notice; the 1st and 3rd to concentrate at Enghien and Braine-le-Comte. The Brunswick Corps was to concentrate on Brussels; the Nassau contingent upon the Louvain road; and the 2nd and 3rd Dutch-Belgic Divisions under Generals Perponcher and d'Aubremé were ordered to concentrate upon Nivelles. His lordship had received no intelligence from Mons, and was still unwilling to do more than to put his Army in a state of readiness to move at a moment's notice. The Quartermaster-General's office became a busy hive, with De Lancey moving about in it with his sheaf of papers, and frowning over his maps as he worked out the details for the movements of the divisions, sending out his messages, and inwardly resolving to be done with the Army when this campaign was over. He was a good officer, but the responsibility of his post oppressed him. Too much depended on his making no mistakes. The Adjutant-General had to deal with the various duties to be distributed, with morning-states of men and horses, and with the discipline of the Army, but the Quartermaster-General's work was more harassing. On his shoulders rested the task of arranging every detail of equipment, of embarkation, of marching, halting, and quartering the troops. It was not easy to move an army; it would be fatally easy to create chaos in concentrating troops that were spread over a large area. De Lancey checked up his orders again, referred to the maps, remembered that such-and-such a bridge would not bear the passage of heavy cavalry, that this or that road had been reported in a bad state. At the back of his busy mind another and deeper anxiety lurked. He would send Magdalene to Ghent, into safety. He hoped she would consent to go; he would know no peace of mind if she were left in this unfortified and perilously vulnerable town.

The stir in the Quartermaster-General's office, the departure of Deputy-Assistants charged with the swift delivery of orders to the divisions of the Army, infected the rest of the Staff with a feeling of expectation and suppressed excitement. A few moderate spirits continued to maintain their belief in the attack's being nothing more than an affair of outposts; but the general opinion was that the Anglo-Allied Army would shortly be engaged. Colonel Audley went to his brother's house at seven, to dress for the ball, and on his way through the Park encountered a tall Rifleman with a pair of laughing eyes, and a general air of devil-may-care. He thrust out his hand. "Kincaid!"

The Rifleman grinned at him. "A Staff Officer with a worried frown! What's the news?"

"There's damned little of it. Are you going to the ball to-night?"

"What, the Duchess of Richmond's? Now, Audley, *do*

246

I move in those exalted circles? Of course I'm not! However, several of ours are, so the honour of the regiment
will be upheld. They tell me there's going to be a war.
A real *guerra al cuchillo!*"

"Where *do* you get your information?" retorted the
Colonel.

"Ah, we hear things, you know! Come along, out with
it! What's the latest from the frontier?"

"*Nada, nada, nada!*" said the Colonel.

"Yes, you look as though there were nothing. All alike,
you Staff Officers: close as oysters! My people have been
singing *Ahé Marmont* all the afternoon."

"There's been no news sent off later than nine this
morning. Are your pack-saddles ready?"

Kincaid cocked an eyebrow. "More or less. They won't
be wanted before to-morrow, at all events, will they?"

"I don't know, but I'll tell you this, Johnny: if you've
any preparations to make, I wouldn't, if I were you, delay
so long. Good-bye!"

Kincaid gave a low whistle. "That's the way it is, is
it? Thank you, I'll see to it!"

Colonel Audley waved to him and strode on. When
he reached Worth's house he found that both Worth and
Judith were in their rooms, dressing for the ball. He ran
up the stairs to his own apartment, and began to strip off
his clothes. He was standing before the mirror in his shirt
and gleaming white net pantaloons, brushing his hair,
when Worth presently walked in.

"Hallo, Charles! So you go to the ball, do you? Is
there any truth in the rumours that are running round the
town?"

"The Prussians were attacked this morning. That's all
we know. The Great Man's inclined to think it a feint.
He doesn't think Boney will advance towards Charleroi:
the roads are too bad. It's more likely the real attack
will be on our right centre. Throw me over my sash,
there's a good fellow!"

Worth gave it him, and watched him swathe the silken
folds round his waist, so that the fringed ends fell gracefully

down one thigh. The Colonel gave a last touch to the black stock about his neck, and struggled into his embroidered coat.

"Are you dining with us?"

"No, I dined early with the Duke. I don't know when I shall get to the ball: we've orders to remain at Head-quarters."

"That sounds as though something is in the wind."

"Oh, there is something in the wind," said the Colonel, flicking one Hessian boot with his handkerchief. "God knows what, though! We're expecting to hear from Mons at any moment."

He picked up his gloves and cocked-hat, charged Worth to make his excuses to Judith, and went back to the Rue Royale.

The Duke was in his dressing-room when, later in the evening, Baron Müffling came round to Headquarters with a despatch from Gneisenau, at Namur, but he called the Baron in to him immediately. The despatch confirmed the earlier tidings sent by Ziethen, and announced that Blücher was concentrating at Sombreffe, near the village of Ligny. General Gneisenau wanted to know what the Duke's intentions were, but the Duke was still obstinately awaiting news from Mons. He stood by the table, in his shirt-sleeves, an odd contrast to the Prussian in his splendid dress-uniform, and said with a note of finality in his voice which the Baron had begun to know well: "It is impossible for me to resolve on a point of concentration till I shall have received the intelligence from Mons. When it arrives I will immediately advise you."

There was nothing for Müffling to do but to withdraw. If he chafed at the delay, he gave no sign of it. He was aware of the Duke's obsession that the attack would fall on his right, and though he did not share this belief he was wise enough to perceive that nothing would be gained by argument. He went back to his own quarters to make out his report to Blücher, keeping a courier at his door to be in readiness to ride off as soon as he should have discovered the Duke's intentions.

The long-awaited news from Mons came in soon after he left the Duke. There had been no further intelligence from Ziethen all day: what had occurred before Charleroi was still a matter for conjecture; and the despatch from Mons contained no tidings from Colonel Grant, but had been sent in by General Dörnberg, who reported that he had no enemy in front of him, but believed the entire French Army to be turned towards Charleroi.

It now seemed certain that a concerted move was being made upon Charleroi, but whether the town had fallen or was still in Prussian hands, how far the French had penetrated across the frontier, was still unknown. After a few minutes' reflection, the Duke sent for De Lancey, and dictated his After-Orders. The dispositions of the Dutch-Belgic Divisions at Nivelles was to remain unchanged; the 1st and 4th British Divisions were ordered to move on Braine-le-Comte and Enghien; Alten's 3rd Division to move from Braine-le-Comte to Nivelles, and all other divisions to march on Mont St. Jean.

The Duke gave his directions in his clear, concise way, finished his toilet, and, a little time before midnight, drove round to General Müffling's quarters. Müffling had been watching the clock for the past hour, but he received the Duke without the least appearance of impatience.

"Well! I've got news from Dörnberg," said his lordship briskly. "Orders for the concentration of my Army at Nivelles and Quatre-Bras are already despatched. Now, I'll tell you what, Baron: you and I will go to the Duchess's ball, and start for Quatre-Bras in the morning. You know all Bonaparte's friends in this town will be on tiptoe. The well intentioned will be pacified if we go, and it will stop our people from getting into a panic."

The ball had been in progress for some time when the Duke's party arrived in the Rue de la Blanchisserie. All the Belgian and Dutch notables were present; the Prince of Orange, the Duke of Brunswick, the British Ambassador, the foreign Commissioners, the Earl of Uxbridge, Lord Hill, and such a host of Generals with their Aides-de-Camp, fashionable young Guardsmen, and officers of

249

Cavalry regiments, that the lilac crapes and figured muslins were rendered insignificant by the scarlet and gold which so overpoweringly predominated. Jealous eyes dwelled from time to time on Barbara Childe, who, with what Lady Francis Webster almost tearfully described as fiendish cunning, had appeared midway through the evening in a gown of unrelieved white satin, veiled by silver net drapery *à l'Ariane.* Nobody else had had such forethought; indeed, complained Lady John Somerset, who but Bab Childe would have the audacity to wear a gown like a bridal robe at a ball? The puces swore faintly at the scarlet uniforms; the celestial blues and the pale greens died; but the white satin turned all the gold-encrusted magnificence into a background to set it off.

"One comfort is that that head of hers positively shrieks at the uniforms!" said a lady in a Spanish bodice and petticoat.

Barbara had come with the Vidals, but Lavisse was missing from her usual escort. None of the officers invited from General Perponcher's division had put in an appearance, a circumstance which presently began to cause a little uneasiness. No one knew just what was happening on the frontier, but wild rumours had been current all day, and the news of the Army's having been put in motion had begun to spread.

It was a very hot night, and the young people, overcoming the prudence of their elders, had had the windows opened in the ballroom. But hardly a breath of air stirred the long curtains, and young gentlemen in tight stocks and high collars had begun to mop their brows and agonize over the possible wilting of the starched points of shirt-collars, so nattily protruding above the folds of their black cravats.

The ballroom formed a wing of its own to the left of the hall, and had an alcove at one end and a small ante-room at the other. It was papered with a charming trellis pattern of roses and had several French windows on each side of it. It opened on to a passage that ran the length of the house, bisecting the hall in the middle. At the back of the hall, and immediately opposite the front door, was the entrance to the garden, with the dining-room on one side of it and two smaller apartments, one of which the Duke of Richmond used as a study, on the other. A fine staircase and a billiard-room flanked the front door. The Duke's study was inhospitably closed, but every other room on the ground floor had been flung open. Candles burned everywhere; and banks of roses and lilies, anxiously sprinkled from time to time by the servants, overcame the hot smell of wax with their heavier scent.

Everything that could make the ball the most brilliant of the season had been done. There was no Catalani in Brussels to sing at the party, but the Duchess had a much more original surprise for her guests than the trills of a mere prima donna. She had contrived to get some of the Sergeants and Privates of the 42nd Royal Highlanders and the 92nd Foot to dance reels and strathspeys to the music of their own pipes. It was a spectacle that enchanted everyone: scarlet, and rifle-green, and the blaze of Hussar jackets were at a discount when the weird sound of the pipes began and the Highlanders came marching in with their kilts swinging, tartans swept over their left shoulders, huge white sporrans bobbing, and the red chequered patterns of their stockings twinkling in the quick steps of the reel. A burst of clapping greeted their appearance; the strathspeys and the sword-dances called forth shouts of Bravo! One daring young lady threw the rose she had been wearing at a blushing private; everyone began to laugh, one or two ladies followed her example, and the Highlanders retired presently, almost overwhelmed by the admiration they had evoked.

But when the skirl of the pipes had died away and the orchestra struck up a waltz, the brief period of forgetfulness left the company. The young people thronged on to the floor again, but older guests gathered into little groups, discussing the rumours, and button-holing every General Officer who happened to be passing. None of the Generals could give the anxious any news; they all said they had

251

heard nothing fresh—even Uxbridge and Hill, who, it was thought, must have received certain intelligence. Hill wore his habitual placid smile; Uxbridge was debonair, and put all questions aside with a light-heartedness he was far from feeling. He had had, earlier in the evening, a somewhat disconcerting interview with the Duke. He stood next to him in seniority, and would have liked a little information himself. He had been warned not to ask questions of the Duke if he wished to avoid a snub, but he had prevailed upon Alava, whom he knew to be a personal friend of Wellington, to pave the way for him. But it had not been very successful. "Plans! I have no plans!" had exclaimed his lordship. "I shall be guided by circumstances." Uxbridge had stood silent. His lordship, using a milder tone, had clapped him on the shoulder, and added: "One thing is certain: you and I will both do our duty, Uxbridge."

The Duke's absence from the ball increased the uneasiness that had lurked in everyone's mind all day. When he arrived, soon after midnight, Georgiana Lennox darted off the floor towards him, dragging Lord Hay by the hand, and demanded breathlessly: "Oh, Duke, do pray tell me! Are the rumours true? Is it war?"

He replied gravely: "Yes, they are true: we are off to-morrow."

She turned pale; his words, overheard by those standing near, were repeated, and spread quickly round the ballroom. The music went on, and some of the dancing, but the chatter died, only to break out again, voices sharper, and a note of excitement audible in the medley of talk. Officers who had ridden in from a distance to attend the ball hurried away to rejoin their regiments, some with sober faces, some wildly elated, some lingering to exchange touching little keepsakes with girls in flower-like dresses who had stopped laughing, and clung with frail, unconscious hands to a scarlet sleeve, or the fur border of a pelisse. One or two General Officers went up to confer with the Duke, and then returned to their partners, saying cheerfully that there was no need for anyone to be alarmed:

they were not going to the war yet; time enough to think of that when the ball was over.

From scores of faces the polite company masks seemed to have slipped. People had forgotten that at balls they must smile, and hide whatever care or grief they owned under bright, artificial fronts. Some of the senior officers were looking grave; here and there a rigid, meaningless smile was pinned to a mother's white face, or a girl stood with a fallen mouth, and blank eyes fixed on a scarlet uniform. A queer, almost greedy emotion shone in many countenances. Life had become suddenly an urgent business, racing towards disaster, and the craving for excitement, the breathless moment compound of fear, and grief, and exaltation, when the mind sharpened, and the senses were stretched as taut as the strings of a violin, surged up under the veneer of good manners, and shone behind the dread in shocked young eyes. For all the shrinking from tragedy looming ahead, there was yet an unacknowledged eagerness to hurry to meet whatever horror lurked in the future; if existence were to sink back to the humdrum, there would be disappointment behind the relief, and a sense of frustration.

The ball went on; couples, hesitating at first, drifted back into the waltz; Sir William Ponsonby seized a girl in a sprigged muslin dress round the waist, and said gaily: "Come along! I can't miss this! It is quite my favourite tune!"

Georgiana felt a tug at her sleeve, and turned to find Hay stammering with excitement, his eyes blazing. "Georgy! We're going to war! Going into action against Boney himself! Oh, I say, come back and dance this! Was there ever anything so splendid?"

"How can you, Hay?" she exclaimed. "You don't know what you are talking about!"

"Don't I, by Jove! Why, we've been living for this moment!"

"I won't listen to you! It's not splendid: it's the most dreadful thing that has ever happened!"

"But, Georgy——!"

253

"Go and find someone else to dance with you!" she said, almost crying, and turned away from him to seek refuge beside Lady Worth.

Hay stared after her in a good deal of astonishment, but was diverted from his purpose of following her to make his peace by having his arm grasped by a kindred spirit. "Hay, have you heard?" said Harry Alastair eagerly. "Ours have been ordered to Braine-le-Comte. I'm off immediately! Are you coming? Oh no, of course! You'll stay for General Maitland. By Jove, won't we give the French a hiding! There's Audley! I must speak to him before I go!"

He darted off to where the Colonel was standing in conversation with Lord Robert Manners, and stood, impatient but decorous, until it should please the Colonel to notice him. This Audley soon did, smiling to see him so obviously fretting to be off.

"Hallo, Harry! You've got your wish, you see!"

"By Gad, haven't I just! I only came up to say good-bye and wish you luck. I'm off to Braine-le-Comte, you know. It's my first engagement! Lord, won't some of the fellows at home be green with envy!"

"Well, mind you capture an Eagle," said the Colonel, holding out his hand. "I daresay I shall run up against you some time or other, but in case I don't, the best of luck to you. Take care of yourself!"

Lord George Alastair came striding out of the ante-room behind them as Harry wrung the Colonel's hand. He merely nodded to the Colonel, but said curtly to his brother: "Are you off, Harry? I'll go with you as far as the centre of the town. I'm for Ninove. Where are you for?"

"Braine-le-Comte. You don't look very cheerful, I must say. Been bidding someone a tender farewell?"

"That's it: come along, now!"

"Wait a bit, here's Bab!"

Colonel Audley turned his head quickly, and saw Barbara coming across the room towards them. Her eyes were fixed on her brothers, but as though she were conscious of his gaze she glanced in his direction, and flushed.

254

Colonel Audley thrust a hand which he found to be shaking slightly in Lord Robert's arm, and walked away with him.

The Duke had gone to sit beside Lady Helen Dalrymple on the sofa. She found him perfectly amiable but preoccupied, breaking off his conversation with her every now and then to call some officer to him to receive a brief instruction. The Prince of Orange and the Duke of Brunswick both conferred with him for some minutes, and then left the ball together, the Prince heedless of everything but the excitement of the moment, the Duke calm, bestowing his grave smile on an acquaintance encountered in the doorway, not forgetting to take his punctilious leave of his hostess.

A few minutes later, Colonel Audley went up to Judith and touched her arm, saying quietly: "I'm off, Judith. Tell Worth, will you? I haven't time to look for him."

She clasped his hands. "Oh, Charles! Where?"

"Only to Ath, with a message, but it's urgent. I'm not likely to return to Brussels to-night. Don't be alarmed, will you? You will see what a dressing we shall give Boney!"

The next instant he was gone, slipping out of the ballroom without any other leave-taking than a word to his hostess. Others followed him, but in spite of the many departures there seemed to be no empty places in the dining-room when the guests presently went in to supper. Tables were arranged round the room; the junior officers, under the wing of Lord William Lennox, with an arm in a sling and bandages and sticking-plaster adorning his head, crowded round the sideboard, and were honoured by Lord Uxbridge's calling out to them, with a brimming glass held in his hand: "A glass of wine with the side-table!"

The Duke sat with Georgiana beside him. He seemed to be in good spirits; his loud laugh kept breaking out; he had given Georgiana a miniature of himself, done by a Belgian artist, and was protesting jokingly at her showing it to those seated near them.

255

Supper had hardly begun when the Prince of Orange came into the room, looking very serious. He went straight to the Duke, and bent over him, whispering in his ear.

A despatch had been brought in by one of his Aides-de-Camp from Baron Constant at Braine-le-Comte. It was dated as late as 10.30 p.m., and reported that Charleroi had fallen not two hours after Ziethen's solitary message had been sent off that morning. The French had advanced twenty miles into Belgian territory. The Prussians had been attacked at Sombreffe by Grouchy, with Vandamme's Corps in support, and had fallen back on Fleurus; Ney had pushed forward on the left to Frasnes, south of Quatre-Bras, with an advance guard of cavalry, but had encountered there Prince Bernhard of Saxe-Weimar, who, taking the law courageously into his own hands, had moved forward from Genappe with one Nassau battalion and a battery of horse artillery. A skirmish had taken place, but Ney had apparently had insufficient infantry to risk an engagement. He had made some demonstrations, but the handful of troops opposed to him had held their ground, and at seven o'clock he had bivouacked for the night. Prince Bernhard had reported the affair to General Perponcher, who, wisely ignoring the Duke's positive orders to assemble his division at Nivelles, had directed it instead on the hamlet and cross-roads of Quatre-Bras.

The Duke listened to these tidings with an unmoved countenance. He saw that everyone in the room was watching him, and said in a loud voice: "Very well! I have no fresh orders to give. I advise your Royal Highness to go back to your quarters and to bed."

The Prince, whose air of suppressed excitement had escaped no one, withdrew; the Duke resumed his conversation. But the impression created by the Prince's reappearance was not to be banished; except amongst those who had no relatives engaged in the operations, conversation had become subdued, and faces that had worn smiles an hour earlier now looked a little haggard in the glare of the candlelight. No one was surprised when the Duke went up to his host, saying cheerfully: "I think it's time for me to go to bed likewise." In the distance could be heard the ominous sound of bugles calling to arms; dancing seemed out of place; the Duke's departure was for most of those present a welcome sign of the party's breaking up. Wives exchanged nods with their husbands; mothers tried to catch heedless daughters' eyes; Georgiana Lennox stole away to help her brother March pack up.

The Duke said under his breath: "Have you a good map in the house, Richmond?"

Richmond nodded, and led him to his study. The Duke shut the door and said abruptly: "Napoleon has humbugged me, by God! He has gained twenty-four hours' march on me."

He walked over to the desk, and bent over the map Richmond had spread out on it, and studied it for a moment or two in silence.

Richmond stood watching him, startled by what he had said and wondering a little that no anxiety should be apparent in his face. "What do you intend doing?" he asked presently.

"I've ordered the Army to concentrate on Quatre-Bras," replied his lordship. "But we shan't stop him there, and if so, I must fight him *here*." As he spoke he drew his thumbnail across the map below the village of Waterloo, and straightened himself. "I'll be off now, and get some sleep."

In the ballroom a few determined couples were still dancing, but with the departure of the officers the zest had gone from the most care-free young female. Ladies were collecting their wraps, carriages were being called for, and a stream of guests were filing past the Duchess of Richmond, returning thanks and taking leave.

Judith, who had gone upstairs to fetch her cloak, was startled, on her way down again, to encounter Barbara, her train caught over her arm, and in her face an expression of the most painful anxiety. She put out her hand impulsively, grasping Judith's wrist, and said in a strangled voice: "Charles! Where is he?"

"My brother-in-law left the ball before supper," replied Judith.

"O God!" The hand left Judith's wrist and gripped the banister-rail. "He is in Brussels? Yes, yes, he is still in Brussels! Tell me, confound you, tell me!"

There was a white agony in her face, but Judith was unmoved by it. She said: "He is not in Brussels, nor will he return. I wish you good-night, Lady Barbara."

She passed on down the stairs to where Worth stood waiting for her. Their carriage was at the door; in another minute they had entered it, and were being driven out of the gates in the direction of the centre of the town.

Judith leaned back in her corner, trying to compose her spirits. Worth took her hand presently, and held it lightly in his own. "What is it, my dear?"

"That woman!" she said in a low voice. "Barbara Childe! She dared to ask me where Charles had gone. I could have struck her in the face for her effrontery! She let Charles go like that—unhappy, all his old gaiety quite vanished!" She found that tears were running down her face, and broke off to wipe them away. "Don't let us speak of it! I am tired, and stupid. I shall be better directly."

He was silent, but continued to hold her hand. After a minute or two she said in a calmer tone: "That noise! It seems to thud in my brain. What is it?"

"The drums beating to war," he replied. "The Reserve is being put into motion at once."

She shuddered. As the carriage drew nearer to the Park, the coachman was obliged to curb his horses to a walk, and sometimes to bring them to a complete standstill. There was scarcely a house in Brussels where soldiers were not billeted; the sound of the trumpets and the drums brought them out, knapsacks slung over their shoulders, coats unbuttoned, and shakos crammed on askew. Some had wives running beside them; others had their arms round Belgian sweethearts; one Highlander was carrying a little boy on his shoulder, while the child's parents, who had been his hosts, walked beside with his knapsack and his musket.

In the great Place Royale a scene of indescribable

confusion reigned. The sky was already paling towards dawn, and in the ghostly gray light men, horses, waggons, gun-carriages seemed to be inextricably mixed. Waggons were being loaded, and commissariat trains harnessed; the air was full of a medley of noises: the stamp of hooves on the cobbles, the rumble of wheels, the jingle of harness, the sudden neigh of a horse and the indistinguishable clatter of many voices. An officer called sharply; someone was whistling a popular air; a mounted man rode past; a Colour waved. Soldiers were sitting on the pavement, some sleeping on packs of straw, others checking the contents of their knapsacks.

Judith, who had been leaning forward in the carriage, intent upon the scene, turned suddenly towards Worth. "Let us get out!"

"Do you care to? You are not too tired?"

"No. I want to see."

He opened the door and stepped down on to the cobbles, and turned to give his hand to her. She stood beside him while he spoke with the coachman, and then took his arm. They made their way slowly across the Place. No one paid any heed to them; occasionally a soldier brushed past them, or they had to draw aside to allow a waggon to go by, or to pick their way through a tangle of ropes, canteens, corn-sacks, bill-hooks, nose-bags, and all the paraphernalia of an army on the move.

They reached the farther side of the Place at length, and stood for some time watching order grow out of the confusion. Regiments were forming one after the other, and marching down the Rue de Namur towards the Namur Gate. The steady tramp of boots made an undercurrent of sound audible through the shrill blare of the trumpets and the ceaseless beat of the drums. Some of the men sang; some whistled; the Riflemen began to form up, and a voice from their ranks shouted: "The first in the field and the last out of it: the bloody, Fighting Ninety-fifth!" A roar went up; hundreds of voices chanted the slogan. Indifferent-eyed Flemish women, driving market-carts full of vegetables into Brussels from the neighbouring countryside, stared incuriously; an order rang out; another regiment moved forward.

Once Worth bent over Judith, asking: "Are you not tired? Shall we go home?"

She shook her head.

At four o'clock the sun was shining. In the Park, the pipes were playing *Hieland Laddie*. The sound of them drew nearer, the tread of feet grew to a rhythmic thunder. The Highland Brigade came marching through the Place in the first rays of the sunlight, Pipe-Majors strutting ahead, ribbons fluttering from the bagpipes, huge fur head-dresses nodding, and kilts swinging.

"Were they some of these men who danced for us to-night?" Judith asked, recognizing a tartan.

"Yes."

She was silent, watching them pass through the Place and out of sight. When the music of the pipes was faint in the distance, she said, with a sigh: "Let us go home now, Julian. I shall remember this night as long as I live, I think."

CHAPTER XVIII

BY eight o'clock in the morning the last of the regiments had marched out of Brussels. A little later the Duke followed, accompanied by his Staff, and a profound silence descended on the city. Judith had fallen asleep some hours before, with the sound of the trumpets and the tread of many feet in her ears. When she awoke the morning was considerably advanced. Her first feeling was of surprise to find everything quiet, for the shouting and the drumming and the bugle-calls had seemed to run through her dreams. She got up, and looked out between the blinds upon a sun-baked street. A cat curled on the steps of a house opposite was the only living thing in sight. No uniforms swaggered down the street, no ladies in muslins and chip hats floated along to pay their morning calls or to promenade in the Park.

She dressed, and went down to the salon on the first floor. Worth had gone out, but he came in presently with the newspapers. It was being reported in the cafés that the Duke had ridden out in high spirits, saying that Blücher would most likely have settled the business himself by that time and that he would probably be back in Brussels for dinner. The general opinion seemed to be that no action would be fought that day. It was thought that the bulk of the British troops could not be brought up in time. Judith did not know whether to be glad or sorry; the suspense would be as hard to bear as the sound of cannon, she thought.

"Quite a number of people are leaving for Antwerp," Worth observed. "Lady Fitzroy has gone, and I met De Lancey just before he went off to join the Army, who told me that he had prevailed upon that poor young wife of his to go, too." He paused, but she made no comment. He smiled. "Well, Judith?"

"*You* would not wish to go if *I* were not here."

"Very true, but that can hardly be said to have a bearing on the case."

"I don't want to run away, if you think it would not be wrong in me to stay. I hope you don't mean to talk to me of defeat, for I won't listen if you do."

"Like you, I'm of a sanguine disposition. But young Julian's nurse beat us both in that respect. She has taken him out into the Park for an airing, and the only emotion roused in her breast by all the racket that went on during the night was a strong indignation at having a child's rest disturbed."

"Ah, she is a phlegmatic Scot! I have no fear of her losing her head."

They were interrupted by the butler's coming into the room with the announcement that Lady Barbara Childe was below and wished to speak to the Earl.

Judith was astounded. She had not thought that after their encounter on the previous night Lady Barbara would dare to accost her again, let alone call at her residence. She looked at Worth, but he merely raised his eyebrows, and said: "Well, I am at home, and perfectly ready to receive visitors. I don't understand why they are left in the hall. Beg her ladyship to come up."

"Yes, my lord," said the butler, his bosom swelling at the reproof. "I should have done so in the first place but that her ladyship desired me to carry the message."

He withdrew, stately and outraged. The door had scarcely shut behind him when Judith's feelings got the better of her. She exclaimed: "I wish you had sent her about her business! I do not see why I should be obliged to receive her in my house! And that you should be willing to do so gives me a very poor opinion of your loyalty to Charles!"

"I cannot think that Charles would thank me for turning Lady Barbara away from my door," he replied.

There was no time for more; the butler opened the door and announced Barbara; and she came into the room with her long, mannish stride.

Judith rose, but before she had time to speak she was forestalled.

"I didn't mean to force myself into your presence," Barbara said. "I am sorry. My business is with your husband." She paused, and a wintry, rueful smile flashed across her face. "Oh, the devil! My curst tongue again! Don't look so stiff: I have not come to wreck *your* marriage." This was said with a good deal of bitterness. She forced herself to speak more lightly, and added, looking in her clear way at Worth: "I couldn't, could I? You at least have never succumbed to my famous charms."

"No, never," he replied imperturbably. "Will you not sit down?"

"No; I do not mean to stay above a minute. The case is that I am in the devil of a quandary over my horses. Would you be so obliging as to house them for me in your stables? There is the pair I drive in my phaeton, and my mare as well."

"Willingly," he said. "But—forgive me—why?"

"My brother and his wife are leaving Brussels this morning. They are gone by this time, I daresay. The house in the Rue Ducale is given up. My own groom is not to be trusted alone, and I do not care to stable the horses at the hôtel. They tell me there is already such a demand for horses to carry people to Antwerp that by nightfall it will be a case of stealing what can't be hired."

"Lord and Lady Vidal gone!" Judith exclaimed, surprised into breaking her silence.

"Oh yes!" Barbara replied indifferently. "Gussie has been in one of her confounded takings ever since the news was brought in last night, and Vidal is very little better."

"But you do not mean to remain here alone, surely?"

"Why not?"

"It is not fit!"

"Ah, you doubt the propriety of it! I don't care for that." Her mouth quivered, but she controlled it. Judith noticed that she had twisted the end of her scarf tightly between her fingers and was gripping it so hard that her gloves seemed in danger of splitting. "Both my brothers are engaged in this war," she said. "And Charles."

"I had not supposed that Charles's fate was any longer a concern of yours," Judith said.

"I am aware of that. But it is my concern, nevertheless." She stared at Judith with haunted eyes. "Perhaps I may never see him again. But if he comes back I shall be here." She drew a sobbing breath, and continued in a hard voice: "That, however, is my affair. Lord Worth, you are very obliging. My groom shall bring the horses round during the course of the day. Good-bye!" She held out her hand, but drew it back, flushing a little. "Oh——! You would rather not shake hands with me, I daresay!"

"I have not the least objection to shaking hands with you," he replied. "But I should be grateful to you if you could contrive to stop being foolish. Now sit down and try to believe that your differences with my brother leave me supremely indifferent."

She smiled faintly, and after a brief hesitation sat down in the chair by the table. "Well, what now?" she asked.

"Are you staying with friends? May I have your direction?"

"I am at the Hôtel de Belle Vue."

"Indeed! Alone?"

"Yes, alone, if you discount my maid."

"It will not do," he said. "If you mean to remain in Brussels you must stay here."

She looked at him rather blankly. "You must be mad!"

"I am quite sane, I assure you. It can never be thought desirable for a young and unprotected female to be staying in a public hotel. In a foreign capital, and in such unsettled times as these, it would be the height of folly."

She gave a short laugh. "My dear man, you forget that I am not an inexperienced miss just out of the school-room! I am a widow, and if it comes to *folly*, why, I make a practice of behaving foolishly!"

"Just so, but that is no reason why you should not mend your ways."

She got up. "This is to no purpose. It is unthinkable that I should stay in your house. You are extremely kind, but——"

"Not at all," he interrupted. "I am merely protecting myself from the very just anger I am persuaded my brother would feel were he to find you putting up at an hôtel when he returns to Brussels."

She said unsteadily: "Please——! We will not speak of Charles. You don't wish me to make a fool of myself, I imagine."

He did not answer; he was looking at Judith. She was obliged to recognize the propriety of his invitation. She did not like it, but good breeding compelled her to say: "My husband is right. I will have a room prepared at once, Lady Barbara. I hope you will not find it very disagreeable: we shall do our best to make your stay comfortable."

"Thank you. It is not I who would find such a visit disagreeable. You dislike me cordially: I do not blame you. I dislike myself."

Judith coloured, and replied in a cool voice: "I have

not always done so. There have been times when I have liked you very well."

"You hated me for what I did to Charles."

"Yes."

"O God, if I could undo—if I could have it back, all this past month! It is useless! I behaved like the devil I am. That wretched quarrel! The very knowledge that I was in the wrong drove me to worse conduct! I have never been answerable to anyone for my misdeeds: there is a fiendish quality in me that revolts at the veriest hint of——but how should you understand? It is not worthy of being understood!"

She covered her face with her hands. Worth walked across the room to the door, and went out.

Judith said in a kinder tone: "I do understand in part. *I* was not always so docile as you think me. But Charles! There is such a sweetness of temper, such nobility of mind——"

"Stop!" Barbara cried fiercely. "Do you think I don't know it? I knew it when he first came up to me, and I looked into his eyes, and loved him. I knew myself to be unworthy! The only thing I did that I am not ashamed of now was to try not to let him persuade me into becoming engaged to him. That impulse was the noblest *I* have ever felt. But he would not believe me when I told him what I was like. Though I knew I should not, I yielded. I wanted him, and all my life I have taken what I wanted, without thought or compunction!" She gave a wild laugh. "You despise me, but you should also pity me, for I have enough heart to wish I had more."

"I do pity you," Judith said, considerably moved. "But having yielded——"

"Yes! Having yielded, why could I not submit? I do not know, unless it be that from the day I married Jaspar Childe I swore I would never do so, never allow myself to be possessed, or governed, or even guided. Don't misunderstand me! I am not trying to find excuses for myself. The fault lies deeper: it is in my curst nature!"

"I have sometimes thought," Judith said, after a short pause, "that the circumstances of your engagement made it particularly trying for you. In this little town we are obliged to live in a crowded circle from which there can be no escape. One's every action is remarked, and discussed. It is as though your engagement to Charles was acted upon a stage, in all the glare of footlights, for the amusement of your acquaintances."

"Oh, if you but knew!" Barbara exclaimed. "You do, in part, realize the evils of my situation but you cannot know what a demon was roused in me by finding myself the object of every form of cheap wit on the one hand, and of benign approval upon the other! It was said that I had met my match, that I was tamed at last, that I should soon settle down to a life of humdrum propriety! *You* would have had the strength to disregard such nonsense: I had not. When I was with Charles it did not signify. Every annoyance was forgotten in his presence; even my damnable restlessness left me. But he was busy; he could not be always at my side; and when he was away from me I was bored. If he had married me when I begged him to! But no! It would not have answered. There must still have been temptation."

"Yes, I am very sensible of that. You are so much admired: it must have been hard indeed to give up your——" She hesitated.

"My flirtations," said Barbara, with a melancholy smile. "It was hard. You know that I did not give them up. When I look back upon the past month it is with loathing, believe me! It was as though I was swept into a whirlpool! I could not be still."

"Oh, do not speak of it! I myself have been conscious of what you describe. There has been no time for reflection, no time for anything but pleasure! It was as though we were all a little mad. But I believe Charles understood how it was. He said once to me that the life we were leading was ruinous. It was very true! I do not deny that your wildness made him anxious; indeed, I have blamed you bitterly for it. But all that was nothing!"

"You are thinking of my having made your brother fall in love with me. It was very bad of me."

"The provocation was severe. I honoured you for coming up to Harriet so handsomely that day. There can be no excuse for her behaviour. It vexed me when you made him go to you at the Richmond's party, but I did not blame you entirely. But afterwards! How could you have let it go on? Forgive me! I did not mean to advert to this subject. It is over, and should be forgotten. I do not know what passed between you and Charles."

"Everything of the most damnable on my part!" Barbara said.

"I daresay you might lose your temper. But your conduct since that night! You left nothing undone that could hurt him."

"Nothing!" Barbara said. "Nothing that could drive him mad enough to come back to me! I would not go to him: he was to come to me—upon my own terms! Folly! He would not do it, nor did I wish him to. The news that war had broken out brought me to my senses. There was no room then for pride. Even if his affections had been turned in another direction—but I could not believe it could be so, for mine were unaltered! He turned from me in the ballroom, but I thought I saw, in his eyes, a look——" Her voice was suspended; she struggled to regain her composure, and after a moment continued: "I tried to find him. Nothing signified but that I should see him before he went away. But he had gone. Perhaps I shall never see him again."

She ended in a tone of such dejection that Judith was impelled to say, with more cheerfulness than she felt: "We shall not think of that, if you please! Recollect that his employment on the Duke's Staff is to his advantage. He will not be in the line. Why, how absurd this is! He has survived too many engagements for us to have the least reason to suppose that he will not survive this one. Indeed, all the Duke's Aides-de-Camp have been with him for a long time now. Depend upon it, they will come riding back in the best of health and spirits.

Meanwhile, I do earnestly beg of you to remain with us!"

"Thank you. I will do so, and try not to disgrace you. You won't be plagued with me too much, I hope. I shall be busy. Indeed, I ought not to be here now. I have promised to go to Madame de Ribaucourt's. She has made herself responsible for the preparations for the wounded, and needs help."

"Oh, that is the very thing!" Judith cried. "To be able to be of use! Stay till I fetch my bonnet and gloves! I would like, of all things, to go along with you."

A few minutes later they left the house together, and set out on foot for their destination. They met few acquaintances on the way; streets which the day before had been full of officers and ladies were now only lined with the tilt-carts designed for the transport of the wounded, and with baggage-waggons, in perfect order, ready to move off at a moment's notice. Flemish drivers were dozing in the carts; a few sentinels were posted to guard the waggons. The Place Royale, strangely quiet after the confusion of the night, had been cleared of all the litter of equipment. There were more waggons and carts there, with a little crowd of citizens standing about, silently staring at them. Horses were picketed in the Park, but a fair number of people were strolling about there, much as usual, except for the gravity of their countenances and the lowered tones of their voices.

At the Comtesse de Ribaucourt's all was bustle and business. Many of Judith's friends were there, scraping lint and preparing cherry-water.

The feeling of being able to do something which would be of use in this crisis did much to relieve the oppression of everyone's spirits. Dr. Brügmans, the Inspector-General of Health, came in at noon for a few minutes, and told of the tents to be erected at the Namur and Louvain Gates for the accommodation of the wounded. Various equipments were needed for them, in particular blankets and pillows. Judith willingly undertook the responsibility of procuring all that could be had from her numerous acquaintances in the town, and lost no time in setting out on a house-to-house visitation.

The hours sped by; she was astonished on returning to Madame Ribaucourt's to find that it was already three o'clock; she was conscious neither of fatigue nor of hunger. She sat down at a table to transcribe the list of equipments she had cajoled from her friends, but was arrested in the middle of this task by a sound that made her look up quickly, her pen held in mid-air.

All conversation was stopped short; every head was raised. The sound was heard again, a dull rumble far away in the distance.

Someone said in an urgent voice: "Listen!" Lady Barbara walked over to the window, and stood there, her head a little bent, as though to hear more plainly.

The sound was repeated. "It's the guns!" said Georgiana Lennox, dropping the lint she was holding.

"No, no, it's only thunder! Everyone says there can be no action until to-morrow!"

"It is the guns," said Barbara. She came away from the window, and quite coolly resumed her work of scraping lint.

The distant cannonading had been heard by others besides themselves. All over the town the greatest consternation was felt. People came running out of their houses to stand listening in the street; crowds flocked to the ramparts; and a number of men set out on horseback in the direction of Waterloo to try to get news.

They brought back such conflicting accounts that it was soon seen that very little dependence could be placed on what they said. They had seen nothing; their only information came from peasants encountered on the road; all that was certain was that an action was being fought somewhere to the south of Brussels.

When Judith and Barbara reached home at five o'clock the cannonading was still audible. Everyone they met was asking the same questions: were the Allied troops separately engaged? Had they joined the Prussians? Where was the action being fought? Could the cavalry have reached the spot? Could the outlying divisions have come up? There could be no answer to such questions; none, in fact, was expected.

Worth was at home when the ladies came in. He had seen Barbara's trunks brought round from the Hôtel de Belle Vue, and had installed her frightened maid in the house. He had driven out, afterwards, a little way down the Charleroi road, but, like everyone else, had been unable to procure any intelligence. The baggage-waggons lined the chaussée for miles, he said, but none of the men in charge of them knew more than himself.

They sat down to dinner presently in the same state of anxious expectation. The sound of the guns seemed every moment to be growing more distinct. Judith found it impossible not to speculate upon the chances of defeat. The thought of her child, sleeping in his cot above stairs, made her dread the more acute. She should have sent him to England with Peregrine's children; her selfishness had made her keep them in Brussels; she had exposed him to a terrible danger.

She managed to check such useless reflections, and to join with an assumption of ease in the conversation Worth and Barbara were maintaining.

Some time after dinner, when the two ladies were seated alone in the salon, Worth having gone out to see whether any news had been received from the Army, a knock sounded on the front door, and in a few minutes they were astonished by the butler's announcing Colonel Canning.

Only one visitor could have been more welcome. Judith almost sprang out of her chair, and started forward to meet him. "Colonel Canning! Oh, how glad I am to see you!"

He shook her warmly by the hand. "I have only dropped in for a few moments to tell you that Charles was well when I saw him last. I have been on a mission to the French King, at Alost, and am on my way back now to Quatre-Bras."

"Quatre-Bras! Is that where the action is being fought? Oh, stay just for a few minutes! We have been without news the whole day, and the suspense is dreadful. Sit down: I will ring for the tea-tray to be brought in directly. But have you dined?"

"Yes, yes, thank you! I dined at Greathed's, in the Park. Seeing me pass by his house, he very kindly called to me to come up and join him. Creevey was there to. I can't tell you much, you know. I was sent off just before 5.0, so I don't know how it has been going. However, by the time I left the Brunswickers and the Nassau contingent had arrived, and Van Merlen's Light Cavalry besides, so you may be sure everything is doing famously."

Barbara said, with a smile: "Confound you, Colonel, you begin at the end! Let us have the start, if you please!"

"By God!" he said seriously, "we have had an escape! You won't blab it about the town, but the fact is Boney took us by surprise, and if Ney had pushed on last night, or even this morning, there's no saying what might not have happened. Prince Bernhard had only a battalion of Nassauers and one horse battery at Quatre-Bras." He gave a chuckle. "We can guess why Ney didn't, of course. The French know the trick the Duke has of concealing the better part of his troops from sight. No doubt Ney was afraid he'd come up against the whole Army, and dared not risk an attack without more infantry. But God knows why he delayed so long to-day! They say the French weren't even under arms at ten o'clock this morning. We arrived at half-past to find Orange there with two of his divisions, and nothing of a force in front of him. Charles arrived from Ath a little while after—still in his ball-dress! He had no time to waste changing it last night, so there he is, in all his splendour. However, he is not the only one. Where was I?"

"You had arrived at Quatre-Bras to find no very startling force opposing you."

"Oh yes! Well, so it was. The Duke inspected the position, saw that Ney was making no move, and rode over with Gordon and Müffling to confer with old Blücher, at Ligny."

"We have not joined the Prussians, then?"

"Oh lord, no! They're seven miles to the east of us, and pretty badly placed, too. I don't know how it has gone with them: they've been engaged all day against Boney himself, but we've had no news. It appears that General Bourmont deserted to Blücher with all his Staff yesterday morning, but the old man would have nothing to do with him! I haven't heard of any other desertions. As for the Prussians to-day, Gordon told me Blücher had his men exposed on the slope of the hill, and that the Duke told Hardinge pretty bluntly that he thought they would be damnably mauled. I daresay they have been. Gniesenau was anxious for the Duke to move to his support, which, I understand from Gordon, he said he would do, if he were not attacked himself. But we were attacked, and there was no question of going to help the Prussians. By the time the Duke got back to our position, somewhere between two and three in the afternoon, the French were in force in a wood in front of us. They started shouting *Vive l'Empereur!* and then we heard Ney go down the line, calling out: '*L'Empereur recompensera celui qui s'avancera!*' We've heard *that* before, and we knew we were in for it. I can tell you, it was a nice situation to be in, with only a handful of Dutch-Belgic troops to hold the position, and no sign of old Picton with the Reserve."

"But how is it possible?" Judith exclaimed. "We saw the regiments march out of Brussels in the small hours!"

"There was some muddle over the orders: they were halted at Waterloo, and only reached Quatre-Bras at about half-past three. By God, we were glad to see them! The French opened the attack on a farm on the main road. I should think Ney had about fifteen or sixteen thousand men opposed to our seven thousand—but that's a guess. The fields are so deep in rye you can't make out the exact positions of anyone, friend or foe. In some places it's above one's head—or it was, till it got trampled down."

He paused, for the tea-tray was just then brought in. Judith handed him a cup, and he gulped some of the tea down. "Thank you. Well, the Dutch were driven out of Bossu Wood, and there was a general advance of the French. I needn't tell you the Duke remained as cool as a cucumber throughout. There never was such a man! He was always in the hottest part of the fight—no one knows better than he how to put heart into the men! They may not worship him, as they say the French worship Boney, but by God, they trust him!"

Judith smiled. "I know how much *you* value him, Colonel. But go on!"

"Well, we couldn't hold the position against such odds, of course. Things were beginning to look devilish black, but Picton came up in the very nick of time, which pretty well doubled our strength. But even so it was a ticklish business. The Highland Brigade were cut to pieces, poor devils, but they didn't yield an inch. However, as I told you the Brunswickers came up from Nivelles, then the Nassauers, and Van Merlen's cavalry. That was when I left." He glanced at the clock on the mantelpiece, swallowed the rest of his tea, and jumped up. "I must get back. You'll be hearing more news, I daresay: some-one is sure to be sent in. Good-bye—don't be alarmed! All's well, you know."

He hurried away, and not long after he had gone the noise of the firing, which had sounded closer in the still-ness of the evening, grew more desultory, and by ten o'clock had ceased. Worth came in, saying that the population of Brussels was still wandering about the ramparts and the Park. Great anxiety was being felt on all sides to know the result of the action. No news had as yet come in; some stout-hearted persons were maintaining that the Allies must have held their ground; others, in a state of growing uneasiness, were preparing to remove instantly to Antwerp.

The ladies gave him an account of Canning's visit, recalling as well as they were able his description of the battlefield. Worth listened intently, exclaiming when Bar-bara spoke of the arrival of the Brunswick and Nassau contingent: "Then none of our cavalry are engaged!"

"No. Colonel Canning mentioned only General Picton's division."

He looked serious, and said briefly: "It is an ill-managed business!"

"The Colonel said the French had taken us by surprise."

273

"It may well have been so. From what De Lancey told me this morning, it is plain that Wellington, as late as then, was expecting the attack to be directed on his right. Do you say the Prussians have also been engaged?"

"Yes, at Ligny, but he could not tell us how the day had gone with them. He said Napoleon himself was opposed to them."

"I would not give a penny for their chances of success!" he said. "The question will be, Can Wellington maintain his communications with Blücher? It is plain Bonaparte has struck this blow in the endeavour to get between our forces. By God, it should be a lesson to those who have been saying he had lost his old genius! It is masterly! The rapidity of his march from Paris, his strategy in launching the attack at our point of junction with Blücher—it is something quite in his old style: one cannot but admire him! If he can succeed in defeating the Prussians, and Ney in carrying our position, it will be a serious business." He observed Judith's pallor, and dropped his hand on her shoulder, saying more quietly: "There is no need for alarm. If the day has gone against us we are bound to hear of it in time for me to drive you and the boy to safety. I have given orders in the stables: you need be under no apprehension."

Barbara, who had walked over to the window, turned, and said in her lively way: "Confound you, are you one of the croakers? I'll tell you what: I have a very good mind to put my horses up for sale, and so burn my boats!"

"I admire your spirit," he said, with a slight smile.

"You need not," she replied. "I have merely a shocking love of excitement. Consider! In spite of all my adventures I was never till now in danger of falling into the hands of the French. It is something quite out of the common way, and therefore enchanting!"

Judith was obliged to smile at her nonsense, but said protestingly: "How can you talk so?"

"The devil! How else should I talk? You know, if the French should come I fancy we shall make a hit with them.

There is no denying that we are a handsome pair. Neither of us, I am persuaded, need look lower than a Marshal at the very least.''

Such raillery, though it might bring a blush to Judith's cheeks, had the effect of relieving the oppression of her spirits. Nothing more was said of the chances of defeat, and presently Worth went out again to see if any further news had arrived from Quatre-Bras.

He came back a little after eleven, and found that Judith and Barbara were still up. "I called at Creevey's," he said. "Hamilton had been in during the evening on a errand for General Barnes, and of course dropped in on Creevey, to see Miss Ord. The result was still uncertain when he left the field, but Creevey got the impression from him that it was going in our favour. Charles was safe when he left the field: he saw him trying to rally the Belgians, who had had enough, just as he came away. Hamilton reports them as having done well at the start, but they won't stand like our own men. The worst, so far, is that the Duke of Brunswick has fallen. He was killed by a ball passing through his hand to his heart. Hamilton did not mention many of the casualties. The Highlanders have suffered most. Fassiefern and Macara have both fallen; young Hay has gone, too; but I heard of no one else whom we know.''

"Hay!" Barbara lifted her hand to shade her eyes for a moment. "That boy!" Ah, how wanton, how damnable! But go on! If Hay was present, Maitland's brigade must have come up. Could you get no news of Harry?"

"No; Creevey was positive Hamilton mentioned only Hay, and one other, whose name I forget.''

Judith said: "Depend upon it, he would have told Mr. Creevey had your brother been killed.''

"He might not know. But never mind that! What else could you discover, Lord Worth? Shall we hold our ground?''

"I see no reason why we should not. It appears that reinforcements have been arriving ever since five o'clock. The most serious part of the business is that we have no cavalry there worth mentioning. The infantry has done magnificently, however: Hamilton told Creevey that nothing could equal their endurance. Only their steadiness under the onslaughts of Kellermann's Cuirassiers saved the day for us at one point. The Belgian and Brunswick cavalry were scattered; our whole position was completely turned, and might have been carried but for the Highlanders—I think he said the 92nd, but I might mistake. The Duke directed them in person, charging them not to fire until he gave the word. They obeyed him implicitly, though he allowed the Cuirassiers to come within thirty paces before giving the order for a volley. The attack was completely repulsed, Kellermann drawing off in a good deal of disorder. Hamilton seems to have been full of enthusiasm for the Duke's coolness. It appears he has been everywhere at once, exposing himself in the most reckless fashion."

"Surely he should not do so!"

"So I think, but you will not get his officers to agree. Even those who dislike him will tell you that the sight of his long nose amongst them does more to steady the troops than the arrival of a division to support them. He seems to bear a charmed life. What do you think of his being nearly taken by a party of Lancers when the Brunswick Hussars broke under the musketry-fire? He was forced to gallop for his life, made for a ditch lined by the Gordon Highlanders, sang out to them to lie still, and cleared the fence, bayonets and all!"

They remained for some time discussing the news, but the clock striking midnight soon recalled them to a sense of the lateness of the hour. All sound of firing had died away at ten o'clock; nothing had been heard of since; and they could not but believe that if a defeat had been suffered news of it must have reached them. Judith and Barbara went up to their rooms, but they had scarcely begun to undress when the noise of heavy carriages rumbling over the cobbles reached their ears. Nothing could be seen from the windows but people running out of doors to find out what was going on. Shouts and cries seemed to come from all parts of the town; and Judith, pausing only to fling a wrap round her shoulders, hurried to find Worth. He had not yet come upstairs, and called to her from the ground-floor to do nothing until he had discovered what was happening. He went out; Barbara joined Judith in the salon, and they sat in a state of apprehension that made it impossible for either to utter anything but a few occasional, disjointed sentences.

They were soon roused from this condition by the necessity of calming the servants, some of whom were hysterical with fright. Barbara went out into the hall amongst them, and very soon restored order. While Judith occupied herself with reassuring those whose alarm had had the effect of bereaving them of all power of speech or of action, she dealt in a more drastic manner with the rest, swearing at the butler, and emptying jugs of water over any *fille de chambre* unwise enough to fall into a fit of hysterics.

By the time Worth returned, the household was quiet, and Barbara had gone back into the salon with Judith, who had temporarily forgotten her own fears in amusement at her guest's ruthless methods.

Worth brought reassuring tidings. The noise they had heard had been caused by a long train of Artillery, passing through the town on its way to the battlefield. The panic had arisen from a false notion having got about that the train was in retreat. People had rushed out of their houses in every stage of undress; a rumour that the French were coming had spread like wildfire; and the greatest confusion reigned until it became evident, even to the most foolish in the crowd, that the Artillery was moving, not away from the field of action but towards it.

"Is that all?" exclaimed Barbara. "Well, if there is no immediate need for us to become heroines we may as well go to bed. I, at any rate, shall do so."

"Oh," said Judith, with a little show of playfulness, "you need not think that I shall be behind you in sang-froid: you have put me quite on my mettle!"

Good-nights were exchanged; both ladies retired again

277

to their rooms, each with a much better opinion of the other than she had had at the beginning of what, in retrospect, seemed to have been the longest day of her life.

CHAPTER XIX

THE night was disturbed. Many of the Bruxellois seemed to be afraid to go to bed, and spent the hours sitting in their houses with ears on the prick, ready to run out into the streets at the smallest alarm. Just before dawn a melancholy cortège entered the town, bearing the Duke of Brunswick's body. Numbers of spectators saw it pass through the streets. The sable uniforms of the Black Brunswickers, the grim skull-and-cross-bones device upon their caps and the grief in their faces, awed the thin crowds into silence. A feeling of dismay was created; when the sad procession had passed, people dispersed slowly, some to wander about in an aimless fashion till daylight, others returning to their houses to lie down fully clothed upon their beds or to drop uneasily asleep in chairs.

Between five and six in the morning, after an interval of quiet, commotion broke out again. A troop of Belgian Cavalry, entering by the Namur Gate, galloped through the town in the wildest disorder, overturning market-carts, thundering over the cobbles, their smart green uniforms white with dust and their horses foaming. They had all the appearance of men hotly pursued, and scarcely drew rein in their race through the town to the Ninove Gate. All was panic; they were shouting: *"Les Français sont ici!"* and the words were immediately taken up by the terrified crowds who saw them pass. The French were said to be only a few miles outside the town, the Allied Army in full retreat before them. Distracted Belgians ran to collect their more precious belongings, and then wandered about, carrying the oddest collection of goods, not knowing where to go, or what to do. Women became hysterical, *filles de chambre* rushing into hotel bedrooms to rouse sleepy visitors

278

with the news that the French were at the gates; mothers clasping their children in their arms and screaming at their husbands to transport them instantly to safety. The drivers of the carts and the waggons drawn up in the Place Royale caught the infection; no sooner had the cavalry flashed through the great square than they set off down every street, rocking and lurching over the pavé in their gallop for the Ninove Gate. In a few minutes the Place was deserted, except for the people who still drifted about it, spreading the dreadful news, or begging complete strangers for the hire of a pair of horses; and for a few market-carts driven into the town by stolid peasants in sabots and red night-caps, who seemed scarcely to understand what all the pandemonium was about.

Many of the English visitors behaved little better. Some of those who, on the night of the 15th, had stoutly declared their intention of remaining in Brussels, now ordered their carriages, or, if they possessed none, hurried about the town trying to engage horses or to procure passages on the canal track-boats. For the most part, however, the flight of a troop of Belgic cavalry did not rouse much feeling of alarm in British breasts. Ladies busied themselves, as they had done the previous day, with preparations for the wounded, and if there were some who thought the cessation of all gun-fire ominous, there were others who considered it to be a sure sign that all must be well.

Judith and Barbara again went to the Comtesse de Ribaucourt's. On entering the house Judith encountered Georgiana Lennox, who came up to her with a white face and trembling lips, trying to speak calmly on some matter of a consignment of blankets. She was scarcely able to control her voice, and broke off to say: "Forgive me, this is foolish! Only it is so dreadful—I don't seem able to stop crying."

Judith took her hand, saying with a good deal of concern: "Oh, my poor child! Your brothers——?"

"Oh no, no!" Georgiana replied quickly. "But Hay has been killed!" She made an effort to control herself. "He was almost like one of my brothers. It is stupid—I know

279

he would not care for that, but I can't get it out of my head how cross I was with him for being so glad to be going into action." She tried to smile. "I scolded him. I wouldn't dance with him any more, and then I never saw him again. He went away so excited, and now he's been killed, and I didn't even say good-bye to him."

Judith could only press her hand. Georgiana said rather tightly: "I can't believe he's dead, you know. He said: 'Georgy! We're going to war! Was there ever anything so splendid?' And I was cross."

"Dearest Georgy, you mustn't think of that. I am sure he did not."

"Oh no! I know I'm being silly. Only I wish I had not scolded him." She brushed her hand across her eyes. "He was General Maitland's Aide-de-Camp, you know. Now that he has been killed William feels that he must rejoin Maitland, and he is not fit to do so."

"Your brother! Oh, he cannot do so. His arm is still in a sling, and he looks so ill!"

"That is what Mama feels, but my father agrees that it is William's duty to go to General Maitland. I do not know what will come of it." Her lips quivered again; she said inconsequently: "Do you remember how beautifully the Highlanders danced at our ball? They are all dead."

"Oh, hush, my dear, don't think of such things! Not all!"

"Most of them. They were cut to pieces by the Cuirassiers. They say the losses in the Highland brigade are terrible."

Judith could not speak. She had seen the Highlanders march out of Brussels in the first sunlight, striding to war to the music of their own fifes, and the memory of that proud march brought a lump into her throat. She pressed Georgiana's hand again, and released it, turning away to hide the sudden rush of tears to her own eyes.

She and Barbara returned home a little after noon, to find that Worth had just come back from visiting Sir Charles Stuart. He was able to tell them that an Aide-de-Camp had ridden in during the morning, having left the field at 4.0 a.m. He reported that after a very sanguinary battle the Allied Army had remained in possession of the ground. Towards the close of the action the cavalry had come up, having been delayed by mistaken orders. It had not been engaged on the 16th, but would certainly be in the thick of it to-day, if the French attack were renewed, as the Duke was confident it would be.

The ladies had hardly taken off their hats when the sound of cheering reached the house; they ran out to the end of the street, where a crowd had collected, and were in time to see a number of French prisoners being marched under guard towards the barracks of Petit Château.

But the heartening effect of this sight was not of long duration. The next news that reached Brussels was that the Prussians had been defeated at Ligny, and were in full retreat. The intelligence brought a fresh feeling of dismay, which was made the more profound by the arrival, a little later, of the first waggon-loads of wounded. In a short time the streets were full of the most pitiable sights. Men who were able to walk had dragged themselves to Brussels on foot all through the night, some managing to reach the town, many collapsing on the way, and dying by the road-side from the effects of their wounds.

Except amongst those whom panic had rendered incapable of any rational action, the arrival of the wounded made people forget their own alarms in the more pressing need to do what they could to alleviate the sufferings of the soldiers. Ladies who had never encountered more unnerving sights than a pricked finger or the graze on a child's knee, went out into the streets with flasks of brandy and water, and the shreds of petticoats torn up to provide bandages; and stayed until they dropped from fatigue, stanching the blood that oozed from ghastly wounds; providing men who were dying on the pavements with water to bring relief to their last moments; rolling blankets to form pillows for heads that lolled on the cobbles; collecting straw to make beds for those who, unable to reach their own billets, had sunk down on the road; and accepting sad, last tokens from dying men who thought of wives, and mothers, and sweethearts at home, and handed to them a ring, a crumpled diary, or a laboriously scrawled letter.

Judith and Barbara were amongst the first to engage on this work. Neither had ever come into anything but the most remote contact with the results of war; Judith was turned sick by the sight of blood congealed over ugly contusions, of the scraps of gold lace embedded in gaping wounds, of dusty rags twisted round shattered joints, and of gray, pain-racked faces lying upturned upon the pavement at her feet. There was so little that could be accomplished by inexpert hands; the patient gratitude for a few sips of water of men whose injuries were beyond her power to alleviate brought the tears to her eyes. She brushed them away, spoke soothing words to a boy crumpled on the steps of a house, and sobbing dryly, with his head against the railings; bound fresh linen round a case-shot wound; spent all the Hungary Water she owned in reviving men who had covered the weary miles from Quatre-Bras only to fall exhausted in the gutters of Brussels.

Occasionally she caught sight of Barbara, her flowered muslin dusty round the hem with brushing the cobbles, and a red stain on her skirt where an injured head had lain in her lap. Once they met, but neither spoke of the horrors around them. Barbara said briefly: "I'm going for more water. The chemists have opened their shops and will supply whatever is needed."

"For God's sake, take my purse and get me more lint —as much of it as you can procure!" Judith said, on her knees beside a lanky Highlander, who was sitting against the wall with his head dropped on his shoulder.

"No need: they are charging nothing." Barbara replied. "I'll get it."

She passed on, making her way swiftly down the street. A figure in a scarlet coat lay across the pavement; she bent over it, saying gently: "Where are you hurt? Will you let me help you?" Then she saw that the man was dead, and straightened herself, feeling her knees shaking, and nausea rising in her throat. She choked it down, and walked on.

A Highlander, limping along the road, with a bandage round his head and one arm pinned up by the sleeve across his breast, grinned weakly at her. She stopped, and offered him the little water that remained in her flask. He shook his head: "Na, na, I'm awa' to my billet. I shall do verra weel, ma'am."

"Are you badly hurt? Will you lean on my shoulder?"

"Och, I got a wee skelp wi' a bit of a shell, that's all. Gi'e your watter to the puir red-coat yonder: *we* are aye well respected in this toon! We ha' but to show our *petticoat*, as they ca' it, and the Belgians will ay gi'e us what we need!"

She smiled at the twinkle of humour in his eye, but said: "You've hurt your leg. Take my arm, and don't be afraid to lean on me."

He thanked her, and accepted the help. She asked him how the day had gone, and he replied, gasping a little from the pain of walking: "It's a bluidy business, and there's no saying what may be the end on't. Oor regiment was nigh clean swept off, and oor Colonel kilt as I cam' awa'. But I doot all's weel."

She supported him to the end of the street, but was relieved of her charge there by a burgher in a sad-coloured suit of broadcloth, who darted up with exclamations of solicitude, and cries to his wife to come at once to the assistance of "*notre brave Écossais.*" He turned out to be the owner of the Highlander's billet, and it was plain that Barbara could relinquish the wounded man to his care without misgiving. He was borne off between the burgher and his comfortable wife, throwing a nod and a wink over his shoulder to Barbara; and she hurried on to fight her way into the crowded chemist's shop.

Nothing could have exceeded the humanity of the citizens. There was hardly a house in the town whose doors were not thrown open to the wounded, whether Dutch, or Belgian, German, Scotch or English. The Belgian doctors were working in their shirt-sleeves with the sweat dripping off their bodies; children, who stared with uncomprehending, vaguely shocked eyes, were bidden by their brisk, shrill mothers to hold umbrellas over men huddled groaning on the pavement under the scorching sun; stout burgomasters and trim gendarmes were busy clearing the wounded off the streets, carrying those who could not walk into neighbouring houses, and directing others with more superficial injuries to places of shelter. Sisters of Mercy were moving about, their black robes and great starched white head-dresses in odd contrast to the frivolous chip-hats and delicate muslin dresses of ladies of fashion who had forgotten their complexions and their nerves, and in all the heat of the noonday sun, and the stench of blood, and dirt, and human sweat, toiled as their scullery-maids had never done.

In one short hour Judith felt her senses to have become numb; the nausea that she had first felt had left her; in the urgent need to give help there was no time for personal shrinking. A Belgian doctor, kneeling beside an infantry-man on a truss of straw in the road, had called to her to aid him; he had told her to hold a man's leg while he dug out a musket-ball from his knee, and roughly bound up the wound. He spoke to her brusquely, and she obeyed him without flinching. A few minutes later she was herself slitting up a coat-sleeve, and binding lint round a flesh-wound that ordinarily would have turned her sick.

At about half-past two, when the news came from the Namur and Louvain Gates that the promised tents were at last ready for the wounded, the sky became suddenly overcast. The relief from the sun's glare was felt by every-one, but in a few minutes the fear of a storm was making it necessary to get all who could be moved under shelter. The blackness overhead was presently shot through with a fork of lightning; almost simultaneously the thunder crashed across the sky, rolling and reverberating in an ominous rumble that died away only an instant before a second flash, and a second clap broke out. By three o'clock the lightning seemed continuous, and the thunder so deafening that the fear of the elements overcame in nearly every breast the lesser fear of a French advance. The lurid light, the flickering flashes in a cloud like a huge pall, the clatter in the sky as of a giant's crockery being smashed, made even the boldest quail, and sent many flying to their homes. Rain began to fall in torrents; in a few minutes the gutters were rushing rivers, and those still out in the streets were soaked to the skin. Rain bounced on the cobbles, and poured off the steep, gabled roofs; it took the starch out of the nuns' stiff caps, made the pale muslins cling to their owners' bodies, and turned modish straw hats into sodden wrecks.

Barbara, helping a man with a shattered ankle to hop up the steps into a house already containing two wounded Belgians, felt her shoulder touched, and looked round to find Worth behind her. He was drenched, and dishevelled; he said curtly: "I'll take him. Go home now."

"Your wife?" she said, her voice husky with fatigue.

"I've sent her home. You have done enough. Go back now."

She nodded, for she was indeed so exhausted that her head felt light, and it was an effort to move her limbs. Worth slipped his arm round the young Scot she had been supporting, and she clung to the railings for a moment to get her breath.

When she reached home she found that Judith had arrived a few moments before her, and had already gone up to strip off her wet and soiled garments. She came out of her bedroom in a wrapper as Barbara reached the top of the stairs. "Barbara!" she said. "Thank God you have come in! Oh, how wet you are! I'll send my woman to you immediately! Yours is in hysterics."

A weary smile touched Barbara's lips. "The confounded wench hasn't ceased having hysterics since the guns were first heard. Is there any news?"

"I don't think so. I've had no time to ask. But don't stand there in those wet clothes!"

"Indecent, aren't they?" said Barbara, with the ghost of a chuckle.

"Shocking, but I'm thinking of the cold you will take. I've ordered coffee to be sent up to the salon. Do hurry!"

Twenty minutes later they confronted one another across

285

a table laid out with cakes and coffee. Judith lifted the silver pot, and found that her hand, which had been so steady, was shaking. She managed to pour out the coffee, and handed the cup to Barbara, saying: "I'm sorry. I've spilled a little in the saucer. You must be very hungry; eat one of those cakes."

Barbara took one, raised it to her mouth, and then put it down. "I don't think I can," she said in rather a strained voice. "I beg your pardon, but I feel quite damnably sick. Or faint—I'm not sure which."

Judith jumped up. "No, no, you are not going to faint, and if you are sick, I'll never forgive you! Wait, I'll get my smelling-salts directly!" She stopped, and said: "No. I forgot. I gave them to that boy whose ear had been shot off. He——oh God, Bab, don't don't!" With the tears pouring down her own face she flung her arms round Barbara, who had broken into a fit of gasping sobs.

They clung together for a few moments, their torn nerves finding relief in this burst of weeping. But presently each made an effort towards self-control; the sobs were resolutely swallowed, and two noses defiantly blown.

"The devil!" Barbara said faintly. "Where's that coffee?"

They smiled mistily at each other. "We're tired," said Judith. "Crying like a couple of vapourish idiots!"

Her teeth chattered on the rim of her cup, but she gulped down a little of the coffee and felt better. Outside, the thunder still crashed and rumbled, and the rain streamed down the window-panes. The butler had lit the candles in the room, and presently, seeing how the flashes of lightning made Judith wince, Barbara got up, and drew the blinds together.

"The troops in this awful storm!" Judith said. "Will the rain never stop?"

"I wonder where they are?"

"The report this morning said that a renewal of the attack was expected."

"I am not afraid. We remained masters of the field last night, and now all the Army is concentrated there."

"Very true: we may hear of a victory at any moment now, I daresay."

They relapsed into silence. The sound of carriage-wheels in the street below roused them. The carriage drew up apparently at the house, and while Judith and Barbara were still looking at each other with a sudden question in their eyes, a double knock fell on the front door. Judith found that she was trembling, and saw that Barbara was gripping the arms of her chair with clenched fingers. Neither seemed capable of moving; each was paper-white, staring at the other. But in another minute the butler had opened the door and announced Miss Devenish and Mr. Fisher.

Judith got up with a shudder of relief, and turned to receive these unexpected guests. Miss Devenish, who was muffled in a long cloak, ran forward, and caught both her friend's arms in a tight clasp. "Oh, have you news?" she panted. "I could bear it no longer! All yesterday and to-day in this terrible uncertainty! I thought you might have heard something, that Colonel Audley might have been here!"

Barbara's hands unclenched. She rose, and walked over to the window under pretext of rearranging the blinds.

"No. We have not seen Charles since he left the ball," Judith replied. "Colonel Canning was in last night, and told us then that up till five o'clock Charles was alive and unhurt. We have had no later tidings."

She disengaged one hand, and held it out to Mr. Fisher, who shook it warmly, and embarked on a speech of apology for having intruded on her at such a time. She cut him short, assuring him that no apology could be thought necessary, and he said, in his unpolished yet kindly way: "That's it: I told my girl here you would be glad to see her. For my part, I'm a plain Englishman, and what I say is, let the Belgians run if they will, for it won't make a ha'porth of odds to our fellows! But the silly miss has been in such a taking, covering her ears every time the cannon sounded, and jumping to the window whenever anyone passed in the street, that in the end I said to her:

287

'Lucy, my pet,' I said, 'rain or no rain, you'll pop on your cloak and we'll drive straight round to your good friend, Lady Worth, and see what she may be able to tell us.' "

"Indeed, you did quite right. I am only sorry that I am unable to give you any news. Since hearing of the Prussian defeat, no tidings of any kind have reached us, except such scraps as we might pick up from the men who have got back from the battlefield."

Lucy, who had sunk into a chair, with her hands kneading one another in her lap, raised her head, and asked in an amazed tone: "You have been out in the streets?"

"Yes, Lady Barbara and I have been doing what we could for the wounded."

Lucy shuddered. "Oh, how I admire you! I could not! The sight of the blood—the wounds—I cannot bear to think of it!"

Judith looked at her for an instant, in a kind of detached wonder. Raising her eyes, she encountered Barbara's across the room. A faint smile passed between them; in that moment of wordless understanding each was aware of the bond which, no matter what might come, could never be quite broken between them.

Mr. Fisher said: "Well, I am sure you are a pair of heroines, no less! But I wonder his lordship would permit it, I do indeed! A lady's delicate sensibilities——"

"This is not a time for thinking of one's sensibilities," Judith interrupted. "But will you not be seated? I am glad to see you have not fled the town, like some of our compatriots."

He said heartily: "No need to do that, I'll be bound! Why, if the Duke can't account for Boney and all his Froggies, he's not the man I take him for, and so I tell my foolish girl here."

"Such sentiments do you credit," said Judith, with mechanical civility. She glanced at Miss Devenish, and added: "Do not be unnecessarily alarmed, Lucy. I believe we must by this time have heard had anything happened to my brother-in-law."

Miss Devenish replied in a numb voice: "Oh yes! It

must be so, of course. Only I hoped he might perhaps have been sent in with a message. It is of no consequence."

Judith could not resist glancing in Barbara's direction. She was standing back against the dark curtains, her eyes fixed on Lucy's face with an expression in them of curious intentness. Judith looked away quickly, and repeated: "I have not seen Charles since the ball."

"No." Miss Devenish looked at Barbara; a little colour crept into her cheeks; she said, stumbling over the words: "And you, Lady Barbara—I do not like to ask you—but you have heard nothing?"

"Nothing at all," Barbara replied.

"No; I quite realize—you must wonder at my asking you, but there are circumstances which——" Her voice failed entirely: indeed, her last words had been almost inaudible. She got up, flushing, and reminded her uncle that they had promised not to leave Mrs. Fisher for more than half an hour.

He agreed that they must be going, and said in a rallying tone, as he shook hands with Judith: "Your ladyship will bear me out in assuring this little puss that there is no need for all this alarm. Ah, you may shake your head as much as you please, Missy, but you won't make your old uncle believe that you haven't lost that soft heart of yours to some handsome officer!"

No answer was vouchsafed; Lucy pressed Judith's hand, bowed slightly to Barbara, and hurried out of the room. Mr. Fisher begged Judith not to think of accompanying them to the door, again thanked her for receiving him, became aware that the butler was holding open the door for him, and bowed himself out.

A long, painful silence fell in the salon. Barbara had parted the curtains and was looking out into the street. "It is still raining," she remarked presently.

"The thunder is less violent, I believe."

"Yes."

Judith sat down, smoothing a crease from her dress. She said, without raising her eyes from her skirt: "I do not believe he cares for her."

It was a moment before Barbara answered. She said then, in a level tone: "If he does, I have come by my deserts."

There could be no gainsaying it. Judith said with a wry smile: "I wanted him to, you know."

"Don't you still?"

"No. These days seem to have altered everything. I did not want to receive you in my house, but your strength has supported me as I would not have believed it could. Whatever has happened in the past, or whatever is to happen in the future, I can never forget the comfort your presence is to me now."

Barbara turned her head. "You are generous!" she said, a note of mockery in her voice. "But the other side of my character is true, too. Don't set me up on a pedestal! I should certainly tumble down from it."

At that moment Worth came into the room. He had changed into dry clothes, and said, in answer to Judith's surprised exclamation, that he had come in while Mr. Fisher and Miss Devenish were sitting with her. The next question was inevitable: "Is there any news?"

"Yes, there is news," he replied. "It is disquieting, but I believe it may be accounted for by the Prussian defeat. The Allied Army is said to be retreating."

Judith gazed at him in horror. Barbara said: "The devil it is! Confound you, I don't believe it!"

"It is a pity your sanguine temperament is not shared by others," he said drily. "The whole town is in an uproar. I am informed on credible authority that as much as a hundred napoleons have been offered for a pair of horses to go to Antwerp." He flicked open his snuff-box and added in a languid tone: "My opinion of the human race has never been high, but the antics that are being performed at this moment exceed every expectation of folly with which I had previously indulged my fancy."

"I hope you observe that we at least are preserving our dignity!" retorted Barbara.

"I do, and I am grateful to you."

"But, Worth! A retreat!" Judith cried.

"Don't disturb yourself, my love. Recollect that Wellington is a master in retreat. If the Prussians have fallen back, we must be obliged to do the same to maintain our communications with them. Until we hear that the retreat is a rout, I must—regretfully, of course—decline to join the rabble on the road to Antwerp."

Judith could not help laughing, but said with a good deal of spirit: "Nothing, indeed, could be more odious. We certainly shall not talk of flight yet awhile."

They dined at an early hour, but although both ladies were very tired from the exertions and the nervous stress they had undergone, neither could think of retiring to bed until further news had been received from the Army. They sat in the salon, trying to occupy themselves with ordinary sewing-tasks, until Worth, with a glance at the clock, got up, saying that he would walk round to Stuart's to discover if anything more had been heard. He left the room, and went downstairs to the hall. At the same moment, the ladies heard a knock on the street door, followed an instant later by the confused murmur of voices in the hall.

CHAPTER XX

JUDITH ran out to the head of the stairs. Worth called up to her: "It is Charles, Judith. All is well!"

"Oh, bring him up! Bring him up!" she begged. "Charles, I am so thankful! Come up at once!"

"I'm in no fit state to enter your drawing-room, you know," Colonel Audley replied in a tired but cheerful voice.

"Good God, what does that signify?" She caught sight of him as she spoke, and exclaimed: "You are drenched to the skin! You must change your clothes immediately, or Heaven knows what will become of you!"

He mounted the stairs, and as he came into the light cast by a sconce of candles Judith saw that his face was gray with fatigue, and his embroidered ball-dress, which he still wore, saturated with rain and mud, a tear in one sleeve and the wrist-band of his shirt stained with blood.

"You are hurt!" she said quickly.

"No, I assure you I am not. Nothing but a cut from a bayonet: it scarcely broke the skin. I am only sleepy, and very hungry, upon my honour!"

"You shall have dinner the instant you are out of those wet clothes," she promised, taking his hand between both hers and clasping it for a moment. "You are worn out! Oh, dear Charles, the relief of knowing you to be safe!"

She could say no more; he smiled, but seemed to have no energy to waste in answering her. Worth took him by the arm and led him towards the second pair of stairs. "Come along!" he said. "The appearance you present is quite appalling, believe me!"

Judith ran back into the salon and tugged at the bell-pull. Barbara was standing just inside the door, watching Colonel Audley as he mounted the stairs to his bedroom. She said with a shaky laugh: "His beautiful ball-dress quite ruined! When I think how smart he was, only two nights ago, it makes me want to weep! Was there ever anything so confoundedly silly?"

Upstairs, Worth rang the bell for his valet, and began to help the Colonel to peel off his sodden coat. Through the torn sleeve of a shirt that was clinging to his body could be seen a strip of sticking-plaster, covering a slash upon the upper arm. The blood had dried upon the shirt-sleeve, and Audley winced a little as he stripped the shirt off.

"I take it that's not serious?" said Worth.

"Good God, no! A scratch."

"How did you come by it?"

"Trying to rally those damned Dutch-Belgians!" replied the Colonel bitterly. He added, with the flash of a smile: "I don't know that I blame them, though, poor devils! They got the brunt of it at the start, and then, to add to their troubles, what must some of our fellows do but mistake a party of them for the French, and open fire on them! It's all the fault of their accursed uniforms, and those bell-topped shakos of theirs."

"Where's the Army?"

"Before Mont St. Jean, rather more than a couple of miles south of Waterloo, bivouacking for the night."

Worth raised his brows. "That seems somewhat close to Brussels."

"No help for it. Old Blücher's gone eighteen miles to his rear, to Wavre. We had to do likewise, of course. But don't worry! We're in a better case than at Quatre-Bras: the ground there was damnable for cavalry."

The valet came into the room just then, and conversation was suspended while the Colonel's mud-caked Hessians were pulled off, his pantaloons peeled from his legs, and warm water fetched to wash away the dirt, and the sweat and the blood-stains from his tired body. By the time he came downstairs again, in his service uniform, a tray had been brought to the salon and a table spread. He walked into the room just ahead of his brother, smiled rather wearily at Judith, and then saw Barbara standing by the fireplace. A frown creased his brow; his eyes, heavy and bloodshot, blinked at her in a puzzled way. His brain felt clogged; he did not know how she came to be there, and felt too tired to speculate much upon the circumstance. A nightmare of estrangement lay between them, but he had been in the saddle almost continuously for two days, had taken part in a fierce battle against superior odds, and knew that perhaps the most serious engagement of his life was ahead of him. His mind refused to grapple with personal considerations; he merely held out his hand, and said: "I didn't know you were here, Bab. How do you do?"

Judith, who had expected some show at least of surprise, and had been prepared to whisk herself and Worth out of the room, felt that this calm greeting must affect Barbara like a douche of cold water. But Barbara just took the Colonel's hand, and answered: "Yes, Charles. I am here. Never mind that now. You are hungry and tired."

"I don't know when I have been more so," he admitted,

turning from her, and seating himself at the table. He accepted a plate of cold beef from Judith, and added: "Both your brothers are safe. I think George got a scratch or two to-day, but nothing serious. I suppose Canning gave you an account of our engagement at Quatre-Bras, Julian?"

"Yes, and I heard more later from Creevey, who had seen Hamilton, of Barnes's Staff."

"Oh, did you?" said the Colonel, his mouth rather full of beef. "Then I expect you know all that happened."

"Very briefly. Hamilton left the field before the engagement ended."

"The Guards settled it. Cooke's division came up at about half-past six, I suppose. Maitland sent Lord Saltoun in with the Light Infantry of the brigade to clear Bossu wood of the French, which he did. I don't really know where Byng's brigade was placed. It was almost impossible to make out anyone's position. One of Halkett's fellows told me they had seen the French actually sending a man galloping ahead to plant a flag as a point for their troops to charge on. You've no idea what the crops are like there. I've never seen rye grown to such a height."

"When did Halkett arrive? I collect you mean Sir Colin, not his brother?"

"Yes, of course. Hew Halkett's Hanoverians weren't at Quatre-Bras at all. Alten brought up the 3rd Division somewhere between four and five in the afternoon, and, by God! they were not a moment too soon. Picton's division was pretty well crippled. I don't know which of the brigades suffered the most, Kempt's or Pack's. To make matters worse, Brunswick had been carried off the field, and his men were badly shaken. Olferman couldn't hold them, and they were retreating in a good deal of haste when old Halkett came up. You know Halkett!—or rather you don't, but he told Olferman without mincing matters what he thought of the retreat, and brought the Bruns-wickers up under cover of a ditch, like the famous old fighter he is!"

"And the Dutch-Belgians?"

The Colonel shrugged. "Well, there's no doubt Perponcher saved the situation by moving on Quatre-Bras as he did, and Prince Bernhard's Nassauers behaved splendidly. They had one Horse Battery with them—Stevenart's, I think—and by Jove, those fellows were heroes! Bylandt's brigade suffered rather severely at the start, and as for the rest—it's a case of the least said the soonest mended."

"How did the Prince of Orange do?"

"Ask Halkett," replied the Colonel, with a wry smile. "Poor Slender Billy! He will get so excited!"

Worth refilled his glass. "At his age that was to be expected. What has he been up to?"

The Colonel drank some of the wine, and picked up his knife and fork again. "Oh, Halkett galloped forward to the front with one of his A.D.C.s, saw a corps of cavalry forming, and of course returned at once to his brigade, and gave the order to form squares. The 69th—that's Colonel Morice's regiment—were in the act of doing so when up came Slender Billy, and wanted to know what the devil they were about. 'Preparing to meet cavalry'—'Oh, cavalry be damned!' says Billy. 'There's none within five miles of you! Form column, and deploy into line at once!' Morice had no choice but to obey, of course. The regiment was actually engaged on the movement when about eight hundred Cuirassiers came charging down on the brigade. The 30th and the 33rd were firmly in square, but the Cuirassiers rode right through the unfortunate 69th, scattered the Belgian and Brunswick cavalry, got as far as Quatre-Bras itself, and completely turned our position. If it hadn't been for the Duke's directing the 92nd Highlanders himself, God knows what might not have happened!"

"Yes, we heard about that, but not about the Prince's folly!"

"You might not. Don't spread the story! I happened to have been sent with a message to Halkett just before the charge, and was in one of the squares beside him. Poor Morice was killed, and scores of others."

"Then you had no cavalry at all to withstand the French attacks?"

"No, that was the devil of it. The Lancers cut up Pack's Highlanders horribly. But you can't shake the Fighting Division. When Picton retired at last, it was in perfect order. But the loss has been shocking in his whole division. By nine o'clock we outnumbered the French. I saw Ney myself, several times. He kept on rallying his infantry and hurling it against us—behaving more like a madman than a Corps Commander, *we* thought. In the end he gave it up, and drew off, and we bivouacked for the night." He pushed his plate aside, and reached out a hand for the cheese. "The Duke spent the night at Genappe. We had no news from the Prussians: Hardinge was badly wounded at Ligny, and is *hors de combat*. It turned out that Blücher did send an officer to us overnight, but he got wounded and never reached us. Gordon was sent off down the Namur road with a half-squadron of the 10th the first thing this morning, to see what intelligence he could gain. He got as far as a place called Tilly, found that the whole Prussian army was retreating on Wavre, and that the French were in force about two miles distant. He got back somewhere about eight o'clock, and that was the first news we had of the Prussian retreat. By that time Ney had been joined by D'Erlon's Corps, and must have been about 40,000 strong. What happened to that Corps yesterday we can't make out. We saw it going off towards Ligny, but it doesn't seem to have been engaged at all. As for us, we had only 25,000, after the flight of the Dutch; but instead of renewing the attack Ney did nothing. At ten o'clock the Duke ordered the infantry to retire in successive brigades through the defile of Genappe, to the position of Mont St. Jean. They did this in perfect order, all except two battalions of the 95th Rifles, which the Duke kept at Quatre-Bras, with all the cavalry." He gave a grin, swallowed a mouthful of bread and cheese, and said: "Old Hookey sat down to read the letters and newspapers from England which had arrived, and then went to sleep by the side of the road, with a paper spread over his face. When he woke up, he had another look at the enemy through his glass, and found them still not under arms.

We began to think they might possibly be retreating. However, about two o'clock, Vivian, who was with the Duke, saw a glitter of steel in the sunlight in the direction of Ligny, and we found that it was caused by huge masses of cavalry moving towards us. At the same time, Ney began to show himself on our front. By the by, it was the most curious effect I ever saw in my life. There was an enormous storm-cloud blowing up from the north. We were all in a sort of twilight, but the sun was still shining on the French. Queerest thing I ever saw. The Duke ordered the cavalry, and the Horse Artillery, and the Rifles, to fall back steadily, and went on ahead to dine at Genappe, leaving Uxbridge to do the business, which he did beautifully, withdrawing the cavalry in three columns, and keeping Norman Ramsay's Troop to guard the rear. We heard the guns in Genappe just about the time the storm burst, and I went back to see what was happening. Apparently the French opened fire on us, but without doing much damage. They seemed to be concentrating their attacks on our centre column—Somerset's and Ponsonby's Heavy Brigades, and a rearguard of the 7th Hussars and the 23rd Light Dragoons. By the time they were drawn up on the high ground beyond Genappe, the French Lancers were in the town. Uxbridge sent in the 7th to clear them out; they were driven back, rallied, went in again gallantly, time after time, but suffered pretty severely. Uxbridge withdrew them at last, and ordered the Light Dragoons to advance, but as they didn't seem to relish the task, he snapped out: 'The Life Guards shall have this honour!' and ordered them up. Of course they asked nothing better than to show us what Hyde Park soldiers could do Uxbridge sent a couple of squadrons into the town. They rode in like thunderbolts—magnificent to watch!—and completely overthrew the Lancers.''

"George?" Barbara said.

He turned his head, as though suddenly recollecting her presence. "Yes, he took part in it. He was not hurt, merely plastered with mud!" He smiled, and said, looking at Worth again: "That was the funniest part of the business, the Life Guards getting tumbled in the mud. I never remember such a storm. Within half an hour the horses were sinking to their knees, and some of the fields looked like lakes. The 95th were watching the Life Guards from beyond the town—you know what the Riflemen are! Kincaid swore that every time one of them suffered a fall he got up covered in mud, and retired to the rear, as though no longer fit to appear on parade! I can tell you, they had to bear a good deal of roasting! Some of the fellows of the 95th shouted to them: 'The uglier, the better the soldier!' which is one of our Peninsular sayings. However, even if they did look absurdly ashamed of their dirt they did famously."

"There was no serious engagement?"

"No, nothing but very pretty manœuvres and skirmishing. Uxbridge is a good man, and, what's more, his work to-day has given his men faith in him. While all the skirmishing was going on, Whinyates began firing off his beloved Rockets, with the idea of amusing our cavalry, drawn up beyond Genappe. The main thing was that it didn't amuse the French at all: they hate Rockets."

"What *are* Rockets?" asked Judith, who was sitting with her chin in her hands, listening to him.

"Well, they're just *Rockets*," replied the Colonel vaguely. "No use asking me: I'm not an artillery man. All I know is that they're fired from a small iron triangle, which is set up wherever you want it. Port-fire is applied, the horrid thing begins to spit sparks, and wriggle its tail as though it were alive, and then suddenly darts off. I'm frightened to death of the things: you never know where they will go! Even Whinyates admits that no two of them ever follow the same course. They go whizzing off, and if you are lucky the shells in their heads burst amongst the French. But they have been known to turn back on themselves, and one fellow swears one chased him about like a squib, and nearly was the end of him." He pushed back his chair from the table, and stood up, and went to the window, drawing back the curtains a little way. The rain still beat against the panes. "A Wellington night!" he said.

and let the curtain fall back into place. He looked over his shoulder at Worth. "I want one of your horses, Julian. My poor brute could scarcely stand up under me when I brought him in."

"You had better take the bay: he's a stayer."

"You may not see him again," said the Colonel, with the flicker of a smile.

"I daresay I shan't. How many have you lost so far?"

"Only one. Judith, will you let me raid the larder? We're devilish short of rations."

"Of course: take what you want," she answered readily. "But must you go back yet? Is it not possible for you to rest for a while?"

He shook his head. "No; I must be back at Head-quarters by midnight, you know. It's nearly ten now, and in this wet and darkness it will take me two hours, or more."

"Where are the Duke's Headquarters?" asked Worth.

"At Waterloo." He picked up his cloak from the chair on which he had laid it, and clasped it round his neck. His cocked-hat in its oilskin cover lay ready to his hand; he tucked it under his arm, and said, with a little hesitation: "Judith, if you should see Miss Devenish——" He paused, as though he did not know how to continue.

"I shall, I expect," she replied. "Do you desire some message to her?"

"No—only that I wish you will tell her that you have seen me to-night, and that all is well."

"Certainly," she said.

"Thank you. Don't forget, will you?" He kissed her cheek in a brotherly fashion, and said, with something of his old gaiety: "You are a capital creature, you know! You understand how important it is to feed a man well!"

"Cold beef!" she protested.

"Nothing could have been better, I assure you. Don't be alarmed if you hear some cannonading to-morrow! We shall have at least one Prussian Corps with us, and we don't mean to lose this war, I promise you." He gave her shoulder a pat, and turned towards Barbara. She was looking pale, but perfectly composed, and held out her hand. He took it. "I don't know why you are here, but I'm glad you are," he said. "Forgive me if I seem dull and stupid. There is so much to say, but I've no time, and this is not the moment. I believe your friend Lavisse to be unhurt. I should have told you before."

"I am glad, but he is not so much my friend that it can concern me."

"Tired of him, Bab?" he said.

She winced. He said at once: "I'm sorry! That was shockingly rude of me." His hand gripped hers more tightly. "Good-bye, my dear. Now, Worth, if you please."

He released her hand, and turned from her to his brother. The corner of his heavy cloak just brushed her dress as he swung round on a spurred heel; he took Worth's arm, and walked to the door with him. "I'll take a couple of bottles of your champagne, Julian," he said, and the next instant was gone from Barbara's sight. She heard his voice on the stairs, as he went down with Worth. "By the by, the 10th did damned well to-day. They might have been on the parade ground. However, the rain put an end to the skirmishing."

Judith walked quickly to the door and shut it. "Skirmishing! Champagne!" she said with a strong indignation. "How can he? As though he had not a thought in his head but of divisions, and brigades, and regiments!"

"He hasn't," said Barbara.

"When I think of the suspense you have been in, what you have suffered from the circumstance of—— And he behaved as though nothing were of the least consequence but this dreadful war!"

Barbara gave a laugh. "Is anything else of consequence? I like him for that!"

"You are made to be a soldier's wife! I was put out of all patience! Oh, Bab, that message! What can he have meant by it?"

Barbara looked at her with glinting eyes, and the lifting smile that meant danger. "I could take him away from that chit in a week. Less! A day!"

"I daresay you might: indeed, I've no doubt of it. But I wish you would not talk so."

"Do not alarm yourself. I shan't do it. If only he comes safe back he may have her—yes, and I'll smile and be glad!" Her face broke up; she cried out: "No, not that! but I won't make mischief—I promise I won't make mischief!"

Twenty minutes later Worth re-entered the room to find both ladies seated on the sofa, in companionable silence. He said in his calm way: "Take my advice, and go to bed. There is no danger to-night, but I may be obliged to convey you to the coast to-morrow. So get what rest you can now."

"Has Charles gone?" Judith asked.

"Yes—and your Sunday dinner with him."

"Oh dear! But it does not signify. I wish it would stop raining! I do not like to think of him riding all that way in this downpour!"

"He will do very well, I assure you. If you wish to be pitying anyone, pity the poor devils who are bivouacking out in the open to-night."

She rose. "I do pity them. Come, Bab! he is right; we should go to bed."

The words were hardly spoken when they heard a knock on the street-door. Even Worth looked a little surprised, and raised his brows. The butler had not yet retired to bed; they heard him go to the door and open it; and a moment later the stairs creaked under his heavy tread. He entered the salon, but before he could announce the visitor, Lucy Devenish had rushed past him into the room.

A wet cloak and hood enveloped her; she was pale, and evidently in great agitation. She looked wildly round the room, and then, fixing her eyes on Judith's astonished countenance, faltered: "My uncle heard that Colonel Audley had been at Sir Charles Stuart's!"

"He has been there, and here, too, but I am afraid he has this moment gone," said Judith. "My dear child, surely you did not come alone, and in this shocking storm? Let me take your cloak! How imprudent this is of you!"

"Oh, I know, I know! But I could not sleep without trying to get news! No one knows that I am not in my bed—it is wrong of me, but indeed, indeed I had to come!"

Judith removed the dripping cloak from her shoulders. "Hush, Lucy! There is no need for this alarm. Charles is safe, and all is well, upon my honour!"

Miss Devenish pushed the hair from her brow with one distracted hand. "I ran the whole way! I hoped to see him —but it is no matter!" She made an effort to be calm, and sank down upon a chair, saying: "I am so glad he is safe! Did he tell you what had been happening? Was there any news? What did he say?"

"Yes, indeed; he has been describing to us how our Army has been obliged to retreat to Mont St. Jean. It appears there has been no very serious fighting to-day: nothing but some cavalry skirmishes, which he said were extremely *pretty*, if you please!"

"Oh——! Please tell me! I—we have heard so little all day, you see," Lucy said, with a forced laugh.

"There was nothing of any consequence, my dear. Indeed, from what he said I gathered that only some Hussars and the Life Guards have been actually engaged with the enemy. Charles himself——"

She stopped, for Lucy had sprung up, her face so ghastly and her manner so distraught that for a moment Judith almost feared that she had taken leave of her senses. "Charles? What is *he* to me?" Lucy said hoarsely. "It is George—George! Was there no word? No message for me? Lady Barbara, for God's sake tell me, or I shall go mad with this suspense!"

"*George?*" gasped Judith, grasping a chair-back for support.

"Yes, George!" Lucy cried fiercely. "I can bear no more! I must know what has become of him, I tell you!"

"He is perfectly safe," said Barbara coolly.

Lucy gave a long sigh and dropped on to the sofa. "Oh, thank God, thank God!" she sobbed. "What I have undergone——! The torture! The suspense!"

Across the room, Barbara's eyes met Judith's for a

moment; then she glanced down at Lucy's bowed head, and said: "Oh, confound you, must you cry because he is safe?"

Judith stepped up to the sofa and laid her hand on Lucy's shoulder. "Lucy, what is this folly?" she asked. "What can Lord George be to you?"

Lucy lifted her face from her hands. "He is my husband!" she said.

A dumbfounded silence fell. Barbara was staring at her with narrowed eyes, Judith in utter incredulity. With deliberation, the Earl polished his quizzing-glass, and raised it, and gazed at Lucy in a dispassionately considering fashion.

"George actually married you?" said Barbara slowly. "When?"

"Last year—in England!" Lucy replied, covering her face with her hands.

"Then all these months——!" Judith ejaculated. "Good God, how is this possible?"

"It is true. I am aware of what your feelings must be, but oh, if you knew how bitterly I have been punished, you would pity me!"

"I do not know what to say! It is not for me to reproach you! But what can have prompted you to commit such an act of folly? Why this long secrecy? I am utterly at a loss!"

"Ah, you are not acquainted with my grandfather!" said Barbara. "The secrecy is easily explained. What, however, passes my comprehension is how the devil you persuaded George into marriage!"

"He loves me!" Lucy said, rearing up her head.

"He must indeed do so. Odd! I should not have thought you the girl to catch his fancy."

"Oh, Bab, pray hush!" besought Judith.

"Nonsense! If Miss Devenish—I beg pardon!—if Lady George has become my sister the sooner she grows accustomed to the language I use the better it will be. So George was afraid to confess the whole to my grandfather, was he?"

"Yes. I cannot tell you all, but you must not blame him! Mine was the fault. I allowed myself to be swept off my feet. The marriage took place in Sussex. George was in the expectation of gaining his promotion——"

"Ah, I begin to understand you! My grandfather was to have given him the purchase-money, eh? Instead he was obliged to spend in hushing up the Carroway affair, and was disinclined to assist George further."

"Yes," said Lucy. "Everything went awry! That scandal—but all that is over now! Indeed, indeed, George loves me, and there can be no more such affairs!"

"My poor innocent! But continue!"

"He said we must wait. His circumstances were awkward: there were debts; and I was unhappily aware of my uncle's dislike of him. I feared nothing but anger could be met with in that quarter. My uncle thinks him a spendthrift, and that, in his eyes, outweighs every consideration of birth or title. To have declared our marriage would have meant George's ruin. But the misery of my position, the necessity of deceiving my uncle and my aunt, the wretchedness of stolen meetings with George—all these led to lowness of spirits in me, and in him the natural irritation of a man tied in such a way to one who——" Her utterance was choked by sobs; she overcame them, and continued: "Misunderstandings, even quarrels, arose between us. I began to believe that he regretted a union entered into so wrongly. When my uncle and aunt decided to come to Brussels in January, I accompanied them willingly, feeling that nothing could be worse than the life I was then leading. But the separation seemed to draw us closer together! When George arrived in this country all the love which I thought had waned seemed in an instant to reanimate towards me! *He* would have declared our marriage then: it was I who insisted on the secret still being kept! Think me what you will! I deserve your censure, but my courage failed. Situated as I was, in the midst of this restricted society, believed by all to be a single woman, I could not face the scandal that such a declaration would have caused! I implored George to wait at least until the war was over; I was even afraid to be seen in his company lest anyone should suspect an attachment to exist between us. All the old wretchedness returned! George—oh, only to tease me into yielding! —began to devote himself to other and more beautiful females. I have come near to putting an end to my existence, even! Then the war broke out. I saw George at the Duchess's ball. Every misunderstanding seemed to vanish, but we had so little time together! He was forced to leave me: had it not been for Colonel Audley's promising to send me word if he could, I must have become demented!"

"Then Charles knew?" Judith exclaimed.

"Yes! On the very night that his engagement was put an end to he found me in great distress, and persuaded me to confide in him. His nature, so frank and upright, must have revolted from the duplicity of mine, but he uttered no word of blame. His sympathy for my situation, the awkwardness of which he understood immediately, his kindness—I cannot speak of it! I had engaged his silence as the price of my confidence. His promise was given, and implicitly kept."

"Good God!" said Judith blankly. She raised her eyes from Lucy's face, and looked at Barbara. She gave an uncertain laugh. "Oh, Bab, the fools we have been!"

"Yes! And the wretch Charles has been! Infamous!" Barbara walked up to the sofa, and laid her hand on Lucy's shoulder. "Dry your tears! Your marriage is in the best tradition of *my* family, I assure you."

Lucy clasped her hand. "Can you ever forgive me?"

"What the devil has my forgiveness to do with it? You have not injured me. I wish you extremely happy."

"How kind you are! I do not deserve to be happy!"

"You are very unlikely to be," said Barbara, somewhat drily. "George will make you a damnable husband."

"Oh no, no! If only he is not killed!" Lucy shuddered.

It was some time before she could regain her composure, and nearly an hour before she left the house. Worth had ordered the horses to be put to, and undertook to escort her to her uncle's lodgings. Judith and Barbara found themselves alone at last.

"Well!" Barbara said. "You will allow that at least I never contracted a secret marriage!"

"I have never been so deceived in anyone in my life!" Judith replied, in a shocked tone.

CHAPTER XXI

COLONEL AUDLEY reached the village of Waterloo a few minutes before midnight. The road through the Forest of Soignes, though roughly paved down the centre, was in a bad state, the heavy rainfall having turned the uncobbled portions on either side of the pavé into bogs which in places were impassable. Waggons and tilt-carts were some of them deeply embedded in mud, and some overturned after coming into collision with the Belgian cavalry in their flight earlier in the day. In the darkness it was necessary for a horseman to pick his way carefully. The contents of the waggons in some cases strewed the road; here and there a cart, with two of its wheels in the air, lay across the pavé; and several horses which had fallen in one of the mad rushes for safety had been shot, and now sprawled in the mud at the sides of the chaussée. The rain dripped ceaselessly from the leaves of the beech trees; the moonlight was obscured by heavy clouds; and only by the glimmer of lanterns slung on the waggons lining the road was it possible to discern the way.

At Waterloo, lights burned in many of the cottage windows, for there was not a dwelling-place in the village, or in any of the hamlets near-by, which did not house a General and his Staff, or senior officers who had been fortunate enough to secure a bed or a mattress under cover. The tiny inn owned by Veuve Bedonghien, opposite the church, was occupied by the Duke, and here the Colonel dismounted. A figure loomed up to meet him. "Is it yourself, sir?" his groom enquired anxiously, holding up a lantern. "Eh, if that's not his lordship's Rufus!"

The Colonel gave up the bridle. "Yes. Rub him down well, Cherry!" The faint crackle of musketry-fire in the distance came to his ears. "What's all this popping?"

Cherry gave a grunt. "Proper spiteful they've been all evening. Pickets, they tell me. 'Well,' I said, 'we didn't do such in Spain, that's all I know.'"

The Colonel turned away and entered the inn. An orderly informed him that the Duke was still up, and he went into a room in the front of the house to make his report.

The Duke was seated at a table, with De Lancey at his elbow, looking over a map of the country. Lord Fitzroy occupied a chair on one side of the fire, and was placidly writing on his knee. He looked up as the Colonel came in, and smiled.

"Hallo, Audley!" said his lordship. "What's the news in Brussels?"

"There's been a good deal of panic, sir. The news of our retreat sent hundreds off to Antwerp," replied the Colonel, handing over the letters he had brought.

"Ah, I daresay! Road bad?"

"Yes, sir, and needs clearing. In places it's choked with baggage and overturned carts. I spoke to one of our own drivers, and it seems the Belgian cavalry upset everything in their way when they galloped to Brussels."

"I'll have it cleared first thing," De Lancey said. "It's the fault of these rascally Flemish drivers! There's no depending on them."

Sir Colin Campbell came into the room, and upon seeing Audley remarked that there was some cold pie to be had; the Duke nodded dismissal, and the Colonel went off to a room upstairs which was occupied by Gordon and Colonel Canning. A fire had been lit in the grate, and several wet garments were drying in front of it. Occasionally it belched forth a puff of acrid wood-smoke, which mingled with the blue smoke of the two officers' cigars, and made the atmosphere in the small apartment extremely thick. Gordon was lying on a mattress in his shirt-sleeves, with his hands linked behind his head; and Canning was sprawling in an ancient arm-chair by the fire, critically inspecting a crumpled coat which was hung over a chair-back to dry.

"Welcome to our humble quarters!" said Canning. "Don't be afraid! You'll soon get used to the smoke."

"What a reek!" said Audley. "Why the devil don't you open the window?"

"A careful reconnaissance," Gordon informed him, "has revealed the fact that the window is not made to open. What are you concealing under your cloak?"

The Colonel grinned, and produced his bottles of champagne, which he set down on the table.

"Canning, tell the orderly downstairs to get hold of some glasses!" said Gordon, sitting up. "Hi, Charles, don't put that wet cloak of yours anywhere near my coat!"

Canning hitched the coat off the chair-back, and tossed it to its owner. "It's dry. We have a very nice billet here, Charles. Try this chair! I daren't sit in it any longer for fear of being too sore to sit in the saddle to-morrow."

Colonel Audley spread his cloak over the chair-back, sat down on the edge of the truckle-bed against the wall, and began to pull off his muddied boots. "I'm going to sleep," he replied. "In fact, I rather think that I'm asleep already. Where's Slender Billy?"

"At Abeiche. Horses at L'Espinettes."

The Colonel wiped his hands on a large handkerchief, took off his coat, and stretched himself full-length on the patchwork quilt. "What do they stuff their mattresses with here?" he enquired. "Turnips?"

"We rather suspect mangel-worzels," replied Canning. "Did you hear the pickets enjoying themselves when you came in?"

"Damned fools!" said Audley. "What's the sense of it?"

"There ain't any, but if the feeling in our lines and the French lines to-night is anything to go by we're in for a nasty affair to-morrow."

"Well, I don't approve of it," said Gordon, raising himself on his elbow to throw the stub of his cigar into the

308

fire. "We used to manage things much better in Spain. Do you remember those fellows of ours who used to leave a bowl out with a piece of money in it every night for the French vedettes to take in exchange for cognac? Now, that's what I call a proper, friendly way of conducting a war."

"There wasn't anything very friendly about our fellows the night the French took the money without filling the bowl," Audley remarked. "Have the French all come up?"

"Can't say," replied Canning. "There's been a good deal of artillery arriving on their side, judging from the rumbling I heard when I was on the field half an hour ago. Queer thing: our fellows have lit camp-fires, as usual, but there isn't one to be seen in the French lines."

"Poor devils!" said Audley, and shut his eyes.

Downstairs, the Duke was also stretched on his bed, having dropped asleep with that faculty he possessed of snatching rest anywhere and at any time. At three o'clock Lord Fitzroy woke him with the intelligence that Baron Müffling had come over from his quarters with a despatch from Marshal Blücher at Wavre.

The Duke sat up, and swung his legs to the ground. "What's the time? Three o'clock? Time to get up. How's the weather?"

"Clearing a little, sir."

"Good!" His lordship pulled on his Hessians, shrugged himself into his coat, and strode into the adjoining room, where Müffling awaited him. "Hallo, Baron! Fitzroy tells me the weather's beginning to clear."

"It is very bad still, however, and the ground in many places a morass."

"My people call this sort of thing 'Wellington weather'," observed his lordship. "It always rains before my battles. What's the news from the Marshal? Hope he's no worse?"

The Marshal Prince had been last heard of as prostrate from the results of having been twice ridden over by cavalry when his horse was shot under him at Ligny. It would not have been surprising had an old gentleman of over seventy years of age succumbed to this rough usage, but Marshal Forwards was made of stern stuff. He was dosing himself with a concoction of his own, in which garlic figured largely, and had every intention of leading his army in person again. He had ordered General Bülow to march at daybreak, through Wavre, on Chapelle St. Lambert, with the II Army Corps in support; and wrote asking for information, and promising support.

After a short conference with the Duke, Müffling went back to his own quarters to send off the intelligence that was wanted, and to represent to General Gneisenau in the plainest language the propriety of moving to the support of the Allied Army without any loss of time.

The Duke, apparently quite refreshed by his short nap, sat down to write letters. *"Pray keep the English quiet if you can,"* he wrote to Sir Charles Stuart. *"Let them all be prepared to move, but neither be in a hurry nor a fright, as all will yet turn out well."*

But his lordship had not forgotten the bugbear of his right wing. Only a few hours earlier, he had sent orders to General Colville, at Braine-le-Comte, to retire upon Hal, and had instructed Prince Frederick to defend the position between Hal and Enghien for as long as possible. It was his opinion that Bonaparte's best strategy would be to outflank him, and seize Brussels by a *coup de main*. *"Il se peut que l'ennemi nous tourne par Hal,"* he wrote to the Duc de Berri. *"Si cela arrive, je prie votre Altesse Royale de marcher sur Anvers et de vous cantonner dans le voisinage."*

His lordship found time to send a note to his Brussels flirt, too. His indefatigable pen warned her that her family ought to make preparations to leave Brussels, but added: *"I will give you the earliest intimation of any danger that may come to my knowledge. At present I know of none."*

His letters all written and despatched, his final dispositions checked, the Duke sent for his shaving water; and Thornhill, his phlegmatic cook, began to prepare breakfast. His lordship was notoriously indifferent to the food he ate (he had, in fact, once consumed a bad egg at breakfast before one of his battles in Spain, merely remarking in a preoccupied tone, when he had finished it: "By the by, Fitzroy, is that egg of yours fresh? for mine was quite rotten"), but Thornhill had his pride to consider, and might be trusted to concoct a palatable meal out of the most unpromising materials.

Just before the Duke left his Headquarters, a Lieutenant of Hussars rode into Waterloo at a gallop, and flung himself out of the saddle at the door of the little inn. His gay dress was generously spattered with mud, but Colonel Audley, leaning against the door-post, had no difficulty in recognizing an officer of his own regiment, and hailed him immediately: "Hallo! Where are you from?"

The Lieutenant saluted. "Lindsay, sir, of Captain Taylor's squadron on picket duty at Smohain. Message for his lordship from General Bülow!"

"Come in, then. What's the news at the front?"

"Nothing much our way, sir. It's stopped raining, but there's a heavy mist lying on the ground. Captain Taylor saw two corps of French cavalry, in close column, dismounted, within a carbine-shot of our vedettes, and a patrol of heavy cavalry moving off to the east: to feel for the Prussians, he supposed. Captain Taylor had just moved our squadron into Smohain village when a Prussian officer with a patrol arrived with the news that General Bülow's Corps was advancing and was three-quarters of a league distant. Captain Taylor sent me off at once with the intelligence."

"You'll be welcome," said the Colonel, and handed him over to Lord Fitzroy.

The Duke set out to join the Army at an early hour, and was accompanied by a numerous suite. In addition to his Aides-de-Camp, a brilliant *Corps Diplomatique* rode with him, in all the splendour of their various uniforms. Prussia, Austria, Russia, Spain, the Netherlands, and little Sardinia were represented in the persons of Barons Müffling and Vincent, Generals Pozzo di Borgo and Alava, Counts van Reede and D'Aglié, and their satellites. Orders and gold lace glittered, and plumes waved about his lordship, a neat plain figure, mounted on a hollow-backed horse of little beauty and few manners.

The Duke, whom his troops had christened Beau Douro, was dressed, with his usual care and complete absence of ostentation, in a blue frock, short blue cloak, white pantaloons, and tasselled Hessians. The only touch of dandyism he affected was a white cravat instead of a black stock. His low-crowned cocked-hat had no plume, but bore beside the black cockade of England, three smaller ones in the colours of Portugal, Spain, and the Netherlands. He held his telescope in his hand, and sat an ugly horse with no particular grace.

His lordship cared nothing for the appearance of his horse. "There may be faster horses, no doubt many handsomer," he said, "but for bottom and endurance I never saw his fellow." Indeed, he had paid a long price for Copenhagen, and had used him continually in Spain. He was an unpleasant brute to ride, but he seemed to delight in going into action, and evinced far more delight at the sight of troops than the troops felt at his too near approach. "Take care of that there 'orse! We know him!" said the Peninsular veterans, keeping wary eyes on his powerful hindquarters. " 'E kicks out!"

The position which the Allied Army had taken up on the previous night was some two miles south of Waterloo, before the village of Mont St. Jean, and immediately in rear of the hollow road which led westward from Wavre to the village of Braine-l'Alleud. The ground had been surveyed the preceding year, and a map drawn of it, and although it was not perhaps ideal, it possessed one feature at least which commended it to the Duke. It fell away in a gentle declivity to the north, which enabled his lordship to keep all but the front lines of his troops out of sight of the enemy. The hollow road, which dipped in some places between steep, hedge-crowned banks, was intersected by the chaussée leading from Brussels to Charleroi, and, farther west, by the main road from Nivelles, which joined the chaussée at Mont St. Jean. In itself it nearly everywhere constituted the front line of the position, but there were several outposts, like bastions, dotted along the position. On the extreme left there were the farm of

Ter La Haye, and the village of Papelotte, occupied by Prince Bernhard of Saxe-Weimar's Nassau troops. On the left centre, situated three hundred yards south of the hollow road, upon the western side of the Charleroi chaussée, was La Haye Sainte, a semi-fortified farm, with a garden and orchard attached; and on the right, where the hollow road took a southerly bend before crossing the Nivelles highway, was the château and wood of Hougoumont, whose main gate gave on to the short avenue leading to the Nivelles road, down which, so short a time before, Lady Worth had driven in an open barouche, on an expedition of pleasure.

The country was undulating, and to the east of the Charleroi road a valley separated the Allied front-line from the ridge, where, as soon as day broke, French troops could be seen assembling. To the west of the chaussée, the banks of the hollow road became less steep; behind Hougoumont, and overlooking it, was a high plateau, bounded on the right by the ravine through which the Nivelles road ran. Across this road, another plateau was occupied by Lord Hill's Corps, drawn back *en potence*, and occupying the villages of Braine-l'Alleud and Merbe Braine.

The Army, retreating to this position through the storm of the previous afternoon, had spent a miserable night, exposed to a downpour that turned the ground into a bog, saturated coats and blankets, and streamed through the canvas tents. Straw, bean-stalks, sheaves of rye and barley had been collected by the men to form mattresses, but nothing could keep the wet out. Gunners sought shelter under the gun-carriages; infantrymen huddled together under the lea of hedges, and many, abandoning all attempt to sleep, sat round the camp-fires, deriving what comfort they could from their pipes, and a comparison of these conditions with those endured in Spain. Peninsular veterans assured the Johnny Newcomes that the miseries they were undergoing were as nothing to the sufferings met with in the Pyrenees. One or two recalled the retreat of Sir John Moore's army upon Corunna, till the raw recruits, listening wide-eyed to the description of forced marches, bare-foot over mountain passes deep in snow, began to feel that they were not so very badly off after all. No rations had been served out overnight, but quite a number of skinny fowls had been looted by seasoned campaigners, and were broiled in kettles over the camp-fires.

The rain ceased shortly before daybreak, but the atmosphere was vapoury, and heavy with damp. Men got up from their sodden beds shaking as though with ague, their garments clammy over their numb bodies, and their teeth rattling in their heads with a chill that seemed to have penetrated into their very bones. A double allowance of gin served out at dawn helped to bring a little warmth to them, but there were some who, lying down exhausted the night before, did not wake in the morning.

The vicious spitting of musketry had sounded up and down the line of pickets at intervals during the night, but with the daylight a general popping began, as the men fired their pieces in the air to clean the barrels of rust. The vedettes and the sentries were withdrawn; optimists declared the weather to be fairing-up; old soldiers became busy drying their clothes and cleaning their arms; young soldiers stared over the dense mist in the valley to the ridge where the French were beginning to show themselves.

At five o'clock, drums, bugles, and trumpets all along the two-mile front sounded the Assembly. Staff Officers were seen galloping in every direction; brigades began to move into their positions: here a regiment of Light Dragoons changed ground; there a battalion of blue-coated Dutch-Belgians marched along the hollow road with their quick, swinging step; or a troop of Horse Artillery thundered over the ground to a position in the front line. A breakfast of stir-about was served to the men; a detachment of Riflemen, posted in a sandpit on the left side of the Charleroi road, immediately south of its junction with the hollow road, began to make an *abattis* across the chaussée with branches of trees.

A tumbledown cottage on the main road, between Mont

St. Jean and the hollow way, had been occupied during the night by the Colonel of the 95th Rifles, and some of his officers and men had kindled a fire against one of its walls, and had boiled a huge camp-kettle full of tea, milk, and sugar over it. The Duke stopped there for a cup of this sticky beverage on his way from Waterloo; and Colonel Audley, standing beside his horse, and also sipping tea from a pannikin, found himself accosted by Captain Kincaid, whose invincible gaiety did not seem to have been in the least impaired by a night spent in the pouring rain. He had slept soundly, waking to find his clothes drenched and his horse, which he had tethered to a sword stuck in the ground, gone.

"Just drew his sword, and marched off!" he said. "Did you ever hear of an Adjutant going into action without his horse? You might as well go without your arms."

"Johnny, you crazy coot!" the Colonel exclaimed, laughing.

"How was I to know the brute had no proper feeling towards me? He's a low fellow: I found him hob-nobbing half a mile off with a couple of artillery horses."

"You know, you have the luck of the devil!" the Colonel told him.

"I have, haven't I? You'd have said I might as well have looked for a needle in a haystack as for one horse in this mob. Have some more tea? That kettle of ours ought to get its brevet for devotion to duty. It has supplied everyone of the big-wigs with tea, from the Duke downwards."

"No, I won't have any more. Where are you stationed?"

"Oh, right in the forefront! Our 2nd and 3rd battalions have been drafted to General Adam, and I believe are over there, on the right wing," replied Kincaid, with an airy gesture to the west. "But the rest of us are going to occupy a snug sand-pit, and the knoll behind it, on the chaussée, opposite to La Haye Sainte. I've had a look at the position: we shall have our right resting on the chaussée and as far as I can see we ought to get the brunt of whatever the French mean to give us."

"Well, that'll give you something to brag about," said the Colonel, handing over his empty pannikin. "Good luck to you, Johnny!"

At nine o'clock, the Duke rode from end to end of the position, inspecting the disposition of the troops and making some final alterations. There being as yet no sign of the Prussians advancing from the east, two brigades of Light Cavalry, Sir Hussey Vivian's Hussars and Sir John Vandeleur's Dragoons, had been posted to guard the left flank until the Prussians should arrive to relieve them. On Vandeleur's right, Prince Bernhard of Saxe-Weimar's brigade of Nassau and Orange-Nassau troops held the advance posts of Papelotte and Ter La Haye. Behind him, Vincke's and Best's Hanoverians were ranged. Next came Pack's Highlanders, a skeleton of the brigade which had marched out of Brussels on the 15th June; and Kempt's almost equally depleted 8th Brigade. These troops, with Vincke's Landwehr battalions, made up the 5th Division under Sir Thomas Picton, and occupied the left centre of the line. In support, some way behind the line, on the downward slope of the ground to the rear, Sir William Ponsonby's Union Brigade of English, Scots, and Irish Dragoons was drawn up, with Ghigny's brigade of Light Cavalry some little way behind them. The hollow road, at this point, dipped between steep banks, crowned on the northern side by straggling hedges which afforded cover for the division. On the southern slope of the bank, closing the interval between Pack's right and Kempt's left, was placed Count Bylandt's brigade of Dutch-Belgians, in an uncomfortably exposed position, looking across the valley to the ridge occupied by the French. Kempt's right lay in the angle formed by the chaussée and the hollow road from Wavre. The 1st battalion of the 95th Rifles was attached to the brigade, and their Light troops were posted in a sand-pit almost opposite La Haye Sainte, and on the knoll behind it, considerably in advance of the line.

La Haye Sainte itself, situated three hundred yards south of the cross-road, abutted directly on to the chaussée and was occupied by the 2nd Light Battalion of Ompteda's

Germans, under Major Baring. Beyond its white walls and blue-tiled roof, the main Charleroi road descended into a valley, and rose again to where, on the southern ridge, the farm of La Belle Alliance could be seen from the Allied line.

The chaussée, cutting through the centre of the Allied line, separated Picton's division from Sir Charles Alten's, drawn up to the west of it. Colonel von Ompteda's brigade of the King's German Legion lay with its left against the chaussée, and with La Haye Sainte in its immediate front; next came Count Kielmansegg's Hanoverian Line battalions; and, west of them, where the hollow road began to curve southwards, was Sir Colin Halkett's brigade of one Highland and three English regiments. From Halkett's right, to where the Nivelles road crossed the hollow way, the ground was strongly held by Cooke's division of British Guards: Maitland, with both battalions of the 1st Guards, lying next to Halkett; and Byng's Coldstream and 3rd Scots Guards occupying the high ground behind and overlooking the château of Hougoumont. Seven companies of the Coldstream, under Sir James Macdonnell, had been thrown into the château, and had been busy all night strengthening the fortifications; while the four Light companies of the division, under Lord Saltoun, were sent forward as skirmishers into the wood and orchard.

In the triangle of ground formed by the junction, at Mont St. Jean, of the two great highways from Charleroi and Nivelles, a number of cavalry brigades were massed behind the infantry, and out of sight of the enemy. In rear of Ompteda, and separated from the Union Brigade of Heavy Cavalry only by the chaussée, was Lord Edward Somerset's Heavy brigade of Household Cavalry: Life Guards, Dragoons and Blues, in magnificent array. Behind them, in reserve, was Baron Collaert's Dutch-Belgic cavalry division, comprising a brigade of Carabiniers, under General Trip; and a brigade of Light cavalry under Baron van Merlen. Immediately to the rear of Kielmansegg were General Kruse's Nassau troops, in reserve, with Colonel Arendtschildt's Light Dragoons and Hussars of the Legion supporting them; and, lying against the Nivelles road, considerably withdrawn from the front, was the Brunswick contingent. Upon the plateau behind the Guards' division were posted Major-General Dörnberg's Light Dragoons; a Hanoverian regiment known as the Cumberland Hussars; and Major-General Grant's Hussar brigade, which lay directly behind Byng's Guards, against the Nivelles road, overlooking the ravine running north to Merbe Braine, and the plateau beyond.

On this plateau, drawn back *en potence* to guard the right flank of the line, was Lord Hill's Second Army Corps. Of this corps, Sir Henry Clinton's division occupied the ground nearest to the highway, Adam's brigade being drawn up immediately to the west of it. The village of Merbe Braine, nestling to the north behind a belt of trees, was occupied by Hew Halkett's brigade of Hanoverian Militia, and Colonel Du Plat's Line battalions of the Legion. Some way to the west, Baron Chassé's Dutch-Belgic division was stationed round Braine-l'Alleud, Colonel Detmer's brigade occupying the village itself and Count d'Aubremé's brigade being posted to the south-west, round the farm of Vieux Foriez, as an Observation Corps. Of General Colville's 4th Division, eight miles away at Hal with Prince Frederick's Corps, only one brigade was present, Colonel Mitchell's, which was formed on the west of the Nivelles road, covering the avenue which led to the great north gate of Hougoumont.

Attached to the divisions and the cavalry brigades were Brigades and Troops of Artillery, those in front line being placed in the intervals of the infantry brigades, and slightly in advance of them. Rogers's Brigade and Ross's Chestnut Troop guarded the Charleroi chaussée; Whinyates was attached to the Union Brigade with his Rockets; Gardiner was with Viviân's Hussars; Stevenart's heroic battery with Prince Bernhard's Nassauers; Rettberg before Best; Byleveld with Count Bylandt's brigade; while, west of the chaussée, in front of Alten's and Cooke's divisions, were ranged Cleeve's and Kuhlmann's German batteries,

Bean's, Webber-Smith's, Ramsay's and Bull's Brigades and Troops, each with six guns, manned by eighty or more gunners and drivers, half a dozen bombardiers, and the usual complement of sergeants, corporals, farriers, and trumpeters. Each Troop came up in subdivisions, an impressive cavalcade with two hundred horses, and a train of forge-carts, spare-wheel carriages and extra-ammunition waggons. Every horse was brought on to the field in the pink of condition, his flanks plumped out with plundered forage. A hard life, the artillery officer's, for while, on the one hand, plundering was strictly forbidden by the Duke, on the other, the allowance of forage was insufficient to put the fat on the horses which his lordship demanded. "Either way you quake in your shoes," declared Captain Mercer bitterly. "Bring your Troop on to the ground with your beasts a shade thinner than the next man's, and that damned cold eye of the Duke's will see the difference in a flash. You won't be asked questions about it, and if you try to defend yourself you won't be attended to. You'll be judged out of hand as unfit for your command, and very likely removed from the Army as well. But if you plunder the poor foreigner's fields, and he reports you to the Duke—whew!"

While the Duke, accompanied by his Military Secretary, his Aides-de-Camp, the Prince of Orange, Lord Uxbridge, the Diplomatic Corps, and their train, was inspecting his position, the French columns were mustering upon the opposite heights. The weather was clearing fast, the mist in the hollows curling away in wreaths; and occasionally a pale shaft of sunlight would pierce through the clouds for a moment or two. The ground, intersected by hedges of beech and hornbeam, was nearly all of it under cultivation, crops of rye, wheat, barley, oats, and clover standing shoulder-high, with here and there a ploughed field showing dark between the stretches of waving grain.

The bulk of the French army had bivouacked about Genappe, but at nine o'clock, just as the Duke started to ride down his lines, the heads of the columns began to appear above the ridge to the south. Drums and trumpets were first heard, and then the music of the bands, playing a medley of martial tunes. Strains of the *Marseillaise*, mingled with *Veillons au Salut de l'Empire*, floated across the valley to the Allied lines. Four columns, destined to form the first line, came marching over the hill, and deployed in perfect order, just as seven others appeared descending the slope. From the Allied lines the whole magnificent spectacle was watched by thousands of pairs of eyes. Knowledgeable gentlemen exclaimed at intervals: "That's Reille's Corps, moving off to their left! . . . that's D'Erlon! . . . those are Kellermann's Cuirassiers!"

The mist still lay white in the valley, but beyond it, less than a mile distant, the ground was gradually becoming covered with dark masses of infantry. As the divisions deployed, the cavalry began to appear. Squadron after squadron of Cuirassiers galloped over the brow of the hill, their steel breast-plates and copper crests occasionally caught by the feeble rays of sunlight trying to pierce through the clouds. The slope was soon vivid with bright, shifting colours, as Chasseurs à Cheval, blazing with green and gold, giant Carabiniers in white, brass-casqued Dragoons, Hussars in every colour, Grenadiers à Cheval in Imperial blue with bearskin shakos, and red Lancers with towering white plumes and swallow-tailed pennons fluttering on the ends of their lances, cantered into their positions.

It was an hour and a half before the movement which brought the French Army into six formidable lines, forming six double W's, was completed, and during that time the Duke of Wellington was employed in inspecting his own position. Sir Thomas Picton, still in his frock-coat and round hat, grimly concealing even from his Aides-de-Camp that an ugly wound, roughly bandaged by his servant after Quatre-Bras, lay beneath his shabby coat, had also inspected it very early in the morning, and had told Sir John Colborne, of Adam's brigade, that he considered it to be the most damnable place for fighting he had ever seen.

Lord Uxbridge, tall and handsome in his magnificent

Hussar dress, preferred the position to that of Quatre-Bras, but was fretted by the impossibility, owing to the suddenness of the order to advance on the 16th June, of forming his cavalry into divisions; and by the circumstance of having been informed by the Duke, at the eleventh hour, that the Prince of Orange desired him to take over the command of all the Dutch-Belgic cavalry. Uxbridge accepted the charge, but was forced to observe that he thought it unfortunate that he should have had no opportunity of making himself acquainted with any of the officers, or their regiments. He was anxiously awaiting the arrival of the Prussian Corps to relieve Vivian's and Vandeleur's much needed brigades on the left flank, and more than once adverted to its non-appearance. The Duke, whose irritability fell away from him the moment he set foot on a battlefield, replied calmly that they would be up presently: the roads were in a bad state, which would account for their delay.

Baron Müffling, knowing the Prussian Chief of Staff's mistrust of the Duke, was also anxious, and had already despatched one of his Jägers to try to get news of Bülow's advance. He knew that the Duke had placed the weakened 5th Division on the left centre in the expectation of its being immediately strengthened by Prussian infantry: and having by this time identified himself far more with the British than with the Prussian Army, Bülow's delay caused him a good deal of inward perturbation. Being a sensible man, he refused to permit his anxiety to oppress him, but fixed his mind instead on the problems immediately before him. He rode beside the Duke, acquainting himself with the disposition of the Allied troops, and occasionally proffering a suggestion. When he went with him into the château of Hougoumont, he felt considerable doubts of the possibility of the post's being held by a mere detachment of British Guards. But the Duke seemed perfectly satisfied. He rode into the courtyard through the great north gate, and was met by Lieutenant-Colonel Sir James Macdonnell, a huge Highlander with narrowed, humorous eyes, a square jowl, and the frame of an ox, whom he greeted in a cheerful tone, and with marked friendliness. Macdonnell took him round the fortifications, showing him the work which the garrison had been engaged on during the night. The brick walls of the garden had been pierced for loop-holes; wooden platforms erected to enable a second firing-line to shoot over the walls; and flagstones, timbers, and broken waggons used as barricades to the various entrances. The Duke gave the whole a hasty survey, and, as he prepared to mount his horse again, nodded to Müffling, and said: "They call me a Sepoy General. Well! Napoleon shall see to-day how a Sepoy General can defend a position!"

Müffling bowed, but thought the chances of holding the château so small that he felt obliged to express his doubts. "It is not, in my opinion, sir, a strong post. I confess, I find it hard to believe that it can be held against a determined assault."

The Duke, swinging himself into the saddle, gave a short laugh, and pointed at the impassive Highlander. "Ah! You do not know Macdonnell!" he said.

Those of his Staff who stood near him laughed; the Duke raised two fingers to his hat, and rode off.

The Baron caught him up on the avenue leading to the Nivelles road, and began to urge the propriety of strengthening the post. His trained eye had instantly perceived that it was of paramount importance, for the possession of it by the French would enable them to enfilade the Allied lines from its shelter. "Even supposing that the garrison should be able to hold it against assault, Duke, how will it be if the enemy advances up the Nivelles road?" he argued.

"We shall see," responded his lordship. "Let us take a look at the ground."

An inspection of the Nivelles road, and the country to the south of it, resulted in his lordship's drawing in his right wing a little, raising a battery to sweep the road, and posting some infantry in the rear. Several Aides-de-Camp went galloping off with brief messages scrawled on leaves torn from his lordship's pocket-book, and the Duke turned his attention to the wood to the south of the château, which was occupied by Saltoun's Light Companies of the Guards. His lordship altered this arrangement, withdrawing the Guards into the garden and orchard, and desiring the Prince of Orange to send orders to Prince Bernhard to despatch a battalion of his Nassau troops to occupy the wood. Colonel Audley was sent at the same time to bring up a detachment of Hanoverians, and rode off in a spatter of mud kicked up by his horse's hooves.

Upon his return to the Duke, who had moved towards the centre of the position, he passed by the 1st Guards, and caught a glimpse of Lord Harry Alastair, looking rather tired, but apparently in good spirits. He called a greeting to him, and Lord Harry came up, and stood for a moment with his hand on the Colonel's saddle-bow. "Enjoying yourself, Harry?" asked Audley.

"Lord, yes! You know we were engaged at Quatre-Bras, don't you? By Jove, there was never anything like it, was there? If only poor Hay——but never mind that!" he added hastily, blinking his sandy lashes. "It's just that he was rather a friend of mine. I say, though, what do you think? I'm damned if William Lennox didn't present himself for duty this morning! Nothing of him to be seen for bandages, and of course General Maitland sent him packing. He's just gone off, he and his father. Devilish sportsmanlike of him to come, I thought!" He detained the Colonel a moment longer, saying: "Have you seen anything of George, sir? They say the Life Guards were engaged at Genappe yesterday."

"Yes, I saw George in the thick of it, but he came out with nothing but a scratch or two!"

"Oh, good! Give him my love, if you should happen to run into him at any time, and tell him I'm in famous shape. Good-bye! the best of luck, Charles!"

"Thanks: the same to you!" said the Colonel, and waved and rode on.

By ten o'clock, the Duke had completed his inspection, but the French Army was still deploying on the opposite heights, and guns, their wheels up to the naves in mud, were being dragged into position along the ridge. A little before eleven o'clock, a Prussian *galopin* arrived with a despatch for General Müffling, who had only a few minutes before rejoined the Duke, after making an examination of the ground beyond Papelotte, on the left wing. He had been driven back by a French patrol coming up from the village of Plancenoit, to the south, but not before he had satisfied himself that a Prussian advance by the plateau of St. Lambert would not only be possible but extremely beneficial. He wrote down his views, read them to the Duke, who said, in his decided way: "I quite agree!" and was in the act of sending an Aide-de-Camp to Wavre, with the despatch, when the Prussian *galopin* found him.

The despatch he had brought was from Marshal Blücher, and was dated 9.30 a.m. from Wavre. "*Your Excellency will assure the Duke of Wellington from me,*" wrote the Marshal Prince, "*that, ill as I am, I shall place myself at the head of my troops, and attack the right of the French, in case they undertake anything against him.*"

There was a postscript subjoined to this missive by another and more cautious hand. General Count von Gneisenau, still convinced that his English ally's early service in India had made him a master in the art of duplicity, entreated the Baron "*to ascertain most particularly whether the Duke of Wellington has really adopted the decided resolution of fighting in his present position: or whether he only intends some demonstration, which might become very dangerous to our Army.*"

To Müffling, who profoundly respected the openness of the Duke's character, and knew how serious the coming engagement was likely to be, this postscript was exasperating. He neither mentioned it to the Duke nor made enquiries of him which he knew to be superfluous. The despatch which he had already written must convince Gneisenau of the seriousness of his lordship's intentions. He gave it to his Aide-de-Camp, telling him to be sure to let General Bülow read it, if, on his way to Wavre, he should encounter him. He could do nothing more to hasten the march of the Prussian IV Corps, and having seen the Aide-de-Camp off, had little else to do but wait, in steadily growing impatience, for news of his compatriots' approach.

The deploying movements of the French had been completed by half-past ten. The music and the trumpet-calls ceased, and the columns stood in a silence that seemed the more absolute from its marked contrast to the medley of martial noises that had been resounding on all sides for the past hour. As the village clocks in the distance struck eleven, the Duke took up a position with all his Staff, near Hougoumont, and looked through his glass at the French lines. A very dark, wiry young officer, with a thin, energetic face in which a pair of deep-set eyes laughed upon the world, came riding up to the Duke, and saluted smartly. The Duke called out: "Hallo, Smith! Where are you from?"

"From General Lambert's brigade, my lord, and they from America!" responded Brigade-Major Harry Smith, with the flash of an impudent grin.

"What have you got?"

"The 4th, the 27th, and the 40th. The 81st remain in Brussels."

"Ah, I know! But the others: are they in good order?"

"Excellent, my lord, and very strong," declared the Major.

"That's all right," said his lordship, "for I shall soon want every man."

"I don't think they will attack to-day," remarked one of his Staff, frowning across the valley.

"Nonsense!" said his lordship, with a snap. "The columns of attack are already forming, and I think I have seen where the weight of the attack will fall. I shall be attacked before an hour. Do you know anything of my position, Smith?"

"Nothing, my lord, beyond what I see—the general line, and the right and left."

"Go back and halt Lambert's brigade at the junction of the two great roads from Charleroi and Nivelles. I'll tell you what I want of you fellows."

He rode a little way with Smith, apprising him of his intentions. The Major, who was one of his lordship's promising young favourites, listened, saluted, and rode off at a canter to the rear. He cut across the slope behind Alten's division, leapt a hedge, and came down on to the chaussée almost on top of Colonel Audley, who, having been sent on an errand to Mont St. Jean, was riding back to the front.

"God damn your—— Harry Smith, by all that's wonderful! I might have known it! When did you arrive? Where's your brigade?"

"At Waterloo. We were held up by the waggons and baggage upset all over the road from Brussels, and when we got to Waterloo we met Scovell, who had been sent by the Duke to see if the rear was clear—which, by God, it was not! He requested us to sweep up the litter before moving on! What's the news with you, old fellow?"

"Oh, famous! How's Juana? You haven't brought her out with you, I suppose?"

"Haven't brought her out with me?" exclaimed the Major. "She was sitting down to dinner with Lambert at some village just the other side of the Forest last night!"

"Good God, you don't mean to tell me she's with the brigade now?"

"No, I've sent her back to Ghent with her groom," replied the Major coolly. "We're in for a hottish day, from the looks of it. I understand my brigade will be wanted to relieve old Picton. Cut up at your little affair at Quatre-Bras, was he?"

"Devilishly. Someone said he himself had been wounded, but he's here to-day, so I suppose he wasn't. I must be off."

"By Jove, and so must I! We shall meet again—here or in hell! *Adiós! Bienes de fortuna!*"

He cantered off; the Colonel set his horse at the bank on the right of the chaussée, scrambled up, and rode past Lord Edward Somerset's lounging squadrons up the slope to the front line.

By the time he had found the Duke it was just past eleven

o'clock. He joined a group of persons gathered about his lordship, and sat with a loose rein, looking along the ridge opposite.

"Heard about Grant?" asked Canning, who was standing next to him.

"No: which Grant?" replied the Colonel absently.

"Oh, not General Grant! Colonel Grant. He did send the information of the French massing on Charleroi on the 15th—the very fullest information, down to the last detail. It's just come to hand!"

"Just come to hand?" repeated Audley. "How the devil did it take three days to reach us?"

"Ask General Dörnberg," said Canning. "It was sent to him, at Mons, and he, if you please, coolly sent it back to Grant, saying that it didn't convince him that the French really intended anything serious! Grant then despatched the information direct to the Duke, but of course, by that time, we were on the march. Good story, ain't it?"

"Dörnberg ought to be shot! Who the devil is he to question Grant's Intelligence?"

"My very words," remarked Gordon, who had come up to them. He glanced towards the French lines, and said, with a yawn: "Don't seem to be in a hurry to come to grips with us, do they?"

The words had scarcely been uttered when the flash of cannon-fire flickered all along the ridge, and the silence that had lain over the field for over an hour was rent by the boom of scores of great guns trained on the Allied position. The scream of a horse, hit by roundshot, sounded from a Troop of artillery close at hand; a cannon-ball buried itself in the soft ground not three paces from where Colonel Audley was standing, and sent up a shower of mud. His horse reared, snorting; he gentled it, shouting to Gordon above the thunder of the guns: "What do you call this?"

"Damned noisy!" retorted Gordon.

The flashes and the puffs of smoke continued all along the ridge; suddenly a deafening crash, reverberating down the Allied line, answered the challenge of the French cannons, and a cheer went up: the English batteries had come into action.

CHAPTER XXII

THE French, after their usual custom, had opened a cannonade over the whole front. Behind the quick-set hedges the first lines of British infantry remained lying down, while the second lines of cavalry, drawn back on the downward slope to the north, suffered little from shot which for the most part fell short of them. The sodden condition of the ground caused many of the shells to explode harmlessly in deep mud, but there were uncomfortable moments when shells with extra long fuses fell amongst the troops, hissing and burning for some time before they burst. Some of the old soldiers lit pipes, and lay smoking and cracking jokes, but every now and then there would be a sob from some man hit by a splinter, or a groan from a boy with a limb shattered by case-shot. In front line, in the intervals between the brigades, the gunners were busy, loading the 9-pounders with round-shot with a case over it, the tubes in the vents, port-fires glaring and spitting behind the wheels.

The Duke was standing by Maitland's brigade on the right, critically observing the effect of the French cannonade. The shots tore up the ground beside him, and hissed over his head, but he merely remarked: "That's good practice. I think they fire better than in Spain."

The cannonade continued until twenty minutes past eleven without any movement of infantry attack being made by the enemy. The hottest fire was being directed upon Hougoumont, but the wood on the southern side of the château to a large extent protected it. At twenty minutes past eleven, Prince Jérôme Bonaparte's division of infantry, belonging to Reille's Corps, on the French left, began to advance in column towards the wood, with a cloud of skirmishers thrown out in front. These were met by a blaze of musketry-fire from the Hanoverian and Nassau troops posted amongst the trees. The Duke shut his telescope with a snap, and galloped down the line, with his Staff streaming behind him, to where Byng's brigade was drawn up on the high ground behind the château. An order was rapped out; Colonel Canning wheeled his horse, and made for the spot where Captain Sandham's Field Battery was stationed. "Captain Sandham! You are wanted immediately in front! Left limber up, and as fast as you can!"

The order was swiftly repeated: "Left limber up! At a gallop, march!"

The horses strained at their collars; the mud gave up its hold on the wheels with a sucking sound; the train moved forward, lurching and clanking over the ground, and came up in grand style, guns loaded with powder, priming wires in the vents to prevent the cartridges slipping forward, slow matches lighted. The leading gun, a howitzer, was quickly unlimbered, and its first shell burst over the head of the French column moving upon the wood of Hougoumont. The other guns followed suit one after the other, as they came into position and unlimbered; and in a few minutes an additional and destructive fire was being directed on the column by Captain Cleeve's battery of the Legion, in front of Alten's division.

The column shuddered under the fire, and checked. In the wood, the skirmishers were already engaged with the Hanoverian and Nassau defenders. Twelve pieces of Horse Artillery of Reille's Corps were pushed forward, and a heavy counter-cannonade was begun. The column of infantry recovered, and pressed on, leaving its dead and wounded lying on the field. A well-directed fire from Sandham's and Cleeve's batteries again threw it into disorder, but it re-formed, and reached the wood, driving the defenders back from tree to tree. The popping of musketry now mingled with the roar of the cannons; and a steady trickle of wounded men began to make their way to the shelter of the British line.

329

Colonel Audley, who had been sent off to the left wing with instructions to Sir Hussey Vivian not to fire on any troops advancing from the west, did not see the start of the fight in Hougoumont Wood. By the time he returned to the Duke, it had been in progress for half an hour, and the Nassauers, after contesting the ground with a good deal of courage, were giving way. More of Reille's Corps had moved to Jérôme's support, and the skirmishers of the Guards, pressed back through the Great Orchard, were being driven into an alley of holly and yew trees separating it from the smaller orchard surrounding the garden.

The Nassauers, retreating in disorder, poured out on to a sunken lane forming the northern boundary of the Hougoumont enclosure. When Colonel Audley rode up, the Duke, spurring forward from his position in front of Byng's brigade, was trying to rally them. But his presence, so invigorating to his own men, had very little effect upon the Nassauers, some of whom, in the panic of the moment, actually fired after him as he rode through their ranks. "Pretty scamps to win a battle with!" he said, with a bark of laughter; and wasting no more time on them, galloped off to where, a few yards from where the Nivelles highway crossed the hollow road to Braine-l'Alleud, Major Bull's Howitzer Troop was drawn up. He brought the Troop up in person, explaining in a few incisive sentences what he wanted done. Major Bull, ordered to clear the wood with shell fire, considered the position calmly for a moment, and gave his gunners their directions. It was a ticklish business, for the château, with its defenders, lay between his Troop and the enemy, and a shell falling short must inevitably drop amongst the British Guards, desperately fighting in the alleys south of the garden wall. The first shell shot up, clearing the enclosures, and exploded over the wood.

"That's right!" said his lordship. "That's good shooting. Well, Audley, any news of the Prussians yet?"

"No, sir. A patrol of French cavalry came up to Colonel Best's people. He formed the brigade in squares, but the cavalry seemed only to be reconnoitring, and drew off again. The French are massing their guns in the centre of the line."

"Oh yes! This is nothing but a diversion," said the Duke, nodding towards Hougoumont. He found that several officers from Byng's brigade had come up to watch the struggle, and told them curtly to get back to the brigade. "You will have the devil's own fire on you immediately!" he said, and, as though to prove the truth of his words, a hurricane of grape and round-shot began to whistle about the position, as Reille's gunners found their range.

The howitzer shells, falling thick in the wood, drove Jérôme back. The swarms of French infantry rallied, and came on again; the Hanoverians were forced back and back, through sheer weight of numbers, into the orchard. A glimpse of red showed through the trees; Jérôme's troops hurled themselves forward at what they believed to be a line of British soldiers, and were brought up short by the brick wall enclosing the garden. They tried to scale it, but the Coldstream Guards, posted on the inner platforms and at the loopholes, poured in such a murderous fire that the blue-coated infantry recoiled. The ditches lining the alley separating the wood from the orchard became choked with dead; in the orchard, Saltoun's Light Companies began to press back the invaders; but the 1st Léger Regiment succeeded in setting fire to a haystack, and, under cover of the black smoke, crept round the western side of the château. A British battery, raking the Nivelles road, was assailed by a storm of *tirailleurs,* and suffered such loss of men and horses that it was forced to retire. A horse battery attached to Piré's Lancers, who had come up as an Observation Corps to the south-west, opened fire on Bull's Troop; and the Guards posted on the avenue leading from the high road to the north gate of the château saw, through the smothering whorls of smoke, hundreds of Jérôme's men advancing on them.

The north gate was open, and it was down the avenue of elm trees that reinforcements of men and ammunition were being passed into the château. The Hanoverians

331

defending the approach to the avenue were overwhelmed and flung back in confusion. The Guards, attacked on all sides, stood shoulder to shoulder, fighting off the waves of the French that broke over them, and retreating, step by step, to the gateway. The French saw Hougoumont almost within their grasp; one of their Generals spurred forward, shouting to his men to prevent the closing of the gates. They surged after him, but a Sergeant of the Coldstream dashed forward, right into the mass of the enemy, and hurled himself at General Cubières. Before the French had had time to realize what was happening, the General had been dragged from his horse, and Sergeant Fraser, brandishing a blood-stained halberd, was up in the saddle, and riding hell-for-leather towards the gate. The momentary check caused by this diversion enabled the handful of Guards to reach the courtyard, but a party of Sapeurs, recovering from their astonishment at Fraser's daring, rushed after him, led by a young Sous-Lieutenant of ferocious mien. The Guards, fighting their way backwards through the gateway, heard above the rattle of musketry and the thunder of artillery a yell of: *"En avant, l'Enfonceur!"* and saw the Sapeurs come charging through the smother of black smoke. They made a desperate attempt to shut the gates, but with a roar of rage and triumph the Sapeurs flung themselves against the heavy doors. The Guards, reduced in numbers, suffocated by the smoke, could not hold them. Amid the crash of timbers and crumbling masonry, the French burst through into the courtyard and fought for possession of the gate-house.

The noise reached the ears of Macdonnell, directing the defence of the garden wall. Shouting to three of his officers who stood nearest to him, he raced, drawn sword in hand, to the inner yard, and across it to the wicket leading to the main courtyard. There the most appalling sight met his eyes. The courtyard was full of Frenchmen; some of the Guards were fighting to defend the cowshed, where their own wounded lay; from every ambush of shed, or window, or cellar, a steady musketry-fire was holding the surge of men through the gateway in check;

while in the château, the Guards besieged on the staircase had hacked away the lower steps, and were firing down upon the French trying to storm up to them. By the gate, the paving-stones were slippery with blood, and cumbered by the dead and wounded who lay there; a heroic little band, under the command of two Sergeants, was still fighting to prevent the gate-house from falling, but in the gateway itself the French were massed, and outside reinforcements were advancing down the avenue.

Roaring at his officers to follow him, Macdonnell launched himself across the courtyard. Hatless, with nothing but a sword in his hand, he fell upon the French in the gateway, and with such force that they broke involuntarily, as they would have broken before the charge of a mad bull. His officers and a few Sergeants rushed to his support. For an instant the French were scattered; and while a couple of Ensigns and two Sergeants held them at bay, Macdonnell and Sergeant Graham set their shoulders to the double-doors, and forced them together, the sweat pouring down their faces and the muscles standing out like corrugations down their powerful thighs.

Yells of fury sounded outside, as Graham, while his Colonel held the doors together against every effort of the Sapeurs to force them open, slammed the great iron cross-bar into position. Bayonets and hatchets beat upon the unyielding timbers; and the French trapped in the court-yard tried to set fire to the barns before being shot or bayoneted by the Guards who were round them.

A few brave men managed to scale the wall, but were shot before they could even leap down into the courtyard. Fresh columns were being moved down by Jérôme, and had carried the avenue. Colonel Audley, his right sleeve torn by a musket-ball, was sent flying to bring up two guns from Bolton's battery, and arrived above the north alley enclosing the orchard just as Colonel Woodford led forward four companies of the Guards to the relief of the garrison.

"There, my lads: in with you! Let me see no more of you!" the Duke called out to them.

The Guards gave him a cheer, and went in at the

charge. They drove the French before them at the point of the bayonet, sweeping them away from the château walls; and Woodford managed to reinforce the garrison through a side-door leading into the alley. The Light Companies reoccupied the ground they had lost, and Jérôme drew off to re-form his mutilated battalions.

Several officers of the Staff Corps had galloped up with messages for the Duke from time to time; of his personal Staff, Lord Arthur Hill and young Cathcart were both mounted on troopers, their horses having been shot under them; and Colonel Audley had suffered a contusion on his right arm from a glancing musket-ball. Fremantle, returning from the left wing, found him trying to tie his handkerchief round the flesh wound with one hand and his teeth, and pushed up to him, saying: "Here, let me do that!"

"Any news of Blücher?" asked Audley.

"Not so much as a sniff of those damned Prussians! My God, you've got a pretty shambles here! What's been going on?"

"We all but lost Hougoumont, that's all. Bull's had to retire. He's been enfiladed by a Troop of horse artillery belonging to the Lancers over there." He jerked his head towards the Nivelles road. "Jérôme's bringing up reserve after reserve. Looks as though he means to take Hougoumont or perish in the attempt. Anything happening anywhere else?"

"Not yet, but we'll be in for it soon, or I'm a Dutchman. Never saw so many guns massed in my life as the batteries they're bringing up in the centre. There you are—all right and tight!"

It was now nearly one o'clock, and for an hour and a half the most bitter struggle had been raging for the possession of Hougoumont. The Duke, who seemed to have been everywhere at once, cantered back to the centre of the position, to where an elm tree stood on the highest point of the ground, to the west of the Charleroi chaussée. He had no sooner arrived there than an artillery officer came up to him in a great state of excitement, stating that he could clearly perceive Bonaparte and all his Staff before the farm of La Belle Alliance, and had no doubt of being able to direct his guns on to them.

This suggestion was met by a frosty stare, and a hasty: "No, no, I won't have it! It is not the business of General Officers to be firing upon each other!"

"Just retire quietly," said Gordon, in the chagrined officer's ear. "Forget that you were born! You had better not have been, you know."

Colonel Fremantle's description of the guns being assembled upon the opposite ridge had not been exaggerated. During the struggle about Hougoumont, battery after battery had been brought up on the French side, covering the whole of the Allied centre, from Colin Halkett's brigade on the right of Alten's division to Prince Bernhard's Nassauers at Papelotte. Nearly eighty guns had been massed upon the ridge, and at one o'clock the most infernal cannonade broke out. Shells screamed through the air, ploughing long furrows in the ground as they fell, blowing the legs off horses, exploding in the Allied lines, and scattering limbs and brains over men crouching behind the meagre shelter of the quick-set hedges. The infantry set its teeth and endured. Young soldiers, determined not to lag behind their elders in courage, gulped, and smiled waveringly as the blood of fallen comrades spattered in their faces; veterans declared that this was nothing, and went on grimly cracking their jokes. On the high ground under the elm tree balls hummed and whistled round the Duke and his brilliant Staff, until he said in his cool way: "Better separate, gentlemen: we are a little too thick here."

Shortly after one o'clock, Reille's guns, away to the right, succeeded in setting fire to the haystack in the yard of Hougoumont. In the centre of the line, smoke was beginning to lie thickly in the valley between the opposing ridges. The air was hot and acrid; and a curious noise, like the hum of a gigantic swarm of bees, was making novices ask anxiously: "What's that? What's that buzzing noise?"

335

Baron Müffling, after a short colloquy with the Duke, rode away to take up his position with the cavalry brigades on the left flank. Messenger after messenger went galloping off to try to gain some intelligence of the Prussian advance, for it was plain that the cannonade was a prelude to an attack upon the Allied centre, which, held by Picton's and Alten's divisions on either side of the chaussée, was the weakest part of the line.

At half-past one, the cannonade slackened, and above the diminishing thunder could be heard the French drums beating the *pas de charge*.

"Here comes Old Trousers at last!" sang out a veteran, uncorking his muzzle-stopper and slipping off his lock-cap. "Now for it, you Johnny Newcomes!"

On the ridge of La Belle Alliance, a huge mass of infantry was forming, flanked by squdarons of Cuirassiers. Sharp-eyed men on the Allied front swore they could discern Bonaparte himself; that he was there was evident from the shouts of "*Vive l'Empereur!*" and the dipping of Colours, as the regiments filed past the group beside the chaussée. The rub-a-dub of drums and the blare of trumpets now mingled with the roar of artillery. Four divisions of infantry, led by Count D'Erlon, began to advance down the slope to the hollow road, in ponderous columns at 400 pace intervals, showing fronts from 160 to 200 files. The battalions of each division were deployed, and placed one behind the other, except on the French left, where Allix's division was formed into two brigades side by side, under Quiot and Bourgeois. These moved forward to encircle the farm of La Haye Sainte, Quiot branching off to the west of the chaussée and Bourgeois advancing to the east of it. A determined musketry-fire from the orchard and the windows of the farm met them, but Baring's Germans were soon driven from the orchard and gardens into the building itself. While the other divisions moved in three columns down the slope towards the Allied left centre, the Lüneberg Field Battalion was detached from Count Kielmansegg's brigade, and sent forward to try to reinforce Baring. These young troops advanced boldly down the slope, but wavered under the French fire. The sight of their own skirmishers falling back took the heart out of them. They began to retreat; the Cuirassiers, covering Quiot's left flank, swept down upon them, and in their disordered state killed and rode over many of them, driving the rest back with great loss to their own lines.

Upon the eastern side of the chaussée the three other columns, led by Donzelot, Marcognet, and Durutte, moved steadily down upon the Allied line. As each column cleared its own guns on the ridge behind it, and descended the slope into the valley, these began firing again, until the thunder and crash of artillery drowned the rool of the drums and the shrill blare of the trumpets.

To the eyes that watched this tidal advance, it seemed as though the whole slope was covered with men. European armies had seen these columns, and had broken and fled before them, appalled by the sheer weight of infantry opposed to them. The British had time and again proved the superiority of Line over Column, but Count Bylandt's Dutch-Belgic brigade, badly placed on the slope confronting the French position, already demoralized by the heavy cannonading, could not stand the relentless march of the columns towards them. They had suffered considerably at Quatre-Bras, had had no rations served out to them since the morning of the previous day, and had seen Count Bylandt carried off the field. The men in their gay uniforms and white-topped shakos began to waver, and before the head of the column immediately in their front had reached the valley below them, they fled. The exertions of their officers, frantically trying to check the rout, were of no avail. The men, some of them flinging down their arms, broke through the hedge in their rear, and retreated in the wildest confusion through the interval between Kempt's and Pack's brigades. Byleveld's battery was swept back in the rush, and a great gap yawned in the Allied line.

The Dutch-Belgians were met by derisive cat-calls from Pack's Highlanders. Not a man in the 5th Division caught the infection of that mad panic; instead, the Scots helped the terrified foreigners to the rear with sly bayonet-thrusts, while the men of Kempt's left, until called to order by their officers, fired musket-balls into the retreating mass.

In the confusion, Colonel Audley, desperately trying with a handful of others to stem the rush, came upon Lavisse, livid and cursing, laying about him with the flat of his sword. "That's no use, man!" he shouted. "Christ, can't you fellows get your men together? Form them up in the rear, and bring them on again, for God's sake! We can't afford this gap!"

"Damn you, do I not know?" Lavisse gasped.

"Och, sir, let the puir bodies gang!" shouted a Sergeant of the Gordons. "*We* dinna want furriners hired to fight for us!"

The three companies of the 95th Rifles, posted on the knoll and in the sandpit in front of Kempt's right, were firing steadily into Bourgeois' and Donzelot's columns, advancing on either side of them; and two of Ross's 9-pounders, guarding the chaussée, caused Bourgeois' brigade to swerve away from La Haye Sainte to its right, where it was thrown against Donzelot's division, and advanced with it in one unwieldy mass. The Riflemen stood their ground until almost hemmed in by the sea of French, but were forced at last to abandon the sand-pit and retreat to the main position.

Bylandt's men had forced their way right to the rear, and although Byleveld's Troop had extricated itself from the mêlée and was in the front line again, firing into the head of the column already starting to deploy in the valley, over two thousand Dutch-Belgians had deserted from the line, leaving three thousand men of Picton's decimated division to face the charge of thirteen thousand Frenchmen.

Picton, wasting no time in trying to bring Bylandt's men to the front again, deployed Kempt's brigade into an attenuated two-deep line, to fill the breach. Below, in the hollow road and the cornfields beyond it, the French columns were also trying to deploy in the constricted space afforded for such a movement. The whole valley swarmed with blue-coated infantry, struggling in the press of their own numbers to get into line. The front ranks charged up the banks of the hedge concealing the British troops, shouting and cheering, confident that the flight of the large body of troops in their front had left the road open to them through the Allied centre. Picton's voice blared above the roar of cannon: "Rise up!"

The men of Kempt's brigade, crouched behind the hedge, leaped to their feet; the French saw the bank crowned by a long line of red, overlapping their column on either side. Every musket was at the present; a volley riddled the advancing mass; and as the French recoiled momentarily under it, Picton roared: "Charge! Hurrah!" and Kempt's warriors, with the British cheer the French had learned to dread, charged with bayonets levelled.

To the east of Donzelot, Marcognet's column was surging up the bank to where Pack's Highlanders waited, a little drawn back from the crest. "Ninety-second! Everything has given way in front of you!" Pack shouted. "You must charge!"

A yell of "Scotland ever!" answered him. The skirl of pipes soared above the din, and the men of the Black Watch, the Royals, and the Gordons, all with the deaths of comrades to avenge, hurled themselves through the hedge at the advancing column.

In Kempt's brigade, the Camerons, attacked by a devastating cross-fire from Bourgeois' column on their right, began to give way. Picton shouted to one of Uxbridge's Aides-de-Camp: "Rally the Highlanders!" The next instant he fell, shot through the right temple. Captain Seymour rode forward to obey this last command, but it was the Duke, watching the crash of the two Armies from the high ground in the centre, who galloped before him into the thick of the fight, and succeeded in rallying the Camerons and the hard-pressed Riflemen.

"Stand fast, Ninety-fifth! We must not be beaten!" he shouted. "What will they say in England?"

A ragged cheer answered him; he re-formed the 79th

himself, and directed them to fire upon the column that had driven them back, only withdrawing out of the heat of the battle when he saw that they stood firm.

The guns on both sides had ceased fire as the French and the British troops met, but in the valley smoke lay thick, and muskets spat and crackled. The French were hampered by the size of their own columns, but although the men of Picton's depleted division had checked their advance by the sheer ferocity of their charge, they could not hope to hold such overwhelming numbers at bay. West of the chaussée, the Cuirassiers, having routed the Lüneberg battalion, re-formed under the crest of the Allied position. Ignorant of what the reverse slope of the ground concealed, they charged up the bank, straight at Ompteda's men, hidden behind it. But the Germans had opened their ranks to permit the passage of cavalry through them. Before the Cuirassiers had reached the crest, they heard the thunder of hooves above them, and the next instant the Household Brigade was upon them, led by Uxbridge himself, at the head of the 1st Life Guards.

With white crests, and horses' manes flying, the Life Guards came up at full gallop and crashed upon the Cuirassiers in flank. The earth seemed to shudder beneath the shock. The Hyde Park soldiers never drew rein, but swept the Cuirassiers from the bank, and across the hollow road in the irresistible impetus of their charge. Swords rang against the cuirasses; someone yelled above the turmoil: "Strike at the neck!" and the Cuirassiers, already a little disorganized by their encounter with the German infantry, were flung back in fighting confusion. The Life Guards and the 1st Dragoon Guards hurled their left flank past the walls of La Haye Sainte in complete disorder, and scattered Quiot's brigade of infantry assailing the farm. The right flank of the Cuirassiers swerved sharply to the east, and plunged down on to the chaussée to escape from the fury of six-foot men on huge horses, who seemed to have no idea of charging at anything slower than a full gallop. Not more than half their number had crossed the chaussée to the valley where Donzelot was driving his congested ranks against Kempt's brigade, when the rest of the Household Cavalry, coming up on the left of the Life Guards, fell upon them in hard-riding squadrons, and crumpled them up. The *abattis*, so painstakingly built up by the Riflemen, was scattered in an instant; the Cuirassiers were cut down in hundreds, and the Dragoon Guards rode over them to charge full tilt into the column of French infantry pressing Kempt's men back.

At the same moment, an Aide-de-Camp rode up from the rear to the hedge beyond which Pack's Highlanders were fighting fiercely with the men of Marcognet's division. For one moment he stood there, closely observing the state of the battle raging in the valley; then he took off his cocked-hat and waved it forwards.

There was a yell of: "Now then, Scots Greys!" and the next instant the whole of the Union Brigade came thundering up the reverse slope. The French, disordered through their inability to deploy their enormous column before the Highlanders charged them, appalled hardly more by the fury of the kilted devils who rushed on them than by the unearthly music of the pipes playing *Scots, Wha' Hae* in the hell of blood and smoke and clashing arms that filled the valley, heard the cavalry thundering towards them, and looked up to see great gray horses clearing the hedge above them.

They fell back. In the valley, officers were shouting to the Gordons to wheel back by sections to let the cavalry pass through. The Scots Greys tightened their grips, and came slipping and scrambling down the bank, shouting: "Hurrah, Ninety-second! Scotland for ever!" as they caught sight of the red-feathered bonnets in the press and the smoke below.

Greys, Royals, and Inniskillings, riding almost abreast, poured over the hedge and down into the seething valley. The Gordons were yelling: "Go at them, the Greys! Scotland for ever!" and snatching at stirrup-leathers as the Greys rode through them, so that they too were borne forwards in this terrific charge. Somewhere, lost in the smoke, a pipe-major was coolly playing *Hey, Johnny Cope*, *are ye waukin' yet?* while all around sounded screams, shouts, musketry-fire, and the clash of steel.

Many of the horses and their riders were brought down by musketry-balls or the desperate thrust of bayonets, but the cavalry charge had caught Marcognet's column unawares and in confusion. The Union Brigade rode over the column, lopping off heads with their sabres, while the Gordons, who had been carried forward with them, did deadly work with the bayonet. To the right, where Donzelot's men had fought their way through Kempt's thin lines to the crest of the position, the Royal Dragoons, unchecked by the frontal fire that met them, charged straight for the leading column of the division. The column faced about and tried to retreat over the hedge, but there was no time to get to safety before the Royals were in their midst, their sabres busy and their horses squealing, biting, and striking out with their iron-shod forefeet. Between the Greys and the Royals, the Inniskillings, with their blood-curdling howl, broke through Donzelot's rear brigades. As the Royals, capturing an Eagle, charged on over the slaughtered leading column to the supporting ones behind it, and the Greys rode down Marcognet's men, the French, utterly demoralized, began throwing down their arms and crying for quarter.

The Household Brigade, having broken the Cuirassiers and smashed their way through Bourgeois' rear column, dashed on, deaf to the trumpets sounding the Rally and to the voices of Uxbridge and Lord Edward trying to recall them, up the slope towards the great French battery on the ridge. The Union Brigade, leaving behind them a plain strewn with dead and wounded, and prisoners being herded to the rear, charged after the Household troops, and galloped up the slope to within half-carbine shot of where Napoleon himself was standing, by the farm of La Belle Alliance.

A Colonel of the Greys shouted: "Charge! Charge the guns!" and his men dashed after him, through a storm of shot, laming the horses, cutting the traces, and sabring the gunners.

The cavalry charge had put almost all Count D'Erlon's Corps d'Armée to rout, but it had been carried too far. Ahead, solid columns of infantry were advancing from the French rear; and behind, from either flank, Lancers and Cuirassiers were riding to cut off the retreat.

A voice cried: "Royals, form on me!" The Greys and the Inniskillings on the ridge, their horses blown, themselves badly mauled, looked round in vain for their officers, and tried to re-form to meet the onset of the French cavalry. The Colonel who had led them in the charge towards the battery had been seen riding amongst the guns like a maniac, with both hands lopped off at the wrists, and his reins held between his teeth; but he had fallen, and a dozen others with him. A Sergeant called out: "Come on, lads! That's the road home!" and the gallant little band rode straight for the oncoming cavalry that separated it from its own lines.

A pitiful remnant broke through. On the Allied left wing, Vandeleur flung forward his Light Dragoons to cover the retreat. They cheered the Heavies as they passed them, caught the Lancers in flank, and drove them back in disorder. The survivors of the Union Brigade reached the shelter of their own lines, having pierced three columns, captured two Eagles, wrecked fifteen guns, put twenty-five more temporarily out of action, and taken nearly three thousand prisoners.

CHAPTER XXIII

THE great infantry attack on the Allied left centre had failed. The Household Brigade had repulsed Quiot from La Haye Sainte; Bourgeois and Donzelot had been forced to retreat with heavy loss; and Marcognet's division was shattered. The remaining column, led by Durutte, had had more success, but was forced to retire in the general retreat. Durutte had advanced against Papelotte, and had driven Prince Bernhard's Nassauers out of the village. These re-formed, and in their turn drove out the French. Vandeleur's brigade of Light Cavalry charged the column, and it drew off, but in good order.

On the Allied side the losses were enormous. Kempt and Pack could no longer hope to hold the line, and Lambert's brigade was ordered up from Mont St. Jean to reinforce them. The Union Brigade had been cut to pieces; the Household troops were reduced to a few squadrons. Of the Generals, Picton had been killed outright in the first charge; Sir William Ponsonby, leading the Union Brigade on a hack-horse, was lying dead on the field with his Aide-de-Camp beside him; and Pack and Kempt, on whom the command of the 5th Division had developed, were wounded. Lord Edward Somerset, unhorsed, his hat gone, the lap of his coat torn off, got to his own lines miraculously unscathed.

Lord Uxbridge, who, when the Life Guards and the Dragoon Guards ignored the Rally, had ridden back to bring up the Blues in support, only to find that they had galloped into first line before ever they had passed La Haye Sainte, listened in contemptuous silence to the congratulations of the Duke's suite upon the brilliant success of his charge. He turned away, remarking to Seymour, with a disdainful curve to the mouth: "That *Troupe dorée* seems to think the battle is over. But had I, when I sounded the Rally, found only four well-formed squadrons coming on at an easy trot we should have captured a score of guns and avoided these shocking losses. Well! I deviated from my own principle: the *carrière* once begun the leader is no better than any other man. I should have placed myself at the head of the second line."

During D'Erlon's attack, the cannonading had been kept up on the other parts of the line, while, round Hougoumont, the struggle still raged with unabated fury, more and more men of Reille's Corps being employed in the attempt to capture the château. The stubborn resistance of the Guards inside the château and garden, and of Saltoun's Light Companies, holding the orchard and the

344

alley to the north in the teeth of all opposition, awoke a corresponding determination in the French generals. No attempt was made to mask the post; Jérôme, Foy and Bachelu were all sent against it; and a howitzer Troop was summoned up to drop shells upon the buildings. At a quarter to three, the roof of the château was blazing, and the Duke, observing it, scrawled one of his brief messages in his pocket-book: "*I see that the fire has communicated from the Haystack to the roof of the Château. You must, however, still keep your men in those parts to which the fire does not reach. Take care that no men are lost by the falling in of the roof or floors. After they will have fallen in, occupy the ruined walls inside the gardens; particularly if it should be possible for the Enemy to pass through the Embers in the inside of the house.*"

He tore out the leaves, and folded them, and handed them to Colonel Audley, with a curt instruction.

The Colonel made his way to the right, behind Alten's division. The going was hard, the ground being heavy from the recent storm, and the smoke from the shells bursting all round making it difficult to see the way. He caught a glimpse of some squadrons of Dutch Carabiniers, drawn up considerably to the rear, with their left against the chaussée, out of range of the cannon-shots; passed by General Kruse's Nassauers, held in reserve; and arrived at length on the plateau overlooking Hougoumont. Skirting a regiment of Dragoons of the Legion, who announced themselves to belong to General Dörnberg's brigade, the Colonel took a deep breath, gave his horse a pat on the neck, saying: "Now for it, my lad!" and plunged forward into the region of shot and shell-bursts. As he rode past Maitland's Guards, lying down in line four-deep above the bend of the hollow road to the south, a cannon-ball screamed past his head, and made him duck involuntarily. An officer commanding a Troop of Horse Artillery, a little to the west of the 1st Guards, saw him, and laughed, shouting: "Whither away, Audley?"

"To Hougoumont. Ramsay, where the devil has Byng's brigade got to?"

"In there, most of 'em," replied Ramsay, pointing to

345

the Hougoumont enclosures. "They tell me the ditches are piled up with the dead: don't add to their number, if you can avoid it!"

"Damn you, I'm shaking with fright already!" called Audley over his shoulder.

Ramsay laughed, and waved him on. The last sight Colonel Audley had of him was sitting his horse beside his guns, as cool as though engaged on field manœuvres, waving his hand, and laughing.

He set spurs to his horse, and galloped forward into the smoke and the heat of the fight round Hougoumont. He found himself soon amongst what seemed to be a steady stream of wounded, making their painful way to the rear. The lane behind the château, which was flanked by ditches and elm trees, was lined with some of the Light Companies of the Guards regiments, and in the orchard beyond a never-ending skirmish was going on. From the cover of the tree-trunks, and the ditches, the Guards, stepping over their own dead, were upholding their proud reputation. The carnage was appalling, but Colonel Audley, making his way to the northern wicket leading into the château, could see no signs of dismay in even the youngest face. When a man fell, with a queer little grunt as the ball struck him, those near him would do no more than glance at him in the intervals of reloading their muskets. They were intent on their marksmanship, their strained eyes staring ahead through the drifting smoke, their muskets at the ready.

Except for a shot which carried away his horse's ear, and caused the poor beast to rear up, snorting and squealing, the Colonel reached the wicket-gate without sustaining any injury, and penetrated into the courtyard.

The scene outside in the enclosures faded to insignificance before the inferno within the walls. The haystack was still blazing, and not only the roof of the château but also a cow-shed where the wounded had been lying, had caught fire. The heat was overpowering; shells were falling on the buildings; horses, caught in flaming stables, were screaming; a few men, unrecognizable in torn and blackened uniforms, were working desperately to drag the last of the wounded out of the cow-shed, while others, forming a chain, were pouring bucketful after bucketful of water on the smoking walls. On every side sounded the crash of falling timbers, the bursting of shells, and the groans of men, who, unable to move for shattered legs or ghastly stomach wounds, were scorched by the fire and driven mad by pain and thirst. A Sergeant of the Coldstream shouted to Audley above the din that Colonel Macdonnell was in the garden, and thither Audley made his way, out of the heat and the fire, into what seemed an oasis set in the middle of hell.

Reille's guns were all trained on the courtyard and the surrounding buildings, and scarcely any shells had fallen in the neat garden which Barbara Childe had planned to visit again in the summer. Roses were blooming in the formal beds; the long turf-walks between were shaded by fruit trees, and perfectly smooth. The Colonel had no time to waste in gazing on this refreshing scene; but its contrast with the horror of the courtyard most forcibly struck him as he strode towards the high brick wall on the southern side. Here the defenders were for the most part gathered, some firing through the rough loopholes, others mounted on the wooden platforms, and firing over the top of the wall into the infantry in the orchard and the fringe of the wood beyond. Colonel Audley soon found Macdonnell, and delivered the Duke's message. The big Scot read it, and gave a short laugh. "He need not worry: we can hold the place. But send more ammunition down to us, Audley, if you can: we're running damned short. How is it going along the rest of the line?"

"The 5th Division and the Heavy Brigades have repulsed an infantry attack on the left centre, sir. No one has it as hot as you, so far."

"Ah! Well, no one has troops like my fellows. Tell the Duke there's no talk of surrender here."

Making his way back again through the house and the courtyard. Colonel Audley once more reached the wicket-gate, and found his horse, which he had tethered there, apparently not much troubled by the loss of his ear. He mounted, and galloped back to the main position, crossing the hollow road just below the spot where the few companies of Byng's brigade not engaged in the struggle about Hougoumont were posted. He did not see Byng himself, but gave Macdonnell's message to a senior officer, who begged him to carry it farther, to the Prince of Orange's Staff. He rode on towards Maitland's brigade, where he was informed the Prince was to be found, but was told there by Maitland himself that the Prince had moved to the left, towards Alten's division.

"I'll send one of my family, if you like," Maitland said. "The trouble is to get the carts through to Hougoumont."

"You have enough on your hands, sir, by the look of it. I must pass Alten's division in any case."

Maitland had his glass to his eye, and replied in a pre-occupied tone: "Very well. I don't like the look of those fellows moving up round the eastern side of Hougoumont. I wonder—no, never mind: off with you!"

The Colonel left him, still watching the stealthy advance of a large body of French Light Troops who were creeping along the eastern hedge of the Hougoumont enclosure with the evident intention of turning Saltoun's left flank, and galloped on towards the centre of the line.

The Prince of Orange, who was surrounded by numerous Staff, was not difficult to pick out. He was wearing his English Hussar dress, with an orange cockade in his hat, and was standing beside Halkett's brigade on the right flank of the division, his glass, like Maitland's, trained on the advancing French skirmishers. The Colonel rode towards him, but arrived in his presence in a precipitate fashion which he did not intend. A shell, bursting within a few yards of him, brought his horse down in mid-gallop; the Colonel was shot over his head, feeling at the same moment something like a red-hot knife sear his left thigh, and fell almost at the feet of Lord March.

The explosion, and the heavy fall, knocked him sense-less for a moment or two, but he soon came to himself, to find March's face bent over him. He blinked at it, recollected his surroundings, and tried to laugh. "Good God, what a way to arrive!"

"Are you hurt, Charles?"

"No, merely dazed," replied the Colonel, grasping his friend's hand, and pulling himself up. "My horse killed?"

"One of the men shot him. His fore legs were blown off at the knees. We thought you were gone. You are hurt! I'll get you to the rear."

"You'll do no such thing!" said the Colonel, feeling his leg through his blood-stained breeches. "I think a splinter must have caught me. I'll get one of Halkett's sawbones to tie it up. I was looking for you fellows. I've been charged by Colonel Macdonnell to see that more ammunition is sent down to him."

"I'll pass the message. Things are looking rather black at the moment." He pointed towards the hedge of Hougoumont.

At that moment the Prince cantered up, looking pale and rather excited. "March! I've ordered the Light Troops not to stir from their position! They were forming to move against those skirmishers who are trying to turn Saltoun's left flank, but I'm sure the Duke will have seen that movement, and will make his own dispositions. You agree?"

"Yes, sir."

"Eh, *mon Dieu*, if one knew what were best to do—but no, I'm right! Charles, go at once to the rear: you are bleeding like a pig! My dear fellow, I have so much on my hands—ah, I was right! I knew it! See there, March! The Guards are moving down to cut off this attempt! All is well then, and it is a mercy I would not permit the Light Troops to go. March, take Charles to the rear, and find him a horse—no, a surgeon! *Au revoir*, Charles. I wish—but you see how it is: I have not a moment!"

He flew off again; Audley's eyes twinkled; he said: "Has he been like this all day?"

March smiled. "This is nothing. But you mustn't laugh at him; he's doing well—quite well, if only he wouldn't

349

get excited. Good, there's one of the assistant-surgeons! Finlayson! Patch Colonel Audley up, will you? I'll get you a trooper from somewhere, Charles. Take care of yourself!"

The Colonel's wound was found to have been caused, as he suspected, by a splinter. This was speedily, if somewhat painfully, extracted, and his leg bound up, by which time one of the Sergeants of the 30th Regiment had come up, leading a trooper. The Colonel mounted, declaring himself to be in splendid shape, and rode off as fast as his heavy steed would bear him.

The Duke was standing on Alten's right flank, on the highest part of the position. The time was a little after three o'clock, and Colonel Audley rejoined his lordship just as the sadly diminished Household Brigade was returning from a charge led by Uxbridge against a French force once more attacking the farm of La Haye Sainte. Baring had been reinforced by two companies after the overthrow of D'Erlon's columns, and the little garrison, in spite of having lost possession of the orchard and garden, was stoutly defending the buildings. The second attack, which was not very rigorously pressed, had been repulsed, and the charge of the Household Cavalry seemed to have succeeded. The French infantry had drawn off again, and except for the continued but not very severe cannonade against the whole Allied front, and the bitter fight about Hougoumont, a lull had fallen on the battle. Colonel Audley seized the opportunity to ride to the rear, where, on the chaussée a little below Mont St. Jean, his groom was stationed with his remaining horses. He fell in with Gordon on the way, and learned from him that the head of Bülow's corps was reported to have reached St. Lambert, five miles to the east of La Belle Alliance.

"Coming along in their own good time, damn them!" said Gordon. "They say the roads are almost impassable, but I'll tell you what, Charles, if we don't get some reinforcements for our left centre before we're attacked again we shall be rompéd."

"Where's Lambert?"

"Just come up into the front line, which means we haven't a single man in reserve on the left—unless you count Bylandt's heroes as reserves."

"I shouldn't care to trust to them," admitted the Colonel. "Did their officers ever succeed in re-forming them?"

"I don't know. Pack's fellows have started a tale that they've all gone off for a picnic in the Forest. I never saw such a damnable rout in all my life! It was God's mercy it happened where it did, and not before some of our raw regiments. You were there, weren't you? Is it true that Picton's rascals fired after them?"

"They tried to, but we restrained them. Does anyone know what is going to happen next?"

"I certainly don't. All I do know is that I wish to God we had some of the fellows stationed at Hal here," replied Gordon candidly.

For over half an hour no sign of a fresh attack was made by enemy. Speculation was rife in the Allied lines; no one could imagine what the next move was going to be, or against what part of the line it would be directed. At Hougoumont, all but two companies of Byng's brigade, which were left to guard the Colours, had been drawn into the fight in the orchards and wood. Colonel Hepburn, whom the Prince of Orange had seen advancing with the remaining companies of the Scots Guards to Lord Saltoun's relief, had taken over the command from him after assisting him to drive Foy's men out of the orchard; and Saltoun had retired to his brigade, with just one-third of the men of the Light Companies whom he had led into action.

The gradual absorption of Byng's entire brigade in the defence of Hougoumont made it imperative to reinforce the right of the line. Shortly before four o'clock, an Aide-de-Camp was sent off to bring up some young Brunswick troops, held in reserve, to fill the gap. This had hardly been accomplished when the firing on the Allied right centre suddenly became so violent that after a very few minutes of it the Duke withdrew his troops farther back from the crest of the position. Old soldiers with a score of battles behind them admitted, as they lay flat on their bellies under the rain of grape, round-shot, and spherical case, that they had never experienced such a cannonading. Occasionally a greater explosion than the rest would roar above the din as an ammunition waggon was struck, and a column of smoke would rise vertically in the air, spreading like an umbrella.

Everyone knew that the cannonade was the prelude to an attack, but when those on the high ground on the right of the Charleroi road saw forming across the valley on the ridge of La Belle Alliance, not infantry divisions but huge masses of cavalry, they were thunderstruck. It soon became evident that the attack was going to be directed against the right centre of the Allied line, for the squadrons, which had first appeared on the east of the Charleroi road, crossed it, obliquing to their left, and advanced slowly but in beautiful order through the fields of deep corn that lay between the advance posts of Hougoumont and La Haye Sainte.

Twenty-four squadrons of Milhaud's Cuirassiers led the cavalcade in first line, their burnished breast-plates and helmets making them look like a wall of steel. They were supported by nineteen squadrons of the Light Cavalry of the Guard: red Lancers with high white plumes, gaudy horse-trappings, and fluttering pennons, in second line; and, in third line, the Chasseurs à Cheval in green dolmans embroidered richly with gold, black bearskin shakos on their heads, and fur-trimmed pelisses swinging from their shoulders.

It was a formidable array, terrifying to inexperienced troops, but regarded by the Staff officers who watched its assembly with a good deal of criticism.

"Good God, this is too premature!" Lord Fitzroy exclaimed. "They cannot mean to attack unshaken infantry with cavalry alone!"

"Perhaps Ney's gone mad," suggested Canning hopefully. "What the devil has he done with his infantry columns?"

"I fancy the Prussians must be at something on the left," said the Duke, overhearing this interchange.

"I shall believe in the Prussians when I see them," remarked Canning to Colonel Audley.

There was no opportunity for further speculation. Orders were sent to the brigade to prepare to withstand cavalry attacks; Aides-de-Camp dashed off through the hail of shot; and the troops lying on the ground beside their arms were quickly formed into two lines of squares, placed chequer-wise behind the crest of the position. In support, all the available cavalry was mustered; the two British Heavy Brigades, now reduced to a few squadrons, under the command of Lord Edward Somerset; Trip's Carabiniers; seven squadrons of Van Merlen's Light Cavalry; a regiment of Brunswick Hussars; Colonel Arendtschildt's brigade of the Legion; and a part of Dörnberg's and Grant's brigades. A demonstration by some French Lancers by the Nivelles road had succeeded in drawing off two of Grant's regiments and one of Dörnberg's, so that of Grant's brigade only the 7th Hussars, who had suffered great loss at Genappe, on the previous day, were left to meet the attack of French cavalry; and of Dörnberg's only the 1st and 2nd Light Dragoons of the Legion. In all, it was a meagre force to throw against the forty-three squadrons assembling between Hougoumont and La Haye Sainte, and the want of the two British brigades guarding the left flank of the line until the Prussians should arrive to relieve them began to be acutely felt.

The Brunswickers, who had been brought up to fill the gap on Maitland's right, were raw troops, and the Duke wisely strengthened them by sending for a regiment from Colonel Mitchell's brigade, posted west of the Nivelles road, and stationing it between their two squares. Light troops were ordered to fall back upon the squares immediately in their rear, irrespective of nation or brigade; the artillery was instructed to keep up a steady fire upon the advancing cavalry until the last possible moment, and then to run for safety to the infantry squares; guns were double-loaded with shot and canister; and the squares formed four-deep, the front ranks kneeling, so that each square presented four faces bristling with bayonets.

The French artillery-fire ceased as the squadrons began to advance, at a slow trot. Owing to the Duke's having withdrawn his right centre slightly down the reverse slope of the position to protect it from the cannonading, the French, advancing to the crest, saw no infantry opposing them. They were met by a devastating fire of artillery, but though their front ranks were disordered by the gaps torn in the lines, they pushed on intrepidly. As the leading squadrons breasted the rise, the trumpeters sounded the Charge, and the Cuirassiers, cheering, and shouting "*En avant!*" spurred forward, and saw ahead of them, not an army in retreat, as they had been led to suppose, but motionless squares, awaiting their charge in grim British silence.

The British gunners, remaining at their posts until almost surrounded by the surge of horsemen, were firing at point-blank range. As the Cuirassiers charged up to the batteries, the terrible case-shot brought them down in tangled heaps of men and horses together. When the muzzles of their guns almost touched the leading squadrons, the artillery men, some detaching the wheels from their guns and bowling them along with them, rushed to the nearest squares and flung themselves down under the bayonets.

In a cacophony of shouts, trumpet-calls, and the discharge of carbines, the Cuirassiers charged down upon the silent squares. When they came to within thirty paces, the order to fire upon them was given, and a storm of bullets rattled against the steel breast-plates, for all the world like hailstones on a glass roof. Those in the rear ranks of the squares were employed in reloading the muskets, and the repeated volleys caused the advancing columns to split, and to swerve off to right and left, only to receive a still more devastating flank-fire from the sides of the squares. In a very few moments all order was lost, the Cuirassiers jostling one another in the spaces between the squares, some riding against the red walls to discharge their carbines and pistols into the set faces upturned behind the gleaming *chevaux de frise* of bayonets; others trotting round and round in an attempt to find a weak spot to break through.

No sooner had the Cuirassiers passed the first line of squares than the artillerymen dashed back to their guns, to meet with renewed fire the second columns of Lancers and Chasseurs, ascending the southern slope in support of the Cuirassiers. The same tactics were repeated, with the same results. The squadrons, already thrown into some disorder by the charges of case-shot exploding amongst them, obliqued before the frontal fire of the squares. Soon the whole plateau was covered with horsemen: Lancers, Chasseurs and Cuirassiers, mixed in inextricable confusion, spreading right up to the second line of squares. Man after man fell in the British ranks, but the gaps were always filled, and the squares remained unbroken. Skirmishers, taking cover behind the carcasses of dead horses, kept up a steady fire on the congested mass of the enemy. Wounded and dead sprawled beneath the hooves; and unhorsed Cuirassiers cast off their encumbering breast-plates to struggle back through the press to the safety of their own lines. When the confusion was at its height, the Allied cavalry charged up from the rear and drove the French from the plateau.

They retired, leaving the ground littered with horses, men, piles of cuirasses, and accoutrements; but no sooner had the last of them disappeared over the crest than the punishing cannonade burst forth again, while Ney re-formed his muddled squadrons in the valley.

The attack, though it had not broken the squares, had considerably weakened them. The Duke, riding down the line, heartening the troops with the sight of his well-known figure and the sound of his loud, cheerful voice, sent Aides-de-Camp galloping off to bring up Clinton's division, in reserve on the west of the Nivelles road.

This consisted of General Adam's British Light Brigade, comprising the 1st battalion of Sir John Colborne's Fighting 52nd, the 71st Highland Regiment, and two battalions of the 95th Rifles; Colonel Du Plat's brigade of the Legion; and Hew Halkett's Hanoverian Landwehr battalions.

Colonel Audley was one of those sent on this errand,

and galloping through the hail of shot, reached the comparative quiet of the ground west of the Nivelles road, to find Lord Hill awaiting the expected instructions to send reinforcements from his Corps into the front line. The Colonel, parched with thirst, coughing from the smoke of the shells, his wounded thigh throbbing, and his horse blown, sketched a salute, and thrust the Duke's message into his hand.

"Having a hot time of it in the centre, aren't you?" said Hill. He cast a glance at the Colonel's face, and added in his kindly way: "You look as though a drink would do you good. Hurt?"

"No, sir!" gasped the Colonel, trying to get the smoke out of his lungs. "But we must have reinforcements before they come on again!"

"Oh yes! you shall have them!" Hill nodded to his younger brother and Aide-de-Camp. "Give Audley some of that wine of yours, Clement."

Audley, gratefully accepting a long-necked bottle, drank deeply, and sat recovering his breath while Lord Hill issued his instructions. It was his task to lead Adam's brigade to a strategic but dangerous position between the north-east angle of Hougoumont and the point on the higher ground behind the hollow road where the Brunswick troops stood huddled in two squares, with one British between. The boys, for they were little more, in their sombre uniforms and death's-head badges, were shaking, kept together only by the exertions of their officers, and the moral support afforded by the sight of the seasoned British regiment separating their squares.

Hew Halkett was brought up in support of the Brunswickers on Maitland's right; Du Plat was formed on the slope behind Hougoumont; and Adam's brigade, forming line four deep, came up to fill the interval between the Brunswickers and Hougoumont. The brigade was met by the Duke in person, who pointed to the cloud of skirmishers assailing the left flank of the Guards defending the orchard, and briefly ordered them to: "Drive those fellows away!"

The artillery-fire, which was mowing the ranks down, ceased, and the men, lying on the ground, were again ordered to form squares. The cavalry came riding over the crest as before, but this time it was seen that a considerable portion of their force was kept in compact order, and took no part in the attempt to break through the infantry squares. These horsemen were evidently formed to attack the Allied cavalry, but no sooner had the previous confusion of squadrons splitting and obliquing to right and left been repeated than the Allied cavalry, not waiting to be attacked, advanced to meet them and again drove them over the crest and down the slope.

The same tactics were repeated time after time, but with the same lack of success. The men forming the squares grew to welcome the cavalry attacks as a relief from the terrible cannonading that filled the intervals between them.

The Duke, who seemed to be everywhere at once, generally riding far ahead of the cortège that still galloped devotedly after him, was pale and abstracted, but gave no other sign of anxiety than the frequent sliding in and out of its socket of his telescope. If he saw a square wavering, he threw himself into it, regardless of all entreaties not to risk his life, and rallied it by the very fact of his presence.

"Never mind! We'll win this battle yet!" he said, and his men believed him, and breathed more freely when they caught a glimpse of that low cocked-hat and the cold eyes and bony nose beneath it. They did not love him, for he did not love them, but there was not a man serving under him who had not complete confidence in him.

"Hard pounding, this, gentlemen," he said, when the cannonade was at its fiercest. "Let's see who will pound the longest."

When the foreign diplomats remonstrated with him, he said bluntly: "My Army and I know each other exactly, gentlemen. The men will do for me what they will do for no one else."

Lord Uxbridge led two squadrons of the Household

357

Brigade against a large body of cavalry advancing to attack the squares, and although he could not drive it back, he managed to hold it in check. Major Lloyd fell, mortally wounded, beside his battery. Sometimes the Cuirassiers succeeded in cutting men off from the angles of the squares, but before they could escape to the rear, Staff Officers galloped after them and got them back to their positions. At times, the squares, growing smaller as the men fell in them, were lost to sight in the sea of horsemen all round them.

Between four and five o'clock, convinced at last that no flanking attack was contemplated on his right, the Duke sent to order Baron Chassé up from Braine-l'Alleud.

Staff Officers were looking anxious; artillerymen, seeing little but masses of enemy cavalry swarming all over the position, waited in momentary expectation of receiving the order to retreat. The heat on the plateau was fast becoming unbearable. Reserves brought up from the rear felt themselves to be marching into a gigantic oven, and young soldiers, hearing for the first time the peculiar hum that filled the air, stared about them fearfully through the smoke, flinching as the shots hissed past their heads, and asking nervously:"What makes that humming noise like bees?"

Colonel Audley, riding back from an errand to the right wing, had his second horse killed under him close to a Troop of Horse Artillery, drawn up in the interval between two Brunswick squares, in a slight hollow below the brow of the position, north of Hougoumont. He sprang clear, but heard a voice call out: "Hi! Don't mask my guns! Anything I can do for you, sir?"

"You can give me a horse!" replied the Colonel, trying to recover his breath. He looked into a lean, humorous face, shaded by the jut of a black, crested helmet, and asked: "Who are you?"

"G. Troop—Colonel Dickson's, under the command of Captain Mercer—at your service!"

"Oh yes! I know." The Colonel's eyes travelled past him to a veritable bank of dead Cuirassiers and horses, not twenty paces in front of his guns. He gave an awed whistle. "Good God!"

"Yes, we're having pretty hot work of it here," replied Mercer. A shell came whizzing over the crest, and fell in the mud not far from his Troop, and lay there, its fuse spitting and hissing. He broke off to admonish his men, some of whom had flung themselves down on the ground. The shell burst at last, without, however, doing much damage; and the nonchalant Captain turned back to Colonel Audley, resuming, as though only a minor inter-ruption had occurred: "—pretty hot work of it here. We wait till those steel-clad gentry come over the rise, and then we give 'em a dose of round-shot with a case over it. Terrible effect it has. I've seen a whole front rank come down from the effects of the case."

"Do you mean that you stand by your guns through-out?"

"Take a look at those squares, sir," recommended Mercer, jerking his head towards the Brunswickers, who were lying on the ground to right and left of his rear. "You can't, at the moment, but if you care to wait you'll see them form squares, huddled together like sheep. If we scuttled for safety amongst them, they'd break and run. They're only children—not one above eighteen, I'll swear. Gives 'em confidence to see us here."

"You're a damned brave man!" said the Colonel, taking the bridle of the trooper which a driver had led up.

"Oh, we don't give a button for the cavalry!" replied Mercer. "The worst is this infernal cannonading. It plays the devil with us. We've been pestered by skirmishers, too, which is a damned nuisance. Only way I can stop my fellows wasting their charges on them is to parade up and down the bank in front of my guns. That's nervous work, if you like!"

"I imagine it might be," said the Colonel, with a grin. "Don't get your Troop cut up too much, or his lordship won't be pleased."

"The artillery won't get any of the credit for this day's work in any case, so what's the odds?" Mercer replied.

"Fraser knows what we're about. He was here a short time ago, very much upset from burying poor Ramsay."

The Colonel had one foot in the stirrup, but he paused and said sharply: "Is Ramsay dead?"

"Fraser buried him on the field not half an hour ago. Bolton's gone too, I believe. Was Norman Ramsay a friend of yours, sir? Pride of our Service, you know."

"Yes," replied Audley curtly, and hoisted himself into the saddle, wincing a little from the pain of his wounded thigh. "I must push on before your steel-clad gentry come up again. Good luck to you!"

"The same to you, sir, and you'd better hurry. Cannonade's slackening."

The pause following the third onset of the cavalry was of longer duration than those which had preceded it. Ney had sent for reinforcements, and was reassembling his squadrons. To Milhaud's and Lefebvre-Desnouettes' original forty-three squadrons were now added both Kellermann's divisions and thirteen squadrons of Count Guyot's Dragoons and Grenadiers à Cheval, making a grand total of seventy-seven squadrons. Not a foot of the ground, a third of a mile in width, lying between Hougoumont and La Haye Sainte, could be seen for the glittering mass of horsemen that covered it. It was an array to strike terror into the bravest heart. They advanced in columns of squadrons: gigantic Carabiniers in white with gold breast-plates; Dragoons wearing tiger-skin helmets under their brass casques, and carrying long guns at their saddle-bows; Grenadiers in Imperial blue, with towering bearskin shakos; steel-fronted Cuirassiers; gay Chasseurs; and white-plumed Lancers, riding under the flutter of their own pennons. They did not advance with the brilliant dash of the British brigades, but at a purposeful trot. As they approached the Allied position the earth seemed to shake under them, and the sound of the horses' hooves was like dull thunder, swelling in volume. Fifteen thousand of Napoleon's proudest horsemen were sent against the Allied infantry squares, to break through the Duke's hard-held centre. They came over the crest in wave upon wave; riding up in the teeth of the guns until the entire plateau was a turbulent sea of bright, shifting colours, tossing plumes, and gleaming sabres. The fallen men and horses encumbering the ground hampered their advance, and once again the musketry-fire from the front faces of the squares caused the squadrons to swerve off to right and left. Lancers, Grenadiers, Dragoons jostled one another in the press, their formation lost; but the tide swept on up to the second line of squares, and surrounded them. Some of the cavalry pushed right down the slope to the artillery-waggons in the rear, and slew the drivers and horses, but though men were dropping all the time in the squares, the gaps were instantly filled, and when a square became disordered, the sharp command: "Close up!" was obeyed before the cavalry could take advantage of the momentary confusion. For three-quarters of an hour the squares were almost swamped by the overwhelming hordes that pressed up to them, fell back again before the fire of the muskets, and rode round and round, striking with swords and sabres at the bayonets, discharging carbines, and making isolated dashes at the corners of the squares.

The French were driven off the plateau, when in hopeless confusion, by the charge of the Allied cavalry, but they retreated only to re-form. The cannonading burst forth again, and the sorely tried infantry, deafened by the roar of artillery, many of them wounded and all of them worn out by the grim struggle to keep their ranks closed, lay down on the torn ground, each man wondering in his heart what would be the end.

When the squadrons came over the crest again, Colonel Audley was nearly caught amongst them. He was mounted on his last horse, the Earl of Worth's Rufus, and owed his preservation to the hunter's pace. He snatched out his sword when he saw the cavalry bearing down upon him, threw off a lance by his right side, and clapping his spurs into Rufus's flanks, galloped for his life. One of Maitland's squares opened its files to receive him, and he rode into the middle of it and the files closed behind him.

"Hallo, Audley!" drawled a tall Major, who was having

sticking-plaster put on a sabre-cut. "That was a near thing, wasn't it?"

"Too damned near for my taste!" replied Audley, sliding out of the saddle and looping Rufus's bridle over his arm. He eased his wounded leg, with a grimace. "Seen anything of the Duke, Stuart?"

"Not quite lately. He went off towards the Brunswickers, I think. Some of those fellows seem to revel in this sort of thing."

"The younger ones don't like it."

The surgeon, having finished his work on the Major's arm, bustled away, and the Major, drawing his tunic on again, said, with a grave look: "What do you make of it?"

Audley returned the look. "Pretty black."

The Major nodded. He buttoned up his coat, and said: "We don't see much of it here, you know. Nothing but smoke and this damned cavalry. One of the artillery fellows who took cover in our square during the last charge said he thought it was all over with us."

"Not it! We shall win through!"

"Oh, not a doubt! But damme, if ever I saw anything like this cavalry affair! Look at them, riding round and round! Makes you feel giddy to watch them." He glanced round the square, and sighed. "God, my poor regiment!" He saw a slight stir taking place in one of the ranks, and hurried off towards the wall of red, shouting: "Close up, there! Stand fast, my lads! We'll soon have them over the hill!"

The inside of the square was like a hospital, with wounded men lying all over the ground amongst the ammunition-boxes and the débris of accoutrements. Those of the doctors attached to the regiment who had not gone to the rear were busy with bandages and sticking-plaster, but there was very little they could do to ease the sufferings of the worst cases. From time to time, a man fell in the ranks, and crawled between the legs of his comrades into the square. The dead lay amongst the living, some with limbs twisted in a last agony, and sightless eyes glaring up at the chasing clouds; others as though asleep, their eyelids mercifully closed, and their heads pillowed on their arms.

Almost at Audley's feet, a boy lay in a sticky pool of his own blood. He looked very young; there was a faint smile on his dead lips, and one hand lay palm upwards on the ground, the fingers curling inwards in an oddly pathetic gesture. Audley was looking down at him when he heard his name feebly called. He turned his head and saw Lord Harry Alastair not far from him, lying on the ground, propped up by knapsacks.

He stepped over the dead boy at his feet, and went to Harry, and dropped on his knee beside him. "Harry! Are you badly hurt?"

"I don't know. I don't think I can be," Harry replied, with the ghost of a smile. "Only I don't seem able to move my legs. As a matter of fact, I can't feel anything below my waist."

The Colonel had seen death too many times not to recognize it now in Harry's drawn face and clouding eyes. He took one of the boy's hands and held it, saying gently: "That's famous. We must get you to the rear as soon as these hordes of cavalry have drawn off."

"I'm so tired!" Harry said, with a long sigh. "Is George safe?"

"I hope so. I don't really know, old fellow."

"Give him my love, if you see him." He closed his eyes, but opened them again after a minute or two, and said: "It's awful, isn't it?"

"Yes. The worst fight I ever was in."

"Well, I'm glad I was in it, anyway. To tell you the truth, I haven't liked it as much as I thought I should. It's seeing one's friends go, one after the other, and being so hellish frightened oneself."

"I know."

"Do you think we can hold out, Charles?"

"Yes, of course we can, and we will."

"By Jove, it'll be grand if we beat Boney after all!" Harry said drowsily. A doctor bent over a man lying beside him. The Colonel said urgently: "Can't you get this boy to the rear when the cavalry draws off again?"

A cursory glance was cast at Harry. "Waste of time," said the doctor. "I'm sorry, but I've enough on my hands with those I *can* save."

The Colonel said no more. Harry seemed to be dropping asleep. Audley stayed holding his hand, but looked up at a mounted officer of the Royal Staff Corps who was standing close by. "What's happening?"

"Our cavalry's coming up. By God, in the very nick of time too! I think Grant must have brought back his fellows from the Nivelles road. Yes, by Jove, those are the 13th Light Dragoons! Oh, well done! Go at them, you devils, go at them!"

His excitement seemed to rouse Harry. He opened his eyes, and said faintly: "Are we winning?"

"Yes, Grant's brigade is driving the French off the plateau."

"Oh, splendid!" He smiled. "I say, you won't be able to call me a Johnny Newcome any longer, will you?"

"No, that I shan't."

Harry relapsed into silence. Outside the dogged square Grant's Light Dragoons had formed, and charged the confused mass of French cavalry, hurling it back from the plateau and pursuing it right the way down the slope to the low ground near the orchard of Hougoumont. In a short while, the plateau, which had seethed with steel helmets, copper crests, towering white-plumes, and heavy bearskin shakos, was swept bare of all but Allied troops, mounds of French dead and wounded, and riderless horses, some of them wandering aimlessly about with blood streaming from their wounds, some neighing piteously from the ground where they lay, others quietly cropping the trampled grass.

The Colonel bent over Lord Harry. "I must go, Harry."

"Must you?" Harry's voice was growing fainter. "I wish you could stay. I don't feel quite the thing, you know."

"I can't stay. God knows I would, but I must get back to the Duke."

364

"Of course. I was forgetting. I shall see you later, I daresay."

"Yes, later," the Colonel said, a little unsteadily. "Goodbye, old fellow!" He pressed Harry's hand, laid it gently down, and rose to his feet. His horse stood waiting, snorting uneasily. He mounted, saluted Harry, who raised a wavering hand in return, and rode away to find the Duke.

CHAPTER XXIV

THE cavalry attacks were abating at last, but under cover of them renewed attempts were being made on La Haye Sainte. Again and again Major Baring sent to his brigade demanding more ammunition. One waggon never reached the farm; another was found to contain cartridges belonging to the Baker rifles used by the 95th, which were of the wrong calibre for the German rifles.

Colonel Audley arrived at the centre, immediately west of the Charleroi chaussée, in time to witness Uxbridge leading the gallant remnant of the Household Brigade against a column of French infantry, covered by cavalry, advancing upon the farm. Their numbers were so diminished that they could make little impression, and were forced to retire. Uxbridge, his Hussar dress spattered with mud and soaked with sweat, went flying past to bring up Trip's Carabiniers, a powerful body of Heavy cavalry, nine squadrons strong, who were drawn up behind Kielmansegg's brigade. He placed himself at their head, gave them the order to charge, and rode forward, only to be stopped by Horace Seymour snatching at his bridle and bellowing: "They don't follow you, sir!"

Uxbridge checked, and rode back, ordering the reluctant Carabiniers with a flood of eloquence to follow the example of the shattered Household Brigade. Nothing could avail, however: the squadrons would not attend to him, but began to retire, sweeping a part of the 3rd Hussars of the Legion before them. Old Arendtschildt's voice could be heard above the bursting shells, raised in a fury of invective; the German Hussars, scattered by the sheer weight of the Carabiniers, were only restrained from engaging with their Dutch allies by the exertions of their officers, who rode amongst them, calling them to order, and re-forming them as the Carabiniers passed through to the rear. The stolid Germans, roused to rage by their forced rout, rallied, and charged down upon the French about La Haye Sainte. They were driven back by the Cuirassiers supporting the infantry column; and the Hanoverian regiment, the Cumberland Hussars, which had been brought up, began to retire. Captain Seymour, despatched by Uxbridge to stop this retreat, thundered down upon them, a giant of a man on a huge charger, and grabbed at the Commanding Officer's bridle, roaring at him to get his men together, and bring them up again. The Hanoverian Colonel, who seemed dead to all feeling of shame, replied in a confused way that he could not trust his men: they were appalled by the repulse of the Household Troops; their horses were their own property; he did not think they would risk them in a charge against such overwhelming odds. He almost cringed under the menace of the English giant who loomed over him, pouring insults on his head, but he would do nothing to stop the retreat. Seymour, abandoning him, appealed to his next in command to supersede him, to any officer who had courage enough to rally his troops and lead them to the charge. It was useless: he galloped back to his Chief, reporting failure.

"Tell their Colonel to form them up out of range of the guns!" Uxbridge ordered.

But the Cumberland Hussars had no intention of taking part in the fight, and by the time Captain Seymour reached the Colonel again, the whole regiment was in full retreat towards Brussels.

Colonel Audley, finding the Duke at last, was sent off immediately with a scrawled message for Uxbridge.

"We ought to have more Cavalry between the two high roads. That is to say, 3 Brigades at least. . . . One heavy and one light Brigade might remain on the left."

This note delivered into Uxbridge's hands, Colonel Audley found himself beside Seymour, still seething with rage at the behaviour of the Hanoverians and the Dutch-Belgians. From him he learned that the head of the Prussian column, coming up to the west of Papelotte, had been sighted at about five o'clock, and that Baron Müffling, almost frantic at the delay, had ridden in person to bring up the reinforcements so desperately needed.

The farm of La Haye Sainte had caught fire from the cannonade directed upon it. Two of the French guns had been brought up to the north of it, and were enfilading Kempt's lines on the west of the chaussée. These were speedily silenced by the 95th Rifles, terribly reduced in numbers but still holding their ground in front of Lambert's brigade; but French skirmishers were now all round La Haye Sainte. A message from General Alten reached Baron Ompteda, requesting him, if possible, to deploy a battalion and send it against these *tirailleurs.* Ompteda, knowing that they were strongly supported by cavalry, sent back this intelligence to his General, but the Prince of Orange, carried away by the excitement of the moment, and forgetful of the disaster attendant upon his interference at Quatre-Bras, impetuously ordered him to advance at once. Ompteda looked at him for one moment; then he turned and gave the command to deploy the 5th Line battalion of the Legion. Placing himself at its head, he led it against the French skirmishers, and drove them back. The Cuirassiers in support charged down upon him; he fell, and half his men with him, cut to pieces by the cavalry. Arendtschildt, watching from the high ground to the north, flung his Hussars into the fray again. They fell upon the Cuirassiers in flank and drove them back, enabling the shattered remnant of the 5th Line battalion to reach the main position. Fresh French cavalry advanced and drove the Hussars back, but the Riflemen, on the knoll above the sand-pit across the road, who had been impatiently awaiting their opportunity, no sooner saw the ground cleared of Ompteda's infantry than they poured in such an accurate fire that the French cavalry was thrown into confusion, and the German Hussars drew off in good order.

The cavalry attacks on the right had almost ceased; the Duke sent to withdraw Adam's brigade from its exposed position on to the high ground on Maitland's right; and despatched Colonel Fremantle to the left wing, where the Prussians were beginning to come up, with a request for reinforcements of three thousand infantry to strengthen the line. The Colonel returned with a message from Generals Bülow and Ziethen that their whole Army was coming up, and they could make no detachment. He was delayed on his way back by finding Prince Bernhard's Nassauers, who had behaved with the greatest gallantry all day, being put to rout by a Prussian battery of eight guns which was busily employed in firing on them in the mistaken belief that they were French troops.

"A pretty way to behave after taking the whole day to come up!" he told Lord Fitzroy wrathfully. "The Prince rallied his fellows a quarter of a mile behind the line, but I had to gallop all the way back to Ziethen to get him to send orders to stop his damned battery!"

"How long before Ziethen can bring his whole force up?" Fitzroy demanded. "Things are looking pretty black."

"God knows! Müffling is doing all he can to hasten them, but there's only some advance cavalry arrived so far. They say they had the greatest difficulty to get here, owing to the state of the roads. Wouldn't have come at all if it hadn't been for old Blücher cheering them on. If it weren't so damned serious it would be comical! No sooner did Ziethen's advance guard get within reach of us than they heard we were being forced to retreat, and promptly turned tail and made off. You can imagine old Müffling's wrath! He went after them like one of Whinyates' Rockets, and ordered them up at once. The main part of the Prussian Army is already engaged round

Plancenoit, if Ziethen is to be believed. If they really are attacking Boney on his right flank, it would account for Ney not bringing infantry up against us. Ten to one, Boney's had to employ most of it against Bülow."

Uxbridge, seeing the Household Cavalry drawn up in a thin, extended line behind Ompteda's and Kielmansegg's brigades, sent Seymour to tell Lord Edward to withdraw his men to a less exposed position. Seymour came back with a grim answer from Lord Edward, still holding his ground: "If I were to move, the Dutch in support of me would move off immediately."

The fire had been extinguished at La Haye Sainte, but the garrison had fired its last cartridge, and was forced, after holding it in the teeth of the French columns all day, to abandon the post. Fighting a hand-to-hand rearguard action against the French breaking in through every entrance, Major Baring got out of the farm, and back to the lines, with forty-two men left of the original four hundred who had occupied the farm.

La Haye Sainte had fallen, and the effects of its loss were at once felt. Quiot, occupying it in force, brought up his guns and opened a crippling fire upon the Allied centre. To the east the smoke hung so thickly that, although not a hundred yards lay between them, the men of the 95th, reduced to a single line of skirmishers, could only see by the flash of their pieces where the French gunners were situated. Their senior officers had all been carried off the field, and the command of the battalion had fallen upon a Captain. Behind the Riflemen, Sir John Lambert was standing staunchly in support, in the angle of the chaussée and the hollow road, with three regiments, two living and one lying dead in square. On the west of the chaussée, the shot and the shells from the French batteries were tearing great rents in already depleted ranks. Alten had fallen; and Ompteda was dead. Staff Officers from the various brigades galloped up from all sides to beg the Duke for orders. "There are no orders," he said. "My only plan is to stand my ground here to the last man."

369

Though his Staff fell about him, he continued to ride up and down his lines, rallying failing troops, restraining men who, maddened by the rain of deadly shot, could hardly be kept from launching themselves through the smoke in a desperate charge against their persecutors. "Wait a little longer, my lads: you shall have at them presently," he promised.

"By God, I thought I had heard enough of this man, but he far surpasses my expectations!" Uxbridge exclaimed. "It is not a man, but a god!"

De Lancey, the Quartermaster-General, was struck by a spent cannon-ball at the Duke's side, and fell, imploring those who hurried to him not to move him, for he was done for. Behind the crumbling ranks of Alten's division was only the extenuated line of Lord Edward's cavalry. The Duke brought up the only remaining Brunswickers in person, and formed them to fill the gap. They marched up bravely, but the sight of the horrors all around them, and the dropping of men in their own ranks, shook them. They broke, and fell back, but shouting to his Aides-de-Camp to rally them, the Duke spurred after them, rounding them up, heartening them by word and gesture. Gordon and Audley raced after him, and the terrified soldiers were re-formed and led up again.

Uxbridge rode off like the wind, to bring up the cavalry from the left wing. He met Sir Hussey Vivian advancing to the centre of his own initiative, learned from him that the Prussians were at last arriving in force, and despatched a message to Vandeleur to move to the centre in Vivian's wake.

A Staff Officer met Vivian's brigade on its way to the centre, and exchanged his own wounded hunter for a trooper belonging to the 18th Hussars. "The Duke has won the battle if only we could get the damned Dutch to advance!" he told one of the officers.

The brigade, coming up behind the infantry lines from their comparatively quiet position on the left flank, could see no sign of victory in the desolation which surrounded them. Dead and dying men lay all over the ground;

mutilated horses wandered about in aimless circles; cannon-balls were tearing up the trampled earth in great gashes; and a pall of smoke hung over all. Vivian led the brigade over the chaussée, and saw Lord Edward Somerset, in a Life Guardsman's helmet, with a bare couple of squadrons drawn up west of the road. He called out; "Lord Edward, where is your brigade?"

"Here," replied Lord Edward.

Audley, engaged in rallying the Brunswickers, heard Gordon's voice raised above the whistle and hum of shot: "For God's sake, my Lord, don't expose yourself! This is no work for you!"

The next instant Audley saw him fall, but he could neither desert his post to go to him nor discover whether he were dead or alive. Gordon was carried off; Bruns-wickers, their panic checked, saw Vivian's Hussar brigade in support of them, and stood their ground; the Duke rode off to another part of the line.

Colonel Audley, his senses deadened to the iron rain about him, struggled after, saw Lord March, dismounted, and kneeling on the ground, supporting a wounded man in his arms, and shouted to him: "March! March! is Gordon alive?"

"Oh, my God, not Gordon too?" March cried out in an anguished tone.

The Colonel pushed up to him, saw that the man in his arms was Canning, and almost flung himself out of the saddle.

A musket-ball had struck Canning in the stomach; he was dying fast, and in agony that made it difficult for him to speak. Some men of the 73rd Regiment had raised him to a sitting position with their knapsacks. He gasped out: "The Duke—is he safe?"

"Yes, yes, untouched!"

A ghastly smile flickered over Canning's mouth; he tried to clasp Audley's hand; turned his head a little on March's shoulder; managed to speak their names; and so died.

An agitated officer from Ghigny's brigade came riding

371

up while March still held Canning's body in his arms. "*Milord, mon Capitaine, je vous en prie! C'est Son Altesse luimême qui est en ce moment blessé! Il faut venir tout de suite!*"

March, lost in grief, seemed not to hear him. Colonel Audley, hardly less distressed, laid a hand on his shoulder. "He's gone, March. Lay him down. Slender Billy's hurt."

March raised his head, dashing the tears from his eyes. "What's that?" He glanced up at the Dutchman standing over them. The message was repeated: the Prince had been hit in the shoulder while leading some of General Kruse's Nassauers to the charge, and had fallen so heavily from his horse that the sense seemed to have been knocked out of him. March laid Canning's body down, and got up. "I'll come at once. Where is he?"

He rode away with the Dutch officer; Colonel Audley, consigning Canning's body to the care of an officer of Halkett's brigade, also mounted, and plunged off through the confusion to find the Duke again.

Vandeleur had come up from the left flank with his brigade of Light Dragoons, and, passing behind Vivian, had formed his squadrons more to the right, immediately in rear of Count D'Aubremé's Dutch-Belgian Line battalions, brought up from Vieux Foriez to fill a gap on the right centre. Here they were exposed to a galling fire, but D'Aubremé's men in their front were weakening, and to have withdrawn out of range of the guns would have left the road open to the Dutch-Belgians for retreat. They closed their squadron intervals, as Vivian had done, to prevent the infantry passing through to the rear, and stood their ground, while Vandeleur, with some of his senior officers, bullied and persuaded the Dutch-Belgians into forming their front again.

At seven o'clock things looked very serious along the Allied front. To the west, only some Prussian cavalry had arrived to guard the left flank; Papelotte and the farm of Ter La Haye were held by Durutte, whose skirmishers stretched to the crest of the Allied position; the gunners and the *tirailleurs* at La Haye Sainte were raking the centre

372

with their fire; and although twelve thousand men of Reille's Corps d'Armée had failed all day to dislodge twelve hundred British Guards from the ruins of Hougoumont, all along the Allied line the front was broken, and in some places utterly disorganized.

The Duke remained calm, but kept looking at his watch. Once he said: "It's night, or Blücher," but for the most part he was silent. An Aide-de-Camp rode up to him with a message from his General that his men were being mowed down by the artillery fire, and must be reinforced. "It is impossible," he replied. "Will they stand?"

"Yes, my lord, till they perish!"

"Then tell them that I will stand with them, till the last man."

Turmoil and confusion, made worse by the smoke that hung heavily over the centre, and the débris that littered the ground from end to end of the line, seemed to reign everywhere. Staff Officers, carrying messages to brigades, asked mechanically: "Who commands here?" The Prince of Orange had been taken away by March; three Generals had been killed; five others carried off the field, too badly wounded to remain; the Adjutant-General and the Quartermaster-General had both had to retire. Of the Duke's personal Staff, Canning was dead; Gordon dying in the inn at Waterloo; and Lord Fitzroy, struck in his right arm while standing with his horse almost touching the Duke's, had left the field in Alava's care. Those that were left had passed beyond feeling. It was no longer a matter for surprise or grief to hear of a friend's death: the only surprise was to find anyone still left alive on that reeking plain. Horse after horse had been shot under them; sooner or later they would probably join the ranks of the slain: meanwhile, there were still orders to carry, and they forced their exhausted mounts through the carnage, indifferent to the heaps of fallen redcoats sprawling under their feet, themselves numb with fatigue, their minds focused upon one object only: to get the messages they carried through to their destinations.

Just before seven o'clock, a deserting Colonel of

Cuirassiers came galloping up to the 52nd Regiment, shouting: *"Vive le Roi!"* He reached Sir John Colborne, and gasped out: *"Napoléon est là avec les Gardes! Voilà l'attaque qui se fait!"*

The warning was unnecessary, for it had been apparent for some minutes that the French were mustering for a grand attack all along the front. D'Erlon's corps was already assailing with a swarm of skirmishers the decimated line of Picton's 5th Division; and to the west of La Haye Sainte, on the undulating plain facing the Allied right, the Imperial Middle Guard was forming in five massive columns.

Colonel Audley was sent on his last errand just after seven. He was mounted on a trooper, and the strained and twisted strapping round his thigh was soaked with blood. He was almost unrecognizable for the smoke that had blackened his face, and was feeling oddly light-headed from the loss of blood he had suffered. He was also very tired, for he had been in the saddle almost continually since the night of the 15th June. His mind, ordinarily sensitive to impression, accepted without revulsion the message of his eyes. Death and mutilation had become so common that he who loved horses could look with indifference upon a poor brute with the lower half of its head blown away, or a trooper, with its fore-legs shot off at the knees, raising itself on its stumps, and neighing its sad appeal for help. He had seen a friend die in agony, and had wept over him, but all that was long past. He no longer ducked when he heard the shots singing past his head; when his trooper shied away, snorting in terror, from a bursting shell, he cursed it. But there was no sense in courting death unnecessarily; he struck northwards, and rode by all that was left of the two Heavy Brigades, drawn back since the arrival of Vivian and Vandeleur some three hundred paces behind the front line. An officer in the rags of a Life Guardsman's uniform, his helmet gone, and a blood-stained bandage tied round his head, rode forward, and hailed him.

"Audley! Audley!"

He recognized Lord George Alastair under a mask of mud, and sweat, and blood-stains, and drew rein. "Hallo!" he said. "So you're alive still?"

"Oh, I'm well enough! Do you know how it has gone with Harry?"

"Dead," replied the Colonel.

George's eyelids flickered; under the dirt and the blood his face whitened. "Thanks. That's all I wanted to know. You saw him?"

"Hours ago. He was dying then, in one of Maitland's squares. He sent you his love."

George saluted, wheeled his horse, and rode back to his squadron.

The Colonel pushed on to the chaussée. His horse slithered clumsily down the bank on to it; he held it together, and rode across the pavé to the opposite bank and scrambled up, emerging upon the desolation of the slope behind Picton's division. He urged the trooper to a ponderous gallop towards the rear of Best's brigade. A handful of Dutch-Belgians were formed in second line; he supposed them to be some of Count Bylandt's men, but paid little heed to them, wheeling round their right flank, and plunging once more into the region of shot and shell bursts.

He neither saw nor heard the shell that struck him. His horse came crashing down; he was conscious of having been hit; blood was streaming down his left arm, which lay useless on the ground beside him, but there was as yet no feeling in the shattered elbow-joint. His left side hurt him a little; he moved his right hand to it, and found his coat torn, and his shirt sticky with blood. He supposed vaguely that since he seemed to be alive this must be only a flesh wound. He desired nothing better than to lie where he had fallen, but he mastered himself, for he had a message to deliver, and struggled to his knees.

The sound of horse's hooves galloping towards him made him lift his head. An Adjutant in the blue uniform and orange facings of the 5th National Militia dismounted beside him, and said in English: "Adjutant to Count

375

Bylandt, sir! I'm directed by General Perponcher to—
Parbleu! it is you, then!"

Colonel Audley looked up into a handsome, dark face bent over him, and said weakly: "Hallo, Lavisse! Get me a horse, there's a good fellow!"

"A horse!" exclaimed Lavisse, going down on one knee, and supporting the Colonel in his arms. "You need a surgeon, my friend! Be tranquil: my General sends to bear you off the field." He gave a bitter laugh, and added: "That is what my brigade exists for—to succour you English wounded!"

"Did you succeed in rallying your fellows?" asked the Colonel.

"Some, not all. Do not disturb yourself, my rival! You have all the honours of this day's encounter. *My* honour is in the dust!"

"Oh, don't talk such damned theatrical rubbish!" said the Colonel irritably. He fumbled with his right hand in his sash, and drew forth a folded and crumpled message. "This has to go to General Best. See that it gets to him, will you?—or, if he's been killed, to his next in command."

A couple of orderlies and a doctor had come up from the rear. Lavisse gave the Colonel into their charge, and said with a twisted smile: "You trust your precious message to me, my Colonel?"

"Be a good fellow, and don't waste time talking about it!" begged the Colonel.

He was carried off the field as the attack upon the whole Allied line began. On the left, Ziethen's advance guard had reached Smohain, and the Prussian batteries were in action, firing into Durutte's skirmishers; while somewhere to the south-east Bülow's guns could be heard assailing the French right flank. Allix and all that was left of Marcognet's division once more attacked the Allied left; Donzelot led his men against Ompteda's and Kielmansegg's depleted ranks; while the Imperial Guard of Grenadiers and Chasseurs moved up in five columns at rather narrow deploying intervals, in echelon, crossing the undulating plain diagonally from the chaussée to the

376

Nivelles road. Each column showed a front of about seventy men, and in each of the intervals between the battalions two guns were placed. In all, some four thousand five hundred men were advancing upon the Allied right, led by Ney, *le Brave des Braves*, at the head of the leading battalion.

The sun, which all day had been trying to penetrate the clouds, broke through as the attack commenced. Its setting rays bathed the columns of the Imperial Guard in a fiery radiance. Rank upon rank of veterans who had borne the Eagles victorious through a dozen fights advanced to the beat of drums, with bayonets turned to blood-red by the sun's last glow, across the plain into the smoke and heat of the battle.

Owing to their diagonal approach the columns did not come into action simultaneously. Before the battalions marching upon the British Guards had reached the slope leading to the crest of the Allied position, Ney's leading column had struck at Halkett's brigade and the Brunswickers on his left flank.

Over this part of the line the smoke caused by the guns firing from La Haye Sainte lay so thick that the Allied troops heard but could not see the formidable advance upon them. Colin Halkett had fallen, wounded in the mouth, rallying his men round one of the Colours; two of his regiments were operating as one battalion, so heavy had been their losses; and these were thrown into some confusion by their own Light troops retreating upon them. Men were carried off their feet in the surge to the rear; the Colonel, on whom the command of the brigade had devolved, seemed distracted, saying repeatedly: "What am I to do? What would you do?" to the Staff Officer sent by the Duke to "See what is wrong there!" The men of the 33rd, fighting against the tide that was sweeping them back, re-formed, and came on, shouting: "Give them the cold steel, lads! Let 'em have the Brummagum!" A volley was poured in before which the deploying columns recoiled; to the left, the Brunswickers, rallied once more by the Duke himself, followed suit, and the Imperial

377

Guard fell back, carrying with it a part of Donzelot's division.

Those of the batteries on the Allied front which were still in action met the advance with a fire which threw the leading ranks into considerable disorder. Many of the British batteries, however, were useless. Some had been abandoned owing to lack of ammunition; several guns stood with muzzles bent down, or touch-holes melted from the excessive heat; and more than one Troop, its gunners either killed or too exhausted to run the guns up after each recoil, had its guns in a confused heap, the trails crossing each other almost on top of the limbers and the ammunition waggons. Ross's, Sinclair's, and Sandham's were all silent. Lloyd's battery was still firing from in front of Halkett's brigade; so was Napier, commanding Bolton's, in front of Maitland; and a Dutch battery of eight guns, belonging to Detmer's brigade, brought up by Chassé in second line, had been sent forward to a position immediately to the east of the Brunswick squares, and was pouring in a rapid and well-directed fire upon the Grenadiers and the men on Donzelot's left flank.

As the Brunswickers and Halkett's men momentarily repulsed the two leading columns, which, on their march over the uneven ground, had become merged into one unwieldy mass, the Grenadiers and the Chasseurs on the French left advanced up the slope to where Maitland's Guards lay silently awaiting them. The drummers were beating the *pas de charge*, shouts of *"Vive l'Empereur!"* and *"En avant à la baïonette!"* filled the air. The Duke, who had galloped down the line from his position by the Brunswick troops, was standing with Maitland on the left flank of the brigade, not far from General Adam, whose brigade lay to the right of the Guards. Adam had ridden up to watch the advance, and the Duke, observing through his glass the French falling back before Halkett's men, exclaimed: "By God, Adam, I believe we shall beat them yet!"

At ninety paces, the brass 8-pounders between the advancing battalions opened fire upon Maitland's brigade. They were answered by Krahmer de Bichin's Dutch

378

battery, but though the grape-shot tore through the ranks of the Guards the Duke withheld the order to open musketry-fire. Not a man in the British line was visible to the advancing columns until they halted twenty paces from the crest to deploy.

"Now, Maitland! Now's your time!" the Duke said at last, and called out in his deep, ringing voice: "Stand up, Guards!"

The Guards leaped to their feet. The crest, which had seemed deserted, was suddenly alive with men, scarlet coats standing in line four-deep, with muskets at the present. Almost at the point of crossing bayonets they fired volley after volley into the Grenadiers. The Grenadiers, in column, had only two hundred muskets able to fire against the fifteen hundred of Halkett's and Maitland's brigades, deployed in line before them. They tried to deploy, but were thrown into confusion by a fire no infantry could withstand.

On Maitland's left, General Chassé had brought up Detmer's brigade of Dutch-Belgians in perfect order. When the word to charge was given, and the sound of the three British cheers was heard as the Guards surged forward, the Dutch came up at the double, and, with a roar of "*Oranje boven!*" drove the French from the crest in their front.

The Guards, scattering the Grenadiers before them, advanced until their flank was threatened by the second attacking column of Chasseurs. The recall was sounded, and the order given to face-about and retire. In the din of clashing arms, crackling musketry, groans, cheers, and trumpet-calls, the order was misunderstood. As the Guards regained the crest, an alarm of cavalry was raised. Someone shrieked: "Square, square, form square!" and the two battalions, trying to obey the order, became intermingled. A dangerous confusion seemed about to spread panic through the ranks, but it was checked in a very few moments. The order to "Halt!—Front!—Form up!" rang out; the Guards obeyed as one man, formed again four-deep, and told off in companies of forty.

In the immediate rear of Maitland's and Halkett's brigades, D'Aubremé's Dutch-Belgians, formed in three squares, appalled by the slaughter in their front, began to retreat precipitately upon Vandeleur's squadrons. The Dragoons closed their ranks until their horses stood shoulder to shoulder; Vandeleur galloped forward to try to stem the rout; and an Aide-de-Camp went flying to the Duke on a foaming horse, gasping out that the Dutch would not stand, and could not be held.

"That's all right," answered his lordship coolly. "Tell them the French are retiring!"

Meanwhile, to the right, where Adam's brigade held the ground above Hougoumont, Sir John Colborne, without waiting for orders, had acted on his own brilliant judgment. As the columns advanced upon Maitland, he moved the 52nd Regiment down to the north-east angle of Hougoumont, and right-shouldered it forward, until it stood in line four-deep parallel to the left flank of the second column of Chasseurs.

Adam, seeing this deliberate movement, galloped up, calling out: "Colborne! Colborne! What are you meaning to do?"

"To make that column feel our fire," replied Sir John laconically.

Adam took one look at the Chasseurs, another at the purposeful face beside him, and said: "Move on, then! the 71st shall follow you," and rode off to bring up the Highlanders.

The Chasseur column, advancing steadily, was met by a frontal fire of over eighteen hundred muskets from the 95th Rifles and the 71st Highlanders, and, as it staggered, the Fighting 52nd, the men in third and fourth line loading and passing muskets forward to the first two lines, riddled its flank. It broke, and fell into hideous disorder, almost decimated by a fire it could not, from its clumsy formation, return. A cry of horror arose, taken up by battalion after battalion down the French lines: "*La Garde recule!*"

Before the column could deploy, Sir John Colborne

swept forward in a charge that carried all before it. The officer carrying the Colour was killed, and a hundred and fifty men on the right wing, but the advance was maintained, right across the ground in front of the Allied line, the Imperial Guard being driven towards the chaussée in inextricable confusion. The 2nd and 3rd battalions of the Rifles, with the 71st Highlanders, followed the 52nd in support; the Imperial Guard, helpless under the musketry-fire, cast into terrible disorder through their inability to deploy, lost all semblance of formation, and retreated *pêle-mêle* to the chaussée, till the ground in front of the Allied position was one seething mass of struggling, fighting, fleeing infantry.

Hew Halkett brought up his Hanoverians into the interval between Hougoumont and the hollow road; the 52nd advanced across the uneven plain until checked by encountering some squadrons of Dörnberg's 23rd Light Dragoons, whom, in the dusk, they mistook for French cavalry and fired upon.

The Duke, who had watched the advance from the high ground beside Maitland, galloped up to the rear of the 52nd, where Sir John, having ordered his Adjutant to stop the firing, was exchanging his wounded horse for a fresh one.

"It is our own cavalry which has caused this firing!" Colborne told him.

"Never mind! *Go* on, Colborne, *go* on!" replied the Duke, and galloped back to the crest of the position, and stood there, silhouetted against the glowing sky on his hollow-backed charger. He raised his cocked-hat high in the air, and swept it forward, towards the enemy's position, in the long-looked-for signal for a General Advance. A cheer broke out on the right, as the Guards charged down the slope. The crippled forces east of the chaussée, away to their left, heard it growing louder as it swelled all along the line towards them, took it up by instinct, and charged forward out of the intolerable smoke surrounding them, on to a plain strewn with dead and dying, lit by the last rays of a red sun, and covered with men flying in confusion towards the ridge of La Belle Alliance.

Cries of: "*Nous sommes trahis!*" mingled with the dismayed shouts of "*La Garde recule!*" Donzelot's division was carried away in the rush of Grenadiers and Chasseurs; the retreat had become a rout. Ney, on foot, one epaulette torn off, his hat gone, a broken sword in his hand, was fighting like a madman, crying: "Come and see how a Marshal of France dies!" and, to D'Erlon, borne towards him in the press: "If we get out of this alive, D'Erlon, we shall both be hanged!"

Far in advance of the charging Allied line, Colborne, having crossed the ground between Hougoumont and La Haye Sainte, had reached the chaussée, and passed it, left-shouldering his regiment forward to ascend the slope towards La Belle Alliance.

To the right, Vivian had advanced his brigade, placing himself at the head of the 18th Hussars. "Eighteenth! You will, I know, follow me!" he said, and was answered by one of his Sergeant-Majors: "Ay, General! to hell, if you'll lead us!"

Taking up his position on the flank of the leading half-squadron, holding his reins in his injured right hand, which, though it still reposed in a sling, was just capable of grasping them, he led the whole brigade forward at the trot. As the Hussars cleared the front on Maitland's right, the Guards and Vandeleur's Light Dragoons cheered them on, and they charged down on to the plain, sweeping the French up in their advance past the eastern hedge of Hougoumont towards the chaussée at La Belle Alliance.

Through the dense smoke lying over the ground the Duke galloped down the line. When the Riflemen saw him, they sent up a cheer, but he called out: "No cheering, my lads, but forward and complete your victory!" and rode on, through the smother, out into the sea of dead, to where Adam's brigade was halted on the ridge of La Belle Alliance, a little way from where some French battalions had managed to re-form.

The Duke, learning from Adam that the brigade had been halted for the purpose of closing the files in, scrutinized the French battalions closely for a moment, and then said decidedly: "They won't stand: better attack them!"

Baron Müffling, looking along the line from his position on the left flank, saw the General Advance through the lifting smoke. Kielmansegg's, Ompteda's and Pack's shattered brigades remained where they had stood all day, but everywhere else the regiments charged forward, leaving behind them an unbroken red line of their own dead, marking the position where, for over eight hours of cannonading, of cavalry charges, and of massed infantry attacks the British and German troops had held their ground.

From Papelotte to Hougoumont the hillocky plain in front was covered with dead and wounded. Near the riddled walls of La Haye Sainte the Cuirassiers lay in mounds of men and horses. The corn which had waved shoulder-high in the morning was everywhere trodden down into clay. On the rising ground of La Belle Alliance the Old Guard was making its last stand, fighting off the fugitives, who, trying to find shelter in its squares, threatened to overwhelm them. These three squares, with one formed by Reille, south of Hougoumont, were the only French troops still standing firm in the middle of the rout. With the cessation of artillery-fire by the hollow road the smoke was clearing away, but over the ruins of Hougoumont it still rose in a slow, black column. Those of the batteries which had been able to follow the advance were firing into the mass of French on the southern ridge; musketry crackled as the Old Guard, with Napoleon and his Staff in the middle of their squares, retreated step by step, fighting a heroic rearguard action against Adam's brigade and Hew Halkett's Hanoverians. Where Vivian, with Vandeleur in support, was sweeping the ground east and south of Hougoumont, fierce cavalry skirmishing was in progress, and the Middle Guard was trying to re-form its squares to hold the Hussars at bay.

Müffling, detaching a battery from Ziethen's Corps, led it at a gallop to the centre of the Allied position. He met

the Duke by La Haye Sainte. His lordship called triumphantly to him from a distance: "Well! You see Macdonnell
has held Hougoumont!"

Müffling, who found himself unable to think of what
the Guards at Hougoumont must have endured without
a lump's coming into his throat, knew the Duke well
enough to realize that this brief sentence was his lordship's way of expressing his admiration, and nodded.

The sun was sinking fast; in the gathering dusk musket-
balls were hissing in every direction. Uxbridge, who had
come scatheless through the day, was hit in the knee by
a shot passing over Copenhagen's withers, and sang out:
"By God! I've got it at last!"

"Have you, by God?" said his lordship, too intent on
the operations of his troops to pay much heed.

Colin Campbell, preparing to support Uxbridge off the
field, seized the Duke's bridle, saying roughly: "This is
no place for you! I wish you will move!"

"I will when I have seen these fellows off," replied his
lordship.

To the south-east of La Belle Alliance, the Prussians,
driving the Young Guard out of Plancenoit, were advancing
on the chaussée, to converge there with the Allied troops.
Bülow's infantry were singing the Lutheran hymn, *Now
thank we all our God*, but as the columns came abreast of
the British Guards, halted by the road, the hymn ceased
abruptly. The band struck up *God Save the King*, and as
the Prussians marched past they saluted.

It was past nine o'clock when, in the darkness, south of
La Belle Alliance, the Duke met Prince Blücher. The
Prince, beside himself with exultation, carried beyond
coherent speech by his admiration for the gallantry of the
British troops and for the generalship of his friend and ally,
could find only one thing to say as he embraced the Duke
ruthlessly on both cheeks: "I stink of garlic!"

When his first transports of joy were a little abated, he
offered to take on the pursuit of the French through the
night. The Duke's battered forces, dog-tired, terribly
diminished in numbers, were ordered to bivouac where

they stood, on the ground occupied all day by the French; and the Duke, accompanied by a mere skeleton of the brilliant cortège which had gone with him into the field that morning, rode back in clouded moonlight to his Headquarters.

Baron Müffling, drawing abreast of him, said: "The Field Marshal will call this battle Belle-Alliance, sir."

His lordship returned no answer. The Baron, casting a shrewd glance at his bony profile, with its frosty eye and pursed mouth, realized that he had no intention of calling the battle by that name. It was his lordship's custom to name his victories after the village or town where he had slept the night before them. The Marshal Prince might call the battle what he liked, but his lordship would head his despatch to Earl Bathurst: "Waterloo".

CHAPTER XXV

FOR those in Brussels the day had been one of increasing anxiety. Contrary to expectation, no firing was heard, the wind blowing steadily from the north-west. The Duke's despatch to Sir Charles Stuart, written from Waterloo in the small hours, reached him at seven o'clock, and shortly afterwards Baron van der Capellan, the Secretary of State, issued a reassuring proclamation. After that no news of any kind was received in the town for many hours.

Colonel Jones, left in Brussels during the Duke's absence as Military Commander, was besieged all the morning by applications for passports. Every track-boat bound for Antwerp was as full as it could hold of refugees; money could not buy a pair of horses in all Brussels. Scores of people drove off at an early hour, with baggage piled high on the roofs of their carriages; the town seemed strangely quiet and deserted; and the church bells ringing for morning service sounded to sensitive ears like a knell.

Both Judith and Barbara had slept the night through,

in utter exhaustion, but neither in the morning looked as though she were refreshed by this deep slumber. Except for discussing in a desultory manner the extraordinary revelation Lucy Devenish had made on the previous evening, they did not talk much. Once Judith said: "If you knew the comfort it is to me to have you with me!" but Barbara merely smiled rather mockingly, and shook her head.

In the privacy of their own bedroom, Judith had remarked impulsively to Worth: "I am out of all conceit with myself! I have been deceived alike in Lucy and in Barbara!"

"You might certainly be forgiven for having been deceived in Lucy," Worth replied. "I imagine no one could have suspected such a melodramatic story to lie behind that demure appearance."

"No, indeed! I was never more shocked in my life. Bab says George will make her a very bad husband, and if it were not unchristian I should be much inclined to say that she will have nothing but her just deserts. But Bab! I could not have believed that she had such strength of character, such real goodness of heart! Have not you been surprised?"

"No," he replied. "I should have been very much surprised had she not, in this crisis, behaved precisely as she has done. My opinion of her remains unchanged."

"How can you talk so? You cannot have supposed from her conduct during these past months that she would behave so well now!"

"On the contrary, I never doubted her spirit. She is, moreover, just the kind of young woman who, under the stress of such conditions as these, is elevated for the time above her ordinary self."

"For the time! You place no dependence on this softened mood continuing, I collect!"

"Very little," he answered.

"You are unjust, Worth! For my part, I am persuaded that she repents bitterly of all that has passed. Oh, if only Charles is spared, I shall be so glad to see him reunited to her!"

386

"That is fortunate, since I have little doubt that you will see it."

"You don't think it will do?"

"I am not a judge of what will suit Charles. It would not do for me. She will certainly lead him a pretty dance."

"Oh no, no! I am sure you are mistaken!"

He smiled at the distress in her face, and pinched her chin. "I daresay I may be. I will admit, if you like, that I prefer this match to the one *you* tried to make for Charles, my dear!"

She blushed. "Oh, don't speak of that! At least there is nothing of that lack of openness in Bab."

"Nothing at all," he agreed somewhat dryly.

She saw that she could not talk him round to her way of thinking, and allowed the conversation to drop.

They had scarcely got up from the breakfast table, a little later, when they received a morning call from Mr. and Mrs. Fisher.

"She has confessed, then!" Judith exclaimed when the visitors' cards were brought to her.

"In floods of tears, I'd lay my last guinea!" said Barbara.

"It is not to be wondered at if she did weep!"

"I abominate weeping females. Do you wish for my support at this interview?"

"Oh yes, they will certainly desire to see you."

"Very well, but I'll be hanged if I'll be held accountable for George's sins."

It was as Judith had supposed. Lucy had confessed the whole to her aunt and uncle. They were profoundly shocked, and Mr. Fisher seemed almost bewildered. He said that he could not understand how such a thing could have come to pass, and so far from blaming Barbara for her brother's conduct, several times apologized to her for it. Mrs. Fisher, torn between a sense of propriety and a love of romance, was inclined to find excuses for the young people, in which occupation Judith gladly assisted her. Mr. Fisher agreed, but with a very sober face, that since the marriage had actually taken place there was nothing to do but to forgive Lucy. Barbara's presence prevented

387

him from expressing his opinion of Lord George's character, but it was plain that this was not high. He sighed deeply several times, and shook his head over his poor girl's chances of happiness. Mrs. Fisher exclaimed, with the tears springing to her eyes: "Oh! if only she is not even now, perhaps, a widow!"

This reflection made them all silent. After a moment, her husband said heavily: "You are very right, Mrs. Fisher. Ah, poor child, who knows what this day may not bring upon her? You must know, Lady Worth, that she is already quite overcome by her troubles, and is laid down upon her bed with the hartshorn."

"I am sure it is no wonder," Judith responded, avoiding Barbara's eye.

The Fishers soon took their leave, and the rest of the morning was spent by Judith and Barbara in rendering all the assistance in their power to those nursing the wounded in the tent by the Namur Gate. Returning together just before four o'clock, they found visitors with Worth in the salon, and walked in to discover these to be none other than the Duke and Duchess of Avon, who had arrived in Brussels scarcely an hour previously.

Barbara stood on the threshold, staring at them. "What the devil——? Grandmama, how the deuce do you come to be here?"

The Duke, a tall man with grizzled hair and fiery dark eyes, said: "Don't talk to your grandmother like that! What's this damnable story I hear about that worthless brother of yours?"

Barbara bent to kiss her grandmother, a rather stout lady, with a straight back, and an air of unshakable imperturbability: "Dear love! Did you come for my sake?"

"No, I came because your grandfather would do so. But this is very surprising, this news of George's marriage. Tell me, shall I like his wife?"

"You'll have nothing to do with her!" snapped his Grace. "Upon my word, I'm singularly blessed in my grandchildren! One is such a miserable poltroon that he takes to his heels the instant he hears a gun fired; another makes herself the talk of the town; and a third marries a damned Cit's daughter. You may as well tell me what folly Harry has committed, and be done with it. I wash my hands of the pack of you! There is no understanding how I came to have such a set of grandchildren."

"Vidal's behaviour is certainly very bad," agreed the Duchess. "But I find nothing remarkable about George's and Bab's conduct, Dominic. Only I'm sorry George should have married in such a hole-and-corner fashion. It will make it very awkward for his wife. You have not told me if I shall like her, Bab."

"You will think her very dull, I daresay."

"You will not receive her at all!" stated his Grace.

The Duchess replied calmly: "Your mother received me, Dominic."

"Mary!"

"Well, my dear, but the circumstances were far more disgraceful, weren't they?"

"I suppose you will say that *I* am to blame for George's conduct?"

"At all events, you are scarcely in a position to condemn him," she said, smiling. "You made a shocking *mésalliance* yourself. Dear me, how rude we are, to be sure! Here is Lady Worth come in, and not one of us pays the least heed! How do you do, my dear child? You must let me thank you for your kindness to my granddaughter. I am afraid she has not used your family very well."

"Oh, ma'am, that is all forgotten!" Judith said, taking her hand. "I cannot find words to express to you what it has meant to me to have her here during this terrible time!" She turned towards the Duke, saying with a quiver in her voice: "This is not a moment for reproaches! If you knew what we have seen—what may even now be happening—forgive me, but every consideration but the one seems so trivial, so——" Her voice failed, she averted her face, groping in her reticule for her handkerchief. She recovered her composure with a strong effort, and said in a low tone: "Excuse me! We have been amongst the wounded the whole morning, and it has a little upset me."

Barbara pushed her into a chair, saying: "Confound you, Judith, if you set me off crying, I'll never forgive you!" She looked at the Duke. "Well, sir, my compliments! You must be quite the only man to come *into* Brussels to-day! Did you come because there was a battle being fought, or in despite of it?"

"I came," replied his Grace, "on account of the intelligence received by your grandmother from Vidal. So you have jilted Charles Audley, have you? I congratulate you!"

"Your congratulations are out of place. I never did anything more damnable in my life."

"Why, Bab, my girl!" said his Grace, surprised. He put his arm round her, and said gruffly: "There, that will do! You are a baggage, but at least you have some spirit in you! When I think of that white-livered cur, Vidal, running for his life——"

"Oh, that was Gussie's doing! Did you meet them on your way here?"

"I? No, nor wish to! We landed at Ostend, and drove here through Ghent. If it had not been for the rabble choking the road we should have been here yesterday."

"Yes," said his wife. "They warned us in Ghent not to proceed farther, as we should certainly be obliged to fly from Brussels, so naturally your grandfather had the horses put to immediately."

He regarded her with a grim little smile. "*You* were not behind-hand, Mary!"

"Certainly not. All this dashing about makes me feel myself a young woman again. Which reminds me that I must call upon my new granddaughter. You will give me her uncle's direction, Bab."

"Understand me, Mary——"

"I will give it to you, ma'am, but you must know that Mr. Fisher regards the match with quite as much dislike as does my grandfather."

This remark brought a sparkle into the Duke's eye. "He does, does he? Go on, Miss! Go on! What the devil has he against my grandson?"

"He thinks him a spendthrift, sir."

"Ha! Damned Cit! He may consider himself lucky to have caught George for his nobody of a niece!"

"As to that, Lucy is his heir. I fancy he was looking higher for her. Her fortune will not be inconsiderable, you know, and in these days——"

"So he was looking higher, was he? An Alastair is not good enough for him! I'll see this greasy merchant!"

The Duchess said in her matter-of-fact way: "You should certainly do so. It will be much more the thing than that wild notion you had taken into your head of riding out with Lord Worth towards the battlefield."

"Fisher can wait," replied his Grace. "I have every intention of going to see what news can be got the instant I have swallowed my dinner."

"Dinner!" Judith exclaimed. "How shocking of me! I had forgotten the time. You must know, Duchess, that here in Brussels we have got into the way of dining at four. I hope you will not mind. You must please stay and join us."

"You should warn them that Charles bore off our Sunday dinner," Barbara said, with a wry smile.

"You may be sure my cook will have contrived something."

The Avons were putting up at the Hôtel de Belle Vue, and the Duchess at once suggested that the whole party should walk round to dine there. It was declined, however; Judith's confidence in her cook was found not to have been misplaced; and in a very few minutes they were all seated round the table in the dining-parlour.

The conversation was mostly of the war. The wildest rumours were current in Ghent, and the Duke was glad to listen to a calm account from Worth of all that had so far passed. When he heard that the Life Guards had driven the French Lancers out of Genappe, he looked pleased, but beyond saying that if George did not get his brevet for this he supposed he would be obliged to purchase promotion for him, he made no remark. As soon as they rose from the table, he and Worth took their departure, to ride towards the Forest of Soignes in search of intelligence, and Judith, excusing herself, left Barbara alone with her grandmother.

"I have surpassed myself, ma'am," Barbara said in a bitter tone. "Did Vidal write you the whole?"

"Quite enough," replied the Duchess. "I wish, dearest, you will try to get the better of this shocking disposition of yours."

"If Charles comes back to me there is nothing I will not do!"

"We will hope he may do so. Your grandfather was very much pleased with the civil letter Colonel Audley wrote to him. How came you to throw him off as you did, my love?"

"O God, Grandmama!" Barbara whispered, and fell on her knees beside the Duchess, and buried her face in her lap.

It was long before she could be calm. The Duchess listened in understanding silence to the disjointed sentences gasped out, merely saying presently: "Don't cry, Bab. It will ruin your face, you know."

"I don't give a damn for my face!"

"I am very sure that you do."

Barbara sat up, smiling through her tears. "Confound you, ma'am, you know too much! There, I have done! You don't wish me to remove to the Hôtel de Belle Vue, do you? I cannot leave Judith at this present."

"By all means stay here, my love. But tell me about this child George has married, if you please!"

"I cannot conceive what possessed George to look twice at her. She is quite insipid."

"Dear me! I had better go and call upon her aunt."

She very soon took her leave, setting out on foot to the Fishers' lodging. Her visit did much to sooth Lucy's agitation; and her calm good sense almost reconciled Mr. Fisher to an alliance which he had been regarding with the deepest misgiving. Neither his appearance nor the obsequiousness of his manners could be expected to please the Duchess, but she was agreeably surprised in Lucy, and although not placing much dependence upon her being able to hold George's volatile fancy, went back presently to her hôtel feeling that things might have been much worse.

Worth returned at about six o'clock, having parted from the Duke at the end of the street. He had very little news to report. He described meeting Creevey in the suburbs, and their mutual surprise at finding the Sunday population of Brussels drinking beer, and making merry, round little tables, for all the world as though no pitched battle were being fought not more than ten miles to the south of them. It had been found to be impossible to penetrate far into the Forest, on account of the baggage choking the road, but they had met with a number of wounded soldiers making their way back to Brussels, and had had speech with a Life Guardsman, who reported that the French were getting on in such a way that he did not see what was to stop them.

"He had taken part in a charge of the whole Household Brigade, and says that they have lost, in killed, wounded, and prisoners, more than half their number. George, however, was safe when the man left the field. A private soldier's opinion of the battle is not to be depended on, but I don't like the look of things."

Scarcely an hour later, the town was thrown into an uproar by the Cumberland Hussars galloping in through the Namur Gate, and stampeding through the streets, shouting that all was lost, and the French hard on their heels. They seemed not to have drawn rein in their flight from the battlefield, and went through Brussels scattering the inhabitants before them.

People began once more to run about, crying: "*Les Français sont ici! Ils s'emparent à la porte de la ville! Nous sommes tous perdus! Que ferons-nous?*" Many people kept their horses at their doors, but no more troops followed the Hussars, and the panic gradually abated. A little later, a large number of French prisoners entered the town under escort, and were marched to the barracks of Petit Château. The sight of two captured Eagles caused

393

complete strangers to shake one another by the hand; more prisoners arrived, and hopes ran high, only to be dashed by the intelligence conveyed by one or two wounded officers that everything had been going as badly as possible when they had left the field. The Adjutant-General's chaise-and-four was seen by Mr. Creevey to set out from his house in the Park and bowl away, as fast as the horses could drag it, to the Namur Gate. More and more wounded arrived in town, all telling the same tale: it was the most sanguinary battle they had ever known; men were dropping like flies: there was no saying in the smoke and the carnage who was still alive or who had been killed: no time should be lost by civilians in getting away.

In curious contrast to this scene of agitation, lights shone in the Théâtre de la Monnaie, where Mlle. Ternaux was playing in *Œdipe à Colonne* before an audience composed of persons who either had no relatives or friends engaged in the battle or who looked forward with pleasure to the entrance of Bonaparte into Brussels.

At half-past eight o'clock, Worth, who had gone out some time before in quest of news, came abruptly into the salon where Judith and Barbara were sitting in the most dreadful suspense, and said, with more sharpness in his voice than his wife had ever heard: "Judith, be so good as to have pillows put immediately into the chaise! I am going at once towards Waterloo: Charles is there, very badly wounded. Cherry has just come to me with the news."

He did not wait, but strode out to his own room, to make what preparations for the journey were necessary. Both ladies ran after him, imploring him to tell them more.

"I know nothing more than what I have told you. Cherry had no idea how things were going—badly, he thinks. I may be away some time: the road is almost blocked by the carts overturned by the German cavalry's rout. Have Charles's bed made up—but you will know what to do!"

"I will have the pillows put in the chaise," Barbara

said in a voice of repressed anguish, and left the room.

The chaise was already at the door, and Colonel Audley's groom waiting impatiently beside it. He was too overcome to be able to tell Barbara much, but the little he did say was enough to appal her.

Colonel Audley had been carried to Mont St. Jean by some foreigners; he did not know whether Dutch or German.

"It does not signify. Go on!"

Cherry brushed his hand across his eyes. "I saw them carrying him along the road. Oh, my lady, in all the years I've served the Colonel I never thought to see such a sight as met my eyes! My poor master like one dead, and the blood soaked right through the horse-blanket they had laid him on! He was taken straight to the cottage at Mont St. Jean, where those damned sawbones—saving your ladyship's presence!—was busy. I thought my master was gone, but he opened his eyes as they put him down, and said to me: 'Hallo, Cherry!' he said, 'I've got it, you see.' "

He fairly broke down, but Barbara, gripping the open chaise door, merely said harshly: "Go on!"

"Yes, my lady! But I don't know how to tell your ladyship what they done to my master, Dr. Hume, and them others, right there in the garden. Oh, my lady, they've taken his arm off! And he bore it all without a groan!"

She pressed her handkerchief to her lips. In a stifled voice, she said: "But he will live!"

"You would not say so if you could but see him, my lady. Four horses he's had shot under him this day, and a wound on his leg turning as black as my boot. We got him to the inn at Waterloo, but there's no staying there: they couldn't take in the Prince of Orange himself, for all he had a musket-ball in his shoulder. Poor Sir Alexander Gordon's laying there, and Lord Fitzroy too. Never till my dying day shall I forget the sound of Sir Alexander's sufferings—him as always was such a merry gentleman, and such a close friend of my master's! Not but what by the time we got my master to the inn he was too far gone to heed. I shouldn't have spoken of it to your ladyship, but I'm that upset I hardly know what I'm saying."

Worth ran down the steps of the house at that moment, and curtly told Cherry to get up on the box. As he drew on his driving-gloves, Barbara said: "I have put my smelling-salts inside the chaise, and a roll of lint. I would come with you, but I believe you will do better without me. O God, Worth, bring him safely back!"

"I shall certainly bring him back. Go in to Judith, and do not be imagining anything nonsensical if I'm away some hours. Good-bye! A man doesn't die because he has the misfortune to lose an arm, you know."

He mounted the box; the grooms let go the wheelers' heads, and as the chaise moved forward one of them jumped up behind.

For the next four hours Judith and Barbara, having made every preparation for the Colonel's arrival, waited, sick with suspense, for Worth's return. The Duke of Avon walked round from the Hôtel de Belle Vue at ten o'clock, and, learning of Colonel Audley's fate from Judith's faltering tongue, said promptly: "Good God, is that all? One would say he had been blown in pieces by a howitzer-shell to look at your faces! Cheer, up Bab! Why, I once shot a man just above the heart, and he recovered!"

"That must have been a mistake, sir, I feel sure."

"It was," he admitted. "Only time I ever missed my mark."

At any other time both ladies would have wished to hear more of this anecdote, but in the agitation of spirits which they were suffering nothing that did not bear directly upon the present issue had the power to engage their attention. The Duke, after animadverting with peculiar violence upon Mr. Fisher's manners and ideals, bade them good-night, and went back to his hôtel.

Hardly more than an hour later, Creevey called to bring the ladies news. His prospective stepson-in-law, Major Hamilton, had brought the Adjutant-General into Brussels a little after ten o'clock, and had immediately repaired to

Mr. Creevey's house to warn him that in General Barnes's opinion the battle was lost, and no time should be wasted in getting away from Brussels.

"I could not go to bed without informing you of this," Creevey said. "I thought it only right that you should know, and decide for yourselves what were best to do under the circumstances."

"Thank you," Judith said. "It was kind of you, but there is now no question of our leaving Brussels. My brother-in-law is severely wounded. Worth has gone to bring him in."

He looked genuinely concerned, and pressed her hand in the most speaking way. "I am excessively sorry to hear of this! But once you have Colonel Audley in your care you will see how quickly he will recover!"

"We hope—— Do you and Mrs. Creevey mean to go to Antwerp?"

"No, it is out of the question to move Mrs. Creevey in her present state of health. I don't scruple to tell you, my dear ma'am, that General Barnes's prognostications do not convince me that all is over. Hamilton tells me he was shot through the body at about five o'clock, and borne off the field. I cannot but feel that if the battle had been lost we must by now have received intelligence of it. Do you know what I judge by? Why, I'll tell you! The baggage-train is still moving *towards* the battlefield! To my mind, that proves that all is well."

"I had not thought of that. Yes, indeed: you must be right. You put us quite at our ease, Mr. Creevey. Thank you again for coming to us!"

He saw that the result of the battle was of less importance to her at the moment than Colonel Audley's fate, and after lingering only for a few moments to express his sympathy, took his leave and went back to the Rue du Musée.

After he had gone, no further interruptions occurred. The evening was mild, with a fitful moonlight shining through the lifting storm-clouds. Barbara had drawn back the blinds and opened one of the windows, and sat by it almost without stirring. In the street below a few people

397

passed, but the sounds that drifted to the salon were muffled, as though Brussels were restless but quiet.

Once Judith said: "Would you like to lie down upon your bed for a little while? I would wake you the instant he comes."

"I could not rest. But you——"

"No, nor I."

The brief conversation died. Another hour crept by. As the church clocks struck the hour of one, the clatter of horses' feet on the cobbles reached the ladies' straining ears. Lanterns, dipping and rocking with the lurch of a chaise, were seen approaching down the street, and in another moment Worth's chaise-and-four had drawn up outside the house.

Barbara picked up the branch of candles from the table. "Go down. I will light the stairs," she said.

Judith ran from the room, feeling her knees shaking under her. The butler and Worth's valet were already at the door: there was nothing for her to do, and, almost overpowered by dread, she remained upon the landing, leaning against the wall, fighting against the nervous spasm that turned her sick and faint. She saw Barbara standing straight and tall in her pale dress, at the head of the stairs, holding the branch of candles up in one steady hand. A murmur of voices reached her ears. She heard the butler exclaim, and Worth reply sharply. A groan, and she knew that Charles lived, and found that the tears were pouring down her cheeks. She wiped them away, and, regaining command of herself, ran back into the salon, and snatching up a companion to the chandelier Barbara held, bore it up the second pair of stairs to the Colonel's room. She had scarcely had time to turn back the sheets from the bed before Worth and Cherry carried Colonel Audley into the room.

Judith could not suppress an exclamation of horror. The Colonel had been wrapped in his own cloak, but this fell away as he was lowered on to the bed, revealing a blood-stained shirt hanging in tatters about him. His white buckskins were caked with mud, and had been slit down the right leg to permit of the flesh wound on his thigh being dressed. His curling brown hair clung damply to his brow; his face, under the blackening of smoke, was ghastly; but worst of all was the sight of the bandaged stump where so short a time ago his left arm had been. He was groaning, and muttering, but although his pain-racked eyes were open it was plain that he was unconscious of his surroundings.

"Razor!" Worth said to his valet, who had followed him up the stairs with a heavy can of hot water. "These boots off first!" He glanced across at the two women. "This is no fit sight for you. You had better go."

"Fool!" Barbara said, in a low, fierce voice.

"As you please," he shrugged, and, taking the razor from his valet's hand, began to slit the seams of the Colonel's Hessians.

While he got the boots off, Barbara knelt down by the bed and sponged away the dirt from the Colonel's livid face. Judith stood beside her, holding the bowl of warm water. Over Barbara's head, she spoke to Worth: "Will he live?"

"He is very ill, but I believe so. I have sent for a surgeon to come immediately. The worst is this fever. The jolting of the chaise has been very bad for him. I thought at one time I should never get through to Waterloo: the road is choked—waggons lying all over it, baggage spilt and plundered, and horses shot in their traces. There was never anything so disgraceful!"

"The battle?"

"I know no more than you. I met Charles in a common tilt-waggon half-way through the Forest, being brought to Brussels with a dozen others. Everything is turmoil on the road: I could come by no certain intelligence; but I conjecture that all must be well, or the French must by now have penetrated at least to the Forest."

He moved up to the head of the bed, and while he and his valet stripped the clothes from the Colonel's body, Barbara poured away the tainted water in the bowl and filled it with fresh. She looked so pale that Judith feared she must be going to faint, and begged her to withdraw. She shook her head. "Do not heed me! I shall not fail."

By the time an over-driven surgeon had arrived, the Colonel was lying between clean sheets, restlessly trying to twist from side to side. At times it needed all Worth's strength to prevent him from turning on to his injured left side; occasionally he made an effort to wrench himself up; once he said quite clearly: "The Duke! I've a message to deliver!" But mostly his utterance was indistinct, and interrupted by deep groans.

The surgeon looked grave, and saw nothing for it but to bleed him. Judith could not help saying with a good deal of warmth: "I should have thought he had lost enough blood!"

She was not attended to; the surgeon had been at work amongst the wounded since the previous morning, and was himself tired and harassed. He took a pint of blood from the Colonel, and it seemed to relieve him a little. He ceased his restless tossing and fell into a kind of coma. The surgeon gave Worth a few directions, and went away, promising to return later in the morning. It was evident that he did not take a very hopeful view of the Colonel's state. He would not permit of the bandages being removed to enable him to inspect the injuries to the thigh and the left side of the body. "Better not disturb him!" he said. "If Hume attended to him, you may depend upon it the wounds have been properly dressed. I will see them later. There is nothing for it now but to keep him quiet and hope for the fever to abate."

He hurried away. Worth bent over the Colonel, feeling his hand and brow. Over his shoulder, he addressed the two women: "Settle it between yourselves, but one of you must go and rest. Charles is in no immediate danger."

"There can be no doubt which of us must go," said Judith. "Come, my poor child!"

"Oh no! You go!"

"No, Bab. It is you Charles will want when he comes to himself, and if you sit up now you will drop in the end, and think how shocking that would be! It is of no use to argue; I am quite determined."

Barbara glanced towards the bed; the Colonel was lying still at last, sunk in a heavy stupor. "Very well," she said in a deadened tone. "I will do as you wish."

Judith led her away, with an arm round her waist. Barbara went unresistingly, but by the time they had reached her room such a fit of shuddering had seized her that Judith was alarmed. She forced her to sit down in a chair, while she ran to fetch her smelling-salts and the hartshorn. When she came back, the shudders had given place to dry sobs that seemed to convulse Barbara's whole body. She contrived to make her swallow a dose of hartshorn and water, and got her upon the bed, and sat with her till she was a little calmer. Barbara gasped: "Oh, do not stay! Go back to him! This is nothing!"

"Worth will send if he needs me. Only tell me where I may find your laudanum drops."

"Never! *He* did not like me to!"

"In such a case as this he could have no objection!"

"No, I tell you! See, I am better; I wish you to go back."

Judith drew the quilt up over her shoulders. "I will go, if it will relieve your mind. There, my dear, do not look like that! He will recover, and you will both be so happy together!" She bent, and kissed Barbara, and had the satisfaction of seeing the dreadful pallor grow less deathly. "I shall come back in a little while to see how you go on," she promised, and, setting the candle where its tongue of light would not worry Barbara's eyes, went softly back to Colonel Audley's room.

Barbara returned to the sick-room shortly after six o'clock. Judith came forward to meet her, saying in a low tone: "We think him better. The pulse is not so tumultuous. There has been a good deal of restlessness, but you see he is quiet now. Oh, my dear, such glorious news! Bonaparte has been utterly overthrown and the whole French Army put to rout! Worth sent round to Sir Charles Stuart's an hour ago, and he had just himself heard from General Alten of our complete victory! You must know that Alten was brought in, severely wounded, very late last night, but had left instructions with one of his Aides-de-Camp to let him know the result of the battle at the earliest opportunity. The news reached him at three o'clock."

"The French Army routed!" Barbara repeated. "Good God, is it possible? Oh, if anything can make Charles recover, it must be that news!"

"You shall tell him when he wakes," Judith said. "I am going to bed for an hour or so. Worth has gone off to shave and change his clothes, but his man is just outside if you should need any assistance. But indeed, my dear, Charles is better."

She went away. Barbara took her vacated chair by the bedside, and sat watching the Colonel. He lay quiet, except for the occasional twitching of his hand. She felt it softly, and found it, though still dry and hot, no longer burning to the touch. Satisfied, she folded her own hands in her lap, and sat without moving, waiting for him to awaken.

A few minutes after seven he stirred. A deep sigh broke the long silence; he opened his eyes, clouded with sleep, and gave a stifled groan. His hand moved; Barbara took it in hers and lifted it to her lips. He looked at her, blankly for a moment, then with recognition creeping into his eyes, and, with it, the ghost of his old smile. "Why, Bab!" he said, in a very faint voice. "You've come back to me!"

Tears hung on her lashes; she slipped to her knees, and laid her cheek against his. "*You* have come back to *me*, Charles. I shall never let you go again."

He put his arm weakly around her, and turned his head on the pillow to kiss her.

CHAPTER XXVI

FOR a minute everything was forgotten in the passing away of all bitterness and grief between them. Neither spoke: explanations were not needed; for each all that signified was that they were together again.

Barbara raised her head at last, and taking the Colonel's face between her hands, looked deep into his eyes, her own more beautiful through the mist of tears that filled them than he had ever seen them. "My darling!" she whispered.

He smiled wearily, but as fuller consciousness returned to him, his thoughts turned from her. "The battle? They were massing for an attack."

"It is over. The French have been overthrown: their whole Army is in full retreat."

A flush of colour came into his drawn face. "Boney's beat! Hurrah!"

She rose from her knees and moved away to measure out the medicine that the surgeon had left for him. When she came back to the bedside the Colonel was lying with his hand across his eyes, and his lips gripped tightly together. Her heart was wrung, but she said only: "Here is a horrid potion for you to swallow, dear love."

He did not answer, but when she slid her arm under him to raise him, he moved his hand from his eyes, and said in a carefully matter-of-fact voice: "I remember now. I've lost my arm."

"Yes, dear."

He drank the dose she was holding to his mouth, leaning against her shoulder. As she lowered him again on to the pillows, he said with an effort: "It's a lucky thing it was only my left. It has been a most unfortunate member. I was wounded in it once before."

"In that case, we will say good riddance to it. Oh, my love, my love, does it hurt you very much?"

"Oh no! Nothing to signify," he answered, lying gallantly.

He seemed as though he would sink back into the half-sleep, half-swoon which had held him for so long, but presently he opened his eyes, and turned them towards Barbara with an expression in them of painful anxiety. "Gordon? Have you heard?"

"Only that he had been wounded."

He was obliged to be satisfied, but she saw that although his eyes were closed again he was fully awake. She said, taking his hand between hers: "We shall know presently."

"Fitzroy, too," he said, in a fretting tone. "You would have heard if the Duke had been hit. But March took Slender Billy away. That was after Canning fell. How many of us are left? They dropped off, man after man— I cannot recall——" He broke off, and drew his hand away, once more covering his eyes with it.

She saw that he was growing agitated, and although she longed to ask for news of her brothers, she remained silent. But after a slight pause, he said abruptly: "George was alive just before I was struck. I saw him."

Her pent-up anxiety found relief in a gaping sigh. She waited for a moment, then whispered: "Harry?"

He shook his head. A sob broke from her; she buried her face in the coverlet to stifle the sound, and presently felt his hand come back to hers, feebly clasping her fingers.

She remained on her knees until she saw that he had dropped into an uneasy sleep. As she rose, Worth came into the room. She laid a finger to her lips, and moved silently to meet him.

"Has he waked?" Worth asked in a low voice.

"Yes. He is quite himself, but I think in a good deal of pain."

"That was bound to be. Go down to breakfast. Your grandmother is here. I will send if he should rouse and wish for you."

She nodded, and slipped away. Judith was asleep on her bed, but breakfast had been laid in the parlour, and the Duchess of Avon was sitting behind the coffee cups.

She greeted her granddaughter with a smile and a tender embrace. "There, dearest! Such a happy morning for you after all! Sit down, and I will give you some coffee."

"Harry is dead," Barbara said.

The Duchess's hand trembled. She set the coffee-pot down, and looked at Barbara.

"Charles told me. George was alive when he left the field."

The Duchess said nothing. Two large tears rolled down her cheeks. She wiped them away, picked up the coffee-pot again, poured a cup out rather unsteadily and gave it to Barbara. After a long pause she said: "Such foolish thoughts keep crossing my mind. One remembers little, forgotten things. He would always call me 'The Old Lady', in spite of your grandfather's disliking it so. Such a bad, merry boy!" She stretched out her hand to Barbara, and clasped one of hers. "Poor child, I wish I could say something to comfort you."

"It seems as though every joy that comes to one must have a grief to spoil it."

"It is so, but think instead, dearest, that every grief has joy to lighten it. Nothing in this world is quite perfect, nor quite unbearable." She patted Barbara's hand, and said in a voice of determined cheerfulness: "When you have eaten your breakfast, I am going to send you round to see your grandfather. A turn in the fresh air will make you feel better."

"I could not leave Charles."

"Nonsense!" said her Grace. "I am going to sit with your precious Charles, my dear. I know far better than you what to do for a wounded man. I have had a great deal of practice, I assure you."

So when Colonel Audley opened his eyes again, it was to see a grey-haired lady, with humorous eyes, bending over him. He blinked, and, since she was smiling, weakly smiled back at her.

"That is much better!" she said. "Now you shall take a little gruel, and be quite yourself again. Worth, be so good as to lift your brother slightly, while I put another pillow beneath his shoulders."

The Colonel turned his head, as Worth came up on the

opposite of the bed, and held out his hand. "Hallo, Julian!" he said. "How did I get here?"

"I brought you in. There! Is that comfortable?"

"Babs was here," said the Colonel, frowning. "She said Boney was beat. I didn't dream that."

"No, certainly you did not. Bab will be back directly. Meanwhile, here is her grandmother come to see you."

"So that is who you are!" said the Colonel, looking up at the Duchess. "But I don't quite understand—am I being very stupid?"

"Not at all. You cannot imagine how I come to be here. Well, I came to see what Bab was about to have jilted you so shockingly, only to find that that was quite forgotten and that you are going to be married after all. So now open your mouth!"

He swallowed the spoonful of gruel put to his lips, but said: "Am I going to be married?"

"Certainly you are. Open again!"

He obeyed meekly. "I should like to see Bab," he said, when the spoon was once more removed.

"So you shall, when you have drunk up all your gruel," promised the Duchess.

The Colonel thought it over, and then said in a firmer tone: "I'll be shaved first."

"My dear fellow, why worry?" Worth said.

"By all means let him be shaved," said the Duchess, frowning at him. "He will feel very much more the thing."

When Barbara came in with her grandfather to be met by the news that Colonel Audley was in the valet's hands, being shaved, she exclaimed: "Shaved! Good God, how came you to let him disturb himself for such a foolish thing?"

"My love, when a man begins to think of shaving you may take it from me that he is on the road to recovery," said the Duchess. She took her husband's hands, and squeezed them. "Bab has told you, hasn't she, Avon? My dear, we must be very proud of our boys, and try not to grieve."

He put his arm round her, saying: "Poor Mary! Depend upon it, we shall soon get news of that scamp George being safe and sound. I have been to Stuart's, and learned from him that the Duke is in the town. Our losses have been enormous, by all accounts, but just think of Bonaparte completely overset! By God, it makes up for all!"

The arrival just then of the surgeon put an end to any further conversation. The Duchess and Worth accompanied him upstairs to the Colonel's room. He admitted that he had not expected to find his patient in such good shape, but pulled a long face over the leg wound, which, from having been so roughly bound upon the battlefield, and chafed by continued exertion, was in a bad state. He took Worth aside, and warned him that he should prepare the Colonel's mind for amputation.

Worth said, with such an icy rage in his voice that the surgeon almost recoiled: "You'll save that leg: do you hear me?"

"Certainly I shall do my utmost," replied the surgeon stiffly. "Perhaps you would like one of my colleagues to see it?"

"I should," said Worth. "I'll have every doctor this town holds to see it before I'll permit you or any other of your kidney to hack my brother about any more!"

"You are unreasonable, my lord!"

"Unreasonable! Get Hume!"

"Dr. Hume has already so much on his hands——"

"Get him!" snapped Worth.

The surgeon bowed, and walked off. The Duchess, who had come out of the Colonel's room, nodded approvingly, and said: "That's right. Don't pay any heed to him! We will apply fomentations, and say nothing at all to the poor boy about amputation. I wish you will ask my granddaughter to find some flannel and bring it to me."

"I will," he said, and went downstairs in search of Barbara.

He met, instead, his wife, who informed him that the Comte de Lavisse had that instant entered the house and was with Barbara in the back-parlour.

He looked annoyed, but she said: "He came, most kindly, to enquire after Charles. Only fancy, Worth! It was he who had Charles carried off the field! I declare, I could almost have embraced him, much as I dislike him!"

"I will see him, and thank him. Will you get the flannel for the fomentations?"

"Yes, immediately," she replied.

Downstairs, the Count faced Barbara across the small room, and said, gripping a chair-back: "I did not think to find you here! I may know what I am to understand, I suppose!"

She said abstractedly: "He is better. He has even desired to be shaved."

"I am delighted to hear it! You perhaps find me irrelevant?"

"Oh no! I am so glad you are safe. Only my mind is so taken up just now——"

"It is seen! By God, I think you are a devil!"

She said rather listlessly: "Yes, I know. It does no good to say I'm sorry, or I would."

He struck the chair-back with his open palm. "In fact, you made a fool of me!"

She replied with a flash of spirit: "Oh, the devil! You at least were fair game!"

He gave a short laugh. "*Touché!* I might have known! I cut an ignoble figure beside your heroic Staff Officer, do I not? You have doubtless heard that my brigade fled—fled without firing a shot!"

"I hadn't heard," she replied. "I am sorry." There did not seem to be anything more to say. She tried to find something, and added: "It was not that. I always loved Charles Audley."

"Thank you! It needs no more! Convey my felicitations to the Colonel: I wish that that shell had blown him to perdition!"

She was spared having to answer him by Worth's entering the room at that moment. The Count, picking up his shako, held out his hand. "*Adieu!* It is unlikely that we meet again."

She shook hands, and went back to the Colonel. Worth attempted to thank the Count for his kind offices the previous day, but was cut short.

"It is nothing. I was, in fact, ordered by my General to do my possible for the Colonel. I am happy to learn that my poor efforts were not wasted. I am returning immediately to my brigade."

Worth escorted him to the door, merely remarking: "You must allow me, however, to tell you that I cannot but consider myself under a deep obligation to you."

"Oh, *parbleu!* It is quite unnecessary!" He shook hands, but paused half-way down the steps, and looked back. "You will tell the Colonel, if you please, that his message was delivered," he said, and saluted, and walked quickly away.

Worth had hardly shut the door when another knock fell upon it. He opened it again to find Creevey on the top step, beaming all over his shrewd countenance, and evidently bubbling with news.

He declined coming in: he had called only to see how Colonel Audley did, and would not intrude upon the family at such a time. "I have just seen the Duke!" he announced. "I have been to his Headquarters, hearing that he had come in from Waterloo, and found him in the act of writing his despatch. He saw me from his window, and beckoned me up straightway. You may imagine how I put out my hand and congratulated him upon his victory! He said to me in his blunt way: 'It has been a damned serious business. Blücher and I have lost thirty thousand men.' And then, without the least appearance of joy or triumph, he repeated: 'It has been a damned nice thing—the nearest run thing you ever saw in your life.' He told me Blücher got so damnably licked on Friday that he could not find him on Saturday morning, and had to fall back to keep up his communications with him. Upon my word, I never saw him so grave, nor so much moved! He kept on walking about the room, praising the courage of our troops, in particular those Guards who kept Hougoumont against the repeated attacks of the French. 'You may depend upon it,' he said, 'that no troops but the British could have held Hougoumont, and only the best of them at that!' Then he said—not with any vanity, you know, but very seriously: 'By God! I don't think it would have done if I had not been there.' "

"I can readily believe that," Worth replied. "Does he anticipate that there will be any more fighting?"

"No, that is the best of all! He says that every French Corps but one was engaged in the battle, and the whole Army gone off in such a perfect rout and confusion he thinks it quite impossible for them to give battle again before the Allies reach Paris."

"Excellent news! I am much obliged to you for bringing it to me."

"I knew you would be glad to hear of it! You'll give my compliments to the ladies, and to poor Audley: I must be off, to catch the mail."

He bustled away, and Worth went upstairs to convey the tidings to his brother, whom he found lying quietly, with his hand in Barbara's. He told him what had passed, and had the satisfaction of seeing the Colonel's eyes regain a little of their sparkle. Lavisse's parting message evoked only a languid: "Poor devil! What a piece of work to make of nothing!" Worth, seeing that he was tired, went away, leaving him to the comfort of Barbara's presence.

The Duchess remained in the house all day, and the Duke, after trying in vain to obtain intelligence of George's fate, and calling at the Fishers' lodging to see Lucy (whom he declared to be a poor little dab of a thing, not worth looking at), took up his quarters in Lady Worth's salon. He was permitted to visit Audley for a few minutes before dinner, and took his hand in a strong hold, saying with a softened expression in his rather hard eyes: "Well, my boy, so you mean to have that vixen of mine, do you? You're deserving of a better fate, but if you're determined you may take her with my blessing."

"Thank you, sir," said the Colonel.

"And mind you keep her this time!" said his Grace. "I won't have her back on my hands again!"

410

His wife and granddaughter, judging that a very little of his bracing personality was enough for the Colonel in his present condition, then sent him away, and he went off to announce to Judith that, whatever he might think of George's choice, he was very well satisfied with Barbara's.

He bore his wife off to the Hôtel de Belle Vue for dinner, promising, however, to permit of her returning to Worth's house later in the evening, to see how the Colonel went on. The fomentations had afforded some relief; there was no recurrence of the fever which had alarmed the ladies earlier in the day; and although the pulse was unsteady, the Duchess was able to inform her granddaughter before leaving the house that she had every expectation of the Colonel's speedy recovery.

He was too weak to wish to indulge in much conversation, but he seemed to like to have Barbara near him. He lay mostly with closed eyes under a frowning brow, but if she moved from her chair it was seen that he was not asleep, for his eyes would open and follow her about the room. She soon found that her absence from his side made him restless, and so placed her chair close to the bed, and sat there, ready in an instant to bathe his brow with vinegar and water, to change the fomentations, or just to smile at him and take his hand.

It was not such a reunion as she had imagined. Her thoughts were confused. Harry's death lay at the back of them, like a bruise on her spirit. She had been prepared to hear that Charles had been killed, but she had never thought that he might come back to her so shattered that he could not take her in his arms, so weak that the smile, even, was an effort. There was much she had wanted to say to him, but it had not been said, and perhaps never would be. No drama attached to their reconciliation: it was quiet, tempered by sorrow.

Yet in spite of all, as she sat hour after hour beside Charles, a contentment grew in her and the vision of the conquering hero, who should have come riding gallantly back to her, faded from her mind. Reality was less romantic than her imaginings, but not less dear; and his feeble laugh and expostulation when she fed him with her grandmother's prescribed gruel were more precious to her than the most ardent love-making could have been.

Her dinner was sent up to her on a tray, and Judith and Worth sat down in the dining-parlour alone. They had not many minutes risen from the table when a knock fell on the street door, and an instant later Lord George Alastair walked into the salon.

Judith exclaimed at the sight of him, for his appearance was shocking. His baggage not having reached Nivelles, where his brigade was bivouacked, he had not been able to change his tattered jacket and mud-splashed breeches. An epaulette had been shot off; a bandage was bound round his head; and he limped slightly from a sabre-cut on one leg. He looked pale, and his blood-shot eyes were heavy and red-rimmed from fatigue. He cut short Judith's greetings, saying curtly: "I came to enquire after Audley. Can I see him?"

"He is better, but very weak. But sit down! You look quite worn out, and you are wounded!"

"Oh, this!" He raised his hand to his head. "That will only spoil my beauty. Don't waste your pity on me, ma'am!"

"Have you dined?" Worth asked.

"Yes: at my wife's!" George replied, flinging the word at him. "I have also seen my grandparents, and have nothing left to do before rejoining my regiment except to thank Audley for his kind offices towards my wife."

"I am very sure he does not wish to be thanked. Oh, how relieved your grandparents must be to know you are safe, to have had the comfort of seeing you!"

He replied, with the flash of his sardonic smile: "Yes, extremely gratifying! It is wonderful what a slash across the brow can do for one. You will be happy to hear, ma'am, that my wife will remain in my grandparents' charge until such time as she may follow me to Paris. May I now see Audley?"

She looked doubtful. He saw it, and said rather harshly:

"Oblige me in this, if you please! What I have to ask him will not take me long."

"To ask him?" she repeated.

"Yes, ma'am, to ask him! Audley saw my brother die, and I want to know where in that charnel-house to search for his body!"

She put out her hand impulsively. "Ah, poor boy! Of course you shall see him! Worth will take you up at once."

"Thank you," he said with a slight bow, and limped to the door, and opened it for Worth to lead the way out.

Judith was left to her own melancholy reflections, but these were interrupted in a very few minutes by yet another knock on the street door. She paid little heed, expecting merely to have a card brought in to her with kind enquiries after the state of Colonel Audley's health, but to her astonishment the butler very soon opened the door into the salon and announced the Duke of Wellington.

She started up immediately. The Duke came in, dressed in plain clothes, and shook hands, saying: "How do you do? I have come to see poor Audley. How does he go on?"

She was quite overpowered. She had never imagined that in the midst of the work in which he must be immersed he could find time to visit the Colonel. She had even doubted his sparing as much as a thought for his Aides-de-Camp. She could only say in a moved voice: "How kind this is in you! We think him a little better. He will be so happy to receive a visit from you!"

"Better, is he? That's right! Poor fellow, they tell me he has had to lose his arm."

She nodded, and, recollecting herself a little, began to congratulate him upon his great victory.

He stopped her at once, saying hastily: "Oh, do not congratulate me! I have lost all my dearest friends!"

She said in a subdued voice: "You must feel it, indeed!"

"I am quite heart-broken at the loss I have sustained," he replied, taking a quick turn about the room. "My friends, my poor soldiers—how many of them have I to regret! I have no feeling for the advantages we have acquired." He stopped, and said in a serious tone: "I have

413

never fought such a battle, and I trust I shall never fight such another. War is a terrible evil, Lady Worth."

She could only throw him a speaking glance; her feelings threatened to overcome her; she was glad to see Worth come back into the room at that moment, and to be relieved of the necessity of answering the Duke. She sank down into a chair while Worth shook hands with his lordship. He, too, offered congratulations and comments on the nature of the engagement. The Duke replied in an animated tone: "Never did I see such a pounding-match! Both were what you boxers call gluttons. Napoleon did not manœuvre at all. He just moved forward in the old style, in columns, and was driven off in the old style. The only difference was that he mixed cavalry with his infantry, and supported both with an enormous quantity of artillery."

"From what my brother has said, I collect that the French cavalry was very numerous?"

"By God, it was! I had the infantry for some time in squares, and we had the French cavalry walking about us as if they had been our own. I never saw the British infantry behave so well!"

"It has been a glorious action, sir."

"Yes, but the glory has been dearly bought. Indeed, the losses I have sustained have quite broken me down. But I must not stay: I have very little time at my disposal, as you may imagine. I came only to see Audley."

"I will take you to him at once, sir. Nothing, I am persuaded, will do him as much good as a visit from you."

"Oh, pooh! nonsense!" the Duke said, going with him to the door. "I shall be in a bad way without him, and the others whom I have lost, I can tell you!"

He followed Worth upstairs to Colonel Audley's room, only to be brought up short on the threshold by the sight of Lord George, standing by the bed. A frosty glare was bent on him; a snap was imminent; but Audley, startled by the sight of his Chief, still kept his wits about him, and said quickly: "Lord George Alastair, my lord, who has been sent in to have his wounds attended to, and has been kind enough to visit me on his way back to his brigade."

"Oh!" said his lordship. "Avon's grandson, are you? I'm glad to see you're alive, but get back to your brigade, sir! There's too much of this going on leave!"

Thankful to have escaped with only this mild reproof, George effaced himself. The Duke stepped up to the bed, and clasped Colonel Audley's hand. "Well! We have given the French a handsome dressing!" he said heartily. "But I'm sorry to see you like this, my poor fellow! Never mind! Fitzroy's had the misfortune to lose his right arm, you know. I've just seen him: he's perfectly free from fever, and as well as anybody could be under such circumstances."

"His right arm!" the Colonel said. "Oh, poor Fitzroy!"

"There, don't distress yourself! Why, what do you think! He's already learning to write with his left hand, and will be back with me again before I've had time to turn round."

Audley struggled up on his elbow. "Sir, what of Gordon?"

A shadow crossed the Duke's face. He said in a broken voice: "Ah, poor Gordon! He lived long enough to be informed by myself of the glorious success of our actions. They carried him to my Headquarters at Waterloo, you know. Hume called me at three this morning to go to him, but he was dead before I got there."

The Colonel gave a groan and sank back upon his pillows. "A little restaurant in Paris!" he whispered. "O God!"

Barbara moved forward, and slid her hand into his. His fingers gripped it feebly; he lay silent, while the Duke, turning to Worth, asked in his blunt fashion: "Who has him in charge? Has Hume been here?"

"Not yet," Worth replied. "I am extremely anxious to get him, but there seems to be no possibility of securing his services."

"Nonsense! I'll send him round at once," said his lordship. "Can't afford to lose any more of my family." He bent over Colonel Audley again, and laid his hand on his right shoulder. "Well, Audley, I must go. You'll be glad to know that we're moving on immediately. Old Blücher took up the pursuit last night, and you may be sure we shan't discontinue our operations till we get to Paris. As for Boney, in my opinion, *il n'a que se pendre*. But I shall be in a bad way without you fellows: take care that you lose no time in rejoining me!"

"I shall report for duty the instant I can stand on my feet, sir. Who takes the despatch to England?"

"Percy, with three Eagles as well. Good-bye, my boy: now, don't forget! I rely on your following me as soon as you may."

He pressed the Colonel's shoulder, and went away, with a nod to Barbara and a brief handshake for Worth.

He was as good as his word in sending Dr. Hume to see the Colonel. The eminent doctor presented himself before an hour had passed, briskly expressing his regret at being kept by a press of work from coming sooner.

His arrival coincided with that of the surgeon who had taken charge of the Colonel's case, and Judith was hard put to it to decide which of the two men she disliked most. Mr. Jones's air of depression might exasperate her, but nothing, to her mind, could have been more out of place than Hume's cheerfulness. His voice was loud, and hearty; as he followed her up the stairs he talked all the way of trivialities; and when he entered the Colonel's room it was in a noisy fashion and with a rallying speech on his lips.

The Duke's visit had considerably tired Audley, but he roused himself when Hume came to the bed, and managed to smile.

"Well, now, and what is all this?" Hume said, taking his pulse. "I thought I had seen the end of you when I packed you off from Mont St. Jean yesterday."

"I am more difficult to kill than you suspected, you see," murmured the Colonel.

"Kill! No such thing! I did a capital piece of work on you, and here you are demanding more of my valuable time! We'll take a look at that leg of yours."

The bandages and the fomentations were removed. The

surgeon said something in a low tone, and was answered by a sharp: "Rubbish! Why do you give up a man with such a pulse, and such a good constitution? He is doing famously! You have been fomenting the leg; excellent! couldn't do better! Now then, Audley, I'll see what I can do to make you easier."

He took off his coat and rolled up his sleeves, while Judith ran to fetch the hot water he demanded. While he worked upon the Colonel's wincing body, he chatted, perhaps with the object of taking his victim's mind off his sufferings, and the Colonel answered him in painful gasps. His matter-of-fact description of the battlefield, literally covered with dead and wounded, shocked Judith inexpressibly, and made her exclaim at the plight of the French soldiers left there until the Allied wounded should have been got in. He replied cheerfully that it was all in their favour to be in the fresh air: provided they were soon moved into the hospitals they would be found to have escaped the fever which had attacked those who were got immediately under cover.

"Do you know how the Prince of Orange is?" asked the Colonel.

"Do I know! Why, I've just been with him! You need not worry your head over him: he's going on capitally. Baron Constant came rushing in this morning while I was with him, shouting out: 'Boney's beat! Boney's beat!' and you never saw anyone more delighted than the Prince was! You heard we were obliged to take Lord Uxbridge's leg off, I daresay? He is as gallant a man as ever I met! What do you think of his telling us he considered his leg a small price to pay for having been in such an action?" He stretched out his hand for some clean lint, and began to bind the Colonel's leg up again. In a graver tone he said: "Our losses have been shocking. The Duke is quite cast-down, and no wonder! He would have me bring him a list of such of our casualties as came within my knowledge last night. I did so, but found him laid down in all his dirt upon the couch, fast asleep, and so set my list down beside him and went away. He had had poor Gordon

417

put into his bed, you know. Ah, that has been a sad business! There was nothing one could do except to wait for death to put a period to his sufferings. The end came at three o'clock. I went to call the Duke, but it was over before he could get there. I never saw him so much affected. People call him unfeeling, but I can tell you this: when I went to him after he had read the list of our casualties there were two white furrows down his cheeks where his tears had washed away the dust. He said to me in a voice tremulous with emotion: 'Well! thank God I don't know what it is to lose a battle, but certainly nothing can be more painful than to win one with the loss of so many of one's friends.' "

Judith saw that Colonel Audley was too much distressed by the thought of Gordon's death to respond, and said civilly: "Nothing, I am sure, could become the Duke more than the way in which he spoke to us of his victory. I have not been used to think him a man of much sensibility, and was quite confounded."

"Sensibility! Ay, I daresay not, but General Alava was telling me it was downright pathetic to watch him, as he sat down to his supper last night, looking up every time the door opened, in the expectation of seeing one of his Staff walk in." He straightened his back, saying with a reversion to his hearty tone: "There! I have done torment-ing you at last! You will be on your feet again as soon as Lord Fitzroy, I promise you."

He turned to give some directions to the other surgeon; recommended the application of leeches, if there should be a recurrence of fever; and took himself off, leaving the Colonel very much exhausted and the ladies quite indignant.

His visit was presently found, however, to have been of benefit to Audley. He seemed easier, and, assisted by a dose of laudanum, passed as quiet a night as could have been expected.

When Barbara came into his room in the morning, she found him being propped up with pillows to partake of a breakfast of toasted bread and weak tea.

He held out his hand to her. The old gaiety was missing from his smile, but he spoke cheerfully. "Good-morning, Bab. You see that I have rebelled against your gruel! Now you shall watch how deedily I can contrive with my one hand."

She bent over him, and to hide her almost overmastering desire to burst into tears, said with assumed raillery: "Ah, you hope to impress me, but I warn you, you won't succeed! You have already had a great deal of practice in the use of one hand!"

He put up the one hand to turn her face towards him and kissed her. "That's too bad! I had hoped to hold you spellbound by my adroitness. Will you oblige me by going to the dressing-table and opening the little drawer under the mirror?"

"Certainly," she replied. "What do you want from it, my darling?"

"You'll see," he said, picking up one of his slices of toast and dipping it in the tea. She opened the drawer, and found a small box in it, containing her engagement-ring. She said nothing, but brought the ring to the Colonel, smiling, but with quivering lips. He took it, and commanded her to hold out her hand. The ring slid over her knuckle, but the Colonel still retained her hand, saying quietly: "That stays there until I give you another in its place, Bab."

She dropped on her knees, burying her face in his shoulder. "Charles, dear Charles, I shall make you such a damnable wife! Oh, only tell me that you forgive me!"

He gave a rather shaky laugh, and put his arm round her. "Who is the 'dear fool' now?" he said. "Oh, Bab, Bab, just look what I have done!"

Judith came in a minute later to find Barbara, between tears and laughter, mopping up the spilt tea on the sheet, and exclaimed: "Well! This does not look like a sick-room!"

Barbara held out her hand. "Congratulate me, Judith! I have just become engaged to your brother-in-law!"

"Oh, my love, of course you have!" Judith cried, embracing her. "Charles, this time I congratulate you with all my heart!"

"Thank you!" he said, with rather a surprised look. "What's the news in the town to-day? How do Fitzroy and Billy go on?"

"I have not heard, but of course we shall call to make enquiries later on. The Duke has driven out in his curricle to rejoin the Army, at Nivelles. We understand he has taken Colonel Felton Hervey on as his Military Secretary, until Lord Fitzroy is well enough to go back."

"A one-armed man!"

"Yes, and that is what touches one so much. There is a delicacy in such a gesture: Lord Fitzroy must be sensible of it, I am sure! I never thought to like the Duke as well as I have done ever since he called here yesterday."

The Colonel smiled, but merely replied: "He must be worse off than ever for Staff Officers. I pity the poor devils remaining: they'll find him damned crusty!"

Judith was quite put out by this proasic remark, but Colonel Audley knew his Chief better than she did.

The Duke, rejoining his disorganized Army at Nivelles, found much to annoy him. He was displeased with the conduct of various sections of his Staff, and quite incensed by the discovery that Sir George Wood, who commanded the Royal Artillery, had, instead of securing the captured French guns, allowed a number of them to be seized by the Prussians. That was a little too much: those guns must be recovered, and there would be no peace for Wood or Fraser till they had been recovered.

His lordship, no longer a demi-god but only a much harassed man, sat down to write his instructions for the movement of his Army. There was no difficulty about that: the instructions were compressed into four succinct paragraphs, and borne off by a trembling young gentleman of the Quartermaster-General's Staff.

His lordship dipped his pen in the ink and began to compose his first General Order since the battle. The pen moved slowly, in stiff, reluctant phrases.

"*The Field Marshal takes this opportunity of returning to the Army his thanks for their conduct in the glorious action fought on the 18th instant, and he will not fail to report his sense of their conduct in the terms which it deserves to their several Sovereigns.*"

His lordship read that through, and decided that it would do. He wrote the figure 3 in the margin, and started another paragraph. His pen began to move faster: "*The Field Marshal has observed that several soldiers, and even officers, have quitted their ranks without leave, and have gone to Bruxelles, and even some to Antwerp, where, and in the country through which they have passed, they have spread a false alarm, in a manner highly unmilitary, and derogatory to the character of soldiers.*"

The pen was flowing perfectly easily now. His lordship continued without a check: "*The Field Marshal requests the General officers commanding divisions in the British Army . . . to report to him in writing what officers and men (the former by name) are now or have been absent without leave since the 16th instant . . .*"

THE END

SHORT BIBLIOGRAPHY

COTTON, Sergt.-Major Edward. *A Voice from Waterloo.* 10 edn. 1913.

CRAAN, W. B. *An Historical Account of the Battle of Waterloo.* 1817.

CREEVEY, Thomas. *A Selection from the Correspondence and Diaries.* Ed., The Rt. Hon. Sir Herbert Maxwell. 1933.

CROKER, John Wilson. *Correspondence and Diaries.* Ed., Louis J. Jennings. 1884.

DALTON, Charles. *The Waterloo Roll Call.*

D'ARBLAY, Mme. *Diary and Letters.* Vol. IV. Ed., Charlotte Barrett.

DE BAS, Col. F., and T'SERCLAES DE WOMMERSON, Col. Ct. J. de. *Campagne de 1815 aux Pays-Bas.* 4 vols. 1908.

DE LANCEY, Lady. *A Week at Waterloo in 1815.* Ed., Major B. R. Ward. 1906.

ELLESMERE, Earl of. *Personal Reminiscences of the Duke of Wellington.* Ed., Alice, Countess of Strafford. 1904.

FORTESCUE, The Hon. Sir John. *A History of the British Army.* Vol. X. 1920.—*Wellington.* 1925.

FRASER, Sir William. *Words on Wellington.* 1900.

GALESLOOT, L. *Le Duc de Wellington à Bruxelles.* 1884.

GLEIG, Rev. G. R. *Story of the Battle of Waterloo.* 1847.— *Personal Reminiscences of the Duke of Wellington.* Ed., Mary E. Gleig. 1904.

GOMM, Sir William Maynard. *Letters and Journals.*

GREVILLE, Charles. *Diary.* 2 vols. Ed., Philip Whitwell Wilson. 1927.

GRIFFITHS, Major Arthur. *The Wellington Memorial.* 1897. —*Wellington and Waterloo.* 1898.

GRONOW, Capt. *Reminiscences and Recollections.* 2 vols. 1892.

GUEDALLA, Philip. *The Hundred Days.* 1934.

HOUSSAYE, Henri. *1815.* 1903.

JACKSON, Lieut.-Col. Basil. *Notes and Reminiscences of a Staff-Officer.* 1903.

JAMES, Lieut.-Col. W. H. *Campaign of 1815*. 1908.

JONES, George. *The Battle of Waterloo, with Those of Ligny and Quatre-Bras*. 1815.

KELLY, Christopher. *The Memorable Battle of Waterloo*. 1817.

KINCAID, John. *Adventures in the Rifle Brigade*. Ed., The Hon. Sir John Fortescue. 1929.—*Random Shots from a Rifleman*. 1835.

LARPENT, F. S. *Private Journal*. 3 vols. Ed., Sir George Larpent. 1853.

LENNOX, Lord William Pitt. *Celebrities I Have Known*. 1876. —(An Ex-Aid-de-Camp.) *Three Years with The Duke, or Wellington in Private Life*. 1853.

LOW, Edward Bruce. *With Napoleon at Waterloo*. Ed., MacKenzie MacBride. 1911.

MALMESBURY, Earl of. *Letters*. Vol. II. 1845.

MAXWELL, The Rt. Hon. Sir Herbert. *Life of Wellington*. 2 vols. 1899.

McGRIGOR, Sir James. *Autobiography*. 1861.

MERCER, General Cavalié. *Journal of the Waterloo Campaign*. 1927.

MÜFFLING, General. *A Sketch of the Battle of Waterloo*. 1830. —*Passages From My Life*. Ed., Col. Philip Yorke. 1853.

NEVILLE, Ralph. *British Military Prints*. 1909.

OMAN, Sir Charles. *Wellington's Army*. 1913.

SHAW KENNEDY, General Sir James. *Notes on the Battle of Waterloo*. 1865.

SIBORNE, Capt. William. *History of the War in France and Belgium in 1815*. 2 vols. 1844.

SIBORNE, Maj.-Gen. H. T. (Ed.) *Waterloo Letters*. 1891.

SIDNEY, Rev. Edwin. *Life of Lord Hill, G.C.B.* 1845.

SMITH, G. C. Moore. *Life of John Colborne, Field-Marshal Lord Seaton*. 1903.

SMITH, Lieut.-Gen. Sir Harry. *Autobiography*. Vol. I. Ed., G. C. Moore Smith. 1901.

STANHOPE, Earl of. *Notes of Conversations with the Duke of Wellington*. 1888.

SWINTON, The Hon. Mrs. J. R. *A Sketch of the Life of Georgiana, Lady de Ros*. 1893.

WELLESLEY, Muriel. *The Man Wellington Through the Eyes of Those Who Knew Him.* 1937.

WELLINGTON, 1st Duke of. *Dispatches.* Ed., Lieut.-Col. John Gurwood. 1838.—*Supplementary Despatches.* Vols. IX and X. Ed., Arthur, 2nd Duke of Wellington. 1863.

WOOD, Sir Evelyn. *Cavalry in the Waterloo Campaign.* 1895.